the Dark Vault

A COLLECTION

ALSO BY **VICTORIA SCHWAB**

The Near Witch

THE ARCHIVED
The Archived
The Unbound

MONSTERS OF VERITY
This Savage Song
Our Dark Duet

VICIOUS
Vicious
Vengeful

SHADES OF MAGIC
A Darker Shade of Magic
A Gathering of Shadows
A Conjuring of Light

VICTORIA SCHWAB

the Dark Vault

A COLLECTION

HYPERION
Los Angeles   New York

First Paperback Edition, August 2018
10 9 8 7 6 5 4 3 2 1
FAC-025438-18180
Printed in the United States of America

This book is set in Perpetua MT Pro/Monotype; DIN Next LT Pro/Linotype
Lettering by Jenna Stempel-Lobell
Designed by Mary Claire Cruz

Library of Congress Control Number for *The Archived* Hardcover: 2012025485
Library of Congress Control Number for *The Unbound* Hardcover: 2013035335

ISBN 978-1-368-02770-0

Visit www.hyperionteens.com

To Patricia, for the shoulder, the ear, and the unwavering faith

To Bob Ledbetter, whose History I'd love to read

*And to Shelley McBurney, who leaves a mark
on everything she touches, and everyone she meets*

Book One

THE ARCHIVED

*Do not stand at my grave and weep
I am not there; I do not sleep.*
—Mary Elizabeth Frye

T HE NARROWS remind me of August nights in the South.

They remind me of old rocks and places where the light can't reach.

They remind me of smoke—the stale, settled kind—and of storms and damp earth.

Most of all, Da, they remind me of you.

I step into the corridor and breathe in the heavy air, and I am nine again, and it is summer.

My little brother, Ben, is sprawled inside by the fan, drawing monsters in blue pencil, and I am on the back porch looking up at the stars, all of them haloed by the humid night. You're standing beside me with a cigarette and an accent full of smoke, twirling your battered ring and telling stories about the Archive and the Narrows and the Outer in calm words, with your Louisiana lilt, like we're talking weather, breakfast, nothing.

You unbutton your cuffs and roll your sleeves up to the elbows as you speak, and I notice for the first time how many scars you have. From the three lines carved into your forearm to the dozens of other marks, they cut crude patterns in your skin, like cracks in old leather. I try to remember the last time you wore short sleeves. I can't.

That old rusted key hangs from its cord around your neck the way it always does, and somehow it catches the light, even though the night is pitch-black. You fidget with a slip of paper, roll it and unroll it, eyes scanning the surface as if something should be written there; but it's blank, so you roll it again until it's the size and shape of a cigarette, and tuck it behind your ear. You start drawing lines in the dust on the porch rail as you talk. You could never sit still.

Ben comes to the porch door and asks a question, and I wish I could remember the words. I wish I could remember the sound of his voice. But I can't. I do remember you laughing and running your fingers through the three lines you'd drawn in the dust on the railing, ruining the pattern. Ben wanders back inside and you tell me to close my eyes. You hand me something heavy and smooth, and tell me to listen, to find the thread of memory, to take hold and tell you what I see, but I don't see anything. You tell me to try harder, to focus, to reach inside, but I can't.

Next summer it will be different, and I will hear the hum and I will reach inside and I will see something, and you will be proud and sad and tired at the same time, and the summer after that you will get me a ring just like yours, but newer, and the summer after that you'll be dead and I'll have your key as well as your secrets.

But this summer is simple.

This summer I am nine and you are alive and there is still time. This summer when I tell you I can't see anything, you just shrug and light another cigarette, and go back to telling stories.

Stories about winding halls, and invisible doors, and places where the dead are kept like books on shelves. Each time you finish a story, you make me tell it back to you, as if you're afraid I will forget.

I never do.

ONE

THERE IS NOTHING fresh about this start.

I lean back against the car and stare up at the Coronado, the hotel-turned-apartment building that my mother and father find "so charming." It stares back, wide-eyed, gaunt. I spent the whole drive twisting the ring on my finger, running my thumb over the three lines etched into its surface, as if the silver band were a rosary or a charm. I prayed for someplace simple, uncluttered, and new. And I got this.

I can see the dust from across the street.

"Isn't it divine?" squeals my mother.

"It's . . . old."

So old that the stones have settled, the cracks deep enough to give the whole facade a tired look. A fist-size piece of stone loosens before my eyes and tumbles down the side of the building.

I look up to find a roof dotted with gargoyles. Not at the corners, where you'd expect gargoyles to be, but perching at random intervals like a line of crows. My eyes slide over rippling windows and down six floors to the carved and cracking stone marquee that tops the lobby.

Mom hurries forward, but stops halfway across the road to marvel at the "antiquated" paving stones that give the road so much "character."

"Honey," calls Dad, following. "Don't stand in the street."

There should be four of us. Mom, Dad, Ben, me. But there's not. Da's been dead for four years, but it hasn't even been a year since Ben died. A year of words no one can say because they call up images no one can bear. The silliest things shatter you. A T-shirt discovered behind the washing machine. A toy that rolled under a cabinet in the garage, forgotten until someone drops something and goes to fetch it, and suddenly they're on the concrete floor sobbing into a dusty baseball mitt.

But after a year of tiptoeing through our lives, trying not to set off memories like land mines, my parents decide to quit, but call it change. Call it a fresh start. Call it just what this family needs.

I call it running.

"You coming, Mackenzie?"

I follow my parents across the street, baking in the July sun. Below the marquee is a revolving door, flanked by two regular ones. A few people—mostly older—lounge around the doors, or on a patio to the side.

Before Ben died, Mom had whims. She wanted to be a zookeeper, a lawyer, a chef. But they were *whims*. After he died, they became something more. Instead of just dreaming, she started doing. With a force. Ask her about Ben and she pretends she didn't hear, but ask her about her newest pet project—whatever it happens to be—and she'll talk for hours, giving off enough energy to power the room. But Mom's energy is as fickle as it is bright. She's started switching careers the way Ben switches—*switched*—favorite foods, one week cheese, the next applesauce. . . . In the past year, Mom's gone through seven. I guess I should be thankful she didn't try to switch lives, too, while she was at it. Dad and I could have woken up one day and found only a note in her nearly illegible script. But she's still here.

Another stone crumbles off the side of the building.

Maybe this will keep her busy.

The deserted space on the first floor of the Coronado, tucked behind the patio and below the awnings, is the future home of my mother's biggest whim—she prefers to call this one her "dream endeavor"—Bishop's Coffee Shop. And if you ask her, she'll tell you this is the only reason we're m̶ ̶·̶ ̶·̶ ̶ ̶ ̶ ̶'hing to do with Ben (only s̶h̶

d lands on
d wavering
The dead are silent,
uiet until you reach
oud. Living people
haven't   s they're a jumble
of mem   'p and held at bay
only by   lps, but it can't
block th

I try   y shoulder, like
Da taugh   barrier, but it doesn't work. The sound is still there, laye   ones and statics, like radios tuned wrong, and after an appropriate number of seconds, I take a step forward, beyond his reach. Dad's hand falls away, and the quiet returns. I roll my shoulders.

"What do you think, Mac?" he asks, and I look up at the hulking shape of the Coronado.

I think I'd rather shake my mother until a new idea falls out and leads us somewhere else.

But I know I can't say this, not to Dad. The skin beneath his eyes is nearly blue, and over the last year he's gone from slim to thin. Mom might be able to power a city, but Dad barely stays lit.

"I think . . ." I say, managing a smile, "it will be an adventure."

I am ten, almost eleven, and I wear my house key around my neck just to be like you.

They tell me I have your gray eyes, and your hair—back when it was reddish brown instead of white—but I don't care about those things. Everyone has eyes and hair. I want the things most people don't notice. The ring and the key and the way you have of wearing everything on the inside.

We're driving north so I'll be home for my birthday, even though I would rather stay with you than blow out candles. Ben is sleeping in the backseat, and the whole way home, you tell me stories about these three places.

The Outer, which you don't waste much breath on because it's everything around us, the normal world, the only one most people ever know about.

The Narrows, a nightmarish place, all stained corridors and distant whispers, doors and darkness thick like grime.

And the Archive, a library of the dead, vast and warm, wood and stone and colored glass, and all throughout, a sense of peace.

As you drive and talk, one hand guides the steering wheel, and the other toys with the key around your neck.

"The only things the three places have in common," you say, "are doors. Doors in, and doors out. And doors need keys."

I watch the way you fiddle with yours, running a thumb over the teeth. I try to copy you, and you catch sight of the cord around my neck and ask me what it is. I show you my silly house key on a string, and there's this strange silence that fills the car, like the whole world is holding its breath, and then you smile.

You tell me I can have my birthday present early, even though you know how Mom likes to do things right, and then you pull a small unwrapped box from your pocket. Inside is a silver ring, the three lines that make up the Archive mark carefully etched into the metal, just like yours.

I don't know what it's for, not yet—a blinder, a silencer, a buffer against the world and its memories, against people and their cluttered thoughts—but I'm so excited I promise I will never take it off. And then the car hits a bump and I drop it under the seat. You laugh, but I make you pull off the freeway so I can get it back. I have to wear it on my thumb because it's too big. You tell me I'll grow into it.

We drag our suitcases through the revolving door and into the lobby. Mom chirps with glee, and I wince.

The sprawling foyer is like one of those photos where you have to figure out what's wrong. At first glance it glitters, marble and crown molding and gilt accents. But at second look the marble is coated in dust, the molding is cracked, and the gilt accents are actively shedding gold onto the carpet. Sunlight streams in through the windows, bright despite the aging glass, but the space smells like fabric kept too long behind curtains. This place was once, undeniably, spectacular. What happened?

Two people mill by a front window, seemingly oblivious to the haze of dust they're standing in.

Across the lobby a massive marble staircase leads to the second floor. The cream-colored stone would probably gleam if someone polished it long enough. Wallpaper wraps the sides of the staircase, and from across the room, I see a ripple in the fleur-de-lis pattern there. From here it almost looks like a crack. I doubt anyone would notice, not in a place like this, but I'm supposed to spot these things. I'm hauling my luggage toward the ripple when I hear my name and turn to see my parents vanishing around a corner. I hoist my bags and catch up.

I find them standing in front of a trio of elevators just off the lobby.

The wrought iron cages look like they might safely hold two. But we're already climbing into one of them, three people and four suitcases. I whisper something halfway between a prayer and a curse as I pull the rusted gate closed and press the button for the third floor.

The elevator groans to life. There might be elevator music, too, but it's impossible to hear over the sounds the machine makes simply hoisting us up. We rise through the second floor at a glacial pace, padded in by luggage. Halfway between the second and third floor, the elevator pauses to think, then heaves upward again. It gives a death rattle at the third floor, at which point I pry the jaws open and set us free.

I announce that I'm taking the stairs from now on.

Mom tries to free herself from the barricade of luggage. "It has a certain . . ."

"Charm?" I parrot, but she ignores the jab and manages to get one leg over the suitcases, nearly toppling as her heel snags on a strap.

"It has personality," adds my father, catching her arm.

I turn to take in the hall, and my stomach drops. The walls are lined with doors. Not just the ones you would expect, but a dozen more—unusable, painted and papered over, little more than outlines and ridges.

"Isn't it fascinating?" says my mother. "The extra doors are from way back when it was a hotel, before they began knocking down walls and combining rooms, converting spaces. They left the doors, papered right over them."

"Fascinating," I echo. And eerie. Like a well-lit version of the Narrows.

We reach the apartment at the end, and Dad unlocks the door—an ornate 3F nailed to its front—and throws it open. The apartment has the same scuffed quality as everything else. Lived-in. This place has marks, but none of them are ours. In our old house, even when you took away the furniture and packed up the *stuff*, there were all these marks. The dent in the wall where I threw that book, the stain on the kitchen ceiling from Mom's failed blender experiment, the blue doodles in the corners of rooms where Ben drew. My chest tightens. Ben will never leave a mark on this place.

Mom *oohs* and *ahhs*, and Dad drifts quietly through the rooms, and I'm about to brave the threshold when I feel it.

The scratch of letters. A name being written on the slip of Archive paper in my pocket. I dig the page out—it's roughly the size of a receipt and strangely crisp—as the History's name scrawls itself in careful cursive.

Emma Claring. 7.

"Mac," calls Dad, "you coming?"

I slide back a step into the hall.

"I left my bag in the car," I say. "I'll be right back."

Something flickers across Dad's face, but he's already nodding, already turning away. The door clicks shut, and I sigh and turn to the hall.

I need to find this History.

To do that, I need to get to the Narrows.

And to do that, I need to find a door.

TWO

I'M ELEVEN, and you are sitting across from me at the table, talking under the sound of dishes in the kitchen. Your clothes are starting to hang on you—shirts, pants, even your ring. I overheard Mom and Dad, and they said that you're dying—not the fast, stone-drop way, there and then gone, but still. I can't stop squinting at you, as if I might see the disease picking you clean, stealing you from me, bite by bite.

You're telling me about the Archive again, something about the way it changes and grows, but I am not really listening. I'm twirling the silver ring on my finger. I need it now. Fractured bits of memory and feeling are starting to get through whenever someone touches me. They're not jarring or violent yet, just kind of messy. I told you that and you told me it would get worse, and you looked sorry when you said it. You said it was genetic, the potential, but it doesn't manifest until the predecessor makes the choice. And you chose me. I hope you weren't sorry. I'm not sorry. I'm only sorry that as I get stronger, you seem to get weaker.

"Are you listening?" you ask, because it's obvious I'm not.

"I don't want you to die," I say, surprising us both, and the whole moment hardens, stops, as your eyes hold mine. And then you soften and shift in your seat, and I think I can hear your bones moving.

"What are you afraid of, Kenzie?" you ask.

You said you passed the job to me and I can't help but wonder if that's why you're getting worse now. Fading faster. "Losing you."

"Nothing's lost. Ever."

I'm pretty sure you're just trying to make me feel better, half expect you to say something like *I'll live on in your heart.* But you would never say that.

"You think I tell you stories just to hear my own voice? I mean what I said. Nothing's lost. That's what the Archive's for."

Wood and stone and colored glass, and all throughout, a sense of peace . . .

"That's where we go when we die? To the Archive?"

"You don't, not exactly, but your History does." And then you start using your "Pay Attention" voice, the one that makes words stick to me and never let go. "You know what a History is?"

"It's the past," I say.

"No, Kenzie. That's history with a little *h.* I mean History with a big *H.* A History is . . ." You pull out a cigarette, roll it between your fingers. "You might think of it as a ghost, but that's not what it is, really. Histories are records."

"Of what?"

"Of us. Of everyone. Imagine a file of your entire life, of every moment, every experience. All of it. Now, instead of a folder or a book, imagine the data is kept in a body."

"What do they look like?"

"However they looked when they died. Well, *before* they died. No fatal wounds or bloated corpses. The Archive

11

wouldn't find that tasteful. And the body's just a shell for the life inside."

"Like a book cover?"

"Yes." You put the cigarette in your mouth, but know better than to light it in the house. "A cover tells you something about a book. A body tells you something about a History."

I bite my lip. "So . . . when you die, a copy of your life gets put in the Archive?"

"Exactly."

I frown.

"What is it, Kenzie?"

"If the Outer is where we live, and the Archive is where our Histories go, what are the Narrows for?"

You smile grimly. "The Narrows are a buffer between the two. Sometimes a History wakes up. Sometimes Histories get out, through the cracks in the Archive, and into those Narrows. And when that happens, it's the Keeper's job to send them back."

"What's a Keeper?"

"It's what I am," you say, pointing to the ring on your hand. "What you'll be," you add, pointing to my own ring.

I can't help but smile. You chose me. "I'm glad I get to be like you."

You squeeze my hand and make a sound somewhere between a cough and a laugh, and say, "Good thing. Because you haven't got a choice."

Doors to the Narrows are everywhere.

Most of them started out as *actual* doors, but the problem is that buildings change—walls go down, walls go up—and these doors, once they're made, don't. What you end up with are cracks, the kind most people wouldn't even notice, slight disturbances where the two worlds—the Narrows and the Outer—run into each other. It's easy when you know what you're looking for.

But even with good eyes, finding a Narrows door can take a while. I had to search my old neighborhood for two days to find the nearest one, which turned out to be halfway down the alley behind the butcher shop.

I think of the ripple in the fleur-de-lis paper in the lobby, and smile.

I head for the nearest stairwell—there are two sets, the south stairs at my end of the hall, and the north stairs at the far end, past the metal cages—when something makes me stop.

A tiny gap, a vertical shadow on the dust-dull yellow wallpaper. I walk over to the spot and square myself to the wall, letting my eyes adjust to the crack that is most definitely there. The sense of victory fades a little. Two doors so close together? Maybe the crack in the lobby was just that—a crack.

This crack, however, is something more. It cuts down the wall between apartments 3D and 3C, in a stretch of space without any ghosted doors, a dingy patch interrupted only by a painting of the sea in an old white frame. I frown and slide the silver ring from my finger and feel the shift, like a screen being removed. Now when I stare at the crack, I see it, right in the center of the seam. A keyhole.

The ring works like a blinder. It shields me—as much as it can—from the living, and blocks my ability to read the impressions they leave on things. But it also blinds me to the Narrows. I can't see the doors, let alone step through them.

I pull Da's key from around my neck, running a thumb over the teeth the way he used to. For luck. Da used to rub the key, cross himself, kiss his fingers and touch them to the wall—any number of things. He used to say he could use a little more luck.

I slide the key into the keyhole and watch as the teeth vanish into the wall. First comes the whisper of metal against metal. Then the Narrows door surfaces, floating like a body up through water until it presses against the yellow paper. Last, a single strand of crisp light draws itself around the frame, signaling that the door is ready.

If someone came down the hall right now, they wouldn't see the door. But they would hear the click of the lock as I turned Da's rusted key, and then they would see me step straight through the yellow paper into nothing.

There's no sky in the Narrows, but it always feels like night, smells like night. Night in a city after rain. On top of that there's a breeze, faint but steady, carrying stale air through the halls. Like you're in an air shaft.

I knew what the Narrows looked like long before I saw them. I had this image in my head, drawn by Da year after year. Close your eyes and picture this: a dark alley, just wide enough for you to spread your arms and skim the rough walls on either side with your fingers. You look up and see . . . nothing, just the walls running up and up and up into black. The only light comes from the doors that line the walls, their outlines giving off a faint glow, their keyholes letting in beams of light that show like threads in the dusty air. It is enough light to see by, but not enough to see well.

Fear floats up my throat, a primal thing, a physical twinge as I step through, close the door behind me, and hear the voices. Not true voices, really, but murmurs and whispers and words stretched thin by distance. They could be halls, or whole territories, away. Sounds travel here in the Narrows, coil through the corridors, bounce off walls, find you from miles away, ghostlike and diffused. They can lead you astray.

The corridors stretch out like a web or a subway, branching, crossing, the walls interrupted only by those doors. City blocks' worth of doors mere feet apart, space compressed. Most of them are locked. All of them are marked.

Coded. Every Keeper has a system, a way to tell a good door from a bad one; I cannot count the number of X's and slashes and circles and dots scribbled against each door and then rubbed away. I pull a thin piece of chalk from my pocket—it's funny, the things you learn to keep on you at all times—and use it to draw a quick Roman numeral I on the door I just came through, right above the keyhole (the doors here have no handles, can't even be tried without a key). The number is bright and white over the dozens of old, half-ruined marks.

I turn to consider the hall and the multitude of doors lining it. Most of them are locked—inactive, Da called them—doors that lead back into the Outer, to different rooms in different houses, disabled because they go places where no Keeper is currently stationed. But the Narrows is a buffer zone, a middle ground, studded with ways out. Some doors lead to and from the Archive. Others lead to Returns, which isn't its own world, but it might as well be. A place where even Keepers aren't allowed to go. And right now, with a History on my list, that's the door I need to find.

I test the door to the right of Door I, and to my surprise it's unlocked, and opens onto the Coronado's lobby. So it wasn't just a ripple in the wallpaper after all. Good to know. An old woman ambles past, oblivious to the portal, and I tug the door shut again and draw a II above the keyhole.

I take a step back to consider the numbered doors, set side by side—my ways out—and then continue down the hall, testing every lock. None of the other doors budge, and I mark each one with an X. There's this sound, a fraction louder than the others, a *thud thud thud* like muffled steps, but only a fool hunts down a History before finding a place to send him, so I quicken my pace, rounding a corner and testing two more doors before one finally gives.

The lock turns and the door opens, this time into a room made of light, blinding and edgeless. I draw back and close the door, blinking away little white dots as I mark its surface with a circle and quickly shade it in. *Returns.* I turn to the next door over and don't even bother to test the lock before I draw a circle, this one hollow. *The Archive.* The nice thing about the Archive doors is that they're always to the right of Returns, so if you can find one, you've found the other.

And now it's time to find Emma.

I flex my hands and bring my fingers to the wall, the silver ring safely in my pocket. Histories and humans alike have to touch a surface to leave an impression, which is why the floors here are made of the same concrete as the walls. So I can read the entire hallway with a touch. If Emma set a foot here, I'll see it.

The surface of the wall hums beneath my hands. I close my eyes and press down. Da used to say there was a thread in the wall, and you had to reach, reach right through the wall until you catch hold of that thread and not let go. The humming spreads up my fingers, numbing them as I focus. I squeeze my eyes shut harder and reach, and feel the thread tickling my palms. I catch hold, and my hands go numb. Behind my eyes the darkness shifts, flickers, and then the Narrows take shape again, a smudged version of the present, distorted. I see myself standing here, touching the wall, and guide the memory away.

It plays like a skipping film reel, winding back from present to past, flickering on the insides of my eyelids. The name showed on my list an hour ago, when Emma Claring's escape was registered, so I shouldn't have to go back far. When I twist the memories back two hours and find no sign of her, I pull away from the wall and open my eyes. The past of the Narrows vanishes, replaced by an only slightly brighter but definitely clearer present. I head down the hall to the next branching corridor and try again: closing my eyes, reaching, catching hold, winding time forward and back, sweeping the last hour for signs of—

A History flickers in the frame, her small form winding down the hall to a corner just ahead, then turning left. I blink and let go of the wall, the Narrows sharpening as I follow, turn the corner, and find . . . a dead end. More accurately, a territory break, a plane of wall marked by a glowing keyhole. Keepers have access only to their own territories, so the speck of light serves as nothing more than a stop sign. But it does keep the Histories from getting too far away; and sitting on the floor right in front of the break is a girl.

Emma Claring sits in the hall, her arms wrapped tightly around her knees. She's not wearing any shoes, only grass-stained shorts and a T-shirt; and she's so small that the corridor seems almost cavernous around her.

"Wake up, wake up, wake up."

She rocks back and forth as she says it, the beat of her body against the wall making the *thud thud thud* I heard earlier. She squeezes her eyes shut, then opens them wide, panic edging into her voice when the Narrows don't disappear.

She's obviously slipping.

"Wake up," the girl pleads again.

"Emma," I say, and she startles.

Two terrified eyes swivel toward me in the dark. The pupils are spreading, the black chewing away the color around them. She whimpers but doesn't recognize me yet. That's good. When Histories slip far enough, they start to see other people when they look at you. They see whomever it is they want or need or hate or love or remember, and it makes the confusion worse. Makes them fall faster into madness.

I take a slow step forward. She buries her face in her arms and continues whispering.

I kneel in front of her. "I'm here to help you," I say.

Emma Claring doesn't look up. "Why can't I wake up?" she whispers. Her voice hitches.

"Some dreams," I say, "are harder to shake."

Her rocking slows, and her head rolls side to side against her arms.

"But do you know what's great about dreams?" I mimic the tone my mother used to use with me, with Ben. Soothing, patient. "Once you know you're in a dream, you can control it. You can change it. You can find a way out."

Emma looks up at me over her crossed arms, eyes shining and wide.

"Do you want me to show you how?" I ask.

She nods.

"I want you to close your eyes"—she does—"and imagine a door." I look around at this stretch of hall, every door unmarked, and wish I'd taken the time to find another Returns door nearby. "Now, on the door, I want you to imagine a white circle, filled in.

And behind the door, I want you to imagine a room filled with light. Nothing but light. Can you see it?"

The girl nods.

"Okay. Open your eyes." I push myself up. "Let's go find your door."

"But there are so many," she whispers.

I smile. "It will be an adventure."

She reaches out and takes my hand. I stiffen on instinct, even though I know her touch is simply that, a touch, so unlike the wave of thought and feeling that comes with grazing a living person's skin. She may be full of memories, but I can't see them. Only the Librarians in the Archive know how to read the dead.

Emma looks up at me, and I give her hand a small squeeze and lead her back around the corner and down the hall, trying to retrace my steps. As we weave through the Narrows, I wonder what made her wake up. The vast majority of names on my list are children and teens, restless but not necessarily bad—just those who died before they could fully live. What kind of kid was she? What did she die of? And then I hear Da's voice, warning about curiosity. I know there's a reason Keepers aren't taught to read Histories. To us, their pasts are irrelevant.

I feel Emma's hand twist nervously in mine.

"It's okay," I say quietly as we reach another hall of unmarked doors. "We'll find it." I hope. I haven't exactly had a wealth of time to learn the layout of this place, but just as I'm starting to fidget too, we turn onto another corridor, and there it is.

Emma pulls free and runs up to the door, stretching her small fingers over the chalk circle. They come away white as I get the key in the lock and turn, and the Returns door opens, showering us both in brilliant light. Emma gasps.

For a moment, there is nothing but light. Like I promised.

"See?" I say, pressing my hand against her back and guiding her forward, over the threshold and into Returns.

Emma is just turning back to see why I haven't followed her when I close my eyes and pull the door firmly shut between us. There's no crying, no pounding on the door; only a deathly quiet from the other side. I stand there for several moments with my key in the lock, something like guilt fluttering behind my ribs. It fades as fast. I remind myself that Returning is merciful. Returning puts the Histories back to sleep, ends the nightmare of their ghostly waking. Still, I hate the fear that laces the younger eyes when I lock them in.

I sometimes wonder what happens in Returns, how the Histories go back to the lifeless bodies on the Archive shelves. Once, with this boy, I stayed to see, waited in the doorway of the infinite white (I knew better than to step inside). But nothing happened, not until I left. I know because I finally closed the door, only for a second, a beat, however long it takes to lock and then unlock, and when I opened it again, the boy was gone.

I once asked the Librarians how the Histories got out. Patrick said something about doors opening and closing. Lisa said the Archive was a vast machine, and all machines had glitches, gaps. Roland said he had no idea.

I suppose it doesn't matter *how* they get out. All that matters is they do. And when they do, they must be found. They must go back. Case open, case closed.

I push off the door and dig the slip of Archive paper from my pocket, checking to make sure Emma's name is gone. It is. All that's left of her is a hand-shaped smudge in the white chalk.

I redraw the circle and turn toward home.

THREE

"**G**ET WHAT YOU WANTED from the car?" asks Dad as
I walk in.

He spares me the need to lie by flashing the car keys, which I
neglected to take. Never mind that, judging by the low light through
the window and the fact that every inch of the room behind him is
covered with boxes, I was gone way too long. I quietly curse the
Narrows and the Archive. I've tried wearing a watch, but it's useless.
Doesn't matter how it's made—the moment I leave the Outer, it
stops working.

So now I get to pick: truth or lie.

The first trick to lying is to tell the truth as often as possible. If
you start lying about everything, big and small, it becomes impossible to keep things straight, and you'll get caught. Once suspicion is
planted it becomes exponentially harder to sell the next lie.

I don't have a clean record with my parents when it comes to
lying, from sneaking out to the occasional inexplicable bruise—some
Histories don't want to be Returned—so I have to tread carefully,
and since Dad paved the way for truth, I roll with it. Besides, sometimes a parent appreciates a little honesty, confidentiality. It makes
them feel like the favorite.

"This whole thing," I say, slumping against the doorway, "it's a lot
of change. I just needed some space."

"Plenty of that here."

"I know," I say. "Big building."

"Did you see all seven floors?"

"Only got to five." The lie is effortless, delivered with an ease that would make Da proud.

I can hear Mom several rooms away, the sounds of unpacking overlapped with radio music. Mom hates quiet, fills every space with as much noise and movement as possible.

"See anything good?" asks Dad.

"Dust." I shrug. "Maybe a ghost or two."

He offers a conspiratorial smile and steps aside to let me pass.

My chest tightens at the sight of the boxes exploding across every spare inch of the room. About half of them just say STUFF. If Mom was feeling ambitious, she scribbled a small list of items beneath the word, but seeing as her handwriting is virtually illegible, we won't know what's in each box until we actually open it. Like Christmas. Except we already own everything.

Dad's about to hand me a pair of scissors when the phone rings. I didn't know we had a phone yet. Dad and I scramble to find it among the packing materials, when Mom shouts, "Kitchen counter by the fridge," and sure enough, there it is.

"Hello?" I answer, breathless.

"You disappoint me," says a girl.

"Huh?" Everything is too strange too fast, and I can't place the voice.

"You've been in your new residence for hours, and you've already forgotten me."

Lyndsey. I loosen.

"How do you even know this number?" I ask. "*I* don't know this number."

"I'm magical," she says. "And if you'd just get a cell . . ."

"I have a cell."

"When's the last time you charged it?"

I try to think.

"Mackenzie Bishop, if you have to think about it, it's been too long."

I want to deliver a comeback, but I can't. I've never needed to charge the phone. Lyndsey is—was—my next door neighbor for ten years. Was—is—my best friend.

"Yeah, yeah," I say, wading through the boxes and down a short hall. Lyndsey tells me to hold and starts talking to someone else, covering the phone with her hand so all I hear are vowels.

At the end of the hall there's a door with a Post-it note stuck to it. There's a letter on it that vaguely resembles an *M*, so I'm going to assume this is my room. I nudge the door open with my foot and head inside to find more boxes, an unassembled bed, and a mattress.

Lyndsey laughs at something someone says, and even sixty miles away, through a phone and her muffled hand, the sound is threaded with light. Lyndsey Newman is made of light. You see it in her blond curls, her sun-kissed skin, and the band of freckles across her cheeks. You feel it when you're near her. She possesses this unconditional loyalty and the kind of cheer you start to suspect no longer exists in the world until you talk to her. And she never asks the wrong questions, the ones I can't answer. Never makes me lie.

"You there?" she asks.

"Yeah, I'm here," I say, nudging a box out of the way so I can reach the bed. The frame leans against the wall, the mattress and box spring stacked on the floor.

"Has your mom gotten bored yet?" Lyndsey asks.

"Sadly, not yet," I say, collapsing onto the bare mattress.

Ben was madly in love with Lyndsey, or as in love as a little boy can get. And she adored him. She's the kind of only child who dreams of siblings, so we just agreed to share. When Ben died, Lyndsey only got brighter, fiercer. An almost defiant kind of optimism. But when my parents told me we were moving, all I could think was, *What about Lynds? How can she lose us both?* The day I told her about the move, I saw her strength finally waver. Something slipped inside her, and she faltered. But moments later, she was back. A nine-out-of-ten smile— but still, wider than what anyone in my house had been able to muster.

"You should convince her to open up an ice cream parlor in some awesome beachside town. . . ." I slide my ring to the edge of my finger, then roll it back over my knuckle as Lynds adds, "Oh, or in, like, Russia. Get out, see the world at least."

Lyndsey has a point. My parents may be running, but I think they're scared of running so far they can't look back and see what they've left. We're only an hour from our old home. Only an hour from our old lives.

"Agreed," I say. "So when are you going to come crash in the splendor that is the Coronado?"

"Is it incredible? Tell me it's incredible."

"It's . . . old."

"Is it haunted?"

Depends on the definition of haunted, really. *Ghost* is just a term used by people who don't know about Histories.

"You're taking an awfully long time to answer that, Mac."

"Can't confirm ghosts yet," I say, "but give me time."

I can hear her mother in the background. "Come on, Lyndsey. Mackenzie might have the luxury of slacking, but you don't."

Ouch. *Slacking.* What would it feel like to slack? Not that I can argue my case. The Archive might take issue with my exposing them just to prove that I'm a productive teen.

"Ack, sorry," says Lyndsey. "I need to go to practice."

"Which one?" I tease.

"Soccer."

"Of course."

"Talk soon, okay?" she says.

"Yeah."

The phone goes dead.

I sit up and scan the boxes piled around the bed. They each have an *M* somewhere on the side. I've seen *M*'s, and *A*'s (my mother's name is Allison) and *P*'s (my father's name is Peter) around the living room, but no *B*'s. A sick feeling twists my stomach.

"Mom!" I call out, pushing up from the bed and heading back down the hall.

Dad is hiding out in a corner of the living room, a box cutter in one hand and a book in the other. He seems more interested in the book.

"What's wrong, Mac?" he asks without looking up. But Dad didn't do this. I know he didn't. He might be running, too, but he's not leading the pack.

"Mom!" I call again. I find her in her bedroom, blasting some talk show on the radio as she unpacks.

"What is it, love?" she asks, tossing hangers onto the bed.

When I speak, the words come out quiet, as if I don't want to ask. As if I don't want to know.

"Where are Ben's boxes?"

There is a very, very long pause. "Mackenzie," she says slowly. "This is about fresh starts—"

"Where are they?"

"A few are in storage. The rest . . ."

"You didn't."

"Colleen said that sometimes change requires drastic—"

"You're going to blame your therapist for throwing out Ben's

25

stuff? Seriously?" My voice must have gone up, because Dad appears behind me in the doorway. Mom's expression collapses, and he goes to her, and suddenly I'm the bad guy for wanting to hold on to something. Something I can read.

"Tell me you kept some of it," I say through gritted teeth.

Mom nods, her face still buried in Dad's collar. "A small box. Just a few things. They're in your room."

I'm already in the hall. I slam my door behind me and push boxes out of the way until I find it. Shoved in a corner. A small *B* on one side. It's little bigger than a shoe box.

I slice the clear packing tape with Da's key, and turn the box over on the bed, spreading all that's left of Ben across the mattress. My eyes burn. It's not that Mom didn't keep anything, it's that she kept the wrong things. We leave memories on objects we love and cherish, things we use and wear down.

If Mom had kept his favorite shirt—the one with the *X* over the heart—or any of his blue pencils—even a stub—or the mile patch he won in track, the one he kept in his pocket because he was too proud to leave it at home, but not proud enough to put it on his backpack . . . but the things scattered on my bed aren't really his. Photos she framed for him, graded tests, a hat he wore once, a small spelling trophy, a teddy bear he hated, and a cup he made in an art class when he was only five or six.

I tug off my ring and reach for the first item.

Maybe there's something.

There has to be something.

Something.

Anything.

• • •

"It's not a party trick, Kenzie," you snap.

I drop the bauble and it rolls across the table. You are teaching me how to read—things, not books—and I must have made a joke, given the act a dramatic flair.

"There's only one reason Keepers have the ability to read things," you say sternly. "It makes us better hunters. It helps us track down Histories."

"It's blank anyway," I mutter.

"Of course it is," you say, retrieving the trinket and turning it over between your fingers. "It's a paperweight. And you should have known the moment you touched it."

I could. It had the telltale hollow quiet. It didn't hum against my fingers. You hand me back my ring, and I slip it on.

"Not everything holds memories," you say. "Not every memory's worth holding. Flat surfaces—walls, floors, tables, that kind of thing—they're like canvases, great at taking in images. The smaller the object, the harder it is for it to hold an impression. But," you add, holding up the paperweight so I can see the world distorted in the glass, "if there is a memory, you should be able to tell with a brush of your hand. That's all the time you'll have. If a History makes it into the Outer—"

"How would they do that?" I ask.

"Kill a Keeper? Steal a key? Both." You cough, a racking, wet sound. "It's not easy." You cough again, and I want to do something to help; but the one time I offered you water, you growled that water wouldn't fix a damn thing unless I meant to drown you with it. So now we pretend the cough isn't there, punctuating your lectures.

"But," you say, recovering, "if a History does get out, you have to track them down, and fast. Reading surfaces has to be second nature. This gift is not a game, Kenzie. It's not a magic trick. We read the past for one reason, and one alone. To hunt."

I know what my gift is for, but it doesn't stop me from sifting through every framed photo, every random slip of paper, every piece of sentimental junk Mom chose, hoping for even a whisper, a hint of a memory of Ben. And it doesn't matter anyway because they're all useless. By the time I get to the stupid art camp cup, I'm desperate. I pick it up, and my heart flutters when I feel the subtle hum against my fingertips, like a promise; but when I close my eyes—even when I reach past the hum—there's nothing but pattern and light, blurred beyond readability.

I want to pitch the cup as hard as I can against the wall, add another scratch. I'm actually about to throw it when a piece of black plastic catches my eye, and I realize I've missed something. I let the cup fall back on the bed and retrieve a pair of battered glasses pinned beneath the trophy and the bear.

My heart skips. The glasses are black, thick-rimmed, just frames, no lenses, and they're the only thing here that's *really* his. Ben used to put them on when he wanted to be taken seriously. He'd make us call him Professor Bishop, even though that was Dad's name, and Dad never wore glasses. I try to picture Ben wearing them. Try to remember the exact color of his eyes behind the frames, the way he smiled just before he put them on.

And I can't.

My chest aches as I wrap my fingers around the silly black frames. And then, just as I'm about to set the glasses aside, I feel it, faint and far away and yet right there in my palm. A soft hum, like a bell trailing off. The tone is feather-light, but it's there, and I close my eyes, take a slow, steadying breath, and reach for the thread of memory. It's too thin and it keeps slipping through my fingers, but finally I catch it. The dark shifts behind my eyes and lightens into gray, and the gray twists from a flat shade into shapes, and from shapes into an image.

There's not even enough memory to make a full scene, only a kind of jagged picture, the details all smeared away. But it doesn't matter, because Ben is there—well, a Ben-like shape—standing in front of a Dad-like shape with the glasses perched on his nose and his chin thrust out as he looks up and tries not to smile because he thinks that only frowns are taken seriously, and there's just enough time for the smudged line of his mouth to waver and crack into a grin before the memory falters and dissolves back into gray, and gray darkens to black.

My heart hammers in my ears as I clutch the glasses. I don't have to rewind, guide the memory back to the start, because there's only one sad set of images looping inside these plastic frames; and sure enough, a moment later the darkness wobbles into gray, and it starts again. I let the stilted memory of Ben loop five times—each time hoping it will sharpen, hoping it will grow into a scene instead of a few smudged moments—before I finally force myself to let go, force myself to blink, and it's gone and I'm back in a box-filled bedroom, cradling my dead brother's glasses.

My hands are shaking, and I can't tell if it's from anger or sadness or fear. Fear that I'm losing him, bit by bit. Not just his face—that started to fade right away—but the marks he made on the world.

I set the glasses by my bed and return the rest of Ben's things to their box. I'm about to put my ring back on when a thought stops me. *Marks.* Our last house was new when we moved in. Every scuff was ours, every nick was ours, and all of them had stories.

Now, as I look around at a room filled not only with boxes but plenty of its own marks, I want to know the stories behind them. Or rather, a part of me wants to know those stories. The other part of me thinks that's the worst idea in the world, but I don't listen to that part. Ignorance may be bliss, but only if it outweighs curiosity. *Curiosity is a gateway drug to sympathy,* Da's warning echoes in my head, and I know, I know; but there are no Histories here to feel sympathy *for.* Which is exactly why the Archive wouldn't approve. They don't approve of any form of recreational reading.

But it's *my* talent, and it's not like a little light goes off every time I use it. Besides, I've already broken the rule once tonight by reading Ben's things, so I might as well group my infractions. I clear a space on the floor, which gives off a low thrum when my fingertips press against the boards. Here in the Outer, the floors hold the best impressions.

I reach, and my hands begin to tingle. The numbness slides up my wrists as the line between the wall and my skin seems to dissolve. Behind my closed eyes, the room takes shape again, the same and yet different. For one thing, I see myself standing in it, just like I was a few moments ago, looking down at Ben's box. The color's been bleached out, leaving a faded landscape of memory, and the whole picture is faint, like a print in sand, recent but already fading.

I get my footing in the moment before I begin to roll the memory backward.

It plays like a film in reverse.

Time spins away and the room fills up with shadows, there and gone and there and gone, so fast they overlap. Movers. Boxes disappear until the space is bare. In a matter of moments, the scene goes dark. Empty. But not ended. Vacant. I can feel the older memories beyond the dark. I rewind faster, searching for more people, more stories. There's nothing, nothing, and then the memories flicker up again.

Broad surfaces hold on to every impression, but there are two kinds—those burned in by emotion and those worn in by repetition—and they register differently. The first is bold, bright, defined. This room is full of the second kind—dull, long periods of habit worn into the surfaces, years pressed into a moment more like a photo than a film. Most of what I see are faded snapshots: a dark wooden desk and a wall of books, a man walking like a pendulum back and forth between the two; a woman stretched out on a couch; an older couple. The room flares into clarity during a fight, but by the time the woman has slammed the door, the scene fades back into shadow, and then dark again.

A heavy, lasting dark.

And yet, I can feel something past it.

Something bright, vivid, promising.

The numbness spreads up my arms and through my chest as I press my hands flush against the floorboards, reaching through the span of black until a dull ache forms behind my eyes and the darkness finally gives way to light and shape and memory. I've pushed too hard, rewound too far. The scenes skip back too fast, a blur, spiraling out of my control so that I have to drag time until it slows, lean into it until it shudders to a stop around me.

When it does, I'm kneeling in a room that is my room and isn't.

I'm about to continue backward, when something stops me. On the floor, a few feet in front of my hands, is a drop of something blackish, and a spray of broken glass. I look up.

At first glance it's a pretty room, old-fashioned, delicate, white furniture with painted flowers . . . but the covers on the bed are askew, the contents of the dresser shelf—books and baubles—are mostly toppled.

I search for a date, the way Da taught me—bread crumbs, book-marks, in case I ever need to come back to this moment—and find a small calendar propped on the table, the word MARCH legible, but no year. I scan for other temporal markers: a blue dress, bright for the faded memory, draped over a small corner chair. A black book on the side table.

A sinking feeling spreads through me as I roll time forward, and a young man stumbles in. The same slick and blackish stuff is splashed across his shirt, painted up his arms to the elbows. It drips from his fingers, and even in the faded world of the memory, I know it's blood.

I can tell by the way he looks down at his skin, as if he wants to crawl out of it.

He sways and collapses to his knees right beside me, and even though he can't touch me, even though I'm not here, I can't help but shuffle back, careful to keep my hands on the floor, as he wraps his stained arms around his shirt. He can't be much older than I am, late teens, dark hair combed back, strands escaping into his eyes as he rocks back and forth. His lips move, but voices rarely stick to memories, and all I hear is a *hushushush* sound like static.

"Mackenzie," calls my mother. The sound of her voice is dis-torted, vague and bent by the veil of memory.

The man stops rocking and gets to his feet. His hands return to his sides, and my gut twists. He's covered in blood, but it's not his. There are no cuts on his arms or his chest. One hand looks sliced up, but not enough to bleed this much.

So whose blood is it? And whose *room* is it? There's that dress, and I doubt that the furniture, dappled with tiny flowers, belongs to him, but—

"Mackenzie," my mother calls again, closer, followed by the sound of a doorknob turning. I curse, open my eyes, and jerk my hands up from the floor, the memory vanishing, replaced by a room full of boxes and a dull headache. I'm just getting to my feet when Mom comes barging in. Before I can get the silver band out of my pocket and around my finger, she wraps me in a hug.

I gasp, and suddenly it's not just noise but *cold cavernous cold hollowed out too bright be bright screaming into pillow until I can't breathe be bright smallest bedroom packing boxes with B crossed out it still shows couldn't save him should have been there should have* before I can shove her tangled stream of consciousness out of my head. I try to force a wall between us, a shaky mental version of the ring's barrier. It is fragile as glass. Pushing back worsens the headache, but at least it blocks out my mother's cluttered thoughts.

I'm left feeling nauseous as I pull away from her hug and maneuver my ring back on to my finger, and the last of the noise drops out.

"Mackenzie. I'm sorry," she says, and it takes a moment for me to orient myself in the present, to realize that she isn't apologizing for that hug, that she doesn't know *why* I hate being touched. To remember that the boy I just saw covered in blood isn't here but years in the past, and that I'm safe and still furious with Mom for throwing away Ben's things. I want to stay furious, but the anger is dulling.

"It's okay," I say. "I understand." Even though it's not okay and I don't understand, and Mom should be able to see that. But she can't.

She sighs softly and reaches out to tuck a stray lock of hair behind my ear, and I let her, doing my best not to tense beneath her touch.

"Dinner's ready," she says. As if everything is normal. As if we're home instead of in a cardboard fortress in an old hotel room in the city, trying to hide from my brother's memories. "Come set the table?"

Before I can ask if she even knows where the table is, she guides me into the living room, where she and Dad have somehow cleared a space between the boxes. They've erected our dining table and arranged five cartons of Chinese food in a kind of bouquet in the center.

The table is the only piece of furniture assembled, which makes us look like we're dining on an island made of packing material. We eat off dishes dug out of a box with a surprisingly informative label: KITCHEN——FRAGILE. Mom coos about the Coronado, and Dad nods and offers canned monosyllables of support; and I stare down at my food and see blurred Ben-like shapes whenever I close my eyes, so I wage a staring contest with the vegetables.

After dinner I put Ben's box in the back of my closet, along with two labeled DA. I packed those myself, offered to make space for them, mostly because I was worried Mom would finally get rid of his things if I didn't find room. I never thought she'd get rid of Ben's. I keep out the silly blue bear, which I set beside the bed, and balance Ben's black glasses on its button nose.

I try to unpack, but my eyes keep drifting back to the center of the room, to the floor where the bloodstained boy collapsed. When I pushed the boxes aside, I could almost make out a few dark stains on the wood, and now it's all I can see each time I look at the floor. But who knows if the stains were drops of his blood. Not *his* blood, I remember. *Someone's.* I want to read the memory again—well, part of me wants to; the other part isn't so eager, at least not on my first night in this room—but Mom keeps finding excuses to come in, half the time not even knocking, and if I'm going to read this, I'd like to avoid another interruption when I do it. It'll have to wait until morning.

I dig up sheets and make my bed, squirming at the thought of sleeping in here with whatever happened, even though I know it was years and years and years ago. I tell myself it's silly to be scared, but I still can't sleep.

My mind swims between Ben's blurred shape and the blood-stained floor, twisting the two memories until Ben is the one surrounded by broken glass, looking down at his red-drenched self. I sit up. My eyes go to the window, expecting to see my yard, and just beyond it the brick side of Lyndsey's house, but I see a city, and in that moment I wish I were home. I wish I could lean out my window and see Lyndsey lounging on her roof, watching stars. Late at night was the only time she let herself be lazy, and I could tell she felt rebellious for stealing even a few minutes. I used to sneak home from the Narrows—three streets over and two up behind the butcher shop—and climb up beside her, and she never asked me where I'd been. She'd stare up at the stars and start talking, pick up midsentence as if I'd been there with her the whole time. As if everything were perfectly normal.

Normal.

A confession: sometimes I dream of being normal. I dream about this girl who looks like me and talks like me, but isn't me. I know she's not, because she has this open smile and she laughs too easily, like Lynds. She doesn't have to wear a silver ring or a rusted key. She doesn't read the past or hunt the restless dead. I dream of her doing mundane things. She sifts through a locker in a crowded school. She lounges poolside, surrounded by girls who swim and talk to her while she flips through silly magazines. She sits engulfed in pillows and watches a movie, a friend tossing up pieces of popcorn for her to catch in her mouth. She misses almost every time.

She throws a party.

She goes to a dance.

She kisses a boy.

And she's so . . . happy.

M. That's what I call her, this normal, nonexistent me.

It's not that I've never done those things, kissed or danced or just "hung out." I have. But it was put-on, a character, a lie. I am so good at it—lying—but I can't lie to myself. I can pretend to be M; I can wear her like a mask. But I can't *be* her. I'll never be her.

M wouldn't see blood-covered boys in her bedroom.

M wouldn't spend her time scouring her dead brother's toys for a glimpse of his life.

The truth is, I know why Ben's favorite shirt wasn't in the box, or his mile patch, or most of his pencils. He had those things with him the day he died. Had the shirt on his back and the patch in his pocket and the pencils in his bag, just like any normal day. Because it was a normal day, right up until the point a car ran a red light two blocks from Ben's school just as he was stepping from the curb.

And then drove away.

What do you do when there *is* someone to blame, but you know you'll never find them? How do you close the case the way the cops do? How do you move on?

Apparently you don't move on; you just move away.

I just want to see him. Not a Ben-like shape, but the real thing. Just for a moment. A glimpse. The more I miss him, the more he seems to fade. He feels so far away, and holding on to empty tokens—or half-ruined ones—won't bring him any closer. But I know what will.

I'm up, on my feet and swapping pajamas for black pants and a long-sleeved T-shirt, donning my usual uniform. My Archive paper sits on the side table, unfolded and blank. I pocket it. I don't care if there are no names. I'm not going to the Narrows. I'm going through them.

To the Archive.

FOUR

BEYOND THE BEDROOM, the apartment is still, but as
I slip into the hall I see a faint line of light along the bottom of
my parents' door. I hold my breath. Hopefully Dad just fell asleep
with his reading light on. The house key hangs like a prize on a hook
by the front door. These floors are so much older than the ones in
our last house that with every step I expect to be exposed, but I
somehow make it to the key without a creak, and slide it from the
hook. All that's left is the door. The trick is to let go of the handle
by degrees. I get through, ease **3F** shut, and turn to face the third-
floor hall.

And stop.

I'm not alone.

Halfway down the corridor a boy my age is leaning against the
faded wallpaper, right beside the painting of the sea. He's staring up
at the ceiling, or past it, the thin black wire from his headphones
tracing a line over his jaw, down his throat. I can hear the whisper of
music from here. I take a soundless step, but still he rolls his head,
lazily, to look at me. And he smiles. Smiles like he's caught me cheating, caught me sneaking out.

Which, in all fairness, he has.

His smile reminds me of the paintings here. I don't think any of
them are hung straight. One side of his mouth tilts up like that, like
it's not set level. He has several inches of spiked black hair, and I'm
pretty sure he's wearing eyeliner.

He closes his eyes and leans his head back against the wall as if to say, *I never saw you.* But that smile stays, and his conspiratorial silence doesn't change the fact that he's standing between me and my brother, his back where the Narrows door should be, the keyhole roughly in the triangle of space between the crook of his arm and his shirt.

And for the first time I'm thankful the Coronado is so old, because I need that second door. I do my best to play the part of a normal girl sneaking out. The pants and long sleeves in the middle of summer complicate the image, but there's nothing to be done about that now, and I keep my chin up as I wander down the hall toward the north stairs (turning back toward the south ones would only be suspicious).

The boy's eyes stay closed, but his smile quirks as I pass by. Odd, I think, vanishing into the stairwell. The stairs run from the top floor down to the second, where they spill me out onto the landing of the grand staircase, which forms a cascade into the lobby. A ribbon of burgundy fabric runs over the marble steps like a tongue, and when I make my way down, the carpet emits small plumes of dust.

Most of the lights have been turned off, and in the strange semi-darkness, the sprawling room at the base of the stairs is draped in shadows. A sign on the far wall whispers CAFÉ in faded cursive. I frown and turn my attention back to the side of the staircase where I first saw the crack. Now the papered wall is hidden in the heavy dark between two lights. I step into the darkness with it, running my fingers over the fleur-de-lis pattern until I find it. The ripple. I pocket my ring and pull Da's key from around my neck, using my other hand to trace down the crack until I feel the groove of the key-hole. I slot the key and turn, and a moment after the metallic click, a thread of light traces the outline of the door against the stairs.

The Narrows sigh around me as I enter, humid breath and words so far away they've bled to sounds and then to hardly anything. I start down the hall, key in hand, until I find the doors I marked before, the filled white circle that designates Returns, and to its right, the hollow one that leads to the Archive.

I pause, straighten, and step through.

The day I become a Keeper, you hold my hand.

You *never* hold my hand. You avoid touch the way I'm quickly learning to, but the day you take me to the Archive, you wrap your weathered fingers around mine as you lead me through the door. We're not wearing our rings, and I expect to feel it, the tangle of memories and thoughts and emotions coming through your skin, but I feel nothing but your grip. I wonder if it's because you're dying, or because you're so good at blocking the world out, a concept I can't seem to learn. Whatever the reason, I feel nothing but your grip, and I'm thankful for it.

We step into a front room, a large, circular space made of dark wood and pale stone. An antechamber, you call it. There is no visible source of light, and yet the space is brightly lit. The door we came through appears larger on this side than it did in the Narrows, and older, worn.

There is a stone lintel above the Archive door that reads SERVAMUS MEMORIAM. A phrase I do not know yet. Three vertical lines, the mark of the Archive, separate the words, and a set of Roman numerals runs beneath. Across the room a woman sits behind a large desk, writing briskly in a ledger, a QUIET PLEASE sign propped at the edge of her table. She sees us and sets her pen down fast enough to suggest that we're expected.

My hands are shaking, but you tighten your grip.

"You're gold, Kenzie," you whisper as the woman gestures over her shoulder at a massive pair of doors behind her, flung open and back like wings. Through them I can see the heart of the Archive, the atrium, a sprawling chamber marked by rows and rows and rows of shelves. The woman does not stand, does not go with us, but watches us pass with a nod and a whispered, cordial "Antony."

You lead me through.

There are no windows because there is no outside, and yet above the shelves hangs a vaulted ceiling of glass and light. The place is vast and made of wood and marble, long tables running down the center like a double spine, with shelves branching off to both sides like ribs. The partitions make the cavernous space seem smaller, cozier. Or at least fathomable.

The Archive is everything you told me it would be: *a patchwork . . . wood and stone and colored glass, and all throughout, a sense of peace.*

But you left something out.

It is beautiful.

So beautiful that, for a moment, I forget the walls are filled with bodies. That the stacks and the cabinets that compose the walls, while lovely, hold Histories. On each drawer an ornate brass cardholder displays a placard with a neatly printed name, a set of dates. It's so easy to forget this.

"Amazing," I say, too loud. The words echo, and I wince, remembering the sign on the Librarian's desk.

"It is," a new voice replies softly, and I turn to find a man perched on the edge of a table, hands in pockets. He's an odd sight, built like a stick figure, with a young face but old gray eyes and dark hair that sweeps across his forehead. His clothes are normal enough—a sweater and slacks—but his dark pants run right into a pair of bright red Chucks, which makes me smile. And yet there's a sharpness to his eyes, a coiled aspect to his stance. Even if I passed him on the street instead of here in the Archive, I'd know right away that he was a Librarian.

"Roland," you say with a nod.

"Antony," he replies, sliding off from the table. "Is this your choice?"

The Librarian is talking about *me*. Your hand vanishes from mine, and you take a step back, presenting me to him. "She is."

Roland arches a brow. But then he smiles. It's a playful smile, a warm one.

"This should be fun." He gestures to the first of the ten wings branching off the atrium. "If you'll follow me . . ." And with that, he walks away. You walk away. I pause. I want to linger here. Soak up the strange sense of quiet. But I cannot stay.

I am not a Keeper yet.

There is a moment, as I pass into the circular antechamber of the Archive and my eyes settle on the Librarian seated behind the desk—a man I've never seen before—when I feel lost. A strange fear takes hold, simple and deep, that my family moved too far away, that I've crossed some invisible boundary and stepped into another branch of the Archive. Roland assured me it wouldn't happen, that each branch is responsible for hundreds of miles of city, suburb, country, but still the panic washes through me.

I look over my shoulder at the lintel above the door, the familiar SERVAMUS MEMORIAM etched there. According to two semesters of Latin (my father's idea), it means "We Protect the Past." Roman numerals run beneath the inscription, so small and so many that they seem more like a pattern than a number. I asked once, and was told that that was the branch number. I still cannot read it, but I've memorized the pattern, and it hasn't changed. My muscles begin to uncoil.

"Miss Bishop."

The voice is calm, quiet, and familiar. I turn back toward the desk to see Roland coming through the set of doors behind it, tall and slim as ever—he hasn't aged a day—with his gray eyes and his easy grin and his red Chucks. I let out a breath of relief.

"You can go now, Elliot," he says to the man seated behind the desk, who stands with a nod and vanishes back through the doors.

Roland takes a seat and kicks his shoes up onto the desk. He digs in the drawers and comes up with a magazine. Last month's issue of some lifestyle guide I brought him. Mom subscribed to them for a while, and Roland insists on staying as much in the loop as possible when it comes to the Outer. I know for a fact he spends most of his time skimming new Histories, watching the world through their lives. I wonder if boredom prompts him to it, or if it's more. Roland's eyes are tinged with something between pain and longing.

He misses it, I think; the Outer. He's not supposed to. Librarians commit to the Archive in every way, leaving the Outer behind for their term, however long they choose to stay, and he's told me himself that being promoted is an honor, to have all that time and knowledge at your fingertips, to protect the past—SERVAMUS MEMORIAM and

43

all—but if he misses sunrises, or oceans, or fresh air, who can blame him? It's a lot to give up for a fancy title, a suspended life cycle, and an endless supply of reading material.

He holds the magazine toward me. "You look pale."

"Keep it," I say, still a little shaken. "And I'm fine. . . ." Roland knows how scared I am of losing this branch—some days I think the constancy of coming here is all that's keeping me sane—but it's a weakness, and I know it. "Just thought for a moment I'd gone too far."

"Ah, you mean Elliot? He's on loan," says Roland, digging a small radio from a drawer and setting it beside the QUIET PLEASE sign. Classical music whispers out, and I wonder if he plays it just to annoy Lisa, who takes the signs as literally as possible. "A transfer. Wanted a change of scenery. So, what brings you to the Archive tonight?"

I want to see Ben. I want to talk to him. I need to be closer. I'm losing my mind.

"Couldn't sleep," I say with a shrug.

"You found your way here fast enough."

"My new place has *two* doors. Right in the building."

"Only two?" he teases. "So, are you settling in?"

I trace my fingers over the ancient ledger that sits on the table. "It's got . . . character."

"Come now, the Coronado's not so bad."

It creeps me out. Something horrible happened in my bedroom. These are weak thoughts. I do not share them.

"Miss Bishop?" he prompts.

I hate the formality when it comes from the other Librarians, but for some reason I don't mind it from Roland. Perhaps because he seems on the verge of winking when he speaks.

"No, it's not so bad," I say at last with a smile. "Just old."

"Nothing wrong with old."

"You'd know," I say. It's a running line. Roland refuses to tell me how long he's been here. He can't be that old, or at least he doesn't look it—one of the perks is that, as long as they serve, they don't age—but whenever I ask him about his life *before* the Archive, his years hunting Histories, he twists the topic, or glides right over it. As for his years as Librarian, he's equally vague. I've heard Librarians work for ten or fifteen years before retiring—just because the age doesn't show doesn't mean they don't feel older—but with Roland, I can't tell. I remember his mentioning a Moscow branch, and once, absently, Scotland.

The music floats around us.

He returns his shoes to the floor and begins to straighten up the desk. "What else can I do for you?"

Ben. I can't dance around it, and I can't lie. I need his help. Only Librarians can navigate the stacks. "Actually . . . I was hoping—"

"Don't ask me for that."

"You don't even know what I was going to—"

"The pause and the guilty look give you away."

"But I—"

"Mackenzie."

The use of my first name makes me flinch.

"Roland. Please."

His eyes settle on mine, but he says nothing.

"I can't find it on my own," I press, trying to keep my voice level.

"You shouldn't find it at all."

"I haven't asked you in weeks," I say. *Because I've been asking Lisa instead.*

Another long moment, and then finally Roland closes his eyes in a slow, surrendering blink. His fingers drift to a notepad the same size and shape as my Archive paper, and he scribbles something on it. Half a minute later, Elliot reappears, his own pad of paper at his side. He gives Roland a questioning look.

"Sorry to call you back," says Roland. "I won't be gone long."

Elliot nods and silently takes a seat. The front desk is never left unattended. I follow Roland through the doors and into the atrium. It's dotted with Librarians, and I recognize Lisa across the way, her black bob disappearing down a side hall toward older stacks. But otherwise I do not look up at the arching ceiling and its colored glass, do not marvel at the quiet beauty, do not linger, in case any pause in my step makes Roland change his mind. I focus on the stacks as he leads me to Ben.

I've tried to memorize the route—to remember which of the ten wings we go down, to note which set of stairs we take, to count the lefts and rights we make through the halls—but I can never hold the pattern in my head, and even when I think I have, it doesn't work out the next time. I don't know if it's me, or if the route changes. Maybe they reorder the shelves. I think of how I used to arrange movies: one day best to worst, the next by color, the next title . . . Everyone in these stacks died in the branch's jurisdiction, but beyond that, there doesn't seem to be a consistent method of filing. In the end, only Librarians can navigate these stacks.

Today Roland leads me through the atrium, then down the sixth wing, through several smaller corridors, across a courtyard, and up a short set of wooden steps before finally coming to a stop in a spacious reading room. A red rug covers most of the floor, and chairs are tucked into corners; but it is, for the most part, a grid of drawers.

Each drawer's face is roughly the size of a coffin's end.

Roland brings his hand gently against one. Above his fingers I can see the white placard in its copper holder. Below the copper holder is a keyhole.

And then Roland turns away.

"Thank you," I whisper as he passes.

"Your key won't work," he says.

"I know."

"It's not him," he adds softly. "Not really."

"I know," I say, already stepping up to the drawer. My fingers hover over the name.

BISHOP, BENJAMIN GEORGE
2003–2013

FIVE

I **TRACE MY FINGERS** over the dates, and it is last year again and I'm sitting in one of those hospital chairs that look like they might actually be comfortable but they're not because there's nothing comfortable about hospitals. Da has been gone three years. I am fifteen now, and Ben is ten, and he's dead.

The cops are talking to Dad and the doctor is telling Mom that Ben died on impact, and that word—*impact*—makes me turn and retch into one of the hospital's gray bins.

The doctor tries to say there wasn't time to feel it, but that's not true. Mom feels it. Dad feels it. I feel it. I feel like my skeleton is being ripped through my skin, and I wrap my arms around my ribs to hold it in. I walked with him, all the way to the corner of Lincoln and Smith like always, and he drew a stick-figure Ben on my hand like always and I drew a stick-figure Mac on his like always and he told me it didn't even look like a human being and I told him it wasn't and he told me I was weird and I told him he was late for school.

I can see the black scribble on the back of his hand through the white sheet. The sheet doesn't rise and fall, not one small bit, and I can't take my eyes off it as Mom and Dad and the doctors talk and there is crying and words and I have neither because I'm focusing on the fact that I will see him again. I twist my ring, a spot of silver above black fingerless knit gloves that run to my elbows because I cannot cannot cannot look at the stick-figure Ben on the back of my hand. I twist the ring and run my thumb over the grooves and tell myself that it's okay. It's not okay, of course.

Ben is ten and he's dead. But he's not gone. Not for me.

Hours later, after we get home from the hospital, three weak instead of four strong, I climb out my window and run down dark streets to the Narrows door in the alley behind the butcher's.

Lisa is on duty at the desk in the Archive, and I ask her to take me to Ben. When she tries to tell me that it's not possible, I order her to show me the way; and when she still says no, I take off running. I run for hours through the corridors and rooms and courtyards of the Archive, even though I have no idea where I'm going. I run as if I'll just know where Ben is, the way the Librarians know where things are, but I don't. I run past stacks and columns and rows and walls of names and dates in small black ink.

I run forever.

I run until Roland grabs my arm and shoves me into a side room, and there on the far wall halfway up, I see his name. Roland lets go of me long enough to turn and close the door, and that's when I see the keyhole beneath Ben's dates. It's not even the same size or shape as my key, but I still rip the cord from my throat and force the key in. It doesn't turn. Of course it doesn't turn. I try again and again.

I bang on the cabinet to wake my brother up, the metallic sound shattering the precious quiet, and then Roland is there, pulling me away, pinning my arms back against my body with one hand, muffling my shouts with the other.

I have not cried at all, not once.

Now I sink down to the floor in front of Ben's cabinet—Roland's arms still wrapped around me—and sob.

. . .

I sit on the red rug with my back to Ben's shelf, tugging my sleeves over my hands as I tell my brother about the new apartment, about Mom's latest project and Dad's new job at the university. Sometimes when I run out of things to tell Ben, I recite the stories Da told me. This is how I pass the night, time blurring at the edges.

Sometime later, I feel the familiar scratch against my thigh, and dig the list from my pocket. The careful cursive announces:

Thomas Rowell. 12.

I pocket the list and sink back against the shelves. A few minutes later I hear the soft tread of footsteps, and look up.

"Shouldn't you be at the desk?" I ask.

"Patrick's shift now," says Roland, nudging me with a red Chuck. "You can't stay here forever." He slides down the wall beside me. "Go do your job. Find that History."

"It's my second one today."

"It's an old building, the Coronado. You know what that means."

"I know, I know. More Histories. Lucky me."

"You'll never make Crew talking to a shelf."

Crew. The next step above Keeper. Crew hunt in pairs, tracking down and returning the Keeper-Killers, the Histories who manage to get out through the Narrows and into the real world. Some people stay Keepers their whole lives, but most shoot for Crew. The only thing higher than Crew is the Archive itself—the Librarian post—though it's hard to imagine why someone would give up the thrill of the chase, the game, the fight, to catalog the dead and watch lives through other people's eyes. Even harder to imagine is that every Librarian was a fighter first; but somewhere under his sleeves, Roland bears marks of Crew just like Da did. Keepers have the marks, too, the three lines, but carved into our rings. Crew marks are carved into skin.

"Who says I want to make Crew?" I challenge, but there's not much fight behind it.

Da worked Crew until Ben was born. And then he went back to being a Keeper. I never met his Crew partner, and he never talked about her, but I found a photo of them after he died. The two of them shoulder to shoulder except for a sliver of space, both wearing smiles that don't quite reach their eyes. They say Crew partners are bonded by blood and life and death. I wonder if she forgave him for leaving.

"Da gave it up," I say, even though Roland must already know.

"Do you know why?" he asks.

"Said he wanted a life. . . ." Keepers who don't go Crew split into two camps when it comes to jobs: those who enter professions benefited by an understanding of objects' pasts, and those who want to get as far away from pasts as possible. Da must have had a hard time letting go, because he became a private detective. They used to joke in his office, so I heard, that he had sold his hands to the devil, that he could solve a crime just by touching things. "But what he meant was, he wanted to stay alive. Long enough to groom me, anyway."

"He told you that?" asks Roland.

"Isn't it my job," I say, "to know without being told?"

Roland doesn't answer. He is twisting around to look at Ben's name and date. He reaches up and runs a finger over the placard with its clean black print—letters and numbers that should be worn to nothing now, considering how often I touch them.

"It's strange," says Roland, "that you always come to see Ben, but never Antony."

I frown at the use of Da's real name. "Could I see him if I wanted to?"

"Of course not," says Roland in his official Librarian tone before sliding back into his usual warmth. "But you can't see Ben, either, and it never stops you from trying."

I close my eyes, searching for the right words. "Da is etched so clearly in my memory, I don't think I could forget anything about him even if I tried. But with Ben, it's only been a year and I'm already forgetting things. I keep forgetting things, and it terrifies me."

Roland nods but doesn't answer, sympathetic but resolute. He can't help me. He *won't*. I've come to Ben's shelf two dozen times in the year since he died, and Roland has never given in and opened it. Never let me see my brother.

"Where is Da's shelf, anyway?" I ask, changing the subject before the tightness in my chest grows worse.

"All members of the Archive are kept in Special Collections."

"Where is that?"

Roland arches an eyebrow, but nothing more.

"Why are they kept separately?"

He shrugs. "I don't make the rules, Miss Bishop."

He gets to his feet and offers me his hand. I hesitate.

"It's okay, Mackenzie," he says, taking my hand; and I feel nothing. Librarians are pros at walling off thoughts, blocking out touch. Mom touches me and I can't keep her out, but Roland touches me and I feel blind, deaf, normal.

We start walking.

"Wait," I say, turning back to Ben's shelf. Roland waits as I pull the key from around my neck and slip it into the hole beneath my brother's card. It doesn't turn. It never turns.

But I never stop trying.

• • •

I'm not supposed to be here. I can see it in their eyes.

And yet here I am, standing before a table in a large chamber off the atrium's second wing. The room is marble-floored and cold, and there are no bodies lining the walls, only ledgers, and the two people on the other side of the table speak a little louder, unafraid to wake the dead. Roland takes his seat beside them.

"Antony Bishop," says the man on the end. He has a beard and small, sharp eyes that scan a paper on the table. "You are here to name your . . ." He looks up, and the words trail off. "Mr. Bishop, you do realize there is an age requirement. Your granddaughter is not eligible for another"—he consults a folder, coughs—"four years."

"She's up for the trial," you say.

"She'll never pass," says the woman.

"I'm stronger than I look," I say.

The first man sighs, rubs his beard. "What are you doing, Antony?"

"She is my only choice," answers Da.

"Nonsense. You can name Peter. Your son. And if, in time, Mackenzie is willing and able, she will be considered—"

"My son is not fit."

"Maybe you don't do him justice—"

"He's bright, but he's got no violence in him, and he wears his lies. He's not fit."

"Meredith, Allen," says Roland, steepling his fingers. "Let's give her a chance."

The bearded man, Allen, straightens. "Absolutely not."

My eyes flick to Da, craving a sign, a nod of encouragement, but he stares straight ahead.

"I can do it," I say. "I'm not the only choice. I'm the best."

Allen's frown deepens. "I beg your pardon?"

"Go home, little girl," says Meredith with a dismissive wave.

You warned me they would resist. You spent weeks teaching me how to hold my ground.

I stand taller. "Not until I've had my trial."

Meredith makes a strangled sound of dismay, but Allen cuts in with, *"You're. Not. Eligible."*

"Make an exception," I say. Roland's mouth quirks up. It bolsters me. "Give me a chance."

"You think this is a sport? A club?" snaps Meredith, and then her eyes dart to you. "What could you possibly be thinking, bringing a child into this—"

"I think it's a job," I cut in, careful to keep my voice even. "And I'm ready for it. Maybe you think you're protecting me, or maybe you think I'm not strong enough—but you're wrong."

"You are an unfit candidate. And that is the end of it."

"It would be, Meredith," says Roland calmly, "if you were the only person on this panel."

"I really can't condone this. . . ." says Allen.

I'm losing them, and I can't let that happen. If I lose them, I lose you. "I think I'm ready, and you think I'm not. Let's find out who's right."

"Your composure is impressive." Roland stands up. "But you are aware that not all Histories can be won with words." He rounds the table. "Some are troublesome." He rolls up his sleeves. "Some are violent."

The other two Librarians are still trying to get a word in,

but I don't hear them. My focus is on Roland. Da told me to be ready for anything, and it's a good thing he did, because between one moment and the next, Roland's posture shifts. It's subtle—his shoulders loosen, knees unlock, hands curl toward fists—but I see the change a fraction before he attacks. I dodge the first punch, but he's fast, faster even than Da, and before I can strike back, a red Chuck connects with my chest, sending me to the floor. I roll back and over into a crouch, but by the time I look up, he's gone.

I hear him the instant before his arm wraps around my throat, and manage to get one hand between us so I don't choke. He pulls back and up, my feet leaving the ground, but the table is there and I get my foot on top and use it as leverage, pushing up and off, twisting free of his arm as I flip over his head and land behind him. He turns and I kick, aiming for his chest; but he's too tall and my foot connects with his stomach, where he catches it. I brace myself, but he doesn't strike back.

He laughs and lets go of my shoe, sagging against the desk. The other two Librarians sit behind him looking shocked, though I can't tell if they're more surprised by the fight or Roland's good humor.

"Mackenzie," he says, smoothing his sleeves. "Do you want this job?"

"She does not truly know what this job *is*," says Meredith. "So she has a mouth on her and she can dodge a punch. She is a child. And this is a joke—"

Roland holds up a hand, and Meredith goes quiet. Roland's eyes do not leave mine. They are warm. Encouraging. "Do you want this?" he asks again.

I do want it. I want you to stay. Time and disease are taking you from me. You've told me, made it clear, this is the only way I can keep you close. I will not lose that.

"I do," I answer evenly.

Roland straightens. "Then I approve the naming."

Meredith makes a stifled sound of dismay.

"She held composure against *you*, Meredith, and that is something," says Roland, and finally his smile breaks through. "And as for her fighting, I'm in the best position to judge, and I say she has merit." He looks past me, to you. "You've raised quite a girl, Antony." He glances over at Allen. "What do you say?"

The bearded Librarian raps his fingers on the table, eyes unfocused.

"You can't actually be considering . . ." mutters Meredith.

"If we do this, and she proves herself unfit in any way," says Allen, "she will forfeit the position."

"And if she proves unfit," adds Meredith, "you, Roland, will remove her yourself."

Roland smiles at the challenge.

I step forward. "I understand," I say, as loud as I dare.

Allen stands slowly. "Then I approve the naming."

Meredith glowers for a moment before standing too. "I am overruled, and as such, I must approve the naming."

Only then does your hand come to rest against my shoulder. I can feel your pride in your fingertips. I smile.

I will show them all.

For you.

SIX

I YAWN AS ROLAND leads me back through the Archive. I've been here for hours, and I can tell I'm running out of night. My bones ache from sitting on the floor, but it was worth it for a little time with Ben.

Not Ben, I know. Ben's *shelf*.

I roll my shoulders, stiff from leaning so long against the stacks, as we wind back through the corridors and into the atrium. Several Librarians dot the space, busy with ledgers and notepads and even, here and there, open drawers. I wonder if they ever sleep. I look up at the arched stained glass, darker now, as if there were a night beyond. I take a deep breath and am starting to feel better, calmer, when we reach the front desk.

A man with gray hair, black glasses, and a stern mouth behind a goatee is waiting for us. Roland's music has been shut off.

"Patrick," I say. Not my favorite Librarian. He's been here nearly as long as I have, and we rarely see eye to eye.

The moment he catches sight of me, his mouth turns down.

"Miss Bishop," he scolds. He's Southern, but he's tried to obliterate his drawl by being curt, cutting his consonants sharp. "We try to discourage such recurrent disobedience."

Roland rolls his eyes and claps Patrick on the shoulder.

"She's not doing any harm."

Patrick glares at Roland. "She not doing any good, either. I should report her to Agatha." His gaze swivels to me. "Hear that? I should report you."

I don't know who this Agatha is, but I'm fairly certain I don't want to know.

"Restrictions exist for a reason, Miss Bishop. There are no visiting hours. Keepers do not attend to the Histories here. You are not to enter the stacks without *good* reason. Are we clear?"

"Of course."

"Does that mean you will cease this futile and rather tiresome pursuit?"

"Of course not."

A cough of a laugh escapes from Roland, along with a wink. Patrick sighs and rubs his eyes, and I can't help but feel a bit victorious. But when he reaches for his notepad, my spirits sink. The last thing I need is a demerit on my record. Roland sees the gesture, too, and brings his hand down lightly on Patrick's arm.

"On the topic of attending to Histories," he offers, "don't you have one to catch, Miss Bishop?"

I know a way out when I see it.

"Indeed," I say, turning toward the door. I can hear the two men talking in low, tense voices, but I know better than to look back.

I find and return twelve-year-old Thomas Rowell, fresh enough out that he goes without many questions, let alone a fight. Truth be told, I think he is just happy to find someone in the dark halls, as opposed to some*thing*. I spend what's left of the night testing every door in my territory. By the time I finish, the halls—and several spots on the floor—are scribbled over with chalk. Mostly X's, but here and there a circle. I work my way back to my two numbered doors, and discover a third, across from them, that opens with my key.

Door I leads to the third floor and the painting by the sea. Door II leads to the side of the stairs in the Coronado lobby.

But Door III? It opens only to black. To nothing. So why is it unlocked at all? Curiosity pulls me over the threshold, and I step through into the dark and close the door behind me. The space is quiet and cramped and smells of dust so thick, I taste it when I breathe in. I can reach out and touch walls to my left and right, and my fingers encounter a forest of wooden poles leaning against them. A closet?

As I slide my ring back on and resume my awkward groping in the dark, I feel the scratch of a new name on the list in my pocket. Again? Fatigue is starting to eat into my muscles, drag at my thoughts. The History will have to wait. When I step forward, my shin collides with something hard. I close my eyes to cut off the rising claustrophobia; finally, my hands find the door a few feet in front of me. I sigh with relief and turn the metal handle sharply.

Locked.

I could go back into the Narrows through the door behind me and take a different route, but a question persists: Where *am* I? I listen closely, but no sound reaches me. Between the dust in this closet and the total lack of anything resembling noise from the opposite side, I think I must be somewhere abandoned.

Da always said there were two ways to get through any locked door: by key or by force. And I don't have a key, so . . . I lean back and lift my boot, resting the sole against the wood of the door. Then I slide my shoe left until it butts up against the metal frame of the handle. I withdraw my foot several times, testing to make sure I have a clear shot before I take a breath and kick.

Wood cracks loudly, and the door moves; but it takes a second strike before it swings open, spilling several brooms and a bucket out onto a stone floor. I step over the mess to survey the room and find a sea of sheets. Sheets covering counters and windows and sections of floor, dirty stone peering out from the edges of the fabric. A switch is set into the wall several feet away, and I wade through the sheets until I get near enough to flip the lights.

A dull buzzing fills the space. The light is faint and glaring at the same time, and I cringe and switch it back off. Daylight presses in with a muted glow against the sheets over the windows—it's later than I thought—and I cross the large space and pull a make-shift curtain down, showering dust and morning light on everything. Beyond the windows is a patio, a set of suspiciously familiar awnings overhead—

"I see you've found it!"

I spin to find my parents ducking under a sheet into the room. "Found what?"

Mom gestures to the space, its dust and sheets and counters and broken broom closet, as if showing me a castle, a kingdom.

"Bishop's Coffee Shop."

For a moment, I am genuinely speechless.

"The café sign in the lobby didn't give it away?" asks Dad.

Maybe if I'd come through the lobby. I am still dazed by the fact that I've stepped out of the Narrows and into my mother's newest pet project, but years of lying have taught me to never look as lost as I feel, so I smile and roll with it.

"Yeah, I had a hunch," I say, rolling up the window sheet. "I woke up early, so I thought I'd take a look."

It's a weak lie, but Mom isn't even listening. She's flitting around the space, holding her breath like a kid about to blow out birthday candles as she pulls down sheets. Dad is still looking at me rather intently, eyes panning over my dark clothes and long sleeves, all the pieces that don't line up.

"So," I say brightly, because I've learned if I can talk louder than he can think, he tends to lose his train of thought, "you think there's a coffee machine under one of these sheets?"

He brightens. My father needs coffee like other men need food, water, shelter. Between the three classes he's set to teach in the history department and the ongoing series of essays he's composing, caffeine ranks way up there on his priority list. I think that's all it took for Mom to get him to support her dream of owning a café: an invitation from the local university and the guarantee of continuous coffee. Brew it, and they will come.

I try to stifle a yawn.

"You look tired," he says.

"So do you," I shoot back, pulling the covers off a piece of equipment that might have once been a grinder. "Hey, look."

"Mackenzie . . ." he presses, but I flip the switch and the machinery does in fact grind to life, drowning him out with a horrible sound like it's eating its own parts, chewing up metal nuts and bolts and gobbling down air. Dad winces, and I turn it off, sounds of mechanic agony echoing through the room, along with a smell like burning toast.

I can't help glancing back at the cleaning closet, and Mom must have followed my gaze, because she heads straight for it.

"I wonder what happened here," she says, swinging the door on its broken hinges.

I shrug and head over to an oven, or something like it, and pry the door open. The inside is stale and scorched.

"I was thinking that we should bake some muffins," says Mom.

"'Welcome' muffins!" She doesn't say it like *welcome* but rather like *Welcome!* "You know, to let everyone know that we're here. What do you think, Mac?"

In response, I nudge the oven door, and it swings shut with a bang. Something dislodges and lands with a *tinktinktinktink* across the stone before rolling up against her shoe.

Her smile doesn't even falter. It turns my stomach, her sickly-sweet-everything's-better-than-fine pep. I've seen the inside of her mind, and this is all a stupid act. I lost Ben. I shouldn't have to lose her, too. I want to shake her. I want to say . . . But I don't know what to say. I don't know how to get through to her, how to make her see that she's making it worse.

So I tell the truth. "I think it's falling apart."

She misses my meaning. Or steps around it. "Well then," she says cheerfully, stooping to fetch the metal bolt, "we'll just use the apartment oven until we get this one in shape."

With that she turns on her heel and bobs away. I look around, hoping to find Dad, and with him some measure of sympathy or at least commiseration, but he's on the patio, staring up at the awnings.

"Chop chop, Mackenzie," Mom calls through the door. "You know what they say—"

"I'm pretty sure no one says it but you—"

"Up with the sun and just as bright."

I look out the window at the light and cringe, and follow.

We spend the rest of the morning in the apartment baking *Welcome!* muffins. Or rather, Dad ducks out to run some errands, and Mom makes muffins while I do my best to look busy. I could really use a few hours of sleep and a shower, but every time I make a move to leave, Mom thinks up something for me to do. While she's distracted pulling a fresh batch from the oven, I dig the Archive list from my pocket. But when I unfold it, it's blank.

Relief washes over me before I remember that there should be a name on it. I could swear I felt the scrawl of a new History being added when I was stuck in the café closet. I must have imagined it. Mom sets the tray of muffins on the counter as I refold the paper and tuck it away. She drapes a cloth over them, and out of nowhere I remember Ben standing on his toes to peek beneath the towel and steal a pinch even though it was always too hot and he burned his fingers. It's like being punched in the chest, and I squeeze my eyes shut until the pain passes.

I beg off baking duty for five minutes just to change clothes—mine smell like Narrows air and Archive stacks and café dust. I pull on jeans and a clean shirt, but my hair refuses to work with me, and I finally dig a yellow bandana out of a suitcase and fashion a head-band, trying to hide the mess as best I can. I'm tucking Da's key beneath my collar when I catch sight of the dark spots on my floor and remember the bloodstained boy.

I kneel down, trying to tune out the clatter of baking trays beyond the door as I slide off my ring and bring my fingertips to the floorboards. The wood hums against my hands as I close my eyes and reach, and—

"Mackenzie!" Mom calls out.

I sigh and blink, pushing up from the floor. I straighten just as Mom knocks briskly on the door. "Have I lost you?"

"I'm coming," I say, shoving the ring back on as her footsteps fade. I cast one last glance at the floor before I leave. In the kitchen, the muffins are already wrapped in blossoms of cellophane. Mom is filling a basket, chattering about the residents, and that's when I get an idea.

Da was a Keeper, but he was a detective too, and he used to say you could learn as much by asking people as by reading walls. You get different answers. My room has a story to tell, and as soon as I can get an ounce of privacy, I'll read it; but in the meantime, what better way to learn about the Coronado than to ask the people in it?

"Hey, Mom," I say, pushing up my sleeves, "I'm sure you've got a ton of work to do. Why don't you let me deliver those?"

She pauses and looks up. "Really? Would you?" She says it like she's surprised I'm capable of being nice. Yes, things have been rocky between us, and I'm offering to help because it helps me—but still.

She tucks the last muffin into a basket and nudges it my way.

"Sure thing," I say, managing a smile, and her resulting one is so genuine that I almost feel bad. Right up until she wraps me in a hug and the high-pitched strings and slamming doors and crackling paper static of her life scratches against my bones. Then I just feel sick.

"Thank you," she says, tightening her grip. "That's so sweet." I can barely hear the words through the grating noise in my head.

"It's . . . really . . . nothing," I say, trying to picture a wall between us, and failing. "Mom," I say at last, "I can't breathe." And then she laughs and lets go, and I'm left dizzy but free.

"All right, get going," she says, turning back to her work. I've never been so happy to oblige.

I start down the hall and peel the cellophane away from a muffin, hoping Mom hasn't counted them out as I eat breakfast. The basket swings back and forth from the crook of my arm, each muffin individually wrapped and tagged. *BISHOP'S*, the tag announces in careful script. A basket of conversation starters.

I focus on the task at hand. The Coronado has seven floors—one lobby and six levels of housing—with six apartments to a floor, **A** through **F**. That many rooms, odds are someone knows something.

And maybe someone does, but nobody seems to be home. There's the flaw in both my mother's plans and in mine. Late morning on a weekday, and what do you get? A lot of locked doors. I slip out of **3F** and head down the hall. **3E** and **3D** are both quiet, **3C** is vacant (according to a small slip of paper stuck to the door), and though I can hear the muffled sounds of life in **3B**, nobody answers. After several aggressive knocks on **3A**, I'm getting frustrated. I drop muffins on each doorstep and move on.

One floor up, it's more of the same. I leave the baked goods at **4A**, **B**, and **C**. But as I'm heading away from **4D**, the door swings open.

"Young lady," comes a voice.

I turn to see a vast woman filling the door frame like bread in a loaf pan, holding the small, cellophaned muffin.

"What is your name? And what is this adorable little treat?" she asks. The muffin looks like an egg, nested in her palm.

"Mackenzie," I say, stepping forward. "Mackenzie Bishop. My family just moved in to **3F**, and we're renovating the coffee shop on the ground floor."

"Well, lovely to meet you, Mackenzie," she says, engulfing my hand with hers. She is made up of low tones and bells and the sound of ripping fabric. "My name is Ms. Angelli."

"Nice to meet you." I slide my hand free as politely as possible.

And then I hear it. A sound that makes my skin crawl. A faint meow behind the wall that is Ms. Angelli, just before a clearly desperate cat finds a crack somewhere near the woman's feet and squeezes through, tumbling out into the hall. I jump back.

"Jezzie," scorns Ms. Angelli. "Jezzie, come back here." The cat is small and black, and stands just out of reach, gauging its owner. And then it turns to look at me.

I hate cats.

Or really, I just hate *touching* them. I hate touching any animal, for that matter. Animals are like people but fifty times worse—all id, no ego; all emotion, no rational thought—which makes them a bomb of sensory input wrapped in fur.

Ms. Angelli frees herself from the doorway and nearly stumbles forward onto Jezzie, who promptly flees toward me. I shrink back, putting the basket of muffins between us.

"Bad kitty," I growl.

"Oh, she's a lover, my Jezzie." Ms. Angelli bends to fetch the cat, which is now pretending to be dead, or is paralyzed by fear, and I get a glimpse of the apartment behind her.

Every inch is covered with antiques. My first thought is, *Why would anyone have so much stuff?*

"You like old things," I say.

"Oh, yes," she says, straightening. "I'm a collector." Jezzie is now tucked under her arm like a clutch purse. "A bit of an artifact historian," she says. "And what about you, Mackenzie—do you like old things?"

Like is the wrong word. They're *useful*, since they're more likely to have memories than new things.

"I like the Coronado," I say. "That counts as an old thing, right?"

"Indeed. A wonderful old place. Been around more than a century, if you can believe it. Full of history, the Coronado."

"You must know all about it, then."

Ms. Angelli fidgets. "Ah, a place like this, no one can know everything. Bits and pieces, really, rumors and tales . . ." She trails off.

"Really?" I brighten. "Anything unusual?" And then, worried my enthusiasm is a little too strong, I add, "My friend is convinced a place like this has to have a few ghosts, skeletons, secrets."

Ms. Angelli frowns and sets Jezzie back in the apartment, and locks the door.

"I'm sorry," she says abruptly. "You caught me on my way out. I've got an appraisal in the city."

"Oh," I fumble. "Well, maybe we could talk more, some other time?"

"Some other time," she echoes, setting off down the hall at a surprising pace.

I watch her go. She clearly knows *something*. It never really occurred to me that someone would know and not want to share. Maybe I should stick to reading walls. At least they can't refuse to answer.

My footsteps echo on the concrete stairs as I ascend to the fifth floor, where not a single person appears to be home. I leave a trail of muffins in my wake. Is this place empty? Or just unfriendly? I'm already reaching for the stairwell door at the other end of the hall when it swings open abruptly and I run straight into a body. I stumble back, steadying myself against the wall, but I'm not fast enough to save the muffins.

I cringe and wait for the sound of the basket tumbling, but it never comes. When I look up, a guy is standing there, the basket safely cradled in his arms. Spiked hair and a slanted smile. My pulse skips.

The third-floor lurker from last night.

"Sorry about that," he says, passing me the basket. "No harm, no foul?"

"Yeah," I say, straightening. "Sure."

He holds out his hand. "Wesley Ayers," he says, waiting for me to shake.

I'd rather not, but I don't want to be rude. The basket's in my right hand, so I hold out my left awkwardly. When he takes it, the sounds rattle in my ears, through my head, deafening. Wesley is made like a rock band, drums and bass and interludes of breaking glass. I try to block out the roar, to push back, but that only makes it worse. And then, instead of shaking my hand, he gives a theatrical bow and brushes his lips against my knuckles, and I can't breathe. Not in a pleasant, butterflies-and-crushes way. I literally cannot breathe around the shattering sound and the bricklike beat. My cheeks flush hot, and the frown must have made its way onto my face, because he laughs, misreading my discomfort, and lets go, taking all the noise and pressure with him.

"What?" he says. "That's custom, you know. Right to right, hand-shake. Left to right, kiss. I thought it was an invitation."

"No," I say curtly. "Not exactly." The world is quiet again, but I'm still thrown off and having trouble hiding it. I shuffle past him toward the stairs, but he turns to face me, his back to the hall.

"Ms. Angelli, in Four D," he continues. "She always expects a kiss. It's hard with all the rings she wears." He holds up his left hand, wiggles his fingers. He's got a few of his own.

"Wes!" calls a young voice from an open doorway halfway down the hall. A small, strawberry-blond head pops out of 5C. I want to be annoyed that she didn't answer when I knocked, but I'm still resisting the urge to sit down on the checkered carpet. Wesley makes a point of ignoring her, his attention trained on me. Up close I can confirm that his light brown eyes are ringed with eyeliner.

"What were you doing in the hall last night?" I ask, trying to bury my unease. His expression is blank, so I add, "The third-floor hall. It was late."

"It wasn't *that* late," he says with a shrug. "Half the cafés in the city were still open."

"Then why weren't you in one of them?" I ask.

He smirks. "I like the third floor. It's so . . . yellow."

"Excuse me?"

"It's yellow." He reaches out and taps the wallpaper with a painted black nail. "Seventh is purple. Sixth is blue. Fifth"—he gestures around us—"is clearly red."

I wouldn't go so far as to say it's clearly any color.

"Fourth is green," he continues. "Third is yellow. Like your bandana. Retro. Nice."

I bring a hand up to my hair. "What's second?" I ask.

"It's somewhere between brown and orange. Ghastly."

I almost laugh. "They all look a bit gray to me."

"Give it time," he says. "So, you just move in? Or do you enjoy roaming the halls of apartment buildings, hocking"—he peers into the basket—"baked goods?"

Wes," the girl says again, stamping her foot, but he ignores her pointedly, winking at me. The girl's face reddens, and she disappears into the apartment. A moment later she emerges, weapon in hand.

She sends the book spinning through the air with impressive aim, and I must have blinked, or missed something, because the next minute, Wesley's hand has come up and the book is resting in it. And he's still smiling at me.

"Be right there, Jill."

He brushes the book off and lets it fall to his side while he peers into the muffin basket. "This basket nearly killed me. I feel I deserve compensation." His hand is already digging through the cellophane, past ribbons and tags.

"Help yourself," I say. "You live here, then?"

"Can't say that I do— Oooooh, blueberry." He lifts a muffin and reads the label. "So you are a Bishop, I presume."

"Mackenzie Bishop," I say. "Three F."

"Nice to meet you, Mackenzie," he says, tossing the muffin into the air a few times. "What brings you to this crumbling castle?"

"My mother. She's on a mission to renovate the café."

"You sound so enthused," he says.

"It's just old . . ." *That's enough sharing,* warns a voice in my head. One dark eyebrow arches. "Afraid of spiders? Dust? Ghosts?"

"No. Those things don't worry me." *Everything is loud here, like you.* His smile is teasing, but his eyes are sincere. "Then what?"

I'm spared by Jill, who emerges with another book. Part of me wants to see this Wesley try to stave off a second blow while holding a book and a blueberry muffin, but he turns away, conceding.

"All right, all right, I'm coming, brat." He tosses the first book back to Jill, who fumbles it. And then he casts one last look at me with his crooked smile. "Thanks for the muffin, Mac." He just met me and he's already using a nickname. I'd kick his ass, but there's a slight affection to the way he says it, and for some reason I don't mind.

"See you around."

Several moments after the door to 5C has closed, I'm still standing there when the scratch of letters in my pocket brings me to my senses. I head for the stairs and pull the paper from my jeans.

Jackson Lerner. 16.

This History is old enough that I can't afford to put it off. They slip so much faster the older they get—distress to destruction in a matter of hours; minutes, even. I get back to the third floor, ditching the basket in the stairwell, and pocket my ring as I reach the painting of the sea. I pull the key's cord over my head, wrapping it several times around my wrist as my eyes adjust to make out the keyhole in the faint wall crack. I slot the key and turn. A hollow click; the door floats to the surface, lined in light, and I head back into the forever night of the Narrows.

I close my eyes and press my fingertips against the nearest wall, reaching until I catch hold of the memories, and behind my eyes the Narrows reappear, bleak and bare and grayer, but the same. Time rolls away beneath my touch, but the memory sits like a picture, unchanging, until the History finally flickers in the frame, blink-and-you-miss-it quick. The first time, I *do* miss it, and I have to drag time to a stop and turn it forward, breathing out slow, slow, inching frame by frame until I see him. It goes like *empty empty empty empty empty empty body empty empty*—gotcha. I focus, holding the memory long enough to identify the shape as a teenage boy in a green hoodie—it must be Jackson—and then I nudge the memory forward and watch him walk past from right to left, and turn the first corner. Right.

I blink, the Narrows sharpening around me as I pull back from the wall, and follow Jackson's path around the corner. Then I start again, repeating the process at each turn until I close the gap, until I'm nearly walking in his wake. Just as I'm reading the fourth or fifth wall, I hear *him*, not the muddled sounds of the past but the shuffling steps of a body in the now. I abandon the memory and track the sound down the hall, whipping around the corner, where I find myself face-to-face with—

Myself.

Two distorted reflections of my sharp jaw and my yellow bandana pool in the black that's spreading across the History's eyes, eating up the color as he slips.

Jackson Lerner stands there staring at me with his head cocked, a mop of messy reddish brown hair falling against his cheeks. Beneath his bright green hoodie, he has that gaunt look boys sometimes get in their teens. Like they've been stretched. I take a small step back.

"What the hell's going on here?" he snaps, hands stuffed into his jeans. "This some kind of fun house or something?"

I keep my tone empty, even. "Not really, no."

"Well, it blows," he says, a thin layer of bravado masking the fear in his voice. Fear is dangerous. "I want to get out of here."

He shifts his weight, as solid as flesh and blood on the stained floor. Well, as solid as flesh, anyway. Histories don't bleed. He shifts again, restless, and then his blackening eyes drift down to my hand, to the place where my key dangles from the cord wrapped around my wrist. The metal glints.

"You got a key." Jackson points, gaze following the key's small, swinging movements. "Why don't you just let me out? Huh?"

I can hear the change in tone. Fear twists into anger.

"All right." Da would tell me to stay steady. *The Histories will slip; you can't afford to.* I glance around at the nearest doors.

But they all have chalk X's.

"What are you waiting for?" he growls. "I said, let me out."

"All right," I say again, sliding back. "I'll take you to the right door."

I steal another step away. He doesn't move.

"Just open this one," he says, pointing to the nearest outline, X and all.

"I can't. We need to find one with a white circle and then——"

"Open the damn door!" he yells, lunging for the key around my wrist. I dodge.

"Jackson," I snap, and the fact that I know his name causes him to pause. I try a different approach. "You have to tell me where you want to go. These doors all go to different places. Some don't even open. And some of them do, but the places they lead are very bad."

The anger written across his face fades into frustration, a crease between his shining eyes, a sadness in his mouth. "I just want to go home."

"Okay," I say, letting a small sigh of relief escape. "Let's go home."

He hesitates.

"Follow me," I press. The thought of turning my back on him sends off a slew of warning lights in my head, but the Narrows are too, well, *narrow* for us to pass through side by side. I turn and walk, searching for a white circle. I catch sight of one near the end of the hall, and pick up my pace, glancing back to make sure Jackson is with me.

He's not.

He's stopped, several feet back, and is staring at the keyhole of a door set into the floor. The edge of an X peeks out beneath his shoe.

"Come on, Jackson," I say. "Don't you want to go home?"

He toes the keyhole. "You aren't taking me home," he says.

"I am."

He looks up at me, his eyes catching the thin stream of light coming from the keyhole at his feet. "You don't know where my home is."

That is, of course, a very good point. "No, I don't." A wave of anger washes over his face when I add, "But the doors do."

I point to the one at his feet. "It's simple. The X means it's not your door." I point to the one just ahead, the filled-in circle drawn on its front. "That one, with the chalk circle. That's your door. That's where we're going."

Hope flickers in him, and I might feel bad about lying if I had any choice. Jackson catches up, then pushes past me.

"Hurry up," he says, waiting by the door, running a finger over the chalk as his gaze continues down the hall. I reach out to slide the key into the lock.

"Wait," he says. "What's that?"

I look up. He's pointing at another door, one at the very end of the hall. A white circle has been drawn above the keyhole, large enough to see from here. Damn.

"Jackson—"

He spins on me. "You lied. You're not taking me home." He steps forward, and I step back, away from the door.

"I didn't—"

He doesn't give me a chance to lie again, but lunges for the key. I twist out of the way, catching his sleeved wrist as he reaches out. I wrench it behind his back, and he yelps, but somehow, by some combination of fighter's luck and sheer will, twists free. He turns to run, but I catch his shoulder and force him forward, against the wall.

I keep my arm firmly around his throat, pulling back and up with enough force to make him forget that he is six inches taller than I am, and still has two arms and two legs to fight with.

"Jackson," I say, trying to keep my voice level, "you're being ridiculous. Any door with a white circle can take you—"

And then I see metal, and jump back just in time, the knife in his hand arcing through the air, fast. This is wrong. Histories never have weapons. Their bodies are searched when they're shelved. So where did he get it?

I kick up and send him reeling backward. It only buys a moment, but a moment is long enough to get a good look at the blade. It gleams in the dark, well-kept steel as long as my hand, a hole drilled in the grip so it can be spun. It is a *lovely* weapon. And there is no way it belongs to a punk teen with a worn-out hoodie and a bad attitude.

But whether it's his, or he stole it, or someone gave it to him—a possibility I don't even want to consider—it doesn't change the fact that right now he's the one holding a knife.

And I've got nothing.

SEVEN

I AM ELEVEN, and you are stronger than you look.
You take me out into the summer sun to show me how to
fight. Your limbs are weapons, brutally fast. I spend hours
figuring out how to avoid them, how to dodge, roll, anticipate,
react. It's get out of the way or get hit.

I'm sitting on the ground, exhausted and rubbing my ribs
where you got a touch, even though I saw you try to pull back.

"You said you'd teach me how to fight," I say.

"I am."

"You're only showing me how to defend."

"Trust me. You need to know that first."

"I want to learn how to attack." I cross my arms. "I'm
strong enough."

"Fighting isn't really about using your strength, Kenzie.
It's about using theirs. Histories will always be stronger. Pain
doesn't stick, so you can't hurt them, not really. They don't
bleed, and if you kill them, they don't stay dead. They die,
they come back. You die, you don't."

"Can I have a weapon?"

"No, Kenzie," you snap. "Never carry a weapon. Never
count on anything that's not attached to you. It can be taken.
Now, get back up."

• • •

There are times when I wish I'd broken Da's rules. Like right now, staring at the sharp edge of a knife in the hands of a slipping History. But I don't break Da's rules, not ever. Sometimes I break the Archive's rules, or bend them a bit, but not his. And they must work, because I'm still alive.

For now.

Jackson fidgets with the knife, and I can tell by the way he holds it he's not used to the weapon. Good. Then at least I stand a chance of getting it away from him. I tug the yellow bandana from my hair and pull it tight between my hands. And I force my mouth to smile, because he might have the advantage as far as sharp things go, but even when the game turns physical, it never stops being mental.

"Jackson," I say, pulling the fabric taut. "You don't need to—"

Something moves in the hall beyond him. A shadow there and then gone, a dark shape with a silver crown. Sudden enough to catch my attention, dragging it from Jackson for only a second.

Which is, of course, the second he lunges.

His limbs are longer than mine, and it's all I can do to get out of the way. He fights like an animal. Reckless. But he's holding the knife wrong, too low, leaving a gap on the hilt between his hand and the blade. The next slice comes blindingly quick, and I lean back but hold my ground. I have an idea, but it means getting close, which is always risky when the other person has a knife. He jabs again, and I try to twist my body to get my arms to one side, one above and one below the knife; but I'm not fast enough, and the blade skims my forearm. Pain burns over my skin, but I've almost got this—and sure enough, on the next try he jabs wrong and I dodge right, lifting one arm and lowering the other so the knife slices into the circle of space made by my limbs and the bandana. He sees the trap too late, jerks back; but I swing my hand down, looping the fabric around the knife, the gap on the hilt. I snap it tight and bring my boot to the front of his green hoodie as hard as I can, and he stumbles, losing his hold on the knife.

The fabric goes slack and the blade tumbles into my grip, handle hitting my palm right as he dives forward, tackling me around the waist and sending us both to the floor. He knocks the air from my lungs like a brick to the ribs, and the blade goes skittering into the dark.

At least it's a fair fight now. He might be strong, made stronger by slipping, but he clearly didn't have a grandfather who saw combat training as a bonding opportunity. I free my leg from under him and manage to get my foot against the wall, for once thankful that the Narrows are so narrow. Pushing off, I roll on top of Jackson, just in time to dodge a clumsily thrown fist.

And then I see it on the floor, right above his shoulder.

A keyhole.

I never marked it, so I don't know where it leads, or if my key will even work, but I have to do something. Ripping my wrist and my key free of his grip, I drive the metal teeth down into the gap and turn, holding my breath until I hear it click. I look down into Jackson's wild eyes just before the door falls open, plunging us both downward.

Space changes, suddenly, and instead of falling down we fall forward, sprawling onto the cold marble of the Archive's antechamber floor.

I can see the front desk in the corner of my eye, a QUIET PLEASE sign and a stack of papers and a green-eyed girl looking over it.

"This is not the Returns room," she says, her voice edged with amusement. She has hair the color of sun and sand.

"I realize that," I growl as I try to pin a hissing, cussing, clawing Jackson to the floor. "A little help?"

I've got him down for all of two seconds before he somehow gets his knee and then his shoe between our bodies.

The young Librarian stands up as Jackson uses his boot to pry me off, sending me backward to the hard floor. I'm still on the ground, but Jackson is halfway to his feet when the Librarian rounds the desk and cheerfully plunges something thin and sharp and shining into his back. His eyes widen, and when she twists the weapon there's a noise, like a lock turning or a bone breaking, and all the life goes out of Jackson Lerner's eyes. She withdraws, and he crumples to the floor with the sickening thud of dead weight. I can see now that what she holds is not a weapon exactly, but a kind of key. It's gleaming gold and has a handle and a stem, but no teeth.

"That was fun," she says.

There's something like a giggle in the corners of her voice. I've seen her around the stacks. She always catches my eye because she is so young. Girlish. Librarian is top rank, so the vast majority are older, seasoned. But this girl looks like she's twenty.

I drag myself to my feet. "I need a key like that."

She laughs. "You couldn't handle it. Literally." She holds it out, but the moment my fingers touch the metal, they go pins-and-needles numb. I pull back, and her laugh trails off as the key vanishes into the pocket of her coat.

"Stumble through the wrong door?" she asks just before the large doors behind the desk fly open.

"What is going on?" comes a very different voice. Patrick storms in, the eyes behind his black glasses flicking from the Librarian to Jackson's body on the floor to me.

"Carmen," he says, his attention still leveled on me. "Please take care of that."

The girl smiles and, despite her size, hauls the body up and through

79

a pair of doors built right into the curving walls of the antechamber. I blink. I never noticed those before. And the moment they've closed behind her, I can't seem to focus on them. My eyes roll off.

"Miss Bishop," Patrick says tersely. The room is quiet except for my heavy breathing. "You're bleeding on my floor."

I look down and realize he's right. Pain rolls up my arm as my eyes slide over the place where Jackson's knife cut through fabric and grazed skin. My sleeve is stained red, a narrow line running down my hand and over my key before dripping to the floor. Patrick is gazing distastefully at the drops as they hit the granite.

"Did you have a problem with the doors?" asks Patrick.

"No," I say, aiming for a joke. "The doors were fine. I had a problem with the *History*."

Not even a smile.

"Do you need medical attention?" he asks.

I feel dazed, but I know better than to show it. Certainly not in front of him.

Every branch staffs a medically trained Librarian in the interest of keeping work-related injuries quiet, and Patrick is the man for this branch. If I say yes, then he'll treat me; but he'll also have an excuse to report the incident, and there won't be anything Roland can do to keep it off the books. I don't have a clean record, so I shake my head.

"I'll live." A swatch of yellow catches my eye, and I recover my bandana from the floor and wrap it around the cut. "But I really liked this shirt," I add as lightly as possible.

He frowns and I think he's going to chew me out or report me, but when he speaks it's only to say, "Go clean up."

I nod and turn back to the Narrows, leaving a trail of red behind.

EIGHT

I **AM A MESS.**

I scoured the Narrows, but Jackson's knife was nowhere to be found. As for the strange shadow I saw during the fight, the one with the silvery crown . . . maybe my eyes were playing tricks on me. That happens, now and then, with the ring off. Press against a surface wrong and you can see the present and past at once. Things can get tangled.

I wince, focusing on the task at hand.

The cut on my arm is deeper than I thought, and it bleeds through the gauze before I can get the bandage on. I toss another ruined wrap into the plastic bag currently serving as the bathroom trash bin and run the cut under cool water, digging through the extensive first-aid kit I've assembled over the years. My shirt is sitting in a heap on the floor, and I take in my reflection, the web of fine scars across my stomach and arms, and the bruise blossoming on my shoulder. I am never without the marks of my job.

Pulling my forearm from the water, I dab the cut, finally getting it gauzed and wrapped. Red drops have made a trail along the counter and into the sink.

"I christen thee," I mutter to the sink as I finish bandaging the cut. I take the trash bag and add it to the larger one in the kitchen, making sure all evidence of my first aid is buried, just as Mom appears, a slightly smooshed but still cellophaned muffin in one hand, and the basket in the other. The muffins inside have cooled, a film of condensation fogging up the wrappers. Damn. I knew I forgot something.

"Mackenzie Bishop," she says, dropping her purse on the dining room table, which is the only fully assembled piece of furniture. "What is this?"

"A Welcome muffin?"

She drops the basket with a thud.

"You said you would *deliver* them. Not drop them on people's doormats and leave the basket in the stairwell. And where have you been?" she snaps. "This couldn't have taken you all morning. You can't just disappear. . . ." She's an open book: anger and worry too thinly veiled behind a tight-lipped smile. "I asked for your help."

"I knocked, but nobody was home," I snap back, pain and fatigue tightening around me. "Most people have jobs, Mom. Normal jobs. Ones where they get up and go to the office and come home."

She rubs her eyes, which means that she's been rehearsing whatever she's about to say. "Mackenzie. Look. I was talking to Colleen, and she said that you'd need to grieve in your own way—"

"You're kidding me."

"—and when you add that to your age, and the natural desire for rebellion—"

"Stop." My head is starting to hurt.

"—I know you need space. But you also need to learn discipline. Bishop's is a family business."

"But it wasn't a family *dream*."

She flinches.

I want to be oblivious to the hurt written on her face. I want to be selfish and young and normal. M would be that way. She would need space to grieve. She would rebel because her parents were simply uncool, not because one was wearing a horrifying happy mask and the other was a living ghost. She'd be distant because she was preoccupied with boys or school, not because she's tired from hunting down the Histories of the dead, or distracted by her new hotel-turned-apartment, where the walls are filled with crimes.

"Sorry," I say, adding, "Colleen's right, I guess." The words try to crawl back down my throat. "Maybe I just need a little time to adjust. It's a lot of change. But I didn't mean to bail."

"Where were you?"

"Talking to a neighbor," I say. "Ms. Angelli. She invited me in, and I didn't want to be rude. She seemed kind of lonely, and she had this amazing place full of old stuff, and so I just stayed with her for a while. We had tea, and she showed me her collections."

Da would call that an extrapolation. It's easier than a straight lie because it contains seeds of truth. Not that Mom would be able to tell if I told her a blatant lie, but it makes me feel a fraction less guilty.

"Oh. That was . . . sweet of you," she says, looking wounded because I'd rather have tea with a stranger than talk to her.

"I should have kept better track of time"—and then, feeling guiltier—"I'm sorry." I rub my eyes and begin to lean toward the bedroom. "I'm going to go unpack a little."

"This will be good for us," she promises. "This will be an adventure." But while it sounded cheerful coming from Dad, it leaves her lips like a breath being knocked out of her. Desperate. "I promise, Mac. An adventure."

"I believe you," I say. And because I can tell she wants more, I manage a smile and add, "I love you."

The words taste strange, and as I make my way to my room and then to my waiting bed, I can't figure out why. When I pull the sheet over my head, it hits me.

It's the only thing I said that wasn't a lie.

I'm twelve, six months shy of becoming a Keeper, and Mom is mad at you because you're bleeding. She accuses you of fighting, of drinking, of refusing to age gracefully. You light a cigarette and run your fingers through your shock of peppered hair and let her believe it was a bar fight, let her believe you were looking for trouble.

"Is it hard?" I ask when she storms out of the room. "Lying so much?"

You take a long drag and flick ash into the sink, where you know she'll see it. You're not supposed to smoke anymore.

"Not hard, no. Lying is easy. But it's lonely."

"What do you mean?"

"When you lie to everyone about everything, what's left? What's true?"

"Nothing," I say.

"Exactly."

The phone wakes me.

"Hey, hey," says Lyndsey. "Daily check-in!"

"Hey, Lynds." I yawn.

"Were you sleeping?"

"I'm trying to fulfill your mother's image of me."

"Don't mind her. So, hotel update? Found me any ghosts yet?"

I sit up, swing my legs off the bed. I've got the bloodstained boy in my walls, but I don't think that's really shareable. "No ghosts yet, but I'll keep looking."

"Look harder! A place like that? It's got to be full of creepy things. It's been around for, like, a hundred years."

"How do you know that?"

"I looked it up! You don't think I'd let you move into some haunted mansion without scoping out the history."

"And what did you find?"

"Weirdly, nothing. Like, *suspiciously* nothing. It was a hotel, and the hotel was converted into apartments after World War Two, a big boom time moneywise. The conversion was in a ton of news-papers, but then a few years later the place just falls off the map . . . no articles, nothing."

I frown, getting up from the bed. Ms. Angelli admitted that this place was full of history. So where is it? Assuming *she* can't read walls, how did she learn the Coronado's secrets? And why was she so defensive about sharing them?

"I bet it's like a government conspiracy," Lynds is saying. "Or a witness protection program. Or one of those horror reality films. Have you checked for cameras?"

I laugh, but silently wonder—glancing at the blood-spotted floor—if the truth is worse.

"Have you at least got tenants who look like they belong in a Hitchcock film?"

"Well, so far I've met a morbidly obese antiques hoarder, and a boy who wears eyeliner."

"They call that guyliner," she says.

"Yes. Well." I stretch and head for the bedroom door. "I'd call it stupid, but he's rather nice to look at. I can't tell if the eyeliner makes him attractive, or if he's good-looking in spite of it."

"At least you've *got* nice things to look at."

I step around the ghostly drops on the floor and venture out into the apartment. It's dusk, and none of the lights are on.

"How are *you* doing?" I ask. Lyndsey possesses the gift of normalcy. I bathe in it. "Summer courses? College prep? Learning new languages? New instruments? Single-handedly saving countries?"

Lyndsey laughs. It's so easy for her. "You make me sound like an overachiever."

I feel the scratch of letters and pull the list from my jeans.

Alex King. 13.

"That's because you *are* an overachiever," I say.

"I just like to stay busy."

Come over here, then, I think, pocketing the list. *This place would keep you busy.*

I distinctly hear the thrum of guitar strings. "What's that noise?" I ask.

"I'm tuning, that's all."

"Lyndsey Newman, do you actually have me on speaker just so you can talk and tune a guitar at the same time? You're jeopardizing the sanctity of our conversations."

"Relax. The parents have vacated. Some kind of gala. They left in fancy dress an hour ago. What about yours?"

I find two notes on the kitchen counter.

My mother's reads: *Store! Love, Mom.*

My father's reads: *Checking in at work. —D*

"Similarly out," I say, "but minus the fancy dress and the togetherness."

I retreat to the bedroom.

"The place to yourself?" she says. "I hope you're having a party."

"I can barely hear over the music and drinking games. I better tell them to quiet down before someone calls the cops."

"Talk soon, okay?" she says. "I miss you." She really means it.

"I miss you, Lynds." I mean it too.

The phone goes dead. I toss it onto the bed and stare down at the faded spots on my floor.

Questions eat at me. What happened in this room? Who was the boy? And whose blood was he covered in? Maybe it's not my job, maybe it's an infraction to find out, a misuse of power, but every member of the Archive takes the same oath.

We protect the past. And the way I see it, that means we need to understand it.

And if neither Lyndsey's search engines nor Ms. Angelli are going to tell me anything, I'll have to see for myself. I tug the ring from my finger, and before I can chicken out, I kneel, press my hands to the floor, and reach.

NINE

THERE IS A girl sitting on a bed, knees pulled up beneath her chin.

I run the memories back until I find the small calendar by the bed that reads MARCH, the blue dress on the corner chair, the black book on the table by the bed. Da was right. *Bread crumbs and bookmarks.* My fingers found their way.

The girl on the bed is thin in a delicate way, with light blond hair that falls in waves around her narrow face. She is younger than I am, and talking to the boy with the bloodstained hands, only right now his hands are still clean. Her words are a murmur, nothing more than static, and the boy won't stand still. I can tell by the girl's eyes that she's talking slowly, insistently, but the boy's replies are urgent, punctuated by his hands, which move through the air in sweeping gestures. He can't be much older than she is, but judging by his feverish face and the way he sways, he's been drinking. He looks like he's about to be sick. Or scream.

The girl sees it too, because she slides from the bed and offers him a glass of water from the top of the dresser. He knocks the glass away hard and it shatters, the sound little more than a crackle. His fingers dig into her arm. She pushes him away a few times before he loses his grip and stumbles back into the bed frame. She turns, runs. He's up, swiping a large shard of glass from the floor. It cuts into his hand as he lunges for her. She's at the door when he reaches her, and they tumble into the hall.

I drag my hand along the floor until I can see them through the doorway, and then I wish I couldn't. He's on top of her, and they are a tangle of glass and blood and fighting limbs, her slender bare feet kicking under him as he pins her down.

And then the struggle slows. And stops.

He drops the shard beside her body and staggers to his feet, and I can see her, the lines carved across her arms, the far deeper cut across her throat. The shard pressed into her own palm. He stands over her a moment before turning back toward the bedroom. Toward me. He is covered in blood. *Her* blood. My stomach turns, and I have to resist the urge to scramble away. He is not here. I am not there.

You killed her, I whisper. Who are you? Who is she?

He staggers into the room, and for a moment he breaks, slides into a crouch, rocking. But then he gets back up. He looks down at himself, the glitter of broken glass at his feet, and over at the body, and begins to wipe his bloody hands slowly and then frantically on his bloody shirt. He scrambles over to the closet and yanks a black coat from a hook, forcing it on and pulling it closed. And then he runs, and I'm left staring at the girl's body in the hall.

The blood is soaking into her pale blond hair. Her eyes are open, and in that moment, all I want is to cross to her and close them.

I pull my hands from the floor and open my eyes, and the memory shatters into the now, taking the body with it. The room is my room again, but I still see her in that horrible light-echo way, like she's burned into my vision. I shove my ring on, tripping over half the boxes as I focus on the simple need to get the hell out of this apartment.

I slam the door to **3F** behind me and sag against it, sliding to the floor and pressing my palms to my eyes, breathing into the space between my chest and knees.

Revulsion claws up my throat and I swallow hard and picture Da taking one look at me and laughing through smoke, telling me how silly I look. I picture the council who inducted me seeing straight through the worlds and declaring me unfit. I am not M, I think. Not some silly squeamish girl. I am more. I am a Keeper. I am Da's replacement.

It's not the blood, or even the murder, though both turn my stomach. It's the fact that he *ran*. All I can think is, did he get away? Did he get away with that?

Suddenly I need to move, to hunt, to do *something*, and I get up, steadying myself against the door, and pull the list from my pocket, thankful to have a name.

But the name is gone. The paper is blank.

"You look like you could use a muffin."

I shove the paper back in my jeans and look up to find Wesley Ayers at the other end of the hall, tossing a still-wrapped *Welcome!* muffin up and down like a baseball. I don't feel like doing this right now, like putting on a face and acting normal.

"You still have that?" I ask wearily.

"Oh, I ate mine," he says, heading toward me. "I swiped this one from Six B. They're out of town this week."

I nod.

When he reaches me, his face falls. "You all right?"

"I'm fine," I lie.

He sets the muffin on the carpet. "You look like you need some fresh air."

What I need are answers. "Is there a place here where they keep records? Logs, anything like that?"

Wesley's head tilts when he thinks. "There's the study. Mostly old books, classics, anything that looks, well, like it belongs in a study.

But it might have something. It's kind of the opposite of fresh air, though, and there's this garden I was going to show——"

"Tell you what. Point me to the study, and then you can show me whatever you want."

Wesley's smile lights up his face, from his sharp chin all the way to the tips of his spiked hair. "Deal."

He bypasses the elevator and leads me down the flight of concrete steps to the grand staircase, and from there down into the lobby. I keep my distance, remembering the last time we touched. He's several steps below me, and from this angle, I can just see beneath the collar of his black shirt. Something glints, a charm on a leather cord. I lean, trying to see——

"Where are you going?" comes a small voice. Wesley jumps, grabs his chest.

"Jeez, Jill," he says. "Way to scare a guy in front of a girl."

It takes me several seconds to find Jill, but finally I spot her in one of the leather high-backed chairs in a front corner, reading a book. The book comes up to the bridge of her nose. She skims the pages with sharp blue eyes, and every now and then turns her attention up, as if she's waiting for something.

"He spooks easily," she calls behind her book.

Wesley runs his fingers through his hair and manages a tight laugh. "Not one of my proudest traits."

"You should see what happens when you really surprise him," offers Jill.

"That's enough, brat."

Jill turns a page with a flourish.

Wesley casts a glance back at me and offers his arm. "Onward?"

I smile thinly but decline to take it. "After you," I say.

He leads the way across the lobby. "What are you looking for, anyway?"

"Just wanted to learn about the building. Do you know much about it?"

"Can't say I do." He guides me down a hall on the other side of the grand stairs.

"Here we are," he says, pushing open the door to the study. It's stuffed to the brim with books. A corner desk and a few leather chairs furnish the space, and I scan the spines for anything useful. My eyes trail over encyclopedias, several volumes of poetry, a complete set of Dickens. . . .

"Come on, come on," he says, crossing the room. "Keep up."

"Study first," I say. "Remember?"

"I pointed it out." He gestures to the room as he reaches a pair of doors at the far side of the study. "You can come back later. The books aren't going anywhere."

"Just give me a——"

He flings the doors open. Beyond them, there's a garden flooded with twilight and air and chaos. Wesley steps out onto the moss-covered rocks, and I drag my attention from the books and follow him out.

The dying light lends the garden a glow, shadows weaving through vines, colors dipping darker, deeper. The space is old and fresh at once, and I forget how much I've missed the feel of green. Our old house had a small yard, but it was nothing like Da's place. He had the city at his front but the country at his back, land that stretched out in a wild mass. Nature is constantly growing, changing, one of the few things that can't hold memories. You forget how much clutter there is in the world, in the people and things, until you're surrounded by green. And even if they don't hear and see and feel the past the way

I do, I wonder if normal people feel this too—the quiet.

"'The sun retreats,'" Wes says softly, reverently. "'The day, out-lived, is o'er. It hastens hence and lo, a new world is alive.'"

My eyebrows must be creeping up, because when he glances over his shoulder at me, he gives me his slanted smile.

"What? Don't look so surprised. Beneath this shockingly good hair is something vaguely resembling a brain." He crosses the garden to a stone bench woven over with ivy, and brushes away the tendrils to reveal the words etched into the rock.

"It's *Faust*," he says. "And it's possible I spend a good deal of time here."

"I can see why." It's bliss. If bliss had gone untouched for fifty years. The place is tangled, unkempt. And perfect. A pocket of peace in the city.

Wesley slides onto the bench. He rolls up his sleeves and leans back to watch the streaking clouds, blowing a blue-black chunk of hair from his face.

"The study never changes, but this place is different every moment, and really best at sun fall. Besides"—he waves a hand at the Coronado—"I can give you a proper tour some other time."

"I thought you didn't live here," I say, looking up at the dimming sky.

"I don't. But my cousin, Jill, does, with her mom. Jill and I are both only children, so I try to keep an eye on her. You have any siblings?"

My chest tightens, and for a moment I don't know how to answer. No one's asked that, not since Ben died. In our old town, everyone knew better, skipped straight to pity and condolences. I don't want either from Wesley, so I shake my head, hating myself even as I do, because it feels like I'm betraying Ben, his memory.

"Yeah, so you know how it is. It can get lonely. And hanging around this old place is better than the alternative."

"Which is?" I find myself asking.

"My dad's. New fiancée. Satan in a skirt, and all. So I end up here more often than not." He arches back, letting his spine follow the curve of the bench.

I close my eyes, relishing the feel of the garden, the cooling air and the smell of flowers and ivy. The horror hidden in my room begins to feel distant, manageable, though the question still whispers in my mind: *Did he get away?* I breathe deep and try to push it from my thoughts, just for a moment.

And then I feel Wesley stand and come up beside me. His fingers slide through mine. The noise hits a moment before his rings knock against mine, the bass and beat thrumming up my arm and through my chest. I try to push back, to block him out, but it makes it worse, the sound of his touch crushing even though his fingers are feather-light on mine. He lifts my hand and gently turns it over.

"You look like you lost a fight with the moving equipment," he says, gesturing to the bandage on my forearm.

I try to laugh. "Looks like it."

He lowers my hand and untangles his fingers. The noise fades, my chest loosening by degrees until I can breathe, like coming up through water. Again my eyes are drawn to the leather cord around his neck, the charm buried beneath the black fabric of his shirt. My gaze drifts down his arms, past his rolled sleeves, toward the hand that just let go of mine. Even in the twilight I can see a faint scar.

"Looks like you've lost a couple fights of your own," I say, running my fingers through the air near his hand, not daring to touch. "How did you get that?"

"A stint as a spy. I wasn't much good."

A crooked line runs down the back of his hand. "And that?"

"Scuff with a lion."

Watching Wesley lie is fascinating.

"And that?"

"Caught a piranha bare-handed."

No matter how absurd the tale, he says it steady and simple, with the ease of truth. A scratch runs along his forearm. "And that?"

"Knife fight in a Paris alley."

I search his skin for marks, our bodies drawing closer without touching.

"Dove through a window."

"Icicle."

"Wolf."

I reach up, my fingers hovering over a nick on his hairline. "And this?"

"A History."

Everything stops.

His whole face changes right after he says it, like he's been punched in the stomach. The silence hangs between us.

And then he does an unfathomable thing. He smiles.

"If you were clever," he says slowly, "you would have asked me what a History was."

I am still frozen when he reaches out and brushes a finger over the three lines etched into the surface of my ring, then twists one of his own rings to reveal a cleaner but identical set of lines. The Archive's insignia. When I don't react—because no fluid lie came to me and now it's too late—he closes the gap between us, close enough that I can *almost* hear the bass again, radiating off his skin. His thumb hooks under the cord around my throat and guides my key out from under my shirt. It glints in the twilight. Then he fetches the key from around his own neck.

"There," he says cheerfully. "Now we're on the same page."

"You knew," I say at last.

His forehead wrinkles. "I've known since the moment you came into the hall last night."

"How?"

"Your eyes went to the keyhole. You did a decent job of hiding the look, but I was watching for it. Patrick told me there would be a new Keeper here. Wanted to see for myself."

"Funny, because Patrick didn't tell *me* there was an old one."

"The Coronado isn't really my territory. It hasn't been anyone's for ages. I like to check in on Jill, and I keep an eye on the place while I'm at it. It's an old building, so you know how it goes." He taps a nail against his key. "I even have special access. Your doors are my doors."

"You're the one who cleared my list," I say, the pieces fitting together. "There were names on my list, and they just disappeared."

"Oh, sorry." He rubs his neck. "I didn't even think about that. This place has been shared for so long. They always keep the Coronado doors unlocked for me. Didn't mean any harm."

A moment of quiet hangs between us.

"So," he says.

"So," I say.

A smile begins to creep up the side of Wesley's face.

"What?" I ask.

"Oh, come on, Mac . . ." He blows at a chunk of hair hanging in his face.

"Come on, what?" I say, still sizing him up.

"You don't think it's cool?" He gives up and fixes his hair with his fingers. "To meet another Keeper?"

"I've never met one except for my grandfather." It sounds naive, but it never occurred to me to think of others. I mean, I knew they existed, but out of sight, out of mind. The territories, the branches of the Archive—I think they're all designed to make you feel like an only child. Unique. Or solitary.

"Me either," Wes is saying. "What a broadening experience this is." He squares his shoulders toward me. "My name is Wesley Ayers, and I am a Keeper." He breaks out into a full grin. "It feels good to say it out loud. Try."

I look up at him, the words caught in my throat. I have spent four years with this secret bottled in me. Four years lying, hiding, and bleeding, to hide what I am from everyone I meet.

"My name is Mackenzie Bishop," I say. Four years since Da died, and not a single slip. Not to Mom or Dad, not to Ben, or even to Lynds. "And I am a Keeper."

The world doesn't end. People don't die. Doors don't open. Crew don't pour out and arrest me. Wesley Ayers beams enough for both of us.

"I patrol the Narrows," he says.

"I hunt Histories," I say.

"I return them to the Archive."

It becomes a game, whispered and breathless.

"I hide who I am."

"I fight with the dead."

"I lie to the living."

"I am alone."

And then I get why Wes can't stop smiling, even though it looks silly with his eyeliner and jet-black hair and hard jaw and scars. I am not alone. The words dance in my mind and in his eyes and against our rings and our keys, and now I smile too.

"Thank you," I say.

"My pleasure," he says, looking up at the sky. "It's getting late. I'd better go."

For one silly, nonsensical moment, I'm scared of his leaving, scared he'll never come back and I'll be left with this, this . . . loneliness. I swallow the strange panic and force myself not to follow him to the study door.

Instead I keep still and watch him tuck his key beneath his shirt, roll his ring so the three lines are hidden against his palm. He looks exactly the same, and I wonder if I do too and how that's possible, considering how I feel—like some door in me has been opened and left ajar.

"Wesley," I call after him, instantly berating myself when he stops and glances back at me.

"Good night," I say lamely.

He smiles and closes the gap between us. His fingers brush over my key before they curl around it, and guide it under the collar of my shirt, the metal cold against my skin.

"Good night, Keeper," he says.

And then he's gone.

TEN

I LINGER A MOMENT in the garden after Wes is gone, savoring the taste of our confessions on my tongue, the small defiance of sharing a secret. I focus on the coolness creeping into the air around me, and the hush of the evening.

Da took me onto the stretch of green behind his house once and told me that building walls—blocking out people and their noise— should feel like this. An armor of quiet. Told me that walls were just like a ring but better because they were in my head, and because they could be strong enough to silence anything. If I could just learn to build them.

But I couldn't. I sometimes think that maybe, if I could remember what it felt like, touching people and feeling nothing but skin . . . But I can't, and when I try to block out their noise, it just gets worse, and I feel like I'm in a glass box under the ocean, the sound and pressure cracking in. Da ran out of time to teach me, so all I have are frustrating memories of him wrapping his arm around people without even flinching, making it look so easy, so normal.

I would give anything to be normal.

The thought creeps in, and I force it away. No I wouldn't. I wouldn't give anything. I wouldn't give the bond I had with Da. I wouldn't give the time I have with Ben's drawer. I wouldn't give Roland, and I wouldn't give the Archive, with its impossible light and the closest thing I've ever felt to peace. This is all I have. This is all I am.

I head for the study doors, thinking of the murdered girl and the bloodstained boy. I have a job. SERVAMUS MEMORIAM. I push the doors open, and stiffen when I see the large woman behind the desk in the corner.

"Ms. Angelli."

Her eyebrows inch into a nest of hair I strongly suspect is a wig, and a moment of surprise passes before recognition spreads across her broad face. If she's upset to see me after this morning, she doesn't show it, and I wonder for once if I read too much into her rush to leave. Maybe she really was late for an appraisal.

"Mackenzie Bishop, of the baked goods," she says. Her voice is quieter here in the study, almost reverent. Several large texts are spread before her, the corners of the pages worn. A cup of tea sits nestled in the space between two books.

"What are you reading?" I ask.

"Histories, mostly." I know she only means the kind in books, the *little h* kind, as Da would say. Still, I flinch.

"Where did they all come from?" I ask, gesturing toward the volumes stacked on the table and lining the walls.

"The books? Oh, they appeared over time. A resident took one and left two behind. The study simply grew. I'm sure they stocked it when the Coronado was first converted, leather-bound classics and atlases and encyclopedias. But these days it's a delightful mix of old and new and odd. Just the other night I found a romance novel mixed in with the directories! Imagine."

My pulse skips. "Directories?"

Something nervous shifts in her face, but she points a ringed finger over her shoulder. My eyes skim the walls of books behind her until they land on a dozen or so slightly larger than the rest, more uniform. In the place of a title, each spine has a set of dates.

"They chronicle the residents?" I ask casually, eyes skimming the years. The dates go all the way back to the earliest parts of the past century. The first half of the books are red. The second half are blue.

"They were first used while the Coronado was still a hotel," she explains. "A kind of guestbook, if you will. Those red ones, those are from the hotel days. The blue ones are from the conversion on."

I round the table to the shelf that bears the books' weight. Pulling the most recent one from the wall and flipping through, I see that each directory comprises five years' worth of residential lists, an ornate page dividing each year. I go to the last divider, the most recent year, and turn until I get to the page for the third floor. In the column for **3F**, someone has crossed out the printed word *Vacant* and added *Mr. and Mrs. Peter Bishop* in pencil. Flipping back through, I find that **3F** has been vacant for two years, and was rented before that to a *Mr. Bill Lighton*. I close the book, return it to the shelf, and immediately take up the previous directory.

"Looking for something?" Ms. Angelli asks. There's a subtle tension in her voice.

"Just curious," I say, again searching for **3F**. Still *Mr. Lighton*. Then *Ms. Jane Olinger*. I pause, but I know from reading the walls that it was more than ten years ago, and besides, the girl was too young to be living alone. I reshelve the book and pull the next one down.

Ms. Olinger again.

Before that, *Mr. and Mrs. Albert Locke*. Still not far enough.

Before that, *Vacant*.

Is this how normal people learn the past?

Next, a *Mr. Kenneth Shaw*.

And then I find what I'm looking for. The wall of black, the dead space between most of the memories and the murder. I run my finger down the column.

Vacant.

Vacant.

Vacant.

Not just one set, either. There are whole books of *Vacant*. Ms. Angelli watches me too intently, but I keep pulling the books down until I reach the last blue book, the one that starts with the conversion: 1950 – 54.

The 1954 book is marked *Vacant*, but when I reach the divider marked *1953*, I stop.

3F is missing.

The entire floor is missing.

The entire *year* is missing.

In its place is a stack of blank paper. I turn back through 1952 and 1951. Both are blank. There's no record of the murdered girl. There's no record of *anyone*. Three entire years are just . . . missing. The inaugural year, 1950, is there, but there's no name written under **3F**. What did Lyndsey say? There was nothing on record. *Suspiciously* nothing.

I drop the blue book open on the table, nearly upsetting Ms. Angelli's tea.

"You look a touch pale, Mackenzie. What is it?"

"There are pages missing."

She frowns. "The books are old. Perhaps something fell out. . . ."

"No," I snap. "The years are deliberately blank."

Apartment **3F** sat vacant for nearly two decades after the mysterious missing chunk of time. The murder. It had to have happened in those years.

"Surely," she says, more to herself than to me, "they must be archived somewhere."

"Yeah, I——" And it hits me. "You're right. You're totally right." Whoever did this tampered with evidence in the Outer, but they can't tamper with it in the Archive. I'm already out of the leather chair. "Thanks for your help," I say, scooping up the directory and returning it to its shelf.

Ms. Angelli's eyebrows inch up. "Well, I didn't really do——"

"You did. You're brilliant. Thanks. Good night!" I'm at the door, then through it, into the Coronado's lobby, and pulling the key from my neck and the ring from my finger before I even reach the door set into the stairs.

"What brings you to the Archive, Miss Bishop?"

It's Lisa at the desk. She looks up, pen hovering over a series of ledgers set side by side behind the QUIET PLEASE sign, which I'm pretty sure is her contribution. Her black bob frames her face, and her eyes are keen but kind—two different shades—behind a pair of green horn-rimmed glasses. Lisa is a Librarian, of course, but unlike Roland, or Patrick, or most of the others, for that matter, she really looks the part (aside from the fact that one of her eyes is glass, a token from her days as Crew).

I fiddle with the key around my wrist.

"Couldn't sleep," I lie, even though it's not that late. It's my default response here, the way people always answer *How are you?* with *Good* or *Great* or *Fine*, even when they're not. "Those look nice," I say, gesturing to her nails. They're bright gold.

"You think so?" she asks, admiring them. "Found the polish in the closets. Roland's idea. He says they're all the rage right now."

I'm not surprised. In addition to his public addiction to trashy magazines, Roland has a private addiction to stealing glances at newly added Histories. "He would know."

Her smile thins. "What can I do for you tonight, Miss Bishop?" she asks, two-toned eyes leveled on me.

I hesitate. I could tell Lisa what I'm looking for, of course, but I've already used up my quota of Lisa-issued rule-bending coupons this month, what with the visits to Ben's shelf. And I don't have any bartering chips, no tokens from the Outer that she might like. I'm comfortable with Lisa, but if I ask her and she says no, I'll never make it past the desk.

"Is Roland around?" I ask casually. Lisa's gaze lingers, but then she goes back to writing in the ledgers.

"Ninth wing, third hall, fifth room. Last time I checked."

I smile and round the desk to the doors.

"Repeat it," orders Lisa.

I roll my eyes, but parrot, "Nine, three, five."

"Don't get lost," she warns.

My steps slow as I cross into the atrium. The stained glass is dark, as if the sky beyond—if there were a sky—had slipped to night. But still the Archive is bright, well-lit despite the lack of lights. Walking through is like wading into a pool of water. Cool, crisp, beautiful water. It slows you and holds you and washes over you. It is dazzling. Wood and stone and colored glass and calm. I force myself to look down at the dark wood floor, and find my way out of the atrium, repeating the numbers *nine three five, nine three five, nine three five*. It is too easy to go astray.

The Archive is a patchwork, pieces added and altered over the years, and the bit of hall I wander down is made of paler wood, the ceilings still high but the placards on the front of the shelves worn. I reach the fifth room, and the style shifts again, with marble floors and a lower ceiling. Every space is different, and yet in all of them, that steady quiet reigns.

Roland is standing in front of an open drawer, his back to me and his fingertips pressed gently into a man's shoulder.

When I enter the room, his hands shift from the History to its drawer, sliding it closed with one fluid, silent motion. He turns my way, and for a moment his eyes are so . . . sad. But then he blinks and recovers.

"Miss Bishop."

"'Evening, Roland."

There's a table and a pair of chairs in the center of the room, but he doesn't invite me to sit. He seems distracted.

"Are you all right?" I ask.

"Of course." An automatic reply. "What brings you here?"

"I need a favor." His brows knit. "Not Ben. I promise."

He looks around the space, then leads me into the hall beyond, where the walls are free of shelves.

"Go on . . ." he says slowly.

"Something horrible happened in my room. A murder."

A brow arches. "How do you know?"

"Because I read it."

"You shouldn't be reading things unnecessarily, Miss Bishop. The point of that gift is not to indulge in—"

"I know, I know. The perils of curiosity. But don't pretend you're immune to it."

His mouth quirks.

"Look, isn't there any way you can . . ." I cast my arm wide across the room, gesturing at the walls of bodies, of lives.

"Any way I can *what?*"

"Do a search? Look for residents of the Coronado. Her death

would have been in March. Sometime between 1951 and 1953. If I can find the girl here in the Archive, then we can read her and find out who she was, and who *he* was—"

"Why? Just to slake your interest? That's hardly the purpose of these files—"

"Then what is?" I snap. "We're supposed to protect the past. Well, someone is trying to erase it. Years are missing from the Coronado's records. Years in which a girl was *murdered*. The boy who killed her *left*. He ran. I need to find out what happened. I need to know if he got away, and I can't—"

"So that's what this is about," he says under his breath.

"What do you mean?"

"This isn't just about understanding a murder. It's about Ben."

I feel like I've been slapped. "It's not. I—"

"Don't insult me, Miss Bishop. You're a remarkable Keeper, but I know why you can't stand leaving a name on your list. This isn't just about curiosity, it's about closure—"

"Fine. But that doesn't change the fact that something horrible happened in my room, and someone tried to cover it up."

"People do bad things," Roland says quietly.

"Please." Desperation creeps in with the word. I swallow. "Da used to say that Keepers needed three things: skill, luck, and intuition. I have all three. And my gut says something is *wrong*."

He tilts his head a fraction. It's a tell. He's bending.

"Humor me," I say. "Just help me find out who she was, so I can find out who *he* was."

He straightens but pulls a small pad from his pocket and begins to make notes.

"I'll see what I can do."

I smile, careful not to make it broad—I don't want him to think he was conned—just wide enough to read as grateful. "Thank you, Roland."

He grunts. I feel the telltale scratch of letters in my pocket, and retrieve the list to find a new name. *Melanie Allen. 10.* I rub my thumb over the number. Ben's age.

"All well?" he asks casually.

"Just a kid," I say, pocketing the list.

I turn to go, but hesitate. "I'll keep you apprised, Miss Bishop," says Roland in answer to my pause.

"I owe you."

"You always do," he says as I leave.

I wind my way back through the halls and the atrium and into the antechamber, where Lisa is flipping through the pages of her ledgers, eyes narrowed in concentration.

"Going so soon?" she asks as I pass.

"Another name," I say. She should know. She gave it to me. "The Coronado is certainly keeping me busy."

"Old buildings—"

"I know, I know."

"We've been diverting traffic, so to speak, as best we could, but it will be better now that you're on the premises—"

"Joy."

"It's safe to say you'll experience a higher number of Histories here than in your previous territory. Maybe two to three times. No more—"

"Two to three *times*?"

Lisa folds her hands. "The world tests us for reasons, Miss Bishop," she says sweetly. "Don't you want to be Crew?"

I hate that line. I hate it because it is the Librarians' way of saying *deal with it.*

She locks eyes with me over her horn-rimmed glasses, daring me to press the issue. "Anything else, Miss Bishop?"

"No," I grumble. It's rare to see Lisa so rigid. "I think that's all."

"Have a nice night," she calls, offering a small, gold-flecked wave before taking up her pen. I head back into the Narrows to find Melanie.

There's this moment when I step into the Narrows, right after the Archive door closes behind me and before I start hunting; this little sliver of time where the world feels still. Not quiet, of course, but steady, calm. And then I hear a far-off cry or the shuffle of steps or any one of a dozen sounds, and all of them remind me it's not the calm that keeps me still. It's fear. Da used to say that only fools and cowards scorned fear. Fear keeps you alive.

My fingers settle on the stained wall, the key on my wrist clinking against it. I close my eyes and press down, reach until I catch hold of the past. My fingers, then palms, then wrists go numb. I'm just about to roll the memories back in search of Melanie Allen, when I'm cut off by a sound, sharp like metal against rock.

I blink and draw back from the wall.

The sound is too close.

I follow the noise down the corridor and around the corner.

The hall is empty.

Pausing, I slide the Archive list from my pocket, checking it again, but ten-year-old Melanie is the only name there.

The sound comes a second time, grating as nails, from the end of the hall, and I hurry down it, turn left and—

The knife comes out of nowhere.

It slashes, and I drop the paper and jerk back, the blade narrowly missing my stomach as it carves a line through the air. I recover and dodge sideways as the knife slices the air again, clumsy but fast. The hand holding the knife is massive, the knuckles scarred, and the History behind the knife looks just as rough. He is height and muscle, filling the hall, his eyes half buried beneath thick, angry brows, the irises fully black. He's been out long enough to slip. Why wasn't he listed? My stomach sinks when I recognize the knife in his hand as Jackson's. A blade of folded metal the length of my hand running into a dark hilt and—somewhere hidden by his palm—a hole drilled into the grip.

He slashes again, and I drop to a crouch, trying to think; but he's fast, and it's all I can do to stay on my feet and in one piece. The hall is too narrow to take out his legs, so I spring up, get a foot on the wall, and push off, crushing his face into the opposite wall with my boot. His head connects with a sound like bricks, but he barely flinches, and I hit the ground and roll just in time to avoid another slice.

Even as I dodge and duck, I can tell I'm losing ground, being forced backward.

"How do you have that key, Abbie?"

He's already slipped. He's looking at me but seeing someone else, and whoever this Abbie is, he doesn't seem too happy with her.

I scan him desperately for clues as I duck. A faded jacket with a small nameplate sewn into the front reads *Hooper*.

He swings the knife like an ax, chopping the air. "Where did you get the key?"

Why isn't he on my list?

"Give it to me," he growls. "Or I'll cut it from your pretty wrist."

He slashes with so much force that the knife hits a door and sticks, the metal embedded in the wood. I seize the chance and kick him as hard as I can in the chest, hoping the momentum will force him to let go of the blade. It doesn't. Pain rolls up my leg from the blow, which knocks Hooper back just hard enough to help him free his weapon from the Narrows wall. His grip tightens on the handle.

I know I'm running out of room.

"I need it," he groans. "You know I need it."

I need to pause this whole moment until I can figure out what a full-grown History is doing in my territory and how I'm going to get out of here without considerable blood loss.

Another step back and a wall comes up to meet my shoulders.

My stomach twists.

Hooper presses forward, and the cool tip of the knife comes up just below my chin, so close that I'm afraid to swallow.

"The key. Now."

ELEVEN

YOU HOLD OUT the slip of paper you keep rolled behind your ear.

I tap the small *7* beside the boy's name. "Are they all so young?"

"Not all," you say, smoothing the paper, an unlit cigarette between your teeth. "But most."

"Why?"

You take the cigarette out, jabbing the air with the unlit tip. "That is the most worthless question in the world. Use your words. Be specific. *Why* is like *bah* or *moo* or that silly sound pigeons make."

"Why are most of the ones that wake so young?"

"Some are—were—troubled. But most are restless. Didn't live enough, maybe." Your tone shifts. "But everyone has a History, Kenzie. Young and old." I can see you testing the words in your mouth. "The older the History, the heavier they sleep. The older ones that wake have something in them, something different, something dark. Troubled. Unstable. They're bad people. Dangerous. They're the ones who tend to get into the Outer. The ones who fall into the hands of Crew."

"Keeper-Killers," I whisper.

You nod.

I straighten. "How do I beat them?"

"Strength. Skill." You run a hand over my hair. **"And luck. Lots of luck."**

My back presses against the wall as the tip of the knife nicks my throat, and I really don't want to die like this.

"Key," Hooper growls again, his black eyes dancing. "God, Abbie, I just want out. I want out and he said you had it, said I had to get it—so give it to me now."

He?

The knife bites down.

My mind is suddenly horribly blank. I take a shallow breath.

"Okay," I say, reaching for the key. The cord is looped three times around my wrist, and I'm hoping that somewhere between untangling it and motioning toward him, I can get the knife away.

I unloop it once.

And then something catches my eye. Down the hall, beyond Hooper's massive form, a shadow moves. A shape in the dark. The form slips silently forward, and I can't see his face, only his outline and a sweep of silver-blond hair. He slides up behind the History as I unloop the cord a second time.

I unloop the cord a final time, and Hooper is snatching the key, the knife retreating a fraction from my throat, when the stranger's arm coils around the History's neck.

The next moment Hooper is slammed backward onto the ground, the knife tumbling from his grasp. The motion is clean, efficient. The stranger catches the blade and drives it down toward the History's broad chest, but he's a beat too slow, and Hooper grabs hold of him and flings him into the nearest wall with an audible crack.

And then I see it, glittering on the floor between us.

My key.

I dive for it as Hooper sees, and lunges too. He reaches it first, but between one blink and the next, the blond man has his hands around Hooper's jaw, and swiftly breaks his neck.

Before Hooper can sag forward, the stranger catches his body and slams it against the nearest door, driving the knife straight through his chest, the blade and most of the hilt buried deep enough to pin his body against the wooden door. I stare at the History's limp form, chin against his chest, wondering how long it will take him to recover from that.

The stranger is staring, too, at the place where his hand meets the knife and the knife meets Hooper's body, the wound bloodless. He curls and uncurls his fingers around the handle.

"He won't stay like that," I say, desperate to keep the tremor from my voice as I rewrap the key cord around my wrist.

His voice is quiet, low. "I doubt it."

He lets go of the knife, and Hooper's body hangs against the door. I feel a drop of blood running down my throat. I wipe it away. I wish my hands would stop shaking. My list is a spot of white on the blackened floor. I recover it, muttering a curse.

Right below Melanie Allen's name sits a new one in clean print.

Albert Hooper. 45.

A little late. I look up as the stranger brings a hand to the slope of his neck and frowns.

"Are you hurt?" I ask, remembering how hard he hit the wall.

He rolls his shoulder first one way and then the other, a slow testing motion. "I don't think so."

He's young, late teens, maybe, whitish blond hair long enough to drift into his eyes, across his cheekbones. He's dressed in all black, not punk or goth, but simple, well-fitting. His clothing blurs into the dark around him.

The moment is surreal. I can't shake the feeling that I've seen him before, but I know I'd remember if I did. And now we're standing in the Narrows, the body of a History hanging like a coat on the door between us. He doesn't seem bothered by that. If his combat skills aren't enough to mark him as a Keeper, his composure is.

"Who are you?" I ask, trying to force as much authority into my voice as possible.

"My name's Owen," he says. "Owen Chris Clarke."

His eyes meet mine as he says it, and my chest tightens. Everything about him is calm, even. His movements when fighting were fluid, efficient to the point of elegant. But his eyes are piercing. Wolfish. Eyes like one of Ben's drawings, sketched out in a stark, pale blue.

I feel dazed, both by Hooper's sudden attack and Owen's equally sudden appearance, but I don't have time to collect myself, because Hooper's body shudders against the door.

"What's your name?" Owen asks. And for some reason, I tell him the truth.

"Mackenzie."

He smiles. He has the kind of smile that barely touches his mouth.

"Where did you come from?" I ask, and Owen glances over his shoulder, when Hooper's eyelids flutter.

The door he's braced against is marked with white, the edge of the chalk circle peering out from his back, and that's all I have time to notice before Hooper's black eyes snap open.

I spring into action, driving the key into the door and turning the lock as I grip the knife in the History's chest and pull. The door falls open and the knife comes out; and I drive my boot into Hooper's stomach, sending him back a few steps, just enough. His shoes hit the white of the Returns, and I catch the door and slam it shut between us.

I hear Hooper beat against it once before falling deathly silent. I spin to face the Narrows, only seconds having passed, but Owen Chris Clarke is gone.

I slump down onto the worn runner of the Coronado's stairs and slide my ring back on, dropping the knife and the list onto the steps beside me. Hooper's name is gone now. Little good it did, since it didn't show up until I was halfway through the fight. I should report it, but to who? The Librarians would probably just turn it into a lecture on making Crew, on being prepared. But how could I have been prepared?

My eyes burn as I replay the fight. Clumsy. Weak. Caught off guard. I should never, ever be off guard. I know he'd lecture, I know he'd scold; but for the first time in years, the memories are not enough. I wish I could talk to Da.

"I nearly lost."

It is a whispered confession to an empty lobby, the strength leaching from my voice. Behind my eyes, Owen Chris Clarke breaks Hooper's neck. "I didn't know how to fight him, Da. I felt helpless." The word scratches my throat. "I've been doing this for years and I've never felt that." My hands tremble faintly.

I turn my thoughts from Hooper to Owen as my fingers drift toward the knife. His fluid movements, the ease with which he handled the weapon and the History. Wesley said the territory had been shared. Maybe Hooper was on Owen's list first. Or maybe Owen, like Wesley, had nothing better to do and happened to be in the right place at the right time.

I turn the knife absently between my fingers, and stop. There's something etched into the metal, right above the hilt. Three small lines. The Archive mark. My stomach twists. The weapon belonged to a member of the Archive—Keeper, Crew, Librarian—so how did it end up in the hands of a History? Did Jackson swipe it when he escaped?

I rub my eyes. It's late. I tighten my grip on the knife. Maybe I'll need it. I drag myself to my feet, and I'm about to go upstairs when I hear it.

Music.

It must have been playing all along. I turn my head from side to side, trying to decipher where it's coming from, and see that a sheet of paper has been tacked beneath the café sign: *Coming Soon!* announced in the cleanest, most legible version of my mother's script. I head for the sign, but then I remember that I'm holding a large, unsheathed, and very conspicuous knife. There's a planter in the corner where the grand stairs meet the wall, and I set the weapon carefully inside before crossing the lobby. The music grows. Into the hall, and it's louder still, then through the door on the right, down a step and through another door, the notes leading me like bread crumbs.

I find my mother kneeling in a pool of light.

It's not light, I realize, but clean, pale stone. Her head is bent as she scours the floor, the tiles of which, it turns out, are not gray at all, but a stunning pearlescent white marble. One section of the counter, too, where Mom has already asserted her cleaning prowess, is gleaming white granite, run through with threads of black and gold. These spots glitter, like gems across coal. The radio blasts, a pop song that peaks then trails off into commercials, but Mom doesn't seem to register anything but the *whoosh* of her sponge and the spreading pool of white. In the middle of the floor, partially revealed, is a rust-colored pattern. A rose, petal after petal of inlaid stone, an even, earthy red.

"Wow," I say.

She looks up suddenly. "Mackenzie, I didn't see you there."

She gets to her feet. She looks like a human cleaning rag, as if she simply transferred all the dirt from the café onto herself. On one of the counters a bag of groceries sits, forgotten. Condensation makes the plastic bag cling to the once-cold contents.

"It's amazing," I say. "There's actually something underneath the dust."

She beams, hands on her hips. "I know. It's going to be perfect."

Another pop song starts up on the radio, but I reach over and turn it off.

"How long have you been down here, Mom?"

She blinks several times, looks surprised. As if she hadn't thought about time and its penchant for moving forward. Her eyes register the darkness beyond the windows, then travel back to the neglected groceries. Something in her sags. And for a moment, I see her. Not the watts-too-bright, smile-till-it-hurts her, but the real one. The mother who lost her little boy.

"Oh, I'm sorry, Mac," she says, rubbing the back of her hand across her forehead. "I completely lost track of time." Her hands are red and raw. She isn't even wearing plastic gloves. She tries to smile again, but it falters.

"Hey, it's fine," I say. I hoist the soap-filled bucket onto the counter, wincing as the weight sends pain through my bandaged arm, and dump its contents into the sink. The sink, by the looks of it, could use it. I hook the empty container on my elbow. "Let's go upstairs."

Mom suddenly looks exhausted. She picks up the groceries from the counter, but I take them from her.

"I got it," I say, my arm aching. "Are you hungry? I can heat you up some dinner."

Mom nods wearily. "That would be great."

"All right," I say. "Let's go home."

Home. The word still tastes like sandpaper in my mouth. But it makes Mom smile—a tired, true smile—so it's worth it.

I'm so tired my bones hurt. But I can't sleep.

I press my palms against my eyes, going through the fight with Hooper over and over and over again, scouring the scene for what I could have—should have—done differently. I think of Owen, the swift, efficient movements, the breaking of the History's neck, the plunging of the knife into his chest. My fingers drift to my sternum, then inch down until they rest on the place where it ends.

I sit up, reach beneath the bed, and free the knife from the lip of bed frame, where I hid it. Once Mom was settled, I went back to the lobby and rescued it from the planter. Now it glints wickedly in the darkened room, the Archive mark like ink on the shining metal. Whose was it?

I slide off my ring, letting it fall to the comforter, and close my hand over the hilt. The hum of memories buzzes against my palm. Weapons, even small ones, are easy to read because they tend to have such vivid, violent pasts. I close my eyes and catch hold of the thread inside. Two memories roll backward, the more recent one with Hooper—I watch myself pressed against the wall, eyes wide— and the older one with Jackson. But before Jackson brought it into the Narrows, there's . . . *nothing.* Only flat black. This blade should be filled to the brim with stories, and instead it's like it doesn't have a past. But the three marks on the metal say otherwise. What if Jackson didn't steal it? What if someone sent him into the Narrows armed?

I blink, trying to dispel my growing unease along with the matte black of missing memories.

The only bright side is that, wherever this weapon came from, it's mine now. I hook my finger through the hole in the handle and twirl the blade slowly. I close my hand around the handle, stopping its path, and the hilt hits my palm with a satisfying snap, the metal tracing the line up my forearm. I smile. It is an amazing weapon. In fact, I'm fairly certain I could kill myself with it. But having it, holding it, makes me feel better. I'll have to find a way to bind it to my calf, to keep it from sight, from reach. Da's warnings echo in my head, but I quiet them.

I put my ring back on and return the knife to its hidden lip beneath the bed, promising myself I won't *use* it. I tell myself I won't need to. I lie back, less shaken, but no closer to sleep. My eyes settle on the blue bear propped on my side table, the black glasses perched on its nose. Nights like this I wish I could sit and talk to Ben, wear my mind out, but I can't go back to the stacks so soon. I think of calling Lyndsey, but it's late, and what would I say?

How was your day? . . . Yeah? Oh, mine?

I got attacked by a Keeper-Killer.

I know! And saved by a stranger who just vanished—

And that guyliner boy, he's a Keeper!

. . . No, Keeper *with a capital* K.

And there's the murder in my room. Someone tried to cover it up, ripped the pages right out of the history books.

Oh, and I almost forgot. Someone in the Archive might be trying to get me killed.

I laugh. It's a strained sound, but it helps.

And then I yawn, and soon, somehow, I find sleep.

TWELVE

THE NEXT DAY *Melanie Allen. 10.* has been joined by *Jena Freeth. 14.* but the moment I emerge from my room to hunt, Mom appears with an apron and a revived high-wattage smile, thrusts a box of cleaning supplies into my hands, and drops a book on top.

"Coffee shop duty!"

She says it like I've been given a prize, a reward. My forearm still aches dully, and the box bulges in my arms, threatening to crumble.

"I have a vague idea of what cleaning supplies do, but what's with the book?"

"Your father picked up your school's reading list."

I look at my mother, then at the calendar on the kitchen wall, then at the sunlight streaming in the window. "It's summer."

"Yes, it's a *summer* reading list," she says cheerfully. "Now, off with you. You can clean or you can read, or you can clean and then read, or read and then clean, or—"

"I got it." I could beg off, lie, but I'm still feeling shaky from last night and I wouldn't mind a couple hours as M right now, a taste of normalcy. Besides, there's a Narrows door *in* the coffee shop.

Downstairs, the overhead lights blink sleepily on. I drop the box on the counter, letting it regain its composure as I dig out the book. Dante's *Inferno*. You've got to be kidding me. I consider the cover, which features a good deal of hellfire and proudly announces that this is the SAT prep edition, complete with starred vocabulary. I turn to the first page and begin to read.

In the midway of this our mortal life, I found me in a gloomy wood, astray . . .

No, thank you.

I toss Dante onto a pile of folded sheets by the wall, where it lands with a plume of dust. Cleaning it is, then. The whole room smells faintly of soap and stale air, and the stone counters and floor make it feel cold, despite the summer air beyond the windows. I throw them open, then switch the radio on, crank up the volume, and get to work.

The soapy mixture I concoct smells strong enough to chew right through my plastic gloves, to peel back skin and polish bone. It is beautiful bluish stuff, and when I smear it across the marble, it shimmers. I think I can hear it chewing away at the grime on the floor. A few vigorous circles and my corner of the floor even begins to resemble Mom's.

"I don't believe it."

I look up to find Wesley Ayers sitting backward on a metal chair, a relic unearthed from beneath one of the folded sheets. Most of the furniture has been moved onto the patio, but a few chairs dot the room, including this one. "There's actually a room under all this dust!" He drapes his arms over the chair and rests his chin on the arching metal. I never heard him come in.

"Good morning," he adds. "I don't suppose there's a pot of coffee down here."

"Alas, not yet."

"And you call yourself a coffee shop."

"To be fair, the sign says 'Coming Soon.' So," I say, getting to my feet, "what brings you to the future site of Bishop's Coffee Shop?"

"I've been thinking."

"A dangerous pursuit."

"Indeed." He raises one eyebrow playfully. "I got it into my head to save you from the loneliness born of rainy days and solitary chores."

"Oh, did you?"

"Magnanimous, I know." His gaze settles on the discarded book. He leans, reaching until his fingertips graze Dante's *Inferno*, still on its bed of folded sheets.

"What have we here?" he asks.

"Required reading," I say, starting to scrub the counter.

"It's a shame they do that," he says, thumbing through the pages. "Requirement ruins even the best of books."

"Have you read it?"

"A few times." My eyebrows arch, and he laughs. "Again with the skepticism. Looks can be deceiving, Mac. I'm not *all* beauty and charm." He keeps turning the pages. "How far in are you?"

I groan, making circular motions on the granite. "About two lines. Maybe three."

Now it's his turn to raise a brow. "You know, the thing about a book like this is that it's meant to be heard, not read."

"Oh, really."

"Honest. I'll prove it to you. You clean, I'll read."

"Deal."

I scrub as he rests the book on the top of the chair. He doesn't start from the beginning, but turns to a page somewhere in the middle, clears his throat, and begins.

"Through me you pass into the city of woe."

His voice is measured, smooth.

"'Through me you pass into eternal pain. . . .'"

He slips to his feet and rounds the chair as he reads, and I try to listen, I do, but the words blur in my ears as I watch him step toward me, half his face in shadow. Then he crosses into the light and stands there, only a counter between us. Up close, I see the scar along his collar, just beneath the leather cord; his square shoulders; the dark lashes framing his light eyes. His lips move, and I blink as his voice dips low, private, forcing me to listen closer, and I catch the end.

"'Abandon all hope, ye who enter here.'"

He looks up at me and stops. The book slips to his side.

"Mackenzie." He flashes a crooked smile.

"Yeah?"

"You're spilling soap on everything."

I look down and realize he's right. The soap is dripping over the counter, making bubble-blue puddles on the floor.

I laugh. "Well, can't hurt," I say, trying to hide my embarrassment. Wesley, on the other hand, seems to relish it. He leans across the counter, drawing aimless patterns in the soap.

"Got lost in my eyes, did you?"

He leans farther forward, his hands in the dry spaces between soap slicks. I smile and lift the sponge, intending to ring it out over his head, but he leans back just in time, and the soapy mix splashes onto the already flooded counter.

He points a painted black nail at his hair. "Moisture messes up the 'do." He laughs good-naturedly as I roll my eyes. And then I'm laughing, too. It feels good. It's something M would do. Laugh like this.

I want to tell Wes that I dream of a life filled with these moments.

"Well," I say, trying to sop up the soap, "I have no idea what you were reading about, but it sounded nice."

"It's the inscription on the gates of Hell," says Wes. "It's my favorite part."

"Morbid, much?"

He shrugs. "When you think about it, the Archive is kind of like a Hell."

The cheerful moment wobbles, cracks. I picture Ben's shelf, picture the quiet, peace-filled halls. "How can you say that?" I ask.

"Well, not the Archive so much as the Narrows. After all, it is a place filled with the restless dead, right?"

I nod absently, but I can't shake the tightness in my chest. Not just at the mention of Hell, but at the way Wesley went from reciting homework to musing on the Archive. As if it's all one life, one world—but it's not, and I'm stuck somewhere between my Keeper world and my Outer world, trying to figure out how Wesley has one foot so comfortably in each.

You use your thumbnail to dig out a sliver of wood from the railing on the porch. It needs to be painted, but it never will be. It's our last summer together. Ben didn't come this year; he's at some sleepaway camp. And when the house goes on the market this winter, the rail will still be crumbling.

You're trying to teach me how to split myself into pieces.

Not messy, like tearing paper into confetti, but clean, even: like cutting a pie. You say that's you how you lie and get away with it. That's how you stay alive.

"Be who you need to be," you say. "When you're with your brother, or your parents, or your friends, or Roland, or a History. Remember what I taught you about lying?"

"You start with a little truth," I say.

"Yes. Well, this is the same." You throw the sliver of wood over the rail and start working on another. Your hands are never still. "You start with you. Each version of you isn't a total lie. It's just a twist."

It's quiet and dark, a too-hot summer even at night, and I turn to go inside.

"One more thing," you say, drawing me back. "Every now and then, those separate lives, they intersect. Overlap. That's when you have to be careful, Kenzie. Keep your lies clean, and your worlds as far apart as possible."

Everything about Wesley Ayers is messy.

My three worlds are kept apart by walls and doors and locks, and yet here he is, tracking the Archive into my life like mud. I know what Da would say, I know, I know, I know. But the strange new overlap is scary and messy and welcome. I can be careful.

Wesley fiddles with the book, doesn't go back to reading. Maybe he can feel it, too, this place where lines smudge. Quiet settles over us like dust. Is there a way to do this? Last night in the dark of the garden it was thrilling and terrifying and wonderful to tell the truth, but here in the daylight it feels dangerous, exposed.

Still. I want him to say the words again. *I am a Keeper. I hunt Histories . . .* I'm about to ask something, anything, to break the quiet, when Wesley beats me to it.

"Favorite Librarian?" As if he's asking about my favorite food, or song, or movie.

"Roland," I say.

"Really?" He drops the book.

"You sound surprised."

"I pictured you as a Carmen fan. But I do appreciate Roland's taste in shoes."

"The red Chucks? He says he found them in the closets, but I'm pretty sure he swiped them from a History."

"Weird to think of closets in the Archive."

"Weird to think of Librarians *living* there," I say. "It just seems unnatural."

"I left a ball of Oreo filling out for months one time," says Wesley. "It never got hard. Lot of unnatural things in the world."

A laugh escapes my lips, echoes off the granite and glass of the hollowed coffee shop. The laugh is easy, and it feels so, so good. And then Wes picks up the book, and I pick up my sponge, and he promises to read as long as I keep cleaning. I turn back to my work as he clears his throat and starts. I scrub the counter four times just so he won't stop.

For an hour, the world is perfect.

And then I look down at the frosted blue of the soap, and my mind drifts, of all things, to Owen. Who is he? And what's he doing in my territory? Some small part of me thinks he was a phantom, that maybe I've split myself into one too many pieces. But he seemed real enough, driving the knife into Hooper's chest.

"Question," I say, and Wes's reading trails off. "You said you covered the Coronado's doors. That this place was shared." Wes nods. "Were there any other Keepers covering it?"

"Not since I got my key last year. There was a woman at first, but she moved away. Why?"

"Just curious," I say automatically.

His mouth quirks. "If you're going to lie to me, you'll have to try a bit harder."

"It's not a big deal. There was an incident in my territory. I've just been thinking about it." My words skirt around Owen and land on Hooper. "There was this adult—"

His eyes go wide. "Adult *History*? Like a *Keeper-Killer*?"

I nod. "I took care of it, but . . ."

He misreads my question about the Keepers on patrol.

"Do you want me to go with you?"

"Where?"

"In the Narrows. If you're worried—"

"I'm not—" I growl.

"I could go with you, for protect—"

I lift the sponge. "Finish that word," I say, ready to pitch it at his head. To his credit, he backs down, the sentence fading into a crooked smile. Just then, something scratches my leg. I drop the sponge back to the counter, tug off the plastic gloves, and dig out the list. I frown. The two names, *Melanie Allen. 10.* and *Jena Freith. 14.* hover near the top of the page, but instead of a third name below them, I find a note.

Miss Bishop, please report to the Archive. —R

R, for Roland. Wesley is lounging in the chair, one leg over the side. I turn the paper for him to see.

"A summons?" he asks. "Look at you."

My stomach sinks, and for a moment I feel like I'm sitting in the back of English class when the intercom clicks on, ordering me to the principal's office. But then I remember the favor I asked of Roland, and my heart skips. Did he find the murdered girl?

"Go on," says Wesley, rolling up his sleeves and reaching for my discarded plastic gloves. "I'll cover for you."

"But what if Mom comes in?"

"I'm going to meet Mrs. Bishop eventually. You do realize that."

I can dream.

"Go on now," he presses.

"Are you sure?"

He's already taking up the sponge. He cocks his head at me, silver glinting in his ears. He paints quite a picture, decked in black, a teasing smile and a pair of lemon-yellow gloves.

"What's the matter?" he asks, wielding the sponge like a weapon. "Doesn't it look like I know what I'm doing?"

I laugh, pocket the list, and head for the closet in the back of the café. "I'll be back as soon as I can." I hear the slosh of water, a muttered curse, the sounds of a body slipping on a slick floor.

"Try not to hurt yourself," I call, vanishing among the brooms.

THIRTEEN

CLASSICAL MUSIC WHISPERS through the circular antechamber of the Archive.

Patrick is sitting at the desk, trying to focus on something while Roland leans over him, wielding a pen. A Librarian I've never spoken to—though I've heard her called Beth—is standing at the entrance to the atrium, making notes, her reddish hair plaited down her back. Roland looks up as I step forward.

"Miss Bishop!" he says cheerfully, dropping the pen on top of Patrick's papers and coming to meet me. He guides me off in the direction of the stacks, making small talk, but as soon as we turn down a wing on the far side of the atrium, his features grow stern, set.

"Did you find the girl?" I ask.

"No," he says, leading me through a tight corridor and up a flight of stairs. We cross a landing and end up in a reading room that's blue and gold and smells like old paper, faded but pleasant. "There's no one in the branch that fits your description or the time line."

"That's not possible; you must not have searched wide—" I say.

"Miss Bishop, I scrounged up whatever I could on every female resident—"

"Maybe she wasn't a resident. Maybe she was just visiting."

"If she died in the Coronado, she'd be shelved in this branch. She isn't."

"I know what I saw."

"Mackenzie—"

She has to be here. If I can't find her, I can't find her killer. "She existed. I *saw* her."

"I'm not questioning that you did."

Panic claws through me. "How could someone have erased her from *both* places, Roland? And why did you call me here? If there's no record of this girl—"

"I didn't find her," says Roland, "but I found someone else." He crosses the room and opens one of the drawers, gesturing to the History on the shelf. From his receding hairline to his slight paunch to his worn loafers, the man looks . . . ordinary. His clothes are dated but clean, his features impassive in his deathlike sleep.

"This is Marcus Elling," Roland says quietly.

"And what does he have to do with the girl I saw?"

"According to his memories, he was also a resident on the third floor of the Coronado from the hotel's conversion in 1950 until his death in 1953."

"He lived on the same floor as the girl, and died in the same time frame?"

"That's not all," says Roland. "Put your hand on his chest."

I hesitate. I've never read a History. Only the Librarians are allowed to read the dead. Only they know *how*, and it's an infraction for anyone else to even try. But Roland looks shaken, so I put my hand on Elling's sweater. The History feels like every other History. Quiet.

"Close your eyes," he says, and I do.

And then Roland puts his hand over mine and presses down. My fingers instantly go numb, and it feels like my mind is being shoved into someone else's body, pushed into a shape that doesn't fit my own. I wait for the memories to start, but they don't. I'm left in total darkness. Typically, memories start with the present and rewind, and

130

I've been told the lives of Histories are no different. They begin with their end, their most recent memory. Their death.

But Marcus Elling has no death. I spin back for ten solid seconds of flat black before the dark dissolves into static, and then the static shifts into light and motion and memory. Elling carrying a sack of groceries up the stairs.

The weight of Roland's hand lifts from mine, and Elling vanishes. I blink.

"His death is missing," I say.

"Exactly."

"How is that even possible? He's like a book with the last pages torn out."

"That is, in effect, exactly what he is," says Roland. "He's been altered."

"What does that mean?"

He scuffs one sneaker against the floor. "It means removing a memory, or memories. Carving the moments out. It's occasionally done in the Outer to protect the Archive. Secrecy, you have to understand, is key to our existence. Only a select few members of Crew are capable of and trained to do alterations, and only when absolutely necessary. It's neither an easy nor a pleasant task."

"So Marcus Elling had some kind of contact with the Archive? Something that merited wiping the end of his memory?"

Roland shakes his head. "No, altering is sanctioned only in the *Outer*, and only to shield the Archive from exposure. If he were dead or dying, there'd be no risk of exposure. In this case, the History was altered *after* he was shelved. The alteration's old—you can tell by the way the edges are fraying—so it was probably right after he arrived."

"But that means that whoever did it wanted Elling's death hidden from people here in the *Archive*."

Roland nods. "And the severity of the implication . . . the fact that this happened . . . it's . . ."

I say what he won't. "Only a Librarian possesses the skills to read a History, so only a Librarian would be able to alter one."

His voice slides toward a whisper. "And to do so goes against the principles of this establishment. Altering is used to modify the memories of the living, not bury the lives of the dead."

I stare down at Marcus Elling's face, as if his body can tell me something his memories couldn't. We now have a girl with no History, and a History with no death. I thought I was being paranoid, thought that Hooper could have been a glitch, that maybe Jackson stole the knife. But if a Librarian was willing to do *this*, to break the cardinal oath of the Archive, then maybe a Librarian was behind the malfunctioning list and the weapon too. But whoever altered Elling would be long gone by now . . . right?

Roland looks down at the body, a deep crease forming between his brows. I've never seen him look so worried.

And yet he is the one who asks me if I'm all right. "You seem quiet," he adds.

I want to tell him about the Keeper-Killer and the Archive knife, but one has been returned and the other is strapped to my calf beneath my jeans, so instead I ask, "Who would do this?"

He shakes his head. "I honestly don't know."

"Don't you have a file or something on Elling? Maybe there are clues—"

"He *is* the file, Miss Bishop."

With that he closes the drawer on Elling and leads me from the reading room back to the stairs.

"I'll keep looking into this," he says, pausing at the top of the steps. "But Mackenzie, if a Librarian was responsible for this, it's possible they were acting alone, defying the Archive. Or it's possible they had a reason. It's even possible they were following orders. By investigating these deaths, we're investigating the Archive itself. And that is a dangerous pursuit. Before we go any further, you need to understand the risks."

There's a long pause, and I can see Roland searching for words. "Altering is used in the Outer to eliminate witnesses. But it's also used on members of the Archive if they choose to leave service . . . or if they're deemed unfit."

My heart lurches in my chest. I'm sure the shock is written on my face. "You mean to tell me that if I lose my job, I lose my *life*?"

He won't look at me. "Any memories pertaining to the Archive and any work done on its behalf—"

"That *is* my life, Roland. Why wasn't I told?" My voice gets louder, echoing in the stairs, and Roland's eyes narrow.

"Would it have changed your mind?" he asks quietly.

I hesitate. "No."

"Well, it would change some people's minds. Numbers in the Archive are thin as it is. We cannot afford to lose more."

"So you lie?"

He manages a sad smile. "An omission is not the same thing as a lie, Miss Bishop. It's a manipulation. You as a Keeper should know the varying degrees of falsehood."

I clench my fists. "Are you trying to make a joke about this? Because I don't find the prospect of being erased, or altered, or whatever the hell you want to call it very funny."

My trial plays back like a reel in my head.

If she proves herself unfit in any way, she will forfeit the position.

And if she proves unfit, you, Roland, will remove her yourself.

Would he really do that to me, carve the Keeper out of me, strip away my memories of this world, of this life, of Da? What would be left?

And then, as if he can read my thoughts, Roland says, "I'd never let it happen. You have my word."

I want to believe him, but he's not the only Librarian here. "What about Patrick?" I ask. "He's always threatening to report me. And he mentioned someone named Agatha. Who is she, Roland?"

"She's an . . . assessor. She determines if a member of the Archive is fit." Before I can open my mouth, he adds, "She *won't* be a problem. I promise. And I can handle Patrick."

I run my fingers through my hair, dazed. "Aren't you breaking a rule just by telling me this?"

Roland sighs. "We are breaking a great many rules right now. That's the point. And you need to grasp that before this goes any further. You can still walk away."

But I won't. And he knows it.

"I'm glad you told me." I'm not, not at all, I'm still reeling; but I have to focus. I have my job, and I have my mind, and I have a mystery to solve.

"But what about Librarians?" I ask as we descend the steps. "You talk about retiring. About what you'll do when you're done serving. But you won't even remember. You'll just be a man full of holes."

"Librarians are exempt," he says when he reaches the base of the steps, but there's something hollow in his voice. "When we retire, we get to keep our memories. Call it a reward." He tries to smile and doesn't quite manage it. "Even more reason for you to work hard and move up those ranks, Miss Bishop. Now, if you're certain——"

"I am."

We head down the corridor back to the atrium.

"So what now?" I ask softly as we pass a QUIET PLEASE sign on the end of a line of stacks.

"*You're* going to do your job. *I'm* going to keep looking—"

"Then I'll keep looking, too. You look here, and I'll look in the Outer—"

"Mackenzie—"

"Between the two of us we'll find out who's—"

The sound of footsteps stops me midsentence as we round a set of stacks and nearly collide with Lisa and Carmen. A third Librarian, the one with the red braid, is walking a few steps behind them, but when we all pull up short, she continues on.

"Back so soon, Miss Bishop?" asks Lisa, but the question lacks Patrick's scorn.

"Hello, Roland," says Carmen, and then, warming when she sees me, "Hello, Mackenzie." Her sun-blond hair is pulled back, and once again I'm struck by how young she looks. I know that age is an illusion here, that she's older now than she was when she arrived, even if it doesn't show, but I still don't get it. I can see why some of the older Librarians choose the safety of this world over the constant danger of Keeper or Crew. But why would she?

"Hello, Carmen," says Roland, smiling stiffly. "I was just explaining to Miss Bishop"—he accentuates the formality—"how the different sections work." He reaches out and touches the name card on the nearest shelf. "White stacks, red stacks, black stacks. That sort of thing."

The placards are color-coded—white cards for ordinary Histories, red for those who've woken, black for those who've made it to the Outer—but I've only ever seen white stacks. The red and black are kept separately, deep within the branch, where the quiet is thick. I've known about the color system for a full two years, but I simply nod.

"Stay out of seven, three, five," says Lisa. As if on cue, there's a low sound, like far-off thunder, and she cringes. "We're having a slight technical difficulty."

Roland frowns but doesn't question. "I was just leading Miss Bishop back to the desk."

The two women nod and walk on. Roland and I return to the front desk in silence. Patrick glances back through the doors and sees us coming, and gathers up his things.

"Thank you," says Roland, "for standing in."

"I even left your music going."

"How kind of you," Roland says, managing a shadow of his usual charm. He takes a seat at the desk as Patrick strides off, a folder tucked under his arm. I head for the Archive door.

"Miss Bishop."

I look back at Roland. "Yes?"

"Don't tell anyone," he says.

I nod.

"And please," he adds, "be careful."

I force a smile. "Always."

I step into the Narrows, shivering despite the warm air. I haven't hunted since the incident with Hooper and Owen, and I feel stiff, more on edge than usual. It's not just the hunt that has me coiled, it's also the new fear of failing the Archive, of being found unfit. And at the same time, the fear of not being able to leave. I wish Roland had never told me.

Abandon all hope, ye who enter here.

My chest tightens, and I force myself to take a long, steadying breath. The Narrows is enough to make me claustrophobic on a good day, and I can't afford to be distracted like this right now, so I resolve to put it out of my mind and focus on clearing my list and keeping my job. I'm about to bring my hands to the wall when something stops me.

Sounds—the stretched-out, far-off kind—drift through the halls, and I close my eyes, trying to break them down. Too abstract to be words; the tones dissolve into a breeze, a thrum, a . . . melody?

I stiffen.

Somewhere in the Narrows, someone is humming.

I blink and push off the wall, thinking of the two girls still on my list. But the voice is low and male, and Histories don't sing. They shout and cry and scream and pound on walls and beg, but they don't sing.

The sound wafts through the halls; it takes me a moment to figure out which direction it's coming from. I turn a corner, then another, the notes taking shape until I round a third and see him. A shock of blond hair at the far end of the hall. His back is to me, his hands in his pockets and his neck craned as if he's looking up at the ceilingless Narrows, in search of stars.

"Owen?"

The song dies off, but he doesn't turn.

"Owen," I call again, taking a step toward him.

He glances over his shoulder, startling blue eyes alight in the dark, just as something slams into me, *hard*. Combat boots and a pink sundress, and short brown hair around huge blackening eyes. The History collides with me, and then she's off again, sprinting down the hall. I'm up and after her, thankful the pink of her dress is bright and the metal on her shoes is loud, but she runs fast. I finally chance a shortcut and catch her, but she thrashes and fights, apparently convinced I'm some kind of monster, which—as I'm half carrying, half dragging her to the nearest Returns door—maybe I am.

I pull the list from my pocket and watch as *Jena Freith. 14.* fades from the page.

The fight has done one thing—scraped the film of fear away, and as I lean, breathing heavy, against the Returns door, I feel like myself again.

I retrace my steps to the spot where I saw Owen, but he's nowhere to be found.

Shaking my head, I go in search of Melanie Allen. I read the walls and track her down, and send her back, all the while listening for Owen's song. But it never starts again.

FOURTEEN

LIST CLEARED, I head back to the coffee shop, ready to save Wesley Ayers from the perils of domestic labor. I use the Narrows door in the café closet, and freeze.

Wesley isn't alone.

I creep to the edge of the closet and chance a look out. He's engaged in lively conversation with my dad, talking about the perks of a certain Colombian coffee while he mops the floor. The whole place glitters, polished and bright. The rust-red rose, roughly the diameter of a coffee table, gleams in the middle of the marble floor.

Dad is juggling a mug and a paint roller, waving both as he sloshes dark roast and finishes a large color swatch—burnt yellow—on the far wall. His back is to me as he chats, but Wesley catches sight of me and watches as I slide from the closet and along the wall until I'm near the café door.

"Hey, Mac," he says. "Didn't hear you come in."

"There you are," says Dad, jabbing the air with his roller. He's standing straighter, and there's a light in his eyes.

"I told Mr. Bishop I offered to cover while you ran upstairs to get some food."

"I can't believe you put Wesley here to work so fast," says Dad. He sips his coffee, seems surprised to find so little left, and sets it down. "You'll scare him off."

"Well," I say, "he does scare easily."

Wesley wears a look of mock affront.

"Miss Bishop!" he says, and I have to fight back a smile. His impersonation of Patrick is spot-on. "Actually," he admits to my father, "it's true. But no worries, Mr. Bishop, Mac's going to have to do better than assign chores if she means to scare me off."

Wesley actually winks. Dad smiles. I can practically see the marquee in his head: *Relationship Material!* Wesley must see it too, because he capitalizes on it, and sets the mop aside.

"Would you mind if I borrowed Mackenzie for a bit? We've been working on her summer reading."

Dad *beams*. "Of course," he says, waving his paint roller. "Go on, now."

I half expect him to add *kids* or *lovebirds*, but thankfully he doesn't.

Meanwhile, Wes is trying to tug off the plastic gloves. One snags on his ring, and when he finally manages to wrest his hand free, the metal band flies off, bouncing across the marble floor and underneath an old oven. Wes and I go to recover it at the same time, but he's stopped by Dad's hand, which comes down on his shoulder.

Wes goes rigid. A shadow crosses his face.

Dad's saying something to Wes, but I'm not listening as I drop to the floor before the oven. The metal grate at the base digs into the cut on my arm as I reach beneath, stretching until my fingers finally close around the ring, and I get to my feet as Wesley bows his head, jaw clenched.

"You okay there, Wesley?" asks Dad, letting go. Wes nods, a short breath escaping as I drop the ring into his palm. He slides it on.

"Yeah," he says, voice leveling. "I'm fine. Just a little dizzy." He forces a laugh. "Must be the fumes from Mac's blue soap."

"Aha!" I say. "I told you cleaning was bad for your health."

"I should have listened."

"Let's get you some fresh air, okay?"

"Good idea."

"See you, Dad."

The café door closes behind us, and Wesley slumps back against it, looking a little pale. I know the feeling.

"We have aspirin upstairs," I offer. Wesley laughs and rolls his head to look at me.

"I'm fine. But thank you." I'm struck by the change in tone. No jokes, no playful arrogance. Just simple, tired relief. "Maybe a little fresh air, though."

He straightens up and heads through the lobby, and I follow. Once we reach the garden, he sinks down on his bench and rubs his eyes. The sun is bright, and he was right, this is a different place in daylight. Not a lesser place, really, but open, exposed. At dusk there seemed so many places to hide. At midday, there are none.

The color is coming back into Wesley's face, but his eyes, when he stops rubbing them, are distant and sad. I wonder what he saw, what he felt, but he doesn't say.

I sink onto the other end of the bench. "You sure you're okay?"

He blinks, stretches, and by the time he's done, the strain is gone and Wes is back: the crooked smile and the easy charm.

"I'm fine. Just a bit out of practice, reading people."

Horror washes over me. "You *read* the living? But how?"

Wesley shrugs. "The same way you read anything else."

"But they're not in order. They're loud and tangled and—"

He shrugs. "They're *alive*. And they may not be organized, but the important stuff is there, on the surface. You can learn a lot, at a touch."

My stomach turns. "Have you ever read *me*?"

Wes looks insulted but shakes his head. "Just because I know how doesn't mean I make a sport of it, Mac. Besides, it's against Archive policy, and believe it or not, *I'd* like to stay on their good side."

You and me both, I think.

"How can you stand to read them?" I ask, suppressing a shudder. "Even with my ring on, it's awful."

"Well, you can't go through life without touching anyone."

"Watch me," I say.

Wesley's hand floats up, a single, pointed finger drifting through the air toward me.

"Not funny."

But he keeps reaching.

"I. Will. Cut. Your. Fingers. Off."

He sighs and lets his hand drop to his side. Then he nods at my arm. Red has crept through the bandage and the sleeve where the bottom of the oven dug in.

I look down at it. "Knife."

"Ah," he says.

"No, it really was a teenage boy with a really big knife."

He pouts. "Keeper-Killers. Kids with knives. Your territory was never that much fun when I worked there."

"I'm just lucky, I guess."

"You sure I can't give you a hand?"

I smile, more at the way he offers this time—tiptoeing through the question—than the prospect; but the last thing I need is another complication in my territory.

"No offense, but I've been doing this for quite a while."

"How's that?"

I should backtrack, but it's too late to lie when the truth is half-way up my throat. "I became a Keeper at twelve."

His brow furrows. "But the age requirement is sixteen."

I shrug. "My grandfather petitioned."

142

Wesley's face hardens as he grasps the meaning. "He passed the job to a kid."

"It wasn't——" I warn.

"What kind of sick bastard would——" The words die on his lips as my fingers tangle in his collar, and I shove him back against the stone bench. For a moment he is just a body and I am a Keeper, and I don't even care about the deafening noise that comes with touching him.

"Don't you dare," I say.

Wesley's face is utterly unreadable as my hands loosen and slide away from his throat. He brings his fingers to his neck but never takes his eyes from mine. We are, both of us, coiled.

And then he smiles.

"I thought you hated touching."

I groan and shove him, slumping back into my corner of the bench.

"I'm sorry," I say. The words seem to echo through the garden.

"One thing's for certain," he says. "You keep me on my toes."

"I shouldn't have——"

"It wasn't my place to judge," he says. "Your grandfather obviously did something right."

I try to shape a tight laugh, and it dies in my throat. "This is new to me, Wes. Sharing. Having someone I *can* share with. And I really appreciate your help—— That sounds lame. I've never had someone like . . . This is a mess. There's finally something good in my life and I'm already making a mess of it." My cheeks go hot, and I have to clench my teeth to stop the rambling.

"Hey," he says, knocking his shoe playfully against mine. "It's the same for me, you know? This is all new to me. And I'm not going anywhere. It takes at least three assassination attempts to scare me off. And even then, if there are baked goods involved, I might come back." He hoists himself up from the bench. "But on that note, I retreat to tend my wounded pride." He says it with a smile, and somehow I'm smiling, too.

How does he do that, untangle things so easily? I walk with him back through the study and into the lobby. As the revolving doors groan to a stop after him, I close my eyes and sink back against the stairs. I've been mentally berating myself for all of ten seconds when I feel the scratch of letters and dig my list from my pocket to see a new name scrawl itself across my paper.

Angela Price. 13.

It's getting harder to keep this list clear. I am heading for the Narrows door set into the side of the stairs when I hear a creak and turn to see Ms. Angelli coming in, struggling with several bags of groceries. For an instant, I'm back in the Archive, watching the last moment of Marcus Elling's recorded life as he performed the exact same task. And then I blink, and the large woman from the fourth floor comes back into focus as she reaches the stairs.

"Hi, Ms. Angelli," I say. "Can I give you a hand?" I hold out my hands, and she gratefully passes two of the four bags over.

"Obliged, dear," she says.

I follow her up, choosing my words. She knows about the Coronado's past, its secrets. I just have to figure out how to get her to share. Coming at it head-on didn't work, but maybe a more oblique path will. I think of her living room, brimming with antiques.

"Can I ask you something," I say, "about your job?"

"Of course," she says.

"What made you want to be a collector?" I understand clinging to one's own past, but when it comes to the pasts of other people, I don't get it.

She gives a winded laugh as she reaches the landing. "Everything is valuable, in its own way. Everything is full of history." *If only she knew.* "Sometimes you can feel it in them, all that life. I can always spot a fake." She smiles, but then her face softens. "And . . . I suppose . . . it gives me purpose. A tether to other people in other times. As long as I have that, I'm not alone. And they're not really gone."

I think of Ben's box of hollow things in my closet, the bear and the black plastic glasses, a tether to my past. My chest hurts. Ms. Angelli shifts her grip on the groceries.

"I haven't got much else," she adds quietly. And then the smile is back, bright as her rings, which have torn tiny holes in the grocery bags. "I suppose that might sound sad. . . ."

"No," I lie. "I think it sounds hopeful."

She turns and heads past the elevators, into the north stairwell. I follow, and our footsteps echo as we climb.

"So," she calls back, "did you find what you were looking for?"

"No, not yet. I don't know if there are other records about this place, or if it's all lost. It seems sad, doesn't it, for the Coronado's history to be forgotten? To fade away?"

She is climbing the stairs, and while I can't see her face, I watch her shoulders stiffen. "Some things should be allowed to fade."

"I don't believe that, Ms. Angelli," I say. "Everything deserves to be remembered. You think so too, or you wouldn't do what you do. I think you probably know more than anyone else in this building when it comes to the Coronado's past."

She glances back, her eyes dancing nervously.

"Tell me what happened here," I say. We reach the fourth floor and step out into the hall. "Please. I know that you know."

She drops her groceries onto a table in the hall and digs around for her keys. I set my bags beside hers.

"Children are so morbid these days," she mutters. "I'm sorry," she adds, unlocking the door. "I just don't feel comfortable talking about this. The past is past, Mackenzie. Let it rest."

And with that, she scoops up her groceries, steps into her apartment, and shuts the door in my face.

Instead of dwelling on the irony of Ms. Angelli telling me to let the past rest, I go home.

The phone is ringing when I get there. I'm sure it's Lyndsey, but I let it ring. A confession: I am not a good friend. Lyndsey writes letters, Lyndsey makes calls. Lyndsey makes plans. Everything I do is in reaction to everything she does, and I'm terrified of the day she decides not to pick up the phone, not to take the first step. I'm terrified of the day Lyndsey outgrows my secrets, my ways. Outgrows me.

And yet. Some part of me—a part I wish were smaller—wonders if it would be better to let it go. Let her go. One less thing to juggle. One less set of lies, or at least omissions. I hate myself as soon as the thought forms. I reach for the phone.

"Hey!" I say, trying to sound breathless. "Sorry! I just walked in."

"Have you been out finding me some ghosts or exploring forbidden corners and walled-up rooms?"

"The search continues."

"I bet you're too busy getting close to Guyliner."

"Oh, yeah. If I could just keep my hands off him long enough to look around . . ." But despite the joke, I smile—a small genuine thing that she obviously can't see.

"Well, don't get too close until I can inspect him. So, how goes it in the haunted mansion?"

I laugh, even as a *third* name scratches itself into the list in my pocket. "Same old, same old." I dig the list out, unfold it on the counter. My stomach sinks.

Angela Price. 13.

Eric Hall. 15.

Penny Walker. 14.

"Pretty boring, actually," I add, running my fingers over the names. "How about you, Lynds? I want stories." I crumple the list, shove it back in my jeans, and head into my room.

"Bad day?" she asks.

"Nonsense," I say, sagging onto my bed. "I live for your tales of adventure. Regale me."

And she does. She rambles, and I let myself pretend we're sitting on the roof of her house, or crashed on my couch. Because as long as she talks, I don't have to think about Ben, or the dead girl in my room, or the missing pages in the study, or the Librarian erasing Histories. I don't have to wonder if I'm losing my mind, dreaming up Keepers, or acting paranoid, twisting glitches and bad luck into dangerous schemes. Because as long as she talks, I can be somewhere else, some*one* else.

But soon she has to leave, and hanging up feels like letting go. The world sharpens the way it does when I pull out of a memory and back into the present, and I examine the list again.

The Histories' ages have been going up.

I noticed it before and thought it was a blip, a rash of double digits, but now everyone on my list is in their teens. I can't afford to wait. I pull on some workout pants and a fresh black shirt, the knife still strapped carefully to my calf. I won't use it, but I can't bring myself to leave it behind. The metal feels good against my skin. Like armor.

I head into the living room right as Mom comes through the front door with her arms full of bags.

"Where are you off to?" she asks, dropping everything on the table as I continue toward the door.

"Going for a run," I say, adding, "Might go out for track this year." If my list doesn't settle down, I'll need a solid excuse for being gone so often anyway, and I used to run, back in middle school when I had spare time. I like running. Not that I actually plan to go running tonight, but still.

"It's getting dark," says Mom. I can see her working through the pros and cons. I head her off.

"There's still a little light left, and I'm pretty out of shape. Won't go far." I pull my knee to my chest in a stretch.

"What about dinner?"

"I'll eat when I get back."

Mom squints at me, and for a moment, part of me begs for her to see through this, a flimsy, half-concocted lie. But then she turns her attention to her bags. "I think it's a good idea, you joining track."

She always tells me she wishes I'd join a club, a sport, be a part of something. But I *am* a part of something.

"Maybe you could use some structure," she adds. "Something to keep you busy."

I almost laugh.

The sound crawls up my throat, a near hysterical thing, and I end up coughing to hold it back. Mom tuts and gets me a glass of water. Staying busy isn't exactly a problem right now. But last time I checked, the Archive didn't offer PE credits for catching escaped Histories.

"Yeah," I say, a little too sharply. "I think you're right."

In that moment, I want to shout.

I want to show her what I go through.

I want to throw it in her face.

I want to tell her the *truth*.

But I can't.

I would never.

I know better.

And so I do the only thing I can.

I walk out.

FIFTEEN

ANGELA PRICE is easy enough to find, and despite her being
very upset, and mistaking me for her dead best friend, which
of course only adds to her distress, I usher her back to Returns with
little more than cunning lies and a few hugs.

Eric Hall is scrawny, albeit a little . . . hormonal, and I get him to
the nearest Returns door with a giggle, a girlish look, and promises
I'll never have to keep.

By the time I finish hunting down and delivering Penny Walker,
I feel like I really have gone for a run. I have a headache from reading walls, my muscles burn from being constantly on guard, and
I think I might actually be able to sleep tonight. I'm making my
way back toward the cluster of numbered doors when something
catches my eye.

The white chalk circle on the front of one of the Returns doors
has been disturbed, altered. Two vertical lines and one horizontal
curve have been drawn into the chalk, turning my marker into a kind
of . . . smiley face? I bring my hand to the door and close my eyes,
and I've barely skimmed the surface of the memories when a form
appears right in front of me, lean and dressed in black, his silvery-
blond hair standing out against the dark.

Owen.

I let the memory roll forward, and his hand dances languidly
across the chalk, drawing the face. And then he dusts the white from
his fingers, puts his hands back in his pockets, and ambles down the

hall. But when he reaches the end, he doesn't continue around the corner. He turns on his heel and doubles back.

What is he doing here? He's not tracking, not hunting. He's . . . pacing.

I watch him come all the way down the hall, toward me, eyes on the floor. He walks until he's inches from my face. And then he stops and looks up, his eyes finding mine, and I can't shake the feeling that he *sees* me even though he's alone in the past and I'm alone in the now.

Who are you? I ask his wavering form.

It doesn't answer, only stares unblinking off into the dark beyond me.

And then I hear it.

Humming. Not the humming of the walls beneath my hands, not the sound of memories, but an actual human voice, somewhere nearby.

I pull away from the door and blink, the Narrows refocusing around me. The melody weaves through the halls, close. It's coming from the same direction as my numbered doors, and I round the corner to find Owen leaning against the door with the I above its handle.

His eyes are closed. But when I step closer, they drift open and turn to consider me. Crisp and blue.

"Mackenzie."

I cross my arms. "I was beginning to wonder if you were real."

An eyebrow arches. "What else would I be?"

"A phantom?" I say. "An imaginary friend?"

"Well then, am I all that you imagined?" The very corner of his mouth curls up as he pushes off the door. "You really doubt my existence?"

I don't take my eyes off him, don't even blink. "You have a way of disappearing."

He spreads his arms. "Well, here I am. Still not convinced?"

My eyes trail from the top of his white-blond hair over his sharp jaw, down his black clothes. Something's off.

"Where's your key?" I ask.

Owen pats his pockets. "I don't have one."

That's not possible.

I must have said it aloud, because his eyes narrow. "What do you mean?"

"A Keeper can't get into the Narrows without a key. . . ."

Unless he's not a Keeper. I close the gap between us. He doesn't retreat, not as I come toward him, and not as I press my hand flush against his chest and see . . .

Nothing. Feel nothing. Hear nothing.

Only quiet. Dead quiet. My hands fall away, and the quiet vanishes, replaced by the low hum of the hall.

Owen Chris Clarke isn't a Keeper. He's not even alive.

He's a *History.*

But that can't be. He's been here for days, and he hasn't started slipping. The blue of his eyes is so pale that I'd notice even the slightest change, and his pupils are crisp and black. And everything about him is level, normal, human. But he's not.

Behind my eyes I see him break Hooper's neck, and I take a step back.

"What's wrong?" he says.

Everything, I want to say. Histories have a pattern. From the moment they wake up, they devolve. They become more distressed, frightened, destructive. Whatever they're feeling at the moment of waking becomes worse and worse. But they never, ever become rational, or self-possessed, or calm. Then how does Owen behave like a person in a hallway rather than a History in the Narrows? And why isn't he on my list?

"I need you to come with me," I say, trying to picture the nearest Returns door. Owen takes a single small step back.

"Mackenzie?"

"You're dead."

His brow creases. "Don't be ridiculous."

"I can prove it to you." Prove it to both of us. My hand itches for the knife that's hidden against my leg, but I think better of it. I've seen Owen use it. Instead I grip Da's key. The teeth are rusted but sharp enough to break the skin, with pressure.

"Hold out your hand."

He frowns but doesn't hesitate, offering his right hand. I press the key against his palm—putting a key in the hands of a History; Da would kill me—and drag it quick across his skin. Owen hisses and pulls back, cradling his hand to his chest.

"Alive enough to feel that," he grumbles, and I'm afraid I've made a mistake until he looks down at his hand and his expression changes, shifts from pain to surprise.

"Let me see," I say.

Owen turns his palm toward me. The slash across his hand is a thin dark line, the skin clearly broken, but the cut doesn't bleed. His eyes float up to mine.

"I don't . . ." he starts, before his gaze drops back to his hand. "I don't understand . . . I felt it."

"Does it still hurt?"

He rubs at the line on his palm. "No." And then, "What am I?"

"You're a History," I say. "Do you know what that means?"

He pauses, looks down over his arms, his wrists and hands, his clothes. A shadow flits across his face, but when he answers, it's with a tight "No."

"You're a record of the person you were when you were alive."

"A ghost?"

"No, not exactly. You——"

"But I *am* a ghost," he cuts in, his voices inching louder, and I brace myself for the slip. "I'm not flesh and blood, I'm not human, I'm not alive, I'm not *real* . . ." And then he checks himself. Swallows hard and looks away. When his eyes find mine, he's calm. Impossible.

"You have to go back," I say again.

"Go where?"

"To the Archive. You don't belong here."

"Mackenzie," he says, "I don't belong there either."

And I believe him. He's not on my list, and if it weren't for the irrefutable proof, I'd never believe he's a History. I force myself to focus. He *will* slip; he has to——and then I'll have to deal with him. I should deal with him now.

"How did you get here?" I ask.

He shakes his head. "I don't know. I was asleep, and then I was awake, and then I was walking." He seems to remember only as he says it. "And then I saw you, and I knew you needed help. . . ."

"I didn't *need* help," I snap, and he does the one thing I've never seen a History do.

He *laughs*. It's a soft, choked sound——but still.

"Yes, well," he says, "you *looked like* you might appreciate a hand, then. How did *you* get here?"

"Through a door."

His eyes go to the numbered ones. "One of those?"

"Yes."

"Where do they go?"

"Out."

"Can *I* go out?" he asks. There's no apparent strain in the question, only curiosity.

"Not through those doors," I say. "But I can take you through one with a white circle—"

"Those doors don't go out," he says shortly. "They go back. I'd rather stay here than go back there." A flicker of anger again, but he's already regaining composure, despite the fact that Histories don't *have* composure.

"You need to go back," I say.

His eyes narrow a fraction.

"I confuse you," he says. "Why is that?"

Is he actually trying to *read* me?

"Because you're—"

The sound of footsteps cuts through the hall.

I pull the list from my pocket, but it's still blank. Then again, I'm standing right beside a History who, according to this same slip of paper, doesn't exist, so I'm not sure how much I trust the system right now.

"Hide," I whisper.

Owen holds his ground and stares past me down the hall. "Don't make me go back."

The steps are getting closer, only a few corridors away. "Owen, hide now."

His gaze shifts back to me. "Promise me you won't—"

"I can't do that," I say. "My job—"

"Please, Mackenzie. Give me one day."

"Owen—"

"You owe me." It's not a challenge. When he says it, there's a careful absence in his voice. No accusation. No demand. Just simple, empty observation. "You do."

"Excuse me?"

"I helped you with that man, Hooper." I can't believe a History is trying to bargain. "Just one day."

The steps are too close.

"Fine," I hiss, pointing to a corridor. "Now, hide."

Owen takes a few silent strides backward, vanishing into the dark as I spin and make my way briskly to the bend in the hall where the steps are growing louder and closer—

And then they stop.

I press myself against the corner and wait, but judging by the way the footsteps paused, the other person is waiting too.

Someone has to move, so I turn the corner.

The fist comes out of nowhere, narrowly missing my cheek. I duck and cross behind my attacker. A pole swipes toward my stomach, but my foot finds its way up at the same time, boot connecting with stick. The pole tumbles toward the damp floor. I catch it and bring it up to the attacker's throat, pinning him against the wall. It's only then that I look at his face, and I'm met by a crooked smile. My grip loosens.

"That's twice in one day you've assaulted me."

I let the pole fall away, and Wesley straightens.

"What the hell, Wes?" I growl. "I could have hurt you."

"Um," he says, rubbing his throat, "you kind of did."

I shove him, but the moment my hands meet his body, his crashing rock band sound shatters into *got to get away from there from her from them massive house giant stairs high laughter and glass escape* before the pressure forces me back, knocking the air from my lungs. I feel ill. With Owen, I forgot about the inextricable link between touch and sight—he may act like a living being, but his quiet says he's not. And Wes is anything but quiet. Did *he* see anything when our skin met? If he did, it doesn't show.

"You know," he says, "for someone who doesn't like touching people, you keep finding ways to put your hands on me."

"What are you even doing here?" I say.

He nods at the numbered doors. "I forgot my bag in the café. Thought I'd run back and get it."

"Using the Narrows."

"How do you think I go back and forth? I live on the other side of the city."

"I don't know, Wes! A cab? A bus? On foot?"

He raps a knuckle against the wall. "Condensed space, remember? The Narrows, fastest transportation around."

I offer up the pole. "Here's your stick."

"*Bō* staff." He takes the pole and twirls it a few times. There's something in his eyes, not his usual grin, but a kind of happiness nonetheless, an excitement. Boys. He flicks his wrist and the pole collapses into a short cylinder, like the batons sprinters pass off in relay races.

He watches, obviously waiting for me to be impressed.

"Ooooooh," I say halfheartedly, and he grumbles and puts the stick away. I turn back toward my numbered doors, eyes scanning the dark beyond for Owen, but he's gone.

"How's the hunting?" asks Wes.

"It's getting worse," I say. I can already feel a new name writing itself on the paper in my pocket. I leave the list there. "Was it this bad when you covered the territory?"

"I don't think so, no. A bit irregular, but never unmanageable. I don't know if I had the full picture, or if I was only being given names here and there."

"Well, it's bad now. I cross one History off my list, and three more show up. It's like that Greek beast . . ."

"Hydra," he answers; then, reading my surprise, adds, "Again with the skepticism. I took a trip to the Smithsonian. You should try it sometime. Get your hands on a few ancient artifacts. Worlds faster than reading books."

"Aren't all those things behind glass?"

"Yes, well . . ." He shrugs as we reach the door. "You done for the night?"

I think of Owen somewhere in the dark. But I already promised him a day. And I really, really want a shower.

"Yeah," I say finally. "Let's go."

Wes and I part ways in the lobby, and I'm about to hit the stairs when I get this gut feeling and find myself making a detour to the study.

Angelli was no help at all, what with her *let the past rest* speech—but I can't, not until I know what happened—and there's got to be something here. I don't know where I'll find it, but I've got an idea where to start.

The directories fill a shelf, a block of red, then a block of blue. I swipe the oldest blue directory, the one from the first years of the conversion, shuffling the books a bit to hide the gap. And then I head upstairs to find Mom experimenting in the kitchen, Dad hiding in a corner of the living room with a book, and a box of pizza open on the table. I field a few questions on the length and quality of my run, finally enjoy a glorious shower, and then sink onto my bed with a slice of cold pizza and the Coronado's log, flipping through as I eat. There has to be *something*. Names fill the inaugural year, but the three missing years that follow are a wall of white in the middle of the book. I scan 1954, hoping that some clue—one of the names, maybe—will catch my eye.

In the end it's not the names that strike me as odd, but the lack of them. In the inaugural year, every room is rented out, and there's a wait list at the back of the section. The year the records come back, the word *Vacant* is written into more than a dozen spots. Was a murder enough to empty the Coronado? What about *two* murders? I think of Marcus Elling on his shelf, the stretch of black where his death should have been. His name is among the ones that fill the original roster. Three years later, his room is among the ones marked *Vacant*. Did people leave in reaction to the deaths? Or could more of them be victims? I dig up a pen and pull my Archive list from my pocket. Turning it over, I scribble out the names of the other residents whose apartments were marked *Vacant* when the records resumed.

I sit back to read over the names, but I've only reached the third one when they begin to *disappear*. One by one, from top to bottom, the words soak into the paper and fade away until the page is blank, erasing themselves the way names do when I've returned the Histories. I've always thought of the paper as a one-way street, a way for the Archive to send notices, not a place for dialogue.

But a moment later, new words write themselves across the page.

Who are these people? —*A*

After a brief period of stunned silence, I force myself to scribble out an explanation of the directory: the missing pages and the vacancies. I watch as each word dissolves into the paper, and hold my breath until Roland responds.

Will investigate.

And then . . .

Paper is not safe. Do not use again. —R

I can feel the end of the discussion in Roland's handwriting as it dissolves. As if he's set the pen aside and closed the book. I've seen the ancient ledger they keep on the front desk, the one they use to send out names and notes and summons, a different page for every Keeper, every Crew. I hold my slip of Archive paper, wondering why I never knew that it could carry messages both ways.

Four years of service, and the Archive is still so full of secrets— some big, like altering; some small, like this. The more of them I learn, the more I realize how little I know, and the more I wonder about the things I *have* been told. The rules I have been taught.

I turn the Archive paper over. There are three new names. None of them is Owen's. The Archive teaches us that Histories share a common want, a need, to get out. It is a primal, vital thing, an all-consuming hunger: as if they are starved and all the food is on the other side of the Narrows' walls. All the air. All the life. That need causes panic, and the History spirals and shatters and slips.

But Owen isn't slipping, and when he asked for one thing, it wasn't a way out.

It was time.

Don't make me go back.

Promise me you won't.

Please, Mackenzie. Give me one day.

I press my palms into my eyes. A History who's not on my list and doesn't slip and wants only to stay awake.

What kind of History is that?

What is Owen?

And then, somewhere in my tangled, tired thoughts, the *what* becomes a far more dangerous word.

Who.

"Don't you ever wonder about the Histories?" I ask. "Who they are?"

"Were," you correct. "And no."

"But . . . they're people . . . were people. Don't you—"

"Look at me." You knock my chin up with your finger. "Curiosity is a gateway drug to sympathy. Sympathy leads to hesitation. Hesitation will get you killed. Do you understand?"

I nod halfheartedly.

"Then repeat it."

I do. Over and over again, until the words are burned into my memory. But unlike your other lessons, this one never quite sticks. I never stop wondering about the *who* and the *why*. I just learn to stop admitting it.

SIXTEEN

I **CAN'T EVEN TELL** if the sun is up yet.
Rain taps against the windows, and when I look out, all I see is gray. The gray of clouds and of wet stone buildings and wet streets. The storm drags its stomach over the city, swelling to fill the spaces between buildings.

I had a dream.

In it, Ben was stretched out on the living room floor, drawing pictures with his blue pencils and humming Owen's song. When I came in, he looked up, and his eyes were black; but as he got to his feet, the black began to shrink, twist back into the centers, leaving only warm brown.

"I won't slip," he said, drawing an *X* on his shirt in white chalk. "Cross my heart," he said. And then he reached out and took my hand, and I woke up.

What if?

It is a dangerous thought, like a nag, like an itch, like a prickle where my head meets my neck, where my thoughts meet my body.

I swing my legs off the bed.

"All Histories slip," I say aloud.

But not Owen, whispers another voice.

"Yet." I say the word aloud and shake away the clinging threads of the dream.

Ben is gone, I think, even though the words hurt. *He's gone.* The pain is sharp enough to bring me to my senses.

I promised Owen a day, and as I get dressed in the half dark, I wonder if I've waited long enough. I almost laugh. Making deals with a History. What would Da say? It would probably involve an admirable string of profanity.

It's just a day, whispers the small, guilty voice in my head.

And a day is long enough for a grown History to slip, growls Da's voice.

I pull my running shoes on.

Then why hasn't he?

Maybe he has. Harboring a History.

Not harboring. He's not on my—

You could lose your job. You could lose your life.

I shove the voices away and reach for the slip of Archive paper on my bedside table. My hand hovers above it when I see the number sandwiched between the other two.

Evan Perkins. 15.

Susan Lank. 18.

Jessica Barnes. 14.

As if on cue, a fourth name adds itself to the list.

John Orwell. 16.

I swear softly. Some small part of me thinks that maybe if I stop clearing the names, they will stop appearing. I fold the list and shove it in my pocket. I know the Archive doesn't work that way.

Out in the main room, Dad is sitting at the table.

It must be Sunday.

Mom has her rituals—the whims, the cleaning, the list-making. Dad has his too. One of them is commandeering the kitchen table every Sunday morning with nothing but a pot of coffee and a book.

"Where are you off to?" he asks without looking up.

"Going for a run." I do a few impromptu stretches. "Might go out for track this year," I add. One of the keys to lying is consistency.

Dad sips his coffee and offers an absent nod and a hollow "That's nice."

My heart sinks. I guess I should be glad he doesn't care, but I'm not. He's *supposed* to care. Mom cares so much, it's smothering; but that doesn't mean he's allowed to do this, to check out. And suddenly I need him to care. I need him to give me something so I know he's still here, still Dad.

"I've been working on those summer reading books." Even though it's a crime against nature to do homework in July.

He looks up, face brightening a little. "Good. It's a good school. Wesley's been helping you, right?" I nod, and Dad says, "I like that boy."

I smile. "I like him too." And since Wes seems to be the trick to coaxing signs of life out of my father, I add, "We've really got a lot in common."

Sure enough, Dad gets brighter still. "That's great, Mac." Now that I've got his attention, it lingers. His eyes search mine. "I'm glad you're making a friend here, honey. I know this isn't easy. None of this is easy." My chest tightens. Dad can't voice what *this* is any more than Mom can, but it's written across his tired face. "And I know you're strong, but sometimes you seem . . . lost."

It feels like the most he's said to me since we buried Ben.

"Are you . . ." he starts and stops, searching for the words. "Is everything . . ."

I spare him by taking a breath and wrapping my arms around his shoulders. Noise fills my head, low and heavy and sad, but I don't let go, not even when he returns the hug and the sound redoubles.

"I just want to know if you're okay," he says, so soft I barely hear it through the static.

I'm not, not at all; but his worry gives me the strength I need to lie. To pull back and smile and tell him I'm fine.

Dad wishes me a good run, and I slip away to find Owen and the others.

According to my paper, Owen Chris Clarke doesn't exist.

But he's here in the Narrows, and it's time to send him back.

I wrap the key cord around my wrist and look up and down a familiar, dimly lit passageway.

It occurs to me that I need to find him first. Which turns out not to be a problem, because Owen isn't hiding. He's sitting on the ground with his back against a wall near the end of the corridor, legs stretched out lazily, one knee bent up to support an elbow. His head is slumped forward, hair falling into his eyes.

He's supposed to be distressed, supposed to be banging on the doors, tearing at himself, at the Narrows, at everything, searching for a way out. He's supposed to be slipping. He's not supposed to be *sleeping*.

I take a step forward.

He doesn't move.

I take another step, fingers tightening around my key.

I reach him, and he still hasn't budged. I crouch down, wondering what's wrong with him, and I'm just about to stand up when I feel something cool against my hand, the one clutching the key.

Owen's fingers slide over my wrist, bringing with them . . . nothing. No noise.

"Don't do that," he says, head still bowed.

I let the key slide from my grip, back to the end of its length of cord, and straighten, looking down at him.

He tips his head up. "Good evening, Mackenzie."

A bead of cold sweat runs down my spine. He hasn't slipped at all. If anything, he seems calmer. Grounded and human and alive. *Ben could be like this,* the dangerous thought whispers through my mind. I push it back.

"Morning," I correct.

He stands then, the motion fluid, like sliding down the wall but in reverse.

"Sorry," he says, gesturing to the space around us. A smile flickers across his face. "It's kind of hard to tell."

"Owen," I say, "I came to . . ."

He steps forward and tucks a stray chunk of hair behind my ear. His touch is so quiet I forget to pull back. As his hand traces the edge of my jaw and comes to rest beneath my chin, I feel that same *silence*. That dead quiet that Histories have . . . I've never paid it any mind, always been too busy hunting. But it's not just the simple absence of sound and life. It is a *silence* that spreads behind my eyes, where memories should be. It is a *silence* that doesn't stop at our skin, but reaches into me, fills me with cottony quiet, spreads through me like calm.

"I don't blame you," he says softly.

And then his hand falls away, and for the first time in years, I have to resist the urge to reach out and touch someone back. Instead, I force myself to take a step away, put a measure of distance between us. Owen turns toward the nearest door and brings both hands up against it, splaying his fingers across the wood.

"I can feel it, you know," he whispers. "There's this . . . sense in the center of my body, like home is on the other side. Like if I could just get there, everything else would be okay." His hands stay up against the door, but he turns his head toward me. "Is that strange?"

The black in the center of his eyes stays contained, the pupils small and crisp despite the lack of light. What's more, there's a careful hollowness in his voice when he speaks about the draw of the doors, as if he's skirting strong emotion, holding on to control, holding on to himself. He looks at the door again, then closes his eyes, brings his forehead to rest against it.

"No," I say quietly. "It's not strange."

It's what all Histories feel. It's proof of what he is. But most Histories want help, want keys, want a way out. Most Histories are desperate and lost. And Owen is nothing like that. So why is he here?

"Most Histories wake up for a reason," I say. "Something makes them restless, and whatever it is, it's what consumes them from the moment they wake."

I want to know what happened to Owen Chris Clarke. Not just why he woke, but how he died. Anything that can shed light on what he's doing in my territory, clear-eyed and calm.

"Is there something consuming you?" I ask gently.

His eyes find mine in the semidark, and for a moment, sadness dulls the blue. But then it's gone, and he pushes off the door. "Can I ask you something?"

He's redirecting, but I'm intrigued. Histories don't tend to care about Keepers. They see us only as obstacles. Asking a question means he's curious. Curious means he cares. I nod.

"I know that you're doing something wrong," he says, his eyes brushing over my skin, working their way up to my face. "Letting me stay here. I can tell."

"You're right," I say. "I am."

"Then why are you doing it?"

Because you don't make sense, I want to say. Because Da told me to always trust my gut. *Stomach tells when you're hungry,* he'd say, *and when you're sick, and when you're right or wrong. Gut knows.* And my gut says there's a reason Owen is here now.

I try to shrug. "Because you asked for a day."

"That man with the knife asked for your key," says Owen. "You didn't give it to him."

"He didn't ask nicely."

He flashes me that ghost of a smile, a quirk of his lips, there and gone. He steps closer, and I let him. "Even the dead can have manners."

"But most don't," I say. "I answered your question. Now answer one of mine."

He gives a slight obliging bow. I look at him, this impossible History. What made him this way?

"How did you die?"

He stiffens. Not much, to his credit; but I catch the glimpse of tension in his jaw. His thumb begins to rub at the line I made on his palm. "I don't remember."

"I'm sure it's traumatic, to think—"

"No," he says, shaking his head. "It's not that. I don't remember. I *can't* remember. It's like it's just . . . blank."

My stomach twists. Could he have been altered, too?

"Do you remember your *life*?" I ask.

"I do," he says, sliding his hands into his pockets.

"Tell me."

"I was born up north, by the sea. Lived in a house on the cliffs in a small town. It was quiet, which I guess means I was happy." I know the feeling. My life before the Archive is a set of dull impressions, pleasant but distant and strangely static, as if they belong to someone else. "And then we moved to the city, when I was fourteen."

"Who's we?" I ask.

"My family." And there's that sadness again in his eyes. I don't realize how close we're standing until I see it, written across the blue. "When I think of living by the sea, it's all one picture. Blurred smooth. But the city, it was fractured, clear and sharp." His voice is low, slow, even. "I used to go up on the roof and imagine I was back on the cliffs, looking out. It was a sea of brick below me," he says. "But if I looked up instead of down, I could have been anywhere. I grew up there, in the city. It shaped me. The place I lived . . . it kept me busy," he adds with a small private smile.

"What was your house like?"

"It wasn't a house," he says. "Not really."

I frown. "What was it, then?"

"A hotel."

The air catches in my chest.

"What was it called?" I whisper.

I know the answer before he says it.

"The Coronado."

SEVENTEEN

I TENSE.
"What is it?" he asks.

"Nothing," I say, a fraction too fast. What are the odds of Owen's managing to make his way here, within arm's reach of the numbered doors that don't just lead out, but lead *home*?

I force myself to shrug. "It's unusual, isn't it? Living in a hotel?"

"It was incredible," he says softly.

"Really?" I ask before I can stop myself.

"You don't believe me?"

"It's not that," I say. "I just can't picture it."

"Close your eyes." I do. "First, you step into the lobby. It is glass and dark wood, marble and gold." His voice is smooth, lulling. "Gold traces the wallpaper, threads the carpet, it edges the wood and flecks the marble. The whole lobby glitters. It gleams. There are flowers in crystal vases: some roses the dark red of the carpet, others the white of stone. The place is always light," he says. "Sun streams in through the windows, the curtains always thrown back."

"It sounds beautiful."

"It was. We moved in the year after it was converted to apartments."

There's something vaguely formal about Owen—there is a kind of timeless grace about him, his movements careful, his words measured—but it's hard to believe he lived . . . and died . . . so long ago. But even more striking than his age is the date he's referring to: 1951. I didn't see the name *Clarke* in the directory, and now I know why. His family moved in during the time when the records are missing.

"I liked it well enough," he's saying, "but my sister loved it."

His eyes take on an unfocused quality—not slipping, not black, but haunted.

"It was all a game to Regina," he says quietly. "When we moved to the Coronado, she saw the whole hotel as a castle, a labyrinth, a maze of hiding places. Our rooms were side by side, but she insisted on passing me notes. Instead of slipping them under the door, she'd tear them up and hide the pieces around the building, tied to rocks, rings, trinkets, anything to weigh them down. One time she wrote me a story and scattered it all across the Coronado, wedged in garden cracks and under tiles, and in the mouths of statues. . . . It took me days to recover the fragments, and even then I never found the ending. . . ." His voice trails off.

"Owen?"

"You said you think there's a reason Histories wake up. Something that eats at them . . . us." He looks at me when he says it, and sadness streaks across his face, barely touching his features and yet transforming them. He wraps his arms around his ribs. "I couldn't save her."

My heart drops. I see the resemblance now, clear as day: their lanky forms, their silver-blond hair, their strange, delicate grace. The murdered girl.

"What happened?" I whisper.

"It was 1953. My family had lived at the Coronado for two years. Regina was fifteen. I was nineteen, and I'd just moved away," Owen says through gritted teeth, "a couple of weeks before it happened. Not far, but that day it might as well have been countries, worlds, because when she needed me, I wasn't there."

The words cut through me. The same words I've said to myself a thousand times when I think about the day Ben died.

"She bled out on our living room floor," he says. "And I wasn't there."

He leans back against the wall and slides down it until he's sitting on the ground.

"It was my fault," he whispers. "Do you think that's why I'm here?"

I kneel in front of him. "You didn't kill her, Owen." I know. I've seen who did.

"I was her big brother." He tangles his fingers in his hair. "It was my job to protect her. Robert was my friend first. I introduced them. I brought him into her life."

Owen's face darkens, and he looks away. I'm about to press when the scratch of letters in my pocket drags me back to the Narrows and the existence of other Histories. I pull the paper out, expecting a new name, but instead I find a summons.

Report at once. —R

"I have to go," I say.

Owen's hand comes to rest on my arm. For that moment, all the thoughts and questions and worries hush. "Mackenzie," he says, "is my day over?"

I stand, and his hand slides from my skin, taking the quiet with it.

"No," I say, turning away. "Not yet."

My mind is still spinning over Owen's sister—their resemblance is so strong, now that I know—as I step into the Archive. And then I see the front desk in the antechamber and come to a halt. The table is covered in files and ledgers, paper sticking out of the towering stacks of folders; and in the narrow alley between two piles, I can see Patrick's glasses. Damn.

"If you're trying to set a record for time spent here," he says without looking up from his work, "I'm pretty sure you've done it."

"I was just looking for——"

"You do know," he says, "that despite my title, this isn't *really* a library, right? We don't lend, we don't check out, we don't even have a reference-only reading area. These constant visits are not only tiresome, they're unacceptable."

"Yes, I know, but——"

"And are you not busy enough, Miss Bishop? Because last time I checked, you had"—he lifts a pad of paper from the table, flicks through several pages—"five Histories on your list."

Five?

"You do know why you *have* a list, correct?"

"Yes," I manage.

"And why it's imperative that you clear it?"

"Of course." There's a reason we constantly patrol, hoping to keep the numbers down, instead of just walking away, letting the Histories pile up in the Narrows. It's said that if enough Histories woke and got into the space between the worlds, they wouldn't need Keepers and keys to get through. They could force the doors open. *Two ways through any lock,* said Da.

"Then why are you still standing in front of——"

"Roland summoned me," I say, holding up my Archive paper.

Patrick huffs and sits back in his seat, examining me for a long moment.

"Fine," he says, returning to his work with little more than a gesture to the doors behind him.

I round the desk, slowing to watch him write in the ancient ledger sprawled open before him, and then, barely lifting his pen, in one of a half dozen smaller books. This is the first time I've ever seen the desk look *cluttered*.

"You seem busy," I say as I pass.

"That's because I am," he answers.

"Busier than usual."

"How astute."

"I'm busier too, Patrick. You can't tell me five names is standard, even for the Coronado."

He doesn't look up. "We're experiencing some minor technical difficulties, Miss Bishop. So sorry to inconvenience you."

I frown. "What kind of technical difficulties?" Glitching names? Armed Histories? Boys who don't slip?

"Minor ones," he snaps, making it clear as day that he's done talking.

I put the list away as I pass through the main doors in search of Roland.

Crossing into the warm light of the atrium, my spirits lift, and I feel that sense of peace Da always spoke of. The calm.

And then something crashes.

Not here in the atrium but down one of the branching halls, the metal sound of a shelf falling to the floor. Several Librarians rise from their work and hurry toward the noise, closing the doors behind them; but I stand very, very still, remembering that I am surrounded by the sleeping dead.

I hold my breath and listen. Nothing happens. The doors stay closed. No sound comes through.

And then a hand lands on my shoulder and I spin, twisting the arm back behind the body. In one fluid move, the arm and body are both gone, and somehow I'm the one being pinned, facedown, against a table.

"Easy, there," says Roland, letting go of my wrist and shoulder.

I take a few steadying breaths and lean against the table. "Why did you summon me? Did you find something? And did you hear that crash—"

"Not here," he murmurs, motioning toward a wing. I follow him, rubbing my arm.

The farther we get from the atrium, the older the Archive seems. Roland leads me down corridors that begin to twist and coil and shrink, laid out more like the Narrows than the stacks. The ceilings shift from arching overhead to dipping low, and the rooms themselves are smaller, cryptlike and dusty.

"What was that sound?" I ask as Roland leads the way; but he doesn't answer, only ducks into an oddly shaped alcove and turns again under a low stone arch. The room beyond is dim, and its walls are lined with worn, dated ledgers, not Histories. It is a cramped and faded version of the chamber in which I faced my trial.

"We have a problem," he says as soon as he's closed the door. "I looked through that list of names you sent. Most of them didn't tell me anything, but two of them did. Two more people died in the Coronado, both in August, both within a month of Marcus Elling. And both Histories were altered, their deaths removed."

I sink into a low leather chair, and Roland begins to pace. He looks exhausted, the lilt in his voice growing stronger as he talks. "I didn't find them at first because they'd been mis-shelved, the entry ledgers saying one place but the catalogs saying another. Someone didn't want them found."

"Who were they?"

"Eileen Herring, a woman in her seventies, and Lionel Pratt, a man in his late twenties. Both lived in the Coronado, and both lived alone, just like Elling, but that's the only connection I can find. I can't even be certain they died *in* the Coronado, but their last intact memories are of the building. Eileen leaving her apartment on the second floor. Lionel sitting on the patio, having a smoke. The moments are mundane to a fault. Nothing about them gives any indication of what caused their deaths, and yet both have been blacked out."

"Marcus, Eileen, and Lionel died in August. But Regina was murdered in March."

His eyes narrow. "I thought you didn't know her name."

The air snags in my lungs. I didn't. Not until Owen told me. But I can't exactly explain that I've been sheltering her brother.

"You're not the only one doing research, remember? I tracked down a resident of the Coronado, Ms. Angelli, who'd heard about the murder."

It's not a lie, I reason. Just a manipulation.

"What else did she know?" he presses.

I shake my head, trying to keep the spin as clean as I can. "Not much. She didn't seem eager to swap stories."

"Does Regina have a last name?"

I hesitate. If I give it, Roland will cross-reference her with Owen, who's notably absent. I know I should tell him about Owen—we're already breaking rules—but there are rules and there are Rules, and while Roland has gone far enough to break the former, I don't know how he'd handle my breaking the latter and harboring a History in the Narrows. And I've still got so many questions for Owen.

I shake my head. "Angelli wouldn't say, but I'll keep pressing." At least that lie will buy me a little time. I try to shift the focus back to the second set of deaths.

"Five months between Regina's murder and these three deaths,

Roland. How do we even know they're related?"

He frowns. "We don't. But it's a suspicious number of filing errors. At first I thought it might be a cleanup, but . . ."

"A cleanup?"

"Sometimes, if things go badly—if a History does commit atrocities in the Outer, and there are victims as well as witnesses—the Archive does what it can to minimize the risk of exposure."

"Are you saying the Archive actively covers up murders?"

"Not all evidence can be buried, but most can be twisted. Bodies can be disposed of. Deaths can be made to appear natural." I must look as appalled as I feel, because he keeps talking. "I'm not saying it's right, Miss Bishop; I'm just saying the Archive cannot afford to have people learning about Histories. About us."

"But would they ever hide evidence from their own?"

He frowns again. "I've seen certain measures taken in the Outer. Surfaces altered. I've known members of the Archive who think the past should be sheltered here, in these walls, but not beyond them. People who think the Outer isn't sacred. People who think there are things that Keepers and Crew should not see. But even they would never approve of this, of altering Histories, keeping the truth from *us*." When he says *us*, he doesn't mean me. He means the Librarians. He looks wounded. Betrayed.

"So someone here went rogue," I say. "The question is why."

"Not just why. *Who*." Roland slides down into a chair. "Remember when I said we had a problem? Right after I found Eileen and Lionel, I went back to review Marcus's History. I couldn't. Someone had tampered with him. Erased him entirely."

I grip the arms of my chair. "But that means it was done by a current Librarian. Someone in the Archive *now*."

Suddenly I'm glad I've kept Owen a secret. If he is connected, then there's one big difference between the other victims and him: he's *awake*. I stand a better chance of learning what he knows by listening than by turning him back into a corpse. And if he *is* connected, then the moment I turn him in, our rogue Librarian will almost certainly erase what's left of his memories.

"And judging by the rush job," says Roland, "they know we're digging."

I shake my head. "But I don't get it. You said that Marcus Elling's death was first altered when he was brought in. That was more than sixty years ago. Why would a current Librarian be trying to cover up the work of an old one?"

Roland rubs his eyes. "They wouldn't. And they're not."

"I don't understand."

"Alterations have a signature. Memories that have been hollowed out by different hands both register as black, but there's a subtle difference in the way they read. The way they feel. The way Marcus Elling's History reads now is the same way it read before. The same way the other two read. They were all altered by the same person."

One person over the course of sixty-five years. "Can Librarians even serve that long?"

"There's not exactly mandatory retirement," he says. "Librarians choose the duration of their term. And since, as long as we're stationed here, we don't age . . ." Roland trails off, and I make a mental list of everyone I've seen in the branch. There have to be a dozen, two dozen Librarians here at any one time. I know only a few by name.

"It's clever," Roland says, half to himself. "Librarians are the one element of the Archive that isn't—can't be—fully recorded, kept track of. If they stayed too long in one place, a rogue action would have drawn attention, but Librarians are in a constant state of flux, of transfer. The staff is never together for very long. People come and go. They move freely through the branches. It's conceivable . . ."

I think of Roland, who's been here since my induction; but the others—Lisa and Patrick and Carmen—all came later.

"You stuck around," I say.

"Had to keep you out of trouble."

Roland's Chucks bounce nervously.

"What do we do now?" I ask.

"*We* aren't going to do anything." Roland's head snaps up. "*You're* going to stay away from this case."

"Absolutely not."

"Mackenzie, that's the other reason I summoned you. You've already taken too many chances—"

"If you're talking about the list of names—"

"You're lucky I'm the one who found it."

"It was an accident."

"It was reckless."

"Maybe if I'd known the paper could do that, maybe if the Archive didn't keep everything so damn secret—"

"Enough. I know you only want to help, but whoever is doing this is dangerous, and they clearly don't want to get caught. It's imperative that you stay out of—"

"—the way?"

"No, the crosshairs."

I think of Jackson's knife and Hooper's attack. *Too late.*

"Please," says Roland. "You have a lot more to lose. Let me take it from here."

I hesitate.

"Miss Bishop . . ."

"How long have you been a Librarian?" I ask him.

179

"Too long," he says. "Now, promise me."

I force myself to nod, and I feel a pinch of guilt as his shoulders visibly loosen because he believes me. He gets to his feet and heads to the door. I follow, but halfway there, I stop.

"Maybe you should let me see Ben," I say.

"Why's that?"

"You know, as a cover-up. In case our rogue Librarian is watching."

Roland almost smiles. But he still sends me home.

EIGHTEEN

MOM SAYS there's nothing a hot shower can't fix, but I've been steaming up the bathroom for half an hour and I'm no closer to fixing anything.

Roland sent me home with a last glance and a reminder not to trust *anyone*. Which isn't hard when you know that someone is trying to bury the past and possibly you with it. My mind immediately goes to Patrick, but as much as I dislike him, the fact is he's a model Librarian, and there are at least a dozen other Librarians in the Archive on a given day. It could be any of them. Where do you even start?

I turn the water all the way hot and let it burn my shoulders. After Roland, I went hunting. I wanted to clear my head. It didn't work, and I only managed to return the youngest two Histories, cutting my list in half for all of five minutes before three new names flashed up.

I hunted for Owen too, but without any luck. I'm worried now that I've scared him away, though *away* is a relative term in the Narrows. There can be only so many places to hide, but I haven't found them yet, and apparently he has. I've never met a History who didn't want to be found. And why shouldn't he hide? His bartered day is up, and I'm the one who means to send him back. And I will . . . but first I need to know what he knows, and to get that, I need to gain his trust.

How do you gain a History's trust?

Da would say you don't. But as the water scalds my shoulders, I think of the sadness in Owen's eyes when he spoke of Regina—not of her death, when his voice went hollow, but the time before, when he talked about the games she'd play, the stories she'd hide throughout the building.

One time she wrote me a story and scattered it all across the Coronado, wedged in garden cracks and under tiles, and in the mouths of statues. . . . It took me days to recover the fragments, and even then I never found the ending. . . .

I snap the water off.

That's my shot at Owen's trust. A token. A peace offering. Something to hold on to. My spirits start to sink. What are the odds of anything left for sixty-five years still being here? And then I think of the Coronado, its slow, unkempt decay, and I realize that maybe, maybe. Just maybe.

I dress quickly, glancing at the Archive paper on my bed (and grimacing at the five names, the oldest—*18*). I used to wait days in hopes of getting a name, relished the moment of reveal. Now I shove the slip into my pocket. A stack of books sits on a large box, Dante's *Inferno* on top of the pile. I tuck the paperback under my arm and head out.

Dad is still at the kitchen table, on his third or fourth cup of coffee, judging by the near-empty pot beside him. Mom is sitting beside him, making lists. She has at least five of them in front of her, and she keeps writing and rewriting and rearranging as if she can decode her life that way.

They both look up as I walk in.

"Where are you off to?" asks Mom. "I bought paint."

One of the cardinal rules of lying is to never, if it can be prevented, involve someone else in your story, because you can't control them. Which is why I want to punch myself when the lie that falls from my lips is, "To hang out with Wesley."

Dad beams. Mom frowns. I cringe, turning toward the door. And then, to my amazement, lie becomes truth when I open it to find a tall, black-clad shape blocking my way.

"Lo and behold," says Wesley, slouching in the doorway, holding an empty coffee cup and a brown paper bag. "I have escaped."

"Speak of the devil," says Dad. "Mac was just on her way——"

"Escaped what?" I ask, cutting Dad off.

"The walls of Chez Ayers, behind which I have been confined for days. Weeks. Years." He rests his forehead against the door frame. "I don't even know anymore."

"I just saw you yesterday."

"Well. It *felt* like years. And now I come begging for coffee and bearing sweets with the intent of rescuing you from your indentured servitude in the pit of . . ." Wesley's voice trails off as he sees my mother, arms crossed, standing behind me. "Oh, hello!"

"You must be the boy," says Mom. I roll my eyes, but Wesley only smiles. Not crookedly, either, but a genuine smile that should clash with his black spiked hair and dark-rimmed eyes, but doesn't.

"You must be the mom," he says, sliding past me into the room. He transfers the paper bag to his left hand and extends his right to her. "Wesley Ayers."

Mom looks caught off guard by the smile, the open, easy way he does it. I know I am.

He doesn't even flinch when she takes his hand.

"I can see why my daughter likes you."

Wesley's smile widens as his hand slips back to his side. "Do you think she's falling for my dashing good looks, my charm, or the fact I supply her with pastries?"

Despite herself, Mom laughs.

"'Morning, Mr. Bishop," says Wesley.

"It's a beautiful day," says Dad. "You two should go. Your mom and I can handle the painting."

"Great!" Wes swings his arm around my shoulder, and the noise slams into me. I push back, try to block him out, and make a mental note to punch him when we're alone.

Mom gets us two fresh coffees and walks us to the door, watching as we go. As soon as the door closes behind us, I knock Wesley's arm off my shoulders and exhale at the sudden lack of pressure. "Ass."

He leads the way down to the lobby.

"You, Mackenzie Bishop," he says as we hit the landing, "have been a very bad girl."

"How so?"

He rounds the banister at the base of the staircase. "You involved me in a lie! Don't think I didn't catch it."

We pass through the study to the garden door, and he throws it open and leads me into the dappled morning light. The rain has stopped, and as I look around, I wonder if Regina would hide a bit of story in a place like this. The ivy is overgrown and might keep a token safe, but I doubt a scrap of paper would survive the seasons, let alone the years.

Wes drops onto the Faust bench and takes a cinnamon roll out of the paper bag. "Where were you *really* going, Mac?" he asks, holding out the bag.

I drag my thoughts back to him, taking a roll as I perch on the arm of the bench.

"Oh, you know," I say dryly, "I thought I'd lie in the sun for a few hours, maybe read a book, savor my lazy summer."

"Still trying to clear your list?"

"Yep." And question Owen. And find out why a Librarian would want to cover up deaths that are decades upon decades old. All without letting the Archive know.

"You brought the book just to throw your folks off the trail? How very thorough of you."

I take a bite of the cinnamon roll. "I am, in fact, a master of deceit."

"I believe it," Wes says, taking another bite. "So, about your list . . ."

"Yes?"

"I hope you don't mind, but I took care of the History in your territory."

I stiffen. *Owen.* Is that why I couldn't find him this morning? Did Wesley already send him back? I force my voice level. "What do you mean?"

"A History? You know? One of those things we're supposed to be hunting?"

I fight to keep my shock from showing. "I told you. I didn't. Need. Help."

"A simple thanks will suffice, Mac. Besides, it's not like I went looking for her. She kind of ran into me."

Her? I dig the list from my pocket. *Susan Lark. 18.* is gone. A sigh of relief escapes, and I sag back against the bench.

"Luckily, I was able to use my charm," he's saying. "That, and she thought I was her boyfriend. Which, I'll admit, facilitated things a bit." He runs his hand through his hair. It doesn't move.

"Thanks," I say softly.

"It's a hard word to say, I know. It takes practice."

I throw the last bite of my roll at him.

"Hey," he warns, "watch the hair."

"How long does it take to make it stick up like that?" I ask.

"Ages," he says, standing. "But it's worth it."

"Is it really?"

"I'll have you know, Miss Bishop, that this"—he gestures from his spiked black hair all the way down to his boots—"is absolutely vital."

I raise an eyebrow and stretch out across the weather-pocked stone. "Let me guess," I say with a pout. "You just want to be seen." I give the line a dramatic flair so that he knows I'm teasing. "You feel invisible in your skin, and so you dress yourself up to get a reaction."

Wes gasps. "How did you know?" But he can't keep the smile off his face. "Actually, much as I love seeing my father's tortured expression, or his trophy soon-to-be wife's disdain, this does serve a purpose."

"And what purpose would that be?"

"Intimidation," he says with a flourish. "It scares the Histories. First impressions are very important, especially in potentially combative situations. An immediate advantage helps me control the situation. Many of the Histories don't come from the here and now. And this"—again he gestures to the length of himself—"believe it or not, can be intimidating."

He straightens and steps toward me, into a square of sunlight. His sleeves are rolled up, revealing leather bracelets that cut through some scars and cover others. His brown eyes are alive and warm, and the contrast between his tawny irises and his black hair is stark but pleasant. Beneath it all, Wesley Ayers is actually quite handsome. My eyes pan down over his clothes, and he catches me before I can look away.

"What's the matter, Mac?" he says. "Are you finally falling victim to my devilish good looks? I knew it was only a matter of time."

"Oh, yeah, that's it. . . ." I say, laughing.

He leans down, rests his hand on the bench beside my shoulder.

"Hey," he says.

"Hey."

"You okay?"

The truth sits on my tongue. I want to tell him. But Roland warned me not to trust anyone; and though it sometimes feels like I've known Wes for months instead of days, I haven't. Besides, even if I could tell Wesley parts but not the whole, partial truths are so much messier than whole lies.

"Of course," I say, smiling.

"Of course," he parrots, and pulls away. He collapses onto his own bench and tosses an arm over his eyes to block the sun.

I look back at the study doors and think of the directories. I've been so focused on the early years, I haven't taken a close look at the current roster. I've been focused on the dead, but I can't forget about the living.

"Who else lives here?" I ask.

"Hm?"

"Here in the Coronado," I press. I might not be able to tell Wes what's going on, but that doesn't mean he can't help. "I've only met you and Jill and Ms. Angelli. Who lives here?"

"Well, there's this new girl who just moved in on floor three. Her family's re-opening the café. I hear she likes to lie, and hit people."

"Oh yeah? Well, there's that strange goth guy, the one who's always lurking around Five C."

"Strangely hot in a mysterious way, though, right?"

I roll my eyes. "Who's the oldest person here?"

"Ah, that distinction goes to Lucian Nix up on the seventh floor."

"How old is he?"

Wes shrugs. "Ancient."

Just then, the study door flies open and Jill appears on the threshold.

"I thought I heard you," she says.

"How goes it, strawberry?" asks Wes.

"Your dad has been calling us nonstop for half an hour."

"Oh?" he says. "I must have forgotten." The way he says it suggests he knows exactly what time it is.

"That's funny," Jill says as Wes drags himself to his feet, "because your dad seems to think you snuck out."

"Wow," I chime in, "you weren't kidding when you said you escaped Chez Ayers."

"Yeah, well. Fix it." Jill turns and closes the study door on both of us.

"She's charming," I say.

"She's like my aunt Joan, but in miniature. It's spooky. All she needs is a cane and a bottle of brandy."

I follow him into the study, but stop, eyes drifting to the directories.

"Wish me luck," he says.

"Good luck," I say. And then, as he vanishes into the hall, "Hey, Wes?"

He reappears. "Yeah?"

"Thanks for your help."

He smiles. "See? It's getting easier to say."

And with that he's gone, and I'm left with a lead. Lucian Nix. How long has he lived in the building? I tug down the most recent directory, flipping through until I reach the seventh floor.

7E. *Lucian Nix.*

I pull down the next directory.

7E. *Lucian Nix.*

And the next.

7E. *Lucian Nix.*

All the way back, past the missing files, to the very first year of the first blue book. 1950.

He's been here all along.

I press my ear against the door of **7E.**

Nothing. I knock. Nothing. I knock again, and I'm about to tug my ring off and listen for the sounds of any living thing when, finally, someone knocks back. There is a kind of scuffle on the other side of the door, joined by muttered cursing, and moments later the door swings open and collides with the metal side of a wheelchair. More cursing, and then the chair retreats enough so that the door can fully open. The man in the chair is, as Wesley put it, ancient. His hair is shockingly white, his milky eyes resting somewhere to my left. A thin stream of smoke drifts up from his mouth, where a narrow cigarette hangs, mostly spent. A scarf coils around his neck, and his clawlike fingers pluck at the fringe on the end.

"What are you staring at?" he asks. The question catches me off guard, since he's clearly blind. "You aren't saying anything," he adds, "so you must be staring."

"Mr. Nix?" I ask. "My name is Mackenzie Bishop."

"Are you a kiss-a-gram? Because I told Betty I didn't need girls being paid to come see me. Rather have no girls at all than that—"

I'm not entirely sure what a kiss-a-gram is. "I'm not a kiss—"

"There was a time when all I had to do was smile. . . ." He smiles now, flashing a pair of fake teeth that don't fit quite right.

"Sir, I'm not here to kiss you."

He adjusts his direction at the sound of my voice, pivoting in his chair until he's nearly facing me, and lifts his chin. "Then what are you knocking on my door for, little lady?"

"My family is renovating the coffee shop downstairs, and I wanted to introduce myself."

He gestures to his wheelchair. "I can't exactly go downstairs," he says. "Have everything brought up."

"There's . . . an elevator."

He has a sandpaper laugh. "I've survived this long. I've no plans to perish in one of those metal death traps." I decide I like him. His hand drifts shakily up to his mouth, removes the stub of his cigarette. "Bishop. Bishop. Betty brought in a muffin that was sitting in the hall. Suppose you're to blame for that."

"Yes, sir."

"More of a cookie person, myself. No offense to the other baked goods. I just like cookies. Well, suppose you want to come in."

He slides the wheelchair back several feet into the room, and it catches the edge of the carpet. "Blasted device," he growls.

"Would you like a hand?"

He throws both of his up. "I've got two of those. Need some new eyes, though. Betty's my eyes, and she's not here."

I wonder when Betty will be back.

"Here," I say, crossing the threshold. "Let me."

I guide the chair through the apartment to a table. "Mr. Nix," I say, sitting down beside him. I set the copy of the *Inferno* on the worn table.

"No *Mr.* Just Nix."

"Okay . . . Nix, I'm hoping you can help me. I'm trying to find out more about a series of"—I try to think of how to put this politely, but can't—"a series of deaths that happened here a very long time ago."

"What would you want to know about that for?" he asks. But the question lacks Angelli's defensiveness, and he doesn't feign ignorance.

"Curiosity, mostly," I say. "And the fact that no one seems to want to talk about it."

"That's because most people don't know about it. Not these days. Strange things, those deaths."

"How so?"

"Well, that many deaths so close together. No foul play, they said, but it makes you wonder. Weren't even in the paper. It was news around here, of course. For a while it looked like the Coronado wouldn't make it. No one would move in." I remember the string of vacancy listings in the directories. "Everyone thought it was cursed."

"You didn't, obviously," I say.

"Says who?"

"Well, you're still here."

"I may be stubborn. Doesn't mean I have the faintest idea what happened that year. String of bad luck, or something worse. Still, it's strange, how badly people wanted to forget about it."

Or how badly the Archive wanted them to.

"All started with that poor girl," says Nix. "Regina. Pretty thing. So cheerful. And then someone went and killed her. So sad, when people die so young."

Someone? Doesn't he know it was Robert?

"Did they catch the killer?" I ask.

Nix shakes his head sadly. "Never did. People thought it was her boyfriend, but they never found him."

Anger coils inside me at the image of Robert trying to wipe the blood off his hands, pulling on one of Regina's coats, and running.

"She had a brother, didn't she? What happened to him?"

"Strange boy." Nix reaches out to the table, fingers dancing until they find a pack of cigarettes. I take up a box of matches and light one for him. "The parents moved out right after Regina's death, but the boy stayed. Couldn't let go. Blamed himself, I think."

"Poor Owen," I whisper.

Nix frowns, blind eyes narrowing on me. "How did you know his name?"

"You told me," I say steadily, shaking out the match.

Nix blinks a few times, then taps the space between his eyes. "Sorry. I swear it must be going. Slowly, thanks be to God, but going all the same."

I set the spent match on the table. "The brother, Owen. How did he die?"

"I'm getting there," says Nix, taking a drag. "After Regina, well, things started to settle at the Coronado. We held our breaths. April passed. May passed. June passed. July passed. And then, just when we were starting to let out our air . . ." He claps his hands together, showering his lap with ash. "Marcus died. Hung himself, they said, but his knuckles were cut up and his wrists were bruised. I know because I helped cut the body down. Not a week later, Eileen goes down the south stairs. Broke her neck. Then, oh, what was his name, Lionel? Anyway, young man." His hand falls back into his lap.

"How did he die?"

"He was stabbed. Repeatedly. Found his body in the elevator. Not much use calling that one an accident. No motive, though, no weapon, no killer. No one knew what to make of it. And then Owen . . ."

"What happened?" I ask, gripping my chair.

Nix shrugs. "No one knows—well, I'm all that's left, so I guess I should say no one *knew*—but he'd been having a hard time." His milky eyes find my face and he points a bony finger up at the ceiling. "He went off the roof."

I look up and feel sick. "He jumped?"

Nix lets out a long breath of smoke. "Maybe. Maybe not. Depends on how you want to spin things. Did he jump or was he pushed? Did Marcus hang himself? Did Eileen trip? Did Lionel . . . well, there ain't much doubt about what happened to Lionel, but you see my point. Things stopped after that summer, though, and never started up again. No one could make sense of it, and it don't do any good to be thinking morbid thoughts, so the people here did the one thing they could do. They forgot. They let the past rest. You probably should too."

"You're right," I say softly, but I'm still looking up, thinking about the roof, about Owen.

I used to go up on the roof and imagine I was back on the cliffs, looking out. It was a sea of brick below me. . . .

My stomach twists as I picture his body going over the edge, blue eyes widening the instant before the pavement hits.

"I'd better be going." I push myself to my feet. "Thank you for talking to me about this."

Nix nods absently. I head for the door, but stop, turn back to see him still hunched over his cigarette, dangerously close to setting his scarf on fire.

"What kind of cookies?" I ask.

His head lifts, and he smiles. "Oatmeal raisin. The chewy kind."

I smile even though he can't see. "I'll see what I can do," I say, closing the door behind me. And then I head for the stairs.

Owen was the last to die, and one way or another, he went off the roof.

So maybe the roof has answers.

NINETEEN

I TAKE THE STAIRWELL up to the roof access door, which looks rusted shut, but it's not. The metal grinds against the concrete frame, and I step through a doorway of dust and cobwebs, past a crumbling overhang, and out into a sea of stone bodies. I had seen the statues from the street, gargoyles perched around the perimeter of the roof. What I couldn't see from there is that they cover the entire surface. Hunching, winged, sharp-toothed, they huddle here and there like crows, and glare at me with broken faces. Half of their limbs are missing, the rock eaten away by time and rain and ice and sun.

So this is Owen's roof.

I try to picture him leaning against a gargoyle, head tipped back against a stone mouth. And I can see it. I can see him in this place.

But I can't see him jumping.

There is something undeniably sad about Owen, something lost, but it wouldn't take this shape. Sadness can sometimes sap the fight from a person's features, but his are sharp. Daring. Almost defiant.

I trail my hand along a demon's wing, then make my way to the edge of the roof.

It was a sea of brick below me. But if I looked up instead of down, I could have been anywhere.

If he didn't jump, what happened?

A death is traumatic. Vivid enough to mark any surface, to burn in like light on photo paper.

I slide the ring from my finger, kneel, and press my hands flat to the weathered roof. My eyes slide shut, and I reach and reach. The thread is so thin and faint, I can barely grab hold. A distant tone tickles my skin, and finally I catch what little is left of the memory. My fingers go numb. I spin time back, past years and years of quiet. Decades and decades of nothing but an empty roof.

And then the rooftop plunges into black.

A flat, matte black I recognize immediately. Someone has reached into the roof itself and altered the memories, leaving behind the same dead space I saw in Marcus Elling's History.

And yet it doesn't *feel* the same. It's just like Roland said. Black is black, but it doesn't feel like the same hand, the same signature. And that makes sense. Elling was altered by a Librarian in the Archive. This roof was altered by someone in the Outer.

But the fact that multiple people tried to erase this piece of past is hardly comforting. What could have possibly happened to merit this?

. . . there are things that even Keepers and Crew should not see. . . .

I rewind past the black until the roof appears again, faded and unchanging, like a photo. And then finally, with a lurch, the photo flutters into life and lights and muddled laughter. This is the memory that hummed. I let it roll forward and see a night gala, with fairy lights and men in coattails and women in dresses with tight waists and A-line skirts, glasses of champagne and trays balanced on gargoyles' wings. I scan the crowd in search of Owen or Regina or Robert, but find none of them. A banner strung between two statues announces the conversion of the Coronado from hotel to apartments. The Clarkes don't live here yet. It will be a year until they move in. Three years until the string of deaths. I frown and guide the memory backward, watching the party dissolve into a faded, empty space.

Before that night there is nothing loud enough to hum, and I let go of the thread and blink, wincing in the sunlight on the abandoned roof. A stretch of black amidst the faded past. Someone erased Owen's death, carved it right out of this place, buried the past from both sides. What could have possibly happened that year to make the Archive—or someone in it—do this?

I weave through the stone bodies, laying my hands on each one, reaching, hoping one of them will hum. But they are all silent, empty. I'm nearly back to the rusted door when I hear it. I pause midstep, my fingers resting on an especially toothy gargoyle to my right.

He's whispering.

The sound is little more than an exhale through clenched teeth, but there it is, the faintest hum against my skin. I close my eyes and roll time back. When I finally reach the memory, it's faded, a pattern of light blurred to nearly nothing. I sigh and pull away, when something snags my attention—a bit of metal in the gargoyle's mouth. Its face is turned up to the sky, and time has worn away the top of its head and most of its features, but its fanged mouth hangs open an inch or two, intact, and something is lodged behind its teeth. I reach between stone fangs and withdraw a slip of rolled paper, bound by a ring.

One time she wrote me a story and scattered it across the Coronado, wedged in garden cracks and under tiles, and in the mouths of statues . . .

Regina.

My hands shake as I slide the metal off and uncurl the brittle page.

And then, having reached the top, the hero faced the gods and monsters that meant to bar his path.

I let the paper curl in on itself and look at the ring that held it closed. It's not jewelry—it's too big to fit a finger or a thumb—and clearly not the kind a young girl would wear anyway, but a perfect, rounded thing. It appears to be made of iron. The metal is cold and heavy, and one small hole has been drilled into the side of it; but other than that, the ring is remarkably undisturbed by scratches or imperfections. I slide it gently back over the paper and send up a silent thank-you to the long-dead girl.

I can't give Owen much time, and I can't give him closure.

But I can give him this.

"Owen?"

I wince at the sound of my own voice echoing through the Narrows.

"Owen!" I call again, holding my breath as I listen for something, anything. Still hiding, then. I'm about to reach out and read the walls—though they failed to lead me to him last time—when I hear it, like a quiet, careful invitation.

The humming. It is thin and distant, like threads of memory, just enough to take hold of, to follow.

I wind through the corridors, letting the melody lead me, and finally find Owen sitting in an alcove, a doorless recess, the lack of key light and outlines rendering the space even dimmer than the rest of the Narrows. No wonder I couldn't find him. My eyes barely register the space. Pressed against the wall, he is little more than a dark shape crowned in silver-blond, his head bowed as he hums and runs his thumb over the small dark line on his palm.

He looks up at me, the song trailing into the nothing. "Mackenzie."

His voice is calm but his eyes are tense, as if he's trying to steel himself. "Has it been a day?"

"Not quite," I say, stepping into the alcove. "I found something." I sink to my knees. "Something of yours."

I hold out my hand and uncurl my fingers. The slip of paper bound by the iron ring shines faintly in the dark.

Owen's eyes widen a fraction. "Where did you . . . ?" he whispers, voice wavering.

"I found it in a gargoyle's mouth," I say. "On the Coronado roof." I offer him the note and the ring, and when he takes it, his skin brushes mine and there is a moment of quiet in my head, a sliver, and then it's gone as he pulls back, examining my gift.

"How did you—"

"Because I live there now."

Owen lets out a shuddering breath. "So that's where the numbered doors lead?" he asks. Longing creeps into his voice. "I think I knew that."

He slides the fragile paper from its ring and reads the words despite the dark. I watch his lips move as he recites them to himself.

"It's from the story," he whispers. "The one she hid for me, before she died."

"What was it about?"

His eyes lose focus as he thinks, and I don't see how he can draw up a story from so long ago, until I remember that he's passed the decades sleeping. Regina's murder is as fresh to him as Ben's is to me.

"It was a quest. A kind of odyssey. She took the Coronado and made it grand, not just a building, but a whole world, seven floors full of adventure. The hero faced caves and dragons, unclimbable walls, impassable mountains, incredible dangers." A faint laugh crosses his lips as he remembers. "Regina could make a story out of anything." He closes his hand over the note and the ring. "Could I keep this? Just until the day's over?"

I nod, and Owen's eyes brighten—if not with trust, then with hope. Just like I wanted. And I hate to steal that flicker of hope from him so soon, but I don't have a choice. I need to know.

"When I was here before," I say, "you were going to tell me about Robert. What happened to him?"

The light goes out of Owen's eyes as if I blew out a candle's flame.

"He got away," he says through clenched teeth. "They let him get away. *I* let him get away. I was her big brother and I . . ." There's so much pain in his voice as it trails off; but when he looks at me, his eyes are clear, crisp. "When I first found my way here, I thought I was in Hell. Thought I was being punished for not finding Robert, for not tearing the world apart in search of him, for not tearing *him* apart. And I would have. Mackenzie, I really would have. He deserved that. He deserved worse."

My throat tightens as I tell Owen what I've told myself so many times, even though it never helps. "It wouldn't bring her back."

"I know. Trust me, I do. And I would have done far worse," he says, "if I'd thought there *was* a way to bring Regina back. I would have traded places. I would have sold souls. I would have torn this world apart. I would have done anything, broken any rule, just to bring her back."

My heart aches. I can't count the times I've sat beside Ben's drawer and wondered how much noise it would take to wake him up. And I can't deny how hard I've wished, since I met Owen, that he wouldn't slip: because if he could make it through, why not Ben?

"I was supposed to protect her," he says, "and I got her killed. . . ."

He must take my silence for simple pity, because he adds, "I don't expect you to understand."

But I do. Too well.

"My little brother is dead," I say. The words get out before I can stop them. Owen doesn't say *I'm sorry*. But he does shift closer, until we're sitting side by side.

"What happened?" he asks.

"He was killed," I whisper. "Hit and run. They got away. I would give anything to rewrite that morning, to walk Ben all the way to school, take an extra five seconds to hug him, to draw on his hand, do anything to change the moment when he crossed the street."

"And if you could find the driver . . ." says Owen.

"I would kill him." There is no doubt in my voice.

A silence falls around us.

"What was he like?" he asks, knocking his knee against mine. There is something so simple in it, as if I am just a girl, and he is just a boy, and we are sitting in a hallway—any hallway, not the Narrows—and I'm not talking about my dead brother with a History I'm supposed to have sent back.

"Ben? He was too smart for his own good. You couldn't lie to him, not even about things like Santa Claus or the Easter Bunny. He'd put on these silly glasses and cross-examine you until he found a crack. And he couldn't focus on anything unless he was drawing. He was really great at art. He made me laugh." I've never spoken this way about Ben, not since he died. "And he could be a real brat sometimes. Hated sharing. Would break something before he'd let you have it. This one time he broke an entire box of pencils because I wanted to borrow one. As if breaking pencils made them useless. So I pulled out this sharpener, one of those little plastic ones, and sharpened all the pencil halves and then we each had a set. Half as long as they were to start, but they still worked. It drove him mad."

A small laugh escapes, and then my chest tightens. "It feels wrong to laugh," I whisper.

"Isn't it strange? It's like after they die, you're only allowed to remember the good. But no one's all good."

I feel the scratch of letters in my pocket, but leave it.

"I've gone to see him," I say. "In the stacks. I talk to him, to his shelf, tell him what he's missing. Never the good stuff, of course. Just the boring, the random. But no matter how I hold on to his memory, I'm starting to forget him, one detail at a time. Some days I think the only thing that keeps me from prying open his drawer, from seeing him, from waking him, even, is the fact it's not him. Not really. They tell me there's no point because it wouldn't be him."

"Because Histories aren't people?" he asks.

I cringe. "No. That's not it at all." Even though most Histories *aren't* people, aren't human, not the way Owen is. "It's just that Histories have a pattern. They slip. The only thing that hurts me more than the idea of the thing in that drawer not being my brother is the idea of its being him, and my causing him pain. Distress. And then having to send him back to the stacks after all of it."

I feel Owen's hand drift toward mine, hover just above my skin. He waits to see if I'll stop him. When I don't, he curls his fingers over mine. The whole world quiets at his touch. I lean my head against the wall and close my eyes. The quiet is welcome. It dulls the thoughts of Ben.

"I don't feel like I'm slipping," says Owen.

"That's because you aren't."

"Well, that means it's possible, right? What if—"

"*Stop.*" I pull free of his touch and push myself to my feet.

"I'm sorry," he says, standing. "I didn't mean to upset you."

"I'm not upset," I say. "But Ben's gone. There's no bringing him back." The words are directed at myself more than at him. I turn to go. I need to move. Need to hunt.

"Wait," he says, taking my hand. The quiet floods in as he holds up the note in his other hand. "If you find any more of Regina's story, would you . . . would you bring it to me?" I hover at the edge of the alcove. "Please, Mackenzie. It's all I have left of her. What wouldn't you give, to have something, anything, of Ben's to hold on to?"

I think of the box of Ben's things, overturned on my bed, my hands shaking as I picked up each item and prayed there would be a glimpse, a fractured moment, anything. Clinging to a silly pair of plastic glasses with nothing more than a single, smudged memory.

"I'll keep an eye out," I say, and Owen pulls me into a hug. I flinch but feel nothing, only steady quiet.

"Thank you," he whispers against my ear, and my face flushes as his lips graze my skin. And then his arms slide away, taking the quiet and the touch, and he retreats into the alcove, the darkness swallowing everything but his silvery hair. I force myself to turn away, and hunt.

As nice as his touch was, it's not what lingers with me while I work. It's his words. Two words I tried to shut out, but they cling to me.

What if echoes in my head as I hunt.

What if haunts me through the Narrows.

What if follows me home.

TWENTY

I PEER OUT the Narrows door and into the hall, making sure the coast is clear before I step through the wall and back onto the third floor of the Coronado, sliding my ring on. I got the list down to two names before it shot back up to four. Whatever technical difficulty the Archive is experiencing, I hope they fix it soon. I am a horrible hollow kind of tired; all I want is quiet and rest.

There is a mirror across from me, and I check my reflection in it before heading home. Despite the bone-deep fatigue and the growing fear and frustration, I look . . . fine. Da always said he'd teach me to play cards. Said I'd take the bank, the way things never reach my eyes. There should be something—a tell, a crease between my eyes, or a tightness in my jaw.

I'm too good at this.

Behind my reflection I see the painting of the sea, slanting as if the waves crashing on the rocks have hit with enough force to tip the picture. I turn and straighten it. The frame makes a faint rattling sound when I do. Everything in this place seems to be falling apart.

I return home to **3F**, but when I step through the door, I stop, eyes widening.

I'm braced for vacant rooms and scrounging through a pile of takeout flyers for dinner. I'm not braced for this. The moving boxes have been broken down and stacked in one corner beside several trash bags of packing material, but other than that, the apartment looks strikingly like, well, an apartment. The furniture has been assembled and arranged, Dad is stirring something on the stove, a book open on the counter. He pauses and pulls a pen from behind his ear to make a margin note. Mom is sitting at the kitchen table surrounded by enough paint swatches to suggest that she thoroughly raided that aisle of the home improvement store.

"Oh, hi, Mac!" she says, looking up from the chips.

"I thought you already painted."

"We started to," says Dad, making another note in his book.

Mom shakes her head, begins to stack the chips. "It's just wasn't quite right, you know? It has to be right. Just right."

"Lyndsey called," says Dad.

"How was Wes?" asks Mom.

"Fine. He's helping me with the *Inferno*."

"Is that what they call it?"

"Dad!"

Mom frowns. "Didn't you have it with you when you left?"

I look down at my empty hands, and rack my brain. Where did I leave it? The garden? The study? Nix's place? The roof? No, I didn't have it on the roof—

"Told you they weren't reading," whispers Dad.

"He has . . . character," adds Mom.

"You should see Mac around him. I swear I saw a smile!"

"Are you actually cooking?" I ask.

"Don't sound so surprised."

"Mac, what do you think of this green?"

"Food's up."

I carry plates to the table, trying to figure out why my chest hurts. And somewhere between pouring a glass of water and taking a bite of stir-fry, I realize why. Because this—the banter and the joking and the food—this is what normal families do. Mom isn't smiling too hard, and Dad isn't running away.

This is normal. Comfortable.

This is us moving on.

Without Ben.

My brother left a hole, and it's starting to close. And when it does, he'll be gone. Really and truly gone. Isn't this what I wanted? For my parents to stop running? For my family to heal? But what if I'm not ready to let Ben go?

"You okay?" asks Dad. I realize I've stopped with the fork halfway to my mouth. I open my mouth to say the three small words that will shatter everything. *I miss Ben.*

"Mackenzie?" asks Mom, the smile sliding from her face.

I blink. I can't do it.

"Sorry," I say. "I was just thinking. . . ."

Think think think.

Mom and Dad watch me. My mind stumbles through lies until I find the right one. I smile, even though it feels like a grimace. "Could we make cookies after dinner?"

Mom's brows peak, but she nods. "Of course." She twirls her fork. "What sort?"

"Oatmeal raisin. The chewy kind."

When the cookies are in the oven, I call Lyndsey back. I slip into my room and let her talk. She tunes her guitar and rambles about her parents and the boy at the gym. Somewhere between her description of her new music tutor and her lament over her mother's attempt to diet, I stop her.

"Hey, Lynds."

"Yeah?"

"I've been thinking. About Ben. A lot."

Oddly enough, we never talk about Ben. By some silent understanding he's always been off-limits. But I can't help it.

"Yeah?" she asks. I hear the hollow thud of the guitar being set aside. "I think about him all the time. I was babysitting a kid the other night, and he insisted on drawing with a green crayon. Wouldn't use anything else. And I thought about Ben and his love of blue pencils, and it made me smile and ache at the same time."

My eyes burn. I reach out for the blue stuffed bear, the pair of black glasses still perched on its nose.

"But you know," says Lyndsey, "it kind of feels like he's not gone, because I see him in everything."

"I think I'm starting to forget him," I whisper.

"Nah, you're not." She sounds so certain.

"How do you know?"

"If you mean a few little things—the exact sound of his voice, the shade of his hair, then okay, yeah. You're going to forget. But Ben isn't those things, you know? He's your brother. He's made up of every moment in his life. You'll never forget all of that."

"Are you taking a philosophy course too?" I manage. She laughs. I laugh, a hollow echo of hers.

"So," she says, turning up the cheer, "how's Guyliner?"

I dream of Ben again.

Stretched out on his stomach on my bedroom floor, drawing with a blue pencil right on the hardwood, twisting the drops of blood into monsters with dull eyes. I come in, and he looks up. His eyes are black, but as I watch, the blackness begins to draw inward until it's nothing but a dot in the center of his bright brown eyes.

He opens his mouth to speak, but he only gets halfway through saying "I won't slip" before his voice fades away. And then his eyes fade, dissolving into air. And then his whole face fades. His body begins to fade, as if an invisible hand is erasing him, inch by inch.

I reach out, but by the time I touch his shoulder, he's only a vague shape.

An outline.

A sketch.

And then nothing.

I sit up in the dark.

I rest my head against my knees. It doesn't help. The tightness in my chest goes deeper than air. I snatch the glasses from the bear's nose and reach for the memory, watching it loop three or four times, but the faded impression of a Ben-like shape only makes it worse, only reminds me how much I'm forgetting. I pull on my jeans and boots, and shove the list in my pocket without even looking at the names.

I know this is a bad idea, a horrible idea, but as I make my way through the apartment, down the hall, into the Narrows, I pray that Roland is behind the desk. I step into the Archive, hoping for his red Chucks, but instead I find a pair of black leather boots, the heels kicked up on the desk before the doors, which are now closed. The girl has a notebook in her lap and a pen tucked behind her ear, along with a sweep of sandy blond hair, impossibly streaked with sun.

"Miss Bishop," says Carmen. "How can I help you?"

"Is Roland here?" I ask.

She frowns. "Sorry, he's busy. I'm afraid I'll have to do."

"I wanted to see my brother."

Her boots slide off the desk and land on the floor. Her green eyes look sad. "This isn't a cemetery, Miss Bishop." It feels weird for someone so young to refer to me this way.

"I know that," I say carefully, trying to pick my angle. "I was just hoping . . ."

Carmen takes the pen from behind her ear and sets it in the book to mark her place, then puts the book aside and interlaces her fingers on top of the desk. Each motion is smooth, methodical.

"Sometimes Roland lets me see him."

A faint crease forms between her eyes. "I know. But that doesn't make it right. I think you should——"

"Please," I say. "There's nothing of him left in my world. I just want to sit by his shelf."

After several long moments, she picks up a pad of paper and makes a note. We wait in silence, which is good, because I can barely hear over my pulse. And then the doors behind her open, and a short, thin Librarian strides through.

"I need a break," says Carmen, rolling her neck. The Librarian—Elliot, I remember—nods obediently and takes a seat. Carmen holds her hand toward the doors, and I pass through into the atrium. She follows and tugs them shut behind her.

We make our way through the room and down the sixth wing.

"What would you have done," she asks, "if I'd said no?"

I shrug. "I guess I would have gone home."

We cross through a courtyard. "I don't believe that."

"I don't believe you would have said no."

"Why's that?" she asks.

"Your eyes are sad," I say, "even when you smile."

Her expression wavers. "I may be a Librarian, Miss Bishop, but we have people we miss, too. People we want back. It can be hard to be so far from the living, and so close to the dead."

I've never heard a Librarian talk that way. It's like light shining through armor. We start up a short set of wooden stairs.

"Why did you take this job?" I ask. "It doesn't make sense. You're so young—"

"It was an honor to be promoted," she says, but the words have a hollow ring. I can see her drawing back into herself, into her role.

"Who did you lose?" I ask.

Carmen flashes a smile that is at once dazzling and sad. "I'm a Librarian, Miss Bishop. I've lost everyone."

Before I can say anything, she opens the door to the large reading room with the red rug and the corner chairs, and leads me to the wall of cabinets on the far side. I reach out and run my fingers over the name.

BISHOP, BENJAMIN GEORGE

I just want to see him. That's all. I *need* to see him. I press my hand flat against the face of the drawer, and I can almost feel the pull of him. The need. Is this the way the Histories feel, trapped in the Narrows with only the desperate sense that something vital is beyond the doors, that if they could just get out—

"Is there anything else, Miss Bishop?" Carmen asks carefully.

"Could I see him?" I ask quietly. "Just for a moment?"

She hesitates. And to my surprise, she steps up to the shelves and produces the same key she used to disable Jackson Lerner. Gold and sharp and without teeth, but when she slides it into the slot on Ben's drawer and turns, there is a soft click within the wall. The drawer opens an inch, and sits ajar. Something in me tightens.

"I'll give you a few minutes," Carmen whispers, "but no more."

I nod, unable to take my eyes off the sliver of space between the front of the drawer and the rest of the stacks, a strip of deep shadow. I listen to the sound of Carmen's withdrawing steps. And then I reach out, wrap my fingers over the edge, and slide my brother's drawer open.

TWENTY-ONE

I'M SITTING ON THE SWINGS in our backyard, rocking from heel to toe, heel to toe, while you pick slivers of wood off the frame.

"You can't tell anyone," you say. "Not your parents. Not your friends. Not Ben."

"Why not?"

"People aren't smart when it comes to the dead."

"I don't understand."

"If you told someone that there was a place where their mother, or their brother, or their daughter, still existed—in some form—they'd tear the world apart to get there."

You chew a toothpick.

"No matter what people say, they'd do anything."

"How do you know?"

"Because I'd do it. Trust me, you'd do it too."

"I wouldn't."

"Maybe not anymore, because you know what a History is. And you know I'd never forgive you if you tried to wake one up. But if you weren't a Keeper . . . if you lost someone and you thought they were gone forever, and then you learned you could get them back, you'd be there with the rest of them, clawing at the walls to get through."

•   •   •

My chest turns to stone when I see him, crushing my lungs and my heart.

Benjamin lies on the shelf, still as he was beneath the hospital sheet. But there's no sheet now, and his skin isn't bruised or blue. He's got the slightest flush in his cheeks, as if he's sleeping, and he's wearing the same clothes he had on that day, before they got ruined. Grass-stained jeans and his favorite black-and-red-striped shirt, a gift from Da the summer he died, an emblematic X over the heart because Ben always used to say "cross my heart" so solemnly. I was with him when Da gave it to him. Ben wore it for days until it smelled foul and we had to drag it off of him to be washed. It doesn't smell like anything now. His hands are at his sides, which looks wrong because he used to sleep on his side with both fists crammed under the pillow; but this way I can see the black pen doodle on the back of his left hand, the one I drew that morning, of me.

"Hi, Ben," I whisper.

I want to reach out, to touch him, but my hand won't move. I can't will my fingers to leave my side. And then that same dangerous thought whispers into the recesses of my mind, at the weak points.

If Owen can wake without slipping, why not Ben?

What if some Histories don't slip?

It's fear and anger and restlessness that make them wake up. But Ben was never afraid or angry or restless. So would he even wake? Maybe Histories who wouldn't wake wouldn't slip if they did . . . *But Owen woke,* a voice warns. Unless a Librarian woke him and tried to alter his memories. Maybe that's the trick. Maybe Owen isn't slipping because he didn't wake himself up.

I look down at Ben's body and try to remember that this isn't my brother.

It was easier to believe when I couldn't see him.

My chest aches, but I don't feel like crying. Ben's dark lashes rest against his cheeks, his hair curling across his forehead. When I see that hair tracing its way across his skin, my body unfreezes, my hand drifting up to brush it from his face, the way I used to do.

That's all I mean to do.

But when my fingers graze his skin, Ben's eyes float open.

TWENTY-TWO

I **GASP AND JERK MY HAND BACK,** but it's too late.
Ben's brown eyes—Mom's eyes, warm and bright and wide—
blink once, twice.

And he sits up.

"Mackenzie?" he asks.

The ache in my chest explodes into panic. My pulse shatters the
calmness I know I need to show.

"Hi, Ben," I choke out, the shock making it hard to breathe, to
speak.

My brother looks around at the room—the stacked drawers
reaching to the ceiling, the tables and dust and oddness—then
swings his legs over the edge of the shelf.

"What happened?" And then, before I can answer: "Where's
Mom? Where's Dad?"

He hops down from the shelf, sniffles. His forehead crinkles. "I
want to go home."

My hand reaches for his.

"Then let's go home, Ben."

He moves to take my hand, but stops. Looks around again.

"What's going on?" he asks, his voice unsteady.

"Come on, Ben," I say.

"Where am I?" The black at the center of his eyes wobbles. *No.*
"How did I get here?" He takes a small step back. Away from me.

"It's going to be okay," I say.

When his eyes meet mine, they are tinged with panic. "Tell me how I got here." Confusion. "This isn't funny." Distress.

"Ben, please," I say softly. "Let's just go home."

I don't know what I'm thinking. I can't think. I look at him, and all I know is that I can't leave him here. He's Ben, and I pinkie-swore a thousand times I'd never let anything hurt him. Not the ghosts under the bed or the bees in the yard or the shadows in his closet.

"I don't understand." His voice catches. His irises are darkening. "I don't . . . I was . . ."

This isn't supposed to happen. He didn't wake himself. He's not supposed to—

"Why . . ." he starts.

I step toward him, kneeling so I can take his hands. I squeeze them. I try to smile.

"Ben—"

"Why aren't you telling me what happened?"

His eyes hover on me, the black spreading too fast, blotting out the warm, bright brown. All I see in those eyes is the reflection of my face, caught between pain and fear and an unwillingness to believe that he's slipping. Owen didn't slip. Why does Ben have to?

This isn't fair.

Ben begins to cry, hitching sobs.

I pull him into a hug.

"Be strong for me," I whisper in his hair, but he doesn't answer. I tighten my grip as if I can hold the Ben I know—knew—in place, can keep him with me; but he pushes me away. A jarring strength for such a small body. I stumble, and another pair of arms catches me.

"Get back," orders the man holding me. Roland.

His eyes are leveled on Ben, but the words are meant for me. He pushes me out of his way and approaches my brother. *No, no, no,* I think, the word playing in my head like a metronome.

What have I done?

"I didn't . . ."

"Stay back," Roland growls, then kneels in front of Ben.

That's not Ben, I think. Looking at the History—its eyes black, where Ben's were brown.

Not Ben, I think, clutching my hands around my ribs to keep from shaking.

Not Ben, as Roland puts a hand on my brother's shoulder and says something too soft for me to hear.

Not Ben. Metal glints in Roland's other hand and he plunges a toothless gold key into Not Ben's chest and turns it.

Not Ben doesn't cry out, but simply sinks. His eyes fall shut and his head falls forward, and his body slumps toward the ground but never hits because Roland catches him, scoops him up, and returns him to his drawer. The pain goes out of his face, the tension goes out of his limbs. His body relaxes against the shelf, as if settling into sleep.

Roland slides the door shut, the dark devouring Not Ben's body. I hear the cabinet lock, and something in me cracks.

Roland doesn't look at me as he pulls a notepad from his pocket.

"I'm sorry, Miss Bishop."

"Roland," I plead. "Don't do this." He scratches something onto the paper. "I'm sorry," I say. "I'm sorry, I'm sorry, but please don't—"

"I don't have a choice," he says as the card on the front of Ben's drawer turns red. The mark of the restricted stacks.

No, no, no come the metronome cries, each one causing a crack that splinters me.

I take a step forward.

"Stay where you are," orders Roland, and whether it's his tone or the fact that the cracks hurt so much I can't breathe, I do as he says. Before my eyes, the shelves begin to shift. Ben's red-marked drawer pulls backward with a hush until it's swallowed by the wall. The surrounding drawers rearrange themselves, gliding to fill the gap.

Ben's drawer is gone.

I sink to my knees on the old wood floor.

"Get up," orders Roland.

My body feels sluggish, my lungs heavy, my pulse too slow. I haul myself to my feet, and Roland grabs my arm, forcing me out of the room into an empty hall.

"Who opened the drawer, Miss Bishop?"

I won't rat out Carmen. She only wanted to help.

"I did," I say.

"You don't have a key."

"'Two ways through any lock,'" I answer numbly.

"I warned you to stay away," growls Roland. "I warned you not to draw attention. I warned you what happens to Keepers who lose their post. What were you *thinking?*"

"I wasn't," I say. My throat hurts, as if I've been screaming. "I just had to see him——"

"You woke a History."

"I didn't mean to——"

"He's not a goddamn puppy, Mackenzie, and he's not your brother. That *thing* is not your brother, and you know that."

The cracks are spreading beneath my skin.

"How can you not know that?" Roland continues. "Honestly——"

"I thought he wouldn't slip!"

He stops. *"What?"*

"I thought . . . that maybe . . . he wouldn't slip."

Roland brings his hands down on my shoulders, hard. "Every. History. Slips."

Not Owen, says a voice inside me.

Roland lets go. "Turn in your list."

If there's any wind left in my lungs, that order knocks it out. "What?"

"Your list."

If she proves herself unfit in any way, she will forfeit the position. And if she proves unfit, you, Roland, will remove her yourself.

"Roland . . ."

"You can collect it tomorrow morning, when you return for your hearing."

He promised me he wouldn't. I trusted . . . but what have I done with *his* trust? I can see the pain in his eyes. I force one shaking hand into my pocket and pass him the folded paper. He takes it and motions toward the door, but I can't will myself to leave.

"Miss Bishop."

My feet are nailed to the floor.

"Miss Bishop."

This isn't happening. I just wanted to see Ben. I just needed—

"Mackenzie," says Roland. I force myself forward.

I follow him through the maze of stacks. There is no warmth and there is no peace. With every step, every breath, the cracks deepen, spread. Roland leads me through the atrium to the antechamber and the front desk, where Elliot sits diligently.

When Roland turns to look at me, anger has dulled into something sad. Tired.

"Go home," he says. I nod stiffly. He turns and vanishes back into the stacks.

Elliot glances up from his work, a vague curiosity in the arch of his brows.

I can feel myself breaking.

I barely make it through the door and into the Narrows before I shatter.

It *hurts*.

Worse than anything. Worse than noise or touch or knives. I don't know how make it stop. I have to make it stop.

I can't breathe.

I can't—

"Mackenzie?"

I turn to find Owen standing in the hall. His blue eyes hangs on me, the smallest wrinkle between his brows.

"What's wrong?" he asks.

Everything about him is calm, quiet, level. Pain twists into anger. I push him, hard.

"Why haven't you slipped?" I snap.

Owen doesn't fight back, not even reflexively, doesn't try to escape, the slightest clenching of his jaw the only sign of emotion. I want to push him over. I want to make him slip. He has to. Ben did.

"Why, Owen?"

I push him again. He takes a step away.

"What makes you so special? What makes you so different? Ben slipped. He slipped right away, and you've been here for days and you haven't slipped at all and it isn't fair."

I shove him again, and his back hits the wall at the end of the corridor.

"It isn't fair!"

My hands dig into his shirt. The quiet is like static in my head, filling the space. It is not enough to erase the pain. I am still breaking.

"Calm down." Owen wraps his hands around mine, pinning them to his chest. The quiet thickens, pours into my head.

My face feels wet, but I don't remember crying. "It's not fair."

"I'm sorry," he says. "Please calm down."

I want the pain to stop. I need it to stop. I won't be able to claw my way back up. There is all this anger and this guilt and—

And then Owen kisses my shoulder. "I'm so sorry about Ben."

The quiet builds like a wave, drowning anger and pain.

"I'm sorry, Mackenzie."

I stiffen, but as his lips press against my skin, the silence flares in my head, blotting something out. Heat ripples through my body, pricking my senses as the quiet deadens my thoughts. He kisses my throat, my jaw. Each time his lips brush my skin, the heat and silence blossom side by side and spread, drowning a little bit of the pain and anger and guilt, leaving only warmth and want and quiet in their place. His lips brush my cheek, and then he pulls back, his pale eyes leveled cautiously on mine, his mouth barely a breath from mine. When he touches me, there is nothing but touch. There is no thought of wrong and no thought of loss and no thought of anything, because thoughts can't get through the static.

"I'm sorry, M."

M. That drags me under. That one little word he can't possibly understand. M. Not Mackenzie. Not Mac. Not Bishop. Not Keeper.

I want that. I need that. I cannot be the girl who broke the rules and woke her dead brother and ruined everything. . . .

I close the gap. Pull Owen's body flush with mine.

His mouth is soft but strong, and when he deepens the kiss, the quiet spreads, filling every space in my mind, washing over me. Drowning me.

And then his mouth is gone, and his hands let go of mine. Everything comes back, too loud. I pull his body against mine, feel the impossibly careful crush of his mouth as it steals the air from my lungs, steals the thoughts from my head.

Owen steps forward, urging my body against the wall, pushing me with his kisses and the quiet that comes with his touch. I am letting it all wash over me, letting it wash away the questions and doubts, the Histories and the key and the ring and everything else, until I am just M against his lips, his body. M reflected in the pale blue of his eyes until he closes them and kisses me deeper, and then I am nothing.

TWENTY-THREE

I CANNOT STAY HERE forever, buried under Owen's touch. At last I push away, break the surface of the quiet, and before I lose my will, before I cave, I leave. I can't hunt, so I spend what's left of the night searching the Coronado, moving numbly from floor to floor, trying to read the walls for any clues, anything the Archive— or whoever in it tried to cover things up—might have missed, but that year is shot full of holes. I run through the time lines, scour the memories for leads, and find only dull impressions and stretches of too-flat black. Elling's old apartment is locked, but I read the south stairs, where Eileen supposedly fell, and even brave the elevators in search of Lionel's stabbing, only to find the unnatural nothing of excavated pasts. Whatever happened here, someone went out of their way to bury it, even from people like me.

A dull ache has formed behind my eyes, and I've lost hope of finding any useful memory intact, but I keep searching. I have to. Because every time I stop moving, the thought of losing Ben—really losing him—catches up, the pain catches up, the thought of kissing Owen— of using a History for his touch—catches up. So I keep moving.

I start searching for more of Regina's story. I put my ring on, hoping to dull the headache, and search the old-fashioned way, thankful for the distraction. I check table drawers and shelves, even though sixty years have passed, and the chances of finding anything are slim. I search for hidden compartments in the study, and take down half the books to check behind them. I remember Owen saying something about garden cracks. I know paper would never last out here, but I still search the mossy stones by feel in the dark, grateful for the quiet predawn air.

The sun is rising as I look behind the counters and around the old equipment in the coffee shop, careful not to touch the half-painted walls. And just as I'm about to abandon the search, my eyes drift to the sheeting thrown over the rose pattern in the floor to keep it safe. *In garden cracks and under tiles,* Owen said. It's a long shot, but I kneel and pull aside the plastic tarp. The rose beneath is as wide as my arm span, each inlaid marble petal piece the size of my palm. I brush my hand back and forth across the rust-colored pattern. Near the center, I feel the subtle shift of stones beneath my touch. One of the petals is loose.

My heart skips as I get my fingers under the lip of the petal. It lifts. The hiding place is little more than a hole, the walls of which are lined with white cloth. And there, folded and weighted down by a narrow metal bar, is another piece of Regina's story.

The paper is yellowing but intact, protected by the hidden chamber, and I lift it to the morning light.

The red stones shifted and became steps, a great flight of stairs that led the hero up and up. And the hero climbed.

The pieces are out of order. The last fragment spoke of facing gods and monsters at the top of something. This one clearly goes before. But what comes after?

My attention shifts to the small bar that had held the note in place. It's roughly the size of a pencil but half the length, one end tapering just like a graphite point. A groove has been cut from the blunt end down, and it's made of the same metal as the ring that held the first note.

For one horrible, bitter moment, I consider putting the pieces back, leaving them buried. It seems so unfair that Owen should have pieces of Regina when I can have none of Ben.

But as cruel as it is that Ben slipped when Owen didn't, it isn't Owen's fault. He's the History, and I'm the Keeper. He couldn't have known what would happen, and I'm the one who chose to wake my brother.

The sun is up now. The morning of my trial. I slip both the paper and the bar into my pocket and make my way upstairs.

Dad is already up, and I tell him I went running. I don't know if he believes me. He says I look tired, and I admit that I am. I shower numbly and stumble through the early hours, trying not to think of the trial, of being deemed unfit, of losing everything. I help Mom settle on new paint chips and pack up half the oatmeal raisin cookies for Nix before I make a lame excuse to leave. Mom is so distracted by the paint dilemma—*it's still not right, not quite right, has to be right*—that she simply nods. I pause in the doorway, watching her work, listening to Dad on a call in the other room. I try to memorize this *before*, not knowing what *after* will be.

And then I go.

I cut through the Narrows, and the memory of last night sweeps over me with the humid air and the far-off sounds. The memory of quiet. And as panic eats through me, I wish I could disappear again. I can't. But there's something I should do.

I find the alcove, and Owen in it, and press the note and the small iron bar into his hands, staying only long enough to steal a kiss and a moment of quiet. The peace dissolves into fear as I reach the Archive door and step through.

I don't know what I expected—a row of Librarians waiting, ready to strip me of my key and my ring? Someone named Agatha waiting to judge me unfit, to carve my job right out of my life, taking my identity with it? A tribunal? A lynch mob?

I certainly don't expect Lisa to look up from her desk, over her green horn-rimmed glasses, and ask me what I want.

"Is Roland here?" I ask unsteadily.

She goes back to her work. "He said you'd stop by."

I shift my weight. "Is that all he said?"

"Said to send you in." Lisa straightens. "Is everything all right, Miss Bishop?"

The antechamber is quiet, but my heart is slamming in my chest so loudly, I think she'll hear. I swallow and force myself to nod. She hasn't been told. Just then, Elliot rushes in, and I stiffen, thinking he's come to tell her, come to collect me; but when he leans over her, he says only, "Three, four, six, ten through fourteen."

Lisa lets out a tight breath. "All right. Make sure they're blacked out."

I frown. What kind of technical difficulty is this?

Elliot retreats, and Lisa looks at me again, as if she'd forgotten I was there.

"Firsts," she says, meaning first wing, first hall, first room. "Can you show yourself?"

"I think I can handle it."

She nods and throws open several massive ledgers on the desk. I step past her into the atrium. Looking up at the vaulted ceiling of stone and colored glass, I wonder if I'll ever feel at peace here again. I wonder if I'll have the chance.

Something in the distance rumbles, followed shortly by an aftershock of sound. Startled, I scan the stacks and spot Patrick on the far side of the atrium, and when he hears the noise, he vanishes down the nearest wing, pulling the doors closed behind him. I pass Carmen standing by a row of stacks before the first hall. She gives me a small nod.

"Miss Bishop," she says. "What brings you back so soon?"

For a moment, I just stare at her. I feel like my crimes are written on my face, but there's nothing in her voice to suggest she knows. Did Roland really say nothing?

"Just here to talk to Roland," I say at last, managing only a ghost of calm. She waves me on, and I turn down the first wing, then the first hall, and stop at the first door. It's closed, a heavy, glassless thing, and I press my fingertips against it and summon the courage to go in.

When I do, two pairs of eyes meet mine: one gray and quite stern; the other brown and rimmed with black.

Wesley perches on a table in the middle of the room.

"I believe you two know each other," says Roland.

I consider lying, based on the gut sense that Keepers are supposed to work alone, to exist alone. But Wes nods.

"Hey, Mac," he says.

"What's *he* doing here?" I ask.

Roland steps up. "Mr. Ayers will be assisting you in your territorial duties."

I turn to him. "You gave me a babysitter?"

"Hey, now," says Wes, hopping down from the table. "I prefer the term *partner.*"

I frown. "But only Crew are partnered."

"I am making an exception," Roland says.

"Come on, Mac," says Wes, "it will be fun."

My mind flicks to Owen, waiting in the dark of the Narrows, but I force the image back. "Roland, what's this about?"

"You've noticed an uptick in your numbers."

I nod. "And ages. Lisa and Patrick both said there was some minor technical difficulty."

Roland crosses his arms. "It's called a disruption."

"A disruption, I take it, is worse than a minor technical difficulty."

"Have you noticed how quiet the Archive is kept? Do you know why that is?"

"Because Histories wake up," says Wesley.

"Yes, they do. When there's too much noise, too much activity, the lighter sleepers begin to stir. The more noise, the more activity, the more Histories. Even deep sleepers wake up."

Which explains the older Histories in my territory.

"A disruption happens when the noise Histories make waking up causes other Histories to wake up, and so on. Like dominoes. More and more and more, until it's contained."

"Or they all fall down," I whisper.

"As soon as it started, we acted, and began blacking out rooms. Lighter sleepers first. It should have been enough. A disruption starts in one place, like a fire, so it has a core. Logic says that if you can douse the hottest part, you can tamp out the rest. But it's not working. Every time we put out a fire, a new one flares up in a perfectly quiet place."

"That doesn't seem natural," says Wes.

Roland shoots me a meaningful glance. *That's because it isn't.*

So, is the disruption a distraction from the altered Histories? Or is it something more? I wish I could ask, but following Roland's lead, I don't want to say too much in front of Wes.

"And the Coronado," Roland continues, "is being hit harder than other territories at the moment. So, Mackenzie, until this *minor technical difficulty* is resolved and your numbers return to normal, Wesley will be assisting you in your territory."

My mind spins. I came in here expecting to lose my job, lose my self, and instead I get a partner.

Roland holds out a folded slip of paper.

"Your list, Miss Bishop."

I take it, but hold his gaze. What about last night? What about Ben? Questions I know better than to ask aloud. So instead I say, "Is there anything else?"

Roland considers me a moment, then draws something from his back pocket. A folded black handkerchief. I take it and frown at the weight. Something is wrapped in the fabric. When I peel back the cloth, my eyes widen.

It's a key.

Not like the simply copper one I wear around my neck, or the thin gold ones the Librarians use, but larger, heavier, colder. A near-black thing with sharp teeth and pricks of rust. Something tugs at me. I've seen this key before. I've felt this key.

Wesley's eyes widen. "Is that a *Crew* key?"

Roland nods. "It belonged to Antony Bishop."

"Why do you have two keys?" I ask.

You look at me like you never thought I'd notice the second cord around your neck. Now you tug it up over your head and hold it out for me, the metal hanging heavy on the end. When I take the key, it is cold and strangely beautiful, with a handle at one end and sharp teeth at the other. I can't imagine a lock in the world those teeth would fit.

"What does it do?" I ask, cradling the metal.

"It's a Crew key," you say. "When a History gets out, you've got to return them, fast. Crew can't waste time searching

for doors into the Narrows. So this turns any door into an Archive door."

"Any door?" I ask. "Even the front door? Or the one to my room? Or the one on the shed that's falling down—"

"*Any* door. You just put the key in the lock and turn. Left for the Librarians, right for Returns."

I run a thumb over the metal. "I thought you stopped being Crew."

"I did. Just haven't brought myself to give it back yet."

I hold up the key, sliding it through thin air as if there's a door with a lock I simply can't see. And I'm about to turn it when you catch my wrist. Your noise washes through my head, all winter trees and far-off storms.

"Careful," you say. "Crew keys are dangerous. They're used to rip open the seams between the Outer and the Archive, and let us through. We like to think we can control that kind of power with left turns and right turns, but these keys, they can tear holes in the world. I did it once, by accident. Nearly ate me up."

"How?"

"Crew keys are too strong and too smart. If you hold that piece of rusted metal up, not to a door, just a bit of thin air, and give it a full turn, all the way around, it'll make a tear right in the world, a bad kind of door, one that leads to nowhere."

"If it leads nowhere," I ask, "then what's the harm?"

"A door that leads nowhere and a door that leads *to* nowhere are totally different things, Kenzie. A door that leads *to* nowhere is dangerous. A door to nowhere is a door into nothing," you say, taking the key back and slipping the cord over your head. "A void."

I look down at the Crew key, mesmerized. "Can it do anything else?"

"Sure can."

"Like what?"

You give a tilted smile. "Make it to Crew and you'll find out."

I chew my lip. "Hey, Da?"

"Yes, Kenzie?"

"If Crew keys are so powerful, won't the Archive notice it's gone?"

You sit back and shrug. "Things get misplaced. Things get lost. Nobody's going to miss it."

"Da gave you his key?" I ask. I'd always wondered what happened to it.

"Do I get a Crew key, too?" asks Wes, bouncing slightly.

"You'll have to share," says Roland. "The Archive keeps track of these. It notices when they go missing. The only reason they won't notice this key is gone is because——"

"It stayed lost," I say.

Roland *almost* smiles. "Antony held on to it as long as he could, and then he gave it back to me. I never turned it in, so the Archive still considers the key lost."

"Why are you giving this to me now?" I ask.

Roland rubs his eyes. "The disruption is spreading. Rapidly. As more Histories wake, and more escape, you need to be prepared."

I look down at the key, the weight of the memory pulling at my fingers. "These keys go to and from the Archive, but Da said they did other things. If I'm going to have it and play Crew, I want to know what he meant."

"That key is not a promotion, Miss Bishop. It's to be used only in case of emergency, and even then, only to go to and from the Archive."

"Where else would I go?"

"Oh, oh, like shortcuts?" asks Wes. "My aunt Joan told me about them. There are these doors, only they don't go to the Narrows or the Archive. They're just in the Outer. Like holes punched in space."

Roland gives us both a withering look and sighs. "Shortcuts are used by Crew to move expediently through the Outer. Some let you skip a few blocks, others let you cross an entire city."

Wes nods, but I frown. "Why haven't I ever seen one? Not even with my ring off."

"I'm sure you have and didn't know it. Shortcuts are unnatural—holes in space. They don't look like doors, just a wrongness in the air, so your eyes slide off. Crew learn to look for the places their eyes don't want to go. But it takes time and practice. Neither of which you have. And it takes Crew years to memorize which doors lead where, which is only one of a dozen reasons why you do *not* have permission to use that key on one if you find it. Do you understand?"

I fold the kerchief over the key and nod, sliding it into my pocket. Roland is obviously nervous, and no wonder. If shortcuts barely register as more than thin air, and Da told me what happens when you use a Crew key *on* thin air, then the potential for ripping open a void in the Outer is pretty high.

"Stick together, no playing with the key, no looking for short-cuts." Wes ticks off the rules on his fingers.

We both turn to go.

"Miss Bishop," says Roland. "A word alone."

Wesley leaves, and I linger, waiting for my punishment, my sentence. Roland is silent until the door closes on Wes.

"Miss Bishop," he says, without looking at me, "Mr. Ayers has been made aware of the disruption. He has not been told of its suspected cause. You will keep that, and the rest of our investigation, to yourself."

I nod. "Is that all, Roland?"

"No," he says, his voice going low. "In opening Benjamin's drawer, you broke Archival law, and you broke my trust. Your actions are being overlooked once and only once, but if you ever, *ever* do that again, you will forfeit your position, and I will remove you myself." His gray eyes level on mine. "*That* is all."

I bow my head, eyes trained on the floor so they can't betray the pain I feel. I take a steadying breath, manage a last nod, and leave.

Wesley is waiting for me by the Archive door. Elliot is at the desk, scribbling furiously. He doesn't look up when I come in, even though the sight of two Keepers has to be unusual.

Wes, meanwhile, seems giddy.

"Look," he says cheerfully, holding out his list for me to inspect. There's one name on it, a kid. "That's mine . . ." He flips the paper over to show six names on the other side. "And those are yours. Sharing is caring."

"Wesley, you *were* listening, weren't you? This isn't a game."

"That doesn't mean we won't have fun. And look!" He taps the center of my list, where a name stands out against the sea of black.

Dina Blunt. 33.

I cringe at the prospect of another adult, a Keeper-Killer, the last one still vivid in my mind; but Wesley looks oddly delighted.

"Come, Miss Bishop," he says, holding out his hand. "Let's go hunting."

TWENTY-FOUR

WESLEY AYERS is being too nice.

"So then this wicked-looking six-year-old tries to take me out at the knees . . ."

Too chatty.

". . . but he's two feet shorter so he just ends kicking the crap out of my shins. . . ."

Too peppy.

"I mean, he was six, and wearing soccer cleats—"

Which means . . .

"He told you," I say.

Wesley's brow crinkles, but he manages to keep smiling. "What are you talking about?"

"Roland told you, didn't he? That I lost my brother."

His smile flickers, fades. At last he nods.

"I already knew," he says. "I saw him when your dad touched my shoulder. I saw him when you shoved me in the Narrows. I haven't seen inside your mother's mind, but it's in her face, it's in her step. I didn't mean to look, Mac, but he's right at the surface. He's written all over your family."

I don't know what to say. The two of us stand there in the Narrows, and all the falseness falls away.

"Roland said there'd been an incident. Said he didn't want you to be alone. I don't know what happened. But I want you to know, you're not alone."

My eyes burn, and I clench my jaw and look away.

"Are you holding up?" he asks.

The lie comes to my lips, automatic. I bite it back. "No."

Wes looks down. "You know, I used to think that when you died, you lost everything." He starts down the hall, talking as he goes, so I'm forced to follow. "That's what made me so sad about death, even more than the fact that you couldn't live anymore; it was that you lost all the things you'd spent your life collecting, all the memories and knowledge. But when my aunt Joan taught me about Histories and the Archive, it changed everything." He pauses at a corner. "The Archive means that the past is never gone. Never lost. Knowing that, it's freeing. It gave me permission to always look forward. After all, we have our own Histories to write."

"God, that's cliché."

"I should write greeting cards, I know."

"I'm not sure they have a section for History-based sentimentality."

"It's too bad, really."

I smile, but I still don't want to talk about Ben. "Your aunt Joan. She's the one you inherited from?"

"Great-aunt, technically. The dame with the blue hair . . . also known as Joan Petrarch. And a frightening woman she is."

"She's still alive?"

"Yeah."

"But she passed the job on to you. Does that mean she abdicated?"

"Not exactly." He fidgets, looks down. "The role can only be passed on if the present Keeper is no longer capable. Aunt Joan broke her hip a few years back. Don't get me wrong, she's still pretty damn fierce. Lightning fast with her cane, in fact. I've got the scars to prove it. But after the accident, she passed the job on to me."

"It must be wonderful to be able to talk to her about it. To ask for advice, for help. To hear the stories."

Wesley's smile falls. "It . . . it doesn't work like that."

I feel like an idiot. Of course she *left* the Archive. She would have been altered. Erased.

"After she passed the job on, she forgot." There's a pain in his eyes, a kind I finally recognize. I might not have been able to share in Wes's clownish smile, but I can share in his sense of loneliness. It's bad enough to have people who never knew, but to have one and lose them . . . No wonder Da kept his title till he died.

Wes looks lost, and I wish I knew how to bring him back, but I don't. And then, I don't have to. A History does it for me. A sound reaches us, and just like that, Wesley's smile rekindles. There is a spark in his eyes, a hunger I sometimes see in Histories. I'll bet he patrols the Narrows looking for a fight.

The sound comes again. Gone are the days, apparently, when we actually had to hunt for Histories. There's enough of them here that they find us.

"Well, you've been wanting to hunt here for days," I say. "Think you're ready?"

Wesley gives a bow. "After you."

"Great," I say, cracking my knuckles. "Just keep your hands to yourself so I can focus on my work instead of that horrible rock music coming off you."

He raises a brow. "I sound like a rock band?"

"Don't look so flattered. You sound like a rock band being thrown out of a truck."

His smile widens. "Brilliant. And for what it's worth, you sound like a thunderstorm. And besides, if my soul's impeccable taste in music throws you off, then learn to tune me out."

I'm not about to admit that I can't, that I don't know how, so I just scoff. The sound of the History comes again, a fist-on-door kind of banging, and I pull the key from around my neck and try to calm the sudden jump in pulse as I wrap the leather cord around my wrist a few times.

I hope it's not Owen. The thought surprises me. I can't believe I'd rather face another Hooper than return Owen right now. It can't be Owen, though. He would never make this much noise . . . not unless he's started to slip. Maybe I should have told Wesley about him, but he's part of the investigation, which puts him under the blanket of things I'm not supposed to speak of. Still, if Wes finds Owen, or Owen finds Wes, how will I explain that I need this one History, that I'm protecting him from the Archive, that he's a clue? (And that's all he is, I tell myself as firmly as possible.)

I can't explain that.

I have to hope Owen has the sense to stay as far away from us as possible.

"Relax, Mac," says Wes, reading the tightness in my face. "I'll protect you."

I laugh for good measure. "Yeah, right. You and your spiked hair will save me from the big bad monsters."

Wes retrieves a short cylinder from his jacket. He flicks his wrist, and the cylinder multiplies, becoming a pole.

I laugh. "I forgot about the stick! No wonder the six-year-old kicked you," I say. "You look ready to break open a piñata."

"It's a *bō* staff."

"It's a stick. And put it away. Most of the Histories are already scared, Wes. You're only going to make it worse."

"You talk about them like they're people."

"You talk about them like they're not. *Put it away.*"

Wesley grumbles but collapses the stick and pockets it. "Your territory," he says, "your rules."

The banging comes again, followed by a small "Hello? Hello?" We round a corner, and stop.

A teenage girl is standing near the end of the hall. She has a halo of reddish hair and nails painted a chipping blue, and she's banging on one of the doors as hard as she can.

Wesley steps toward her, but I stop him with a look. I take a step toward the girl, and she spins. Her eyes are flecked with black.

"Mel," she says. "God, you scared me." She's nervous but not hostile.

"This whole place is scary," I say, trying to match her unease.

"Where have you been?" she snaps.

"Looking for a way out," I say. "And I think I finally found one."

The girl's face floods with relief. "About time," she says. "Lead the way."

"See?" I say, resting against the Returns door once I've led the girl through. "No stick required."

Wesley smiles. "Impressive——"

Someone screams.

One of those horrible asylum sounds. Animal. And close.

We backtrack, reach a T, and turn right, to find ourselves sharing the stretch of hall with a woman. She's gaunt, her head tilted to the left. She's a hair shorter than Wesley, her back is to us, and judging by the sound that just came out of her mouth, which was insane but undeniably adult, I'm willing to bet she's *Dina Blunt. 33.*

"My turn," whispers Wesley.

I slip back into the stem of the T, out of sight, and hear him hit the wall with a sharp clap. I can't see the woman, but I imagine her whipping around to face Wes at the sound.

"Why, Ian?" she whimpers. The voice grows closer. "Why did you make me do it?"

I press myself against the wall and wait.

Something moves in my section of hall, and I turn in time to see a shock of silver-blond hair move in the shadows. I shake my head, hoping Owen can see me, and if he can't, hoping he knows better than to show himself right now.

"I loved you." The words are much, much closer now. "I loved you, and you still made me do it."

Wesley takes a step and slides into view, his eyes flicking to me before leveling on the woman, whose footsteps I can now hear, along with her voice.

"Why didn't you stop me?" she whines. "Why didn't you help me?"

"Let me help you now," says Wesley, mimicking my even tone.

"You made me. You made me, Ian," she says as if she can't hear him, can't hear anything, as if she's trapped in a nightmarish loop. *"It's all your fault."*

Her voice is high and rising with each word, until the words draw into a cry, then a scream, and then she lunges into view, reaching for him. They both move past me, Wesley stepping back and her stepping forward, pace for pace.

I slip into the hall behind her.

"I can help you," says Wes, but I can tell from the tension around his eyes that he's not used to this level of disorientation. Not used to using words instead of force. "Calm down," he says finally. "Just calm down."

"What's wrong with *her*?" The question doesn't come from Wesley or me, but from a boy behind Wes at the end of the hall, several years younger than either of us.

Wes glances his way for a blink, long enough for Dina Blunt to lunge forward. As she grabs for his arm, I reach for hers. Her balance is off from panic and forward momentum, and I use her strength instead of mine to swing her back, get my hands against her face, and twist it sharply.

The snap of her neck is audible, followed by the thud of her body collapsing to the Narrows floor.

The boy makes a sound between a gasp and a cry. His eyes go wide as he turns and sprints away, skidding around the nearest corner. Wesley doesn't chase him, doesn't even move. He's staring down at Dina Blunt's motionless form. And then up at me.

I can't decide whether the look is solely dumbfounded or admiring as well.

"What happened to the humanitarian approach?"

I shrug. "Sometimes it's not enough."

"You are crazy," he says. "You are a crazy, amazing girl. And you scare the hell out of me."

I smile.

"How did you do that?" asks Wes.

"New trick."

"Where did you learn it?"

"By accident." It's not a total lie. I never meant for Owen to show me.

The History's body shudders on the floor. "It won't last long," I say, taking her arms. Wes takes her legs.

"So this is what the adults are like?" he asks as we carry her to the nearest Returns door. Her eyelids flutter. We walk faster.

"Oh, no," I say when we reach the door. "They get much worse." I turn the key and flood the hall with light.

Wes smiles grimly. "Wonderful."

Dina Blunt begins to whimper as we push her through.

"So," Wesley says as I tug the door shut and the woman's voice dies on the air, "who's next?"

Two hours later, the list is miraculously clear, and I've managed to go, well, one hour and fifty-nine minutes without thinking about Ben's shelf vanishing into the stacks. One hour and fifty-nine minutes without thinking about the rogue Librarian. Or about the string of deaths. The hunting quiets everything, but the moment we stop, the noise comes back.

"All done?" asks Wes, resting against the wall.

I look over the blank slip of paper and fold the list before another name can add itself. "Seems so. Still wish you had my territory?"

He smiles. "Maybe not by myself, but if you came with it? Yeah."

I kick his shoe with mine, and apparently two boots make enough of a buffer that almost none of Wesley's noise gets through. A little flare of feedback—but it's growing on me, as far as sound goes.

We trace our way back through the halls.

"I could seriously go for some Bishop's baked goods right now," he adds. "Think Mrs. Bishop might have something?"

We reach the numbered doors, and I slide the key into I—the one that leads to the third-floor hall—even though it's lazy and potentially public, because I really, really, really need a shower. I turn the key.

"Will oatmeal raisin do?" I ask, opening the door.

"Delightful," he says, holding it open for me. "After you."

It happens so fast.

The History comes out of nowhere.

Blink-and-you-miss-it quick, the way moments play rewinding memory. But this isn't memory, this is now, and there's not enough time. The body is a blur, a flash of reddish-brown hair and a green sweatshirt and lanky teenage limbs, all of which I distinctly remember *returning*. But that doesn't stop sixteen-year-old Jackson Lerner from slamming into Wesley, sending him back hard. I go to shut the door, but Jackson's foot sails through the air and catches me in the chest. Pain explodes across my ribs, and I'm on the ground, gasping for air, as Jackson's fingers catch the door just before it shuts.

And then he's gone.

Through.

Out.

Into the Coronado.

TWENTY-FIVE

For one terrible, terrifying moment, I don't know what to do.

A History is out, and all I can think about is forcing air back into my lungs. And then the moment ends, and the next one starts, and Wes and I are somehow on our feet again, rushing through the Narrows door and onto the third floor of the Coronado. The hall is empty.

Wes asks me if I'm okay, and I take a breath and nod, pain rippling through my ribs.

My ring is still off, but I don't need to read the walls to find Jackson, because his green sweatshirt is vanishing through the north stairwell door near my apartment. I sprint after him, and Wes turns and launches down the hall toward the south set of stairs beyond the elevators. Steps echo in the stairwell below, and I plunge down to the second floor as the door swings shut. I'm out in time to see Jackson skid to a stop halfway down the hall, Wesley rushing forward to block the landing to the grand stairs and the lobby and the way *out*.

The History is trapped.

"Jackson, stop," I gasp.

"You lied," he growls. "There is no home." His eyes are wide and going black with panic, and for a moment it's as if I'm back in front of Ben, terrified, and my feet are glued to the ground as Jackson turns and kicks in the nearest apartment door, smashing the wood and charging through.

Wes dashes forward, shocking me into motion, and I run as Jackson vanishes into the apartment.

Beyond the broken door of 2C, the apartment is modern, spare, but very clearly occupied. Jackson is halfway to the window when Wes darts forward and over a low couch. He catches Jackson's arm and spins him back toward the room. Jackson dodges his grasp and cuts to the side down a hall, but I catch up and slam him into the wall, upsetting a large framed poster.

The shower in the bathroom at the end of the hall is going, and someone is singing off-key but loudly as Jackson shoves me away and rears back to kick. I spin as the rubber heel of his shoe lodges in the drywall, and grab his wrist while he's off balance, pulling him toward me, my forearm slamming into his chest and sending him to the floor. When I try to pin him, he catches me with a glancing kick, and pain blossoms across my chest, forcing me to let go.

Wesley is there as Jackson scrambles to his feet and into the living room. Wes swings his arm around Jackson's throat and pulls hard, but Jackson fights like mad and forces him several steps back. A glass coffee table catches Wesley behind the knees, and he loses his balance. The two go down together. The shower cuts off as they crash in a wave of shattered glass. Jackson is up first, a shard jutting from his arm, and he's out the door before I can stop him.

Wesley is on his feet, his cheek and hand bleeding, but we tear into the second-floor hall. Jackson, in his panic, has stormed past the entrance to the landing and toward the elevator. We close in as he rips the glass from his arm with a hiss and forces the grille open. The dial above the cage door says the elevator is sitting on the sixth floor. The lobby is two stories tall. Which means two stories *down*.

"It's over," calls Wesley, stepping toward him.

Jackson stares at the elevator shaft, then back at us.

And then he jumps.

Wes and I groan together and turn, racing for the stairs.

Histories don't bleed. Histories can't die. But they do feel pain. And that jump had to hurt. Hopefully it will at least slow him down.

A scream cuts through the air, but not from the elevator shaft. Someone in 2C lets out a strain of words between a cry and a curse as we hit the landing. Halfway down the main staircase we see Jackson clutching his ribs—serves him right—and making a limping but determined beeline for the front doors of the Coronado.

"Key!" shouts Wes, and I dig the black handkerchief from my pocket.

"Right for Returns," I say as he grabs it, gets a foot up on the dark wood railing and jumps over, dropping the last ten feet and somehow landing upright. I hit the base of the stairs as Wes catches Jackson and slams him against the front doors hard enough to crack the glass. And then I'm there, helping hold the thrashing History against the door as Wes gets the Crew key into the lock and turns hard to the right. The scene beyond the glass is sunlight and streets and passing cars, but when Wes turns the key, the door flies open, ripped from his grip as if by wind, and reveals a world of white beyond. Impossible white, and Jackson Lerner falling through it.

The door slams shut with the same windlike force, shattering the already cracked glass. The Crew key sits in the lock, and through the glassless frame, a bus rambles past. Two people across the street have turned to see what reduced the door to littered shards and wood.

I stagger back. Wesley gives a dazed laugh just before his legs buckle.

I crouch beside him even though the motion sends ripples of pain through my ribs.

"Are you all right?" I ask.

Wes stares up at the broken door. "We did it," he says brightly. "Just like Crew."

Blood is running down his face from the gash along his cheekbone, and he's gazing giddily at the place where the door to Returns formed. I reach out and slide the key from the lock. And then I hear it. Sirens. The people from across the street are coming over now, and the wail of a cop car is getting more and more distinct. We have to get out of here. I can't possibly explain all this.

"Come on," I say, turning toward the elevator. Wes gets shakily to his feet and follows. I hit the call button, cringing at the thought of using this death trap, but I don't exactly want to retrace the path of our destruction right now, especially with Wes covered in blood. He hesitates when I pull open the grille, but climbs in beside me. The doors close, and I punch the button for the third floor and then turn to look at him. He's smiling. I can't believe he's smiling. I shake my head.

"Red looks good on you," I say.

He wipes at his cheek, looks down at his stained hands.

"You know, I think you're right."

Water drips from the ends of my hair onto the couch, where I'm perched, staring down at the Crew key cupped in my hands. I listen to the *shhhhhhh* of the shower running, wishing it could wash away the question that's nagging at me as I turn Da's key over and over in my hands.

How did Roland know?

How did he know that we'd need the key today? Was it a coincidence? Da never believed in coincidence, said chance was just a word for people too lazy to learn the truth. But Da believed in Roland. I believe in Roland. I know Roland. At least, I think I know him. He's the one who first gave me a chance. Who took responsibility for me. Who bent the rules for me. And sometimes broke them.

The water shuts off.

Jackson was returned. I returned him myself. How did he escape a second time in less than a week? He should have been filed in the red stacks. There's no way he would have woken twice. Unless someone woke him and let him out.

The bathroom door opens, and Wesley stands there, his black hair no longer spiked but hanging down into his eyes, the eyeliner washed away. His key rests against his bare chest. His stomach is lean, the muscles faint but visible. Thank god he's wearing pants.

"All done?" I ask, pocketing the Crew key.

"Not quite. I need your help." Wesley retreats into the bathroom. I follow.

An array of first-aid equipment covers the sink. Maybe I should have taken him to the Archive, but the cut on his face isn't so bad— I've had worse—and the last thing I want to do is try to explain to Patrick what happened.

Wesley's cheek is starting to bleed again, and he dabs at it with a washcloth. I fish around in my private medical stash until I find a tube of skin glue.

"Lean down, tall person," I say, trying to touch his face with only the swab and not my fingers. It makes my grip unsteady, and when I slip and paint a dab of the skin glue on his chin, Wes sighs and takes my hand. The noise flares through my head, metal and sharp.

"What are you doing?" I ask. "Let go."

247

"No," he says, plucking the swab and the skin glue from my grip, tossing both aside and pressing my hand flat against his chest. The noise grows louder. "You've got to figure it out."

I cringe. "Figure what out?" I ask, raising my voice above the clatter.

"How to find quiet. It's not that hard."

"It is for me," I snap. I try to push back, try to block him out, try to put up a wall, but it doesn't work, only makes it worse.

"That's because you're fighting it. You're trying to block out every bit of noise. But people are made of noise, Mac. The world is full of noise. And finding quiet isn't about pushing everything out. It's just about pulling yourself in. That's all."

"Wesley, let go."

"Can you swim?"

The rock-band static pounds in my head, behind my eyes. "What does that have to do with anything?"

"Good swimmers don't fight against the water." He takes my other hand, too. His eyes are bright, flecked with gold even in the dim light. "They move with it. Through it."

"So?"

"So stop fighting. Let the noise go white. Let it be like water. And float."

I hold his gaze.

"Just float," he says.

It goes against every bit of reason in me to stop pushing back, to welcome the noise.

"Trust me," he says.

I let out an unsteady breath, and then I do it. I let go. For a moment, Wesley washes over me, louder than ever, rattling my bones and echoing in my head. But then, little by little, the noise

evens, ebbs. It grows *steadier*. It turns to white noise. It is everywhere, surrounding me, but for the first time it doesn't feel like it's
in me. Not in my head. I let out a breath.

And then Wesley's grip is gone, and so is the noise.

I watch him fight back a smile and lose. What comes through
isn't smug, or even crooked. It's proud. And I can't help it. I smile
a little too. And then the headache hits, and I wince, leaning on the
bathroom sink.

"Baby steps," says Wes, beaming. He offers me the tube of skin
glue. "Now, if you wouldn't mind fixing me up? I don't want this to
scar."

"I won't be able to hide this," he says, examining my work in the
mirror.

"Makes you look tough," I say. "Just say you lost a fight."

"How do you know I didn't win?" he asks, meeting my eyes in
the glass. "Besides, I can't pull the fight card. It's been used too many
times."

His back is to me. His shoulders are narrow but strong. Defined.
I feel my skin warm as my gaze tracks between his shoulder blades
and down the slope of his back. Halfway down the curve of his spine
is a shallow red cut, glittering from the sliver of glass embedded in it.

"Hold still," I say. I bring my fingertips against his lower back.
The noise rushes in, but this time I don't push. Instead I wait, let it
settle around me, like water. It's still there, but I can think through it,
around it. I don't think I'll ever be the touchy-feely type, but maybe
with practice I can at least learn to float.

Wes meets my gaze in the mirror, and quirks a brow.

"Practice makes perfect," I say, blushing. My fingers drift up his spine, running over his ribs till I reach the shard. Wesley tenses beneath my touch, which makes me tense too.

"Tweezers," I say, and he hands me a pair.

I pinch the glass, hoping it doesn't go deep.

"Breathe in, Wes," I say. He does, his back expanding beneath my fingers. "Breathe out."

He does, and I tug the glass out, his breath wavering as it slides free. I hold up the fragment for him to see. "Not bad." I put a small bandage over the cut. "You should keep it."

"Oh, yeah," he says, turning to face me. "I think I should wash it off and make a little trophy out of it, 'Courtesy of an escaped History and the coffee table in Two C' etched into the stand."

"Oh, no," I say, depositing the shard in his outstretched hand. "I wouldn't wash it off."

Wes drops it onto the top of a small pile of glass, but keeps his eyes on mine. The crooked smile slides away.

"We make a good team, Mackenzie Bishop."

"We do." We *do*, and that is the thing that tempers the heat beneath my skin, checks the flutter of girlish nerves. This is Wesley. My friend. My partner. Maybe one day my Crew. The fear of losing that keeps me in check.

"Next time," I say, pulling away, "don't hold the door open for me."

I clean off the cluttered sink and leave Wes to finish getting dressed, but he follows me down the hall, still shirtless.

"You see what I get for trying to be a gentleman."

Oh, god—he's flirting.

"No more gentlemanly behavior," I say, reaching my room. "You're clearly not cut out for it."

"Clearly," he says, wrapping an arm loosely around my stomach from behind.

I hiss, less from the noise than the pain. He lets go.

"What is it?" he says, suddenly all business.

"It's nothing," I say, rubbing my ribs.

"Take off your shirt."

"You'll have to try a hell of a lot harder to seduce me, Wesley Ayers."

"*My* shirt's already off," he counters. "I think it's only fair."

I laugh. It hurts.

"And I'm not trying to seduce you, Mackenzie," he says, straightening. "I'm trying to help. Now, let me see."

"I don't want to see," I say. "I'd rather not know." I managed to shower and change without looking at my ribs. Things only hurt more when you can see them.

"That's great. Then you close your eyes and I'll see for you."

Wesley reaches out and slips his fingers around the edge of my shirt. He pauses long enough to make sure I won't physically harm him, then guides my top over my head. I look away, intending to educate myself on the number of pens in the cup on my desk. I can't help but shiver as Wesley's hand slides feather-light over my waist, and the noise of his touch actually distracts me from the pain until his hand drifts up and—

"Ouch." I look down. A bruise is already spreading across my ribs.

"You should really have that looked at, Mac."

"I thought that's what you were doing."

"I meant by a medical professional. We should get you to Patrick, just to be safe."

"No way," I say. Patrick's the last person I want to see right now. "Mac—"

"I said no." Pain weaves between my ribs when I breathe, but I *can* breathe, so that's a good sign. "I'll live," I say, taking back my shirt.

Wes sags onto my bed as I manage to get the shirt over my head, and I'm tugging it down when there's a knock on my door, and Mom peeks in, holding a plate of oatmeal-raisin cookies.

"Mackenz— Oh."

She takes in the scene before her, Wesley shirtless and stretched out on my bed, me pulling my shirt on as quickly as possible so she won't see my bruises. I do my best to look embarrassed, which isn't hard.

"Hello, Wesley. I didn't know you were here."

Which is a a bald-faced lie, of course, because my mother loves me, but she doesn't show up with a tray of cookies and a pitcher and her sweetest smile unless I've got company. When did she get home?

"We went for a run together," I say quickly. "Wes is trying to help me get back in shape."

Wesley makes several vague stretching motions that make it abundantly clear he's not a runner. I'll kill him.

"Mhm," says Mom. "Well, I'll just . . . put these . . . over here."

She sets the tray on an unpacked box without taking her eyes off us.

"Thanks, Mom."

"Thanks, Mrs. Bishop," says Wesley. I glance over and find him eyeing the cookies with a wolfish smile. He's almost as good a liar as I am. It scares me.

"Oh, and Mac," adds Mom, swiping one of the cookies for herself.

"Yeah?"

"Door open, please," she chirps, tapping the wooden door frame as she leaves.

"How long have we been running together?" asks Wes.

"A few days." I throw a cookie at his head.

"Good to know." He catches and devours the cookie in a single move, then reaches over and lifts Ben's bear from the bedside table. The plastic glasses are no longer perched on its nose but folded on the table, where I dropped them last night before I went to find my brother. My chest tightens. *Gone gone gone* thuds in my head like a pulse.

"Was this his?" Wes asks, blind pity written across his face. And I know it's not his fault—he doesn't understand, he can't—but I can't stand that look.

"Ben hated that bear," I say. Still, Wesley sets it gently, reverently, back on the table.

I sink onto the bed. Something digs into my hip, and I pull the Crew key out of my pocket.

"That was close today," says Wes.

"But we did it," I say.

"We did." Halfway to a smile, his mouth falls. I feel it too.

Wes reaches for his Archive paper as I reach for mine, and we both unfold the lists at the same time to find the same message scrawled across the paper.

Keepers Bishop and Ayers:
Report to the Archive.
NOW.

TWENTY-SIX

I KNOW THIS ROOM.
The cold marble floors and the walls lined with ledgers and the
long table sitting in the middle of the chamber: it's the room where
I became a Keeper. There are people seated behind that table now,
just as there were then, but the faces—most of them, at least—have
changed. And even as we gather, I can hear the distant sounds of the
disruption spreading.

As Wesley and I stand waiting, my first thought is that I avoided
one tribunal only to end up in another. This morning's would have
been deserved. This afternoon's makes no sense.

Patrick sits behind the table, glowering, and I wonder how long
he's been making that face, waiting for us to walk in. It is, for a
moment, absurdly funny, so much so that I'm worried I'll laugh.
Then I take in the rest of the scene, and the urge dies.

Lisa sits beside Patrick, her two-toned eyes unreadable.

Carmen is beside Lisa, clutching her notepad to her chest.

Roland heads the table, arms folded.

Two more people—the transfer, Elliot, and the woman with
the braid, Beth—stand behind those seated. The expressions in the
room range from contempt to curiosity.

I try to catch Roland's eye, but he's not watching me. He's watching them. And it clicks: Wesley and I are not the only ones on trial.

Roland thinks it's one of them who has been altering Histories.
Is this his way of rounding up suspects? I scan their faces. Could

one of these people be wreaking so much havoc? Why? I scour my memories of them, searching for one that lights up, any moment that makes one of them seem guilty. But Roland is like family; Lisa is sometimes stern but well-meaning; Carmen has confided in me, helped me, and kept my secrets. And little as I like Patrick, he's a stickler for rules. But the two people standing behind them . . . I've never spoken to the woman with the braid, Beth, and I know nothing about Elliot other than the fact that he transferred in just before the trouble started. If I could spend some time with them, maybe I could tell—

A shoe knocks against mine, and a tiny flare of metal and drums cuts through my thoughts. I steal a glance at Wesley, whose forehead is crinkling with concern.

"I still can't believe you told my mother we were going on a date," I say under my breath.

"I told her we were going out. I couldn't exactly be more specific, could I?" Wesley hisses back.

"That's what lying's for."

"I try to keep lies to a minimum. Omissions are much less karmically damaging."

Someone coughs, and I turn to find two more people sidling into the chamber, both in black. The woman is tall, with a ponytail of blue-black hair, and the man is made of caramel—gold skin and gold hair and a lazy smile. I've never seen them before, but there is something lovely and frightening and cold about them, and then I see the marks carved on their skin, just above their wrists. Three lines. They're Crew.

"Miss Bishop," says Patrick, and my attention snaps back to the table. "This is not your first infraction."

I frown. "What infraction have I committed?"

"You let a History escape into the Outer," he says, taking off his glasses and tossing them to the table.

"We also caught him," says Wesley.

"Mr. Ayers, your record has been, before today, impeccable. Perhaps you should hold your tongue."

"But he's right," I say. "What matters is that we caught the History."

"He shouldn't have gotten into the Coronado in the first place," warns Lisa.

"He shouldn't have gotten into the Narrows at all," I answer. "I returned Jackson Lerner this week. So tell me how he managed to wake, find his way back into my territory, and avoid my list? A product of the disruption?"

Roland shoots me a look, but Patrick's eyes flick down to his desk. "Jackson Lerner was a filing error."

I bite back a laugh and he gives me a warning glare, as does Lisa. Carmen avoids eye contact and chews the side of her lip. She's the one who took Jackson from me. She was supposed to return him.

"It was my . . ." she says softly, but Patrick doesn't give her the chance.

"Miss Bishop, this was a filing error precipitated by your incorrect delivery of the History in question. Is it not true you returned Jackson Lerner to the Archive's antechamber, as opposed to the Returns room?"

"I didn't have a choice."

"Jackson Lerner's presence in the Narrows is not the most pressing issue," says Lisa. "The fact that he was allowed into the Outer . . ." *Allowed,* she says, like we just stepped aside. *Allowed,* because we were still alive when he got through. "The fact that two Keepers were patrolling the same territory and yet neither—"

"Who authorized that, anyway?" Patrick cuts in.

"I did," says Roland.

"Why not just give them a Crew key and a promotion while you're at it?" snaps Patrick.

Da's Crew key weighs a thousand pounds in my boot.

"The status of Miss Bishop's territory necessitated immediate aid," says Roland, meeting Patrick's gaze. "Mr. Ayers's territory has yet to experience any increase. Whereas the Coronado and surrounding areas are, for *some* reason, suffering the greatest damage during this disruption. The decision was well within my jurisdiction. Or have you forgotten, Patrick, that I am the highest-ranking official not only in this branch but in this state, and in this region, and, as such, your director?"

Roland? The highest ranking? With his red Chucks and his lifestyle magazines?

"How long have Miss Bishop and Mr. Ayers been paired?" asks Lisa.

Roland draws a watch from his pocket, a grim smile on his lips. "About three hours."

The man in the corner laughs. The woman elbows him.

"Miss Bishop," says Patrick, "are you aware that once a History reaches the Outer, it ceases to be the Keeper's task, and becomes that of the Crew?" On the last word, he gestures to the two people in the corner. "Imagine the level of confusion, then, when the Crew arrives to dispatch the History, and finds it gone."

"We did find some broken glass," offers the man.

"Some police, too," adds the woman.

"And a lady in a robe going off about vandals——"

"But no History."

"Why is that?" asks Patrick, turning his attention to Wesley.

"When Lerner escaped, we went after him," says Wes. "Tracked him through the hotel, caught him before he exited the building, and returned him."

"You acted out of line."

"We did our job."

"No," snaps Patrick, "you did the Crew's job. You jeopardized human lives and your own in the process."

"It was dangerous for you two to pursue the History once it reached the Outer," amends Carmen. "You could have been killed. You're both remarkable Keepers, but you're not Crew."

"Yet," says Roland. "But they certainly demonstrated their potential."

"You cannot be encouraging this," says Patrick.

"I sanctioned their partnership. I should hope I wouldn't do that without believing them capable." Roland stands. "And to be frank, I can't see how reprimanding Keepers for returning Histories is a good use of our time given the current . . . circumstances. And given those circumstances, I believe Mr. Ayers should be allowed to continue assisting Miss Bishop, so long as his own territory does not suffer for it."

"That is not how the Archive functions—"

"Then for now the Archive must learn to be a little more flexible," says Roland. "But," he adds, "if any evidence presents itself that Mr. Ayers is unable to keep his own numbers down, the partnership will be dissolved."

"Granted," says Lisa.

"Very well," says Carmen.

"Fine," says Patrick.

Neither Elliot nor Beth have said a single thing, but now each gives a quiet affirmation.

"Dismissed," says Roland. Lisa stands first and crosses to the doors, but when she opens them, another wave of noise—like metal shelves hitting stone floors—reaches us. She draws her key from her pocket—thin and gleaming gold, like the one Roland drove into Ben's chest—and hurries toward the sound. Carmen, Elliot, and Beth follow. The Crew is already gone, and Wesley and I make our own way out; but Roland and Patrick stay behind.

As I approach the door, I hear Patrick say something to Roland that makes my blood run cold. "Since you are the *director*," he mutters, "it's my duty to inform you that I've asked for an assessment of Miss Bishop."

He says it loud enough for me to hear, but I won't give him the satisfaction of looking back. He's just trying to rattle me.

"You will not bring Agatha into this, Patrick," says Roland, more quietly, and when Patrick answers, it's nothing more than a whisper.

I pick up my pace and force my eyes forward as I follow Wesley out. The numbers of Librarians in the atrium seems to have doubled in the last day. Halfway to the desk, we pass Carmen giving orders to a few unfamiliar faces, listing the wings, halls, rooms to be blacked out. When they peel away, I tell Wes to go on ahead, and stop to ask Carmen something.

"What does that mean, 'blacking out' rooms?"

She hesitates.

"Carmen, I already know what a disruption is. So what does this mean?"

She bites her lip. "It's a last resort, Miss Bishop. If there's too much noise, too many Histories waking, blacking out a room is the fastest way to kill the disturbance, but . . ."

"What is it?"

"It kills the content, too," she says, looking around nervously.

"Blacking out a room blacks out everything inside. It's an irreversible process. It turns the space into a crypt. The more rooms we have to black out, the more content we lose. I've seen disruptions before, but never like this. Almost a fifth of the branch has already been lost." She leans in. "At this rate, we could lose everything."

My stomach drops. Ben is in this branch. Da is in this branch.

"What about the red stacks?" I press. "What about Special Collections?"

"Restricted stacks and Archive members are vaulted. Those shelves are more secure, so they're holding for now, but—"

Just then, three more Librarians rush toward her, and Carmen turns away to speak with them. I think she's forgotten me altogether, but as I turn to go, she glances my way and says only, "Be safe."

"You look sick," says Wes once we're back in the Narrows.

I feel sick. Ben and Da are both in a branch that is crumbling, a branch that someone is trying to topple. And it's my fault. I started the search. I dug up the past. I pushed for answers. Tipped the dominoes . . .

"Talk to me, Mac."

I look at Wesley. I don't like lying to him. It's different lying to Mom and Dad and Lyndsey. Those are big, blanket lies—easy, all-or-nothing lies. But with Wes, I have to sift out what I can say from what I can't, and by *can't* I mean *won't*, because I *could*. I *could* tell him. I tell myself I *would* tell him, if Roland hadn't warned me not to. I *would* tell him everything. Even about Owen. I tell myself I would. I wonder if it's true.

"I've got a bad feeling," I say. "That's all."

"Oh, I don't see why you would. It's not like they just put us on trial, or our branch is falling down, or your territory is out of control in a seriously suspicious way." He sobers. "Frankly, Mac, I'd be worried if you had a *good* feeling about any of this." He glances back at the Archive door. "What's going on?"

I shrug. "No idea."

"Then let's find out."

"Wesley, in case you haven't noticed, I can't afford to get in any more trouble right now."

"I have to admit, I never pegged you as such a delinquent."

"What can I say? I'm the best of the worst. Now, let the Librarians do their job, and we'll do ours. *If* you can handle another day of it."

He smiles, but it seems thinner. "It'll take more than an overflowing Narrows, an escaped History, a glass table, and a tribunal to get rid of me. Pick you up at nine?"

"Nine it is."

Wes veers off into the Narrows toward his own home. I watch him go, then squeeze my eyes shut. What a mess, I think, just before a kiss lands like a drop of water on the slope of my neck.

I shiver, spin, and slam the body into the nearest wall. The quiet floods in where my hand meets his throat. Owen raises a brow.

"Hello, M."

"You should know better," I say, "than to sneak up on someone." I slowly release my hold on him.

Owen's hands drift up to touch mine, then past them to my wrists. In one fluid motion, I'm the one against the wall, my hands pinned loosely overhead. The thrill of warmth washes over my skin, while the quiet courses under it, through my head.

"If I remember correctly," he says, "that's exactly how I saved you."

I bite my lip as he leans in to kiss my shoulder, my throat—heat and silence thrumming through me, both welcome.

"I didn't need saving," I whisper. He smiles against my skin, his body pressing flush with mine. I wince.

"What's wrong?" he asks, lips hovering beneath my jaw.

"Long day," I say, swallowing.

He pulls back a fraction, but doesn't stop brushing me with kisses, leaving a trail of them up my cheek to my ear as his fingers tangle through mine above my head, tighten. The quiet gets stronger, blotting out thoughts. I want to escape into it. I want to vanish into it.

"Who was the boy?" he whispers.

"He's a friend."

"Ah," Owen says slowly.

"No, not 'ah,'" I say defensively. "Just a friend."

Willingly, necessarily just a friend. With Wesley, there is too much to lose. But with Owen, there is no future to be lost by giving in. No future at all. Only escape. Doubt whispers through the quiet. Why does he care? Is it jealousy that flickers across his face? Curiosity? Or something else? It is so easy for me to read people and so hard for me to read him. Is this how people are supposed to look at each other? Seeing only faces, and none of the things behind?

He can read me well enough to know that I don't want to talk about Wesley, because he lets it drop, wraps me in silence and kisses, draws me into the dark of the alcove where we sat before, and guides me to the wall. His hands brush over my skin too gingerly. I pull his body to mine despite the ache in my ribs. I kiss him, relishing the way the quiet deepens when his body is pressed to mine, the way I can blot thoughts out simply by pulling him closer, kissing him harder. What beautiful control.

"M," he moans against my neck. I feel myself blush. In all the strangeness, there's something about the way he looks at me, the way he touches me, that feels so incredibly . . . normal. Boy-and-girl and smiles-and-sideways-glances and whispers-and-butterflies normal. And I want that so, so badly. I can feel the scratch of letters in my pocket, now constant. I leave the list where it is.

A faint smile tugs at the corner of Owen's mouth as it hovers above mine. We are close enough to share breath, the quiet dizzying but not quite strong enough. Not yet. Thoughts keep trickling through my head, warnings and doubts, and I want to silence them. I want to disappear.

As I run my fingers through his hair and pull his face to mine, I wonder if Owen is escaping too. If he can disappear into my touch, forget what he is and what he's lost.

I am blotting out pieces of my life. I am blotting out everything but this. But him. I exhale as he brushes against me, my body beginning to uncurl, to loosen at his fingertips. I am letting him wash over me, drown every part of me that I don't need in order to kiss or to listen or to smile or to want. *This* is what I want. This is my drug. The pain, both skin-deep and deeper, is finally gone. Everything is gone but the quiet.

And the quiet is wonderful.

"Why do you smoke, Da?"

 "We all do things we shouldn't, things that harm us."

 "*I* don't."

 "You're still young. You will."

 "But I don't understand. Why hurt yourself?"

 "It won't make sense to you."

"Try me."

You frown. "To escape."

"Explain."

"I smoke to escape from myself."

"Which part?"

"Every part. It's bad for me and I know it and I still do it, and in order for me to do it and enjoy it, I have to *not* think about it. I can think about it before and after, but while I'm doing it, I stop thinking. I stop being. I am not your Da, and I am not Antony Bishop. I am no one. I am nothing. Just smoke and peace. If I think about what I'm doing, then I think about it being wrong and I can't enjoy it, so I stop thinking. Does it make sense now?"

"No. Not at all."

"I had a dream last night. . . ." says Owen, rolling the iron ring from Regina's note over his knuckles. "Well, I don't know if it was night or day."

We're sitting on the floor. I'm leaning against him, and he has one arm draped over my shoulder, our fingers loosely intertwined. The quiet in my head is like a sheet, a buffer. It is water, but instead of floating, like Wes taught me, I am drowning in it. This is a thing like peace but deeper. Smoother.

"I didn't know Histories could dream," I say, wincing when it comes out a little harsh, making Histories into an *it* instead of a *him* or *you*.

"Of course," he says. "Why do you think they—we—wake up? I imagine it's because of dreams. Because they're so vivid, or so urgent, that we cannot sleep."

"What did you dream about?"

He navigates the iron ring to his palm, folds his fingers over it.

"The sun," he says. "I know it seems impossible, to dream of light in a place as dark as this. But I did."

He rests his chin on my hair. "I was standing on the roof," he says. "And the world below was water, glittering in the sun. I couldn't leave, there was no way off, so I stood and waited. So much time seemed to pass—whole days, weeks—but it never got dark, and I kept waiting for something—someone—to come." The fingers of his free hand trace patterns on my arm. "And then you came."

"What happened then?" I ask.

He doesn't speak.

"Owen?" I press, craning to look at him.

Sadness flickers like a current through his eyes. "I woke up."

He pockets the iron ring and produces the iron bar and the second piece of the story, the one I handed him before the trial.

"Where did you find this?" he asks.

"Under a marble rose," I say. "Your sister picked some clever hiding places."

"The Even Rose," he says softly. "That was the name of the café back then. And Regina was always clever."

"Owen, I've looked everywhere, and I still haven't found the ending. Where could it be?"

"It's a large building. Larger than it looks. But the pieces of the story seem to fit where they've been hidden. The Even Rose fragment spoke of climbing out of stones. The fragment from the roof spoke of reaching the top, battling the monsters. The ending will fit its place, too. The hero will win the battle—he always does—and then . . ."

"He'll go home," I finish quietly. "You said it was a journey. A quest. Isn't the point of a quest is to get somewhere? To get home?"

He kisses my hair. "You're right." He twirls the trinket piece. "But where is home?"

Could it be **3F**? The Clarkes lived there once. Could the ending to Regina's story be hidden in their home? In mine?

"I don't know, M," he whispers. "Maybe Regina won this last game."

"No," I say. "She hasn't won yet."

And neither has the rogue Librarian. Owen's quiet calms my panic and clears my head. The more I think about it, the more I realize that there's no way this disruption is just a distraction from the dark secrets of the Coronado's past. It's something more. There was no need to shatter the peace of the Archive after erasing evidence in both the Archive and the Outer. No, I'm missing something; I'm not seeing the whole picture.

I disentangle myself from Owen and turn to face him, forfeiting the quiet to ask a question I should have asked long ago. "Did you know a man named Marcus Elling?"

A small crease forms between Owen's eyes. "He lived on our floor. He was quiet but always kind to us. Whatever happened to him?"

I frown. "You don't know?"

Owen's face is blank. "Should I?"

"What about Eileen Herring? Or Lionel Pratt?"

"The names sound familiar. They lived in the building, right?"

"Owen, they all died. A few months after Regina." He just stares at me, confused. My heart sinks. If he can't remember anything about the murders, about his own death on the roof . . . I thought I was protecting him from the Archive, but what if I'm too late?

What if someone's already taken the memories I need? "What *do* you remember?"

"I . . . I didn't want to leave. Right after Regina died, my parents packed up everything and ran away, and I couldn't do it. If there was any part of her left in the Coronado, I couldn't leave her. That's the last thing I can remember. But that was days after she died. Maybe a week."

"Owen, you died five *months* after your sister."

"That's not possible."

"I'm sorry, but it's true. And I've got to find out what happened between her death and yours." I drag myself to my feet, pain rippling through my ribs. It's late, it's been a hell of a day, and I have to meet Wesley in the morning.

Owen stands too, and pulls me in for a last, quiet kiss. He leans his forehead against mine, and the whole world hushes. "What can I do to help?"

Keep touching me, I want to say, because the quiet soothes the panic building in my chest. I close my eyes, relish the moment of nothingness, and then pull away. "Try to remember the last five months of your life," I say as I go.

"The day's almost over, isn't it?" he asks as I reach the corner.

"Yeah," I call back. "Almost."

TWENTY-SEVEN

WESLEY IS LATE.

He was supposed to pick me up at nine. I woke at dawn and spent the hour before Mom and Dad got up scouring the apartment for loose boards and any other hiding places where Regina could have hidden a scrap of story. I dragged the boxes from my closet, pulled half the drawers from the kitchen, tested every wooden plank for give, and found absolutely nothing.

Then I put on a show for my parents, doing stretches as I told them how Wes was on his way, how we were planning to hit Rhyne Park today (I found a map in the study, and the splotch of green labeled RHYNE seemed to be within walking distance). I mentioned that we'd grab lunch on the way back, and shooed my parents to their respective work with promises that I'd stay hydrated, wear sunscreen.

And then I waited for Wes, just like we'd agreed.

But nine a.m. came and went without him.

Now my eyes flick to the tub of oatmeal raisin cookies on the counter, and I think of Nix and the questions I could be asking him. About Owen and the missing months.

I give my partner another ten minutes, then twenty.

When the clock hits nine thirty, I grab the tub and head for the stairs. I can't afford to sit still.

But halfway down the hall, something stops me—that gut sense Da was always talking about, the one that warns when something is off. It's the painting of the sea. It's crooked again. I reach out and straighten the frame, and that's when I hear a familiar rattling sound, like something is sliding loose inside, and everything in me grinds to a halt.

I was born up north, by the sea, said Owen.

My heart pounds as I carefully lift the painting from the wall and turn it over. There's a backing, like a second canvas, one corner loose, and when I tip the painting in my hands, something falls free and tumbles to the old checkered carpet with a whispered thud. I return the painting to the wall and kneel, retrieving a piece of paper folded around a chip of metal.

I unfold the paper with shaking hands, and read. . . .

He fought the men and he slayed the monsters and he bested the gods, and at last the hero, having conquered all, earned the thing that he wanted most. To go home.

The end of Regina's story.

I read it twice more, then look closer at the bit of dark metal it was wrapped around. It's the thickness of a nickel and about as large, if a nickel were hammered into a roughly rectangular shape. The two sides opposite each other are regular and straight, but the other two are off. The top side has a notch cut out, as if someone ran a knife across the stone just below the edge. The notch is on both sides. The bottom side of the square has been filed till it is sharp enough to cut with, the metal tapering to a point.

There's something familiar about it, and even though I can't place it, a small sense of victory flutters through me as I pocket the metal and the paper scrap and head upstairs.

On the seventh floor I knock, wait, and listen to the sound of the wheelchair rolling across the wood. Nix maneuvers the door with even less grace than the first time. When he's got it open, his face lights up.

"Miss Mackenzie."

I smile. "How did you know it was me?"

"You or Betty," he says. "And she wears perfume thick as a coat." I laugh. "Told her to stop bathing in it."

"I brought the cookies," I say. "Sorry it took so long."

He pivots the wheelchair and lets me guide him back to the table.

"As you can see," he says as he waves a hand at the apartment, "I've been so busy, I've hardly noticed."

It looks untouched, like a painting of the last visit, down to the cigarette ash and the scarf around his neck. I'm relieved to see he didn't set the thing on fire.

"Betty hasn't been in to clean up," he says.

"Nix . . ." I'm afraid to ask. "Is Betty still around?"

He laughs hoarsely. "She's no dead wife, if that's what you think, and I'm too old for imaginary friends." A breath of relief escapes. "Comes 'round to check on me," he explains. "Dead wife's sister's daughter's friend, or something. I forget. She tells me my mind is going, but really I just don't care enough to remember." He points to the table. "You left your book here." And sure enough, the *Inferno* is sitting where I left it. "Don't worry. Not like I peeked."

I consider leaving it again. Maybe he won't notice. "Sorry about that," I say. "Summer reading."

"What do schools do that for?" he grumbles. "What's the point of summer if they give you homework?"

"Exactly!" I set him up at the table and put the Tupperware in his lap.

He rattles it. "Too many cookies here for just me. You better help."

I take one and sit down across from Nix. "I wanted to ask you—"

"If it's about those deaths," he cuts in, "I've been thinking about 'em." He picks at the raisins in his cookie. "Ever since you asked. I'd almost forgotten. Scary, how easy it is to forget bad things."

"Did the police think the deaths were connected?" I ask.

Nix shifts in his seat. "They weren't certain. I mean, it was suspicious, to be sure. But like I said, you can connect the dots or you can leave them be. And that's what they did, left 'em random, scattered."

"What happened to the brother, Owen? You said he stayed here."

"You want to know about that boy, you know who you should ask? That antiques collector."

I frown. "Ms. Angelli?" I remember the not-so-subtle gesture of her door shutting in my face. "Because she has a thing for history?"

Nix takes a bite of cookie. "Well, that too. But mostly because she lives in Owen Clarke's old place."

"No," I say slowly, "I do. Three F."

Nix shakes his head. "You live in the Clarke *family's* old place. But they moved out right after the murder. And that boy, Owen, he couldn't go, but he couldn't stay either, not there where his sister was . . . Well, he moved into a vacant apartment. And that Angelli woman lives there now. I wouldn't have known it if she hadn't come up to see me, a few years back when she moved in, curious about the history of the building. You want to know more about Owen, you should talk to her."

"Thanks for the tip," I say, already on my feet.

"Thanks for the cookies."

Just then the front door opens and a middle-aged woman appears on the mat. Nix sniffs the air once.

"Ah, Betty."

"Lucian Nix, I know you're not eating sugar."

Betty makes a beeline for Nix, and in the scramble of cookies and curses, I duck out and head downstairs. Names are still scratching on the list in my pocket, but they'll have to wait just a little longer.

When I reach the fourth floor, I run through the spectrum of lies I could use to get Angelli to let me in. I've only passed her once since she shut the door in my face, and earned little more than a curt nod.

But when I reach her door and press my ear to the wood, I hear only silence.

I knock and hold my breath and hope. Still silence.

I test the door, but it's locked. I search my pockets for a card or a hairpin, or anything I can use to jimmy the lock, silently thanking Da for the afternoon he spent teaching me to do that.

But maybe I won't need to. I step back to examine the door. Ms. Angelli is a bit on the scattered side. I'm willing to bet that she's a touch forgetful, and with the amount of clutter in her apartment, the odds of misplacing a key are high. The door frame is narrow but wide enough to form a shallow shelf on top, a lip. I stretch onto my toes and brush my fingertips along the sill of the door. They sweep against something metal, and sure enough, a key tumbles to the checkered carpet.

People are so beautifully predictable. I take up the key and slide it into the lock, holding my breath as I turn it and the door pops open, leading into the living room. Across the threshold, my eyes widen. I'd nearly forgotten how much stuff was here, covering every surface, the beautiful and the gaudy and the old. It's piled on shelves and tables and even on the floor, forcing me to weave between towers of clutter and into the room. I don't see how Ms. Angelli can walk through without upsetting anything.

The layout of **4D** is the same as **3F**, with the open kitchen and the hallway off the living room leading to the bedrooms. I slowly make my way toward them, checking each room to make sure I'm alone. Every room is empty of people and full of things, and I don't know if it's the clutter or the fact that I've broken in, but I can't shake the feeling that I'm being watched. It trails me through the apartment, and when a small crash comes from the direction of living room, I spin, expecting to see Ms. Angelli.

But no one's there.

And that's when I remember. The cat.

Back in the living room, a few books have been toppled, but there's no sign of Angelli's cat Jezzie. My skin crawls. I try to convince myself that if I stay out of her way, she'll stay out of mine. I shift the stack of books, a stone bust, and the edge of the carpet out of the way, clearing a space so I can read.

I take a deep breath, slide off my ring, and kneel on the exposed floorboards. But the moment I bring my hands to the wood, before I've even reached for the past, the whole room begins to hum against my fingers. Shudders. Rattles. And it takes me a moment to realize that I'm not feeling the weight of the memory in the floor alone, that there are so many antiques in this room, so many things with so many memories, that the lines between the objects are blurring. The hum of the floor touches the hum of things sitting on the floor, and so on, until the whole room sings, and it hurts. A pins-and-needles numb that climbs my arms and winds across my bruised ribs.

It's too much to read. There is too much *stuff* in here, and it fills my head the way human noise does. I haven't even started reaching past the hum to whatever memories are beyond it; I can hardly think through the noise. Pain flickers behind my eyes, and I realize I'm pushing back against the hum, so I try to remember Wesley's lessons.

Let the noise go white, he said. I crouch in the middle of Angelli's apartment with my eyes squeezed shut and my hands glued to the floor, waiting for the noise to run together around me, for it to even out. And it does, little by little, until I can finally think, and then focus, and reach.

I catch hold of the memory, and time spirals back, and with it the clutter shifts, changes, then lessens, piece after piece vanishing from the room until I can see most of the floor, the walls. People slide through the space, earlier tenants—some of the memories dull and faded, others bright—an older man, a middle-aged woman, a family with young twins. The room clears, morphs, until finally it is Owen's space.

I can tell even before I see his blond head flicker through the room, moving backward because I'm still rewinding time. At first I'm filled with relief that there *is* a memory to read, that it hasn't been blacked out along with so much of that year. And the memory suddenly sharpens, and I swear I see—

Pain shoots through my head as I slam the memory's retreat to a s top, and let it slide forward.

In the room with Owen, there is a girl.

I only catch a glimpse before he blocks my view. She's sitting in a bay window, and he's kneeling in front of her, his hands up on either side of her face, his forehead pressed to hers. The Owen I know is calm to a fault, composed, and sometimes, though I wouldn't tell him, ghostly. But this Owen is alive, full of restless energy woven through his shoulders and the way he's subtly rocking on his heels as he speaks. The words themselves are nothing more than a murmur, but I can tell they are low and urgent; and as suddenly as he knelt, he's up, hands falling from the girl's face as he turns away. . . . And then I'm not looking at him anymore, because I'm looking at *her*.

She's sitting with her knees drawn up just the way they were the night she was killed, blond hair spilling over them, and even though she's looking down, I know exactly who she is.

Regina Clarke.

But that's not possible.

Regina died before Owen ever moved into this apartment.

And then, as if she knows what I'm thinking, she looks up, past me, and she is Regina and not Regina all at once, a twisted version. Her face is tight with panic and her eyes are too dark and getting darker, the color smudging into—

A screaming sound tears through my head, high and long and horrible, and my vision plunges into color, then black, then color as something shoves up against my bare arm. I jerk back, out of the memories and away from the floor, but the stone bust catches my heel and sends me backward to the carpet, hard. Pain cuts across my ribs as I land, and my vision clears enough to take in the *thing* that attacked me. Jezzie's small black form bobs toward me, and I scoot back, but—

A high-pitched howl grates against my bones as another cat, fat and white with an encrusted collar, wraps its tail around my elbow. I wrench free and—

A third cat brushes my leg, and the world explodes into keening and red and light and pain, metal dragging beneath my skin. Finally I tear free and scramble backward out into the hall, and force the door shut.

My back hits the opposite wall, and I slide to the floor, my eyes watering from the headache that's as sudden and brutal as the cats' touch. I need quiet, true quiet, and I reach into my pocket to fetch my ring, but my fingers meet with nothing.

No.

I look at the door to **4D**. My ring must still be in there. I curse not so softly and put my forehead against my knees, trying to think through the pain and piece together what I'd seen before the onslaught of cats.

Regina's eyes. They were going dark. They were smudging into black, like she was *slipping*. But only Histories slip. And only a History could be sitting in her brother's apartment *after* she died, and that means it wasn't Regina, in the way that the body in Ben's drawer wasn't Ben, and that means she got *out*. But how? And how did Owen find her?

"Mackenzie?"

I glance up to see Wes coming down the hall.

He quickens his step. "What's wrong?"

I return my forehead to my knees. "I will give you twenty dollars if you go in there and get my ring."

Wesley's boots come to a stop somewhere to the right of my leg. "What's your ring doing in Ms. Angelli's place?"

"Please, Wes, just go get it for me."

"Did you break in——"

"Wesley." My head snaps up. "Please." And I must look worse than I feel, because he nods and goes inside. He reappears a few moments later and drops the ring to the carpet, at my feet. I pick it up and slide it on.

Wesley kneels down in front of me. "You want to tell me what happened?"

I sigh. "I was attacked."

"By a *History*?"

"No . . . by Ms. Angelli's cats."

The corner of his mouth twitches.

"It's not funny," I growl, and close my eyes. "I'm never going to live this down, am I."

"Never. And damn, way to give a guy a scare, Mac."

"You scare too easily."

"You haven't seen yourself." He fetches a compact from one of the many pockets of his pants, and flicks it open so I can see the ribbon of blood running from my nose down over my chin. I wipe it away with my sleeve.

"Okay, that's terrifying. Put it away," I say. "So the cats won that round."

I lick my lips, taste blood. I push myself to my feet. The hall sways slightly. Wesley reaches for my arm, but I wave him off and head for the stairs. He follows.

"What were you doing in there?" he asks.

The headache makes it hard to focus on the nuances of lying. So I don't.

"I was curious," I say as we descend the stairs.

"You had to be pretty damn curious to break into Angelli's apartment."

We reach the third floor. "My inquisitive nature has always been a weakness." I can't stop seeing Regina's eyes. How did she get out? She wasn't a Keeper-Killer, wasn't a monster. She wasn't even a punk, like Jackson. She was a fifteen-year-old girl. The murder could have been enough to unsettle her mind, even cause her to wake, but she never should have made it through the Narrows.

I step out of the stairwell, but when I turn to face Wes, he's frowning at me.

"Don't look at me like that with those big brown eyes."

"They're not just brown," he says. "They're hazel. Can't you see the flecks of gold?"

"Good god, how much time do you spend looking at yourself in the mirror each day?"

"Not enough, Mac. Not enough." But the laughter is gone from his voice. "You're clever, trying to distract me with my own good looks, but it won't work. What's going on?"

I sigh. And then I *really* look at Wesley. The cut on his cheek is healing, but there's a fresh bruise blossoming against his jaw. He's guarding his left arm in a way that makes me think he took a hit, and he looks utterly exhausted.

"Where were you this morning?" I ask. "I waited."

"I got held up."

"Your list?"

"The names weren't even *on* my list. When I got into the Narrows . . . I didn't have enough hands. I didn't have enough time. I barely got through in one piece. Your territory's bad, but mine is suddenly impassable."

"Then you shouldn't have come." I turn and walk down the hall.

"I'm your partner," he says, trailing me. "And apparently that's the problem. You were there at the trial, Mac. You heard the caveat. We could only be partners as long as my territory stayed clear. Someone *did* this. And I've been trying to understand all morning why a member of the Archive wouldn't want us working together. All I can think is that I'm missing something." Halfway down the hall he catches my arm, and I force myself not to pull back as the noise floods through me. "*Am* I missing something?"

I don't know how to answer. I don't have a truth or a lie that will fix anything. I've already put him in danger just by having him near, already painted a target on his back. He'd be safer if he just stayed away. If I could keep him away from this mess. Away from me.

"Wesley . . ." Everything else is falling apart. I don't need this to crumble, too.

"Do you trust me?" His question is so sudden and honest that I'm caught off guard.

"Yeah. I do."

"Then talk to me. Whatever's going on, let me help. You're not alone, Mackenzie. Our whole lives are about lying, keeping secrets. I just want you to know that you don't have to keep them from me."

And that breaks my heart. Because I know he means every word. And because I can't confide in him. *I won't.* I won't tell him about the murders or the altered Histories or the rogue Librarian or Regina or Owen. And it's not some noble endeavor to keep him out of harm's way—there is no such thing right now. The truth is I'm scared.

"Thank you," I say, and it has all the terrible awkwardness of someone responding to a heartfelt *I love you* with an *I know*. So I add, "We're a team, Wes."

I hate myself as I watch his shoulders slacken. His hand drops, leaving a quiet that's even heavier than noise. He looks tired, his eyes ringed dark even beyond the makeup.

"You're right," he says hollowly. "We are. Which is why I'm giving you one last chance to tell me exactly what's going on. And don't bother lying. Right before you lie, you test out the words and your jaw shifts a fraction. You've been doing it a lot. So just *don't.*"

And that's when I realize how tired I am, of lies and omissions and half-truths. I put Wes in danger, but he's still here—and if he's willing to brave this chaos with me, then he deserves to know what I know. And I'm about to speak, about to tell him that, tell him everything, when he brings his hand to the back of my neck, pulls me forward, and kisses me.

The noise floods in. I don't push back, don't block it out, and for one moment, all I can think is that he tastes like summer rain.

His lips linger on mine, urgent and warm.

Lasting.

And then he pulls away, breath ragged.

His hand falls from my skin, and I understand.

He's not wearing his ring.

He didn't just kiss me.

He *read* me.

Wesley's face is bright with pain, and I don't know what he saw or what he felt, but whatever he read in me, it's enough to make him turn and storm out.

TWENTY-EIGHT

WESLEY SLAMS the stairwell door, and I turn and punch the wall, hard enough to dent the faded yellow paper, pain rolling up my hand. My reflection stares at me from the mirror on the opposite wall, and it looks . . . lost. It's finally showing in my eyes. Da's eyes. I hold my gaze and search for some of him in me, search for the part that knows how to lie and smile and live and be. And I don't see any of it.

What a mess. Truths are messy and lies are messy, and I don't care what Da said, it's impossible to cut a person into pielike pieces, neat and tidy.

I shove off the wall, the anger coiling into something hard, stubborn, restless. I've got to find Owen. I turn for the Narrows door, pulling the key from around my neck and the list from my pocket. My stomach sinks when I unfold it. The scratch of letters has been near constant, but I didn't expect the paper to be *covered* with names. My feet slow, and for a moment I think it's too many, that I shouldn't go alone. But then I think of Wesley, and speed up. I don't need his help. I was a Keeper before he even knew what Keepers were. I slide off my ring and step into the Narrows.

There is so much noise.

Footsteps and crying and murmurs and pounding. Fear runs through me but doesn't fade, so I hold on to it, use it to keep me sharp. The movement feels good, the pulse in my ears its own white noise, blotting out everything but instinct and habit and muscle memory as I cross through the Narrows in search of Owen.

I can't seem to cover more than a hall without trouble, and I dispatch two feisty teens. But by the time the door to the Returns room shuts, more names flash up to fill their spots. A bead of sweat runs down my neck. The metal of the knife is warm against my calf, but I leave it there. I don't need it. I fight my way toward Owen's alcove.

And then Keeper-Killers begin to blossom across my list.

Two more Histories.

Two more fights.

I brace myself against the Returns door, breathless, and look at the paper.

Four more names.

"Damn it." I slam my fist against the door, still out of air. Fatigue is starting to creep in, the high of the hunt brought down by the fact that the list is matching me one for one, and sometimes two or three for one. It's not possible to dent the list, let alone clear it. If it's this bad here, what's happening in the Archive?

"Mackenzie?"

I spin to find Owen. He wraps his arms around me, and there's a moment of relief and quiet, but neither is thick enough to block out the hurt I saw in Wesley's eyes, or the pain or guilt or anger at him, myself, everything.

"It's falling apart," I say into his shoulder.

"I know," Owen answers, laying a kiss on my cheek, then one on my temple before resting his forehead there. "I know."

Quiet blossoms and fades, and I think of him holding Regina's face, pressing his forehead to hers, the low static of his voice as he spoke to her. But what was she doing there? How did he find her?

Did he even know what she was? Is that why they carved it out of his memory?

But it doesn't add up. The walls of the Coronado and the minds of the Histories were altered by different people, but in both cases the excavations were meticulous, and the time missing from the walls seems to nearly match the time missing from the people's minds. But Angelli's place was left unaltered, which means they missed a spot, or it didn't need to be erased. So why would it be gone from Owen's mind? On top of that, the other altered Histories had *hours* erased, a day or two at most. Why would Owen be missing *months*?

It doesn't make sense. Unless he's lying.

As soon as I think it, the horrible gut feeling that I'm right hits in a wave, like it's been waiting. Building.

"What's the last thing you remember?" I ask.

"I already told you . . ."

I pull free. "No, you told me what you felt. That you didn't want to leave Regina there. But what's the last thing you *saw*? The very last moment of your life?"

He hesitates.

In the distance, someone cries.

In the distance, someone screams.

In the distance, feet are stomping and hands are pounding, and it is all getting closer.

"I don't remember. . . ." he starts.

"This is important."

"You don't believe me?"

"I want to."

"Then do," he says softly.

"Do you want to know the end of your story, Owen?" I say, the gut sense twisting inside me. "I'll tell you what I've pieced together, and maybe it will jog your memory. Your sister was murdered. Your parents left, and you didn't. Instead you moved into another apartment, and then Regina came back, only it wasn't Regina, Owen. It was her History. You knew she wasn't normal, didn't you? But you couldn't help her. So you jumped off the roof."

For one long moment, Owen just looks at me.

And then he says in a calm, quiet voice, "I didn't want to jump."

I feel ill. "So you do remember."

"I thought I could help Regina. I really did. But she kept slipping. I never wanted to jump, but they gave me no choice."

"Who?"

"The Crew who came to take her back. And arrest me."

Crew? How would he know that word unless . . .

"You were part of it. The Archive."

I want him to deny it, but he doesn't.

"She didn't belong there," he says.

"Did you let her out?"

"She belonged with me. She belonged home. And speaking of home," he says, "I think you have something of mine."

My hand twitches toward the last piece of the story in my pocket. I catch myself, too late.

"I'm not a monster, Mackenzie." He takes a step toward me as he says it, hand drifting toward mine, but I step away. His eyes narrow, and his hand drops back to his side. "Tell me you wouldn't have done it," he says. "Tell me you wouldn't have taken Ben home."

Behind my eyes I see Ben, moments after he woke, already slipping, and me, kneeling before him, telling him it would be okay, promising to take him home. But I wouldn't have. I wouldn't have gone this far. Because the moment he pushed me away, I saw the truth in the spreading black of his eyes. It wasn't my brother. It wasn't Ben.

"No," I say. "You're wrong. I wouldn't have gone that far."

I take another step back, toward a bend in the hall. Owen is blocking the way to the numbered doors, but if I can get to the Archive . . .

"Mackenzie," he says, reaching out again, "please don't—"

"What about those other people?" I ask, retreating. "Marcus and Eileen and Lionel? What happened to *them*?"

"I didn't have a choice," he says, following. "I tried to keep Regina in the room, but she was upset—"

"She was slipping," I say.

"I tried so hard to help her, but I couldn't always be there. Those people saw her. They would have ruined everything."

"So you *murdered* them?"

He smiles grimly. "What do you think the Archive would have done?"

"Not this, Owen."

"Don't be naive," he snaps, anger flashing through his eyes like light.

The bend in the hall is only a few steps behind me, and I break into a run as he says, "I wouldn't go that way," and I don't grasp why until I round the corner and come face-to-face with a vicious-looking History. Beyond him there are a dozen more. Standing, staring, black-eyed.

"I told them they had to wait," he says as I retreat into his stretch of hall, "and I would let them out. But they must be losing patience. So am I." He extends his hand. "The ending, please."

He says it softly, but I can see his stance shifting, the series of minute changes in his shoulders and knees and in his hands. I brace myself.

"I don't have it," I lie.

Owen lets out a low, disappointed sigh.

And then the moment collapses. In a blink, he closes the gap between us, and I crouch, free the knife from my leg, and bring it up to his chest as his hand catches my wrist and slams it into the wall hard enough to crack the bones. He catches my free hand, and before I can get my boot up, he forces me against the wall, his body flush with mine. My ribs ache beneath his weight. The quiet pushes in, too heavy.

"Miss Bishop," he says, tightening his grip on my hands. "Keepers should know better than to carry weapons." Something crunches inside my wrist, and I gasp as my grip gives way, the knife tumbling toward the floor. Owen lets go of me, and I lunge to the side, but he catches the falling knife with one hand and my arm with the other, and rolls me back into his arms, bringing the blade up beneath my chin. "I'd stay still, if I were you. I haven't held my knife in sixty years. I might be a little rusty."

His free hand runs over my stomach and down the front of my jeans, sliding into the pocket. His fingers find the note and the metal square, and he sighs with relief as he pulls both free. He kisses the back of my hair, the knife still against my throat, and holds the two things up so I can see. "I was beginning to worry that the painting wasn't there anymore. I didn't expect to be gone so long."

"You hid the story."

"I did, but it's not the *story* I was trying to hide."

The knife vanishes from my throat and he shoves me forward. I spin and find him putting away the note, and lining up the metal pieces in his palm. A ring, a bar, a square.

"Want to see a magic trick?" he asks, gesturing to the pieces.

He palms the square and holds up the ring and the bar. He slides the tapered point of the bar into the small hole drilled into the ring and twists the two pieces together. He produces the square and slides the notched edge of it along the groove in the bar.

And then he holds it up for me to see, and my blood runs cold. It's not as ornate as the one Roland gave me, but there's no mistaking what it is.

The ring, the bar, the square.

The handle, the stem, the teeth.

It's a Crew key.

"I'm not impressed," I say, cradling my wrist. When I flex my fingers, pain sears through my hand. But my key hangs around my good wrist, and if I can find a Returns door . . . I scan the hall, but the nearest white chalk circle is several yards behind Owen.

"You should be," he says. "But if it's credit you want, I'm happy to give it. I couldn't have done it without you."

"I don't believe that," I say.

"I couldn't risk it myself. What if the Crew found me before I found the pieces? What if the pieces weren't where they should be? No, this"—he holds up the key—"this was all you. You delivered the key that makes doors between worlds, the key that will help me tear the Archive down, one branch at a time."

Anger ripples through me. I wonder if I can break his neck before he stabs me. I chance a step forward. He doesn't move.

"I won't let that happen, Owen." I have to get the key back before he starts throwing open doors. And then, as if he can read me from here, the key vanishes into his pocket.

"You don't have to stand in my way," he says.

"Yes I do. That is exactly my job, Owen. To stop the Histories, however *deranged* they are, from getting out."

"I just wanted my sister back," he says, still spinning his knife. "They made it worse than it had to be."

"It sounds like you made it pretty bad yourself." I steal another step toward him.

"You don't know anything about it, little Keeper," he growls. Good. He's getting mad, and angry people make mistakes. "The Archive takes *everything* and gives nothing back. I just wanted one thing—"

The sound of a scuffle echoes down the hall, a shout, a scream, and Owen's attention wavers for an instant. I attack, shifting my weight forward. The toe of my boot catches the bottom of his knife midspin and sends it up into the ceilingless dark of the Narrows. My next kick knocks him backward as the knife falls and clatters to the floor several feet behind me. Owen hits the ground, too, and rolls over into a crouch, somehow straightening in time to dodge another blow. He catches my leg, pulls me forward, and brings his arm to my chest, slamming me to the floor. Pain burns across my injured ribs.

"It's too late," he says as I try to force air back into my lungs. "I will tear the Archive down."

"The Archive didn't kill Regina," I gasp, rolling up onto my hands and knees. "Robert did."

His eyes darken. "I know. And I made him pay for that."

My stomach turns. I should have known.

He got away. They let him get away. I let him get away. I was her big brother. . . .

Owen took everything I felt and mimicked it, twisted it, used it. Used *me*.

I spring to my feet, lunging for him, but he's too fast, and I barely touch him before his hand wraps around my throat and he slams me back into the door. I can't breathe. My vision blurs as I claw at his arm. He doesn't even flinch.

"I didn't want to do this," he says.

And then his free hand drifts to the leather cord around my wrist. My key. He pulls sharply, snapping the cord, and drives the key into the door behind me.

He turns it, and there's click before the door swings open behind me, showering us both in crisp white light. And then he leans in close enough to rest his cheek on mine as he whispers in my ear.

"Do you know what happens to a living person in the Returns room?"

I open my mouth, but no words come out.

"Neither do I," he says, just before he pushes me back, and through, and slams the door.

TWENTY-NINE

THE WEEK before you die, I can see it coming. I see the good-bye in your eyes. The too-long looks at everything, as if by staring you can make memories strong enough to last you through.

But it's not the same. And those lingering looks scare me.

I am not ready.

I am not ready.

I am not ready.

"I can't do this without you, Da."

"You can. And you have to."

"What if I mess up?"

"Oh, you will. You'll mess up, you'll make mistakes, you'll break things. Some you'll be able to piece together, and others you'll lose. That's all a given. But there's only one thing you have to do for me."

"What's that?"

"Stay alive long enough to mess up again."

The moment the Returns door closes, there is no door, and the white is so bright and shadowless that it makes the room look like infinite space: no floor, no walls, no ceiling. Nothing but dizzying white. I know I have to focus, have to find the place where the door was and get out and find Owen——and I can do that, the rational Keeper part of me reasons, if I can just breathe and make my way to the wall.

I take a step, and that's when the white on every side explodes into color and sound and life.

My life.

Mom and Dad on the porch swing of our first house, her legs draped across his lap and his book propped against her legs, and then the new blue house with Mom too big to fit through the door, and Ben climbing the stairs like they were mountain rocks, and Ben drawing on walls and floors and anything but paper, and Ben turning the space under the bed into a tree house because he was scared of heights, and Lyndsey hiding there with him even though she barely fit, and Lyndsey on the roof and Da in the summer house teaching me to pick a lock, to take a punch, to lie, to read to be strong, and hospital chairs and too-bright smiles and fighting and lying and bleeding and breaking into pieces, and moving and boxes and Wesley and Owen, and it all pours out of me and onto every surface, taking something vital with it, something like blood or oxygen because my body and mind are shutting down more and more with every frame extracted from my head.

And then the images begin to fold inward as the white recovers the room square by square by square, blotting out my life like screens being switched off. I sway on my feet. The white spreads, devouring, and I feel my legs buckle beneath me. The images blink out one by one by one, and my heartbeat skips.

No.

The air and the light are thinning.

I squeeze my eyes shut and focus on the fact that gravity tells me I'm on the floor. Focus on the fact that I have to get up. I can hear the voices now. I can make out Mom's voice chirping about the coffee shop; Dad's telling me it will be an adventure; Wesley's saying he's not going anywhere; Ben's asking me to come see; and Owen's telling me it's over.

Owen. Anger flares strong enough to help me focus, even as the voices weaken. Eyes still shut, I beg my body to stand. It doesn't, so I focus on crawling, on making my way to the wall I know exists somewhere in front of me. The room is becoming too quiet, and my mind is becoming too slow, but I keep crawling forward on my hands and knees—the pain in my wrist a reminder that I am still alive—until my fingers skim the base of the wall.

My heart skips again, falters.

My skin is going pins-and-needles numb as I manage to reach into my boot and pull Da's Crew key out. I use the wall to get myself up, brace myself when my body sways, and run my hands over the surface until I catch the invisible lip of a door frame.

The scenes have all gone quiet now except for one with Da.

I can't make out the words, and I can't tell anymore if my eyes are open or closed, and it's terrifying, so I focus on the smooth Louisiana lilt in Da's voice as he talks, and I bring my hands back and forth, back and forth, until my fingers graze the keyhole.

I get the key into the lock and turn hard to the left as Da's voice stops. Everything goes black a moment before the lock clicks and the door opens. I stumble through, gasping for air, every muscle shaking.

I'm back in the Narrows. Crew keys aren't even supposed to lead here. Then again, I'm pretty sure Crew keys aren't supposed to be used from *within* a Returns room. As I force my body to its feet, my pulse pounds in my ears. I'm thankful to still have a pulse. A scrap of paper is crumpled on the floor. My list. I lift it, expecting names, but there are no names at all, only an order.

Get out of the Narrows. Stay out of the Narrows. It's too late. —R

I look around.

The Narrows are empty and painfully quiet, and when I round the corner I see that my cluster of numbered doors have all been flung open. The rooms beyond are cast in shadow, but I can hear shouting in the lobby and the coffee shop—orders, the cold, composed kind given by members of the Archive, not Histories or residents. Only the third floor is quiet. Something in me twists, whispers *wrong wrong wrong*, and I shut the other two doors and step out into the hall.

The first thing I see is the red streaking across the faded yellow wallpaper.

Blood.

I drop to my knees and say a prayer even as I touch the floor and reach. The memory hums into my bones and numbs my hands as I roll it back. The scene is right at the top, and it skips away too fast, a blur of black-spiked hair and metal and red. Everything in me tightens. I slam the memories to a stop, and play them forward.

Anger washes over me as I watch Owen step out from the Narrows door and pull a pen and slip of paper from his pocket. It's the same size as the one with my list. Archive paper. There's a muffled sound down the hall, like knocking, as Owen leans the page against the mirror and writes one word. *Out.*

Moments later, a hand writes back. *Good.*

Owen smiles and pockets the slip.

The knocking stops, and I see Wesley standing by my door. He turns, his fist slipping back to his side; and judging by the way he's looking at Owen, he saw quite enough when he read my skin.

Owen only smiles. And then he says something. The words are nothing more than a hush, a murmur, but Wesley's face changes. His lips move, and Owen's shoulders shrug, and then the knife appears in his hand. He slips his finger into the hilt's hole, twirls the blade casually.

Wesley's hand curls into a fist, and he swings at Owen, who smiles, dodges fluidly, and follows upward with his knife. Wesley leans back just in time, but Owen spins the blade in his fingers at the top of its arc and swings down. This time Wesley isn't fast enough. He gasps and staggers back, gripping his shoulder. Owen strikes again, and Wes avoids the blade but not Owen's free hand, now a fist, as it comes down across his temple. One knee buckles to the floor, and before Wes can get up, Owen slams him back into the wall. Wes's shoulder leaves a blossom of red against one of the hall's ghosted doors, and the left side of his face is stained with blood, a gash on his forehead spilling down like a mask over his left eye. He collapses to the floor, and Owen vanishes into the stairwell.

Wesley staggers to his feet and follows.

And so do I.

I spring up from the floor, the past vanishing into present as I race down the hall and up the stairs. I'm close. I can hear the foot-steps floors above. I vault up past the sixth floor—more blood on the steps. Above me, I hear the roof door slam shut, and the sound is still echoing as I reach it and stumble through into the garden of stone demons.

And there they are.

Wesley catches Owen once across the jaw. Owen's face flicks sideways, and the smile sharpens before Wes throws another fist, and Owen catches his hand, pulls him forward, and plunges the knife into his stomach.

THIRTY

A SCREAM RISES in my throat as Owen pulls the knife free and Wesley collapses to the concrete.

"I'm impressed, Miss Bishop," Owen says, turning toward me. The sun is sinking, the gargoyles multiplied by shadows.

Wesley coughs, tries to move, can't.

"Hang in there, Wes," I say. "Please. I'm sorry. Please." I step forward, and Owen holds the knife over Wes in warning.

"I tried to miss the vital organs," he says. "But I told you, I'm rusty."

He extends one foot toward the ledge of the roof as he looks down, the blood-soaked knife hanging lazily from his fingers.

"It's a long way down, Owen. And there are plenty of Crew at the bottom."

"And they're going to have their hands full with the Histories," he says. "Which is why I'm up here."

He pulls the Crew key from his pocket and reaches out, slides it through the air as if there were . . . a door. My eyes slip off it several times before I can find the edges.

A *shortcut.*

The teeth vanish into the door.

"Is that why you were on the roof last time? To get away?"

"If they'd caught me alive," he says, still gripping the key, "they would have erased my life."

I have to get him away from that door before he goes through.

"I can't believe you're running away," I say, making the disgust in my voice clear.

And sure enough, his hand slips from the key. It hangs in the air as his foot slides from the ledge. "How did you get out?" he asks.

"It's a secret." I pivot and step back, the weight of my Crew key heavy in my coat. I have an idea. "There's something I don't get. So what if you were Crew—you're still a History." I take another step. "You should have slipped."

He pulls the key out of the air and pockets it as he steps over Wesley's body toward me.

"There's a reason Histories slip," he says. "It's not anger, or even fear. It's confusion. Everything is foreign. Everything is frightening. It's why Regina slipped. It's why Ben slipped."

"Don't talk to me about my brother." I take another step back, and nearly stumble on the base of a statue. "You knew what would happen."

Owen steps over a broken statue limb without looking down. "Confusion tips the scale. And that's why all members of the Archive are kept in the Special Collections. Because *our* Histories don't slip. Because we open our eyes and know where we are. We're not simple and scared and easily stopped."

I slip through a gap between the statues, and Owen falls out of sight. Moments later he reappears, following me through the maze of gargoyles. Good. That means he's away from his shortcut. Away from Wes.

"But other Histories aren't like us, Owen. They *do* slip."

"Don't you get it? They slip because they're lost, confused. Regina slipped. Ben slipped. But if we had been allowed to tell them about the Archive when they were still alive, maybe they would have made it through."

"You don't know that," I say, vanishing just long enough to pull the Crew key from my pocket, guard it against my wrist.

"The Archive owed us a chance. They take everything. We deserve something back. But no, it would be against the rules. Do you know why the Archive has so many rules, Miss Bishop? It's because they're afraid of us. Terrified. They make us strong, strong enough to lie and con and fight and hunt and kill, strong enough to rise up, to break free. All they have are their secrets and their rules."

I hesitate. He's right. I've seen it, the Archive's fear, in their strictures and their threats. But that doesn't mean what he's *doing* is right.

"Without the rules," I force myself to say, "there would be chaos." I step back, feel the front of a gargoyle come up against my shoulders. I slip sideways, never taking my eyes off Owen. "That's what you want, isn't it? Chaos?"

"I want freedom," he says, stalking me. "The Archive is a prison, and not only for the dead. And that's why I'm going to tear it down, shelf by shelf and branch by branch."

"You know I won't let you."

He steps forward, knife hanging loosely at his side. He smiles. "You wanted this to happen."

"No, I didn't."

He shrugs. "It doesn't matter. That's how the Archive will see it. And they will carve you up and throw you away. You're nothing to them. Stop running, Miss Bishop. There's nowhere to go."

I know he's right. I'm counting on it. I'm standing in a ring of winged statues, their faces crumbling with age, their bodies set too close. Owen looks at me as if I'm a mouse he's cornered, his eyes bright despite the dusk.

"I'll stand trial for my mistakes, Owen, but not for yours. You are a monster."

"And you aren't? The Archive makes us monsters. And then it breaks the ones who get too strong, and buries the ones who know too much."

I dart sideways as his hand flies forward. I pretend to notice too late, pretend to be too slow. He catches my elbow and forces me back against a demon, his arms caging me. And then he smiles, pulls me toward him just enough to rest the tip of the bloodstained knife between my shoulder blades.

"I wouldn't be so quick to pass judgment. You and I are not so different."

"You twisted it so I would think so. You conned my trust, made me think we were the same, but I am *nothing* like you, Owen."

He presses his forehead against mine. The quiet slides through me, and I hate it.

"Just because you can't read me," he whispers, "doesn't mean I can't read you. I've seen inside you. I've seen your darkness and your dreams and your fears, and the only difference between us is that I know the true extent of the Archive and its crimes, and you are only just learning."

"If you're talking about my inability to quit, I already know."

"You know *nothing*," Owen hisses, forcing my body against his. I wrap my empty hand around his back for balance, and bring the one with the key up behind him.

"But I could show you," he says, softening. "It doesn't have to end like this."

"You used me."

"So did they," he says. "But I'm giving you the one thing they never have, and never will. A choice."

I slide the key through the empty air behind his back and begin to turn. Da said it had to make a full circle, but halfway through the turn, the air *resists* and coalesces around the metal like a lock forming. A strange sense bleeds up the key into my fingers as the door takes shape out of nothing, barely visible and yet there, a shadow hovering in the air behind Owen. I look into his eyes, hold their focus. They are so cold and empty and cruel. No butterflies, no shoulders-to-shoulders, knees-to-knees, no sideways smiles. It makes this easier.

"I'd never help you, Owen."

"Well, I'll help you," he says. "I'll kill you before they do."

I hold fast to the key, but let my other arm fall away from his back. "Don't you see, Owen?"

"See what?"

"The day's over," I say, turning the key the rest of the way.

His eyes widen with surprise as he hears the click behind him, but it's too late. The moment the key finishes the full turn, the door opens backward with explosive force, not onto the dark halls of the Narrows or the white expanse of the Archive, but a cavernous black, a void, like space without stars. A nothing. A nowhere. Just like Da warned. But Da didn't convey the crushing force, the pull, like air being sucked out of an open plane door. It rips Owen and the knife backward, the void at once swallowing him and wrenching me forward to follow; but I cling to the broken arms of a gargoyle with all that's left of my strength. The violent wind within the doorway twists and, having devoured the History, reverses, slamming the door shut in my face.

It leaves nothing. No door, nothing but the key Roland lent me, which hangs in the air, still jammed in the invisible lock, its cord swaying from the force.

My knees buckle.

Then someone lets out a shuddering cough.

Wesley.

I pull the key free and run, weaving through the gargoyles and back to the edge of the roof where Wesley is lying, curled, red spreading out beneath him. I drop to the ground beside him.

"Wes. Wes, please, come on."

His jaw is clenched, his palm pressed against his stomach. I'm still not wearing my ring, and as I take his arm and try to wrap it around my shoulders, he gasps, and it's *pain fear worry anger pacing the hall not home where is she where is she I shouldn't have left and something tight like panic* before I can focus on getting him to his feet.

"I'm sorry," I whisper, dragging him up, his fear and pain washing over me, his thoughts running into mine. "I need you to stand. I'm sorry."

Tears escape down his cheeks, dark from the eyeliner. His breath is ragged as I lead him, too slowly, to the roof door. He leaves a trail of red.

"Mac," he says between gritted teeth.

"Shhh. It's okay. It's going to be okay." And it's such a bad lie, because how can it possibly be okay when he's losing this much blood? We'll never make it down the stairs. He won't last long enough for an ambulance. He needs medical attention. He needs Patrick. We reach the roof door, and I get the Crew key into the lock.

"I'll kick your ass if you die on me, Wes," I say, pulling him close as I turn the key left and drag him through into the Archive.

THIRTY-ONE

T HE DAY BEFORE YOU DIE, I ask if you're afraid.
"Everything ends," you say.

"But are you scared?" I ask.

You are so thin. Not brittle bone so much as barbed wire, your skin like paper over the top.

"When I first learned about the Archive, Kenzie," you say, smoke leaking out of the corner of your mouth, "every time I touched something, someone, I thought, That's going to be recorded. My life is going to be a record of every moment. It can be broken down like that. I relished the logic of it, the certainty. We are nothing but recorded moments. That's the way I thought."

You put the cigarette out on Mom's freshly painted porch rail.

"Then I met my first Histories, face-to-face, and they weren't books, and they weren't lists, and they weren't files. I didn't want to accept it, but the fact is, they were people. Copies of people. Because the only way to truly record a person is not in words, not in still frames, but in bone and skin and memory."

You use the cigarette to draw those same three lines in ash.

"I don't know whether that should terrify or comfort me, that everything is backed up like that. That somewhere my History is compiling itself."

You flick the cigarette butt into Dad's bushes but don't brush away the ash on the rail.

"Like I said, Kenzie. Everything ends. I'm not afraid to die," you say with a wan smile. "I just hope I'm smart enough "to stay dead."

The first thing I notice is the noise.

In a place where quiet is mandatory, there is a deafening clatter, a banging and scraping and slamming and crashing loud enough to wake the dead. And clearly it *is* waking them. The doors behind the desk have been flung back to reveal the chaos beyond, the vast peace shattered by toppled stacks, people rushing, breaking off in teams down halls, shouting orders, and all of them too far away. Da is in there. Ben is in there. Wes is dying in my arms, and there is no one at the desk. How can there be no one at the desk?

"Help!" I shout, and the word is swallowed by the sound of the Archive crumbling around me. "Someone!" Wesley's knees buckle beside me, and I slide to the ground under his weight. "Come on, Wes, *please.*" I shake him. He doesn't respond.

"Help!" I shout again as I feel for a pulse, and this time I hear footsteps and look up to see Carmen striding through the doors. She closes them behind her.

"Miss Bishop?"

"Carmen, I'm so glad to see you."

She frowns, looks down at Wesley's body. "What are you doing here?"

"Please, I need you to——"

"Where's Owen?"

Shock hits, and the whole world slows. And stops.

It was Carmen all along.

The Archive knife in Jackson's hands.

Hooper's name showing up late on my list.

Jackson escaping a second time.

The disruption spreading through the stacks.

Altering Marcus Elling and Eileen Herring and Lionel Pratt.

Flooding Wesley's territory after the trial.

Writing back to Owen the moment he got out.

It was all her.

Beneath my hands, Wesley gasps and coughs blood.

"Carmen," I say, as calmly as I can, "I don't know how you know Owen, but right now we have to get Wesley help. I can't let him—"

Carmen doesn't move. "Tell me what you did with Owen."

"He's going to die!"

"Then you'd better tell me quickly."

"Owen is nowhere," I snap.

"What?"

"You'll never find him," I say. "He's gone."

"No one's ever *gone*," she says. "Look at Regina."

"You're the one who woke her."

Carmen's brow knits. "You really should be more sympathetic. After all, you woke Ben."

"Because you both manipulated me. And you betrayed the Archive. You covered up Owen's murders. You altered *Histories*. Why? Would you do that for him?"

Carmen holds up the back of her hand to show the three lines of the Archive carved into her skin. Crew marks. "We were together, once upon a time. Before I got promoted. You're not Crew. You've never had a partner. If you had, you'd understand. I'd do anything for him. And I did."

"Wes is the closest thing I have to a partner," I say, running my fingers over his jacket until I find the collapsed *bō* staff. "And you're *killing* him."

I drag myself to my feet, vision blurring as I stand. With a flick of my wrist, the staff expands. It gives me something to hold on to.

"You can't hurt me, Miss Bishop," Carmen says with a withering look. "You think I'm here by choice? You think anyone would give up a *life* in the Outer for this place? They wouldn't. They don't."

And for the first time I notice the scratches on her arms, the cut on her cheek. Each mark is little more than a thin, bloodless line.

"You're dead."

"Histories are *records* of the dead," she says. "But yes, we're all Histories here." She comes toward me, blocking my path to the doors and the rest of the Archive. "Appalling, isn't it? Think about it: Patrick, Lisa—even your Roland. No one told you."

I ignore my lurching stomach. "When did you die?"

"Right after Regina. Owen was so broken without his sister, and so angry at the Archive. I just wanted to see him smile again. I thought Regina would help. In the end, he made such a mess, I couldn't save him." And then her green eyes widen. "But I knew I could bring him back."

"Then why did you wait so long?"

She closes in. "You think I wanted to? You think I didn't miss him every day? I had to transfer branches, had to wait for them to forget, to lose track of me, and then"—her eyes narrow—"I had to wait for a Keeper to take over the Coronado. Someone young, impression-able. Someone Owen could use."

Use. The word crawls over my skin.

The crashing of the Archive mounts behind her, and she glances back. "Amazing how easy it is to make a little noise."

In that moment, when she looks away, I make a run for the doors. I push as hard as I can before her hand grabs my arm and she wrenches me backward to the stone floor. The doors open, chaos and noise flooding in, but before I can get up, Carmen is straddling me, holding the staff across my throat.

"Where. Is. Owen?" she asks.

A few feet away, Wesley groans. I can't reach him.

"Please," I gasp.

"Don't worry," says Carmen. "It'll be over soon, and then he'll come back. The Archive doesn't let you go. You serve until you die, and when you do, they wake you on your shelf and they give you a choice, a one-time offer. Either you get up and work, or they close the drawer on you forever. Not much of a choice, is it?" She presses down on the staff. "Can't you see why Owen hates this place so much?"

Over her shoulder and through the doors I can see people. I get my fingers between the pole and my throat, and shout for help before Carmen cuts me off.

"Tell me what you've done with Owen," she orders.

People are coming through the doors, past the desk, but Carmen doesn't see, because all of her fear and anger and attention is focused on me.

"I sent him home," I say. And then I manage to get my foot between us and kick, and Carmen stumbles back into Patrick and Roland.

"What the hell?" growls Patrick as they wrestle her arms behind her back.

"He'll come back," she shrieks as they force her to her knees. "He would never leave me here—" Her eyes go wide as the life goes out of them. The Librarians let go, and she crumples to the floor with the sickening sound of dead weight. Patrick's key, gleaming and gold, is clutched in his grip.

I cough, gasping for breath as the room fills with sound—not just the chaos of the Archive pouring in through the doors, but with people shouting.

"Patrick! Hurry!"

I turn to see Lisa and two other Librarians kneeling over Wesley. He's not moving. I can't look at his body, so I look through the doors at the Archive, at the people hurrying about, barricading doors, making so much noise.

I hear Patrick ask, "Is there a pulse?"

My hands won't stop shaking.

"It's slowing. You have to hurry."

I feel like I should be breaking down, but there's nothing left of me to break.

"He's lost so much blood."

"Get him up, quickly."

A Librarian I've never met takes me by the elbow, guides me to the front desk and a chair. I slip into it. She has a deep scratch on her collar. There's no blood. I close my eyes. I know I'm hurt but I can't feel it anymore.

"Miss Bishop." I blink and find Roland kneeling beside my chair.

"Who are all those people?" I ask, focusing on the crumbling world beyond the antechamber.

"They work for the Archive. Some are Librarians. Some are higher up. They're trying to contain the disruption."

Another deafening crash.

"Mackenzie . . ." Roland grips the arm of the chair. There's blood on his hands. Wesley's. "You have to tell me what happened."

I do. I tell him everything. And when I'm done, he says, "You should go home."

I look at the slick of red on the floor. Behind my eyes I see Wes collapsing on the roof, see him storming away, see him sitting on the floor outside Angelli's, teaching me to float, hunting with me, reading to me, draped over a wrought iron chair, showing me the gardens, leaning in the hall in the middle of the night with his crooked smile.

"I can't lose Wes," I whisper.

"Patrick will do everything he can."

I look back at Wes's body. It's gone. Carmen's body is gone. Patrick is gone. I look down at my hands. Dried blood is flaking from my palms. I blink, focus on Roland. His red Chucks and his gray eyes and that accent I could never place.

"Is it true?" I ask.

"Is what true?" asks Roland.

"That all Librarians . . . that you're dead?"

Roland's face sinks.

"How long have you been . . ." I trail off. What word do I even want? *Dead?* We're trained to think of a History as something other, something less than a person, but how could Roland ever be less?

He smiles sadly. "I was about to retire."

"You mean, go back to being dead." He nods. I shudder. "There's an empty shelf here with your name and dates?"

"There is. And it was beginning to sound nice. But then I got called in to this meeting. An induction ceremony. Some crazy old man and his granddaughter." He stands, guides me up beside him. "And I don't regret it. Now, go home."

Roland walks me toward the Archive door. A man I don't know comes over and begins to speak to him in hushed, hurried tones.

He tells him that the Archive is hemorrhaging, but more staff have been called in from other branches. Sections are still being sealed off to stem the flow. Almost half of the standard stacks had to be sealed. Red stacks and Special Collections were spared.

Roland asks and confirms that Ben and Da are safe.

The Crew appears, the cocky smiles from the trial replaced by grim, tired frowns. They report that the Coronado has been contained. No casualties. Two Histories made it out, but both are being pursued.

I ask about Wesley.

They tell me I'll be summoned when they know.

They tell me to go home.

I ask again about Wesley.

They tell me again to go home.

THIRTY-TWO

THE DAY YOU DIE, you tell me I have a gift. The day you die, you tell me I am a natural. The day you die, you tell me I am strong enough. The day you die, you tell me it will be okay. None of that is true.

In the years and months and days before, you teach me everything I know. But the day you die, you don't say anything.

You flick away your cigarette, put your hollow cheek against my hair and keep it there until I began to think you've gone to sleep. Then you straighten and look me in the eye, and I know in that moment that you are going to be gone when I wake up.

There is a note on my desk the next morning, pinned beneath your key. But the note is blank, save for the mark of the Archive. Mom is in the kitchen, crying. Dad, for once, is home from the school and sitting by her. As I press my ear to my bedroom door, trying to hear over my pulse, I wish that you had said something. It would have been nice, to have words to cling to, like all those other times.

I lie awake for years and re-imagine that good-bye, rewrite that note, and instead of the heavy quiet, or the three lines, you tell me exactly what I need to hear, what I need to know, in order to survive this.

• • •

Every night I have the same bad dream.

I'm on the roof, trapped in the circle of gargoyles, their claws and arms and broken wings holding me in a cage of stone. Then the air in front of me shivers, ripples, and the void door takes shape, spreading across the sky like blood until it's there, solid and dark. It has a handle, and the handle turns, and the door opens, and Owen Chris Clarke stands there with his haunted eyes and his wicked knife. He steps down to the concrete roof, and the stone demons tighten their grip as he comes toward me.

"I will set you free," he says just before he buries the knife in my chest, and I wake up.

Every night I have that dream, and every night I end up on the roof, checking the air in the circle of demons for signs of a door. There is almost no mark of the void I made; nothing but the faintest ripple, like a crack in the world; and when I close my eyes and press my hands against the space, they always go straight through.

Every night I have that dream, and every day I check my list for signs of a summons. Both sides of the paper are blank, and have been since the incident, and by the third day I'm so scared that the list is broken that I dig out a pen and write a note, not caring who finds it.

Please update.

I watch the words dissolve into the page.

No one answers.

I ask again. And again. And again. And every time I'm met with silence and blank space. Panic chews through my battered body. As my bruises lighten, my fear gets worse. I should have heard by now. I should have heard.

On the third morning, Dad asks about Wes, and my throat closes up. I can barely make it through a feeble lie. And so when, at the end of the third day, a summons finally writes itself across my paper . . .

Please report to the Archive. —A

I drop everything and go.

I tug my ring off and pull the Crew key from my pocket—Owen took my Keeper key with him into the void—and slide it into the lock on my bedroom door. A deep breath, a turn to the left, and I step through into the Archive.

The branch is still recovering, most of the doors still closed; but the chaos has subsided, the noise diminished to a dull, steady din, like a cooling engine. I'm not even over the threshold when I open my mouth to ask about Wes. But then I look up, and the question catches in my throat.

Roland and Patrick are standing behind the desk, and in front of it is a woman in an ivory coat. She is tall and slim, with red hair and creamy skin and a pleasant face. A sharp gold key hangs on a black ribbon around her throat, and she's wearing a pair of black fitted gloves. There is something calm about her that clashes with the lingering noise of the damaged Archive.

The woman takes a fluid step forward.

"Miss Bishop," she says with a warm smile, "my name is Agatha."

THIRTY-THREE

AGATHA, THE ASSESSOR.

Agatha, the one who decides if a Keeper is fit to serve, or if they should be dismissed. Erased. Her expression is utterly unreadable, but the stern look on Patrick's face is clear, as is the fear in Roland's eyes. I suddenly feel like the room is filled with broken glass and I'm supposed to walk across it.

"Thank you for coming," she says. "I know you've been through a lot recently, but we need to talk—"

"Agatha," says Roland. There is a pleading in his tone. "I really think we should leave this—"

"Your parental sense is admirable." Agatha gives a small, coaxing smile. "But if Mackenzie doesn't mind . . ."

"I don't mind at all," I say, mustering a calm I don't feel.

"Lovely," says Agatha, turning her attention to Roland and Patrick. "You're both excused. Surely you've got your hands full right now."

Patrick leaves without looking at me. Roland hesitates, and I beg him with a look for news of Wes, but it goes unanswered as he retreats into the Archive and closes the doors behind him.

"You've had quite an exciting few days," says Agatha. "Sit."

I do. She sits down behind the desk.

"Before we begin, I believe you have a key you shouldn't have. Please place it on the desk."

I stiffen. There's only one way out of the Archive—the door at my back—and it requires a key. I force myself to take Da's old Crew key from my pocket and set it on the desk between us. It takes all my strength to withdraw my hand and leave the key there.

Agatha folds her hands and nods approvingly.

"You don't know anything about me, Miss Bishop," she says, which isn't true. "But I know about you. It's my job. I know about you, and about Owen, and about Carmen. And I know you've discovered a lot about the Archive. Most of which we'd rather you'd learned in due course. You must have questions."

Of course I have questions. I have nothing but questions. And it feels like a trap to ask, but I have to know.

"A friend of mine was wounded by one of the Histories involved in the recent attacks. Do you know what happened to him?"

Agatha offers an indulgent smile. "Wesley Ayers is alive."

These are the four greatest words I've ever heard.

"It was close," she adds. "He's still recovering. But your loyalty is touching."

I try to soothe my frayed nerves. "I've heard it's an important quality in Crew."

"Loyal and ambitious," she notes. "Anything else you want to ask?"

The gold key glints on its black ribbon, and I hesitate.

"For instance," she prompts cheerfully, "I imagine you're wondering why we keep the origin of the Librarians a secret. Why we keep so many things a secret."

Agatha has a dangerous ease about her. She's the kind of person you *want* to like you. I don't trust it at all, but I nod.

"The Archive must be staffed," she says. "There must always be Keepers in the Narrows. There must always be Crew in the Outer. And there must always be Librarians in the Archive. It is a choice,

Mackenzie, do know that. It's simply a matter of when the choice is given."

"You wait until they're dead," I say, straining to keep the contempt from my voice. "Wake them on their shelves when they can't say no."

"*Won't*, Mackenzie, is a very different thing from *can't*." She sits forward in her chair. "I'll be honest with you. I think you deserve a bit of honesty. Keepers worry about being Keepers, and rest assured that they'll learn about being Crew if and when the time comes. Crew worry about being Crew, and rest assured that they'll learn about being Librarians if and when the time comes. We've found that the easiest way to keep people focused is to give them one thing to focus on. The question is, given the influx of distraction, will you be able to continue focusing?"

She's asking me, but I know my fate doesn't lie in my decision. It lies in hers. I'm a loose thread. Owen is gone. Carmen is gone. But I'm here. And even after everything, or maybe because of everything, I need to remember. I don't want to be erased. I don't want to have the Archive cut out of my life. I don't want to die. My hands start shaking, so I hold them beneath the edge of the table.

"Mackenzie?" nudges Agatha.

There's only one thing I can do, and I'm not sure I can pull it off, but I don't have a choice. I smile. "My mother says there's nothing that a hot shower can't fix."

Agatha laughs a soft, perfect laugh. "I can see why Roland fights for you."

She stands, circles the desk, one hand brushing its surface.

"The Archive is a machine," she says. "A machine whose purpose is to protect the past. To protect knowledge."

"Knowledge is power," I say. "That's the saying, right?"

"Yes. But power in the wrong hands, in too many hands, leads to danger and dissent. You've seen the damage caused by two."

I resist the urge to look away. "My grandfather used to say that every strong storm starts with a breeze."

She crosses behind me, and I curl my fingers around the seat of the chair, pain screaming through my wounded wrist.

"He sounds like a very wise man," she says. One hand comes to rest on the back of the chair.

"He was," I say.

And then I close my eyes because I know this is it. I picture the gold key plunging through the chair, the metal burying itself in my back. I wonder if it will hurt, having my life hollowed out. I swallow hard and wait. But nothing happens.

"Miss Bishop," says Agatha, "secrets are an unpleasant necessity, but they have a place and a purpose here. They protect us. And they protect those we care about." The threat is subtle but clear.

"Knowledge is power," she finishes, and I open my eyes to find her rounding the chair, "but ignorance can be a blessing."

"I agree," I say, and then I find her gaze and hold it. "But once you know, you can't go back. Not really. You can carve out someone's memories, but they won't be who they were before. They'll just be full of holes. Given the choice, I'd rather learn to live with what I know."

The room around us settles into silence until, at last, Agatha smiles. "Let's hope you're making the right choice." She pulls something from the pocket of her ivory coat and places it in my palm, closing my fingers over it with her gloved hand.

"Let's hope I am, too," she says, her hand over mine. When she pulls away, I look down to find a Keeper's key nestled there, lighter than the one Da gave me, and too new, but still a handle and a stem and teeth and, most of all, the freedom to go home.

"Is that all?" I ask quietly.

Agatha lets the question hang. At last she nods and says, "For now."

THIRTY-FOUR

BISHOP'S IS PACKED with people.
It's only been two days since my meeting with Agatha, and the coffee shop is nowhere near finished—half the equipment hasn't even been delivered—but after the less-than-successful *Welcome!* muffins, Mom insisted on throwing a soft opening for the residents, complete with free coffee and baked goods.

She beams and serves and chats, and even though she's operating at her suspiciously bright full-wattage, she does seem happy. Dad talks coffee with three or four men, leads them behind the counter to see the new grinding machine Mom broke down and got for him. A trio of kids, Jill among them, sits on the patio, dangling their legs in the sun and sipping iced drinks, sharing a muffin between them. A little girl at a corner table doodles on a paper mat with blue crayons. Mom only ordered blue. Ben's favorite. Ms. Angelli admires the red stone rose set in the floor. And, miracle of miracles, Nix's chair is pulled up to a table on the patio, my copy of the *Inferno* in his lap as he flicks ash onto a low edge when Betty looks away. The place is brimming.

And all the while, I cling to the four words—*Wesley Ayers is alive*—because I still haven't seen him. The Archive is still closed and my list is still blank, and all I have are those four words and Agatha's warning buzzing around in my head.

"Mackenzie Bishop!"

Lyndsey launches herself at me, throws her arms around my neck, and I stagger back, wincing. Beneath my long sleeves and my apron, I am a web of bruises and bandages. I could hide most of the damage from my parents, but not the wrist. I claimed it was a bad fall on one of my runs. It wasn't one of my strongest lies, but I am so tired of lying. Lyndsey is still hugging me. With my ring on, she sounds like rain and harmony and too-loud laughter, but the noise is worth it, and I don't pull back or push away.

"You came," I say, smiling. It feels good to smile.

"Duh. Nice apron, by the way," she says, gesturing to the massive *B* on its front. "Mom and Dad are around here somewhere. And good job, Mrs. Bishop, this place is full!"

"Free caffeine and sugar, a recipe for making friends," I say, watching my mother flit between tables.

"You'll have to give me a proper tour later— Hey, is that Guyliner?"

She cocks her head toward the patio doors, and everything stops.

His eyes are tired, his skin a touch too pale, but he's there with his spiked hair and his black-rimmed eyes and his hands buried in his pockets. And then, as if he can feel my eyes on him, Wes finds my gaze across the room, and beams.

"It is," I say, my chest tightening.

But rather than cross the crowded café, Wes nods once in the direction of the lobby and walks out.

"Well, go on, then," says Lynds, pushing me with a giggle. "I'll serve myself." She leans across the counter, swipes a cookie.

I pull off the apron, tossing it to Lyndsey as I trail Wes through the lobby—where more people are milling about with coffee—down the hall and past the study and out into the garden. When we reach the world of moss and vine, he stops and turns, and I throw my arms around him, relishing the drums and the bass and the metal rock as they wash over me, blotting out the pain and guilt and fear and blood of the last time we touched. We both wince but hold on. I listen to the sound of him, as strange and steady as a heartbeat, and then I must have tightened my grip, because he gasps and says, "Gently, there," and braces himself against the back of a bench, one palm gingerly against his stomach. "I swear, you're just looking for excuses to get your hands on me."

"You caught me," I say, closing my eyes when they start to burn. "I'm so sorry," I say into his shirt.

He laughs, then hisses in pain. "Hey, don't be. I know you can't help yourself."

I laugh tightly. "I'm not talking about the hug, Wes."

"Then what are you apologizing for?"

I pull back and look him in the eyes. "For everything that happened." His brow creases, and my heart sinks.

"Wes," I say slowly, "you do remember, don't you?"

He looks at me, confused. "I remember making a date to hunt with you. Nine sharp." He eases himself onto the stone bench. "But to be honest, I don't remember anything about the next day. I don't remember being stabbed. Patrick said that's normal. Because of trauma."

Everything aches as I sink down onto the bench beside him. "Yeah . . ."

"What *should* I remember, Mac?"

I sit and stare at the stones that make up the garden floor.

Knowledge is power, but ignorance can be a blessing.

Maybe Agatha is right. I think of that moment in the stacks when Roland told me about altering, when he warned me what happened to those who failed and were dismissed. That moment when I hated him for telling me, when I wished I could go back. But there is no going back.

So can't we just go forward?

I don't want to hurt Wes anymore. I don't want to cause him pain, make him relive the betrayal. And after Agatha's unfriendly meeting, I have no desire to disobey the Archive. But what sets me over the edge is the fact that there, in my mind, louder than all those other thoughts, is this:

I don't want to confess.

I don't want to confess because *I* don't want to remember. But Wesley doesn't have that choice, and the only reason he's missing that time is because of me.

The truth is a messy thing, but I tell it.

We sit in the garden as the day stretches out, and I tell him everything. The easy and the hard. He listens, and frowns, and doesn't interrupt, except to punctuate with a small "Oh" or "Wow" or "What?"

And after all of it, when he finally speaks, the only thing he says is, "Why couldn't you come to me?"

I'm about to tell him about Roland's orders, but that's only a partial truth, so I start again.

"I was running away."

"From what?"

"I don't know. The Archive. That life. This. Ben. Me."

"What's so wrong with you?" he asks. "I quite like you." And then, a moment later, he adds, "I just can't believe I lost to a skinny blond guy with a knife."

I laugh. Pain ripples through me, but it's worth it. "It was a very big knife," I say.

Silence settles over us. Wes is the one to break it.

"Hey," he says.

"Hey."

"Are you going to be okay?"

I close my eyes. "I don't know, Wes. Everything hurts. I don't know how to make it stop. It hurts when I breathe. It hurts when I think. I feel like I'm drowning, and it's my fault, and I don't know how to be okay. I don't know if I *can* be okay. I don't know if I should be *allowed* to be okay."

Wesley knocks his shoulder against mine.

"We're a team, Mac," he says. "We'll get through this."

"Which part?" I ask.

He smiles. "All of it."

And I smile back, because I want him to be right.

Book Two

THE UNBOUND

In three words I can sum up everything
I've learned about life: it goes on.
—Robert Frost

ONE

MY BODY BEGS for sleep.
I sit on the roof of the Coronado, and it pleads with me, begs me to climb down from my perch on the gargoyle's broken shoulder, to creep back inside and down the stairs and through the still-dark apartment into my bed—to *sleep*.

But I can't.

Because every time I sleep, I dream. And every time I dream, I dream of Owen. Of his silvery hair, his cold eyes, his long fingers curling casually around his favorite knife. I dream of him dragging the jagged side of the blade across my skin as he murmurs that the "real" Mackenzie Bishop must be hidden somewhere under all that flesh.

I'll find you, M, he whispers as he cuts. *I'll set you free.*

Some nights he kills me quickly, and some nights he takes his time; but every night I bolt up in the dark, clutching my arms around my ribs, heart pounding as I search my skin for fresh cuts.

There aren't any, of course. Because there is no Owen.

Not anymore.

It's been three weeks, and even though it's too dark to make out anything more than outlines on the night-washed roof, my eyes still drift to the spot—a circle of gargoyles—where it happened. Or, at least, where it *ended*.

Stop running, Miss Bishop. There's nowhere to go.

The memory is so vivid: Wesley bleeding out on the other side of the roof while Owen pressed the blade between my shoulders and gave me a choice that wasn't really a choice because of the metal biting into my skin.

It doesn't have to end like this.

Words, promises, threats that hung between us only long enough for me to turn the key in the air behind his back and make a tear in the world, a door out of nothing, to nothing—to *nowhere*—and send him through.

Now my eyes find the invisible—*impossible*—mark. It's barely a scratch on the air, all that's left of the void door. Even though I can't *see* the mark, I know exactly where it is: the patch of dark where my eyes slide off, attracted and repelled at once by the out of place, the unnatural, the *wrong*.

The void door is a strange, corrosive thing.

I tried to revisit that day, to read what happened in the statues on the roof, but the memories were all ruined. The opening of the void had overexposed them like film, eaten through solid minutes—the most important of my life—and left only white noise.

But I don't need to read the images in the rocks: I *remember*.

A stone crumbles off a statue on the far side of the roof and I jump, nearly losing my balance on top of the gargoyle. My head is starting to feel heavy in that dangerous, drifting-off way, so I get down before I *fall* down, rolling my neck as the first slivers of light creep into the sky. I tense when I see it. I am in no way ready for today, and not just because I haven't slept. I'm not ready for the uniform hanging on my chair, or the new face I'll have to wear with it. I'm not ready for the campus full of bodies full of noise.

I'm not ready for Hyde School.

But the sun keeps rising anyway.

Several feet away, one of the gargoyles stands out from the others. Its stone body is bundled in old cushions and duct tape, the former stolen from a closet off the Coronado lobby, the latter from a drawer in the coffee shop. It's a poor substitute for a boxing dummy, but it's better than nothing—and if I can't sleep, I might as well train.

Now, as dawn spills over the roof, I gingerly unwind the boxing tape that crisscrosses both my hands, wincing as the blood returns to my right wrist. Pain, dull and constant, radiates down into my fingers. It's another relic from that day. *Owen's grip like a vise, tightening until the bones crack and the knife in my fingers clatters to the Narrows floor.* My wrist would probably heal faster if I didn't spend my time punching makeshift dummies, but I find the pain strangely grounding.

I'm almost done rolling up the tape when I feel the familiar scratch of letters on the piece of paper in my pocket. I dig the slip out and in the spreading light of day I can just make out the name in the middle of the page.

Ellie Reynolds. 11.

I run my thumb over the name, as if expecting to feel the grooves made by the pen, but the strange writing never leaves a real impression. A hand in the Archive writes in a book in the Archive that echoes its words onto the paper here. Find the History, and the name goes away. (No lasting mark. I thought of keeping a list of the people I'd found and returned, but my grandfather, Da, would have told me there's no point in dwelling. *Stare too long at anything,* he'd say, *and you start to wonder. And where does wondering get you? Nowhere good.*)

I head for the rusty rooftop door. Finding Ellie Reynolds should keep me busy, at least until it's a more acceptable hour to be awake. If I told my parents how I'd been spending my nights— half in nightmares and half up here on the roof—they'd send me to a shrink. Then again, if I told my parents how I'd spent the last four and a half years of my life—hunting down and returning the Histories of the dead—they'd lock me in a psych ward.

I make my way down four flights of concrete stairs, intensely aware of the silence and the way my steps knife through it. At the third floor, the stairwell spits me out into a hall adorned with worn yellow wallpaper and dusty crystal lights. Apartment **3F** waits at the far end, and part of me wants so badly to go home and sleep, but another part of me isn't willing to risk it. Instead I stop halfway, just past the metal cage-like elevators at the spot framed between an old mirror and a painting of the sea.

Next to the painting, I can make out the crack, like a ripple in the wallpaper, simultaneously pushing and pulling my gaze. It's a pretty easy way to tell if something doesn't belong, when your eyes can't quite find it because it's something you're not supposed to see. Like on the roof. But *unlike* on the roof, when I slide the silver ring off my finger, the discomfort disappears and I can see the shape crystal clear in the middle of the crack.

A keyhole.

A door to the Narrows.

I run my fingers over the small, dark spot, hesitating a moment. The walls between worlds used to feel like they were made of stone—heavy and impenetrable. These days, they feel too thin. The secrets, lies, and monsters bleed through, ruining the clean lines.

Keep your worlds apart, warned Da. *Neat and even and solidly separate.*

But everything is messy now. My fear follows me into the Narrows. My nightmares follow me out.

I fetch the leather cord from around my neck, tugging it over my head. The key on the end shines in the hallway's artificial light. It isn't mine—isn't Da's, that is—and the first time I used it to open a Narrows door, I remember feeling bitter that it could so easily replace my grandfather's key. As if they were the same.

I weigh this one in my palm. It's too new and a fraction too light, and it's not just a piece of metal, but a symbol: a warning that keys and freedom and memories and lives can all be taken away. Not that I need a reminder. Agatha's interrogation is carved into my memory.

It had only been a few days. Enough time for the bruises to color on my skin, but not enough for my wrist to heal. Agatha sat there in her chair, smiling pleasantly, and I sat in mine, try-ing not to let her see how badly my hands were shaking. I had no key—she'd taken it—and no way out of the Archive without it. The problem, as Agatha explained it, was that I'd seen behind the curtain, seen the system's cogs and cracks. The question was, should I be allowed to remember? Or should the Archive carve out everything I'd ever seen and done within its jurisdiction, leaving me full of holes, free of the weight of it all?

Given the choice, I'd told her, *I'd rather learn to live with what I know.*

Let's hope you're making the right choice, she'd said, placing the new key in my palm. She curled my fingers over it and added, *Let's hope I am, too.*

Now, standing in the hall, I slide Agatha's key into the mark on the yellow wallpaper and watch the shadows spread out from the keyhole, soaking like ink into the wall as the door takes shape. When it's finished forming—its edges marked by light—I will myself to turn the key. But for a second, I can't. My hand starts to shake, so I tighten my grip on the key until the metal bites into my skin and the pain jogs me free, and then I shove open the door and step through into the Narrows.

As the door closes behind me, I hold my breath the way kids do when they pass a graveyard. It's superstitious—just some silly hope that bad things won't happen unless you breathe them in. I force myself to stand there in the dark until my body recognizes that Owen's not here, that it's just me and, somewhere in the maze of halls, Ellie Reynolds.

She turns out to be a simple return, once I finally find her.

Histories are easier to track down when they run, because they cast memories like shadows over every inch of ground they cover. But Ellie stays put, huddled in a corner of the Narrows near the edge of my territory. When I find her, she goes without a fight, and it's a good thing—as I lean back against the dank wall, it's all I can do to keep my eyes open. I drag myself back toward the numbered doors that lead home, yawning as I reach the door with the Roman numeral I chalked onto its front. I step back into the Outer, relieved to find the third floor hall as quiet as when I left it. It's too easy to lose track of time in the Narrows, where clocks and watches don't work, and today of all days, I can't afford to be late.

Sunlight is flooding through the apartment windows as I inch the door closed and cross the living room, steps masked by the sound of coffee brewing and the low hum of the TV. Below the date and time stamp on the screen—six fifteen a.m., Wednesday—a news anchor prattles on about traffic and the sports roundup before changing gears.

"Up next," he says, shuffling papers, "the latest on a crime that has everyone stumped. A missing person. A scene in disarray. Was it a break-in, an abduction, or something worse?"

The anchor delivers the line with a little too much enthusiasm, but something about the still frame hovering behind him catches my attention. I'm halfway to the TV when the muffled sound of my parents' footsteps in their room reminds me I'm standing in the middle of the apartment, still wearing my black, close-fitting Keeper clothes, at six in the morning.

I duck into the bathroom and snap on the shower. The water's hot, and it feels wonderful. The heat loosens my shoulders and soothes my sore muscles, the sound of the water filling the room with white noise, steady and soothing. My eyes drift shut, and then . . .

I sway and catch myself the instant before I fall forward into the wall. Pain zings up my bad wrist as I push off the tile and swear under my breath, snapping the lever to cold. The icy water hits my skin, the shock of it leaving me miserable but awake.

I'm towel-clad and halfway to my bedroom, the Keeper clothes bundled beneath my arm, when my parents' door opens and Dad pops out. He's clutching a coffee mug and exuding his usual air of underslept and overcaffeinated.

"Morning," I mumble.

"Big day, sweetheart." He plants a kiss on my forehead, and his noise—the static every living person carries with them, the sound of their thoughts and memories—crackles through me, the images themselves held back only by the Keeper's ring on my finger. "Think you're ready?" he asks.

"Doubt it," I say, resisting the urge to point out that I don't have a choice. Instead, I listen to him tell me I'll rise to the challenge. I even manage to smile and shrug and say "I'm sure" before escaping into my room.

The cold water may have been enough to wake me up, but it's hardly enough to prepare me for the school uniform waiting on my chair. Water drips from my hair into my eyes as I consider the black cotton polo—long-sleeved, piped with silver, and sporting a crest over the chest pocket—and the plaid skirt, its pattern made up of black, silver, green, and gold. Hyde School colors. In the catalog, boys and girls study under hundred-year-old oaks, a wrought-iron fence to one side and a moss-covered building to the other. A picture of class and charm and sheltered innocence.

I reach for my newly charged cell phone and shoot Wesley a quick text.

> I'm not ready for this.

Wesley Ayers, who labeled himself in my phone as *Wesley Ayers, Partner in Crime*, has been gone for almost a week; he left right after his father's wedding for a "family bonding edition" honeymoon. Judging by how often he's been texting, I'd say he's opted out of most of the bonding.

A moment later, he texts back.

> You're a Keeper. You hunt down the animated records of the dead in your spare time. I'm pretty sure you can handle private school.

I can picture Wesley tucking his hands behind his head as he says it, one brow arching, his hazel eyes warm and bright and lined with black. I chew my lip as a small smile breaks through. I'm trying to think of something clever to say back when he texts again.

> What are you wearing?

My face flushes. I know he's just teasing me—he saw the uniform before he left—but I can't help remembering what happened in the garden last week, on the day of the wedding. The way his lips smiled against my jaw, his now-familiar noise—that cacophony of drums and bass—pressing through me with his touch before I could find the strength to tell him no. The hurt in his eyes once I did—so well concealed that most people wouldn't even notice. But I did. I saw it in his face as he drew back, and in his shoulders as he pulled away, and in the corners of his mouth as he told me it was fine. *We* were fine. And I wanted to believe him, but I didn't. I don't.

Which is why I'm still standing here in my towel, trying to think of what to text back, when I hear the apartment's front door open and slam. A second later, a breathless voice calls my name, and then there's a knock on my bedroom door. I toss the phone aside.

"I'm getting dressed."

As if that's an invitation, the door starts to swing open. I catch it with my palm, forcing it shut again.

"*Mackenzie,*" my mom says with a huff. "I just want to see how the uniform fits."

"And I'll show you," I snap, "just as soon as I'm *wearing* it."

She goes quiet, but I can tell she's still standing there in the hall beyond the door. I pull the polo over my head and button the skirt. "Shouldn't you be down in the café," I call, "getting ready to open?"

"I didn't want to miss you," she says through the wood. "It's your first day. . . ."

Her voice wavers before trailing off, and I sigh loudly. Taking the hint, she retreats down the hall, her footsteps echoing behind her. When I finally emerge, she's perched at the kitchen table in a Bishop's apron, flipping through the pamphlet on Hyde School dos and don'ts. (Students are encouraged to be helpful, respectful, and well-mannered, but discouraged from makeup, piercings, unnaturally dyed hair, and raucousness. The word *raucousness* is actually in the pamphlet. I highlighted the bits I think Lyndsey will like; just because she's an hour away doesn't mean she can't get a good laugh at my expense.)

"Well?" I ask, indulging my mom with a slow twirl. "What do you think?"

She looks up and smiles, but her eyes are shining, and I know we've entered fragile territory. My stomach twists. I've been doing my best to think *around* the issue, but seeing Mom's face—the subtle war of sadness and stubborn cheer—I can't help but think of Ben.

My little brother was killed last year on his way to school, just a couple of weeks before summer break. The dreaded day last fall when I went back to class and Ben didn't will go down as one of the darkest in my family's history. It was like bleeding to death, except more painful.

So when I see the strain in Mom's eyes, I'm just thankful we've gained the buffer of a year, even if it's thin. I allow her to run her fingers over the silver piping that lines the shoulders of my polo, forcing myself to remain still beneath the grinding sound that pours from her fingers and through my head with her touch.

"You'd better get back to the coffee shop," I say through clenched teeth, and Mom's hand slips away, mistaking my discomfort for annoyance.

She manages a smile anyway. "You ready to go?"

"Almost," I say. When she doesn't immediately turn to leave, I know it's because she wants to see me off. I don't bother to protest. Not today. Instead I just do a quick check: first the mundane—backpack, wallet, sunglasses—and then the specific—ring around my finger, key around my neck, list in my . . . No list. I duck back into my room to find the piece of Archive-issued paper still shoved in the pocket of my pants. My phone's there, too, lying at the foot of my bed where I tossed it earlier. I transfer the slip—blank for now—into the front pocket of my shirt and type a quick answer to Wesley's question . . .

> What are you wearing?

>> Battle armor.

. . . before dropping the phone into my bag.

On our way out, Mom gives me the full spiel about staying safe, being nice, playing well with others. When we reach the base of the lobby's marble stairs, she plants a kiss on my cheek (it sounds like breaking plates in my head) and tells me to smile. Then an old man calls over from across the lobby, asking if the café is open, and I watch her hurry away, issuing a trill of morning cheer as she leads him into Bishop's.

I push through the Coronado's revolving doors and head over to the newly installed bike rack. There's only one bike chained to it, a sleek metal thing marred—Wes would say *adorned*—by a strip of duct tape on which the word *DANTE* has been scrawled in Sharpie. I knew a car was out of the question—all our money is feeding into the coffee shop right now—but I'd had the foresight to ask for the bike. My parents were surprised; I guess they figured I'd just take the bus (local, of course, not school; Hyde wouldn't deign to have its name stenciled on the side of some massive yellow monstrosity, and besides, the average student probably drives a Lexus), but buses are just narrow boxes crammed with bodies full of noise. The thought makes me shudder.

I dig a pair of workout pants out of my bag, tugging them on under my skirt before unlocking Dante. The café's awning flaps in the breeze, and the rooftop gargoyles peer down as I swing my leg over and push off the curb.

I'm halfway to the corner when something—some*one*—catches my eye, and I slow down and glance back.

There's someone across the street from the Coronado, and he's watching me. A man, early thirties, with gold hair and sun-touched skin. He's standing on the curb, shielding his eyes against the sun and squinting up at the old hotel as if it's intensely interesting. But a moment earlier as I zipped by, I could swear he was looking at me. And even now that he's not, the feeling lingers.

I stall at the corner, pretending to adjust the gears on my bike as I watch him not-watch me. There's something familiar about him, but I can't place it. Maybe he's been to Bishop's while I was on shift, or maybe he's friends with a Coronado resident. Or maybe I've never seen him before, and he just has one of those familiar faces. Maybe I just need sleep. The moment I let in the doubt, it kills my conviction, and suddenly I'm not even sure he was looking at me in the first place. When he crosses the street a moment later and vanishes through the front doors of the Coronado without so much as a glance my way, I shake it off and pedal away.

The morning is cool, and I relish the fresh air and the wind whistling in my ears as I weave through the streets. I mapped out the route yesterday—drew it on my hand this morning to be safe—but I never look down. The city unfolds around me, a vast and sunlit grid, a stark contrast to the dark tangle of corridors I'm used to.

And for a few minutes, as the world blurs past, I almost forget about how tired I am and how much I'm dreading today. But then I round the corner and the moment ends as I find myself face-to-face with the moss-slick stones, ivy-strewn walls, and iron gates of Hyde School.

TWO

MY FAMILY is about to run away. Ben's been dead for almost a year, and our home has somehow become a house, something kept at arm's reach. They say the only way around is through, but apparently that's not true. The other option, I know now, is to turn and run. My parents have started packing; things are vanishing, one by one, into boxes. I try not to notice. Between struggling to survive sophomore year and keeping my list of Histories clear, I've done a pretty good job of ignoring the Ben-shaped hole—but eventually even I can't help but see the signs.

Mom quits another job.

Dad starts going on trips in his most collegiate suits.

The house is more often empty than full.

And then one day, when I'm sitting at the kitchen table, studying for finals, Dad gets back from a trip—an interview, it turns out—and places a booklet in front of me. I finish the paragraph I'm reading before letting my gaze wander over to the glossy paper. At first glance it looks like a college packet, but the people splashed across the cover in studious poses wear uniforms of black and green and silver and gold, and most of them look a shade too young for university. I read the name printed in gothic capitals across the top: *HYDE SCHOOL.*

I should say no. Blending in is hard enough in a school of fifteen hundred, and between the Ben-shaped hole and the Archive's ever-filling page, I'm barely keeping up my grades.

But Dad has that horrible, hopeful look in his eyes, and he skips the speech about how it will "enrich my academic portfolio," doesn't bother to tell me that it is "a smaller school, easier to meet people," and goes straight for the kill. The quiet, questioning, "It will be an adventure."

And maybe he's right.

Or maybe I just can't stand our home-turned-house.

Maybe I want to run away, too.

I say yes.

I should have said no.

That's all I can think as I straddle the bike and stare up at Hyde School. The campus is tucked behind a wrought iron fence, and the lot in front is filled with fancy cars and peppered with students who look like they came straight out of that catalog Dad brought home last spring. There is a bike rack, too—but the only students around it are clearly freshmen and sophomores. I can tell by the color of the piping on their uniform shirts. (According to the brochure, freshmen are marked by a glossy black, sophomores by green, juniors by silver, seniors by gold.)

I hover at the edge of the lot, leaning the bike against a tree as I dig out my phone and reread Wesley's text.

> I'm pretty sure you can handle private school.

Letting my gaze drift back up, I'm not so confident. It's not the uniforms that have me thrown, or even the obvious old-money air—I wouldn't be much of a Keeper if I couldn't blend in. It's the fact that I could count the number of students here in less than a minute if I wanted to. There are few enough to make me think I could come to know their names and faces. Which means they could come to know mine. My last school was large enough to afford a certain degree of anonymity. I'm sure there *was* a radar, but it was easy to stay off it—and I did. But here? It's hard enough keeping my second life a secret with only a few people to con. In an "intimate atmosphere"—the brochure's words, not mine—people are going to notice if I slip up.

What difference does it make? I tell myself. *Just a few more people to lie to.*

It's not like I'll be selling different lies to different crowds here. I just have to convince everyone of one simple thing: that I'm normal. Which would, admittedly, be easier if I'd slept more than a couple of hours at a time in the last three weeks, and if I weren't being haunted by the memory of a History who tried to kill me. But hey. No such thing as a perfect scenario.

Most of the students have gone onto campus by now, so I cross the lot, chain Dante to the bike rack, and tug off the workout pants from underneath my skirt. When I get to the front gate, I can't help but smile a little. A massive metal *H* has been woven through the bars. I snap a photo on my phone and send it to Wes with the caption *Abandon all hope, ye who enter here* (the inscription on the gates of Hell in Dante's *Inferno*, and Wesley's favorite passage). A moment later he responds with a single smiley face, which is enough to make me feel a little less alone as I step onto campus.

Hyde is made of stone and moss, most of the buildings laid out around a quad. It's all linked by paths and bridges and halls—a miniature version of the university where Dad works now. (I guess that's the idea behind a college preparatory school.) All I can think as I make my way down a tree-lined path to the administration building, with its ivy-strewn facade and clock tower, is how much Lyndsey would love it here. I send her a text telling her so, and a few seconds later she texts back.

Who is this?

Ha. Ha.

The Mackenzie Bishop I know doesn't charge her phone, let alone text.

People evolve.

You did it for Guyliner, didn't you?

No.

It's okay, I forgive you.

I roll my eyes and pocket my phone before taking a last, deep breath and pushing open the doors of the admin building. I'm deposited in a large glass lobby with corridors trailing off in several directions. I manage to find the main office and retrieve my final schedule and room assignments from a woman with a frighteningly tight bun, but instead of backtracking, I'm then sent through a separate set of doors that lead into a large hall crowded with students. I have no idea what to do next. I do my best to stay out of the way as I internally repeat the phrase *I will not pull out a map, I will not pull a map, I will not pull out a map*. I studied the layout of campus, I really did. But I'm tired. And even with a solid sense of direction, it's like the Narrows, where you have to learn the grid by moving through it.

"It's one building over, second hall, and third room on the left."

The voice comes from right behind me, and I turn to find a senior (gold stripes trace across the black of his uniform) looking down at me.

"Excuse me?"

"Precalc with Bradshaw, math hall, room 310," he says, pointing at the paper in my hands. "Sorry, didn't mean to look over your shoulder. You just seemed a little lost."

I fold the paper and shove it back into my bag. "That obvious?" I ask, trying to keep my voice light.

"Standing in the middle of the admin building with a class schedule and a daunted look?" he says. "Can't blame a guy for wanting to help." There is a kind of warmth to him, from his dark hair and deep tan to his broad smile and gold eyes. And then he goes and ruins it by adding, "After all, the whole thing does have an air of 'damsel' to it."

The air ices over.

"I'm not a damsel." There's no humor in my voice now. "And I'm really not in distress, if that's where you were going next."

He flinches; but instead of retreating, he holds his ground, his smile softening into something more genuine. "I sounded like an ass just then, didn't I? Let me start again." He holds out a hand. "I'm Cash."

"Mackenzie," I say, bracing myself as I slide my hand into his. The sound that fills my head is loud—the noise of the living is *always* loud—but strangely melodic. Cash is made of jazz and laughter. Our hands fall apart and the sound fades away, replaced a moment later by the first bell, which echoes through the halls from the clock tower.

And so it begins.

"Let me walk you to class," he says.

"That's not necessary."

"I know. But I'd be happy to do it all the same."

I hesitate, but there's something about him that reminds me of Wes—maybe the way he stands or how easily he smiles—and at this point I'd probably attract more attention by saying no; people are already casting glances as they hurry past us to class. So I nod and say, "Lead the way."

Within moments I regret it.

Having Cash as an escort not only results in a halting pace—he stops to say hello, hug, or fist-bump *everyone*—but also more attention than I ever wanted to garner, since he introduces me every single time. And despite the fact that the first bell's already rung and the halls are emptying, everyone takes the time to say hello back, walking with us a few feet while they chat. By the time Cash finally guides me through one of the elevated halls that bridge the buildings into the math hall and deposits me at room 310, I feel dazed from the attention.

And then he just disappears with little more than a smile and a "Good luck!"

I don't even have a chance to thank him, let alone ask for a clue about where I'm headed next. Sixteen pairs of eyes shift up as I walk in, sporting the usual spectrum of interest. Only the teacher's attention stays trained on the board as he scribbles out instructions below the header *Precalculus*. Most of the seats are already taken; in some strange and twisted version of the high school dynamic, I'm left with the back row instead of the usually shunned front. I slide into the last empty seat as the teacher starts, and my chest finally begins to loosen.

Waiting for something to start is always worse than when it does.

As the lesson begins, I'm relieved to find that underneath the moss and stone and uniforms, school still kind of feels like school. You can dress it up, but it doesn't change much from place to place. I wonder what class Lyndsey has first. She'll be sitting in the front row, of course. I wonder who will sit next to her on the left, who will reach over and doodle in the margins of her books when she's not looking. I start to wonder what Ben would be studying, but then I catch myself and turn my thoughts to the equations on the board.

I've always been good at math. It's straightforward, black-and-white, right and wrong. Equations. Da thought of people as books to be read, but I've always thought of them more as formulas—full of variables, but always the sum of their parts. That's what their noise is, really: all of a person's components layered messily over one another. Thought and feeling and memory and all of it unorganized, until that person dies. Then it all gets compiled, straightened out into this linear thing, and you can see exactly what the various parts add up to. What they equal.

Tick. Tick. Tick.

I notice the sound in the lull between two of Bradshaw's explanations. It's a clock on the back wall, and once I start to notice it, I can't stop. Even with Bradshaw's expert projection (I wonder if he took a speech class or used to act, and how he ended up teaching precalc instead), there it is: low and constant and clear. Da used to say you could isolate the sounds in the Narrows if you tried, pluck out notes and pull them forward, letting the rest sink back. I tug on the *tick tick tick*, and soon the teacher's voice fades and the clock is all I can hear, quiet and constant as a pulse.

Tick. Tick. Tick.

Tick. Tick.

Tick . . .

And then, between one tick and the next, the lights go off.

All at once the whole set of soft fluorescents on the ceiling flickers and goes out, plunging the classroom into darkness. When the lights come back on, the room is *empty*. Sixteen students and a teacher all gone in a blink, leaving only vacant desks and the ticking clock and a knife resting, gentle as a kiss, against my throat.

THREE

"**O**WEN."

It comes out barely a whisper, my voice tight with fear. *Not here. Not now.*

He lets out a low breath behind me, and then I feel his lips brush against my ear. "Hello, M."

"Don't——" I start, but the words die as the knife presses into my throat.

"Look at you," he says, using the metal to lift my chin. "Putting on a show. Smiling and nodding and trying to pass for normal."

The knife falls away, and a moment later he's there—rounding my chair, clucking his tongue as he perches on top of the desk in front of mine, hunched forward, resting his elbows on his knees. His silvery hair is swept back, and his eyes hang on me, wild and wolfish and blue.

"Do they know you're broken?" he asks, twirling the blade between his fingers. "They will, soon enough. Should we show them?"

I grip the desk. "You don't exist."

"And yet I could break you," he says softly, "in front of all of them. Crack you open, let them see all the monsters you're made of. I could set them free. Set *you* free." He sits up straight. "You don't belong here."

"Where do I belong?"

In a blink he's gone from the other desk and standing next to

346

mine. He rests the knife against my desk, its tip inches from my ribs. His other hand comes down on my shoulder, holding me in my chair as he leans close and whispers, "With me."

He drives the knife forward and I gasp and jerk upright in my seat, catching my rib cage on the edge of my desk as the bell rings. Owen is gone, and the room is full of students scraping their chairs back and hoisting their bags onto their shoulders. I sag back again, rubbing my ribs, then haul myself to my feet and slide my too-blank notebook into my bag, trying to shake off the dregs of the nightmare. I'm almost to the door when Mr. Bradshaw stops me.

"Miss Bishop?" he says, straightening his desk.

I turn back to him. "Yes, sir?"

"Did I bore you?"

I cringe. "No, sir."

"Well, that's a relief," he says, adjusting his glasses. "I do so worry about boring my students."

"Oh, you shouldn't," I say. "You're a very good speaker. Drama training?"

I curse myself before the words have even left my lips. Mouthing off in the Archive is one thing, but Mr. Bradshaw's not a Librarian, he's a teacher. Luckily, he smiles.

"I'll assume then that, despite outward appearances, you were listening to my lecture with rapt attention. Still, perhaps in the future you could listen with your eyes open. Just so I know for sure."

I manage a weak smile, a nod, and another "Yes, sir" before heading into the hall in search of Literary Theory and Analysis—I don't see why they can't just call it English. But before I can orient myself, someone clears his throat loudly. I turn to see Cash leaning against the door, waiting. He's got a coffee in each hand, and he holds one out to me.

"Still trying to play the knight?" I ask, reaching reflexively for the cup.

"Your English class with Wellson is on the other side of the quad," he says. "Five minutes isn't enough time, unless you know the way."

As soon as I take the coffee, he sets off down the hall. It's all I can do to keep up and not spill the drink all over myself as I swerve to avoid being hit by shoulders and the noise that comes with them.

"Before you ask how I knew about Wellson," he says, "I don't have a thing for preying on new students." He taps the side of his head. "Just a photographic memory."

"That has to come in handy in a school like this."

His smile widens. "It does."

As he leads me through the building, I try to commit the route to memory.

"You'll learn it backward and forward in no time."

I'll have to. One of the "innovative learning tactics" mentioned in the brochure is the scheduling. Semesters at Hyde are made up of five classes: three before lunch, two after. Every other day the schedule is reversed, so whatever class came first goes last, last first, etc., etc. So Mondays, Wednesdays, and Fridays look like this: Precalc, Literary Theory, Wellness, (lunch), Physiology, Government. Tuesdays and Thursdays look like this: Government, Physiology, Wellness, (lunch), Literary Theory, Precalc.

The brochure contained a lengthy, case study–supported explanation of *why* it works; right now it feels like just another hoop to jump through.

Cash leads the way through a set of doors, out onto an inner quad that's ringed with buildings. Then he veers down a path to the right. Along the way, he drinks his coffee and cheerfully tosses out fun facts about Hyde: It's been around since 1832; it used to be two schools (one for guys and one for girls), but they consolidated; one of the founders was a sculptor, and the campus is studded with statues, fourteen in all, though the number is always up for debate. Cash rambles on, waving whenever someone shouts his way (which is surprisingly often) without so much as a pause in his speech.

Luckily he doesn't stop to chat with anyone this time, and we reach my class right as the second bell rings. He smiles triumphantly, turning away—but not before I can say thanks this time. He offers a salute that sweeps into a bow, and then he's gone. I finish my coffee, trash the cup, and push the door open. Students are still taking their seats, and I snag one two rows back as a middle-aged woman with strikingly good posture—I assume she's Ms. Wellson—writes in perfect print across the board. When she steps aside and I see the words, I can't help but smile.

DANTE'S INFERNO.

It is summer, and I'm searching for a coffee shop beneath layers of dust, while Wesley Ayers sits backward on a metal chair. I can see the outline of a key beneath his shirt. The shared secret of our second lives hangs between us, not like a weight, but like a lifeline. I clean, and he rescues a book from a pile of sheets beside the chair.

"What have we here?" he asks, holding up the text.

Dante's *Inferno.*

"Required reading," I tell him.

"It's a shame they do that," he says, flipping through the unread pages. There's a reverence in the way he handles it, his eyes skimming the words as if he knows them all by heart. "Requirement ruins even the best of books."

I ask him if he's read it, and he says he has, and I admit I haven't, and he smiles and tells me that books like this are meant to be heard.

"I'll prove it to you," he says, flashing me a crooked smile.. "You clean, I'll read."

And he does. That first day, and for the rest of the summer. And I remember every word.

When the bell rings again, I've aced a pop quiz—the other students didn't even have the decency to look annoyed when Ms. Wellson announced it—and gone a whole class period without a nightmare, thanks to Cash and his coffee. I expect to find him waiting for me in the hall, but there's no sign of him. (I'm surprised to feel a small pang of disappointment as I survey the stream of students in black and green, silver and gold, and come up empty.) The silvers and golds, however, all seem to be heading in the same direction, and since I know from the brochure that juniors and seniors all have Wellness—which as far as I can tell is just a pretentious way of saying *gym*—together before lunch, I decide to follow the current.

It leads out and across the lawn, beyond the ring of buildings to another majestic structure, this one all ancient stone and gothic accents. I finally catch sight of one of the sculptures Cash mentioned, a stone hawk perched on the mantel over the doors.

"The Hyde School hawk," he says, appearing beside me out of nowhere, and a little out of breath. "It's our mascot. Said to represent insight, initiative, and ingenuity."

A cluster of junior girls are on the path several feet ahead of us; as Cash talks, one of them looks back and rolls her eyes. "Cassius

Arthur Graham, I keep telling you, you can't woo girls with school facts. Hyde history is never going to be a turn-on."

I feel my face go warm, but Cash doesn't color at all, only smiles broadly. "It may surprise you, Safia, but not *all* of us open our mouths with the sole intention of getting into someone's pants."

Her friends laugh, but the girl's eyes narrow with the kind of irritation usually reserved for exes and younger siblings. Judging by her features—she has the same dark hair as Cash, hers pulled back into a ponytail, and the same gold eyes—I'm guessing she's the latter. Cash's comment seems to have hit a nerve, because Safia links her arm through her friend's, shoots back a short string of nasty words, and hurries into the Wellness Center. Cash shrugs, unfazed.

"Sister," he confirms as we pass through the doors. "*Anyway*, sorry I was late. Mr. Kerry went off on one of his tangents—be glad you've got a year before you're subjected to him—and kept us after. Have I sacrificed my knighthood? Or did my valiant display in the face of fire-breathing dragons just now win me some credit?"

"I think you can keep your shield."

"What a relief," he says, nodding toward his sister as her ponytail vanishes into the locker room. "Because I think I'll need it later."

By the time I find my locker, preassigned and prestocked with workout shorts and a T-shirt—I cringe at the sight of short sleeves, thankful I'm largely bruise-free (if not scar-free) at the moment—I've knocked into three different girls by accident and managed to avoid several dozen others. School is like a minefield: so many people, so little personal space. Locker rooms are even worse, but I make it through with only a dull headache.

I watch the other girls peel off their necklaces and rings—what little jewelry Hyde allows—and stash them in their lockers before getting changed. I'm not about to relinquish my ring, but I fumble with the key around my neck, knowing it will draw more attention. If someone calls me out on the necklace, they're bound to demand the rest of my jewelry comes off, too. I slide the key over my head and set it on the shelf, feeling too light without it.

I'm just tugging on my workout shirt when I hear someone shout, "Come on, Saf!"

"I'll be right there," comes a now-recognizable voice. I look over to see Safia lacing up her sneakers at the end of the bench. She doesn't look up, but there's no one else around, so I know she's talking to me when she speaks.

"You know it's his job, right?" she asks, cinching her shoes.

"Excuse me?"

She straightens, tightening her ponytail before leveling her gaze on me. "My brother is a school ambassador. Showing you around, making you feel welcome—it's just another one of his duties. A *job*. I thought you should know."

She wants it to sting, and it does. But hell if I'll give her the benefit of letting it show.

"Well, that's a relief," I say brightly. "He's been so clingy, I was starting to think I'd led him on." I shut my locker firmly and stride past her. "Thanks," I add, patting her shoulder as I go. (It's worth the sound of ripping metal in my head to feel her tense beneath my touch.) "I feel *so* much better now."

The outside of Hyde's Wellness Center may sport the same old stone-and-moss facade as the rest of campus, but beyond the locker rooms—which act as gatekeepers to the gym—the inside is all whitewashed wood and glass and steel. There are smaller rooms branching off to one side and a pool branching off to the other, but the main training room is a massive square. It's subdivided into quadrants by black stripes on the floor and ringed by a track. I can't help but brighten a little at the sight of the glittering equipment. It's a pretty big step up from my makeshift gym on the Coronado roof.

I hug the perimeter, taking in the scene. A group is playing volleyball, another jogging around the track. Half a dozen students are breaking into fencing bouts; Safia stands with them, fastening her glove and flexing her sword. I've never fenced before, but I'm half tempted to try, just for the chance to hit her. I smile and take a few steps toward her when a shout goes up from the far side of the room.

On a raised platform near the edge of the massive center, two students are sparring.

They're standing in a kind of boxing ring minus the rope—both seniors, judging by the gold stripes that mark their gym clothes where the fabric peeks out from behind the pads. The gold is all I can see, since the rest of them is buried beneath padding; even their faces are masked by the soft helmets. A handful of students— I can just make out Cash among them, a fencing mask tucked under his arm—and a burly middle-aged teacher stand around, watching as the two boys bounce on their toes, punching, kicking, and blocking. The shorter of the two seems to be working a lot harder.

The taller one moves with fluid grace, easily avoiding most of the jabs. And then, between one blink and the next, he acts instead of reacts, thrusting one foot forward and low before planting his shoe at the last moment, turning on it, and delivering a round-house kick to the other boy's head.

The boy ends up on his back, dazed but unhurt. I doubt anyone else noticed his opponent slowing his motion just before his foot connected, easing the blow. The teacher sounds a whistle, the students applaud, and the victor helps the defeated to his feet. He gives the shorter boy a quick pat on the back before the loser hops down from the platform.

I've managed to make my way across the fitness hall while watching the bout, and I've just reached the edge of the group of spectators when the victor gives a theatrical bow, clearly relishing the attention.

Then he tugs his helmet off, and I find myself looking up at Wesley Ayers.

FOUR

WESLEY AYERS is the stranger in the halls of the Coronado.

He is the Keeper in the garden who shares my secret.

He is the boy who reads me books.

He is the one who teaches me how to touch.

And today, he is the guy on the stone bench, wearing a tux.

It's the end of summer, and we're sitting in the Coronado garden. I'm perched on one of the benches in workout pants and a long-sleeve shirt pushed up to the elbows, and Wesley is stretched out on the other in his best black and white. There's only an hour or two left until his father's wedding, but he's still here.

Something is eating at him, I can tell. Something has been since he showed up, and I stupidly assume it's just the fact that he hates his father's fiancée, or at least what she means for his family. But he doesn't offer any of his usual acerbic remarks, doesn't even acknowledge the wedding or the tux. He just slumps down onto his bench and starts reciting the last of my required reading as if it's any other day.

And then, somewhere between one line and the next, his voice trails off. I glance over, wondering if he's asleep, but his eyes are neither closed nor unfocused. They're leveled on me. I return the look.

"You okay there?" I ask.

A smile flickers across his face. "Just thinking."

He sets the book aside and pushes up from his bench, smoothing the front of his rumpled tux as he closes the gap between us.

"About what?" I ask, shifting to make room as he settles down beside me. He comes close, close enough to touch, his folded arm knocking against my shoulder, his knee against mine. I take a breath as his rock band sound washes over me, loud but familiar.

"About us."

At first, I barely recognize him.

Wesley's hazel eyes are free of the eyeliner I've seen him wear all summer; his hair is still black, but instead of standing up, it's stuck to his forehead with sweat; every bit of silver is missing from his ears. All his little quirks are stripped away, but he's got those proud shoulders and that crooked smile, and his whole face is lit up from the fight. Even without the bells and whistles, it is still undeniably Wesley Ayers. And now that I see him, I don't know how I didn't see him earlier.

Maybe because Wesley Ayers—*my* Wesley—is supposed to be on some beach, bonding with his family.

My Wesley wouldn't be here at this stuck-up school, wouldn't lie to me about going here, and certainly wouldn't look like he *belongs* here.

"Who's next?" he asks, eyes glittering.

"I am," I shout back.

The spectators—all boys—turn collectively, but my gaze

is leveled firmly on Wes. The corner of his mouth tilts up. Of course he's not surprised to see *me*. He's known for weeks where I was enrolled. He never said anything. No "Oh great, we can stick together." No "Don't worry, you won't be alone." Not even a "Well, what a coincidence." Why? Why didn't he tell me?

"Now, young lady, I don't think——" starts the burly gym teacher as I approach the platform and begin strapping on pads.

"I signed the waivers," I cut in, tugging on forearm guards, wondering if there even *are* waivers for this class. It seems like that kind of school.

"It's not about that," says the teacher. "This is hand-to-hand combat, and it's important to match the students in terms of——"

"How do you know we're not well matched?" I shoot back, cinching down a shin guard. "Unless you're assuming that because I'm a girl." I look the teacher in the eyes. "Are you assuming that, sir?" I don't wait for him to answer. I step up onto the platform, and he doesn't stop me, which is good enough.

"Give the guy hell!" shouts Cash as I pull the helmet on.

Oh, I think, *I will.*

"Hey, you," says Wesley as I meet him in the center of the platform.

"Hey, you," I mimic bitterly.

"I can explain——" he starts, but he's cut off by the sound of the whistle.

I kick forward hard and fast, catching Wesley high in the chest before the shrill metallic cry has even stopped. The crowd gives a gasp as he falls, hitting the floor for only a moment before rolling over and pulling himself to his feet. I attack with another kick, which he blocks. Out of the corner of my eye, I can see we're gaining a crowd. He throws a punch, which I dodge, followed by an uppercut, which I don't. The wind rushes out of my lungs, but I don't let it stop me from grabbing his fist and his wrist—pain thrumming up my own—and turning fast, flipping him over my shoulder.

He should hit the mat flat on his back, but somehow he twists midair and lands in a crouch, elegant as a cat. In a blink he's up again and closing the gap between us. I arch back just in time to avoid a hit and recover fast enough to see an opening—left side, stomach—but I don't take it. It's been three weeks since Owen stabbed Wesley. Even though it doesn't show in his stance, I know it still hurts him. I've seen the laughs cut short by a wince, the ginger way he stands and sits.

My hesitation earns me a swift kick to the chest, and I've got just enough time to hook my foot behind his knee and wrap my hand around his chest plate before I go down, taking him with me. I hit the mat hard and brace myself for Wesley's weight to land on top of me; but his palms hit the floor before his body hits me, and he manages to catch himself.

He hovers inches over me, breathing hard. Then his mouth quirks into a crooked smile, a *familiar* smile, and he knocks his helmet playfully against mine.

"Miss me?"

The garden is silent except for the sound of my pulse.

Wesley leans across the stone bench and brings his lips featherlight against my temple. Then against my cheekbone. Against my jaw. A trail of kisses that makes me suck in a short breath, because the only time Wesley has ever kissed me—truly kissed me—he did it to read my memories. That was an angry kiss, forceful and firm. But these kisses are different. These kisses are cautious, hopeful.

"Wes," I warn.

His forehead comes to rest against my shoulder. "You sound like thunderstorms and heavy rain, did you know that?" He lets out a soft, low laugh. "I never liked bad weather. Not until I met you."

His voice has its usual easy charm, but now it's also threaded through with longing.

"Say something, Mac."

Wesley's body rests against mine. The combat padding acts as a buffer, and for a moment all I hear are the sounds of his breathing and my heart. How strange. It's so . . . quiet. I've gotten used to the sound of Wesley's noise—learned to float in it instead of drowning—but even the relative quiet of the familiar can never match this. His body on mine. Simple as skin.

My pulse quickens, and I have to remind myself that I pushed him away. *I* pushed *him* away. Now, looking up through Wes's face mask into his eyes—his lashes darkened with sweat—I will myself to do it again.

"What are you doing here?" I hiss, trying to hide the hurt in my voice.

"This might not be the best time to—"

"Tell me."

He opens his mouth. "Mac—"

And then the whistle blows.

"All right, enough of that," calls the teacher. "Both of you, up."

Wesley closes his mouth but doesn't move. I realize my hand

is still hooked around his chest plate, holding him there. I let go quickly, and he winks before springing to his feet. He offers me his gloved hand, but I'm already standing. I tug my helmet off, smooth my hair, and scan the crowd of students that gathered while we fought.

They stare at me and seem . . . stunned. Confused. Impressed. But they *stare*. Great. More eyes.

"We'll talk later," says Wes under his breath. "Promise." Before I can reply, he's heading for the edge of the platform and tugging off his gear.

"Hey, wait," I call after him. He hops down, and I'm about to follow when the burly gym teacher bars my path.

"One of you has to stay on," he says as Wesley tosses his equipment into the pile. Cash slings an arm around his neck and says something I can't hear. It sends both of them into laughter. Who is this boy? He looks so much and nothing like my Wesley.

"Normally it's the winner," the teacher continues, "but truth be told, I'm not entirely sure who won that match."

I'm about to say that I don't want to stay on, but Wesley is already weaving through the crowd, and the next student, a stocky junior, is hoisting himself onto the platform. I don't want the teacher to think I'm beat after a single fight, so I sigh, readjust my helmet, and wait for the whistle as Wesley's form vanishes from sight.

Wesley lifts his forehead from my shoulder and shifts his eyes to meet mine. "Please, say something."

But what can I say? That when Wesley touches me like this, I think of the way Owen forced me back against the

360

Narrows wall, twisting my want into fear as he tightened his grip? That when I feel Wesley's lips and my heart flutters, I think of him kissing me in the Coronado hall, reading me, and then pulling sharply away, eyes full of betrayal? That when I think of what I feel for him, I see him bleeding to death on the roof—and the pain that comes with caring about him is enough to stop me cold?

What I say instead is this: "Life is messy right now, Wes."

"Life is always messy," he says, meeting my gaze. "It's supposed to be."

I sigh, trying to find the words. "Two months ago, I'd never met another Keeper. I didn't have someone in my life I could talk to, let alone trust. And maybe it's selfish, but I can't bear the thought of losing you now."

"You're not going to lose me, Mac."

"You walked away," I say softly.

His brow furrows. "What?"

"When you found out about Owen, you walked away. I know you don't remember it, and I'm not blaming you—I know it was my fault for lying—but watching you go . . . I've been alone in this for so long, and I've always managed because I've never had anyone. But having you and losing you . . . For the first time, I *felt* alone, Wes. Having something and losing it, it's so much crueler than never having had it."

Wesley looks down at his hands. "Does it make you wish we'd never met?"

"No. God, no. But what we have now is still new to me. The sharing, the trust. I'm not ready for more." *I'll just ruin it,* I think.

"I understand." His voice is soft, soothing. He plants a

light kiss on my shoulder, like a parting gift, and pulls away.

"It's all new to me, too, remember?" he says a few minutes later. "I'd never met another Keeper before you. And having you in my life is terrifying and addictive, and I'm not going to lie and tell you it doesn't make my heart race. It does." I wonder if he can feel my own pounding pulse through my noise as he tangles his fingers through mine. "But I'm here. No matter what happens with us, I'm here."

He lets go and slumps back into the corner of the bench. He doesn't pick up the book, just tilts his head back and stares up at the clouds. Silence settles over us, heavier than usual.

"Are we good, Wes?" I ask.

"Yeah," he says, flashing a smile that's almost strong enough to hide the lie. "We're good."

By the time I finish showering, the locker room is mercifully empty, no prying eyes to watch as I loop the key back over my head, tucking it under my collar. My chest loosens as soon as the weight settles there. It feels wrong to be without it, even though this key isn't really mine.

I'm tugging on my polo when I feel the scratch of letters like a pin through my shirt pocket. I dig my list out to find a name:

Harker Blane. 13.

But I'm nowhere near my territory—I don't even know whose territory Hyde School falls in, or where the nearest Narrows door is hidden, and even if I could find it, my key wouldn't work, since

I'm not authorized to use it here—and I've got half a day of school to go, so Harker will have to sit tight. I don't like to make Histories wait; the longer they do, the more they suffer, and the more dangerous they get. I will Harker to hold on and hope he doesn't start to slip.

My stomach growls as I hoist my bag onto my shoulder and set out to find lunch.

Instead I find Wesley. At least, the newest version of him.

He's sitting cross-legged on a stone bench halfway to the dining hall with a book in his lap. He looks like a stranger. He's missing the black polish that usually graces his nails, his hair is swept neatly back, and he looks . . . *elegant* in his uniform, all black but for the gold thread tracing the edges.

I see him, but he doesn't see me—not at first—and I can't help but stare. Only his silver ring and the faint outline of his key beneath his polo mark him as the same guy I met this summer. It's like he's wearing a disguise, only it fits so well that I wonder if my Wesley—the one with spiked hair and lined eyes and that constant, mischievous smile—was the act. My stomach twists at the thought.

And then his eyes drift up from the book and settle on me, and something in him shifts again, and suddenly I see both of them at once: the affluent student and the edgy boy who likes to fight and fits his rock band noise so well. He's still under there somewhere, my Wes, but I can't help but wonder as he hops down from the sculpture and straightens, waiting for me to reach him: how many faces does Wesley Ayers have?

"I was hoping you'd come this way," he says, putting the book away and slinging his bag onto his shoulder.

"I don't know any of the other ways."

"Come on," he says, tipping his head down the path. "I'll show you."

We start walking toward the dining hall, but then we reach a split. Even though I can see the highly trafficked main building rising on our right, Wes veers left down a narrow, vacant path. Despite my rumbling stomach, I follow. I can't stop looking at him, focusing and unfocusing my eyes to find both versions.

"Go ahead." He keeps his eyes on the path ahead. "Say it."

I swallow. "You look different."

He shrugs. "Hyde has a dress code. They discourage eccentricity, which is unfortunate since, as we both know, I'm quite a fan." He looks at me then, as intensely as I'm looking at him. "You look tired, Mac. Are you sleeping?"

I shrug. I don't want to talk about it.

I mentioned my nightmares a while back, but when they didn't go away I decided to stop talking about them. It's bad enough having my parents coat me with their worry. The last thing I need is someone who knows the truth pitying me. And maybe Wes would have bad dreams, too, if he could remember that day; but he has a twenty-four-hour stretch of black in his mind and only my account and a scar from Owen's knife to go on. I envy him until I remember that I wanted to remember. I chose.

"Is there anything I can do to help or—"

"How long have you been back?" I cut in. "Or did you even go away?"

His brow furrows. "I got in last night. Haven't even had a chance to unpack, let alone come by and check on you. Or Jill. You been keeping an eye on the brat for me?"

I ignore his deflection. "Why didn't you tell me you went to school here?"

He shoves his hands in his pockets and shrugs. "At first it was just a reflex. I didn't know how to handle the fact that you were going to cross more than one of my paths, so I kept it to myself."

"I get that, Wes, I do." The Archive teaches us to break our lives into pieces and to keep those pieces secret, separate. "But what about later?" I ask, the words barely a whisper. "Is it because of what happened in the garden?"

"No," he says firmly. "It doesn't have anything to do with that."

"Then why?" I snap. "You spent the last few weeks reading me books you already knew because you read them here last year. You watched me stress out about this place, and you never spoke up."

His mouth twitches playfully. "Would you believe me if I said I just wanted to surprise you?"

I give him a long, hard look. "Well, you succeeded. But I have a hard time believing you lied to me for weeks just to see the look on my face—"

"I didn't lie," he says shortly. "You never asked me where I went."

The words hit like a dull punch. I didn't ask that specific question, he's right. But only because Wesley never wants to talk about his life. It's not that I don't want to be a part of his; I've just grown used to him being a part of *mine*.

"I told myself," continues Wes, "that if you asked, I'd tell you. But you didn't. You made an assumption, and I didn't correct you."

"Why not?"

He pulls his hand from his pocket and runs it through his hair. It's so strange to see it move through his fingers—soft, black, ungelled. I want to touch it myself, but I stifle the urge.

"I don't know," he continues. "Maybe I thought if you knew I went here, you'd think differently of me."

"But why would I judge you for going here?" I ask, gesturing down to my uniform. "I go here, too."

"Yeah, but you hate it," he snaps, coming to a stop. "You don't even know this place and you hate it. You've spent weeks dreading it, mocking it. . . ." I cringe, regretting the time I decided to don a posh accent and do a dramatic reading of a few key passages from the handbook. "But I grew up here. I didn't choose it, and I can't help it, but I did. And I was afraid you'd judge *me* if you knew." He laughs nervously, his eyes focused on the path instead. "Big surprise, Mac, I care what you think of me."

I feel the heat spreading across my face as he adds, "But I'm sorry. I knew you were stressed about Hyde, and I could have made it better and I didn't. I should have told you."

And he should have. But I think of all the times I kept things from Wes in the beginning, either out of habit or fear, and how it took him nearly dying and the Archive stealing his memories for me to finally tell him the truth. I feel my anger diminishing.

"So you have a preppy schoolboy alter ego," I say. "Anything else you want to tell me?"

The relief that sweeps across his face is obvious—relief that we're okay—but he doesn't miss a beat. "I really hate eggplant."

"Seriously?" I ask.

"Seriously," he replies, bouncing a little on his toes. "But I also hate explaining that it's because of the name and the fact that I grew up thinking it was a plant made of eggs, so instead I just tell people I'm allergic."

I laugh, and his smile broadens—and just like that, my Wesley is back. Doling out jokes and crooked grins, eyes glittering even without the makeup.

We start off again down the path.

"I'm happy you're here," I say under my breath, but he doesn't seem to hear me. I raise my voice, but instead of repeating myself, I simply ask, "Where are we going?"

He glances back and quirks a brow. "Isn't it obvious?" he asks. "I'm leading you astray."

FIVE

A DOZEN STRIDES LATER, the tree-lined path dead-ends at a stone courtyard. It's raised a few steps off the ground, each of its four corners marked by a pillar. Three students are lounging on the platform, and in the very center of it stands a statue of a man in a hooded cloak.

"It's the only human sculpture on campus," explains Wesley, " so it's probably meant to be Saint Francis, the patron saint of animals. But everyone calls him the Alchemist."

I can see why. Standing in his shrouds, the statue looks more like a druid than a priest. His elbows are tucked in and his palms are turned up, his head bowed as if focusing on a spell. The mystique is only slightly diminished by the fact that his stone hands are currently holding aloft a pizza box.

"This," says Wes, gesturing to the platform, "is the Court."

The students look up at the sound of Wesley's voice. One of them I've already met. Cash is sitting with his legs stretched out on the stairs.

"Mackenzie Bishop," he calls as we make our way up to the platform. "I will never again make the mistake of calling you a damsel."

Wesley frowns a little. "You two have met?"

"I tried to save her," says Cash. "Turned out she didn't need my help."

Wesley glances my way and winks. "I think Mac can take care of herself."

Cash's smile is surprisingly tight. "You seem awfully friendly toward a girl who just kicked your ass. I take it you know each other?"

"We met over the summer," Wes answers, climbing the steps. "While you and Saf were off boating in—where was it, Spain? Portugal? I can never keep the Graham family excursions straight."

It's brilliant, watching Wesley work other people, twisting the conversation back toward them. Away from himself.

"Don't be bitter," says Cash. "You know you've got an open invitation."

Wesley makes a noncommittal sound. "I don't like boats," he says, retrieving a slice of pizza from the statue's outstretched arms, nodding for me to join him.

"The *Saint-Marie*," says Cash with a flourish, "isn't just a *boat*."

"So sorry," says Wes, mimicking the flourish. "I don't like *yachts*."

I can't tell if they're joking.

"I see you've already begun defacing our poor Alchemist again," adds Wes, waving the pizza slice at the statue.

"Just be glad Safia hasn't *played dress-up* with him," says a girl's voice, and my attention shifts to a pair of students sitting on the platform steps: a junior boy sitting cross-legged, and a redheaded senior with her head in his lap.

"Very true," says Cash as the girl shifts up onto one elbow and looks at me.

"You've brought a stray," she says, but there's no malice in her voice, and her smile quirks in a teasing way.

"She's not a stray, Amber," says the boy she's been using as a pillow. "She's a junior."

He looks up at me then, and my stomach drops. There's a silver stripe across his uniform, but he looks like he can't be more than fifteen. He's small and slim, dark hair curling across his forehead, and between the pair of black-framed glasses perched on his nose and the notes scribbled on the backs of his hands, he looks so much like my brother that it hurts. If Ben had lived—if he had been given five more birthdays—he might have looked just like this.

He looks away and I blink, and the resemblance thins to nearly nothing. Still, it leaves me shaken as I head up the steps and join Wesley by the statue. He grabs a soda from the Alchemist's feet and gestures toward the other students.

"So you've met Cassius," he says.

"Dear god, please don't call me that," says Cash.

"That's Gavin with the glasses," continues Wes, "and Amber is in his lap."

"Amber Kinney," she corrects. "There are two gold Ambers at Hyde and one silver, and it's not a name that lends itself to shortened forms, trust me, so if you hear someone use the name Kinney—which I hate, by the way, never do it—that's me."

I take a soda. "I'm Mackenzie Bishop. New student."

"Of course you are," says Gavin, and I blush until he adds, "Because it's a small school and we know everybody else."

"Yeah, well, you can call me Mackenzie or Mac, if you want. Just not Kenzie." Kenzie was Da's word; it sounds wrong on everyone else's lips. "Or M." M was the name I'd dreamt of being called for years. M was the version of me that didn't hunt Histories or read memories. M was the person I could have been if I hadn't joined the Archive. And M was ruined by Owen when he whispered it in my ear like a promise, right before he tried to kill me.

"Well, Mackenzie," says Gavin, emphasizing each of the three syllables evenly, just the way Ben did, "welcome to Hyde."

"Mackenzie, will you help me?"

We're sitting at the table, Ben and I, while Mom hums in the background, making dinner. I'm twirling my silver ring and reading a passage for my freshman English class, and Ben's trying to do his fourth-grade math, but it's not his best subject.

"Mackenzie . . . ?"

I've always loved the way Ben says my name.

He was never one of those kids who couldn't speak, who skipped syllables and squeezed words down into sounds. By the time he was four, he prided himself on pronouncing everything. Mom was never *Mama*, Dad was never *Daddy*, Da was never *Da* but *Da Antony*, and I was never *Muh-ken-zee* or *Mc-kin-zee*, and certainly not *Kenzie*, but always *Mah-Ken-Zee*, the three beats set like stones in order.

"Will you show me how to do this problem?"

At nine, even his questions are precise. He has this obsession with being a grown-up; not just wearing one of Dad's ties or holding his knife and fork like Mom, but putting on airs, mimicking posture and attitude and articulation. He has the makings of a Keeper, really. Da didn't live long enough to see him taking shape, but I can see it.

I know I already took Da's spot, but I often wonder if the Archive could make a place for Ben, too.

It's a selfish wish, I know. Some might even call it a

wrong wish. I should want to protect him from everything, including—no, *especially*—the Archive. But as I sit there, turning my silver ring and watching Ben work, I think I might give anything to have him beside me.

I get why Da did it. Why he chose me. I get why everyone chooses someone. It's not just so that someone takes their place. It's so that—at least for a little while—they don't have to be alone. Alone with what they do and who they are. Alone with all those secrets.

It is selfish and it is wrong and it is human, and as I sit there, watching Ben work, I think that I would do it. I would choose him. I would take my little brother with me. If they'd let me.

Of course, I never find out.

In truth, Gavin looks very little like Ben. I know because I've been staring at him—and then trying not to stare—for the last fifteen minutes. Luckily, between a long shower and the walk with Wes, fifteen minutes is all I have before the bell rings.

It turns out that even though we're a grade apart, Amber and I have Physiology together. She tells me on the way how it's all part of her pre-premed plan, how her grandmother was some incredible war surgeon behind the blood-slicked camp curtains, and how she has steady hands just like her. Between the Court and the science hall—marked by a statue of a snake—I discover my favorite thing about Amber Kinney.

She likes to talk.

She likes to talk even more than Lyndsey, and as far as I can tell it's not out of a need to fill the quiet so much as a simple lack of filter between her brain and mouth—which is fine with me, because she's surprisingly interesting. She tells me random facts about the school, and then about each member of the Court: Gavin won't eat anything green and has a brother who sleepwalks; Cash speaks four languages and tears up at sappy commercials; Safia— because apparently Amber is actually *friends* with her—used to be so shy she barely spoke, and still hasn't quite figured out how to speak *nicely*; Wesley is a sarcastic flirt and allergic to eggplant and . . .

Amber trails off. "But you already know Wesley," she says.

"Not as well as you'd think," I say carefully.

Amber smiles. "Join the club. I've known Wes for *years*, and there are times I still don't feel like I *know* him. But I think he likes it that way—an air of mystery—so we all let him have his secrets."

I wish everybody felt the way Amber Kinney does about secrets. My life would be a lot easier.

"So," I say, "Wesley's a flirt?"

Amber rolls her eyes and holds the door open for me. "Let's just say that air of mystery tends to work in his favor." I feel the heat creeping into my face as she glances my way. "Don't tell me you've already fallen for it."

I chuckle. "Hardly." And that much is true. After all, it's not Wesley's *secrets* that make my pulse climb. It's the fact that we have the same ones. Or, at least, most of the same ones. I can't help but wonder, after the shock of seeing him here, what else I don't know.

His voice echoes in my head: *You didn't ask.*

We reach the Physiology room and snag two seats side by side as the bell rings. A surprisingly young woman named Ms. Hill walks us through our syllabus, and I spend the next few minutes flipping through the textbook, trying to figure out which bones

Owen snapped inside my wrist. It's funny—looking at the maps of bone and muscle and nerve, the diagrams of body flexion and movement and potential—how much of this I've learned already. More through trial and error and application than assigned reading, but it's still nice to find that some of the knowledge translates. I run my fingertips lightly over the illustrated fingers on the page.

I make it through the lecture, and Amber points me in the direction of my last class: Government. It's taught by Mr. Lowell, a man in his fifties with a mop of graying curls and a soft, even voice. I'm prepared to have to stab myself with my pen to stay awake, but then he starts talking.

"Everything that rises will fall," he says. "Empires, societies, governments. None of them lasts forever. Why? Because even though they are the products of change, they become resistant *to* change. The longer a society survives, the more it clings to its power, and the more it resists progress. The more it resists progress—resists *change*—the more its citizens demand it. In response, the society tightens its grip, desperate to maintain control. It's afraid of losing its hold."

I stiffen in my seat.

Do you know why the Archive has so many rules, Miss Bishop? Owen asked me on the roof that day. *It's because they're afraid of us. Terrified.*

"Societies are afraid of their citizens," echoes Mr. Lowell. "The more a society tightens its grip, the more the people fight that grip." He draws a circle in the air with his index finger, going around and around, and each time he does, the circle gets smaller. "Tighter and tighter, and the resistance grows and grows until it spills over into action. That action takes one of two forms."

He writes two words on the board: *REVOLUTION* and *REFORM*.

"The first segment of this class," says Mr. Lowell, "will be dedicated to the language of revolution; the second segment will be dedicated to the language of reform." He erases the word *REFORM* from the board.

"You've all heard the language of revolution. The rhetoric. For instance, a government can be called corrupt." He writes the word *corrupt* on the board. "Give me some other words."

"The government is rotten," says a girl at the front of the class.

"The company is abusing power," says a boy.

"The system is broken," adds another.

"Very good, very good," says Mr. Lowell. "Keep going."

I cringe as Owen's voice echoes in my head. *The Archive is a prison.*

"A prison," I say, my voice carrying over the others before I even realize I've spoken out loud. The room quiets as the teacher considers me. Finally he nods.

"Rhetoric of imprisonment and, conversely, the call for freedom. One of the most classic examples of revolutionary thought. Well done, Miss . . ."

"Bishop."

He nods again and turns his attention back to the class. "Anyone else?"

By the time school lets out, my edges are starting to fray.

The morning coffee and lunch soda can't make up for the days—weeks, really—without sleep. And having Owen in my head for most of last period hasn't helped my nerves. A shaky yawn escapes as I push open the outer doors of the history hall and step into the afternoon sun, abandoning the crowded path for a secluded patch of grass where I can stop and soak up the light and clear my head. I free my Keeper list from my shirt pocket and am relieved to see that there's still only one name on the page.

"Who's Harker?" asks Cash over my shoulder. I jump a little at the sound of his voice, then unfold the paper slowly, careful to seem unconcerned.

"Just a neighbor," I say, tucking the paper back into my pocket. "I promised to pick up some info on the school for him. He's thinking about it for next year." The lie is easy, effortless, and I try not to relish it.

"Ah, well, we can swing by the office on the way to the parking lot." He sets off down the path.

"You really don't have to escort me," I say, following. "I'm sure I can find my way."

"I have no doubt, but I'd still like——"

"Look," I cut him off. "I know you're just doing your job."

He frowns, but doesn't slow his pace. "Saf tell you that?" I shrug. "Well, yes, okay. It's my job, but I chose it. And it's not like I was assigned to you. I could be imposing my assistance on any of the unsuspecting *freshman*. I'd rather be accompanying you." He chews his lip and squints up toward the summer sun before he continues. "If you'll let me."

"All right," I agree with a teasing smile. "But just to spare those other unsuspecting students."

He laughs lightly and waves to someone across the grass.

"So," I say, "Cassius? That's quite a name."

"Cassius Arthur Graham. A mouthful, isn't it? That's what you get when your mother's an Italian diplomat and your father's a British linguist." The ivy-coated stone back of the main building comes into sight. "But it's not nearly as bad as Wesley's."

"What do you mean?" I ask.

Cash gives me a look, like I should know. Then, when it's obvious I don't, he starts to backtrack.

"Nothing. I forgot you two haven't known each other that long."

My steps slow on the path. "What are you talking about?"

"Well, it's just . . . Wesley's name isn't really Wesley. That's his middle name."

I frown. "Then what's his first name?"

Cash shakes his head. "Can't say."

"That bad?"

"*He* thinks so."

"Come on, I've got to have *some* ammunition."

"No way, he'd kill me."

I laugh and let it drop as we reach the admin building's doors. "You guys seem close," I say as he holds them open for me.

"We are," says Cash with a kind of simple certainty that makes my stomach hurt.

With Wes haunting the Coronado halls all summer, I just assumed that he lived the way I did: at a distance. But he has a *life*. Friends. Good friends. I have Lyndsey, but we're close because she doesn't make me lie. She never asks questions. But I should have asked Wes. I should have wondered.

"We grew up together," explains Cash as we make our way toward the glass lobby. "Met him at Hartford. That's the K-through-eight that leads into Hyde. Saf and I showed up in the fourth grade—third for her—and Wes just kind of took us in. When things started going south with his parents a few years back, we tried to return the favor. He's not very good at taking help, though."

I nod. "He always bounces it back."

"Exactly," he says, sounding genuinely frustrated. "But then his mom left and things went from bad to worse."

"What happened?" I press.

The question jars him, and he seems to realize he shouldn't be sharing this much. He hesitates, then says, "He went to stay with his aunt Joan."

"Great-aunt," I correct absently.

"He told you about her?"

"A little," I say. Joan was the woman who passed her key and her job on to Wesley. The one the Archive cut full of holes when she retired just to make sure its secrets were safe. The fact that I've heard of Joan seems to satisfy something in Cash, and his reluctance dissolves.

"Yeah, well, he was supposed to go stay with her for the summer," he says, "to get away from the divorce—it was brutal—but Hyde started back up in the fall, and he wasn't here. Our whole sophomore year, it was like he didn't exist. You have to understand—he didn't call, didn't write. There was just this void." Cash shakes his head. "He's loud in that way you don't really notice till he's gone. Anyway, sophomore year comes and goes without him. And then summer break comes and goes without him. And finally junior year comes around, and there he is at lunch, leaning up against the Alchemist like he never left."

"Was he different?" I ask as we reach the office door at the mouth of the glass lobby. That was the year he became a Keeper.

Cash stops with his fingers on the handle. "Apart from the black eye I gave him? Not really. If anything, he seemed . . . *happier*. And

I was just glad to have him back, so I didn't pry. Wait here, I'll grab you some prospective student pamphlets."

He vanishes into the office, and I glance absently around the hall. It's covered in photographs—though *covered* suggests chaos, and these are all immaculately hung, each frame perfectly level and perfectly equidistant from the others. Each one has a small, elegant date etched into the top. In every picture, a group of students stands, shoulders touching, in several even rows. Senior classes, judging by the gold stripes in the more recent color photos. The years count backward along both walls, with the most recent years here by the mouth of the lobby and the older ones trailing away down the hall. Like most of the posh private schools, Hyde hasn't always been coed. As I backtrack through the years, the girls vanish from the group photos, appearing in their own set and then disappearing altogether, along with the reds and blues and golds, leaving only boys in black and white. I let my eyes wander the walls, not knowing what I'm looking for until I find it. When I do, everything in me tenses.

He could have gone to any of the schools in the city, but he didn't. He went here.

In the frame marked *1952*, several dozen boys stand in rigid rows, stern, well-groomed, elegant. And there, one row down and several students in, is Owen Chris Clarke.

His silver-blond hair registers as white in the colorless photo, and that, plus the shocking paleness of his eyes, makes him look like a flare of light in the wash of black uniforms. The ghost of a smile brushes his lips, like he knows a secret. And maybe he does. This would have been before—before he graduated, before he was made Crew, before Regina was murdered, before he brought her back, before he killed the Coronado residents and jumped from

379

the roof. But at the time of the photo, he was already a Keeper. It shows in his eyes, in his taunting smile, and in the hint of a ring on the hand resting on another student's shoulder . . .

"You ready?"

I pull away from the photograph to find Cash standing there, holding a short stack of pamphlets.

"Yeah," I say, my voice a little shakier than I'd like, as I cast another glance at the photo.

You and I are not so different.

I frown. So what if Owen went here? He's gone. This is nothing more than a faded photograph, a glimpse of the past—a perfectly reasonable place for a dead boy to be.

"Let's go," I say as I take the papers.

Cash walks me out.

"Where's your car?" he asks, surveying the parking lot, which has already emptied out quite a bit.

I cross to the bike rack and give Dante a sweeping gesture. "My ride."

He blushes. "I didn't mean to assume—"

I wave him off. "It's like a convertible, really. Wind through my hair. Leather seats . . . well, seat." I dig my workout pants out of my bag and tug them on under my skirt.

He smiles, gold eyes drifting down to the sidewalk. "Maybe we could do this again tomorrow."

"You mean school?" I ask, unlocking the bike and swinging my leg over. "I think that's the idea. Doesn't work very well if you only go once." I try to say it straight-faced, but the smile slips through.

Cash breaks into a warm laugh as he turns to go. "Welcome to Hyde, Mackenzie Bishop."

His easy joy is contagious, and I feel myself still grinning as I watch him retreat through the gates. Then I look back out over the parking lot and all the warmth goes cold.

The man from this morning, the one with gold hair and gold skin, is leaning back against a tree at the edge of the lot, sipping coffee out of a to-go cup, and he's looking at me. This time he doesn't even try to hide it. The sight of him is like a brick through a glass window, shattering the mundane. It's a reminder that life couldn't be further from normal. Normal is a thing I might dream about, if I weren't too busy having nightmares.

There's one thing scarier than the fact I'm being followed. And that's *who* is following me. Because there's only one possible answer: the Archive. The thought makes my blood run cold. I can't imagine it's a *good* thing, being tailed by Crew. And that's exactly what he is. What he has to be.

The way he sips his coffee and shifts his weight and his unguarded body language create an illusion of boredom that's dampened only by his gaze, which is sharp, alert. But that's not what gives him away. It's the confidence. A very specific and dangerous kind of confidence. The same kind Owen had.

The confidence exuded by someone who knows they can hurt you before you hurt them.

The golden man's eyes meet mine, and he smiles with half his mouth. He takes another sip of his coffee, and I take a step toward him just as a horn goes off in the parking lot. The sound steals my attention for a second, even less, but by the time I look back at the man, he's gone.

Great.

I wait a second to see if he'll reappear, but he doesn't, and I'm left with only a sinking feeling in my stomach and the nagging question: *why* is the Archive having me followed?

The worry eats at the last of my energy as I pedal home. By the time I get there, my vision is starting to blur from fatigue. When I dismount, the world rocks a little. I have to stand still a moment, wait for the dizziness to pass before I drag myself through the doors and up the stairs.

I want sleep.

I need sleep.

Instead, I go hunting.

SIX

I STIFLE ANOTHER yawn as I step out of the stairwell and into the third floor hall, grateful that Harker's still the only name on my list. After stashing my skirt in my schoolbag and shoving that behind a table halfway down the hall, I straighten my ponytail in the mirror above the table and fetch the key out from under my collar. The transformation is complete: student to Keeper in under a minute.

Across from the mirror is a painting of the sea, and just beside that is a crack in the wall. A seam where the worlds don't quite line up. No one else sees it, but I do, and when I tug off my ring, the crack becomes clearer, the keyhole tucked into the fold. I slot my key, and the Narrows door blossoms like a stain, the faded wallpaper darkening as the frame presses against the surface. A thread of light carves the outline of the door, and I turn the key, hear the hollow click, and step through into the dark. I'm lifting my fingers to the nearest wall, about to read the surface for signs of Harker, when I think I hear it.

Humming.

My heart starts to race as I pull away from the wall and turn toward the noise, panic flooding through me. And then between one pulse—one step—and the next, the world disappears.

Everything goes away.

Goes black.

And then, just as suddenly, it comes back—*I come back*—and the humming is gone and my head is killing me and I'm running. Sprinting. *Chasing.* A boy sprints several yards ahead of me.

"Harker, stop!" The words tumble out before I even realize they're mine. "There's nowhere to run!" I add, which isn't strictly true, since we're both covering plenty of ground. There's just nowhere to run *to*.

My lungs are burning and my legs ache and I don't have enough sleep in my bones for this, but adrenaline fills in the place where sleep should be as the Narrows echo with the sounds of the hunt. Heavy breath and pumping limbs and shoes hitting hard against the concrete, his as he flees, mine as I chase.

And I'm catching up.

The kid loses a stride when he looks back, and then another when he takes a corner too fast and slides into the wall. Harker springs off, keeps going. I cut the corner sharp, too, shoes skidding a fraction on the slick ground of the Narrows, but I know these halls, these walls, these floors, and I'm off again, closing the gap.

He's between one sprinting step and the next when my hand finally tangles in his collar, catching him off balance. I pull hard, and Harker goes sprawling backward to the floor, a few feet from the nearest Returns door, marked by a white chalk circle shaded in. He starts to scramble away, but I haul him to his feet and pin him back against the wall as I get my key into the lock and turn. The door opens, showering us both in glaring white light.

I get a good look at his eyes as they go wide—the pupils wavering, about to slip—right before I shove him into the glaring white, but it's not until after he's through the door, the light is gone, and I'm left alone in the dark with my slamming pulse that I process the look he gave me and realize what it was.

Fear.

Not of the Narrows or of the glaring Returns, but of *me.*

It's like being doused with cold water, that thought, and it leaves me feeling breathless and dizzy. I bring a hand up to the wall for balance. A shallow pain draws my eyes to my arm, and for the first time I see the scratches there, raked across my skin, and a sick feeling spreads through me.

When did this happen?

When did Harker fight back?

I rack my brain, trying to rewind my own mind, trying to remember when he scratched me, or what made him run in the first place, or how we met, and panic coils around me as I realize that I *can't.*

I remember stepping through the door and into the Narrows. I remember the sound of humming, and then . . . nothing. Nothing until halfway through the chase. The time between is just *missing.* I squeeze my eyes shut, scrambling for the memories and finding only a blur. I sink down to the floor and rest my forehead against my knees, forcing air into my lungs.

One of Da's lessons plays in my head, his voice low and steady and smooth: *Keep your head on, Kenzie. Can't think straight when you're all worked up. Histories panic. Look at all the good it does them.*

I take another breath and try to calm down. What was I doing? I was reading the walls . . . I was about to read the walls when I heard the humming, and then . . . and then I lick my lips and taste blood, and just like that, the memories rush back.

Someone was humming.

Just like Owen used to do. My heart started to race as I followed the melody through the halls. It sounded so much like humming at first, but then it didn't—the Narrows does distort things—growing louder and harsher until it wasn't anything like humming, wasn't music at all, but a hard and steady thud thud thud.

Harker kicking a door halfway down the hall, so loud he didn't hear me coming until I was there behind him, head pounding, and then he spun and, before I could even lie my way into his good graces, caught me off guard with his fist.

It comes back like still frames, glimpses in a strobe.

My hand tangled in his shirt.

Shoving him back.

A mess of thrashing limbs.

His shoe coming up against my stomach.

His hands clawing his way free.

Both of us running.

I feel sick with relief. The memory's shaky, but it's there.

As I pull the list from my pocket and watch Harker's name bleed off the page, one question claws its way through my spinning thoughts: why did I black out in the first place?

If I had to guess, I'd say sleep. Or rather, the lack of it.

This—blacking out, losing time, whatever it is—happened once before. A few days after Owen. Last time—which was the first time, and I'd hoped the *only* time—I hadn't been sleeping, either. I was so tired, I could barely see straight. One moment I was trying to talk down a History, a teenage girl, and the next I was alone in the hall and my knuckles were raw and her name was gone from my list. When I finally calmed down, the memories came back, blurry and stilted, but there. She'd already slipped, thought I was someone else. Called me M (probably Em, like Emily or Emma). That's all it had taken to make my hands shake and my heart race and my mind skip. A sliver of Owen.

I told myself then it wasn't a big deal. It only happened once—unlike the nightmares that came every night like clockwork—so I didn't tell Roland. I didn't want him to worry. Da used to say you had to see patterns, but not go looking for them, and I didn't want to make something out of nothing. But Da also used to say that one mistake was an accident, but two was a problem.

As I look down at the scratches on my arms, I know.

This is officially a problem.

I will myself to get back to my feet. I consider the door beside the one I just sent Harker through, the one marked with the hollow white circle I use to denote the Archive. I should tell Roland. And I will—later. Right now, I have to get home. Last time I lost a minute, maybe two, but now I can tell I've lost more than that. I dig my nails into my palms, hoping the sting will keep me awake as I head back for the numbered doors.

The key dangles from its cord around my wrist, and I swing it up into my grip and slide the teeth into the lock on the door that leads back to the third floor. It opens, the hall beyond nothing but shadow from this side, and my shoe is halfway through when I hear a familiar voice on the other side and jerk back sharply, heart hammering in my chest.

Stupid, stupid mistake.

The doorway isn't visible to normal people. If I'd passed through into the Coronado, I would have walked straight through the wall itself—at least it would have appeared that way—and into my mother.

"It's going well, I think. . . ." The Coronado may be lost from sight, but her voice reaches through the veiled space, muffled, yet audible. "Right, it takes time, I know."

I can hear her coming down the hall, nearing the Narrows door as she talks, the long pauses making it clear she's on the phone. And then her footsteps stop right in front of me. Maybe she's looking in the mirror across from the invisible door. I think of the schoolbag stashed behind the table under the mirror, and hope she hasn't discovered it.

"Oh, Mackenzie?"

I stiffen, until I realize she's answering the person on the line.

"I don't know, Colleen," she says.

I roll my eyes. Her therapist. Mom's been seeing Colleen since Ben died last year. I'd hoped the sessions would end with the move. Apparently, they haven't. Now I brace my hands on either side of the doorway and listen to one half of the conversation. I know I shouldn't leave the Narrows door open, but my list is clear and my curiosity is piqued.

"It hasn't come up," says Mom. "Yes, okay, I haven't *brought* it up. But she seemed better. Seems. Seemed. It's so hard to tell with her. I'm her mother. I should be able to tell, and I can't. I can tell something's wrong. I can tell she's wearing this mask, but I can't see past it." My chest tightens at the pain in her voice. "No. It's not drugs."

I clench my teeth against a curse. I hate Colleen. Colleen's the one who told Mom to throw out Ben's things. The one time we met face-to-face, she saw a scratch on my wrist from a pissed-off History and was convinced I did it to myself to *feel things*.

"I know the symptoms," says Mom, ticking off a list that pretty well sums up my current behavior—evasion, moodiness, troubled sleep, being withdrawn, inexplicable disappearances . . . though in my defense, I do my best to explain them. Just not using the truth. "But it's not. Yes, I'm sure." I'm glad she's sticking up for me, at least on this front. "Okay," she says after a long pause, starting down the hall again. "I will. I promise." I listen to her trail off, wait for the jingling sound of her keys, the apartment door opening and closing, and then I sigh and step out into the hall.

The Narrows door dissolves behind me as I slide my ring back on. The skirt and the bag seem undisturbed behind the table, and in a few short steps I've transformed back into an ordinary Hyde School junior. My reflection stares back at me, unconvinced.

I can tell something's wrong. I can tell she's wearing this mask, but I can't see past it.

I practice my smile a few times, checking my mask to make sure it's free of cracks before I turn down the hall and head home.

That evening, I put on a show.

I picture Da clapping in his slow, lazy way as I tell Mom and Dad about my day, injecting as much enthusiasm into my voice as I can without tipping my parents from pleasant surprise to suspicion.

"Hyde's pretty incredible," I say.

Dad lights up. "I want to hear all about it."

So I tell him. I'm basically feeding the pamphlet propaganda back to him, line by line, but while I may be amping up the excitement, the sentiment isn't a total lie. I *did* enjoy it. And it feels good to tell something that even vaguely resembles the truth.

"And you'll never guess who goes there!" I say, stealing a carrot as Mom chops them.

"You can tell us during dinner," she says, shooing me away with a pile of placements and silverware. "Set the table first." But she smiles as she says it.

Dad clears some books from the table so I can set it and retreats to the couch to watch the news.

"Who's closing the coffee shop tonight?" I ask.

"Berk's got it."

Berk is Betty's husband, and Betty is Nix's caretaker. Nix is ancient and blind and lives up on the seventh floor and won't come down because he's wheelchair-bound and doesn't trust the rickety metal elevators.

Berk and Betty moved into one of the vacants on the sixth floor two weeks ago after Nix finally succeeded in lighting his scarf on fire with his cigarette. I was shocked—not about the fire, that was inevitable, but that they would move in for him, not being related in any way. But apparently Nix was like a father to Betty once, and now she's acting like a daughter. It's sweet, and it all worked out because Berk—who's a painter—was looking for a social fix, and Mom was looking for a hand at Bishop's. She can't pay him yet, but he doesn't seem to mind. He only asked to be able to hang his pieces in the coffee shop for sale.

"I'll take him down some dinner later," says Mom, setting aside a plate.

I'm carrying water glasses to the table when the headline on the TV catches my attention, and I look over Dad's shoulder at the screen. It's the same news story from early this morning, about the missing person. A room in disarray flashes across the screen, and I'm about to ask Dad to turn the volume up when Mom says, "Turn that off. Dinner's ready."

Dad obediently clicks the TV off, but my eyes linger on the blackened screen, holding the image of the room in my mind. It looked familiar. . . .

"Mackenzie," Mom warns, and I blink, losing the image as I turn to find my parents both already at the table. They look like they've been waiting.

I shake my head and manage a smile. "Sorry. Coming."

But sitting down turns out to be a bad idea.

The moment I do, the fatigue catches back up, and I spend most of dinner rambling about Hyde just to stay awake. As soon as the dishes are cleared, I retreat to my room in the name of homework, but I've barely gotten through a page of reading before my eyes unfocus, the words on the paper blurring together. I try standing, then I try pacing while holding my textbook, but my mind can't seem to grab hold of anything. I feel like my bones are made of lead.

My gaze wanders to the bed. All I can think of is how much I want to lie down . . .

The book slips through my fingers, hitting the ground with a soft thunk.

. . . how badly I want to sleep . . .

I reach the bed.

. . . how certain I am . . .

I tug back the covers.

. . . that when I do . . .

I sink into the sheets.

. . . I won't dream of anything.

SEVEN

THE ROOF IS full of monsters, and they are all alive.

They perch on stone claws and watch with stone eyes as Owen stalks me through the maze of bodies.

"Stop running, Miss Bishop," his voice echoes across the rooftop.

And just like that, the concrete floor crumbles beneath me and I plunge seven stories through the bones of the building to the Coronado lobby, hitting the floor so hard my bones sing. I roll onto my back and look up in time to see the gargoyles tumbling toward me. I throw my hands up, bracing for the weight of stone. It never comes. I blink and find myself in a cage made from the broken statues, a web of crossing arms and legs and wings. And standing in the middle is Owen, his knife dangling from his fingers.

"The Archive is a prison," he says calmly.

He comes toward me, and I scramble to my feet and back away until I'm pressed up against the stone bodies. Their limbs jerk to life and shoot forward, grabbing my arms and legs, snaking around my waist. Every time I struggle the limbs tighten, my bones cracking under their grip. I bite back a scream.

"But don't worry." Owen runs a hand over my head before tangling his fingers in my hair. "I will set you free."

He draws the flat side of the knife down my body, bringing

the tip to rest between my ribs. He puts just enough weight on the blade to slice through my shirt and nick my skin, and I squeeze my eyes shut, trying to get away, trying to wake up, but the hand tangled in my hair tightens.

"Open your eyes," he warns.

I drag them open and find his face inches from mine. "Why?" I growl. "So I can see the truth?"

His smile sharpens. "No," he says. "So I can watch the life go out of them."

And then he drives the knife forward into my chest.

I sit up in the dark, one hand clutching at my shirt, the other pressed over my mouth to stifle the cry that's already escaped. I know it's a dream, but it is so terrifyingly real. My whole body aches from the fall and the gargoyles' grip, and the place on my chest where the knife drove in burns with phantom pain.

My face is damp, and I can't tell if it's from sweat or tears or both. The clock says twelve forty-five, and I draw up my knees and rest my head against them, taking a few slow, steadying breaths.

A moment later, there is a knock on my door.

"Mackenzie," comes my father's quiet voice. I look up as the door opens and I can see his outline in the light spilling from my parents' bedroom into the hall behind him. He comes to sit on the edge of my bed, and I'm grateful to the dark for hiding whatever is written across my face right now.

"What's going on, hon?" he whispers.

"Nothing," I say. "Sorry if I woke you guys up. Just had a bad dream."

"Again?" he asks gently. We both know it's been happening too often.

"It's no big deal," I say, trying to keep my voice light.

Dad tugs his glasses from his face and cleans them on his T-shirt. "You know what your Da used to tell me about bad dreams?"

I know what Da used to tell *me*, but I doubt it's the same thing he told my father, so I shake my head.

"He used to tell me there were no bad dreams. Just dreams. That when we call them good or bad, we give importance to them. I know that doesn't make it better, Mac. I know it's easy to talk like that when you're awake. But the fact is, dreams catch us with our armor off."

Not trusting myself to speak, I nod.

"Do you want to . . . talk to someone about it?" He doesn't mean talk to him or talk to Mom. He means a therapist. Like *Colleen*. But I've got more than enough people trying to get inside my head right now.

"No. Really, I'm fine."

"You're sure?"

I nod again. "Trust me."

My heart sinks, because I can see in my father's eyes that he wants to, but doesn't. Da used to say that lies were easy, but trust was hard. Trust is like faith: it can turn people into believers, but every time it's lost, trust becomes harder and harder to win back. I've spent the last four and a half years—since I became a Keeper— trying to cling to my parents' trust, watching doubt replace it little by little. And doubt, Da warned, is like a current you have to swim against, one that saps your strength.

"Well, if you change your mind . . ." he says, sliding to his feet.

"I'll let you know," I say, watching him go.

He's right. I should talk to someone. But not Colleen.

I listen to the sound of his receding steps after he's closed the door, and to the murmur of my mother's voice when he returns to their room. I let the whole apartment go quiet and dark, and only when I'm sure that they're asleep do I get up, get dressed, and sneak out.

I step into the Archive, and I shiver.

My sleep hasn't been the only thing affected by Owen and Carmen's recent attack. The Archive has changed, too. It has always been marked by quiet, but where the lack of noise used to feel peaceful, now it feels coiled and tense. The silence is heavier, enforced by hushed voices and warning looks. The massive doors behind the antechamber's desk have been pinned back like butterfly wings, held open to make sure that the newly installed sentinels have full visibility and immediate access to the atrium and the network of halls beyond. The two figures are the most striking addition—and the most loathsome. Dressed in solemn black, they flank the entrance to the Archive. The sentinels are Histories, like everyone else who works within the Archive walls; but unlike the Librarians, they wear no gold keys and do not seem fully *awake*.

Roland told me that they've been implemented in every branch in his jurisdiction, though he himself had no say in the matter of their presence. The order for increased security came from over his head. I'm guessing that means it came from Agatha.

Agatha, the assessor, who I haven't *seen* again since the interrogation, but whose presence seems to haunt this place the way Owen's haunts me.

Roland wasn't happy about it. As far as I can tell, no one was. The Librarians are not used to feeling watched. Agatha can claim the sentinels are there in case of another Owen; the fact is, they're also there in case of another *Carmen*. It's one thing to be betrayed by a known traitor. It's another to be betrayed by someone you thought was a loyal servant.

The sentinels' eyes follow me as I step through into the antechamber.

I force myself not to look at them. I don't want them to see that they give me the creeps. Instead I focus on the desk and how relieved I am to see Lisa sitting there behind it with her black bob and her green horn-rimmed glasses. Lately it feels like a gamble every time I step through. Will I be met by Roland's calm gray eyes or Lisa's cautious smile, or will I be confronted with Patrick's disapproving glare? Or will Agatha herself be waiting?

But tonight, I'm lucky enough to have Lisa. Her head is bent forward over the Archive's ledger, and I can't help but wonder who she's writing *to*. The book that always sits on the desk holds a page for every Keeper and every Crew in the branch, the partner to the paper in my pocket, and its thickness is a strange reminder that even though I often feel alone, I'm not. I'm only one page in a thick old book.

Lisa stops writing and looks up long enough to see my tired eyes. The strain of the past few weeks shows in her eyes, too, the way they flick to the figures behind me before coming back to me. She gives me a nod and says only, "He's in the atrium, toward the back."

Bless her for not making me stand there and state my business in front of the sentinels, who may look like statues, but no doubt hear and see everything that happens here and feed it all back to Agatha.

I mouth the words *thank you* and round the desk, passing through the archway and into the atrium. The central room is still as grand as ever, the high, arching ceilings and stained glass of a church, broken by aisles of shelves instead of pews, ten halls branching off like spokes.

I cross the vast hall in silence and find Roland tucked in between two aisles, his red Chucks a spot of color on the pale floors. His back is to me, head bowed as he looks over a folder. There's tension in his shoulders, and I can tell from his stillness that he's stopped scanning the page and is now staring past it, lost in thought.

I've had four and a half years to study Roland's postures and moods, ever since Da offered me into his care and he accepted. The constancy of him—his tall, thin, unchanging form—has always been a comfort, but now it's also a reminder of what he is. The Archive tells us that Librarians don't change as long as they're here, their suspended age a trade for their time, their service. And up until a few weeks ago, I bought it. And then Carmen told me the truth: that Roland, along with every other Librarian who staffs the Archive, comes not from the Outer, but from the shelves here. That they are all Histories, those of past Keepers and Crew woken from their sleep to serve again. It's still so hard for me to believe that he's *dead*.

"Miss Bishop?" he says without looking up. "You should be in bed." His voice is soft, but even at a whisper I can hear the lilt in it. He closes the folder before turning toward me. His gray eyes travel over my face, and his brow furrows.

"Still not sleeping?"

I shrug. "Maybe I just wanted to tell you about my first day of school."

He hugs the folder to his chest. "How was it? Learn anything useful?"

"I learned that Wesley Ayers goes there, too."

A raised brow. "I assumed you already knew that."

"Yeah, well . . ." I say, trailing off into a yawn.

"How long has it been, Mackenzie?"

"Since what?"

"Since you slept," he says, looking at me hard. "Really slept."

I run a hand through my hair and tally up the time since the rogue History of a deceased Crew member tricked me into trusting him, stole my key, threw me into a Returns room, stabbed Wesley, tried to kill me, and nearly succeeded (with a Librarian's help) in tearing the entire branch of the Archive down. "Three weeks, two days, and six hours."

"Since Owen," says Roland.

I nod and echo, "Since Owen."

"It's showing."

I cringe. I'm trying so hard, but I know he's right. And if he can see it, Agatha could, too.

My head starts to hurt.

Roland cranes his neck, looking up at the stained glass that interrupts the highest part of the walls and trails like smoke onto the ceiling. The Archive is always bright, lit by some unseen source, but the shifting light beyond the windows is an illusion, a way to suggest change in a static world. Right now, the windows are dark, and I wonder if Roland sees something in them I don't, because when his eyes sink back to mine he says, "We have some time."

"For what?" I ask, but he's already walking away.

"Follow me."

EIGHT

I'M THIRTEEN, covered in blood, and sitting cross-legged on a table in a sterile room. I've been a Keeper for less than six months, and this isn't the first time I've landed in the medical wing of the Archive. Roland stands out of the way, arms crossed over his chest while Patrick prepares a cold pack.

"He was twice my size," I say, clutching a bloody cloth to my nose.

"Isn't everyone?" asks Patrick. He's only been at the branch a couple weeks. He doesn't like me very much.

"You're not helping," says Roland.

"I thought that's exactly what I was doing," snaps Patrick. "Helping. You called in a favor, and here I am, patching up your little pet project off the books."

I murmur something unkind behind the cloth, one of the many phrases I picked up from Da. Patrick doesn't hear it, but Roland must, because he raises a brow.

"Miss Bishop," he says, addressing Patrick, "is one of our most promising Keepers. She wouldn't be here if the council had not voted her through."

Patrick gives Roland a weighted look. "Did they vote her through, or did you?"

Roland's gray eyes narrow a fraction. "I would remind you who you're speaking to."

Patrick lets off a short sigh like steam and turns his attention back to me, pulling the cloth from my grip to examine the damage over his glasses. It hurts like hell, but I try not to let it show as he presses the cold pack against my face and repositions my hand over it.

"You're lucky it's not broken," he says, peeling off a pair of plastic gloves.

Roland winks. "Our girl, she's made of steel."

I smile a little behind the cold pack. I like the idea of that. Being a girl of steel.

"Hardheaded," says Patrick. "Keep it iced and try not to get punched in the face again."

"I'll do my best," I say, the words muffled by the cold pack. "But it's so much fun."

Roland chuckles. Patrick packs up his things and leaves, muttering something that sounds like *useless* under his breath. I watch him go.

"You threw your arms up when the History took a swing at you," says Roland casually. "Is that what happened?"

I look down and nod. I should have known better. Da taught me better, but it was like two different lessons, in practice and in truth, and I wasn't ready. Da said the right moves have to be like reflex, not just learned but known, and now I see why. There was no time to think, only act. React. My arms came up and the History's fist hit them and they hit me. Heat spreads across my cheeks, even under the cold pack.

"Hop down," he says, uncrossing his arms. "And show me what you did."

I get off the table and set the cold pack aside. Roland throws a punch, slow as syrup, and I bring my arms up, crossed at the wrists. His fist comes to rest lightly against them, and he considers me over my raised hands.

"There is no right pose to strike, no position to take. The worst thing you can do in a fight is stop moving. When someone attacks, they create force, movement, momentum, but you'll be okay as long as you can see and feel the direction of that force and travel with it." He puts some weight behind his fist, shifting to one side as he leans forward. I let myself shift to the same side and back, and his fist slides away. He nods. "There we go. Now, better get that ice back on your face."

Steps echo in the hall beyond the room, and Roland's gray eyes flick to the door.

"I should go," I say, taking the cold pack with me. But when I get to the door, I hesitate. "Do you regret it?" I ask. "Voting me through?"

Roland folds his arms across his chest. "Not at all," he says with a smile. "You make things infinitely more interesting."

"Where are we going?" I ask under my breath. Roland doesn't answer, only leads me out of the aisle and down the sixth hall that branches off the atrium. The Archive is a network of mismatched spaces, branching and intersecting in a system only the Librarians seem able to comprehend. Every time I follow someone through the maze, I struggle to keep hold of my bearings as I count the turns. But tonight, instead of guiding me on a winding path across landings, down corridors, through rooms, Roland goes straight, straight to the very end of the very long hall and through a smaller set of doors set into the end.

We end up in another hallway, one much shorter, narrower, and dimly lit. He hesitates, glancing around to see and hear if we're alone.

"Where are we?" I ask when it's clear that we are.

"Librarians' quarters," he answers before setting off again. Halfway down the hall, he reaches a simple dark-paneled door and stops. "Here we go."

The door opens into a cozy room with pale striped walls, sparsely furnished with a daybed, a low-backed leather chair, and a table. Classical music whispers from a device on the wall, and Roland moves through the small space with the comfort of someone who knows every inch of it.

He crosses to the table and absently drops the folder he's been carrying into a drawer before pulling something shiny from his pocket. He runs his thumb over the surface once before setting it on top of the table. The gesture is at once worn and gentle, reverent. When he pulls his hand away, I see that the object is a silver pocket watch. It's old, and I can't keep my pulse from quickening when my eyes settle on it. The only objects that come into the Archive arrive on the bodies of Histories. Either he snagged the watch from a body or it came in with his.

"It doesn't work anymore," says Roland, sensing my interest. "Not here." He gestures to the daybed. "Sit."

I sink onto the soft cushion and run a hand over a black blanket folded on the bed beside me. "I didn't think you needed sleep," I say, feeling awkward. It's still so hard to process the idea that he's . . . not alive.

"Need is a strange thing," he says, methodically rolling up his sleeves. "Physical needs make you feel human. The lack of them can make you feel less so. I don't sleep, no, but I rest. I go through the motions. It provides a psychological relief rather than a physical one. Now try to get some rest."

I shake my head, even as my body begs me to lie down. "I can't," I say quietly.

Roland sits down in the low-backed leather chair opposite, his gold Archive key gleaming against the front of his shirt. Keeper keys unlock doors to the Narrows; Crew keys unlock shortcuts in the Outer; Archive keys unlock Histories, turning them on and off like appliances, not people. I wonder what it would feel like to turn a life off with a single twist of metal. I remember Carmen holding hers out to me, remember the pins-and-needles numbness that shot up my hand when I tried to wrap my fingers around it.

"Miss Bishop," says Roland, his voice drawing my attention up. "You have to try."

"I don't believe in ghosts, Roland. But it's like he's haunting me. Every time I close my eyes, he's there."

"He's gone," says Roland simply.

"Are you sure?" I whisper, thinking of the fear and the pain that follow me out of my nightmares. "It's like there's a part of him that dug its nails into my head and held on. I see him when I close my eyes, and he feels so *real*. . . . I feel like I'm going to wake up and he'll still be there."

"Well," says Roland, "you sleep, and I'll keep an eye out for him."

I laugh sadly, but don't lie down. I need to tell him about the blackouts. It would be so much easier *not* to tell him—he's already worried, and it will only make things worse—but I need to know if I'm losing it, and since I'm the one shot through with nightmares and missing moments, I don't think I'm the best judge.

"Something happened today," I say quietly. "In the Narrows."

Roland steeples his fingers. "Tell me."

"I . . . I lost time."

Roland sits forward. "What do you mean?"

"I was hunting, and I . . . It was like I blacked out." I roll my bad wrist. "I was awake, but one minute I was one place, and the next I was somewhere else, and I couldn't remember how I'd gotten there. It was just blank. It came back, though," I add, "after I calmed down."

I don't say how shaky the memory was and how I had to fight to recover it.

Roland's gray eyes darken. "Is this the first time?"

In response, my gaze escapes to the floor.

"How many times?" he asks.

"Just once. A couple weeks ago."

"You should have told me."

I look up. "I didn't think it would happen again."

Roland shoves up from his chair and begins to pace. He should tell me it's going to be okay, but he doesn't bother lying. Bad dreams are one thing. Blacking out on the job is another. We both know what happens to a member of the Archive if they're deemed unfit. There is no such thing as a leave of absence here.

I look up at the cream-colored ceiling.

"How many Keepers lose their minds?" I ask.

Roland shakes his head. "You're not losing your mind, Mackenzie."

I give him a skeptical look.

"You've been through a lot. What you're experiencing, it

sounds like residual trauma and extreme fatigue, paired with the influx of adrenaline, are triggering a kind of tunnel vision. It's a feasible reaction."

"I don't care if it's feasible. How do I make sure it doesn't happen again?"

"You need rest. You need to *sleep*," he says, a note of desperation working its way into his voice as he slumps back down in his chair. His gray eyes are worried, a paler version of the fear that flashed through them when Agatha first summoned me to be assessed. "Please try."

I hesitate, but finally nod, slide off my shoes, and curl up on the daybed, resting my head on the folded blanket. I consider telling him that I think I'm being followed, too, but I can't will the words out.

"Do you regret it yet?" I ask. "Voting me through?"

His mouth twitches, but I don't hear his answer, because my body is already betraying me, dragging me down into sleep.

When I wake, the room is empty, and for a split second I can't remember where I am or how I got here. But then I hear the whisper of classical music from the device on the wall and remember that I'm in the Archive, in Roland's quarters.

I blink away sleep, marveling at the fact it doesn't cling to me. No dreams. No nightmares. For the first time in days. Weeks. I allow a small, breathless laugh to escape. My eyes burn from the sheer relief of a few hours' sleep without Owen and his knife.

I fold the blanket Roland let me borrow and return it to the corner of the daybed before getting up. I switch the music off as I pad across the cloisterlike space. Behind a door left ajar on the far wall, I find several versions of his self-assigned uniform: slacks and sweaters and button-down shirts. I look around for a clock even though I know there isn't one. My eyes go to the silver pocket watch, still on top of the side table. It doesn't work, but I find myself reaching absently for it when my attention slides to the drawer beneath.

It is barely ajar, just enough for me to see another glint of metal, and when I take the drawer in both hands and slide it open—the wood utters a soft hush—I find two worn silver coins and a notebook no larger than my palm. I lift the notebook. The paper edges are yellowed and fragile, and when I peel the cover back, I find a date written in elegant script in the bottom corner.

1819

The next several pages are filled with notes too small and old to read, and mingled with them, pencil sketches. A stone facade. A river. A woman. The name *Evelyn* runs in his careful script under her throat.

The journal sings beneath my fingers, brimming with memories, and I hesitate to put the book back. Roland has always been a mystery. He never wanted to talk about the life he'd left behind, the one he claimed he'd go back to when he was done serving. But now I know he didn't leave a life behind at all, not willingly, and he'll never go back to it.

The question "Who is Roland?" has become "Who *was* Roland?" and before I can stop myself, I close my eyes and reach for the thread of memory in the notebook. I catch hold, and time turns back. It rolls away, and darkness ripples into an alleyway at night: a young, smudged Roland standing beneath a pool of flickering lamplight. He's cradling the notebook in one hand as he shades in the woman's hair with a short stub of pencil and pins a slip of paper to the opposite page with his thumb. As he draws, letters bleed onto the slip. A name. He snaps the notebook shut and checks his pocket watch, three Crew lines spreading like a shadow across the inside of his wrist.

The sound of voices draws me out of the memory, and I set the notebook back into the table drawer as the door groans a little under someone's weight, but doesn't open.

I hold my breath as I ease the drawer shut and step toward the door and the voices on the other side. When I press my ear against it, I can hear his melodic voice and just the edges of Lisa's soft, even tone. And then my chest tightens as I realize they're talking about *me*.

"No," says Roland quietly, "I realize it's not a permanent solution. But she just needs time. And rest," he adds. "She's been through a lot."

Another murmur.

"No," replies Roland. "It hasn't come to that yet. And it won't."

I force myself away from the door as he echoes, "I know, I know."

When Roland comes back into the room, I'm sitting on the floor, lacing up my shoes.

"Miss Bishop," he says. "How are you feeling?"

"Like a new person," I say, getting to my feet. "How long was I out?"

"Four hours."

Four hours, and I want to cry. How mended could I feel with eight? "It's amazing," I say. "The difference. To be free of Owen for a night."

Roland crosses his arms and looks down at them. "You could be free of him for longer." His gray gaze slides up. "You don't have to live with it, the weight of what you've been through. There are options. Alterations——"

"*No.*" *Alterations.* The word for when the Archive carves out memories from someone's mind. Cuts their life full of holes. I think of Wesley, missing a day of his life. I think of his great-aunt, Joan, stripped of years when she retired, just as a *precaution.*

"Miss Bishop," he says, reading my disgust, "alterations are not carried out solely on those who leave, or those who need to be kept in the dark about the Archive's existence."

"No, they're also for those deemed unfit——"

"And for those who *want* to forget," counters Roland. "There's no shame in it, Mackenzie. Wanting to be free of certain memories. The bad ones."

"The bad ones?" I echo. "Roland, they're all tangled up. Isn't that the idea? Life is messy. And even if it weren't, I said no." The truth is, I don't trust them to stop with the memories I'm willing to lose. And even if I did, it feels like running. I need to remember. "We've had this conversation already."

"Yes, we have, back when you were only fighting bad dreams. But if you keep having tunnel moments——"

"Then we'll handle it," I say, making it clear the conversation is over.

Roland's shoulders slump, his arms falling back to his sides. "Very well." He lifts his silver watch from the side table and slips it back into his pocket. "Come on, I'll lead you out." I notice, as I follow him, that the halls don't seem to shift around us. Unlike the twisting corridors of the stacks, the path to the Librarians' quarters is a straight and steady line.

We reach the front desk, and I cringe when I see Patrick sitting there. His eyes flick up, cold behind their black-framed glasses, and his mouth draws into a tight line. Roland anticipates a remark and speaks first.

"It's come to my attention that Miss Bishop's predecessor did not adequately prepare her before his demise."

"Pray tell," says Patrick, "in what ways is she lacking?"

I frown. Nobody likes being talked about like they're not in the room, especially when the talk centers on their shortcomings.

"Stillness," says Roland. "She's more than competent when it comes to combat, but lacks the patience and conservation of energy that comes with proper training."

"And how do you plan to assist her?"

"Meditation," answers Roland. "It'll benefit her, anyway, when she makes Crew and—"

"*If* she makes Crew," corrects Patrick, but Roland continues.

"—and she's a quick learner, so it shouldn't take long for her to pick it up. In the meantime, when she comes, send her back." He straightens, flaunting his full height. "And do it without interrogation, please. I'd like to make the most of *everyone's* time."

I forget sometimes what a good liar Roland is.

Patrick considers us both, clearly trying to pick apart the ruse, but in the end his mouth only twists into a mean smile, his eyes hanging on me as he addresses Roland. "If you think you can teach Miss Bishop to be quiet and still for once, then best of luck."

I bite my tongue as Roland nods to us both and vanishes back into the atrium, leaving me alone with the sentinels and Patrick, who appraises me coldly. Neither one of us has forgotten that he was the one who summoned Agatha in the first place. That he petitioned to have me removed. Now he says nothing, not until I've passed between the sentinels to the Archive door and my key is slotted in the lock. Only then does Patrick add a low but audible, "Sleep tight."

I'm halfway back to my numbered doors, trying to swallow the bad taste Patrick always leaves in my mouth, when my eyes drift to a chalk marking on the wall.

It's not on one of the doors, but on a stretch of dark stone. I drew it two and a half weeks ago to mark the spot where it happened. Some days I walk past it, but others I stop and force myself to remember. To *relive*. Roland would be furious. I know I should be moving on, should be doing everything I can to put the memory behind me, or let the Archive take it away, but I can't. It's already scarred into my mind a dozen ways, all of them twisted, and I need to remember—not the nightmarish distortions that have followed, but what actually happened. I need to remember so I can be better, stronger. Da used to say mistakes were useless if you tried to forget them. You had to remember and learn.

My hand drifts to the wall, and I barely have to reach before the memories rush up beneath my fingers. I spin them back, away, until I find that day—and even then, past the blinding light of the Returns door being thrown open, past our tangling bodies and the key and all the way back to the moment when I thought I had a chance. I know exactly where it is and when to stop, because I've watched the scene so many times, studying his strength and my weakness. Watching myself lose.

I drag the memory to a stop and hold it there, in the second before the fight starts. Owen's hand is outstretched as he asks for the ending of the story; my hand is about to reach for my hidden knife. I know what's going to happen.

And then it does.

There is no sound, no color, only a blur of motion as I go for the knife against my leg and Owen lunges forward. Before my blade can reach his chest, his hand closes around my wrist. He slams it back into the wall, forcing his body against mine.

Phantom pain drifts into my fingers as I watch his grip tighten. The knife tumbles to the floor. I try and fail to get free as he catches the blade and spins my body back against his, the glinting metal coming to rest beneath my chin.

He frees the final piece of the story—and with it the final piece of his key—from my pocket and shoves me away so he can assemble it. I don't run. I don't do anything but stand and watch and cradle my broken wrist. Because I still think I'm going to win.

I attack and manage to send the knife skating into the dark—even manage to send Owen backward, too. But then he's up again, catching my leg and slamming me back onto the hard floor. I curl in on myself in pain, struggling to force air back into my lungs.

It's obvious now that Owen was playing with me.

My recovery is too slow, but he waits for me to get to my feet. He wants me to believe that if I can, I stand a chance.

But when I finally summon the strength, he is there: too fast, a blur as he wraps his hand around my throat and pins me against the nearest door. I watch myself gasp and claw at his grip as he reaches up and takes hold of the key wrapped around my good wrist, snapping the cord with a single sharp tug. He unlocks the door behind me and showers both of us in glaring white light. I watch him lean in, watch his lips move, and I don't need sound to know what he's saying. I remember just fine.

"Do you know what happens to a living person in the Returns room?"

That's what his lips are mouthing. And then, when I don't answer—can't answer—he adds, "Neither do I," before he shoves me backward into the blinding white, closes the door, and walks away.

My hand slips from the wall. A now-familiar numbness spreads through me in the memory's wake.

The Owen in my nightmares is drawn in color and sound, and even when I know I'm dreaming, it feels so unbearably real, here and now and terrifying. But watching us this way, I don't feel any of the fear. Frustration and anger and regret, maybe, but not fear. This scene is faded and gray like an old movie, so clearly a moment in the past. It doesn't even feel like *my* past, but one that belongs to someone else. Someone weaker.

I think of Roland's offer—of letting the Archive go in and hollow out everything that Owen touched and ruined—and I can't help but wonder if this is how I'd feel about him after that. If he were only this, a memory in someone else's life, would he be able to hurt me in my sleep? Or would I be free?

I shove the thought away. I'm not going to run away. That isn't the way to be free. And I'm never going to let the Archive into my head, when it would be so easy for them to erase more of me. Erase everything.

I need to remember.

NINE

I FETCH THE discarded book from my bedroom floor and manage to finish the reading for my government class as the Thursday morning sun peeks over the horizon. *At least it will be fresh in my mind,* I reason as I pack up my school bag. As long as I can get through three chapters of lit theory and a section of precalc during lunch, I'll avoid falling behind on the *second day* of school.

Dad knocks short and crisp on my door and says, "Up!" and I do my best to sound groggy as I call back and zip my bag closed. I'm halfway through the living room when the TV catches my eyes. It's that *same* story. Only this time, in addition to the photo of the trashed room, there's a title in bold on the bottom of the screen.

Retired Judge Phillip Missing

A photo goes up beside the anchor's face, and I get a sinking feeling in my stomach. I recognize the room now, because I *know* the man they're talking about.

I met him two days ago.

Mr. Phillip likes to keep things neat.

I notice before he even lets me in. His welcome mat is straight, and the planters on the porch are evenly spaced, and when he opens the door I can see the order carrying through into the entryway, where three pairs of shoes are lined up, laces out.

"You must be from Bishop's," he says, gesturing to the box tucked under my arm. It has a blue cursive *B* on the top. Until school starts, Mom has me running deliveries as payment for the new bike. Not that I mind. The fresh air helps me stay awake, and the riding helps me learn the city grid—which isn't a grid at all here on the edges, but a mess of veering streets and neighborhoods, apartments and parks.

"Yes, sir," I say, holding out the box. "A dozen chocolate chip."

He nods and takes the box, patting his back pocket and then frowning a little. "Wallet must be in the kitchen," he says. "Come on in."

I hesitate. I was raised not to take candy from strangers or climb into vans or follow older men into their homes, but Mr. Phillip hardly looks threatening. And even if he is, I'm willing to bet I could take him.

I roll my wrist, listening to the bones crack as I cross the threshold. Mr. Phillip is already in the kitchen—which is clean enough to make me think he doesn't use it—arranging the cookies on a plate. He leans in and inhales, and his eyes turn sad.

"Something wrong?" I ask.

"Not the same," he says softly.

He tells me about his wife. She's dead. He tells me how, before, the house always seemed to smell like cookies. He doesn't even like to eat them. He just misses the smell. But it's not the same.

We stand there in this unused kitchen, and I don't know what to do. Part of me wishes Mr. Phillip had never asked me to come in, because I don't need his feelings on top of mine. But I'm here now and I might be able to fix him, or at least glue a couple pieces back together. Finally I hold out my hand.

"Give me the box," I say.

"Excuse me?"

"Here," I say, taking the empty container from his hands and dumping the tray of cookies inside. "I'll be back."

An hour later I'm there again, and instead of a box I'm holding a Tupperware of cookie dough: about twelve cookies' worth. I show him how to heat the oven, and I scoop a few clumps of dough onto a sheet and slide the sheet in. I set the timer and tell Mr. Phillip to follow me outside.

"You'll notice the smell more," I say, "when you go back in."

Mr. Phillip seems genuinely touched.

"What's your name?" he asks as we stand on the porch.

"Mackenzie Bishop," I say.

"You didn't have to do this, Mackenzie," he says.

I shrug. "I know."

Da wouldn't like it. He wasn't a fan of looking back, not when time was still rolling forward, and I know at the end of the day I haven't done anything but give a man in an empty kitchen a way of clinging to the past. But people like me can reach out and touch memories with only our fingers, so we can't really fault everyone else for wanting to hold on, too.

The truth is, I get it. If someone could give me back the

way our house felt when Ben was home, even a shred of it, I'd give them anything. People are made up of so many small details. Some—like the smell of cookies baking—we can recreate. Or at least try.

The timer goes off inside the house. Mr. Phillip opens the door, takes a deep breath, and smiles. "Perfect."

Mr. Phillip liked to keep things neat. But on the screen, his apartment is in disarray. The room shown is one I only saw in passing on the way from the entry to the kitchen, an open living room with a wall of windows that look out onto a small, immaculate garden. But now the glass is shattered and the room is trashed, and Mr. Phillip is missing.

I turn the volume up, and the reporter's voice spills into the living room.

"Well-known civil servant and recently retired judge Gregory Phillip is now considered a missing person, as well as the potential victim of an abduction."

"Mackenzie," cuts in Dad, striding through the room. "You're going to be late."

I hear the door close after him, but don't take my eyes from the screen.

"As you can see behind me," continues the reporter, "this room of his house was found in a state of chaos—paintings ripped from the walls, books strewn across the floor, chairs toppled, windows shattered. Are these the signs of a violent struggle, or a robber trying to cover his tracks?"

The camera cuts to a press conference, where a man with cropped reddish hair and a stern jaw issues a statement. A bar

across the bottom of the screen identifies him as Detective Kinney.
I wonder if he's related to Amber.

"There's no denying the signs of foul play," says Detective
Kinney. His voice is low, gruff. "And at this time, we are treating
the case as an abduction." The camera cuts back to the still frame
of the trashed room, but the detective's voice plays eerily on. "We
are investigating all possible leads, and anyone with information
should contact—"

I shut the TV off, but Mr. Phillip and the trashed room linger
in my mind like echoes. What happened? *When* did it happen? Was
I the last person to see him alive? Should I tell the police? What
would I tell them? That I helped the man's house smell like cookies?

I can't go to the cops. The last thing I need is more attention.
Whatever happened to him, it's tragic . . . but it's got nothing to
do with me.

My phone goes off, and I realize I'm still standing in the empty
living room, staring at the darkened screen. I dig it out of my bag
to find a text from Wesley.

> Got your battle armor on?

I smile, haul my bag onto my shoulder, and text back:

> Can't decide what to wear over it.

The conversation follows me down to the lobby.

> What are your choices?

> Black, black, or black?

> My favorite color. You shouldn't have.

> Slimming.

> Sexy.

> Sensible.

> And good for hiding bloodstains.

I smile and pocket the phone as I reach Bishop's. Mom is busy talking to Ms. Angelli, a cat-happy antiques dealer from the fourth floor, and I swipe a muffin and a coffee and head out, feeling more awake than I have in weeks. *Four hours of sleep,* I marvel as I unchain Dante and pedal off.

I keep my eyes peeled for the golden man from yesterday, but he's nowhere to be seen, and I actually start to wonder if he was ever there or if he was just another side effect of the sleeplessness. I hope for the latter, not wanting to think about what the former could mean.

The morning is cool, and I balance my coffee on the handlebars with one hand and steer with the other. As I ride, something fills my chest. Not fear or fatigue, but something lovely and light: hope. I was beginning to think I'd never find dreamless sleep again; but if I could find it in Roland's daybed, then it's possible to find it elsewhere, too. Right now, high on those four small hours of rest, possibility is enough.

When I get to Hyde, I find Cash leaning up against the bike rack, holding two coffees and shooing freshmen away like flies from the spot he's saving me near the front gate. He smiles when he sees me, a broad grin that brightens the morning and helps push any lingering thoughts of Mr. Phillip from my mind. He scoots aside so I can park Dante.

"I wasn't going to wait for you," he explains, "but you see, the schedule flips. I showed you the route for the A block, but not the B block."

"Isn't it just the A block in reverse?"

"Well, yes," he says, offering me one of the coffees. I take it, even though I just finished mine. "But I wanted to make sure you knew that. I didn't want you to think me a negligent ambassador."

"That would be a travesty," I say, tugging off the workout pants beneath my skirt.

"Truly," he says, sipping his drink. "I'm going to lose points as it is for not being able to show you to your morning classes. I'm on the opposite side of campus, and the teachers around here will lock you out if you're late."

"I won't fault you." I get the first pant leg off.

"Good. There are feedback cards around here somewhere, you know."

"I'll be sure to fill one out. . . ." My shoe catches on the second pant leg; when I try to tug it free, my backpack shifts from my other shoulder and my balance falters. Cash's hand comes up to steady me, and his noise—all jazz and laughter and pulse—pounds through my head, loud enough to make me flinch and pull away, toppling the other direction, straight into the metallic rock band sound of Wesley Ayers.

He smiles, and I can't tell if it's my rare moment of clumsiness or the fact I lean into his noise instead of away from it that makes his eyes glitter.

"Steady there," he says as I finally free the fabric from my shoe. I get both feet back on the ground, but his touch lingers a moment before sliding away, taking the thrum of music with it.

"Morning, Ayers," says Cash with a nod.

"Where did you come from, Wes?" I ask.

He tips his head back down the sidewalk.

"What, no fancy car?" I tease.

"Ferrari's in the shop," he shoots back without missing a beat.

"And the Lexus?" chirps Cash.

Wesley rolls his eyes and shifts his attention to me. "Is this one giving you trouble?"

"On the contrary," I say, "he's been a perfect gentleman. One might even say a knight."

"In shining armor," adds Cash, gesturing to his gold stripes.

"He brought me coffee," I say, holding up my cup.

Wes runs a hand through his black hair and sighs dramatically. "You never bring *me* coffee, Cassius."

And then, out of nowhere, a girl swings her arm around Wesley from behind. He doesn't even tense at the contact—I do—only smiles as she puts her manicured hands over his eyes.

"Morning, Elle," he says cheerfully.

Elle—a pretty little thing, bird-thin with bottle-blond hair—actually *giggles* as she pulls away.

"How did you know?" she squeaks.

Because of your noise, I think drily.

Wesley shrugs. "What can I say? It's a gift."

"All the cool powers were taken," mutters Cash, half into his coffee.

The girl is still hanging on Wesley. *Perching* on him. Like a bird on a branch. She's chirping on about some fall dance when the bell finally rings, and I realize I've never been so happy to go to class.

It's a good thing I've had two coffees to go with my four hours of sleep, because Mr. Lowell kicks off the day with a documentary on revolutionaries. And whether it's the healthy dose of caffeine or the strange way the subject sinks its nails in, I manage to stay awake.

"The thing to remember about revolutionaries," says Lowell, killing the video and flicking on the lights, "is that, while they may be viewed as terrorists by their oppressors, in their own eyes, they are champions. Martyrs. People willing to do what others won't, or can't, for the sake of whatever it is they believe in. In a way, we can see them as the most extreme incarnations of a society's discontent. But just as people elevate their revolutionaries to the station of gods, avenging angels, heroes, so those revolutionaries elevate themselves. . . ."

As he continues, I picture Owen Chris Clarke, eyes blazing on the Coronado roof as he spoke of monsters and freedom and betrayal. Of tearing down the Archive, one branch at a time.

"But the mark of a revolutionary," continues Lowell, "is the fact that cause comes first. No matter how elevated the revolutionary becomes in the eyes of others—and in his own eyes—his life will always matter less than the cause. It is expendable."

Owen jumped off a roof. Took his own life to make sure the Archive couldn't take his mind, his memories. To make sure that if—when—his History woke, he would remember everything. I have no doubt that Owen would have given or taken his life a hundred times to see the Archive burn.

"Sadly," adds Lowell, "revolutionaries often find the lives of others equally expendable."

Expendable. I write the word in my notebook.

Owen definitely saw the lives of others as expendable. From those he murdered to keep his sister a secret, to those he *tried* to murder—Wesley bleeding out so Owen could make a point—to me. Owen gave me the chance to come with him instead of standing in his way. As soon as I refused, I was worthless to him. Nothing more than another obstacle.

If Owen was a revolutionary, then what does that make me? Part of the machine? The world isn't that black-and-white, is it? It doesn't all boil down to with or against. Some of us just want to stay alive.

TEN

AMBER'S LATE TO PHYSIOLOGY, so she has to snag a seat in the back and I have to spend the period studying the nervous system and trying to stay awake. As soon as the bell rings, I'm out of my chair and standing by hers.

"That eager to get to gym?" she asks, packing up her bag.

"Question," I say casually. "Is your dad a cop?"

"Huh?" Amber's strawberry eyebrows go up. "Oh, yeah. Detective." She hoists the bag onto her shoulder and we head into the fray. "Why?"

"I just saw him on the news this morning."

"Kind of sad, isn't it?" she says. "*I* didn't get to see my dad this morning."

Treading dangerous waters, then. "He works a lot?"

Amber sighs. "On a light day. And the Phillip case is killing him." She almost smiles. "My mom hates it when I use words like *killing* in casual conversation. She thinks I'm becoming desensitized to death. I hate to tell her she's too late."

"My grandfather was a detective, too." Well, a private eye, and mostly under the table work at that, but close enough.

Her eyes light up. "Really?"

"Yeah. I grew up around it. Bound to make you a little morbid." Amber smiles, and I take my shot. "Do they have any idea what happened to that guy, Mr. Phillip?"

Amber shakes her head and pushes the door open. "Dad won't

423

talk about it around me." She squints into the late morning light. "But the walls in our house are pretty thin. From what I've heard him say, none of it adds up. You've got this one room, and it's trashed, and the rest of the house is spotless. Nothing missing."

"Except for Mr. Phillip."

"Exactly," she says, kicking a loose pebble down the path, "but nobody can figure out why. He was apparently one of the nicest guys around, and he was retired."

"A judge, right? Do they think someone might have been angry with a sentence or something?"

"Then why not kill him?" says Amber, pushing open the gym doors. "I know that's cold, but if you have a vendetta, you usually have a body. They don't have one. They don't have anything. He just vanished. So my question is, who would go to all the trouble to make someone disappear and then leave a mess like that? Why not make it look like he just walked away?"

She has a point. She has a lot of points.

"You're really good at this," I say, following her into the locker room.

She beams. "Crime dramas and years of eavesdropping."

"What are you two going on about?" asks Safia, dropping her bag on the bench. I hesitate, but Amber surprises me by giving a nonchalant shrug and lying through her teeth. "Arteries and veins, mostly."

Saf screws up her nose. "Ewww." She keys in her locker code and starts to change, but Amber smiles and keeps going. "Did you know that veins move around beneath your skin?"

"Stop," says Saf, paling.

"And did you know——" Amber continues.

"Amber, *stop*," says Saf, tugging on her workout clothes.

"—that the brachial artery," she says, poking Saf's arm for emphasis, "is the first place blood goes after being pumped through your heart, so if you sever it, you could conceivably lose all five liters of blood in your body? Your heart would just pump it right out onto the floor—"

"Gross, gross, *stop*," snaps Saf, slamming her locker and storming away toward the gym doors.

Amber looks back at me with a smile after Safia has stormed out. "She gets squeamish," she says cheerfully.

"I can see that." I'd be lying if I said it didn't lighten my mood. "Hey, will you let me know if they find anything?"

She nods a little reluctantly. "Why so interested in the case?"

I flash a smile. "You're not the only one who grew up on crime shows."

Amber smiles back, and I make a mental note to spend more time watching television.

There's a nervous energy in my bones. I want to run—want to *sprint* until it dissipates—but I'm terrified of triggering another tunnel moment, so I spend the first half of gym walking on the track, trying to clear my head. Amber and Gavin are "stretching" on a mat across the room, trying to hide a magazine on the floor between them. Safia is fencing—she's actually *good*, in an obnoxious way—and Cash is on the weight machines with a few other guys. And Wesley is . . . right beside me. One moment I'm alone, and the next he's fallen casually into step next to me. I count the number of strides we walk in silence—eleven—before Wesley feels the need to break it.

"Did you know," he asks, affecting an accent that I think is *supposed* to be Cash's, "that the hawk, which is Hyde's mascot, is known for performing dazzling aerobatic feats to impress prospective mates?"

I can't help but laugh. Wes smiles, and slips back into his own voice. "What's on your mind?"

"Crime scenes," I say absently.

"Never a dull answer, I'll give you that. Care to be more specific?"

I shake my head.

"Bishop! Ayers!" shouts the gym teacher near the sparring platform. "Come show these idiots how to fight."

Wesley knocks his shoulder against mine—a ripple of bass through two thin layers of fabric—and we make our way to the mat and suit up. I roll my wrist, testing.

"Do you really have a Ferrari?" I ask as I cinch my gloves.

He gives me a withering look. "For your information, Miss Bishop," he says, pulling on his helmet, "I don't own a car."

We go to the center of the platform.

"Shocking," I say as the whistle blows.

Wes throws a punch, and I dodge and catch his wrist.

"Waste of gas," he says, before I turn and flip him over my shoulder. Instead of resisting, he moves with the flip, lands on his feet, and throws a kick my direction. I lunge backward. We dance around each other for a moment.

"So you live in walking distance?" I ask, throwing a punch. He catches it—his grip oddly gentle around my bad wrist—and rolls my body in against his, one arm snaking around my shoulders.

"I use the Narrows," he says in my ear. "Fastest transportation around, remember?" He shoves me forward before I can try to flip him again. I spin to face him and catch him in the stomach, on his good side.

"You could only do that if Hyde School was in your territory," I say, blocking two back-to-back shots.

"It is," he says, clearly trying to focus on the match.

I smile to myself. That means he lives nearby—and the only houses nearby are mansions, massive properties on the land that rings the campus. I try to picture him at a party on one of the stone patios that accent many of the mansions, staff flitting about with trays of champagne. While I'm busy picturing that, Wesley fakes a punch and takes out my legs. I go down hard.

The whistle blows, and this time when Wesley tries to help me up, I let him.

"That's how it's done," says the gym teacher, shooing us off the mat. "A little less chitchat would have been nice, but that's the idea."

I tug my helmet off and toss it into the equipment stack. Wesley's hair is slick with sweat, but I'm still picturing him with a butler. And maybe a pipe. On the Graham family yacht.

"What are you grinning about?" he asks.

"What's your real name?" The question tumbles out. There, in the sliver of time after I ask it and before Wes answers, I see another one of his faces. This one is pale, raw, and exposed. And then it's gone, replaced by a thinner version of his usual ease.

"You already know my name," he says stiffly.

"Cash said Wesley is your middle name, not your first."

"Well, aren't you and Cash just thick as thieves?" he says. There's a tightness in his voice. He's a good enough liar to hide discomfort, so the fact that he's letting a fraction of it show makes me wonder if he wants me to see. He strides away across the gym, and I rush to follow.

"And for the record," he says without looking back, "it's still real."

"What?"

"My name. Just because it's not my first doesn't mean it's not real."

"Okay," I say, trying to keep up, "it's real. I just want to know your *full* name."

"Why?" he snaps.

"Because sometimes I don't feel like I know the full *you*," I say, grabbing his sleeve. I drag him to a stop. His eyes are bright, reflecting specks of mottled brown and green and gold. "The other girls here might think your air of mystery is cute, but I know what you're doing—showing everybody different pieces and keeping the whole secret. And I thought . . ." I trail off. *I thought if you could be honest with anyone, it would be me.* It's what I want to say, but I bite back the words.

Wesley squints at me a little. "You're one to talk about secrets, Mackenzie Bishop," he says. But the words are playful. He turns to face me and surprises me by bringing his hands to rest firmly on my shoulders. My head fills with the cluttered music of his noise.

"You want to know my full name?" he asks softly. I nod. He brings his forehead to rest against mine and talks into the small window of space between our lips. "When Crew are paired up," he says, his voice easy and low over the sound of his noise, "there's a ceremony. That's when they have their Archive marks carved into their skin. Three lines. One made by their own hand. One made by their partner. One made by the Archive." His eyes look down into mine. His words are little more than a breath between us. "The Crew make their scars and take their vows to the Archive and to each other. The vows start and end with their names. So," he whispers, "when we become Crew, I'll tell you mine."

And then the bell echoes through the gym, and he smiles and pulls away. "About time," he says cheerfully, heading for the locker rooms. "I'm starving."

Da won't talk about his Crew partner.

He once said he'd tell me anything if I asked the right question, but somehow I never ask the right one to get him to tell me about Meg. He doesn't even tell me her name; I learn it later, after he's gone and I'm packing up his things.

They all fit into one box.

There's a leather jacket, a wallet, a few letters—to Dad, mostly (and one to Patty, my grandmother, who left him before I was born). There are only three photos in with the letters (Da was never very sentimental). The first one is of him as a young man, leaning up against an iron fence, looking lean and strong and a little arrogant—really the only difference between young Da and old Da is the number of wrinkles on his face.

The second one is of him with Mom and Dad and me and Ben.

And the third one is of him with Meg.

They stand close, shoulder to shoulder but for a small gap, Da tilting his head slightly toward hers. His sleeves are rolled down, but hers are rolled up, and I can see, even in the faded photo, the three parallel scars of the Archive carved into her forearm. It's a mirror image of the one etched into Da's skin, the two of them bonded by scars and oaths and secrets.

Neither one of them is smiling in the photo, but they both look like they're about to, and all I can think is that they fit. It's not just the way their bodies nest, even without touching. It's the knowing way they share the space, sensing where the other ends. It's their mirrored almost-smiles, the closest I have ever seen Da to happy. I know so little of this woman, of Da's days as Crew—only that he left. He told me he wanted to live long enough to train me himself (what would have happened if he'd died first? Would someone else have come?), but seeing him—this strange, vibrant, happier version of my grandfather—it hurts to think he gave her up for me.

"Do you think they were in love?" I ask Roland, showing him the photo.

He frowns, running a thumb over the worn edges.

"Love is simple, Miss Bishop. Crew isn't." His eyes are proud and sad at the same time, and I remember that underneath the sleeves of his sweater, he bears the scars as well. Three even lines.

"How so?" I press.

"Love breaks," he says. "The bond between Crew doesn't. It has love in it, though, and transparency. Being Crew with someone means being exposed, letting them read you—your hopes and wants and thoughts and fears. It means trusting them so much that you're not only willing to put your life in their hands, but to take their life into yours. It's a heavy burden to bear," he says, handing the picture back, "but Crew is worth it."

ELEVEN

I **TAKE A LONG,** cold shower.

Wesley's touch lingers on my skin. His music echoes through my head. I remind myself as I scrub my skin that we are both liars and con artists. That we will always have secrets, some that bind us and some that cut between us, slicing us into pieces. That we will never see each other whole . . . until we become Crew. But I don't know if I want to be Crew with Wesley. I don't know if I'm willing to let him see all the pieces.

I try to put his promise from my mind. It doesn't matter right now. A world stands between me and Crew: a world of nightmares and trauma and *Agatha*. How do I tell Wesley that I might not make it to the ceremony, let alone the naming? Crew are selected. They are assessed. They are found fit.

If Agatha got her hands on my mind right now, I would never be found fit. Which means I need to keep her from getting her hands on me until I find a way to fix whatever's happening.

I have to hope there is a way to fix it.

A way that doesn't involve letting the Archive inside my head to cut out memories. If I let them in, they'll see the damage Owen did. The damage he continues to do.

I snap the water off and begin to get dressed. The lockers have emptied out by now, but as I slip the key back over my head, shivering a little when the metal comes to rest against my sternum,

Safia rounds the corner, focused on the braid she's weaving with her hair. Until she sees me. Her eyes narrow even more than usual.

"What's that?" she asks as I pull my shirt on over the key.

"A key," I say as casually as I can.

"Obviously," she says, finishing her braid and crossing her arms. "Did he give that to you?"

I frown. "Who?"

"Wesley." Her voice tightens a fraction when she says his name. "Is it his?"

My hand goes to the metal through my shirt. I could say yes. "No."

"They look the same," she presses.

They don't, actually. Wesley's is darker and made of a different metal. "It's just a stupid trinket," I say. "A good luck charm." I hold her gaze, waiting to see if she buys it. She doesn't seem convinced. "I read it in some book when I was a kid. This girl wore a key around her neck, and wherever she went, the doors all opened for her. Maybe Wesley read the same book. Or maybe he kept losing his keys so he put them around his neck. Ask him yourself," I say, because I can tell she won't.

Safia shrugs. "Whatever," she says, tugging on one of her earrings. They look like real gold. "If you guys want to wear ratty old keys, that's your choice. Try not to get tetanus." With that, she turns and strolls out.

My stomach growls, and I'm about to follow her when a sliver of metal catches my eye from beneath the bench. I kneel down and find a necklace: a round silver pendant on a simple chain. The pendant has been rubbed so much that the ornate *B* etched into its front is barely visible. I weigh it in my palm, knowing I should just leave it and hope whoever it belongs to comes looking for it. It's not my problem. But the level of wear on the pendant suggests that it's important to someone. It also means there's a good chance a memory or two has been worn in to it. Object memories are fickle—the smaller the object, the harder for memories to stick—but they're usually imprinted by either repetition or strong emotion, and this kind of token sees a fair amount of both. It can't hurt to look.

I glance around the locker room, making sure I'm alone before I pocket my ring. Instantly, the air in the room changes—doesn't thicken or thin, exactly, but shifts—my senses sharpening without the metal buffer. Curling my fingers over the pendant, I can feel the subtle hum of memories tickling my palm, and I close my eyes and reach—not with my skin, but with the thing beneath it. My hand goes numb as I catch hold of the thread, and the darkness behind my eyes dissolves into light and shadow and, finally, into memory.

A girl—tall, thin, blond, classically pretty—sits in a parked car in the dark, face wet from crying, with one hand wrapped, knuckles tight, on the wheel and the other clutching the pendant at her throat. As I roll time back, the memory skips from the car to a marble kitchen counter. This time, the girl is on one side of the counter clutching her pendant, and a woman old enough to be her mother is on the other, gripping a wineglass. I let the memory roll forward, and a moment later the girl shouts something—her words nothing more than static—and the woman pitches the wineglass at the girl's head. The girl cuts to the side and the glass strikes the cabinet behind her and shatters, and I swear I can feel the anger and the hurt and the sadness worn into the surface of the pendant.

I'm about to rewind further when the sharp slam of the locker room door causes me to drop the thread. I blink, pulling myself out of the past just as Amber rounds the corner. I frown and straighten, slipping the necklace into my shirt pocket and sliding my ring back on as she says, "There you are! We were beginning to wonder if you'd snuck out a back door."

And before I can ask who *we* is, she leads me out into the lobby, where Wes and Cash and Gavin are waiting.

"I'm sorry," I say. "I didn't realize anyone was waiting for me."

"Wouldn't be much of an ambassador——" starts Cash, but Wes cuts in.

"Thought you should probably know where they keep the food."

"The pizza yesterday was my treat," adds Amber. "First day tradition. But the rest of the time we have to make do."

Gavin chuckles, and a few minutes later, once they've ushered me across the lawn to the cafeteria—or the dining hall, as Hyde prefers to call it—I understand why.

"Make do"? Hyde has one of the most extensive kitchens I've ever seen. Five stations, each with a course—each course with a regular, healthy, vegetarian, and vegan option. Appetizer through dessert, and a station dedicated to drinks. The only major failing, I realize as another yawn escapes, is the lack of soda. The lack, in fact, of *anything* caffeinated. My body's beginning to slow, and as I load up my tray I can only hope there's some kind of black market caffeine business happening on campus. I ask Cash as much while we're waiting to check out.

"Alas," he says, "Hyde School is *technically* caffeine-free."

"What about the coffees you brought yesterday?"

"Swiped them from the teacher's lounge. Don't tell."

Looks like I'm on my own. It's not so bad, I tell myself. I'll be fine. I just need to eat something. And eating helps, for a little while, but half an hour later, when our trays are stacked on the Alchemist's outstretched arms and I'm wading through a chapter of precalc, Owen's voice begins to whisper in my head. It *hums*. The song reaches up from the back of my mind, out of my nightmares and into my day, wrapping its arms around me in an effort to drag me down into the dark. I close my eyes to clear it, but my head feels heavy, Owen's voice twisting the melody into words and—

"Is that today's homework?"

My head snaps up, and I find Gavin taking a seat on the step above me. I look down at the open math book in my lap and nod.

"I take it that's not," I say, gesturing to the book in his hands.

He shrugs. "You learn to work ahead here whenever you can. Because at some point, you'll invariably fall behind."

I hold up my own work. "Does that point usually come in the first week?"

He laughs. It's a quiet, gentle laugh, not much more than an exhale, but it brightens his face. He pushes the glasses up his nose, and my chest tightens when I see a set of numbers drawn in Sharpie on the back of his hand. It's such a stupid little thing, but it makes me think of Ben. Ben who drew a stick figure on my hand when I dropped him off at the corner near his school the day he died, who let me draw a stick-figure me on his hand to match before I let him go.

So many students make notes on their skin; so few of them look like my brother. "Mackenzie," says Gavin, articulating each syllable.

"Yeah?"

"It's not a big deal or anything, but you're kind of staring at me."

My gaze drops down to my work. "Sorry. You just remind me of someone."

He cracks open his book and takes the pen from behind his ear. "Well, I hope it's someone nice."

Ben takes shape behind my eyes—not the way he was before he died, but the way he was the night I brought him back, the night Carmen opened his drawer and I woke him from his sleep. I see his warm brown eyes turning black as he slips, see him shoving me away with the strength not of a boy, but of a History. I see him crumple to the floor, a gold Archive key gleaming from his back, before Roland returns his small body to its shelf. I see the drawer closing and me on my knees, begging Roland to stop, but it's too late, and the bright red Restricted bar paints itself across the drawer's face before the wall of the Archive swallows my brother.

The math problems on the page blur a little. Fatigue is catching up with me, weakening my walls. Everything is beginning to ache.

"Mackenzie?" presses Gavin softly. "Is it someone nice?"

And I somehow manage to smile and nod. "Yeah," I say softly. "It is."

I can't breathe.

Owen's hand is a vise around my throat.

"Hold still," he says. "You're making it worse."

He's pinning me to the cold ground, one knee on my chest, the other digging into my bad wrist. I'm trying to fight back, but it doesn't help. It never helps. Not here, not like this, when he's taking his time.

And he is. He's carving lines across my body. Ankles to knees, knees to hips, hips to shoulders, shoulders to elbows, elbows to wrists.

"There," he says, dragging the knife from my elbow down to my wrist. "Now we can see your seams." If I could breathe, I would scream. My uniform is dark and wet with blood. It shows up red against the black fabric, like paint—splashed across my front, pooling beneath my body.

"Almost done," he says, lifting the blade to my throat.

And then someone scrapes her chair against the floor and I snap back to English.

Only a few minutes have passed—the teacher's attention is still on the essay she's reading aloud—but it was long enough that my hands are trembling and I can taste the blood in my mouth from biting down on my tongue.

At least I didn't scream, I think as I grip the desk and try to shake the last of the nightmare off. My heart is slamming in my chest. I know it's not real. Just my imagination—today the role of Mackenzie Bishop's fears will be played by the History who tried to kill her in a variety of ways. I still spend the rest of the day picturing Roland's room in the Archive—the daybed with the black blanket, the violin whispering from the wall, the promise of dreamless sleep—and digging my fingernails into my palms to stay awake.

By the time school lets out, there are red crescents across both palms, and I shove through the doors of the building and onto the path, gasping for air. I close my eyes and take a few deep breaths. I feel like I'm cracking. Everything aches, the pain drawing itself into phantom lines.

Ankles to knees, knees to hips, hips to shoulders, shoulders to elbows, elbows to wrists.

"Hey, Mac!"

I open my eyes to find Wesley a little ways down the path, a sports bag slung over his shoulder. I must not be hiding the frayed nerves well enough, because he frowns. Cash is only a few strides behind him, talking to another senior guy.

"All good?" asks Wes as casually as possible.

"All good," I call back.

Cash and the other guy catch up. They're both carrying sports bags.

"Hey, Mac," Cash says, shifting the bag on his shoulder. "Think you can find your way without me?"

"I think I can manage," I reply. "The parking lot is that way, right?" I point in the opposite direction of the lot. Cash laughs. Wesley's eyes are still hovering on me. I flash him a smile, Cash knocks his shoulder, and the three head off toward the fields.

I take a last, steadying breath and head through campus to the front gate and the bike rack. I unlock Dante and swing my leg over the bike, and I'm just about to head home when I see a girl in the lot.

I recognize her. It's the girl from the pendant I found in the locker room. The one who clutched a steering wheel in a driveway at night sobbing and dodged the glass her mother threw at her head.

She's a senior—gold stripes—and she's standing with a group of girls in the lot, leaning up against a convertible and smiling with perfect teeth. Every inch of her has that manicured look that so often comes with money, and it's hard to line this girl up with the one in the memories, even though I know they're the same. Finally she waves to the others and strides up onto the sidewalk, walking away from Hyde's campus.

Before I even realize it, I'm following her. Every step she takes away from Hyde seems to weigh her down, changing her a fraction from the girl in the lot to the girl in the memories. I remember the anger and sadness worn into the pendant, and I will myself to call out. She turns around.

"Sorry," I say, pedaling up to her, "this is going to sound really random, but is this yours?"

I pull the necklace from my pocket and hold it up. Her eyes widen and she nods.

"Where did you find it?" she asks, reaching out.

"The locker room," I say, dropping the silver piece into her palm.

Her perfectly plucked eyebrows draw together. "How did you know it was mine?"

Because I read the memories, I think, *and you keep bringing your hand to the place where it should be.*

"Been asking around all afternoon," I lie. "One of the seniors in the lot just now said they thought it was yours and pointed me in this direction."

She looks down at the pendant. "Thanks. You didn't have to do that."

"It wasn't a problem," I say. "It seemed like something someone would miss." The girl nods, staring down at the metal. "What's the *B* stand for?"

"Bethany," she says. "I really shouldn't care so much about it," she adds. "It's just a piece of junk. Worthless, really." But her thumb is already there again, wearing away the front.

"If it matters to you, then it's not worthless."

She nods and rubs the pendant absently, and we stand there a moment, awkward and alone on the sidewalk, before I finally say, "Hey . . . is everything okay?"

She stiffens and stands straighter. I can see her mentally adjusting her mask.

"Of course." She flashes me a perfect, practiced smile.

Smiling is the worst thing you can do if you want the world to think you're okay when you're not. Some people can't help it——it's like a tic, a tell——and others do it on purpose, thinking people will buy whatever they're selling if it comes with a flash of teeth. But the truth is, smiling only makes a lie harder to pass off. It's like a giant crack in the front of a mask. But I don't know Bethany, not really, and she doesn't know what I saw. And since she's doing a pretty decent impression of a healthy person——much better than mine——I say, "Okay. Just checking."

I'm about to pedal off when she says, "Wait. I've never seen you at Hyde."

"New student," I tell her. "Mackenzie Bishop."

Bethany chews her lip, and I can imagine her mom yelling at her for such a nasty habit.

"Welcome to Hyde," she says, "and thanks again, Mackenzie. You're right about the necklace, you know. It's not worthless. I'm really glad you found it."

"So am I," I say. I feel like I should say something else, something *more*, but I can't, not without sounding trite or creepy, so I just say, "See you tomorrow?"

"Yeah," she says, "see you."

We head our separate ways. When I reach the main road, I think for a second I see the golden man standing at the corner, but by the time I cross the street and steal a glance back, there's no one there.

I'm just parking Dante in front of the Coronado when I feel the scratch of letters in my pocket and find a new name on my list, but I don't get the chance to hunt it down, because Mom heads me off in the lobby.

"Oh, good, you're home," she says, which is never a good opening line, because it means she needs something. Considering she's got a bakery box, a slip of paper, and a frazzled look, I'd say it's a guarantee.

"I am," I say cautiously. "What's up?"

"Last-minute delivery," she says.

My bones groan in response. "Where's Berk?"

She blows a stray chunk of hair out of her eyes. "He's got some kind of art opening, and he already left. I know you've got homework and I wouldn't normally ask, but with the business being so new, I really need every order I can get and . . ."

A headache is starting to form behind my eyes, but the way I see it, anything that convinces Mom I am *okay* and *normal* and a *good daughter* is worth it. I take the box and the slip of paper from her hands, and she responds in the worst way possible. She throws her arms around my neck, engulfing me in a hug full of breaking glass and twisting metal and boxes of plates being pushed down stairs and all the other piercing sounds that make up her noise. My headache instantly gets worse.

"I'd better get going," I say, pulling away.

Mom nods and bounces back toward the coffee shop, and I drag myself back toward Dante, reading over the slip of paper. Beneath the order name, Mom has drawn a rudimentary map. The delivery is only a few miles away, if her chicken scratch can be trusted, but I've never been to that part of the city before.

For the first time in ages, I get lost.

I zone out a little while riding and end up overshooting the apartment complex by several blocks, and I'm forced to double back. By the time I've found the right building, climbed several flights of stairs—the elevator is broken—dropped off the bakery box to a housewife, and gotten back to my bike, the sun is sinking. My whole body is starting to ache from fatigue.

I swing my leg over the bike and hope Mom's on the phone with Colleen right this moment, telling her how *okay* I am.

But as I speed toward the Coronado, I don't feel very okay. My hands are shaking and I just want to get home and through tonight and back to Roland's room, so I take a shortcut through a park. I don't know the park, but if the map in my head is even close to correct, it'll be faster than the streets.

It *is* faster, until I see a guy crouching in the middle of the path and have to hit the brakes hard to keep from slamming into him. I nearly lose my balance as the bike comes to a jarring stop a few feet in front of him.

The moment I put my foot on the ground, I know I've made a mistake. Something moves behind me, but I don't dare take my eyes off the guy in front of me as he straightens and pulls one hand from the pocket of his hoodie. I hear a metal *snick* sound, and a switchblade flashes in his fingers.

"Hey there, pretty thing," he coos.

I bring my foot back to the pedal, but it doesn't move; I twist in my seat to find a second guy with a pipe threaded through my back wheel, pinning it still. His breath smells like oil.

"Let go," I say, using the tone Da taught me to use with difficult Histories. But these aren't Histories, they're humans—and they're both armed.

One of them chuckles. The other one whistles.

"Why don't you come off that toy and play with us instead?" says the one with the knife. He saunters forward, and the one

. holding the wheel reaches for my hair. I'm at enough of a disadvantage without straddling a bike, so I dismount.

"See?" says the one with the pipe. "She *wants* to play."

"There's a good girl," coos the one with the knife.

"Good *school*girl," chimes the other.

My pulse is starting to race.

. . . residual trauma and extreme fatigue, paired with the influx of adrenaline . . .

"Get out of my way," I say.

The one with the knife wiggles the blade back and forth like a finger, tsk-tsking.

"You should ask nicely. In fact," he says, taking another step forward, "maybe you should beg."

"Get out of my way, *please*," I growl, my pulse thudding in my ears.

The one with the pipe chuckles behind me.

The one with the knife smiles.

They keep shifting so I can only see one of them at a time. When I try to cheat a step to the side, the pipe appears, barring my path.

"Where you going, sweetheart?" says the one with the knife. "The fun hasn't even started yet."

They're both closing in.

My head is pounding and my vision is starting to blur, and then the one with the pipe shoves me forward into the one with the knife, and he grabs my bad wrist *hard*, and the pain shoots through me like a current—and then it happens.

The world stops.

Vanishes.

Goes black.

A long, lovely, silent moment of black.

And then it comes back, and I'm standing there in the park, just like before, and my head is killing me and my hands feel damp, and when I look down at them, I see why.

They're covered in blood.

TWELVE

THE MAN with the knife is lying at my feet.

His nose is broken. Blood is gushing down his face, and one of his legs looks like it's bent at the wrong angle. His switchblade is jutting out of his thigh. I don't remember stabbing him or even touching him, but my hands say I did. My knuckles are torn up, and I have a shallow cut on one palm—probably from the switchblade. At first, I'm only aware of how numb I feel and how slowly time is moving. And then it slams into me, along with the pain radiating across my hands and through my head. *What have I done?* I close my eyes and take a few steadying breaths, hoping the body will just disappear—this will all just disappear—but it doesn't, and this time the breathing doesn't help me remember. There's just more panic and a wall of black.

And then I hear sounds of a struggle and remember the guy with the metal pipe, and I turn to see him being strangled by the golden man.

The golden man is standing there with his arm calmly wrapped around the thug's throat, pulling back and up until his shoes skim the ground. The thug is flailing silently, swinging his arms—the pipe is lying on the path a few feet away—as he runs out of breath. As the golden man tightens his grip, his sleeve slides up and I can see three lines cut into his skin.

Crew marks.

I was right. . . . Oh, god, I was *right.* And that means a member of Crew just saw me do . . . this. I don't even know what I did, but he saw it. Then again, he's currently strangling someone in front of me. But I bet he at least remembers doing it.

The thug stops struggling, and the golden man lets his body fall to the ground.

"I hate fighting humans," he says, brushing off his pants. "You have to work so hard not to kill them."

"Who are you?" I ask.

His brow crinkles. "What, not even a *thanks?*"

"Thanks," I say shakily.

"Welcome. Wouldn't be much of a gentleman if I didn't lend a hand." His eyes drift down to the man at my feet. "Not sure you needed it, though. That was quite a show." *Was it?* He reaches out. "Let me see those hands."

His fingers nearly brush my skin when I jerk away. He's not wearing a ring.

"Ah," he says, reading my distrust. He produces a silver band from his pocket, holding it up so I can see the three lines etched on its surface before he slides it on. This time when he holds out his hands, I reluctantly give him mine. His noise is low and steady as a heartbeat through my head.

"How did you know?" he asks, turning over my hands to check for broken bones.

"Posture. Attention. Ego."

He smiles that half smile. "And here I figured you just saw the marks." He runs his thumbs over my knuckles. "Or, you know, there's the fact that we've met."

I wince as he traces the bones in my hands.

"In your defense," he adds, "we weren't formally introduced."

And suddenly it clicks. When Wesley and I were summoned to the Archive last month to explain how we'd allowed a teenage History to escape into the Coronado, the golden man was there. He came in late and flashed me a lazy smile. When he heard how long Wesley and I had been paired up before we let the History escape—three hours—he actually *laughed*. The woman with him didn't.

"I recognized you," I lie.

"No you didn't," he says simply, testing my fingers. "You thought I looked familiar, but there's a big difference between knowing a face and placing it. Stare at anyone long enough and you'll start to think you've seen them before. The name's Eric, by the way." He lets go of my hands. "And nothing's broken."

"Why have you been following me?"

He arches a brow. "Just be glad I was."

"That's not a good enough answer," I snap. "Why have you been following me?"

Again, that lazy smile. "Why does anyone do anything for the Archive? Because they're told to."

"But why?" I press. "And who told you to?"

"Miss Bishop, I don't think now's the time for an interrogation," he says, gesturing to the bodies and then back to me. I look down again at my blood-covered hands. They're shaking, so I curl them into fists, even though it sends sparks of pain across my skin.

"I want an answer."

Eric shrugs. "Even if it's a lie?"

The man with the knife in his leg begins to stir.

"You should go home now," says Eric, fetching the piece of pipe and wiping the prints with his sleeve before tossing it back to the ground. "I'll take care of these two."

"What are you going to do with them?"

He shrugs. "Make them disappear." He rights my bike and walks it toward me.

"Go," he says. "And be careful."

My hands are still shaking as I wipe them on my shirt, mount the bike, and leave.

On the way home, as my body calms and my mind clears, the memories begin to trickle back in flashes of color and sound.

The crack of bone as my free palm came up under his nose.

The cry and the cursing and the blind slashing of the switchblade.

The snap of his knee as my shoe slammed into the side of it.

The silent moment when the switchblade tumbled from his hand into mine.

The scream as I drove it down into his thigh.

The crunch of my fist across his face as he crumbled forward. Again. And again.

Seconds, I marvel. It took only seconds to break so many things.

And even though I couldn't remember at first, I'm not sorry I did it. Not even a little. I *wanted* to hurt him. I wanted to make him regret the way he looked at me, like I wouldn't be able to fight back, like I was weak. I look down at my raw knuckles as I ride. I'm not weak anymore . . . but what am I becoming instead?

"What happened to your hands?" shrieks Mom when I walk into the apartment. She has her phone to her ear and she says a hurried "We'll talk later" to whoever's on the other end before hanging up and rushing over.

"Biking accident," I say tiredly, shrugging off my bag. It's not a total lie, and I'm not about to tell her that I got assaulted on the way back from *her* delivery. She'd implode.

"Are you all right?" she asks, taking my arm. I wince, less from my wounded hands than the sudden high-pitched crackle that comes with her touch. Still, I manage not to pull free as she guides me into the kitchen.

"I'm fine," I lie, holding my hands under the sink while she pours cool water over them. I managed to wipe off most of the blood, but the knuckles are red and raw. "You're home early," I say, changing the subject. "Slow day at the coffee shop?"

Mom gives me a quizzical look. "Mackenzie," she says, "it's nearly seven o'clock."

My eyes drift to the windows. It's halfway to dark. "Huh."

"You were late, and I started to get worried. Now I see I had a good reason to be."

"I'm fine, really."

She cuts off the water and sets to towel-drying my hands, tutting as she unearths a bottle of rubbing alcohol from beneath the sink. It feels nice—not the rubbing alcohol, that hurts like hell, but having Mom patch me up. When I was little, I came home with all kinds of scrapes—the products of more normal childhood escapades, of course—and I'd sit on the counter and let Mom fix them. Whatever it was, she could fix it. After I became a Keeper and started hiding my wounds instead of proudly presenting them, I'd watch her fix Ben, the same worshipping expression in his eyes as she tended to his battle scars.

These days, I'm so used to hiding my cuts and bruises—so used to telling Mom I don't need her and telling her I'm fine when I'm not—that it's a relief not being able to hide an injury. Even if I have to lie about how it happened.

Then Dad walks in.

"What happened?" he asks, dropping his briefcase. It's almost funny, in a sick way, their level of concern over a few cut knuckles. I hate to think how they'd react if they could see some of my larger scars, what they'd say if they knew the truth behind my broken wrist. I nearly laugh before I remember that it's not *that* kind of funny.

"Biking accident," I repeat. "I'm fine."

"And the bike?" he asks.

"The bike's fine, too."

"I'd better check it out," he says, turning toward the door.

"Dad, I said it's fine."

"No offense, Mac, but you don't know much about bikes, and—"

"Leave it," I snap, and Mom looks up from her first aid kit long enough to give me a warning look. I close my eyes and swallow. "The paint might be nicked in a couple places"—I had the sense to scuff it up on the sidewalk—"but it'll live to ride another day. I took the worst of it," I say, displaying my hands.

For once, Dad's not having it. He crosses his arms. "Explain to me the physics of this biking accident."

And doubt, Da said, *is like a current you have to swim against.*

"Peter," starts Mom, but he puts up a hand to stop her.

"I want to know exactly how it happened."

My heart is pounding as I hold his gaze. "The sidewalk was cracked," I say, fighting to keep my voice steady. "The front wheel of the bike caught. I threw my hands out when I went down, but rolled and caught the street with my knuckles instead of my palms. Now, if the Inquisition and the infirmary are both done," I finish, pulling free of Mom and pushing past Dad, "I have homework."

I storm down the hall and into my room, slamming the door

for good measure before slumping against it as the last of the fight goes out of me. It feels like a poor take on a teen tantrum, but apparently it works.

Neither one of them bothers me the rest of the night.

Roland frowns. "What happened to your hands?"

He's waiting in the atrium, perched on the edge of a table with his folder in his lap. When I walk up, his eyes go straight to my knuckles.

"Biking accident," I say automatically.

Something flashes in his eyes. Disappointment. Roland pushes off the table. "I'm not your parents, Miss Bishop," he says, crossing the room. "Don't insult me by lying."

"Sorry," I say, following him out of the atrium and down the hall toward the Librarians' quarters. "There was an incident."

He glances back over his shoulder. "With a History?"

"No. A human."

"What kind of incident?"

"The kind that's taken care of." I consider telling Roland about Eric, but when I form the words in my head—*someone in the Archive is having me followed*—they make me sound cracked. Paranoid. The worry's already showing in Roland's eyes. The last thing I want is to make it worse. Plus, I can't prove anything, not without letting Roland into my head, and if I do that, if he sees the state I'm in, he'll . . . No, I won't rat out Eric, not until I know what he was doing there or why he's been following me.

"Did our lovely new doormen see your hands?"

"The sentinels? No." Patrick did, though. He didn't say anything, just looked at me like I was that useless kid again. *Bloody nose or bloody knuckles, can't hold her own.* If only he knew how the other guy looked.

"Was it another tunnel moment?" asks Roland.

I look down at my hands. "I remember what happened."

We walk the rest of the way to his room in silence. He lets me in, and I see him pull his watch from his pocket and run his thumb over the surface once before setting it on top of the table. Something tugs at me. It's the same set of motions he did last night. The exact same set. It's so hard to think of Roland as a History, but the repetition reminds me that his appearance isn't the only static thing about him.

He gestures to the daybed, and I sink gratefully onto the soft surface, my body begging for rest.

"Sleep well," he says, folding into his chair. I close my eyes and listen to the sound of him making notes, the scratch of letters on paper low and comforting, like rain. I feel myself sinking, and there's a moment—one brief, terrifying moment—where I remember the nightmares that wait. But then the moment is gone and I'm drawn down into sleep.

The next thing I feel is Roland shaking me awake.

I sit up, stiff from the fight and from sleep. I study the fresh bruises that color my hands as Roland moves about the room. The relief at having slept is dampened by dread as I think of the slice of conversation I overheard beyond the door.

It's not a permanent solution.

Roland's right. I cannot keep doing this. I cannot come here every night. But it's the only place the nightmares don't follow me.

"Roland," I say softly. "If it keeps getting worse . . . if *I* keep getting worse . . . will Agatha . . . ?"

"As long as you keep doing your job," he says, "she can't hurt you."

"I want to believe you."

"Miss Bishop, Agatha's job is to *assess* members of the Archive. Her greatest concern is making sure that things run smoothly, that everyone is doing his job. She is not the bogeyman. She cannot just sweep down and snatch you up and take your mind away. Even though she'd like you to think that."

"But last time——"

"Last time you confessed to involvement in a *crime*, so yes, your future was left to her discretion. This is different. She cannot even look inside your mind without permission, let alone take your memories."

"Consent. How forward-thinking." But something eats at me. "Did Wesley give permission?"

Roland's brow crinkles. "What?"

"That day . . ." We both know which day I'm talking about. "He doesn't remember it. Any of it." Did he want to forget? Or was he made to? "Did he give the Archive permission to take those memories?"

Roland seems surprised to hear this. "Mr. Ayers was in very bad shape," he says. "I doubt he was conscious."

"So he couldn't give permission."

"That would have broken protocol." Roland hesitates. "Maybe it wasn't the Archive's doing, Miss Bishop. You know more than most what trauma does to the mind. Maybe he does remember. Or maybe he's chosen to forget."

I cringe. "Maybe."

"Mackenzie, the Archive has rules, and they are followed."

"So as long as I don't grant Agatha permission, I'm supposedly safe? My mind is my own?"

"For the most part," says Roland, perching on the edge of his chair. "As with any system, there are ways around and through. You're not the only one who can *grant* permission. If you denied Agatha access to your mind and she had good reason to believe it harbored guilt, she could petition the board of directors. She wouldn't do it, not unless she had a strong case—evidence that you had committed a crime or that you could no longer perform your job or be trusted with the things you know—but if she had one . . ." He trails off.

"If she had a strong case . . ." I prompt.

"We mustn't let it come to that," says Roland. "Every time the board has granted her access to someone's mind, they've been found unfit and been removed from service. Her record means she won't make the request lightly, but it also means the board will never deny her if she does. And once she has access to your mind—through your permission or theirs—anything she finds there can be used against you. If she found you unfit, you would be sentenced to alteration."

"*Execution.*"

Roland cringes, but doesn't contradict me. "I would challenge the ruling, and there would be a trial, but if the board stands behind her, there is nothing I can do. It is very literally in the directors' hands. You see, only they are authorized to carry out alterations."

Da only told me one thing about the board of directors, and that's that you never want to meet one of them. Now I understand why.

Roland frowns, deep in thought. "But it will not come to that," he adds. "Agatha is the one who pardoned you in the first place. I doubt she's looking for reasons to reverse that decision."

I think of Eric following me. *Someone* told him to. "Maybe Agatha's not," I say, "but what if someone else is? Someone who disagreed with her ruling? Like Patrick. Would he go this far? And if someone handed her a case, would she overlook it?"

"Miss Bishop," says Roland. "These are not the thoughts to be filling your head with right now. Don't give her a reason to question her ruling. Just do your job and stay out of trouble, and you'll be okay."

His words are calm, but his voice is laced with cracks and his brow is furrowed.

"Besides," he adds softly, crossing to the side table to fetch his watch, "I promised your grandfather I would look after you." He slides the silver watch into his pocket. "That's a promise I intend to keep."

As I follow him out the door and through the twisting, turning halls, I can't help but remember that he made a promise to the Archive, too, the day of my initiation.

If we do this, and she proves herself unfit in any way, said a member of the panel, *she will forfeit the position.*

And if she proves unfit, said another, *you, Roland, will remove her yourself.*

THIRTEEN

ROLAND LEAVES ME at the mouth of the antechamber. I nod at the Librarian behind the desk—we've only met in passing—but she doesn't even look up from the ledger, and again I find myself thinking that the book is very large and I am only one page. How many of those pages belong to Keepers? How many to Crew? And why have I never seen any of them in the Archive? I grew up here. Did no one else? Am I really so different? Is that why Patrick hates me?

The eyes of the sentinels follow me out.

On my way home, I dispatch a name on my list with little pretense. The boy takes one look at my battered knuckles and shrinks away, but doesn't run, and I'd be lying if I didn't say that, for once, the fear in his eyes felt gratifying. It is so much easier to handle him with intimidation than by spinning tales and earning trust.

I roll the stiffness from my shoulders as I return home and shower. I'm out and pulling on my uniform when there's a knock on my bedroom door, and Dad calls out, "You better hurry up or we're going to be late."

I finish tugging on my shirt and nearly forget to tuck the key under my collar before opening the door. "What are you talking about?"

Dad flashes his keys. "I'm driving you to school."

"No, you're not."

"I don't mind," he says.

"I do."

He sighs and heads for the kitchen to fill his travel mug with coffee. "I thought you might be nervous about riding your bike."

"Well, I'm not." I frown and follow. "And isn't there a saying about horses and getting back on?"

"Well, yes, but——"

"I'll be *fine*," I say, swinging my bag over my shoulder. His eyes go to my knuckles.

"And you're sure the bike's in working shape?"

"The bike is fine, too. But if you're so worried, why don't you come check it out?"

That seems to pacify him a little, and we head downstairs. I duck into the café and grab a coffee and a muffin while he looks over Dante. Bishop's is busy in the morning, and Mom doesn't even see me come or go. Berk passes me a to-go cup and a paper bag and shoos me away.

"Well, it looks all right," says Dad, brushing off his hands as I join him on the curb. "You sure you don't want a lift?"

"Positive," I say, swinging my leg easily up over the bike to show him how comfortable I feel. "See? Just like a horse."

Dad frowns. "Where's your helmet?"

"My what?" Dad's look turns positively icy, and I'm opening my mouth to say I don't need it when I realize that that's probably a bad line after last night; instead I tell him where it's been since the day he bought it for me. "Under my desk."

"Don't. Move." Dad vanishes back through the doors and I sigh and stand there, straddling the bike with my coffee balanced on the handlebars. I give the street a quick scan, but there's no sign of Eric. I don't know whether that makes me feel better or worse, now that I know he's real. I still don't know why he's been following me.

Maybe it's standard procedure. A checkup. Or maybe he's looking for evidence. Cracks.

Dad reappears and tosses me the helmet. I pluck it out of the air and snap it on. At least it's not pink or covered in flowers or anything.

"Happy now?" I ask. Dad nods, and I pedal off before he can decide the coffee on my handlebars is a safety hazard.

The morning's cool, and I breathe deeply and try to shake off Roland's worry and Dad's distrust as the world blurs past. I'm halfway to school when I round the corner and hop onto a stretch of sidewalk that lines a park, stretching ahead a couple of blocks to form a straight and empty path. In a moment of weakness—or cockiness, or fatigue, maybe—I let myself close my eyes. It's nothing more than a long blink, a second, two tops, but when I open them there's just enough time to see the runner cut out of the park and into my way, and not enough time to swerve.

The collision is a tangle of handles and wheels and limbs, and we both go down hard on the concrete. My head bounces off the sidewalk. The helmet absorbs the worst of it—I'm sure Dad would be thrilled—and I manage to free my leg from under the bike and get to my feet, pain burning through my sleeve and sweatpants. I decide not to look at the damage.

A few feet away, the runner is slower to recover. He gets to his hands and knees and pauses, checking himself before he stands all the way up. I hurry over and offer my hand since I'm the one who technically hit him, even though he's the one who came out of nowhere.

"Are you all right?" I ask. "Anything broken?"

"Nah, I'm okay," he says, getting to his feet. He's not very old—maybe twenty—and he's a little scuffed, but looks otherwise unscathed. Except for the fact that he's *covered* in my coffee.

He looks down and notices it for the first time.

"Huh," he says. "I smell better than I did before."

I groan. "I'm really sorry."

"I think it was my fault," he says, rolling his neck.

"I know it was," I say. "But I'm still sorry I hit you. You came out of nowhere."

He rubs his head. "I guess I got a little lost in the music," he says, gesturing to the earbuds hanging around his neck. He smiles, but seems a little unsteady on his feet.

"Are you sure you're okay?"

He nods cautiously. "Yeah, yeah, I think so. . . ."

"Do you know your name?"

His brow crinkles. "Jason. Do you know *your* name?"

"I didn't hit my head."

"Well, can *I* know your name?" he asks. I think he might be flirting with me.

"Mackenzie. Mackenzie Bishop." I hold up four fingers. "How many fingers do you see?"

"Seven." I'm about to tell him he needs a doctor when he says, "Kidding. Kidding. What happened to your hands, Mackenzie?"

"A bike accident," I say without thinking. "You shouldn't joke when people are trying to determine if you're okay."

"Wow, how many bike accidents have you been in this week?"

"Bad week," I tell him, righting Dante. The bike's a little bruised, but it'll work; I'm relieved, because if I'd broken it, I don't know what I would have told my parents. Not the truth. Even though it *is* the truth this time.

"You're pretty."

"You hit your head."

"That is true. But you're probably still pretty."

"Mm-hmm."

"Mackenzie Bishop," he says, sounding out every syllable. "Pretty name."

"Yeah." I drag my phone from my pocket to check the time. If I don't go, I'm going to be late. "Look, Jason, are you going to be okay?"

"I'm okay. But I feel like we should trade insurance info or something. Do they have that, for bike-body collisions? Do you have bike insurance? If you're getting into this many accidents maybe you should—"

"Do you have a phone?"

He looks at me like he doesn't know what that is. Or why I'm asking.

"A phone," I say again, "so I can give you my number. So you can text me when you get home. So I know you're okay."

He pats his pockets. "I don't run with it."

I shuffle through my backpack and dig out a Sharpie and a scrap of paper and write my number on it. "Here. Take it. Text me," I say, trying to make it as clear as possible that this is a here's-my-number-civic-duty and not a here's-my-number-call-me-hotstuff kind of situation.

Jason takes the piece of paper, and I'm about to get back on the bike when he plucks my phone from my hand and starts typing away. When he passes it back, I see he's programmed his number in with the title *Jason the runner you ran over*.

"Just to be safe," he says.

"Yeah, okay, sure," I reply, and before the moment can get any more awkward, I climb back on Dante—horses, falling off, getting back on, etc.—and pedal off. (I wish Eric could have witnessed my stellar Samaritan behavior and reported *that* back to the Archive, but of course *now* he's nowhere to be seen.) I look back once at the corner to make sure Jason is still standing (he is), and then I head to school.

By the time I get there, the lot is filling up and Wesley is leaning back against the bike rack. Another girl—a silver-striped one this time—is hanging off his shoulder, whispering in his ear. Whatever she's saying, it must be good; he's looking down, chewing his lip, and smiling. My chest constricts, even though it shouldn't because I shouldn't care. He can flirt if he wants to. I hop down from the bike and walk it over. His eyes drift lazily up to find mine, and he straightens.

The girl on his shoulder nearly falls off.

I can't help but grin. He says something, and her flirty little smile fades. By the time I reach the bike rack, she's vanished through the gates—but not before shooting a dark look my way.

"Hey, you," he says cheerfully.

"Hey," I say; then, because I can't help myself, I look around and add, "Where's Cash?"

The blow sticks, and Wesley's good humor thins. Then his eyes wander down to my hands, and it dissolves entirely. "What happened?"

I almost lie. I open my mouth to feed him the same line I've fed everyone else, but I stop. I have a rule about lying to Wesley. I don't do it anymore. I can justify evasions and omissions, but I won't lie outright—not after what happened this summer. But I'm also not going to relive last night here on the steps of Hyde, so I say, "It's a funny story. I'll tell you later."

"I'll hold you to it," he says, and then he looks past me. "There you are. Mackenzie here was beginning to worry."

461

I turn to find Cash striding up the curb, a set of car keys in one hand and a paper bag in the other.

"Morning, lovelies," he says, opening the bag and producing three coffees in a to-go tray. Wesley's eyes light up at the sight of the third drink. He reaches for it, but before his fingers touch the paper cup, Cash pulls it out of reach.

"You can't say I never do nice things for you."

"Statement retracted."

Cash offers me one of the coffees, and I take a long, savoring swallow, since I only got a taste of this morning's cup before I spilled it all over Jason the runner.

"Sorry for the delay," says Cash. "They kept getting the order wrong."

"How hard is it to make three black coffees?" asks Wes.

"Not hard at all," says Cash. "But the order was for two black coffees"—he takes the second coffee—"and a soy hot chocolate caramel whip." He turns the tray in his hand, offering Wesley the last, fancy drink.

Wes scowls.

Cash continues to hold out the tray. "If you're going to be a girl about these things, you're going to get a girly drink. Now be gracious."

"My hero," grumbles Wesley, reaching for the cup.

"And don't pretend you don't like it," adds Cash. "I distinctly remember you ordering it last winter."

"Lies."

Cash taps his temple. "Photographic memory."

Wesley mumbles something unkind into his soy hot chocolate.

The three of us linger at the gates of Hyde, sipping our drinks and watching the flow of students, enjoying the time before the bell rings. And then Cash breaks the peace with one small question, lobbed at Wes.

"Did you hear about Bethany?"

The coffee freezes in my throat. "The blond senior? What about her?"

Cash looks surprised by the fact I know who she is. "Her mom said she never came home yesterday. They haven't been able to find her anywhere." He looks at Wes. "You think she finally ran away?"

"I guess it's possible," he says. He looks upset.

"You okay?" asks Cash. "I know you two—"

"I'm fine," Wes cuts him off, even though I'd really like to hear the end of that sentence. "Just sorry to hear it," he adds.

"Yeah," adds Cash. "Though I can't say I'm surprised."

"Why's that?" I ask.

Behind my eyes, the memory from the pendant echoes: a distraught Bethany clutching the steering wheel, willing herself to go. But what happened? What led up to that moment?

Cash hesitates, then looks to Wes, who says only, "She was having a hard time at home."

And then, before any of us can say more, the bell rings, and we pour through the gates with the rest of the students. Cash and Wes branch off and the conversation dies, but the questions follow me to class. Did Bethany really run away? Why? And if she did, why did she wait until now? She had all summer. What was it about yesterday?

A darker thread runs through my thoughts.

First Mr. Phillip, and now Bethany.

They both have something in common. *Me.*

A sinking feeling follows me through the halls and into class.

Da said you had to see patterns but not go searching for them. Am I drawing lines where they shouldn't be, or am I missing something right in front of me?

No text from Jason.

I check my phone before Precalc and then again before Lit Theory. Finally, on my way to Wellness, I shoot him a message.

> Did you get home safe?

I try to calm my nerves as I shove my phone and my bag into my locker, aware that the noise in the room is different. It's still loud, still full of slamming metal and the shuffle of bodies and voices, but those voices aren't full of laughter. They're full of gossip, and gossip is the kind of thing told in fake whispers rather than shouts, lending the locker room a kind of false quiet.

I only catch snippets of the gossip itself, but I know who it's about.

Bethany.

Popular girl. Small school. The students are latching on to the story. A clump of juniors thinks she was kidnapped for ransom. Another thinks she ran away with a boy. A handful of seniors echo Wes and Cash, saying they're not surprised, after what happened— but they never say exactly what happened. Instead they trail off into silence. One junior thinks she got pregnant. Another thinks she's dead. A few talk under their breaths and shoot dirty looks at the girls who don't have the grace to gossip quietly.

Whatever the story, one thing's for sure: Bethany is missing.

"I don't think it's that simple," says Amber, turning the corner.

"You can't turn everything into a crime," says Safia, following on her heels. "It's morbid."

They slump down onto the bench beside me while I tug on my workout shirt, wishing it were long-sleeved so I could hide my cut-up knuckles. Instead I shove my hands into the pockets of my workout shorts.

"I'm just saying—there's evidence, and it contradicts."

"Admit it, you just want it to be more dramatic than it is."

"I'd say it's already dramatic enough. Bethany's life was like a bad soap opera."

"Ugh," says Safia, shuddering. "You just said *was*. Like she's dead. Don't do that."

"You're talking about that girl who ran away?" I ask as casually as possible.

Amber nods. "*If* she ran away."

I frown. "What makes you think she didn't?"

"Because that wouldn't be as exciting," says Safia, rolling her eyes.

Amber waves her away. "There's evidence that she was *going to* run away, I'll give you that. But there's also evidence that something happened. That she changed her mind."

"What do you mean?" I ask, closing my locker.

"Well, my dad told me that—"

"They got your dad involved? Already?"

"Not *officially*," says Amber. "But he knows Bethany's mom, so he agreed to look into it."

My chest tightens. Make that two things the cases have in common. Me. And the detective. *It's nothing,* I tell myself as I follow Amber and Safia into the gym. *It's nothing, because I didn't do anything. I was nice. I was helpful. I made two people's days better. And those two people just happened to disappear.*

"Anyway," says Amber, "Bethany's backpack and purse were missing, too. But the car was still there, and there was a suitcase tucked in the back, and the car door was open. Either she was grabbed, or she got halfway through leaving and then decided to just walk away instead."

She and Safia head for the mats, and even though I want to run—want to do something to clear my head and calm my nerves—I follow.

"Which would be smart," Amber is saying, "if she really wanted to disappear, since cars are so easy to track."

"Why is everyone convinced she wanted to disappear?" I ask, sinking down onto the mat. "People keep saying they're not surprised, that it was only a matter of time. What do they mean?"

Amber sighs. "Over the summer, my dad was called out to Bethany's house on a noise complaint. There'd been a screaming match, and when he got there, he found Bethany in the driveway with all her things."

"Back up," says Safia. "You're skipping all the good bits." She turns to me. "Okay, so Bethany's mom is a leech. That's what we call it when you only marry someone for their money. Then Beth's dad's company hits a bump or something, and her mom drops him like that." She snaps her fingers. "Takes as much as she can, including the house, and then turns around and finds this new beau to leech off of. He moves in after, like, three weeks."

"Girls," shouts one of the gym teachers. "More work, less chat."

"Stretching is an essential part of wellness!" Safia shouts back. She proceeds to exaggerate every one of her motions, which almost makes me smile.

"So," she continues, "sleazy dude has been there all of a week when he's home alone with Bethany and takes a go at her."

My stomach turns. "What happened?"

"She did what any self-respecting Hyde School girl would do. She punched him in the face. But when she tried to tell her mom what happened, she said it was *Bethany's* fault."

Behind my eyes the woman pitches the glass at Bethany's head.

"And the sleaze totally twisted it to fit," says Safia. "He claimed Bethany tried to seduce *him*. I'm surprised Bethany didn't leave that night. I know she thought about it."

"Dad reported it, but it was word against word. Nothing happened. *But* he told Bethany to call him if the jerk ever tried anything again. If she didn't feel safe."

"So your dad believed her."

Amber's forehead crinkles. "Of course. He's not an idiot. We all thought Bethany would bail, but she didn't. I guess I get it. She just had to get through this year, and then she'd be free." She shakes her head. "I don't know what happened. But it feels off. And why was that suitcase still in the back?"

Safia chews her lip. "Bethany told Wesley once that she kept a bag ready. In case she couldn't take it anymore. That when it got bad she'd sit out in the car, all ready to go. I heard him tell Cash. That still doesn't explain why she left it."

"Did Wes and Bethany have a thing?" I ask.

Safia arches a perfect eyebrow. "Why? Jealous?"

"I'm just trying to get on the same page."

"They had as much of a thing as Wesley has with anyone," says Amber. "Which is not much."

"He's a jerk and a tease," says Safia, even as her gaze wanders over to the track where he and a handful of other guys are running.

She gets to her feet. "Look, not that this hasn't been morbid, girl-bonding fun, but I've got to scout a date for Fall Fest so I don't die alone. Cheers, kids."

Safia bounces off across the gym. Amber watches her go. She looks as unsettled as I feel.

"You don't think she ran away."

Amber shakes her head. "I know it's really early to jump to conclusions, I just have a bad feeling."

"Is the sleazy guy a suspect?" I ask.

"He alibied out, but it's not like he hasn't bought his way out of trouble before. I just . . . I don't trust anything about this. Do you ever get that gut feeling that something's off?"

"All the time."

"Yeah, well, I have it now. And it's not the car abandoned in the driveway, or the fact her mom and Mr. Sleaze pretended to care she was gone," says Amber, pushing to her feet. "It's something else, and it's going to sound small, or stupid, but she had this neck-lace, and she always wore it."

My blood runs cold. "What about the necklace?"

"They found it on the driver's seat."

Lunch, and still no text from Jason.

I send him another message and lean back against the Alchemist statue in the Court. The rest of the group talks about Fall Fest next week and college applications and the Nazi gym teacher, but I can't stop thinking about Mr. Phillip and Bethany. Two people who went missing right after I saw them.

I grip my phone.

What if it's about to be three? What if it already is?

I try to clear the thought. It's ridiculous. This doesn't have any-thing to do with me. I didn't *know* these people. We crossed paths. People cross paths all the time. Bethany could have run away. Maybe something spooked her—a call from her mom, a passing car—and she gave up on the suitcase and the car and bolted on foot before she lost her nerve. It's easy enough to disappear if you have the money and the need.

But she wouldn't leave the necklace. She'd leave the house and the car and the life, but not the piece of silver. I know that just from holding it.

So if she didn't leave it, what happened? Another abduction?

"Waiting for a call?"

Wesley sits down beside me. I put the phone away.

"I'm sorry about Bethany."

"Me too," says Wes. "Did you two meet?"

"Once. Do you really think she ran away?"

"Do you think she didn't?"

I take a deep breath. "It's just . . . it's the second time this week someone's gone missing."

"It's a city, Mac. Bad things happen."

"Yeah, I know," I say softly. "But these two bad things have something in common."

"What's that?"

"Me." I look down at my hands. "I think I was the last person to see them. Both of them."

He frowns, and I explain about Mr. Phillip and the cookies, and about Bethany and the necklace. And then I dig out my phone and tell him about the runner this morning.

"So you meet these people, and then they just, what? Vanish? Why? How?"

"I don't *know*. But this is a bad case of coincidence, Wes."

"This is really bugging you, isn't it?"

I tug my sleeves over my hands.

"Look," he says. "It's weird, the way it lines up, but the simple fact is none of this is your fault. You haven't done anything wrong. Pretty sure you'd remember if you had."

A dark pit forms in the center of my stomach.

Would I?

I spend the rest of the day racking my brain for lost time, trying to remember if I've forgotten anything, which is as hard as it sounds. While Mr. Lowell goes on about social unrest, I scour my memory for patches of mental black ice, chunks of missing time, but I can't find any.

I went straight home from Mr. Phillip's.

I went straight home after meeting Bethany.

I came straight to school from the bike accident with Jason.

So why are they disappearing?

"These are the building blocks of revolution," says Mr. Lowell, tapping the board. "It's not enough to engender discontent, to weaken the people's faith. A revolution isn't a game of might so much as a game of skill. There has to be a strategy . . ."

It just doesn't make any sense.

". . . a method . . ."

I don't *know* these people. We just crossed paths.

". . . a plan of attack."

And then a dark thought occurs to me.

What if I'm being set up? What if these people are being targeted *because* I crossed paths with them?

But why?

Roland's words echo through my head.

For someone to deem you unfit, they would need a case. They would need evidence.

I swallow hard and dig my nails into my palms. I'm jumping again, drawing threads where maybe I shouldn't; it's getting me so tangled, I nearly miss the simple solution.

Start at the beginning.

Judge Gregory Phillip.

Nobody knows what happened to him, but I can find out. After all, the abduction happened inside his house, in a room with four walls. Walls that I can *read.*

All I have to do is break into the crime scene.

FOURTEEN

AS SOON AS the bell rings, I'm out the doors and making my way toward the parking lot. But I pull up short when I reach the gates and see Eric standing at the corner, past the last row of cars, pretending to read a book. Great. *Now* he shows up.

He hasn't seen me yet, and I shuffle back several feet, bumping into students and getting caught in the tide of their grinding static as I retreat through the gates and out of his line of sight.

I don't know what's happening to these people, but whether or not Eric's looking for proof, the last thing I need is the Archive watching while I break into a crime scene. I leave Dante in its place at the bike rack and go in search of another route home, wondering how long Eric will stick around waiting for me to show.

Mr. Phillip's house is only a few blocks past the Coronado, so I can make it there on foot once I'm home. And luckily for me, I know someone who can get me there.

I just hope he's still *here*.

I weave through the main building with its glass lobby and walls of former students, forcing my eyes to skim over Owen's photo, and check the dining hall and the Court, but both are empty. Then I remember the boys dragging sports equipment toward the gym. Halfway down the path to the Wellness Center, I see a shoe-worn trail branching off the main one, and I follow it around the back of the building to find the outdoor fields.

There in the middle of the green, kicking a soccer ball around with a dozen other seniors, is Wesley.

All the guys are dressed in the same black-and-gold school clothes—half still in full uniform and half only in slacks—all moving and shouting, lobbing good-natured insults, calling for the ball. Even though I only get a look at his shirtless back, I recognize him instantly.

Not just by his height or the slope of his shoulders or the tapering muscles of his back—I vividly remember running my fingers down the curve of his spine, pulling slivers of glass from his skin—but by the way he moves. The fluid ease with which he sways and feints, calm giving way to sudden bursts of speed and dissolving back to calm. He plays the way he fights: always in control.

There's a set of low metal bleachers at the edge of the field, and I hop up onto a bench and dig the phone out of my bag. Still no text from Jason. I take a long, steadying breath, then dial his number. It rings and rings and rings, and as it does, the maybes play through my head.

Maybe Jason gave me the wrong number by accident.

Maybe Bethany dropped the necklace, like she did in the locker room.

Maybe Mr. Phillip made enemies.

Maybe—

And then the phone cuts to voice mail and I hear Jason's voice telling me to leave a message, and the maybes come falling down. I slide the phone into my shirt pocket and notice Cash down on the field, less elegant than Wes, and louder. He beams as he steals the ball, bounces it into the air, and drives it toward a makeshift goal. But Wesley is there at the last moment, lunging into the ball's path and plucking it out of the air with his hands. Cash laughs and shakes his head.

"What the hell was that, Ayers?" demands one of the other boys.

He shrugs. "We needed a goalie."

"You can't play all the parts," calls Cash, and for some reason that makes me laugh. It's the smallest sound—there's no way anyone could have heard it—but at that moment, Wesley's eyes flick up past the players to the metal bleachers. To me. He smiles, and punts the ball back into play before abandoning the pickup match and jogging over to the bleachers. A moment later, Cash ducks out, too.

"Hey, you," says Wes, running a hand through his hair to slick it back. Muscles twine over his narrow frame—*Look up, Mac, look up*—and the scar on his stomach is healing fast and well. It's now little more than a dark line.

Before I can tell him why I'm here, Cash catches up.

"Have to admit, Mackenzie," says Cash, "you never struck me as a bleacher girl."

I raise a brow. "What? I don't look like a sports fan to you?"

Wes laughs. "Bleacher girls," he says, gesturing down the metal rows to a cluster of green- and silver-striped girls, eyes trained hungrily on the pickup match and the collection of shirtless and otherwise sweaty seniors. A couple of faces have drifted over to me. Or rather, to Wes and Cash. I roll my eyes.

"No offense, boys, but I'm not here to fawn over you."

Cash clutches a hand to the school emblem over his heart. "Hopes dashed."

Wes brings his shoe up to the lowest bleacher and leans forward, resting his elbow on his knee. "Then what *are* you doing here?"

"I came to find *you*," I say; this time, Cash seems to genuinely deflate a little.

Wes, on the other hand, gives me a strangely guarded look, as if he thinks it's a trap. "Because . . . ?"

"Because you told me to," I lie, adding an impatient sigh for good measure. "You said I could borrow your *Inferno*, since it's a better version than mine."

Wesley relaxes visibly. Now that we're both back in our element—both lying—he knows what to do. And I have to hand it to him. Even without knowing what I really want or where I'm going with this, he doesn't miss a beat.

"If by 'better version,'" he says, "you mean it's marked up based on past pop quizzes, tests, and final exams, then yes. And sorry, I totally forgot. It's in my locker."

Cash frowns and opens his mouth, but Wes cuts him off.

"It's not cheating, Mr. Student Council. Everyone knows they change the tests each year. It's just a very thorough study aid."

"That wasn't what I was going to say," snaps Cash. "But thank you for clarifying."

"Apologies, Cassius," says Wesley, digging his bag out from under the bleachers. "Continue."

Cash toes the grass. "I was just going to point out that Wes copied off me for half that class—"

"Lies," says Wes, aghast. "False accusations, all."

"—so if you want any help—"

"Really, as if I wouldn't find more creative ways to cheat," continues Wes.

"—I'm probably your best bet."

I smile and push to my feet. "That's very good to know."

Wes is still grumbling as the soccer ball gets lobbed our way and Cash plucks it out of the air. "Just here to help," he says brightly, turning back toward the field.

"I'll add it to your feedback card," I call after him as he jogs away. My attention drifts back to Wes, who is standing there, shirtless and staring.

"I'm going to need you to put your shirt back on," I say.

"Why?" he says, arching a brow. "Having trouble concentrating?"

"A little," I admit. "But mostly you're just sweaty."

His smile goes mischievous.

"Ugh no, wait—" I start, but it's too late. He's already closing the gap between us, snaking his arms around my back and pulling me into a hug. I manage to get my hands up as he wraps himself around me, and my fingers splay across his chest, the rock band sound washing over me, pouring in wherever our skin meets. And through his chest and his noise—or maybe *in* it—I can feel his heart beating, the steady drum of it hitting my palms. And as it echoes through my own chest, all I can think is: *Why can't things be this simple?*

I mean, nothing is ever going to be *simple* for us—not the way it is for other people—but couldn't we have this? Couldn't *I* have this? A boy and a girl and a normal life?

He brings his damp forehead against my dry one, and a bead of sweat runs down my temple and cheek before making its way toward my chin.

"You are so gross," I whisper. But I don't pull away. In fact, I have to fight the urge to slide my hands down his chest, over his bare stomach, and around his back. I want to pull our bodies closer and stretch onto my toes until my lips find his. I don't have to read his mind to know how badly he wants to kiss me, too. I can feel it in the way he tenses beneath my touch, taste it in the small pocket of air that separates his mouth from mine.

I force myself to remember that I'm the one who said no. That I'm the thing keeping us apart. Not because I don't feel what he feels, but because I'm afraid.

I'm afraid I'm losing my mind.

Afraid the Archive will decide I'm not worth the risk and erase me.

Afraid I will give Wesley a part of me he can't keep.

Afraid that if we go down this road, it will ruin us.

I will ruin him.

"Wes," I plead, and he spares me the pain of pulling away by letting go. His arms slip back to his sides and he retreats a step, taking his music with him as he crouches and digs his key out of his bag. He slips the metal back around his neck before he straightens, polo in hand.

"So," he says, tugging the shirt over his head. "Why did you really come?"

"Actually, I was hoping you could give me a ride home."

His brow crinkles. "I wasn't joking, Mac. I don't have a car."

"No," I say slowly, "but you have something better. Fastest way around the city, you told me, and I happen to know it leads right to my door."

"The Narrows?" His hand drifts to the key against his sternum. "What's wrong with Dante?"

"Nothing." *Except for the bike's current proximity to Eric.* I tilt my head back. "It just looks like rain." To be fair, it is kind of cloudy.

He looks up, too. "Uh-huh." Not *that* cloudy. His eyes drop back to mine. "Be honest. You just want to get inside my halls."

"Oh, yeah," I say, teasing. "Creepy corridors are *such* a turn-on."

The corner of his mouth tugs up. "Follow me."

Wes leads me around the back of campus to an abandoned building. *Abandoned* might be too severe a phrase; the building is small and old and elegant and draped with ivy, but it doesn't look anywhere near structurally sound, let alone usable. Wes makes another sweeping gesture at the door set into the building's side.

"I don't understand," I say. "Your nearest Narrows door is . . . an *actual* door?"

Wes beams. "Beautiful, isn't it?"

The paint has all flaked off, and the small glass inserts that once occupied the upper middle have broken and been replaced by cobwebs. Even so, it is strange and lovely. I knew that Narrows doors all started out as real doors—wood and hinges and frames—but over time, walls change, buildings come down, and the portals stay. Every Narrows door I've ever seen has been nothing more than a crack in the world, a seam you can barely see. An impossible entrance that takes shape only when summoned by a key.

But here this is: this small, wood-and-metal door. I tug off my ring, the world shifting subtly around me as I tuck the metal band into my skirt pocket and reach out. Pressing my palm flat against the door, I can feel the strangeness, the hum of two worlds meeting and reverberating through the wood. It makes my fingertips go numb. Wesley fishes his key out from under his polo; he slides it into the rusted lock—a real, metal lock—and turns.

"Anything I should know about?" I ask as the door swings open onto darkness.

"Keep your eyes peeled for someone named Elissa," he says. I cast a last glance around for Eric, then follow Wesley through.

The Narrows are the Narrows are the Narrows.

The fact that Wesley's territory looks and smells and sounds like mine—dark and dank and full of distant echoes, like groaning pipes—is just a reminder of how vast the Archive system is. The only differences are the markings he's made on the doors—I use *X*s and *O*s, but Wes has drawn broad red slashes over every locked door, green checks over every usable one. And of course there's the fact I have no idea where I'm going. It looks so much like my territory that I feel like I should know every turn, but the halls and doors are a disorienting almost-mirror.

"Which way home?"

"*Your* home is this way," he says, pointing down the hall.

"And yours?" I ask.

He gestures vaguely behind him.

Curiosity tugs at me. "Can I see?"

"Not today," says Wes, his voice strangely tense.

"But we're so close. How can I pass up the opportunity to see inside the life of the mysterious Wesley Ayers?"

"Because I'm not offering," he says, rubbing his eyes. "Look, it's a big house. Soulless. And I hate it. That's all you need to know." He seems genuinely annoyed, so I let it go. He's so quick to defend the school, even with all its pretention, but whatever's at his house must be worse. The image of Wesley sitting on some grand patio with a butler shudders and breaks.

He starts walking away, and I follow. We move in silence through the Narrows, our senses tuned to the dimly lit corridors around us. I try to make a mental map of these new halls. It's not enough to know the number of rights and lefts—Da taught me how to learn a space, make a memory of it so I could find my way through in both directions and correct my course if I strayed. It's harder this time, since there's already a nearly identical territory mapped in my head.

"Are you going to tell me what happened to your hands?" asks Wes.

"Nothing I couldn't handle."

"You promised me a story."

"It isn't a very nice one," I say, but I still tell him. His steps slow. Even in the dark, I can see him pale as he listens.

"I would have killed them," he says under his breath.

"I nearly did," I say. I carved Eric out of the story. I don't want Wesley to worry, not until there's a good reason to. Luckily the appearance of the territory wall saves me from having to say more.

The boundary between Wesley's territory and mine looks like a dead end, bare except for the keyhole set into it. It's strange, I think, how separate Keepers are kept. Crew may be paired up, but we're isolated. Each on his own page.

Wes slides his key into the small, glowing mark on the otherwise bare wall; as he does, the door takes shape around the lock, the stony surface rippling into wood. The lock turns over with a soft metallic click, and he pulls the door open to reveal my section of the Narrows. The same—a mirror image—and yet different. More familiar.

I free my own key from under my collar and wrap the cord around my wrist. Wes smiles and gives a sweeping bow before stepping aside to let me pass.

"Be safe," he says, holding the door open as I cross through.

I hear it swing shut behind me; by the time I look back, there is nothing but a smooth stone wall and a tiny keyhole filled with light. A shadow crosses it briefly, and then it's gone, and when I press my ear to the wall, I imagine I can hear Wesley's footsteps fading. I feel the scratch of letters on my list, but I don't pull the paper out. The History will have to wait. It might not be happy or sane, but I'll deal with it when I get back.

I head straight through the territory to the numbered doors, my mind already on Mr. Phillip's house as I slot the key into the first door and step out onto the third floor hall, and stop.

Eric is leaning up against the faded yellow wallpaper, reading his book.

"If I didn't know better," he says, turning a page, "I'd think you were avoiding me."

"Flat tire," I say, sliding my ring back on as the Narrows door dissolves behind me.

"I'm sure." He closes the book and pockets it.

"You know," I say, "there's a word for guys who lurk outside schools."

Eric almost smiles. "When you sneak off, it makes one think you're up to no good."

"When you follow people without telling them why, it makes one think the same."

Eric winks. "How are your hands?"

I hesitate. He sounds like he actually cares. Maybe I was wrong about him. I hold them up for his inspection.

"Good," he says. "Fast healer."

"Comes in handy."

"Thank your genes, Miss Bishop. Your recovery rate comes with the territory, just like your sight."

I look down at my mending knuckles. I'd never thought much about it before, but I guess it makes sense.

Just then, the stairwell door bangs open and a woman strides through, a Crew key dangling from her fingers. She's tall, her black eyes fringed with dark lashes, a black ponytail plunging between her shoulders and down her back, straight and knife-sharp. In fact, everything about her is sharp, from the line of her jaw and her shoulders to her fingernails and the heeled boots at the ends of her long, thin legs. I recognize her from that day in the Archive.

Eric's partner.

"There you are," she says, eyes flicking between us.

"Sako, my love." There's a warmth to his voice that matches the cold in hers. "I've just been educating our young Keeper here. They don't teach them anything these days."

I'm willing to bet I know more than Eric thinks about the ways of the Archive, but I hold my tongue.

"Well, school's out. We have work to do."

Eric smiles, his eyes alight. "Wonderful."

My chest loosens. Wonderful indeed. That should keep him off my tail long enough for me to pay Mr. Phillip's house a visit.

He starts toward Sako, and I'm halfway through letting out a breath of relief when he stops and glances back at me.

"Miss Bishop?"

"Yeah?"

"Do try to stay out of trouble."

I smile and spread my arms. "Do I look like a troublemaker to you?"

Sako snorts and vanishes into the stairwell, Eric on her heels.

The moment they're gone, I duck into my apartment and unearth Da's box of things from the back of my closet, rooting around until I find what I'm looking for: a lock pick set. I ditch the school skirt for a pair of jeans and pocket the metal picks, and I'm halfway back to the front door when my phone goes off.

My heart lurches.

In the second between hearing the sound and digging the phone out of my pocket, all my fears feel suddenly silly.

The text will be from Jason, telling me he's fine, and he's sorry his phone was dead, and that he couldn't find the cord, and I'll realize how much I was making out of nothing, piling theory on theory on theory when for once Da was wrong, and it was in fact all coincidence. Maybe Bethany just found the strength to leave her necklace along with the rest of her life. Maybe Eric was hired to protect me, not get me erased. Maybe Mr. Phillip . . . But that's the problem. There is no explanation for Mr. Phillip.

And the text isn't from Jason.

It's from Lyndsey, just saying hi.

My hope collapses, because there are no easy outs—only more questions. And only one place to go. A place that has to have answers.

I take the steps two at a time all the way down to the lobby. Then I cut right down the hall beside the staircase, through the study, and into the garden. I hoist myself up and over the stone wall, hit the pavement in a crouch, and take off running.

FIFTEEN

D A AND I are walking back to his house one scorching summer day, eating lemon ices, when he gets a call. His phone makes that certain sound it only makes when he's being called to a scene. Unofficially, of course—Da never does anything on the books—and he hands me the last of his lemon ice and says, "You go on, Kenzie. I'll catch up." So of course I dump both ices and follow at a distance. He makes his way three streets over to a house that's roped off, but clearly unattended. He goes to the back door, not the front, and proceeds to stand there until I get within earshot. Then he says, without turning, "Your ears broken? I told you to go on home."

But when he glances back, he doesn't look angry, only amused. He knows I'm good at keeping my hands to myself, so he nods me up onto the step and tells me to watch closely. Then he pulls a set of picks from his back pocket and shows me how to line them up, one above the other, and lets me press my ear to the lock to listen for the clicks. Da says every lock will speak to you, if you listen right. When he's done, he rests his hand on the knob and says, "Open sesame." The door swings open.

He tugs off his boots and knots the laces and hangs them on his shoulder before stepping in. I do everything he does and nothing he doesn't, and together we head inside.

It's a crime scene.

I can tell because everything is very still.

Still in that undisturbed-on-purpose way.

I stand by the door and watch him work, amazed by the way he touches things without leaving any mark.

From the street, Mr. Phillip's house looks almost normal.

The plants are still in their pots, the doormat still clean and even at the top of the steps, and I'm willing to bet that inside the door, several pairs of shoes are lined up against the wall. But the illusion of calm order is interrupted by the bright strip of yellow tape criss-crossing the front door and the police cruiser parked on the street.

I'm leaning against a fence a few houses down, assessing the situation. There's one cop in the cruiser, but his seat's kicked back and his hat is over his eyes. Halfway down the block a woman is walking a dog; other than that, the street is empty.

There's a high wooden fence jutting out to either side of Mr. Phillip's house, but his neighbor's lawn is open, and I make my way across the street behind the cop car and into the yard, heading for their backyard like it's my own. Luckily, they're not home to contradict me—as soon as I'm out of the cop car's line of sight, I press my ear to Mr. Phillip's fence and listen. Nothing. The wood barely groans as I hoist myself up and over and land in a crouch in the manicured backyard.

Plastic has been taped over the two shattered windows at the back of the house, and the grass beneath them is sprinkled with glass, which is strange itself. Normally in a break-in, the windows would be broken inward, but the glass out here suggests the windows were broken from the inside *out*.

I keep my eyes on the ground, careful to step where others have obviously stepped rather than in the untouched patches.

When I reach the back door, I press my ear to the wood and listen. Still nothing—no voices, no footsteps, no sounds of life. I check the lock, but it doesn't budge, so I pull the set of picks from my backpack and kneel in front of the lock. From there I maneuver the two metal bars until the lock shifts and clicks under my touch.

"Open sesame," I whisper.

I turn the handle and the door falls open. I slip the lock pick set back into my pocket and step inside, tugging the door shut behind me. At first, everything looks normal—a small room with a tiled floor, a pair of shoes neatly by the door, an umbrella in a holder, that same sense of everything in its place. Then I look into the room on my left and see the damage. The plastic on the windows has left the space dark, but even without the light I can make out the debris scattered across the hardwood floor. A set of floor-to-ceiling bookcases are built into the wall opposite the broken windows. Most of the debris seems to have come from there—the shelves are practically empty, and a trail of books and odd trinkets litters the floor, thinning as it nears the windows.

I hold my breath. There's a horrible stillness to the room. It's only been three days, but the air is starting to feel stale. It's eerie—a crime scene without a body, like a movie set without the actors.

I tug off my ring and set it on the table by the door. The air shifts around me, humming faintly with life. I'm just bringing my hand to the nearest wall when something happens.

I let my gaze slide over the room. Near the windows, *it slides off*. My chest tightens. A *shortcut*? Here?

And then a pit forms in my stomach as I realize it isn't a short-cut. Shortcuts—the invisible doors Crew use to cheat their way across space—disturb the air, but they are smooth, and this is jagged, snagging my gaze and repelling it at once. My heart starts to race.

A shortcut wouldn't do that.

But a *void* would.

Voids are illegal, tears made in the world, doors to nowhere. The last—and only—time I saw a void was the day I *made* one. The day Owen broke free and the fight spilled out of the Narrows and into the Coronado, through the halls and up the stairs and onto the roof.

I squeeze my eyes shut and can feel Owen's grip tighten around me, his knife between my shoulder blades, his cold blue eyes full of anger and hate as I lift the Crew key behind his back. I turn the key in the air and there is a click and a crushing wind, and Owen's eyes widen as the void opens and rips him backward into the darkness.

And then it closes an instant later, leaving only a jagged seam in its wake.

A seam, just like the one in front of me now. My pulse pounds in my ears. That's why there's debris and broken glass but no body. Voids only open for an instant, long enough to devour the nearest living thing. A perfect crime, when you consider no one can see the method, the mark.

But who would do this? There's only one tool in the world that can make a void door.

A Crew key.

And then it hits me: Eric.

What was it he said in the park last night?

What are you going to do with them?

Make them disappear.

Mr. Phillip and Bethany and Jason. They all went missing after

I crossed paths with them. Eric hasn't been following me to look for evidence. He's been *planting* it. Setting me up.

Panic chews through me as I bring a trembling hand to the nearest wall, already knowing what I will find. *Nothing.* The same white-noise nothingness that I found on the Coronado roof that day. Voids cover their own tracks, eat through time and memory and make it all unreadable. But I have to try to see, so I close my eyes and let the memories float toward my fingers. I reach out, taking hold of them and rolling time back. The room flickers into sight. At first it is empty; then, bit by bit, it fills with people: officers and men taking photographs. The images spin away and the room empties again, and for a moment I think I might see something. I can feel the void hovering beyond the quiet.

The memory brushes against my fingers.

And then it *explodes.*

My vision floods with white and static and pain. The room vanishes around me into light, and I wrench my hand away from the door, my ears ringing as I blink away the blinding white.

Ruined. It's all ruined. Whoever did this, they knew they wouldn't show up. They knew the void would hide their presence. But they can't hide the void itself. Not that anyone's going to see *that* evidence. No, the only evidence anyone will see is mine. My prints somewhere in Mr. Phillip's kitchen and on Bethany's necklace, my number in Jason's phone.

I tug my sleeves over my hands and rub any fresh marks from the wall.

And then I hear the car door slam.

The sound makes me jump. I knock into the table by the door, and my silver ring rolls off, hitting the hardwood floor and rolling into the debris as footsteps and muffled voices sound from the front path.

I drop to a crouch and scramble forward, kneeling on an open book. I knock aside a binder and a heavy glass ornament as I grasp for the ring. The smooth metal circle fetches up against a toppled chair, and I grab it and shove it back onto my finger just as the front door opens down the hall. I freeze, but the glass ball continues to roll across the hardwood floor with a steady, heavy sound before coming to rest against the wall.

I hear it, and so do the cops.

One of them calls out, "Hey, someone here?"

I hold my breath, weaving my way silently between pieces of debris toward the wall, where I press myself back against it like it'll do a damn bit of good if they decide to come in.

"Probably just a cat," says the other, but I hear a gun slide from a holster and the heavy tread of approaching boots. They're coming this way. I scan the room, but there's nothing large enough to hide behind, and there are only two ways out: the hall the cops are coming down and the back door I first came through. I gauge how much time it will take to reach it. I don't have a choice.

I take a deep breath and run.

So do the cops.

They're halfway through the house when I crash through the back door. I take three sprinting steps toward the fence and then a wall of a man comes out of nowhere and catches me around the shoulders. The moment I try to twist free, the officer spins me, wrenches my arms behind my back, and forces me to the ground, where he kneels on my shoulder blades. I wince as the metal of the handcuffs digs into my bad wrist. My vision starts to blur and my pulse pounds in my ears, and I have to squeeze my eyes shut and beg my mind to *stay here stay here stay here* as the tunnel moment tries to fill my head like smoke. I force air into my lungs and try to stay calm—or as calm as I can with a police officer pinning me to the ground.

But as he drags me to my feet, I'm still me. It's a thin grip, but I hold on. And then I recognize him from the TV.

Detective Kinney.

He pushes me into the house—around the crime scene—and through the front doors. We're tracking dirt, and it's ridiculous, but I pause to think about how put out Judge Phillip would be just before Detective Kinney slams my back up against the cruiser door.

"Name," he barks.

I nearly lie. It's right there on my lips. But a lie will only make this worse. "Mackenzie Bishop."

"What the hell were you doing in there?"

I'm a little dazed by his force and the anger in his voice. Not a professional kind of gruff, but actual rage. "I just wanted to see—"

"You broke into a private residence and contaminated an active investigation. . . ." I cheat a look to either side, searching for signs of Eric, but Detective Kinney grabs my jaw and drags my face back toward his. "You better focus and tell me what *exactly* you were doing in there."

I should have grabbed something. It's easier to sell the cops on a teen looter than a teen sleuth.

"I saw the story on the news and thought maybe I could—"

"What? Thought you'd play Sherlock and solve it yourself? That was a goddamn *closed crime scene*, young lady."

I frown. His tone, the way his eyes keep going to the Hyde crest on my shirt—it's like he's talking to Amber, not me. Amber, who likes to play detective. Amber, who I'm willing to bet has gotten in the way of work before.

"I'm sorry," I say, doing my best impression of a repentant daughter. I'm not used to being yelled at. Mom runs away to Colleen, and Dad and I haven't had a real fight since before Ben. "I'm really sorry."

"You should be," he growls. One of the cops is still inside, no doubt assessing for damage, and the other is standing behind Kinney, wearing a smug smile. I bet he thinks I'm just some rich girl looking for a thrill.

"This kind of stunt goes on your record," Detective Kinney is saying. "It hurts *everything*, *everyone*. It could sure as hell get you kicked out of that fancy school."

It could do a lot worse, I think, *depending on how much evidence you've found.*

"You want me to take her to the station and book her?" asks the other cop, and my chest starts to tighten again. Booking means taking prints, and if they take mine and add them to the system, they'll find a match here at Judge Phillip's, and maybe even on Bethany's necklace—unless she rubbed the marks away.

"No," says Kinney, waving him away. "I'll handle this."

"Look," I say, "I know it was really stupid, *I* was really stupid. I don't know what I was thinking. It will never ever happen again."

"I'm glad to hear that," he says, opening the cruiser door. "Now, get in the car."

SIXTEEN

DA NEVER LIKED the word *illegal*. Semantics. There was no line between *legal* and *illegal*, he'd say, only between *free* and *caught*.

And I'm caught at the station, handcuffed to a chair next to Detective Kinney's desk. My fingertips are stained black from ink, and Kinney's holding up the page with my prints.

"This right here," he says, waving the sheet, "isn't just a piece of paper. This is the difference between a clean record and a rap sheet."

My eyes hover on the ten black smudges. Then he folds the page and slides it into his desk drawer. "This is your one and only warning," he says. "I'm not going to book you today, but I want you to think about what would happen if I did. I want you to think about the ripple effect. I want you to take this seriously."

Relief pours over me as I drag my eyes from the drawer to his face. "I promise you, sir, I take it very seriously."

The detective sits back in his chair and considers the contents of my pockets on the table in front of him. My cell phone. My house key (he left the one around my neck). Da's lock pick set. And my Archive list. I hold my breath as he takes up the paper, running his thumb against it as his eyes skim the name—*Marissa Farrow. 14.*—before he drops it back on the desk, face up. He takes up Da's lock pick set instead.

"Where did you get this?" he asks.

"It was my grandfather's."

"Was he a deviant, too?"

I frown. "He was a private eye."

"What happened to your hands?"

"Street fight," I say. "Isn't that what deviants do?"

"Don't talk back to me, young lady."

My head is starting to hurt, and I ask for water. While Kinney's gone, I consider the drawer with the page of prints, but I'm sitting in the middle of a police station, surrounded by cops and cuffed to the chair, so I'm forced to leave it there.

Kinney comes back with a cup of water and the news that my parents are on their way.

Terrific.

"Be glad they're coming," scolds Kinney. "If you were my daughter, I'd leave you in a cell for the night."

"She goes to Hyde, doesn't she? Amber?"

"You know her?" he asks, his voice gruff.

I hesitate. The last thing I want is for Amber to hear about this incident, especially since I'll need her case updates more than ever. "It's a small school," I say with a shrug.

"Kinney," calls one of the other officers. He strides toward us.

"Partial prints are back on the Thomson girl's necklace," says the officer.

Thomson. That must be Bethany's last name.

"And?"

"No match."

Kinney slams his fist on the desk, nearly upsetting the cup of water. I almost feel bad for him. These are cases he's never going to close, and I can only hope I catch whoever's doing this before they strike again.

"And the mother's boyfriend?" asks Kinney under his breath.

"We rechecked the alibi, but it holds water."

My gaze drifts down to Kinney's desk. And that's when I see the second name writing itself on the Archive paper.

Forrest Riggs. 12.

Kinney's attention is just drifting back to the table when I rattle my handcuff loudly, hoping he reads my panic as natural teenager-in-trouble panic and not don't-look-at-that-paper panic.

"Sorry," I say, "but do you think you could take these off before my parents get here? My mom will have a stroke."

Kinney considers me a moment, then gets up and wanders off, leaving me chained to the seat.

Ten minutes later, Mom and Dad arrive. Mom takes one look at me cuffed to the chair and nearly loses it, but Dad sends her outside, instructing her to call Colleen. Dad doesn't even look at me while Kinney explains what happened. They talk like I'm not sitting right there.

"I'm not pressing charges, Mr. Bishop, and I'm not booking her. This time."

"Oh, I assure you, Detective Kinney, this will be the *only* time."

"Make sure of it," says Kinney, unlocking the cuff and pulling me to my feet, his heavy static only making the headache worse. He hands me back my things, and Dad ushers me away before Kinney can change his mind.

I try to wipe the ink from the fingerprint kit on my skirt. It doesn't come off.

I feel the eyes on me as soon as I'm through the doors and look up expecting to see Eric watching. Instead, I see Sako. She's on a bench across the street, and her black eyes follow me beneath their fringe. Her gaze is hard to read, but her mouth is smug, almost cruel.

Maybe Eric's not the one I should be worried about.

My steps have slowed, and Dad gives me a nudge toward the car. Mom's in the front seat on the phone, but she ends the call as soon as she sees us. Across the street, Sako gets to her feet, and I clear my throat.

"See Dad?" I say, loud enough for her to hear. "I told you it was all just a misunderstanding."

"Get in the car," says Dad.

On the way home, I almost wish I could have another tunnel moment, lose time. Instead, I'm aware of every single second of weighted silence. The only sounds in the car are Mom's heavy sighing and the tap of my phone as I delete the texts I sent to Jason. I can't erase the prints from Judge Phillip's kitchen or Bethany's necklace, and I can't unsend the texts or unmake the calls, but I can at least minimize the evidence. I whisper a silent apology as I erase his number.

Dad parks the car, and Mom gets out and slams her door, breaking the quiet for an instant before it resettles, following us up the stairs and into our apartment.

Once inside, it shatters.

Mom bursts into tears, and Dad starts to shout.

"What the hell has gotten into you?"

"Dad, it was an accident—"

"No, it was an accident that you got caught. But you broke into a crime scene. I come home and find your schoolbag here and your bike missing, and then I get a call from the police telling me you've been arrested!"

"It doesn't count as an arrest if they don't process you. It was just a conversation with——"

"Where is this *coming* from Mackenzie?" pleads my mother.

"I just thought I might be able to help——"

He throws the lock pick set onto the table. "With those?" he growls. "What are you *doing* with them?"

"They were Da's——"

"I know who they belonged to, Mackenzie. He was my father! And I won't have you ending up like *him*."

I pull back. If he'd struck me, it would have hurt less.

"But Da was——"

"You don't know *what* he was," snaps Dad, running his hands through his hair. "Antony Bishop was a flake, and a criminal, and a selfish asshole who cared more about his secrets and his many lives than his family. He cheated and he stole and he lied. He only cared about himself, and I'll be *damned* if I see you behaving like him."

"Peter——" says Mom, reaching for him, but he shrugs her off.

"How could you be so *selfish*, Mackenzie?"

Selfish? *Selfish?* "I'm just trying to——" I bite back the words before they escape.

I'm just trying to *do my job.*

I'm just trying to *keep everything together.*

I'm just trying to *stay alive.*

"You're just trying to what? Get kicked out of Hyde? Ruin your future? Honestly, Mac. First your hands, and now——"

"That was a bike accident——"

"*Enough,*" snaps Dad. "Enough *lies.*"

"Fine," I growl, throwing up my hands. "It wasn't an accident. Do you want to know what really happened?" I shouldn't be talking, not right now, not when I'm tired and angry, but the words are already spilling out. "I got lost coming back from one of Mom's errands, and it was getting dark, so I cut through a park, and two guys jumped me." Mom sucks in a breath, and I look down at my bruised knuckles. "They cut me off . . ." It feels so strange, telling the truth. ". . . and forced me off the bike . . ." I wonder what it would feel like to tell them about my wrist. About Owen and all the different ways he broke me. ". . . and I didn't have a choice . . ."

Mom grabs me by the shoulders, her noise scraping against my bones. "Did they hurt you?"

"No," I say, holding up my hands. "I hurt them."

Mom lets go and sinks onto the edge of the couch, her hand to her mouth.

"Why would you lie about that?"

Because it's easier.

Because it's what I do.

"Because I didn't want you to be upset," I say. "I didn't want you to feel guilty. I didn't want you to worry."

The anger bleeds away, leaving me bone-tired.

"Well, it's too late for that, Mackenzie," she says, shaking her head. "I *am* worried."

"I know," I say.

I'm worried, too. Worried I can't keep doing this. Can't keep playing all the parts.

My head is pounding, and my hands are shaking, and there are two names on my list, and all I want to do is go to sleep but I can't because of the boy with the knife waiting in my dreams.

I turn away.

"Where are you going?" asks Dad.

"To take a bath," I say, vanishing into the bathroom before any-one can stop me.

I find my gaze in the mirror and hold it. Cracks are showing. There's a glass beside the sink, and I dig a few painkillers out of my medical stash under the counter and wash them down before snapping the water on in the tub.

What a mess, I think as I sink to the tile floor, draw my knees up, and tip my head back against the wall beside the tub, waiting for the bath to fill. I try to count the different things Da would give me hell for—not hearing the cops in time, getting caught, taking a full two days to notice I was being set up—but then again, it sounds like Da wasn't as good at separating his lives as he thought.

He only cared about himself, and I'll be damned if I see you behaving like him.

Is that how Dad really saw him? Is that how my parents see *me*?

The sound of the running water is steady and soothing, and I close my eyes and focus on the *shhhhhhhhhhhhhh* it makes. The steady hush loosens my muscles, clears my cluttered head. And then, threaded through the static, I hear another sound—like metal tapping against porcelain.

I open my eyes to find Owen sitting on the counter, bouncing the tip of his knife against the sink.

"So many lives. So many lies. Aren't you tired yet?"

"Go away."

"I think it's time," he says, tapping to the rhythm of a clock.

"Time for what?" I ask slowly.

"Time to stop hiding. Time to stop pretending you're all right." His smile sharpens. "Time to show them how broken you really are."

His fingers flex on the knife, and I spring to my feet, bolting for the door as he jumps down from the counter and blocks my path.

"Uh-uh," he says, wagging the knife from side to side. "I'm not leaving until we show them."

His knife slides back to his side, and I brace myself for an attack, but it doesn't come. Instead, he sets the weapon down on the counter, halfway between us. The instant he withdraws his hand, I lunge for the blade; my right hand curls around the hilt, but before I can lift it Owen's fingers fold over mine, pinning me to the counter. In a blink he's behind me, his other hand catching my free wrist, wrapping himself around my body. His hands on my hands. His arms on my arms. His chest against my back. His cheek pressed to mine.

"We fit together," says Owen with a smile.

"Let go of me," I growl, trying to twist free, but his grip is made of stone.

"You're not even trying," he says into my ear. "You're just going through the motions. Deep down, I know you want them to see," he says, twisting my empty hand so the wrist faces up. "So show them."

My sleeve is rolled up, my forearm bare, and I watch as six letters appear, ghostlike on my skin.

B R O K E N

Owen tightens his grip over my knife-wielding hand and brings the tip of the blade to the skin just below the crook of my left elbow, to the top of the ghosted *B*.

"Stop," I whisper.

"Look at me." I lift my gaze to the mirror and find his ice blue eyes in the reflection. "Aren't you tired, M? Of lying? Of hiding? Of everything?"

Yes.

I don't know if I think the word or say it, but I feel it, and as I do, a strange peace settles over me. For a moment, it doesn't feel real. None of it feels real. It's just a dream. And then Owen smiles and the knife bites down.

The pain is sudden and sharp enough to make me gasp as blood wells and spills over into the blade's path, and then my vision blurs and I squeeze my eyes shut and grip the counter for balance.

When I open my eyes a second later, Owen is gone, and I'm standing there alone in front of the mirror, but the pain is still there and I look down and realize that I'm bleeding.

A lot.

His knife is gone, and the drinking glass is lying in glittering pieces on the counter, my hand wrapped around the largest shard. Blood runs between my fingers where I've gripped it and down my other arm where I've carved a single deep line. There's a rushing in my ears, and I realize it's the sound of the bathwater *shhhhhhhhhh*ing in the tub, but the tub is overflowing and the floor is soaked, drops of blood staining the shallow water.

Someone is knocking and saying my name, and I have just enough time to drop the shard into the sink before Mom opens the door, sees me, and screams.

SEVENTEEN

G ROWING UP, I have bad dreams.

My parents leave the lights on. They close the closet door. They check under the bed. But it doesn't help, because I am not afraid of the dark or the closet or the gap between the mattress and the floor, places where monsters are said to lurk. I never dream of monsters, not the kind with fangs or claws. I dream of people. Of bad people dropped into days and nights so simple and vivid that I never question if any of it's real.

One night in the middle of summer, Da comes in and perches on the edge of my bed and asks me what I'm so afraid of.

"That I'll get stuck," I whisper. "That I'll never wake up."

He shrugs. "But you will."

"How do you know?"

"Because that's the thing about dreams, Kenzie. Whether they're good or bad, they always end."

"But I don't know it's a dream, not until I wake up."

He leans in, resting his weathered hand on the bed. "Treat all the bad things like dreams, Kenzie. That way, no matter how scary or dark they get, you just have to survive until you wake up."

• • •

This is a bad dream.

This is a *nightmare*. Dad is speeding, and Mom is sitting in the backseat putting pressure on my arm and I'm squeezing my eyes shut and waiting to wake up.

It *was* a dream. I was dreaming. It wasn't real. But the cut *is* real, and the pain *is* real, and the blood still streaked across our bathroom sink *is* real.

What's happening to me?

I am Mackenzie Bishop. I am a Keeper for the Archive and I am the one who goes bump in the night, not the one who slips. I am the girl of steel, and this is all a bad dream and I have to wake up.

How many Keepers lose their minds?

"We're almost there," says Mom. "It's going to be okay."

It's not. No matter what, it's not going to be okay.

I'm not okay.

Someone is trying to frame me, and they don't even have to, because I'm not fit to serve. Not like this. I'm trying so hard to be okay, and it's not working.

Aren't you tired?

I squeeze my eyes shut.

I don't realize until Mom presses a hand to my face that there are tears streaming down it. "I'm sorry," I whisper under the sound of her noise against my skin.

Fourteen stitches.

That's how many it takes to close the cut in my arm (the marks on my right hand from holding the glass are shallow enough to be taped). The nurse—a middle-aged woman with steady hands and a stern jaw—judges me as she sews, her lips pursed like I did it for attention. And the whole time, my parents are standing there, watching.

They don't look angry. They look sad, and hurt, and scared—like they don't know how they went from having two functioning children to one broken one. I open my mouth to say something—*anything*—but there's no lie I can tell to make this better, and the truth will only make everything worse, so the room stays silent while the nurse works. Dad keeps his hand on Mom's shoulder, and Mom keeps her hand on her phone, but she has the decency not to call Colleen until the nurse finishes the stitches and asks them to step outside with her. There's a window in the room, and through the blinds I can see them walk away down the hall.

They've made me wear one of those blue tie-waisted smocks, and my eyes travel over my arms and legs silently assessing not only the most obvious damage, but the last four years' worth of scars. Each one of them has a story: skin scraped off against the stone walls of the Narrows, Histories fighting back tooth and nail. And then there are the scars that leave no mark: the cracked ribs and the wrist that won't heal because I keep rolling it, listening to the *click click click*. But contrary to Colleen's theories, the cut along my arm—the one now hidden under a bright white bandage—is the first I've ever given myself.

I didn't, I think. *I don't—*

"Miss Bishop?" says a voice, and my head snaps up. I didn't hear the door open, but a woman I've never seen before is standing in the doorway. Her dirty blond hair is pulled back into a messy ponytail, but her perfect posture and the way she pronounces my name send off warning bells in my head. Crew? Not one I've ever met, but the ledger's full of pages, and I only know a few. Then I read the name tag on her slim-cut suit, and I almost wish she *were* Crew.

Dallas McCormick, Psychologist. She has a notebook and a pen in one hand.

"I prefer Mackenzie," I say. "Can I help you?"

A smile flickers on her face. "I should probably be the one asking that question." There's a chair beside the bed, and she sinks into it. "Looks like you've had a rough day," she says, pointing to my bandaged arm with her pen.

"You don't know the half of it."

Dallas brightens. "Why don't you tell me?"

I stare at her in silence. She stares back. And then she sits forward, and the smile slides from her face. "You know what I think?"

"No."

Dallas is undeterred. "I think you're wearing too much armor," she says. I frown, but she continues. "The funny thing about armor is that it doesn't just keep other people out. It keeps us in. We build it up around us, not realizing that we're trapping ourselves. And really, you end up with two people. That shiny metal one . . ."

The girl of steel.

". . . and the human one inside, who's falling apart."

"I'm not."

"You can't be two people. You end up being neither."

"You don't know me."

"I know you made that cut on your arm," she says simply. "And I know that sometimes people hurt themselves because it's the only way to get through the armor."

"I'm not a cutter," I say. "I didn't mean to do this to myself. It was an accident."

"Or a confession." My stomach turns at the word. "A cry for help," she adds. "I'm here to help."

"You can't." I close my eyes. "It's complicated."

Dallas shrugs. "Life is complicated."

Silence settles between us, but I don't trust myself to say any more. Finally Dallas stands back up and tucks the notebook she brought and never opened under her arm.

"You must be tired," she says. "I'll come back in the morning."

My chest tightens. "They finished stitching me up. I thought I'd be able to go."

"Such a rush," she says. "Got somewhere to be?"

I hold her gaze. "I just hate hospitals."

Dallas smiles grimly. "Join the club." Then she tells me to get some rest and slips out.

Yeah, rest. Since that seems to be making everything better.

Dallas leaves, and I'm about to look away when I see a man stop her in the hall. Through the blinds, I watch them talk for a moment, and then he points at my door. At me. His gold hair glitters, even under the artificial hospital lights. Eric.

Dallas crosses her arms as they talk. I can't read her lips, so I can only imagine what she's telling him. When she's done, he glances my way. I expect him to look smug, like Sako—*the Keeper is digging her own grave*—but he doesn't. His eyes are dark with worry as he nods once, turns, and walks away.

I bring my hand to my chest, feeling my key through the too-thin hospital smock as the nurse appears with two little pills and a white paper cup filled with water.

"For pain," she says. I wish I could take them, but I'm worried that "for pain" also means "for sleep." Thankfully she leaves them on the table, and I pocket them before my parents can see.

Mom spends the rest of the night on the phone with Colleen, and Dad spends it pretending to read a magazine while really watching me. Neither one of them says a word. Which is fine with me, because I don't have words for them right now. When they finally drift off, Dad in a chair and Mom on a cot, I get up. My clothes and cell are sitting on a chair, and I get changed, pocket the phone, and slip out into the hall. The hospital is strangely quiet as I pad through it in search of a soda machine. I'm just loading a bill into the illuminated front of one when I feel the scratch of letters in my pocket and pull out the list as a fourth name adds itself to my list.

Four names.

Four Histories I can't return. Roland's warning echoes in my head.

Just do your job and stay out of trouble, and you'll be okay.

I take a deep breath and dig my cell out of my other pocket.

> Hey, partner in crime.

A second later, Wesley writes back.

> Hey, you. I hope your night's not as boring as mine.

> I wish.

I think about typing the story into the phone, but now is not the time to explain.

> I need a favor.

Name it.

I chew my lip, thinking of how to say it.

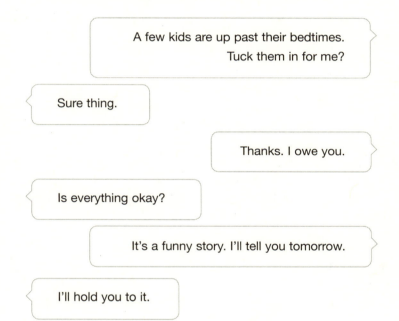

A few kids are up past their bedtimes.
Tuck them in for me?

Sure thing.

Thanks. I owe you.

Is everything okay?

It's a funny story. I'll tell you tomorrow.

I'll hold you to it.

I pocket the phone and the list and dig the soda out of the machine, slumping onto a bench to drink it. It's late and the hall is quiet, and I replay Judge Phillip's crime scene in my head. I know what I saw. The void was real. I have to assume there are two more: one in Bethany's driveway and another wherever Jason vanished. Three innocent people gone. If there's any upside to my being stuck here, it's that no one else should get hurt.

I finish the soda and get to my feet. The local anesthetic has worn off, and the pain in my arm is bad enough to make me con-sider the pills in my pocket. I throw them away to be safe and head back to my room and climb into bed. I'm not feeling anywhere close to sleep, but I'm also not feeling anywhere close to normal. I think of Lyndsey, who always makes me feel a little bit closer to okay, and text her.

> Are you awake?

Stargazing.

I picture her sitting on her roof, cross-legged with a cup of tea and an upturned face.

You?

> Grounded.

Shocker!

> That I did something wrong?

No. That you got caught. ;)

I let out a small, sad laugh.

> Night.

> Sleep sweet.

The clock on the wall says eleven forty-five. It's going to be a long night. I unfold the list in my lap and watch as, over the next hour, the names go out like lights.

EIGHTEEN

IT HAPPENS AT FIVE A.M.

At first I think it's just another name, but I soon realize it's not. It's a note. A *summons*. The words write themselves onto the Archive paper.

Please report to the Archive. —A

I know what the *A* stands for. Agatha. It was only a matter of time. Even with Wesley picking up my slack in the Narrows, he can't cover the incident with the cops, or this. Did Eric tell her I was here? If she knows, then she *knows* I can't answer the summons. Is that what she's counting on? Denying a summons from the Archive is an infraction. Another tally against me.

I'm reading the note for the seventeenth time, trying to decide what to do, when the door opens and Dallas comes in. I force myself to fold the paper and put it away as she says good morning and introduces herself to my parents, then asks them to wait outside.

She sinks into the chair by the bed. "You look like hell," she says—which doesn't strike me as the most professional way to start, but at least it's accurate.

"Couldn't sleep," I say. "They're going to let me go home today, right?" I ask, trying to mask the urgency in my voice.

"Well," she says, tilting her head back, "I suppose that's up to me. Which means it's up to you. Do you want to talk?"

I don't respond.

"Do you dislike me because I'm standing in your way," she asks, "or because I'm a therapist?"

"I don't dislike you," I say evenly.

"But I'm both," observes Dallas. "And most people generally dislike both."

"I dislike *hospitals*," I explain. "The last time my family was in one, my brother had just been killed by a car on his way to school. And I dislike therapists because my mother's told her to throw out all of his things. To help her move on."

"Well then," she says, "I'm afraid your mother's therapist and I wouldn't get along."

"That's a solid tactic," I say.

Dallas raises a brow. "Excuse me?"

"The enemy of my enemy is my friend. It's a good approach."

"Why, thank you," she says cheerfully. "You get away with this a lot, don't you? Deflecting."

I pick at the bandages on my hand. The shallow cuts are healing well. "Most people would rather talk about themselves anyway."

She smiles. "Except therapists."

Dallas doesn't act like a shrink. There's no "How does that make you feel?" or "Tell me more" or "Why do you think that is?" Talking with her is like a dance or a sparring match: a combination of moves, verbal actions and reactions strung together. Her eyes go to my arm. They took the bandages off so it could breathe.

"That looks like it hurts."

"It was a nightmare," I say carefully. "I thought someone else was doing it to me, and then I woke up and it was still there."

"A pretty dangerous twist on sleepwalking."

Her voice is light, but there's no mockery in it.

"I'm not crazy," I whisper.

"Crazy never crossed my mind," she says. "But I was talking to your parents, about Da, and about Ben, and about this, and it seems like you've been exposed to a lot of trauma for someone your age. Have you noticed that?"

Have I? Da's death. Ben's murder. Owen's attack. Wesley's stabbing. Carmen's assault. Archive secrets. Archive lies. Violent Histories. Voids. Countless scars. Broken bones. Bodies. Tunnel moments. Nightmares. This.

I nod.

"Some people crumble under trauma," she says. "And some people build armor. And I think you've built some amazing armor, Mackenzie. But like I said last night, it can't always protect you from yourself." She sits forward. "I'm going to say something, and I want you to listen carefully, because it's kind of important."

She reaches out and brings her hand to rest over mine, and her noise is like an engine, low and humming and steady. I don't pull away.

"It's okay to not be okay," she says. "When you've been through things—whatever those things are—and you don't allow yourself to *not* be okay, then you only make it worse. Our problems will tear us apart if we try to ignore them. They demand attention because they need it. Now, are you okay?"

Before I even realize it, my head is turning side to side. Dallas smiles a little.

"See? Was that so hard to admit?"

She gives my hand a small squeeze, and my gaze drops to her fingers. I stiffen.

Dallas has a dent on her ring finger.

"Divorced," she says, catching my look. "I'm starting to think the mark won't ever fade."

She pulls away and rubs at the spot between her knuckles, and I force myself to breathe, to remember that normal people wear rings, too—and that normal people take them off. Besides, her sleeves are pushed up and her forearms are free of Crew marks.

Dallas gets to her feet.

"I'm going to release you, on the condition that you attend counseling at Hyde. Will you do that for me?"

Agatha's summons burns a hole in my pocket. "Yes," I say quickly. "Fine. Okay."

"Are you sure this is a good idea?" asks Mom when Dallas tells her the news. "I mean, she tried to . . ."

"Not to be crude, ma'am," says Dallas, "but if she'd wanted to kill herself, she would have cut down the road, not across the street. As it is, she's several blocks up."

Mom looks horrified. I almost smile. She's certainly no Colleen.

The nurse rewraps my left arm, and I change back into my school shirt, tugging the sleeve down over the bandage. I can't hide the tape from the glass on my right palm, but that might work to my advantage. Misdirection. The worst of last night's self-pity is gone, and right now I need to focus on surviving long enough to find out who's framing me. *Owen hasn't won yet,* I think, and then I remind myself that Owen didn't do this. I did. Maybe Dallas was right. Maybe I need to stop denying I'm broken and work on finding the pieces.

Speaking of Dallas, she gives me a small salute on the way out and tells me to loosen the armor. The nurse who stitched and bandaged me up seems surprised by Dallas's order to release me, but doesn't question it—only fires off cleaning instructions and tells my parents to keep an eye on me and make sure I get some rest. She leans in and confides in my mother, loud enough for me to hear, that she doesn't think I ever went to sleep.

Great.

There's no sign of Eric or Sako in the hospital lobby or in the lot, and I realize with a sinking feeling that their faces are the only two I'd recognize. I know that a Crew member made the void, but I don't know which one. The Archive keeps its members isolated— each an island—but that means I don't know how many Crew there are in my branch, let alone what they look like.

"Come on, Mac," calls Dad, and I realize I'm standing on the sidewalk staring at the street.

On the drive home, I feel the scratch of more letters in my pocket, and by the time we get back to the Coronado, the summons has repeated itself on the page, the letters darker, as if someone's pressing down harder on the ledger. I turn the paper over and write the words *unable to report*, watching as they bleed into the page. I wait for a reply, a pardon, but the original summons only rewrites itself on the page. The message is clear, but I'm not allowed to close my bedroom door or go to the bathroom without an escort, let alone slip off to the Archive for a good old-fashioned interrogation. I don't even have the excuse of school, since it's Saturday. When I ask if I can go for a walk to get some fresh air, Mom looks at me like I've lost my mind.

And maybe I have, but after an hour of trying to do homework in spite of the hovering and heavy quiet, I can't take it anymore. I break down and text Wesley.

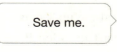

Save me.

Mom won't stop pacing, and Dad finally cracks and sends her down to the café to work off some of her stress. Five minutes after that, there's a knock on the door and Wesley's there with a bag of pastries and a book, looking like himself—well, his summer self: black jeans, lined eyes, spiked hair—for the first time in weeks. When Dad answers the door, I watch the war between what he's supposed to say—*No visitors*—and what he wants to say—*Hi, Wes!* What finally comes out is, "Wesley, I'm not sure now's a good time."

Even though Wes frowns and asks, "Has something happened?" I can tell he's not totally in the dark. If I had to guess, I'd say he's aware of the part where I got picked up by the cops, but not the part where I landed myself in the self-harm section of the hospital. His eyes go to my bandaged hand, and I can see the questions in them.

Dad casts a glance back at the table where I'm nursing a cup of coffee and trying not to look as tired as I feel and says, "Actually, why don't you come in?"

Wesley takes a seat next to me, and Dad stands by the door, clearly debating his next move.

"Dad," I say, reaching out and taking Wesley's hand with my unbandaged one. The steady beat of his rock music fills my head. "Could we have a moment?"

Dad hovers there, looking at us.

"I'm not going anywhere," I promise.

"I'll keep her out of trouble, Mr. Bishop," says Wes.

Dad smiles sadly. "I'm holding you to that," he says. "I'll go down and check on your mom. You've got ten minutes."

When the door closes, Wes gives my fingers a small squeeze before letting go. "Did you hurt your wrist again?" he asks, nodding at my other hand.

I shake my head. "Did Amber tell you?"

"That you got arrested? Yeah."

"It doesn't count as an arrest unless they book you."

Wesley arches a brow. "Spoken like a true criminal. What did you get picked up for?"

"Oh, Amber didn't share that part?"

"She didn't know."

"Ah, well. Remember the guy who disappeared before Bethany? Judge Phillip? I went back to check out his house, since that's where he vanished from. And I might have entered the place using less than legal methods."

Wes hits the table. "You broke into a crime scene *without me?*"

"Be glad, Wes, or we both would have been caught."

"We're a team, Mac. You don't go committing a crime without your *partner in crime.* Besides, if I'd been with you, we probably wouldn't have been caught. I could have stood at the door and made wild bird sounds or something when the cops came back. And if we did get caught, our mug shots would look fabulous."

I can't help but smile at the thought.

"Tell me you at least found something."

The smile slides off my lips. "I did," I say slowly. "A void."

Wesley's brow knits. "I don't understand."

"A void. Like the one on the roof."

"In the middle of Phillip's living room? That doesn't make any sense. The only way there'd be a void there is if someone *made* one. And they'd need a Crew key to do that."

"Exactly." I run my good hand through my hair and tell him about breaking into Judge Phillip's and seeing the void, and the way it made the memories unreadable. I tell him about Eric and

Sako following me. I tell him what Roland said about evidence, and that I know it sounds crazy, but I think I'm being set up.

"You have to tell the Archive," he says.

"I know." I *know*. But tell them what? I know how ludicrous it all sounds. I can see the skepticism in Wesley's eyes, and he's far more forgiving than Agatha will be. I can't just walk in there and announce they have another traitor in their midst. Not after what happened with Owen and Carmen. I need to talk to Roland, but I'll have to get past Agatha first. I know I can't keep ignoring the summonses, but after everything I've put my parents through, I can't just disappear. I think about sending Wesley to the Archive on my behalf, but the last thing I want to do is get him tangled up in this, especially now that Agatha's involved. Besides, we're not really partners. Wesley's not supposed to be helping me.

He looks at me hard. "You didn't feel like mentioning any of this last night?"

I pick at a fraying bit of tape on my hand. "It wouldn't translate well to text," I say. "And I was a little busy."

He reaches out and takes my wrapped hand and runs his fingers lightly over the tape. "What happened, Mac?"

I pull away and roll up my left sleeve for him to see the bandage. I unwrap it so he can see the fourteen little red *X*'s beneath.

"Who did this to you?" he growls.

I wish that were an easier question to answer. I take a breath and hold it for several long seconds before finally saying, "I did."

Confusion flickers across Wesley's face, followed by worry. I go to push my sleeve back down, but he catches my hand and draws my arm closer. His fingers hover over the cut. "I don't understand."

"I didn't mean to do it," I explain. "It started as a dream. Owen was . . . He was the one with the knife, and then I . . ." Wesley pulls me into a hug. He holds me so tight it hurts, so tight his noise pounds through my head, but I don't pull away.

"I don't know what's happening to me," I whisper into his shirt.

Wes pulls back just enough to look at me. "Tell me how I can help."

Go away, I think. *Stay away from me and whatever bad is circling.* But I know him well enough to know that he won't. "For one, you could ask Amber not to tell the whole school I got arrested."

"It doesn't count as an arrest unless they book you," echoes Wes, adding, "She won't tell anyone."

"She told you."

"Because she knows I . . ." He trails off.

"You what?"

"She knows I care," says Wes. "About you. By the way, you look like hell. Have you slept at *all* since . . ."

I rub my eyes. "I can't."

"You can't stay awake forever, Mac."

"I know . . . but I'm scared." Words Da taught me never to say. He thought saying it was halfway to surrendering. Now the confession hangs between us. The room settles and thickens, and I can feel the cracks in my armor as it loosens around me.

Wes pushes up from the table. He pours himself a cup of coffee and rests against the counter.

"Okay," he says. "If you're determined to stay awake, I can help. But this"—he gestures down at the spread of precalc and lit theory on the table—"isn't going to do." He digs the physiology book out from the bottom of the pile and flashes me a mischievous smile. "Here we go."

By the time Dad gets back, Wes has managed to cover himself

in an impressive number of Post-it notes, each labeling a muscle (I don't have the heart to tell him we're studying blood flow right now). Dad takes one look at him and *almost* smiles. And when it takes Wes half a dozen tries to affix a yellow sticker to the place between his shoulders, I end up laughing until my chest hurts, and for a while I forget how much trouble I'm in and how tired I am and how much my arm hurts.

I make it to dusk, but even with Wesley's company, I'm starting to fade. Mom is back home and making no attempt to hide the fact that she's hovering. Every time I yawn, she tells me I should go to bed. Tells me I need to sleep. But I can't. I know Dallas said I had to confront my problems, but I just don't have the strength to face another nightmare right now. Especially now that I know I'm capable of doing actual damage to myself. And maybe to others. I would rather be exhausted and awake than a danger and asleep, so I brush off her concern and crack open a soda. It's halfway to my lips when she catches my hand, filling my head with her high, worried static as she pries the can away and replaces it with a glass of water.

I sigh and take a long sip. She passes the soda to Wes, who makes the mistake of yawning as he takes it.

"You should head home," Mom tells him. "It's getting late, and I'm sure your father is wondering where you are."

"I doubt that," he says under his breath, then adds, "He knows I'm over here."

"Mom," I say, finishing the glass of water, "he's helping me study."

"Does he know you're *here* here?" she presses, ignoring me. "Or does he think you're upstairs with Jill?"

Wesley's brow furrows. "Frankly, I don't think he cares."

"Parents always care," she snaps.

"Honey," says Dad, looking up from a book.

They're talking, all three of them, but the words begin to run together in my ears. I'm just thinking about how strange it is when my vision slides out of focus.

The room sways, and I grip the counter.

"Mac?" Wes's voice reaches me. "Are you okay?"

I nod and set the glass down; or at least I mean to, but the countertop's not where I thought it was, and the glass goes crashing to the floor. It shatters. The sound is far away. At first I think I'm about to have another blackout, but those happen fast, and this is slow like syrup.

"What have you done?" Wes snaps, but I don't think he's talking to me.

I close my eyes, but it doesn't help. The world sways even in darkness.

"The doctor said she needed to—"

Everything else is far away.

"*Allison*," growls Dad. I drag my eyes open. "How could you—"

And then my legs go out from under me, and I feel Wesley's arms and his noise wrap around me before the world goes black.

NINETEEN

AT FIRST, everything is dark and still.
Dark and still, but not peaceful.

The world is somehow empty and heavy at the same time, the nothing weighing me down, pinning my arms and legs. And then, little by little, the details begin to come back, to descend, rise up, wrap around me.

The open air.

My racing heart.

And Owen's voice.

"There's nowhere to run."

Just like that, the darkness thins from absolute black into night, the nothingness into the Coronado roof. I am racing through the maze of gargoyles, and I can hear Owen behind me, the sound of his steps and the grind of metal on stone as he drags his blade along the statues. The roof stretches to every side, forever and ever, the gargoyles everywhere, and I am running.

And I am tired of it.

I have to stop.

The moment the thought hits me, I slam to a halt on the rooftop. My lungs burn and my arm aches, and I look down to find the full word—*B R O K E N*—carved in bloody, bone-deep letters from elbow to wrist. I search my pockets and come up with a piece of cloth, and I'm halfway through tying it around my forearm, covering the cuts, when I realize how quiet the roof has gotten. The footsteps have stopped, the metallic scratching has stopped, and all I can hear is my heart. Then, the knife.

I turn just in time to dodge Owen's blade as it slashes through the air, putting a few desperate steps between our bodies. The gargoyles have shifted to form walls, no gaps to get through: no escape. And that's okay, because I'm not running.

He slashes again, but I grab his wrist and twist hard, and the knife tumbles from his grip into mine. This time I don't hesitate. As his free hand goes for my throat, I bury the blade in Owen's stomach.

The air catches in his throat, and I think it's finally over—that I've finally done it, I've beat him, and it's going to be okay. I'm going to be okay.

And then he looks down at me, at the place where my hand meets the knife and the knife meets his body. He brings his hand to mine and holds the knife there, buried to the hilt, and smiles.

Smiles as his hair goes black, and his eyes go hazel, and his body becomes someone else's.

"No!" I cry out as Wesley Ayers gasps and collapses against me, blood spreading across his shirt. "Wesley. Wesley, please, please don't . . ." I try to hold him up, but we both end up sinking to our knees on the cold concrete, and I feel the scream rising in my throat.

And then something happens.

Wesley's noise—that strange chaotic beat—pours into the dream like water, washing over his body and mine and the rooftop, filling it up until everything begins to dim and vanish.

I'm plunged into a new kind of darkness, warm and full and safe.

And then I wake up.

It's the middle of the night, and Wesley's hand is tangled with mine. He's in a chair pulled up to my bed, slumped forward and fast asleep with his head cradled on his free arm on the comforter. The memory of him crumpling to the concrete almost makes me pull away. But here, now, with his hand warm and alive in mine, the scene on the roof *feels* like it was just a dream. A horrible dream, but a dream—already fading away as his noise washes over me softer and steadier than usual, but still loud enough to quiet everything else.

My head is still filled with fog, and the hours before the nightmare trickle back first in glimpses.

Mom pushing the water into my hand.

The tilting room.

The breaking glass.

Wesley's arms folding around me.

I look down at him, sleeping with his head on my covers. I should wake him up. I should send him home. I slide my fingers from his, and for a moment he rouses, drags himself from sleep long enough to mutter something about storms. Then he's quiet again, his breathing low and even. I sit there, watching him sleep, discovering yet another of his many faces: one without armor.

I decide to let him sleep, and I'm just about to lie back down when I hear it: the sound of someone in the room behind me. Before I can turn, an arm wraps around my shoulders, and a woman's hand closes over my mouth.

Her noise crashes through my head, all metal and stone, and all I can think as her grip tightens is that it takes a cruel person to sound like this. It's how I imagine Owen would have sounded when he was alive, before his life was compiled and his noise replaced by silence.

When she leans in to whisper in my ear, I catch sight of the blue-black fringe that sweeps just above her black eyes. Sako.

"Don't scream, little Keeper," she whispers as she hauls me backward, out of the bed and to my feet. "We don't want to wake him."

Her hand falls away from my mouth, her arm away from my shoulders, and I spin on her in the dark.

"What the hell are you doing here?" I hiss, almost soundless, still dizzy from whatever Mom put in my water.

"Trust me," growls Sako as she grabs my arm and drags me across the room. "I'd rather be a thousand other places."

"Then get out," I snap, pulling free. "Shouldn't you be hunting down Histories?"

"Haven't you figured it out yet, little Keeper?" she says, driving her Crew key into my closet door. "We hunt down *people* for the Archive. Only some of them are Histories."

I barely have time to pull off my ring before she turns the key, opens the door, and shoves me into darkness.

Agatha is waiting.

She's sitting behind the front desk in her cream-colored coat, her red hair sweeping perfectly around her face. One gloved hand turns through the ledger like it's a magazine, while Roland stands at her side, looking stiff and pale. His attention snaps up when Sako drags me in, but Agatha continues to play with the pages of the massive book.

"See, Roland?" she says, the heavy paper crinkling under her touch. "I told you Sako would find her."

Sako nods a fraction. Her hand is still a vise on my shoulder, but nothing filters in with her touch now. The silent buffer of the Archive surrounds us. Only the Librarians can read people here.

"She was asleep," says Sako. "With a boy."

Agatha raises a brow. "I'm so sorry to disturb you," she says in that milky voice.

"Not at all," I say tightly. "I would have come sooner, but I was indisposed, and my doors were out of reach." Only Crew can turn any door into an Archive door. I turn to Sako. "Thanks for the lift."

Sako smiles darkly. "Don't mention it."

Roland's eyes have locked onto the bandage wrapping around my right hand and up my wrist—*You should see my other arm,* I think—and they hover there as Agatha quietly shuts the ledger and rises to her feet.

"If you'll excuse us, I think it's time for Mackenzie and me to have a little chat."

"Requesting permission to be present," says Roland.

"Denied," she says casually. "Someone needs to watch the front desk. And Sako, please stay. You might be needed." Agatha points to one of the two sentinels by the door. "With me, please." I stiffen.

"I really don't think that's necessary," says Roland as one of the two black-clad figures steps forward. It's the first time I've ever seen one move.

"I hope it's not," says Agatha, "but one should always come prepared."

She turns toward the open doors behind the desk, and I scramble to pull my thoughts together as I follow. Roland catches my shoulder as I pass.

"Do not grant her permission," he whispers before the sentinel gives me a push through the doors.

I pad barefoot through the atrium of the Archive, the white of Agatha's coat in front of me, the black of the sentinel's cloak trailing behind, and for the first time, I feel like a prisoner. As we turn down one of the halls, I catch sight of Patrick standing at the edge of a row of stacks. His eyes follow us—curious, but otherwise unreadable.

Agatha leads me into a room with no shelves and two chairs.

"Have a seat," she tells me, waving at one as she takes the other. When I hesitate, the sentinel forces me down. His hands stay pressed onto my shoulders, holding me in place until Agatha says, "That won't be needed," and then he takes a step back. I can feel him looming like a shadow behind the chair.

"Why am I here?" I ask.

Agatha crosses her legs. "It's been nearly a month since our last meeting, Miss Bishop. I thought it time for a checkup. Why?" she says, tilting her head innocently. "Can you think of any other reasons I'd summon you?"

A pit forms in my stomach as she pulls a small black notebook from the pocket of her coat and opens it with a small sigh.

"Preceding the obvious failure to report when summoned . . ." I bite back the urge to cut in, to call her out on the fact she *knew* I couldn't come. ". . . I've compiled a rather concerning list of irregularities," she says, dragging a gloved finger down the page. "We have nights spent in the Archive."

"Roland's been training me."

"The assault of two humans in the Outer."

"They assaulted *me*. I merely defended myself."

"And the Archive had to clean up the mess."

"I didn't ask the Archive to."

She sighs. "An arrest for breaking and entering a crime scene?"

526

"I was never processed."

"Then how about crimes more pertinent to the Archive?" she challenges. "Such as failure to return Histories." I open my mouth, but she holds up a hand. "Do not insult me by claiming you were the one to send those lost souls back, Miss Bishop. I happen to know that Mr. Ayers's key was used to access the Returns in your territory. The simple fact is that you have been neglecting your *job*."

"I'm sorry. I was indisposed."

"Oh, I know. Hospitalized. For self-harm." She taps the paper thoughtfully. "Do you understand why I find that so troublesome?"

"It's not what you——"

"This is a stressful job, Miss Bishop. I am aware of that. The mind bears as many scars as the body. But the mind also keeps our secrets. A weak mind is a threat to the Archive. It is why we alter those who leave. And those who are removed." Agatha's eyes hold mine. "Now tell me, what happened?"

I take a deep breath in. Most people do before telling a lie——it's an almost automatic physical preparation and one of the hardest tells to break——but I make sure to let it out before starting, hoping the hesitation passes for embarrassment. And then I hold out my right hand. The cuts from the glass are shallow, but I've made sure they're covered, and the bandages wrap down around my wrist.

"Last month," I start, "when I tried to stop Owen, he broke a few of the bones in my wrist." I think back to my physiology textbook. "He cracked the radius and crushed the scaphoid, lunate, and part of the triquetrum." I point out the rough placement of each. "The last two didn't set properly. There were a few small pieces of bone that never re-fused. They were getting in the way, so I did my best to take them out." Her eyes drift to the bandages that circle my wrist as she leans forward, closing the narrow gap between us. It's exactly what I want, her to focus on the hand. She need never know about the bandages on my other arm.

"Why not go to the hospital?" she asks.

"I didn't want my parents to worry."

"Why not have *Patrick* see to it?"

"He's not my biggest fan," I say, "and I thought I could see to it myself. But I'm afraid the thing about being a teenager is that people tend to notice when you take a knife to yourself, no matter the reason."

A sad smile touches her lips, and I'm beginning to think she actually bought the lie when she says, "Roll up your sleeves."

I hesitate, and that brief pause is enough to give me away. Agatha rises to her feet, and I move to rise, too, but the sentinel holds me in my seat as she leans forward and guides up my sleeve—not my right one, but my left—exposing the bandage that winds around my forearm.

"Tell me," says Agatha, running a finger gingerly over the tape, "did pieces of bone wander into this arm, too?"

"I can—"

But she lifts a finger to silence me.

"I asked you once," she says, "if you wanted to remember all that had happened to you. I gave you a chance to forget. I fear I might have erred in doing so. Bad memories left in weak minds are like rot. They spread and ruin."

I grip the chair even though it sends pain up my arm. "I assure you, Agatha, I am not ruined."

"No," she says, "but you may be *broken*."

I cringe. "I am not. You have to believe me."

"Actually," she says, tugging on the fingers of one black glove, "I don't. Not when I can see for myself."

The sentinel's grip tightens on my shoulders, and Roland's voice rushes in my ears. *Once she has access to your mind, anything she finds there can be used against you. If she found you unfit, you would be sentenced to alteration. . . . Do not grant her permission.*

"No," I say, the words brimming with panic. "You can't."

Agatha pauses, her eyes narrowing. "Excuse me?"

"You don't have my permission," I say, reminding myself that this is law, even though it feels like suicide. Agatha's false warmth dissolves, and she considers me coldly.

"You are denying me access to your mind." It is not a question. It is a challenge.

I nod. "It is my right."

"Only the guilty plead the Fifth, Miss Bishop. I strongly advise you to reconsider."

But I can't. I have chosen my path, and she must respect it. She can't hurt me, at least not right now. It may only be a reprieve, but it's better than a sentence. I roll my sleeve down over the bandages, and she reads the gesture for the denial it is.

The sentinel's grip retreats from my shoulders, and I'm about to push myself to my feet when she says, "We are not done." My stomach twists as she rounds her chair and curls her gloved hands around the back. "You still haven't explained the crime scene or what you were doing there."

Lie, lie, lie pounds my heart. But a lie has to be as quick as truth, and the fact I've paused yet again means I won't be able to sell a line. She'll see through it. If I was standing on ice before, my refusal has driven cracks into it.

"Someone I met was abducted," I say, the words coming out too cautiously. "I thought I might be able to see something the cops had missed. The man, Gregory Phillip, went missing from his home.

The room where the abduction took place was trashed, and the police didn't have any leads. They couldn't make sense of the evidence, couldn't figure out how the man had vanished. Because they couldn't see it. But when I broke in, I saw it clearly."

"Saw what, Miss Bishop?"

"Someone had made a void."

Agatha's eyes narrow. "That," she says, "is a very serious accusation."

It is. Voids can only be made using Crew keys, the only people given Crew keys are Crew, and Agatha is personally responsible for every member of this branch, Keeper and Crew alike. Which is why she should be more interested in finding the person behind this than in burning me.

"I understand the severity—"

"Do you?" she says, rounding her chair. "Do you truly know what you're suggesting? Voids are tears in the world. Every time one is created, it puts the Outer and the Archive at risk. As such, the intentional creation of one is punishable by alteration. And you think that a member of Crew would disobey the Archive—disobey *me*—and create such a tear in the Outer in order to dispose of *one human?*"

"Three," I correct. "There have been three disappearances in the last week, and I believe voids were created in every instance. And I'm not convinced the Crew responsible is doing it for themselves. I think it's possible that someone in the Archive has given them the order."

"And why on earth would someone do that?"

"I think"—god, I sound mad; I can barely will the words out—"someone's trying to frame me." Agatha's eyebrows go up as I add, "I crossed paths with each victim before they vanished."

"And who would want to frame you?" she asks, her voice drip-ping with condescension.

"There are members of the Archive," I say, "who disapprove of your initial ruling. Those who are opposed to my continued service."

Agatha sighs. "I'm well aware of Patrick's feelings toward you, but you honestly believe he would break Archival law to see you terminated?"

I hesitate. I'm not sure I do. It was easy to believe he would send Eric to find evidence, but I have a harder time believing he would *plant* it.

"I don't know," I say, trying hard not to waver. "I'm only telling you what I found."

"You must be mistaken."

"I know what I saw."

"How can you?" she counters. "Voids are not *truly* visible, to anyone. You got a bad feeling, you thought your eyes slid off a bit of air, and you assumed—"

"I *read the wall*. The memories surrounding the creation of the void were all ruined. Whited out."

She shakes her head. "Even if there was a void, how do I know *you* aren't to blame? Do you have any idea how rare a void door *is*? You've already been tied to one—"

"I was doing my job."

"—and now this. You yourself said three disappearances, and you crossed paths with each."

"I don't have a Crew key."

"There was another one, was there not? On the roof? The one belonging to that traitorous History? What happened to it?"

My mind spins. "It got sucked into the void," I say, "along with Owen."

"How convenient."

"I could have lied, Agatha," I say, trying to stay calm, "and I did not. I told you the truth. Someone is defying you. Defying the Archive."

"Do you think I would allow such crimes and conspiracies to happen under my nose?"

I stiffen. "With all due respect, less than a month ago a Librarian plotted to unleash a restricted History into the Outer and tear down an entire branch from the inside, and she nearly succeeded. All of it under the *Archive's* nose."

In a flash, Agatha is upon me, pinning me to the chair, her fingers digging into my wounded forearm. Tears burn my eyes and I squeeze them shut, fighting back the dizzying dark of a tunnel moment.

"Which is more likely?" she says, her voice a low growl. "That a member of the Archive is conspiring against you—out of personal distaste or retribution, fashioning some elaborate scheme to have you found unfit, constituting treason—or that you're simply delusional?"

I take a few shaky breaths as the pain sears across my skin. "I know . . . you don't want . . . to believe—"

Agatha's nails dig into my arm. "My position is not built on what I *want* to believe, Miss Bishop. It is based on truth and logic. It is a very complicated machine I help to run. And when I find a broken piece, it is my job to fix or replace it before it can damage any other parts."

She lets go and turns away.

"I'm not broken," I say under my breath.

"So you claim. And yet the things that come out of your mouth are madness. Am I correct," she says, turning back to me, "in assuming that you still refuse to grant me access to your mind? That you make this *claim* against the Archive, against Crew, against *me*, and yet you deny me the ability to find you innocent or guilty of the charges you put on those around you?"

I feel sick. If my theory is wrong, then I've also signed my execution, and we both know it. I force myself to nod. Agatha looks past me to the sentinel.

"Go get Sako," she says.

A moment later, I hear the door close. Agatha and I are alone.

"I will start with the Crew then," she says, "because none of them would be foolish enough to deny me permission. And when I've scoured their minds and found each and every one of them loyal and innocent, I will tear your life apart, moment by moment, to uncover your guilt. Because you have proven one thing tonight, Miss Bishop: you are guilty of something." She takes my chin in one gloved hand. "Maybe it's the voids, or maybe it's madness, but whatever it is, I will find out." Her hand drifts down my jaw to my collar. "In the meantime," she says, guiding the key out from under my shirt, "I suggest you keep your list clear."

The threat is clear and cold as ice. *If you wish to remain a Keeper.*

The door opens, and Sako stands there waiting.

"Take Miss Bishop home," says Agatha smoothly, her hand abandoning my collar. "And then come back. We need to talk."

Something flits across Sako's face—curiosity, confusion, a shade of fear?—and then it's gone and she nods. She slides her key straight into the door behind her, takes my elbow, and pushes me through.

An instant later, we are standing in my bedroom again, Wesley asleep with his head on the bed and Sako's noise rattling through my body. Her metal and stone clanging become *coiled annoyance waste of space what did she do guarded what does Agatha want now could have a night with Eric his arms wrapped around warm golden and strong and safe*, and when she lets go of my arm, I'm surprised by how strong Sako's feelings are for him.

"Get out of my head, little Keeper," she growls.

I slide my ring back on, wondering how much of *my* mind *she* saw. She turns on her heel and vanishes the way she came, and I'm left standing there in the dark.

My arm aches, but I can't bring myself to inspect the damage, so I sink onto the bed and rest my head in my good hand. I wish that Da were here to tell me what to do. I've run out of his pre-packaged wisdom, his lessons on hunting and fighting and lying. I need *him*.

As the quiet settles around me, the panic creeps in. What have I done? Bought myself a few days, but at what cost? I've made an enemy of Agatha, and even if my theory's sound and the Crew behind the voids is found, she will not forget my refusal. And if my theory's wrong? I squeeze my eyes shut. *I know what I saw. I know what I saw. I know what I saw.*

Music fills my head, strong and steady, and I look down to see Wesley's hand wrapped around mine, his eyes bleary but open. He must misread the shock and fear in my eyes for the echoes of a nightmare—how I wish this were still a bad dream—because he doesn't ask what's wrong. Instead he climbs onto the bed beside me and rolls me in against him, his arms wrapped around my waist.

"I won't let anyone hurt you," he whispers sleepily into my hair. And all I can think as his music plays in my head is that this is how

Sako saw Eric in her mind: like a shield, strong and safe. This is how Crew partners feel about each other. But we are not Crew. We may never be now. But tonight, I let myself pretend. I hold on to his rock sound and his touch. I let it surround me.

Ten minutes later, the first name appears on my list.

TWENTY

WHEN I WAKE UP, Wesley's gone. There's nothing but a dent on the comforter to show that he was ever here. It's late, light streaming in through the windows, and I lie there for a moment, sleep still clinging to me—dreamless, easy sleep, filled only with music—and savor the calm. And then I move, and pain ripples sharply down my arm and dully through my shoulders, and I remember.

What have I done?

What I had to, I tell myself.

The Archive paper sits on my side table, tucked beneath *The Inferno.* At least there's still only the one name.

Abigail Perry. S.

I pocket the list. The smell of coffee drags me out of bed, and my hand's on the door before I notice there's dried blood staining my sleeve. I tug out of the shirt; the outline of Agatha's grip is nearly visible in the stain. I unwrap the dressing as quickly as possible—my eyes sliding off the gash as if it is a void, something wrong, unnatural, drawing and repelling my gaze at once—and pull a clean shirt on before heading into the kitchen. Dad's already there, brewing a pot of dark roast.

"I sent Wes home," he says in lieu of a good morning.

"I'm amazed you let him stay," I say, gingerly tugging the clean shirtsleeve down over the stitches. Maybe out of sight will turn into out of mind.

"Actually, he kind of refused to leave." Dad pours me a cup. "After what happened."

I take the mug and drag through my thoughts. Past Agatha's interrogation and Owen's nightmare to the room tipping and the water glass shattering on the hardwood floor. "How could she, Dad?"

He rubs his eyes and takes a long sip. "I don't condone what your mother did, Mackenzie. But you have to understand, she was only trying to—"

"Don't tell me she was trying to help."

He sighs. "We're *all* trying to help, Mac. We just don't know how." I look down at my coffee. "And for the record, that was a one-time deal, having your boyfriend stay the night."

"Wesley's not my boyfriend."

He arches a brow over his coffee. "Does he know that?"

My eyes escape to the coffee cup as I remember his arms folding around me, the comforting blanket of his noise.

"Caring about someone is scary, Mac. I know. Especially when you've lost people. It's easy to think it's not worth it. It's easy to think life will hurt less if you don't. But it's not life unless you care about it. And if you feel half of what he feels for you, don't push him away."

I nod distantly, wishing I could tell him that I do feel half, more than half, maybe even all of what Wesley feels, but that it's not that simple. Not in my world. I lean my elbows carefully on the counter. "What are you up to today?" I ask lightly.

"I have to go to the university for a bit. Left some work there that I didn't get to yesterday."

Because you were playing warden. "And Mom?"

"Down in the café."

I sip my coffee. "And me?" I ask cautiously. The list is like a weight in my pocket.

"You'll be with her," he says. What he means is, *She'll be watching you.*

"I still have some homework to do," I lie.

"Take it down there," he says. His tone is gentle, but the message is clear. I won't be left unattended. The love is there, the trust is gone.

I tell Dad I need to take a shower first, and he nods for me to go. A small part of me marvels at the fact I'm allowed to bathe without supervision, until I see that they've already taken every remotely sharp object out of the bathroom.

I'm hoping he'll go on ahead to work and I'll be able to make a quick detour into the Narrows on my way downstairs, but by the time I'm out of the shower and dressed and my arm and hand are freshly wrapped, he's waiting for me by the door.

He ushers me down to the coffee shop like a prisoner, passing me over to my mother's care. She won't look at me. I won't talk to her. I know she wanted to help, but I don't care. I'm not the only one in this place capable of losing someone's trust.

For a woman who won't look me in the eyes, it's amazing how she manages to never let me out of her sight. Thankfully the coffee shop is pretty full, and I welcome the lack of eye contact for the first hour as I clear tables and ring up drinks. Berk's working today, too, which helps. He has a kind of infectious cheer and a hatred for quiet, so he makes enough small talk to cover up the fact that Mom and I haven't said a word to each other.

"I hope the guy deserved it," says Berk when I reach out to take a coffee and he sees my bandaged palm and healing knuckles. "Is that the reason you two are fighting?" he asks, gesturing with a pair of tongs to Mom, who's retreated by now to the patio to chat with a woman in the corner table, her eyes flicking in my general direction every few moments.

"One of many," I say.

Thankfully he doesn't ask more about it—doesn't even assume it's all my fault. He just says, "They mean well, parents," and then tells me to take out the trash, adding, "You look like you could use a little fresh air."

I weigh my odds for escaping to the Narrows, but they aren't good. There's a door in the closet at the back of the café, but that's not exactly inconspicuous, and my other two doors—the one in the lobby and the one on the third floor—aren't in easy reach. As for Mom, well, Berk's barely handed me the bag before her eyes dart my way. I hoist up the trash for her to see and point to the back door. Her eyes narrow and she starts heading toward me, but gets snagged by another table halfway. She flashes me three fingers.

Three minutes.

Fine. Abigail Perry will have to wait, but at least I'll prove to Mom that I can be left alone. I duck out the back door, relishing my three minutes of privacy and sunlight. As soon as I'm outside, I let my steps slow, savoring every second of freedom.

I've just finished loading the bags into the bin when a hand tangles in my shirt and slams me up against the Coronado wall, *hard.*

"How dare you?" growls Sako, her harsh metallic noise scraping through my bones.

"What are you talking ab——" Her other fist connects with my ribs, and I hit the alley floor, gasping.

"You've really made a mess of things. You never should have gone to Agatha."

"What's the matter?" I cough, getting to my feet. "Do you have something to hide?"

She grabs me again and slams me back against the stone side of the Coronado.

"I'm loyal to the Archive, you little shit. A fact Agatha can attest to, because thanks to your cracked little head and its paranoid delusions, I just spent the night letting her claw through my life." She leans in, her face inches from mine. Her black eyes are bloodshot, and dark circles stand out against the pale skin beneath them. "Do you have any idea what that feels like?" she hisses. "Because you *will*. Once she runs out of Crew, she'll come for you. And I hope she tears you apart one memory at a time until there's nothing left."

I'm still reeling from the fact that Sako's innocent when she shoves away from me and says, "She still has Eric. She's been with him for hours. And if she punishes him because of you, I will tear your throat open with my fingernails."

"He shouldn't have been following me," I say.

Sako makes an exasperated noise. "He was only following you because Roland asked him to. To keep you *safe*." The last word comes out in a hiss. I feel like I've been hit again, the air rushes from my lungs as she adds, "Though what Roland sees in you, I have no idea."

Sako smooths her blue-black hair, her Crew key glittering against her wrist. "Maybe I should tell Agatha about your little boyfriend, Wesley. Maybe *he* should be a suspect. Couldn't hurt for her to take a look."

"Wes has nothing to do with this," I say through gritted teeth, "and you know it."

"Do I?" asks Sako. She turns away. "Enjoy your freedom while it lasts, little Keeper. It'll be your turn soon enough. And when it is, I hope Agatha lets me drag you in myself."

She storms away, and I'm left sagging against the wall, winded and worried. Sako and Eric are both innocent?

Cracked little head, echoes Sako in my ears.

Broken, echoes Owen in my mind.

I squeeze my eyes shut and wait for the voices to quiet. I know what I saw. I saw a void. Voids are made by Crew keys, so it had to be Crew. Eric and Sako are not the only pages in the ledger. I try to picture the book on the Archive desk, turn through it in my mind. There's a master page, a table of contents, and then one page for each person who serves in the branch. How many pages total? A hundred? More? Our branch serves a territory with a diameter of two to three hundred *miles.* How many cities fall within that circle? How many pages of the book could be dedicated to *this* city? And how many of those pages belong to Crew? How many people for Agatha to go through? Four? Eight? Twelve? I crossed paths with the victims, but have I crossed paths with the criminal?

I take a deep breath, checking myself again for blood before I go back inside.

"There you are," says Berk. "I was beginning to think I'd lost you."

"Sorry," I say, ducking behind the counter. "I ran into a friend."

Mom's on the patio serving some new customers, and I catch her stealing a glance through the glass to make sure I'm back. She taps her watch, but my attention shifts past her as Sako saunters down the curb. She's talking on the phone now, her head tipped lazily back as if soaking up the sun, and I realize something. Moments ago she was a monster, an animal, all teeth and bite. And now, impossibly, she looks *normal*. Crew look *normal*. They have the ability to blend in. Even Eric, made of gold. I didn't notice him until he wanted me to. Crew could be anyone. What if whoever's doing this doesn't stand out? What if they blend right in? What if they've slipped into my life unnoticed?

Berk laughs and chats with a customer at the end of the counter. My eyes go to his hands, and I tense when I see that they're bare but for a single silver thumb ring. He's only been here for a couple weeks. But his sleeves are rolled up and free of marks. I scan the coffee shop, searching for regulars. I'm looking for people on the periphery of my life, close enough to watch me without being noticed. But no one stands out. And that's exactly the problem.

Just then, a second name scrawls itself on the list in my pocket—*Bentley Cooper. 12.*—and I start to wish I'd risked Mom's wrath to find Abigail. I'm going to have my work cut out for me later.

"Hey, Mac," calls Berk, nodding at the door. "Customer."

I pocket the paper and turn, expecting a stranger, and find Cash instead.

Wesley may trade in his preppy schoolboy persona for guyliner and silver studs, but Cash's weekend look is still solidly Hyde. His dark-wash jeans and crisp white polo make me feel dingy in my Bishop's apron.

His gold eyes light up when he sees me. He crosses the café and hops up onto a stool. "So this is where you live!" he says cheerfully.

"This is where I *work*," I say, drying a mug. "Upstairs is where I live."

He spins around on his stool and leans his elbows back on the counter while he surveys the café.

"Enchanting."

When he turns back around, I've already poured him a drink.

"And enchanted," he says, gesturing at the cup.

"I figured it was my turn to provide the coffee," I say. "So, what are you doing here?"

He takes a slow sip. "I brought your bike. I saw that you left it at school."

"Wow," I say, "you take your ambassador role very seriously."

"Indeed," he says with a sober nod. "But if I'm being honest, the bike was an excuse to come say hi."

I feel myself blushing. "Oh really?"

He nods. "I was worried. Seniors are in charge of organizing Fall Fest, and Wesley bailed on prep yesterday. When I asked where he was, he said with you, and I was about to give him hell for it, as is my friendly obligation, but he told me you'd had a bit of a scrape. So I thought I'd look you up and come make sure you were all right."

"Oh," I say. "You didn't have to, really. I'm fine."

"We must have different definitions of fine," he says, nodding at my bandaged hand. "What happened?"

"It's stupid, really. This old building," I say, showing him my taped palm. "I put my hand against a window and it broke. It's not a big deal," I add, the fourteen stitches aching under my other sleeve. "I'll live."

Cash brings his fingertips to my hand, so light I barely hear the jazz and laughter in his touch. "Glad to hear it," he says, sounding strangely sincere. He rests his elbows on the counter, looking down into his drink. "Hey, so I've been thinking—"

Someone clears their throat, interrupting Cash, and I look up to see Wes standing a foot away, considering us. Or more precisely, considering Cash's hand, which is still touching mine. I pull away.

"Well, this is a surprise," he says. He looks freshly showered, dressed in simple black, his hair slicked back and still wet, his eyes rimmed with dark.

"Testing out your Fall Fest costume?" teases Cash.

Wes ignores the jab. "Am I interrupting something?" he asks.

"No," I say at the same time Cash mutters, "Not at all."

"Cash was just bringing me my bike."

Wes arches a brow. "The student council is far more involved than it used to be."

Cash's eyes narrow even as he smiles. "Quality assurance," he says.

A moment of tense silence falls over us. When it's clear Wesley is here to stay, Cash hops down from his stool. "Speaking of," he says, "I'd better get back to Hyde. I left a huddle of freshmen hanging ribbons, and I just don't trust that lot with ladders." He turns his attention to Wesley. "Are you coming by later?"

Wes shakes his head. "Can't," he says, pointing upstairs. "Got to look after Jill for a bit. I'll stay late tomorrow."

"You better. Senior pride is on the line." He heads for the door. "Thanks for the coffee, Mackenzie."

"Thanks for the bike," I say. "And the chat."

"Any time."

Wesley watches Cash go. "You like him," he says quietly.

"So do you," I say. "He's a nice guy."

"That's not what I mean."

"I know what you mean." I do like Cash. He's normal. And when he's around, I almost forget that I'm not.

"I would have been here sooner," says Wes, "but it appears my access to your territory has been revoked. Any idea why?"

I frown. Agatha.

"Maybe they decided it was time to hand me the reins," I say as casually as possible. "How did you get here, then? Did you drive?"

"For your information, I took the bus."

I shudder at the thought. So many people in such a tiny box. But Wes has always been better with contact than I am. After all, he's the one who taught me how to let the noise wash over me, how to float instead of drown in the current of people's lives.

"Talk and work, kids. Talk and work," calls Berk from the other end of the counter. Wesley smiles and ducks under the bar.

"So," he asks, softer, "how did you sleep last night?"

The rooftop and the gargoyles and Owen's knife all flash through my mind.

"Awful at first," I say. "But then . . ." I feel my face warming. "I heard your noise, filling my head, and the nightmare just kind of fell apart."

"I wasn't sure what to do," he says, pouring himself a drink. "You called my name."

"Oh," I say, as he takes a sip, "that's because I killed you."

Wes nearly chokes on his coffee.

"It was an accident," I add. "Promise."

"Great," he says, knocking his shoulder against mine, briefly filling my head with rock and bass and drum. "Let's see if we can keep you nightmare-free." He pulls back a little. "Oh, and I talked to Amber. I asked her to let me know if Detective Kinney gets any leads. She said he's gotten really tight-lipped, but that she'll try to keep me posted. I think she thought I wanted to know because of Bethany. . . ."

I'd nearly forgotten about their history. "I'm sorry about her," I say. A void is a rip in the world. It only stays open long enough to drag something—*someone*—through, and then it seals. Once a person is gone . . .

"Yeah. Well. I don't understand the *why*, but you're right about the *what*," says Wes. "I swung by her house to see if anything stood out."

"And?" I ask.

"Something's definitely off. It's in the driveway, right next to the car. I couldn't look right at it."

A breath of relief escapes. I didn't realize how badly I needed someone else to see the voids. Just then, my mother comes over. "Wesley," she says by way of hello as she scoops up two drinks from the counter.

Wes ducks back under the counter and nods. "Hi, Mrs. Bishop."

She seems nervous, and he seems tense, and I remember him growling at her last night, when the world began to tilt.

What have you done?

But in the unbalance, I see an opening. "Hey, Wes is going to watch Jill for a while. Can I go with him?"

It's the first thing I've said to her since last night, and I can see the struggle play out across her face as her eyes flick from Wesley to me (or at least to my apron, my collar, my jaw). She doesn't want to let me out of her sight. But if she says no, it'll only cement her as the villain. We're teetering at the edge of something high and steep, and neither of us wants to go over. Part of me thinks that after last night, Mom has already jumped, but I'm offering a rope, a chance to climb back up onto the ledge.

I can tell she wants to take it, but something stops her. I wonder if it's Colleen's voice in her head, warning against the pitfalls of lenient parenting and encouraging vigilance.

"I'm not sure that's a good idea. . . ." Mom looks around the café, but Colleen's an hour away, Berk's staying out of our family drama, and Dad's not here to back her up. If he were, I'm pretty sure he'd side with me.

"I'll keep her out of trouble, Mrs. Bishop," offers Wesley, flashing her a small, genuine smile. If he's surprised by my inviting myself along, he never shows it. "Promise."

Mom shifts her weight, fingers curled around the coffee cups. A man at a corner table flags her over. "Okay," she says at last, still not looking at me. "But be back down in an hour," she adds. "In case it gets busy."

"Sure thing," I say, ducking under the counter before she can see the relief splashed across my face.

"And Mac," she says when Wes and I are nearly to the door.

"Yeah?"

I'm sorry. I can see the words on her lips as she looks at the space a foot to my left, but she can't say them. "One hour," she says again for emphasis. I nod and follow Wes out.

TWENTY-ONE

"**Y**OU'RE IN A HURRY,**"** says Wes once we're on the grand stairs.

"Things to do, dear Wesley."

"I'm intrigued," he says. "But you know, when I said I was going to watch Jill, I didn't intend it as a euphemism. Not that I'm averse, it's just——"

"There are two Histories on my list," I cut in. "And my parents have been playing warden and watch all weekend. I needed an excuse to get away so I could track the names down."

"Is that all my company is to you?" he asks with mock affront. "An excuse?"

We reach the top of the stairs, and I take his chin in my hand, rock music singing through my fingers. "If it makes you feel better," I say teasingly, "you're a very pretty excuse."

His brow crinkles. "I would have preferred *dashing*, but I'll take it."

My hand starts to slide away, but he catches it, holding it gently against his jaw. He gazes down through his black lashes, flashing me a sultry look. Even though I know he's playing, I can feel the heat rising in my cheeks. Finally his hand slips away; but as it does, his fingers graze my forearm and I pull back, wincing.

Wesley's flirting dissolves into a frown. "I don't think you should be hunting."

I sigh and head into the stairwell. "I don't have a choice."

"I could do it for you."

I shake my head. "You no longer have access to my territory."

"You could loan me your key."

"No," I say simply, pushing open the door to the third floor and heading down the hall. "I need to do it myself."

"Wait," he says. "Just wait." I drag myself to a stop beside the painting of the sea. My hour of freedom ticks away inside my head. Wes runs a hand through his hair. "You've been through a lot," he says. "Just give yourself a break."

"I can't," I say simply. "The Archive won't. I have to do this. It's my job. If I can't hunt, then I don't deserve to be a Keeper." I realize with a sinking feeling that it's true. I have to prove that I can do this, that I'm not broken. Agatha's not convinced, and right now, neither am I. But I can't give up. As badly as I want a normal life, I don't want to lose this. Lose myself. Lose Wes.

"I won't be long," I say. As I tug my ring off and pocket it, my senses adjust to the hall, to the keyhole now visible in the wallpaper crease, and to the closeness of Wesley's body, humming with life.

He frowns, tugging off his own ring. "I'm going with you."

"What about Jill?"

He waves a hand. "It's Jill. She's got her nose in some book. She couldn't care less if I'm there to watch her turn the pages."

"You don't have to come," I say, sliding my key over my head and slotting it in the wall.

"But I am," he says matter-of-factly as the Narrows door spreads, stainlike, over the wallpaper beside us. "Listen. I get that you need to do this, but it's been a bad few days, and I don't want you going in there by yourself, okay? Besides, I told your mom I'd keep you out of trouble, and this has trouble written all over it. So if you're determined to go stomping around the Narrows, then

I'm going with you." His crooked smile flickers back to life. "And if you try to stop me—well then, I'll scream."

"You wouldn't," I gasp.

"I would. And you'd be surprised how far my voice carries."

"Fine. You can come." I sigh and turn the key in the Narrows door. "But don't get in my way."

Wes starts forward and then stops, remembering something. "What about your summons?" he asks. "Don't you need to report?"

I hesitate. "I already did," I say slowly. "I spoke to Agatha last night."

"And? Did you tell her about the voids? Your theory?"

I nod, half expecting Wes to tell me I should have kept my mouth shut, but he doesn't. He doesn't know Agatha, not the way I do. To him, she is the assessor. The authority. The Archive. It probably wouldn't occur to him to keep it a secret.

"She wasn't very happy," I add.

"I bet," says Wes. "What did she say?"

I will tear your life apart, moment by moment, to uncover your guilt. Because you have proven one thing tonight, Miss Bishop: you are guilty of something. Maybe it's the voids, or maybe it's madness, but whatever it is, I will find out.

"She said she'd take care of it."

"Well . . ." Wes rubs his neck. "I guess that's a relief? I mean, this is Agatha. She'll get to the bottom of it, one way or another."

"Yeah," I say, opening the door. I have a sickening feeling he's right.

On good days, the stale, twisting corridors of the Narrows put me on edge. Today, they make my skin crawl. Every little sound twists itself into a set of footsteps. A door knock. A distant voice. My pulse inches up before the door to the Outer is even closed, before the little light that snuck through the boundary between worlds is snuffed, plunging us into the key-lit dark.

My wounded arm hangs at my side, aching dully. I force myself to focus on the task at hand instead of the way the pain creeps through my senses, threatening to drag me into a darker place. I can almost feel Owen pinning me against him, his hands over my hands over the knife. . . .

"Mac?" asks Wes under his breath. I shake myself free of the thoughts. I cannot afford to lose myself here, not with names on my list and Wesley at my back. I can feel him behind me, so close I can almost feel his life radiating off of him like heat. He's keeping his body tensed as if he thinks I'll fall, as if he'll need to catch me.

Two names. Two Histories. That's all. It ought to be routine. Anger prickles through me. If I can't do this, I don't deserve to be called a Keeper.

"I'm okay," I say, pressing my hand to the nearest wall to hide the fact it's shaking. I squeeze my eyes shut momentarily. Taking hold of the thread of time, I turn it back, and the Narrows flickers up again in my mind. I roll it backward until a boy flashes into sight. He's there and then gone just as quickly, but I know where to go next. That's all I need. One step at a time, one foot in front of the other. I pull away and follow his path around the corner, weaving deeper into the Narrows. Soon I find my stride and forget about the pain in my arm and the whisper in my head that says *broken broken broken* in Owen's voice.

"See?" I say, pulling away from another wall. "I told you I'd be—"

I'm halfway through the word *fine* when I round the corner and nearly collide with a body. Instinct kicks in, and I slam the form back against the Narrows wall before I've even registered how small it is, or the fact that it's not fighting back. The girl's shoes dangle off the ground, and she looks at me with wide, terrified eyes, her pupils wavering.

Abigail Perry. 8.

The look in her eyes is like cold water. The spell of the Narrows breaks, the nightmarish echoes retreat, and I remember my job. Not to frighten or fight, but to return. To set right.

"Please don't hurt me," she whispers.

I lower the girl's shoes to the ground, loosening my grip without letting go.

"I'm sorry," I say as gently as possible. "I didn't mean to grab you. It's just, you scared me."

Her eyes widen a little more, the pupils settling. "I'm scared, too," she says.

Her gaze drifts to Wesley behind me. "Are you?" she asks him, and Wes, who's always been more of a return-first-talk-later kind of Keeper, kneels in front of Abigail and says, "I am, but Mac here, she's going to show us the way out."

She looks up at me expectantly, and I nod. "That's right," I say, still shaky. "Let's get out of here."

I find the nearest Returns door and send her through. And in that instant before I close the door—when the hall fills with white light—I think of the day I got trapped in that blinding room and my life played all over the walls before folding in square by square, taking my breath and heartbeat with it. I wonder for an instant if that's what it's like to be erased.

But I have no desire to find out.

Two halls away, we run into *Bentley Cooper. 12.* He throws his fists up when he sees us. The kid is all skin and bones and fear, and I can't help but wonder what kind of short life he had to leave him so defensive. The question softens something in me. I know I shouldn't wonder; Da used to scold me for my curiosity, but I'm starting to think he was wrong. Caring is what keeps me human. I know caring is also the reason Owen haunts my dreams—if I didn't let things in, they couldn't hurt me—but maybe Dad was right. It's not life unless you care about it.

I put my hands up, like I'm surrendering, and the boy's come down, and within minutes he's been led into the light. By the time Wes and I step back into the yellow-papered hallway of the third floor, my list and my head are both clearer. The relief I feel at making it through such a small task is sickening—I hope Wes doesn't see it. I slide my ring on and sink back against the wall, feeling more like myself than I have in weeks.

"Well, that was fun," he says casually as he returns his own ring to his finger. "Truth be told, I kind of miss the days when your territory was full of burly knife-wielding convicts. And remember that boy?" he adds nostalgically. "The one who took a jog through the Coronado?"

"Vividly," I say drily. "I picked the broken glass out of your back. Right before we got chewed out for not letting Crew handle it."

Wes sighs. "Crew have all the fun. One day . . ." He trails off, dragging his attention back. "Well, Miss Bishop, your list is clear, and your mother probably thinks we've spent the last"—he checks his watch—"fifty-two minutes engaged in any number of nefarious activities." He reaches out and messes my hair a little, rock music playing through my head with his fingers.

"Wes," I groan, trying to smooth it.

"What? I'm only adding authenticity. Your parents already think we're dating."

"I told them we're not. They don't seem to believe me."

Wes shrugs. "I don't care," he lies. "Gives you a good excuse."

"You're not just an excuse, Wes."

"No, I'm a pretty one," he says with a wink. "I should probably get going, though. Make sure Jill isn't trying to act out any of the things in those books of hers. She's on a pirate kick right now. Made one of Angelli's cats walk a makeshift plank . . ." He turns toward the stairs, but stops after a few feet and casts a mischievous glance back my way. "But I could come by later . . . if you want."

The thought of a full night of sleep, wrapped in nothing but his noise, makes my heart ache, but I force myself to shake my head. "They're not going to let you stay a second time."

"Who says they have to know?" he asks.

"Sneaking into a girl's room?" I ask with mock surprise. "That sounds like something a boyfriend would do."

Wesley's smile tilts. "Just leave the window open."

I make it back to the café with five minutes to spare, catching Mom's eye on the way in. If I'm expecting a smile, a welcome back, or an apology, I'm disappointed. Mom's efficient glance from clock to me to clock to work makes it clear: it's going to take a lot more than an hour without broken promises to piece our family back together.

The first thing I do when I get back upstairs is slide my bedroom window open (if my parents ask, I can say something about needing fresh air, since this seems like the only way I'll ever get any), but when I pause to look out and *down*, I realize there's no way Wes is going to get inside tonight. I rest my elbows on the window and consider the drop until I hear a nervous squeak and turn to see Mom standing in the doorway, looking at me like she thinks I'll jump.

"Nice night," I say, pulling my head back in.

"Dinner's ready," she says, nearly making eye contact before retreating into the kitchen. Progress.

Dad has insisted on cooking, as if that will mend things. He even makes my favorite—spaghetti with meatballs from scratch— but we still spend most of the meal in a silence broken only by scraping knives and forks. Dad won't look at Mom, and Mom won't look at me. All I can think as we sit in silence is that if my life ended right now, there would be this trail of destruction, a wake of ruined trust, and it leaves me feeling empty. Did Da ever feel this way?

Antony Bishop was a flake, and a criminal, and a selfish asshole who cared more about his secrets and his many lives than his family.

Is that how Dad really saw his father? Is that what he was? What I am? Something that rends the family instead of gluing it together? Ben was our glue. Have we been weakening without him? Or have I been prying us apart?

Halfway through the meal, I feel the scratch of letters on my list again, and my heart sinks. I excuse myself and escape to my room, my father's command to leave the door open trailing like a weight behind me.

The silence is worse when I'm alone, quickly filling up with *how*s and *why*s and *what if*s. How is Agatha's search going? Why is someone doing this? What if my theory is wrong? I switch the radio on and unfold the Archive paper. Another name.

Henry Mills. 14.

I slump down on my bed, tossing my good arm over my eyes. Even if I weren't being watched like a hawk, it would be hard to keep up with names appearing at this rate. Keepers are encouraged to deal with them as quickly as possible, to keep the list from getting long and to keep the Histories from slipping into madness, since they're harder to handle once they have. But they're not expected to spend every waking moment standing near a Narrows door, waiting for the call. Then again, their jobs and their lives don't hang in the balance. Someone else may be able to let the names sit. I can't. Not with Agatha looking for any signs of weakness.

I sit up, considering the open window. Can Wes really get in? And if so, can I get out?

Eventually Mom and Dad go to bed with their door open, but I'm allowed to close mine, probably because they figure the only way I can get out is through the window, and nobody would be crazy enough to try that. Nobody except Wesley, apparently, who appears around midnight sitting like a specter in the window frame.

I look up from the bed as he slips into the room, offering a silent and dramatic bow before crossing to me.

"Color me impressed," I whisper under the music on the radio. "Do I want to know how you did that?"

"I said I was a good climber," he whispers. "Never said I had to climb *up*." He points a finger at the ceiling. "4F is vacant."

"Well," I say, getting to my feet, "I'm really glad you made it."

Wesley's eyes light up. "Yeah?"

"Yeah," I say, tugging on my boots.

Wes's brow knits. "Going somewhere?"

"I assume if you got in, you know how to get back out."

"Well, yeah, in theory. But I kind of thought I wouldn't have to test it till morning."

"There's another name on my list."

"So?"

I go to the window and peer out and up, considering the rock walls of the Coronado. Not the easiest ascent, especially with one good arm. "I need to clear it."

"Mac," whispers Wes, joining me by the window. "I'm all for efficiency, but this is bordering on obsessive. It's only one name. Leave it till tomorrow."

"I *can't*," I say, swinging my leg out the window.

He catches my elbow to steady me, the beat of his life sliding through my shirt and under my skin. "Why not?"

I don't want to lie, not to Wes, but I don't want him to worry, either. I'm worried enough for the both of us, and there's nothing he can do right now except show me how to climb out of this room. "Because it's a test." It's not a lie. Agatha *is* testing me.

"What?" Wesley's eyes darken.

"An evaluation," I say. "After everything that's happened, I guess they—Agatha—wants to make sure . . ." My eyes slide down to my sleeve, the bandages peeking out around the wrist.

"Sure of what?" snaps Wes, and I hear something new in his voice. Anger, directed at the Archive. "Jesus, after everything you've been through, everything you're *going* through—"

I swing my leg back into the room and take Wesley by the shoulders, my eyes sliding past him to the door, worried someone will hear the commotion. "Hey," I say, making sure to talk under the sound of the radio. "It's okay. I don't blame them. But I need to keep the list clear. And to do that, I need your help."

"Is this why they locked me out of your territory?"

I nod, and he lets out a low oath before pulling himself together. "What they're doing," he says, shaking his head as if to clear it, "I'm sure it's just protocol." He doesn't sound like he believes it, but I can tell he wants to.

"I'm sure," I say. I wish I could believe it, too.

He steps up to the window, gripping the sill. After a long breath, he says, "Are you sure you can climb?"

"I'll manage," I say stiffly.

"Mac—"

"I'll manage, Wes. Just show me what to do."

He sits on the sill and brings one leg up, resting his shoe on the wood as he takes hold of the open window over his head and then, in one fluid motion, stands, coming to his feet outside. He keeps one hand curled under the window for support as he shimmies to the side and steps off the sill and onto a thin outcrop of rock, vanishing from sight. When I stick my head out, I see him scaling the side of the Coronado, thin bit of stone to thin bit of stone until he reaches an open window roughly ten feet overhead. He hoists himself up into the window and sits there, elbows on his knees, looking down at me.

"Tell me that was more fun than it looks," I say.

"Loads," says Wes as I take a deep breath and climb out onto the frame, following his lead. My arm aches dully as I grip the bottom edge of the window for support, eyeing the surfacing stones that stand between me and **4F**. They are not flat and smooth but jagged, worn away by time and weather like the gargoyles on the roof. Each is somewhere between a brick and a cinder block; as I reach for the first one, a pebble crumbles off overhead and skitters down the wall.

I am going to die. I always thought that if something in the Coronado killed me, it would be the elevators, but no. It will be this.

I take a deep breath and step off the windowsill onto the stones. I will myself not to look down; instead I focus on the number of stones between me and safety, counting down. Eight . . . seven . . . six . . . five . . . four . . . three . . .

"This isn't so bad," I say when I'm nearly to Wes.

. . . two . . . one.

And that's when my toes come down on a moss-slick bit and I slip, plunging a foot before a hand wraps vise-tight around my bad wrist. Pain rips up my arm, sudden and bright, and my vision falters, tunneling. Wesley says something, but his voice is far away and then gone altogether. I feel the darkness folding around me, trying to drag me down, but I cling to his hand and the heavy drum of his noise. I focus on that, not the strange distance or the sense of time skipping like a stone. I focus on the music until I can see the wall in front of me, until I can hear Wesley's words, begging for my other hand.

And just like that, time snaps back into motion, and I grab hold of his arm with both hands, and he hauls me up and through the window. We both hit the floor in the empty apartment and lie there a moment, gasping with relief.

"See?" pants Wes, rolling onto his back on the hardwood floor. "That was fun."

"We really need to discuss your idea of fun." I drag myself into a sitting position, wincing, then get to my feet and look around at the apartment, or at least try. It's pitch-black, the only light streaming in through the window off the street, but I can tell there's nothing here. It has that hollow, echoing feel that comes with empty space, and the only break in the dust on the floor is clearly from Wesley earlier tonight. He brushes himself off and leads me through the bones of **4F**.

"It's been vacant for nearly a decade," he explains. "You will appreciate, though, that according to the walls, the last person who lived here had no fewer than *five* cats."

I shudder. I hate cats, and Wesley knows it. He's the one who found me sitting on the floor outside Angelli's place after being assaulted by her feline horde.

"So who are we looking for?" asks Wes, heading for the front door.

"Henry Mills. Age fourteen."

"Splendid," says Wes, opening the door and showering us in hall light. "Maybe if we're lucky, he'll put up a fight."

Wesley gets his wish.

In the short time Henry's been out, he's slipped enough that when he looks at us he doesn't see *us*, he sees something he's afraid of—in this case, cops—and Wes and I end up chasing him through half the territory before we manage to corner him. It's not the most delicate return—we drag him kicking and screaming through the nearest door—but it gets the job done.

It's nearly three a.m. by the time we get back to **4F** and make the terrifying descent into my room—this time without incident. I sink onto the bed, exhausted. Wesley makes his way to the nearby chair, but I catch his hand, music flaring through me as I draw him to the bed. I let go and scoot back to make room for him. He hovers there a moment, knees against the mattress.

"Beds are for boyfriends," he says.

"And for people who don't like sleeping in chairs," I say. Something like sadness flashes in his eyes before he smiles, sinking onto the comforter beside me. He snaps the bedside light off, and we lie there inches apart in the dark. Wesley offers his hand, and when I take it, he presses my palm to the front of his shirt. His noise pours through me, loud and welcome.

"Good night, Wesley," I whisper.

"Sleep well," he whispers back.

And somehow, I do.

TWENTY-TWO

"IT'S A HEAVY burden to bear," says Roland, handing the picture back, "but Crew is worth it."

I look down at the picture of Da and his partner, Meg. I can't imagine fitting with someone the way they do, so close they almost touch, even though they're not wearing silver bands. Is that what love is for people like us? Being able to share space? Without our rings, we wear our lives on our sleeves. Our thoughts and wants and fears. Our weaknesses. I can't bear the thought of someone seeing mine.

"How?" I ask. "How can it be worth it?" I run my thumb over Da's face. This isn't the Da I knew. My Da had far more wrinkles and far less ease. My Da has been in the ground six months. "Letting people in, loving them—it's a waste. In the end it just hurts more when you lose them."

Roland leans back against a shelf, a History's dates printed just above his shoulder. He looks out past me, his gray eyes unfocused.

"It's worth it," he says, "to have someone from whom you hide nothing. The weight of secrets and lies starts heavy, and it only gets harder. You build walls to keep the world out. Crew is the small part of the world you let in.

"It's worth it," says Roland again. "One day, when you're surrounded by those walls, you'll see."

• • •

Wesley is gone by the time I wake up.

It's a good thing, because Mom is bustling around my room, closing the window, tidying stacks of paper, gathering up pieces of laundry from the floor. Apparently privacy went out the window with trust. She tells the desk it's time to get up, tells the laundry in her hands that breakfast is ready. We seem to have taken a step back.

The Archive list is tucked under the phone on my bedside table, and when I go to check it, I see there's a text from Wesley.

> I dreamed of thunderstorms. Did you dream of concerts?

In truth, I didn't dream of anything, and the feeling of dreamless sleep on my bones is glorious. No nightmares. No Owen. I look down at my arm and wonder how it went that far. I feel so much closer to sane after a few hours of rest.

I'm about to reply when I see a conversation with Lyndsey. One I never had. It's from Saturday night, when Mom spiked my water and Wes first stayed over.

> Earth to Mac!

> Earth to Mac!

> The HOTTEST boy is in this coffee shop.

I need you to be awake so you can vicariously appreciate it.

And he has a violin case. A VIOLIN CASE. *swoon*

Sorry, Mac is sleeping.

Then how is she texting?

Is she a sleep-texter?

GASP.

IS THIS GUYLINER?

The very same.

She charged her phone for you. I hope you're worth it.

I hope so, too.

I almost smile, but then a knot forms in my stomach. *Worth it. Crew is worth it,* echoes Roland.

I put the phone away and begin to get dressed. The cut on my hand is healing well. My forearm, on the other hand, is killing me after last night's adventures; I'm worried I might have ripped the stitches. I flex gingerly and wince, then check my list. There's already another name on it.

Penny Ellison. 13.

"Mackenzie." Mom's standing in the doorway. Her eyes get as close as my cheek. "We're going to be late."

"We?" I ask.

"I'm driving you to school."

"Like hell—"

"*Mackenzie,*" warns Mom. "It's not negotiable. And before you go running to your father, you should know that it was his idea. He doesn't want you using the bicycle with your arm in that condition, and I agree."

I obviously shouldn't have left them alone at the table last night. So much for clearing Penny before heading to Hyde.

I get ready and follow Mom downstairs, and we're through the front doors when Berk shows up on the patio and waves her over, spouting something about an espresso emergency.

My eyes go to Dante, leaning up against the bike rack. "I could—"

"No," says my mom. "Stay here. I'll be *right* back."

I sigh and sink against the patio wall to wait, picking at the tape on my palm. Someone casts a shadow over me, and a moment later, Eric sits down on the low wall a few feet away, resting a Bishop's to-go cup on his knee.

"I didn't know about Roland," I say.

"I didn't tell you," he says simply. I look over. He looks tired, but otherwise unscathed. "Agatha is running out of Crew."

I swallow hard. "How much time do I have?"

"Not enough," he says, sipping his coffee. "Are you innocent, Miss Bishop?" I hesitate, then nod. "Then why would you refuse her?"

"I was afraid I'd fail an assessment."

"But you just said—"

"A mental assessment," I clarify. Silence falls between us. "Do you ever wish you'd gone a different way?" I ask after a minute.

Eric gives me a guarded look. "I'm honored to serve the Archive," he says. "It gives me purpose." And then he softens a little. "There have been times when I've wavered. When I thought maybe I wanted to be normal. But the thing is, what we do, it's in our blood. It's who we are. Normal wouldn't fit us, even if we wanted to wear it." He sighs and gets to his feet. "I'd tell you to stay out of trouble," he says, "but it just seems to find you, Miss Bishop."

Mom reappears with two to-go cups, and there's this split second as she hands me one when she finally looks me in the eye. Then she sees the man standing beside me.

"Good morning, Eric!" she says brightly. "How's that dark roast?"

He gives her his best smile. "Worth crossing the city for, ma'am," he says before heading off down the sidewalk.

"Eric's become a bit of a regular," explains Mom as we walk to her car.

"Yeah," I say drily. "I've seen him around."

. . .

Mom has the decency to drop me off a block and a half from school and out of the line of sight of the parking lot. As the car pulls away, I look down at my arm, hoping I can get through one day without an incident. Maybe Eric's right. Maybe normal doesn't suit us, but I'd be willing to pretend.

I catch sight of Cash, resting against the bike rack with coffee and a smile. Cash, who always makes me *feel* normal. But the moment I reach him, I can see something's off.

His dark hair trails across his cheekbones, but it can't entirely hide the cut beside his eye or the bruise darkening his jaw.

"Looks like I'm not the only one to get into a scrape," I say. "Soccer? Or did you and Wes go a few rounds on the mat?"

"Nah," he says. But he doesn't seem eager to say any more.

"Well, come on," I say as he hands me a fresh coffee. "I told you my clumsy story. It's only fair you tell me yours."

"I wish I could," he says, furrowing his brow, "but I'm not exactly sure what happened."

I frown, taking a sip. "What do you mean?"

"Well, I was heading back from your place yesterday—I was going to take the bus, but it was a nice day, so I decided to walk. I was almost back to the school, when all of a sudden there's this crashing sound behind me, and before I can turn to see what happened, someone pulls me backward *hard*."

The coffee goes bitter in my mouth.

"It was insane," he says. "One minute I'm minding my own business, and the next I'm laid out on the sidewalk." He brings his fingertips to the cut beside his eye. "I caught myself on a bench on the way down. I couldn't have been out for more than a minute or two, but by the time I got up, there was no one else around."

"What did it sound like?" I ask slowly. "The noise behind you."

"It was loud, like a crash, or a tear, or a whoosh. Yeah, a whoosh. And that's not even the strangest part." He curls his fingers around the cup. "You'll think I'm crazy. Hell, *I* think I'm crazy. But I swear there was a guy walking maybe a few strides behind me right before it happened. I thought he might have been the one to grab me, but by the time I got back up he was gone." He straightens and chuckles. "God, I sound like a nut job, don't I?"

"No," I say, gripping the paper cup. "You don't."

A ripping sound, a force hard enough to slam Cash backward, and no visible trace? All the markings of a void. Was the man behind him Crew? Or a fourth victim?

"What did the other guy look like?"

Cash shrugs. "He looked normal."

I frown. It doesn't make sense. If someone was trying to attack Cash, they missed, and I don't see why they'd attack him in the first place—not while I was under lock and key. There would be nothing to tie me to this crime, so why do it?

"Did you see anyone else besides the other guy?" I ask, stepping closer.

He shakes his head, and I grab his arm, his noise singing through me. "Can you remember *anything* about the moments before it happened? Anything at all?"

Cash's gaze goes to the ground. "You."

I pull back a fraction. "What?"

"I wasn't paying attention, because I was thinking about you." My face goes warm as he gives a small, stifled laugh. "Truth be told, I can't *stop* thinking about you."

Then, out of nowhere, Cash takes my face in his hands and kisses me. His lips are warm and soft, and my head fills with jazz and laughter; for an instant, it feels sweet and safe and simple. But my life is none of those things, and I realize as the kiss ends that I don't want to pretend it is, and that there is only one person I want to kiss me like this.

Someone by the gate whistles, another cheers, and I pull away sharply.

"I can't," I say, my face on fire. It feels like everyone in the lot is looking at us.

Cash immediately retreats, trying not to look stung. "It's Wes, isn't it?"

Yes. "It's life."

"Way to be broad," he says, slouching back against the bike rack. "It's a lot easier to hate a *person.*"

"Then it's me. Look, Cash, you're amazing. You're sweet and clever, and you make me smile. . . ."

"I sound pretty awesome."

"You are," I say, stepping away. "But my life right now is . . . complicated."

Cash nods. "Okay. Understood. And who knows," he says, brightening, "maybe one day it will be simpler."

I manage a thin smile. *Maybe.*

And then someone calls Cash's name, and his face lights up as he turns and shouts back, and it's like nothing happened. I have to wonder if he has masks he wears, too. Maybe we all do.

Wes shows up a few minutes later in his senior black-and-gold, looking like he spent the weekend lounging by a pool instead of scaling Coronado walls and warding off my nightmares. Cash gets dragged into a conversation with a nearby group, and Wes knocks his shoulder against mine and whispers, "No nightmares?"

"No nightmares," I say. And that's something to be thankful

for. That is progress—small, fractional, but it is something. It is me clawing my way back to sanity.

The bell rings, and we all head through the gate. Whatever Fall Fest is, it's starting to take over campus. The bones of it are scattered in the stretches of grass between buildings, massive ribbons in black and green and silver and gold are rolled and waiting, and everyone seems oddly cheerful for a Monday morning.

Every moment without the watch and the warden and the constant reminders that I'm *not* okay makes me feel closer to normal. By ten thirty in Lit Theory, I'm feeling positively mundane. And then Ms. Wellson drags her chalk across the board and the sound is too sharp, like metal on stone.

Metal on stone, I think. And as I think it, my body stiffens and stops. The rest of the room doesn't. Wellson keeps talking, but her voice seems suddenly dull and far away. I desperately try to move the pen in my hand, but my hand refuses. My whole body refuses.

"Did you really think," comes a voice from behind me, "that a little sleep could fix the ways you're broken?"

No. I close my eyes. *You're not real.*

But a moment later I *feel* Owen's arms wrap around my shoulders, *feel* his hand brush the line he carved into my arm.

"Are you sure about that?" He presses down. Pain flares across my skin, and the air catches in my throat as I jerk to my feet, my body suddenly unfreezing. The entire class turns to look at me.

"Miss Bishop?" asks Ms. Wellson. "Is something wrong?"

I murmur something about feeling unwell, then grab my bag and race into the hall, reaching the bathroom just in time to retch. My shoulders shudder as I forfeit breakfast and two cups of coffee, then slump back against the stall, resting my forehead against my knees.

This shouldn't be happening. I'm supposed to be getting better. *Did you really think that a little sleep could fix the ways you're broken?*

My eyes start to burn and I squeeze them shut, but a few tears still escape down my cheeks.

"Hangover?" comes a voice from the next stall. Safia. "Morning sickness?" I force my eyes open and drag myself to my feet. She walks out of the stall and over to the sink as she adds, "Eating disorder?"

I rinse my mouth out as she joins me, hopping up onto the counter. "Food poisoning," I lie blandly.

"Less exciting," she says, producing a small container of mints and offering me one. "I'm always telling Cash he shouldn't buy that cheap coffee from the corner store. Honestly, who knows what's in it? I guess it's a nice gesture, though."

"I'm sure he's just doing his job," I mutter, splashing water on my face.

Safia rolls her eyes. She hops down off the counter and turns to go.

"Safia," I say as she reaches the door. "Thanks."

"For what?" she asks, crinkling her nose. "I offered you a mint. That's, like, common decency, not social bonding."

"Well, thanks for being commonly decent, then."

The edge of her mouth quirks, and then she's gone.

The moment the door's shut, I slump back against the brick wall beside the sink and wrap my hands around my ribs to keep them from shaking. Just when I think things can't get worse, I feel the scratch of letters in my pocket. I dig the Archive paper out as a second name—*Rick Linnard. 15.*—writes itself below *Penny Ellison. 13.*

Two names, and it isn't even lunch. Could Agatha be doing this on purpose? Would she go that far to prove a point? I don't know. I don't know what to believe anymore. But it doesn't matter how the names got there; I have to handle them. Besides, clearing this list is the only thing still in my control. My mind spins. The class bell rings in the distance. Wellness. I'll skip. I know where the nearest Narrows door is now. The only problem is my key won't work. It's not my territory. And with Wesley's access to *mine* revoked, even if he lets me in to his, I can't cross the divide.

I find a pencil in my bag and spread the paper out on the sink, tapping the eraser several times against it before finally writing a message.

Requesting access to adjacent territory: Hyde School.

I stand at the sink and stare down at the page, waiting and hoping for a response. I count out the time it will take to get to the door, cross Wesley's territory into my own, and find and return Rick and Penny.

And then the answer comes. One small, horrible word: *Denied.*

It's not signed, but I recognize Agatha's script. Frustration wells up in me, and I slam my hand into the nearest thing, which happens to be a metal tissue holder. It goes crashing to the floor.

"Mackenzie?" asks a voice from the door. I turn to find a woman standing there. She looks exactly like she did in the hospital, from the messy ponytail to the slacks, but she's traded a name tag that reads *Psychologist* for one that reads *Hyde School Counselor.*

"Dallas?" I ask, crumpling the Archive paper before she can see it. The question and answer have both bled away, but the names are still there. "What are you doing here?"

"We had a deal, remember?" She bends down to fetch the dented tissue box and sets it back on the edge of the counter. "I figured I'd meet you at the Wellness Center, but I ran into Miss Graham and she pointed me in this direction. Is everything . . . ?" She trails off, and I appreciate not having to answer the question when it's obvious that, no, everything's not. "Do you need a moment?" she asks. I nod, and Dallas vanishes back through the door to wait.

I check my reflection in the mirror. Blue-gray eyes stare back at me—Da's eyes—but their once-even gaze is now unsure, the blue made brighter by the red ringing them. My cracks are showing. I splash water on my face to cool my cheeks and rinse away any trace of tears, then smooth out the Archive paper and refold it properly before slipping it into the pocket of my shirt.

A few minutes later, when I step out into the hall, I at least *look* the part of a normal junior. Dallas is eating an apple and pretending to be interested in a Fall Fest flyer on the wall. Cash is front and center in the photo, wearing cat ears, dipping a senior girl with one hand and holding a sparkler aloft with the other.

"When you had me agree to therapy," I say, tugging my sleeves down over my hands, "I didn't realize it would be with you."

"Is that going to be a problem?" she asks, ditching the apple core in the nearest trash bin. "Because it's me or a middle-aged guy named Bill who's nice enough, but kind of smells."

"I'll stick with you."

"Good choice," she says, leading me through a pair of doors and across the quad. The Fall Fest materials are scattered everywhere, and we have to weave through them just to get to the Wellness Center.

"I just didn't realize you worked here, too," I say as we reach the building and go in. Instead of heading toward the lockers, she leads me down a hall to a row of offices.

"Most nights and weekends I belong to the hospital," she tells me as we reach an office with her name on it and go inside. There's a chair and a couch and a coffee table. "During the week, I'm here. As long as we're meeting, I'll be taking the place of your Wellness class, since this is, in fact, addressing wellness of another sort."

"And how long are we meeting?" I ask.

"I suppose that depends on you." She slumps into the chair and retrieves a notebook from the coffee table. "How are the battle scars?"

"Healing," I say as I sit down.

"And how are *you*?"

How am I? Three—possibly four—people have been dragged into voids because of me, my only theory as to why is crumbling, the assessor of the Archive is determined to find me unfit, and my nightmares are becoming real. But of course I can't tell Dallas any of this.

"Mackenzie?" she prompts.

"I've been better," I say quietly. "I think I might be losing my mind." It is the most honest thing I've said aloud in days.

She frowns a little. "Still having bad dreams?"

"These days, everything feels like a bad dream," I say. "I just want to wake up."

TWENTY-THREE

BY THE TIME I get to lunch, everyone else's trays are stacked in the Alchemist's outstretched arms and they're sitting in a circle, chatting about Fall Fest. I'm surprised to see Safia on the steps, Amber's elbow locked through hers as if holding her hostage.

"Hey, we missed you in Wellness," says Cash as I climb the steps. "What happened?"

"I had a meeting," I say, sitting down in the gap between Amber and Gavin. I pick at my food, watching bits of rice slide through the tines of my fork. "What did I miss?"

"Let's see," says Gavin, who usually spends most of Wellness stretched out on a weight bench, people-watching. "Amber tried to teach Cash yoga, Wesley boxed, and Saf flirted with a senior running on the track and nearly face-planted."

Safia pitches an empty soda can at his head.

"I'm so sorry I missed that," I say with a small smile. And then, in response to her gold-eyed death glare, I add, "I mean *all* of it. I'm having trouble picturing Cash in any of those poses."

"I'll have you know that I do a mean sun salutation." He proceeds to hop up and demonstrate something that I can only imagine is loosely related to yoga. Everyone laughs and cheers him on, but Wesley finds my eyes across the circle and gives me a questioning look, so I dig my phone out of my bag and text him one word.

Therapy.

Cash has taken his seat again after collecting a healthy amount of applause, and the group is back to talking about Fall Fest.

"What is it exactly?" I ask.

"It's just a dance," says Wes.

"*Just* a dance?" says Cash with mock affront.

"It sets the tone for the *entire* year," adds Safia.

"It's the official back-to-school party," explains Gavin. "Tomorrow night. It's always the first of September, and the senior class is in charge of organizing it."

"And it's going to be a blast," says Cash. "There's music, and food, and dancing, and we're going to end the night with fireworks."

"Of course it's Hyde," cuts in Safia, "so the dress code's killer strict. Most people just stay in uniform."

"But there are no rules for hair and makeup," says Gavin. "Some people treat it like a contest to see how strange you can get without breaking dress code."

"Last year Saf and Cash both went with bright blue hair," says Amber. "And Wes embraced his inner goth boy."

"Seriously?" I say. Wesley winks at me, and I laugh. "I can't imagine that."

"Crazy, right?" she says. "Anyway, you can wear wacky jewelry or weird makeup or neon leggings."

"It's kind of awesome to see everyone as a stranger version of themselves," says Gavin.

"You're going, right, Mackenzie?" asks Amber.

I shake my head. "Sorry, don't think so." I'm pretty sure my house arrest doesn't have a school dance loophole.

"Hey," says Gavin, addressing me. "Is everything okay?"

"Why wouldn't it be?" I ask.

"I heard you had to leave class."

Wesley's brow creases with concern. "You okay?"

"Wow," I say, glancing at Safia, "word *does* travel fast around here."

"Don't look at me," she says. "To talk about it I'd have to care, which I don't. But I *did* hear a rumor about you and Cash this morning in front of the——"

"What happened?" cuts in Amber. "In class?"

"Nothing," I say. "I didn't feel well, so I left."

"Cash's crappy coffee," offers Saf.

"Hey," snaps Cash, "I only buy gourmet."

"The corner store doesn't *have* gourmet, and you know it."

Saf and Cash start bickering, but Wes isn't so quick to drop the subject. *Are you all right?* he mouths at me across the circle, giving me a weighted look. I force myself to nod. He looks skeptical, but then Cash turns to him and says, "Have you decided yet if you're taking Elle or Merilee or Amber?"

Wesley, still considering me, says, "I'm not taking any of them."

Safia gasps. "Wesley Ayers, going stag?"

He shrugs, finally turning his attention back to the group. "I didn't want to pick just one and deprive the others of my company." He flashes a crooked smile when he says it, but the line rings hollow.

"No one's taking anyone," announces Amber. "We'll go as a group."

"Screw your group," says Safia. "I've already got a date."

"You've been working hard enough to get one," says Cash.

Saf throws a book at his head. It nearly hits Gavin, and the rest of lunch is a blur of chattering, bickering, and festival prep.

I barely hear a word they say.

As the lunch bell rings, I scribble another plea to the Archive. Again it's denied.

"When did Safia decide to join the Court?"

Amber and I are walking to Physiology, our shoes echoing against the science hall's marble entryway.

"Ah, the migration," says Amber cheerfully. "A time-honored tradition, really. Saf starts the school year determined to make a name for herself, climb the social ladder, build an entourage of minions—god knows enough of the first and second years are willing—and then she realizes something."

"What's that?"

Amber smiles and lifts her chin. "That the Court is, in fact, infinitely cooler than anyone else she'll find at Hyde. She usually comes around before Fall Fest, and we welcome her back as though she never left. I'm sure she'd rather just ditch the act, but she'll never admit she actually wants to hang out with Cash."

And I'm sure Wesley *has nothing to do with it,* I think as Amber squints at me.

"Speaking of Cash——" she starts.

"Any new leads on the Judge Phillip case?" I say, changing the subject as obviously as possible. "Or Bethany?" Amber sighs, but takes the bait and shakes her head. "I haven't seen Dad this stressed in ages. They put a new case on his plate this weekend. Another unsolvable. This one doesn't even have a crime scene or a point of departure. Some guy just went for a morning run and never came back. The brother finally reported him missing."

My stomach twists. Jason.

"How can they possibly expect him to solve that?" I ask.

Amber shrugs. "It's his job, I guess. They act like he's some miracle-worker. Trust me, he's not." Halfway up the stairs, she says, "Hey, can I ask you a question?"

"Sure thing."

I expect her to ask why her father picked me up this weekend, but instead she asks, "How long have you known Wesley?"

"A couple months," I say, rounding up. It certainly feels like longer.

"And how long do you think he's been in love with you?"

I feel the heat creeping into my face. "We're just friends." Amber makes a sound of disbelief. "I mean, we're close," I add. Bonded by secrets and scars. "But we're not . . . I don't . . . I care about Wesley, and he cares about me."

"Look," she says as we reach the classroom, "I just met you, but I've known Wesley for ages. I can tell you that 'he cares' is an understatement." Amber steps out of the way to let someone get to class. "Did you really kiss Cash this morning?"

"He kissed *me*," I clarify, "and it ended right there."

Amber waves a hand. "I don't care about the details. The point is, I don't want you playing games with Wes. He's been through a lot, and I think he's finally in a good place, and—"

"And you don't think I'm good for him."

The words hit like a blow, even though they're mine. Because they're true. I'm not good for him. At least, I haven't been. I want to be. But how can I? I feel like a bomb waiting to go off; I don't want him holding on to me when it does. But he won't let go, and I can't seem to, either.

"I didn't say that," says Amber. "It's just . . . Gavin and Saf and Cash and I, we work really hard to *keep* him in that good place. He may live in a big house on a hill, but *we're* his family. I don't know how much you know about his life before you came into it, but he's been hurt by a fair number of people. He may have put himself back together decently, but he's not all the way there. And it's obvious he cares about you *a lot*; so all I'm saying is, don't hurt him, okay? Because it's obvious you're going through some things, too, and I want you to be really sure before you let him fall any harder for you. Be sure that you're good for him."

She opens the door. "And if you're not, don't let him fall at all."

Mr. Lowell's out, and the sub in Government spends the first half of the period reading everything Lowell's already taught us straight off a handout, then decides that revolution is too heavy for a Monday and mercifully lets us go early. There's a text from Mom saying she's going to be late picking me up—I'm hoping I can use it as leverage when the topic of transport comes up again tomorrow morning—which leaves me with half an hour or so to kill. I send a third request to the Archive, then wander out onto the quad to wait for the reply.

Even though the bell hasn't rung yet, a dozen gold-striped seniors are scattered around the quad assembling tents. I spot Wesley at the northern edge of the green, hammering steel rods into the grass.

Not the Wesley who hunts Histories, or the one who lies in bed with me, drowning my nightmares with his noise, but one who laughs and smiles and looks *happy*. It's not that he doesn't look that way when we're together, but there's an edge to him when I'm around. The strain of scars and shared secrets and worry shows in his face even when he smiles, even when he sleeps. I weigh him down.

A bone-deep sadness spreads through me as I realize something.

Wesley may be worth it, worth loving and worth letting in, but I can't do it. I won't. Not as long as there's a target on my back. I can't drag him into this mess. Amber was right. The last time he got pulled into my fight, he lost a day of his life. I won't let him lose more, not because of me.

I retreat through campus, weaving from one path to another, the urge to move stronger than the desire to go anywhere in particular. *Restless bones*, that's what Ben used to call it. I have never been able to sit still. Maybe Eric's right, and being a part of the Archive isn't just a job. Maybe it's in my bones. Maybe I couldn't be normal, even if I had a chance to try. Normal is like stillness: uncomfortable, unnatural. So I walk. And as I walk, a word scratches itself onto the paper in my palm.

Denied.

The answer hits like a dull blow as my feet carry me down the path. I don't even realize I've heading for the Wellness Center until I look up and see the stone mantel. I pass through the lockers and into the massive gym.

With everyone either still in class or setting up for Fall Fest, the gym is a hollow white hull—similar to a Returns room, but vast and walled and full of equipment. It's strange being in here alone, and yet it's peaceful. Like the Archive used to be. The quiet here might not be as reverent, but it's all-encompassing, and it reminds me of a time years ago when I was normal—or closer to it—and running was the nearest thing I had to peace.

When I ran, I lost myself.

I have been afraid of losing myself lately. Afraid of pushing too hard. Afraid of letting my guard down. Of letting go.

Now I step onto the track with a kind of abandon and start to run. At first it's a jog, but then I go faster and faster, until I break into a full sprint, giving it everything I have. I haven't run like this in days, weeks, years.

I run until the world blurs. Until I can't breathe, can't hear, can't think. Until Owen is gone and the voids are gone and Agatha is gone and the Archive is gone and Wesley is gone and there is nothing but the sound of my shoes on the track and my pulse in my ears. I run until all my fears—the fear of losing my mind, my memories, my life—have bled away.

Time begins to slip, and for once, I don't try to catch it.

I run until I feel like myself again.

I run until I find peace.

When my shoes finally slow and stop, I bend over my knees, breathing shallowly. Then I pace slowly in a circle, waiting for my heart to slow, my eyes closed in the middle of the empty gym. I focus on the sound of my pulse.

"Miss Bishop?" calls a gruff voice, and I drag my eyes open to find the gym teacher—the one who oversees the sparring ring, I think his name is Metz—trotting over with a clipboard.

"Sorry," I say. "Am I not supposed to be here?"

Coach Metz waves the clipboard. "Whatever. None of the sports have started yet. Speaking of, you're quite the runner. Have you considered track?" I shake my head. "You should," he says. "You're a natural."

"Not sure I have the time, sir."

"Gotta make time for the important things, Bishop. Tryouts are next week. Can I at least put your name down?"

I hesitate. Where will I be next week? Hunting Histories in the Narrows, or strapped to a chair having my memories carved out? What if next week this is all a bad dream and I'm alive and still me?

"We could use someone like you," he adds.

"Okay," I say. "Sure. Count me in." It's so small, but it's something to cling to. A sliver of normal.

Coach Metz passes me the clipboard, and I write out my name and hand it back. He offers me a gruff nod of approval as he reads my name and makes a few notes in the margin.

"Good, good," he grumbles. "Hyde honor at stake, need the speed . . ." And then he trots away, disappearing through a door at the other end of the gym marked OFFICES.

I sink onto the mats to stretch out. My muscles ache from the sudden burst of activity, but it's a welcome pain. I lie down on the mat, going through my stretches; then I stare up at the ceiling and breathe, wondering: If the Archive came for me, would I run? Will it come to that?

My theory is getting thinner by the day. Everything pointed to a setup until Cash. Was the attack on him a mistake? A message? A punishment? Did they miss on purpose? Or were they trying to interrupt the pattern and weaken the theory? Questions trickle through me, and at the heart of all the *hows* and *whys*, the biggest question is *who*.

You're getting tangled, Da would say. *Most problems are simple at their center. You just gotta find the center.*

What's at the center of this problem?

The key.

You don't technically have to be Crew to make a void—I wasn't—so long as you have the right kind of *key*. But Crew are the only ones issued those keys, so the person making the voids is either Crew or someone who's been given a Crew key. Roland gave me Da's, so I know it's possible. Would a Librarian really smuggle one out? Give it to a Keeper to bury the trail of guilt? What if Owen had other allies in the Archive besides Carmen? Could one of them be trying to get revenge? Librarians are Histories; can they be read like Histories? Is there some kind of postscript that records the time they've been in the service of the Archive after their lives have been compiled?

Would Agatha ever consider reading *them*? Or would she just pin the crimes on me instead? It wouldn't fix the problem, wouldn't change the fact that someone is doing this, but it would give her an out, a person to blame. And after our latest meeting, I have no doubt she plans to find me guilty of something. Why wouldn't she sink me for this? It would be easy. All she has to do is claim I have Owen's key.

I sit up, inhaling sharply.

Owen's key. He had it on him when he went into the void. Agatha accused me of having it and I don't, but he did. Maybe he still *does*.

It's the one option I haven't considered. Haven't wanted to consider. Is it even possible? A void is a door to nowhere, but it's still a *door*. And every door has two sides. What if the voids aren't being opened from *this* side? What if someone isn't throwing people in? What if they're just trying to get *out*?

What if Owen's trying to get to me?

No.

I fall back against the mat and force myself to breathe.

No. I have to stop. I have to stop seeing Owen in everything. I have to stop looking for him in every moment of my life. Owen Chris Clarke is gone. I have to stop bringing him back.

I close my eyes and take a deep breath. And then I feel the scratch of letters on the list and take it out, expecting another name. Instead I find a message:

Access granted. Good luck. —R

Roland. Something untangles in my chest. A thread of hope. A fighting chance. I get to my feet, and I'm nearly to the locker rooms when I hear the crash.

TWENTY-FOUR

IT CAME FROM somewhere across the gym.

The crash was far enough away to sound low, loud enough for it to echo around me, but it started in the far corner, the same direction Coach Metz went. I sprint across the gym floor and through the door marked OFFICES, only to find myself in a small hallway full of trophy cases. None of them seem disturbed, and besides, the crash was deep, like something heavy falling—not high, like breaking glass. Doorways stud the hall, each with a glass window insert; I make my way down the corridor, glancing in each room to see if anything's off.

Three doors in, I look through the window and slam to a stop.

Beyond the glass is a storage room. Inside, it's too dark to make out much more than the metal shelves, half of which have toppled over. I pull my sleeve down over my hand and test the door. It's unlocked.

I step through, flicking on one of the three wall switches, illuminating the space just enough to better see the shelves. Two of them have fallen forward and caught each other on the way down. Balls and bats and helmets are now scattered across the storage room floor.

I'm so focused on not tripping on any of the equipment that I nearly slip on the blood.

I catch myself midstep and retreat from the fresh, wet slick on the concrete. I look up at the air above the blood, and my eyes *slide off* of a new void. The air catches in my throat as I listen for sounds of life around me, hearing only the thudding of my pulse.

But this scene is different from the others.

There was no blood at Judge Phillip's house. None in Bethany's driveway.

An aluminum baseball bat rests on the ground beside my shoe; I crouch and grab it (careful to keep my sleeve between the metal and my fingers to avoid leaving prints), then stand and turn in a slow circle, scanning the darker corners of the room for movement. I'm alone. It doesn't *feel* like it, but that strange sense of wrong must be coming from the void door, because there's no one here. My eyes flick back to the blood. *Not anymore, at least.*

I notice a clipboard resting facedown a foot away from the blood. When I turn it over with my shoe, I see my name written in my own hand, and my stomach twists. With a concerning clarity I realize this is evidence. I reach down and free the paper, pocketing it with a silent apology to the coach.

I clear the debris from the floor and kneel a foot or so behind the bloodstain, setting the bat to the side as I tug the ring from my finger and place it on the concrete. The void door will have burned through most of the memory, but maybe there's *something.* I press my palm to the cold concrete, and the hum drifts up toward my hand. Then I stop.

Because something in the storage room *moves.*

Right behind me.

I feel the presence a second before I catch the movement in my periphery, first only a shadow, and then the glint of metal. I will myself to stay crouched and still, one hand pressed to the floor as the other drifts toward the bat a few inches from my grasp.

My hand wraps around the bat at the same instant the shadow

surges toward me from behind, and I spring up and turn in time to block the knife that slices down through the air, the sound of metal on metal high and grinding.

My gaze goes over the bat and the blade to the figure holding it, taking in the silver-blond hair and the cold blue eyes that have haunted me for weeks. He smiles a little as he drags the knife along the aluminum.

Owen.

"Miss Bishop," he says, sounding breathless. "I've been looking for you."

He slices the knife down the length of the bat toward my hand, forcing me to shift my grip. As soon as I do, his shoe comes up sharply beneath the metal and sends it sailing into the air between us. In the time it takes the bat to fall, his knife vanishes into a holster against his back and he catches my boot with his bare hands as it connects with his chest. He twists my foot hard to the outside, knocking me off balance long enough to pluck the falling bat out of the air and swing it at my free leg. It catches me behind the knee, sending me backward onto the concrete.

I hit the ground and roll over and up onto my feet again as he lunges forward and I lunge back. Or at least I mean to, but I misjudge the distance and the toppled shelves come up against my shoulders an instant before he forces the bat beneath my chin. I get my hands up at the last second, but it's all I can do to keep him from crushing my throat. For the first time I see the blood splashed against his fingers.

"Either you've gotten stronger," he says, "or I'm worse off than I thought."

"You're not real," I gasp.

Owen's pale brow crinkles in confusion. "Why wouldn't I be?" And then his eyes narrow. "You're different," he says. "What's happened to you?" I try to force him off me, to get leverage on the bat, but he pins me in place and presses his forehead against mine. "What have they done?" he asks as the quiet—*his* quiet—spills through my head. Tangible in a way it never was in my dreams. No. No, this isn't real. *He* isn't real.

But he's not like the Owen from my nightmares, either. When he pulls back, he looks . . . *tired*. The strain shows in his eyes and the tightness of his jaw, and this time when I try to fight back, it works.

"Get off of me," I growl, driving my knee into his chest. He staggers backward, rubbing his ribs, and I grab the nearest bat and swing it at his head. But he catches it the instant before it can connect and rips the metal from my grip. It goes clanging across the concrete floor, bouncing through the pool of blood on its way and leaving a streak of red in its path.

"The least you could do is ask me how my trip was," he says coldly, twirling the bat still in his hand.

He's not real. He can't be real. This is only happening because I thought of it. This is a hallucination . . . isn't it? It has to be, because the alternative is worse.

Owen stops spinning the bat and leans on it. "Do you have *any* idea how much energy it takes to tear open a void from the other side?"

"Then how did you get out?"

"Perseverance," he says. "The problem with these things . . ." He nods at the rip in the air and makes a small, exasperated sound. "Is they don't stay open very long. As soon as someone gets dragged in, they snap shut. I couldn't seem to get out first. I couldn't go around them. Finally, I decided I had to go *through* them." His eyes flick toward the blood. I think of Coach Metz's body, floating in the void, torn in two by Owen's knife, and my stomach twists. I curl my fingers around the metal shelf behind me.

"Messy business," he says, running his blood-streaked fingers through his silver hair. "But here I am, and the question is——"

Owen doesn't get a chance to finish. I pull the shelf as hard as I can, twisting out of the way just before it comes crashing down on top of him. But even in his current shape, he's too fast. He darts out of the way, and the metal rings out against the concrete. A second later, the lights go out, plunging the storage room into darkness.

"Feistier than ever." His voice wanders toward me. "And yet . . ."

I take a step back and his arm snakes around my throat from behind. "Different." He pulls me sharply back and up, and I gasp for breath as my shoes lift off the floor.

"I should kill you," he whispers. "I could." I writhe and kick, but his hold doesn't loosen. "You're running out of air." My chest burns, and my vision starts to blur. "It's not such a bad way to go, you know. But the question is, is this how Mackenzie Bishop wants to die?"

I can't get enough air to make the word, but I mouth it, I think it, with every fiber of my being.

No.

Just like that, Owen's grip vanishes. I stagger forward and land on my hands and knees on the concrete, gasping, inches away from the streak of Metz's blood.

My silver ring glints on the floor, and I grab the metal band

and shove it on as I stagger to my feet and spin. But Owen's no longer there. The signs of him—the toppled shelves, the blood— are there, but I'm alone. A door in the distance closes, and I storm through it into the brightly lit trophy hall . . . but there's no sign of him. No sign at all. I hurry through the outer door and into the afternoon light. Again, nothing. Only the distant laughter of students setting up Fall Fest. The green is dotted with a huddle of sophomore girls. A freshman boy. A pair of teachers.

But Owen is gone.

I spend ten minutes in the girls' locker room, washing the coach's blood off my skin.

I didn't track any of it out of the storage room, but there are traces on me—my arm, my hand, my throat—from Owen's grip, and I scrub everywhere he touched. When I'm done, I wash my face with cold water over and over and over, as if that will help.

I can't bring myself to go back.

There are no prints, nothing to tie me to the room—the *crime scene,* I realize with a shiver—and the longer it's there, the greater chance of somebody finding it. I can't have them finding me with it.

Mom sends a text that says she's waiting in the lot, and I force my legs to carry me away from the scene and through campus, past students who have no idea that Metz is nothing more than a drying red slick on a concrete floor. Or that it's my fault.

Sako is leaning up against a tree nearby, and her eyes follow me as I pass. She's not just watching anymore. She's *waiting.* Like a hunting dog, kept back until the gun goes off. I know how much she *wants* to hear the bang. A new wave of nausea hits me as I realize that if Owen *is* real, she'll get her chance. Agatha *will* run out of Crew. What am I supposed to tell her when she does? That I know who made the void doors? That the History *I sent* into the abyss clawed his way back into the Outer using the key I helped him assemble? The only reason she pardoned me before was because Owen was gone.

He was supposed to stay gone.

He *is* gone.

He wasn't real.

But the blood—the blood is real, isn't it? I saw it.

Just like I saw *Owen*.

"Is everything okay?" Mom asks as I slump into the passenger seat.

"Long day," I murmur, thankful for once that we're not really on speaking terms. Numbness has crept through my chest and settled there, solidifying. I know distantly that it's a bad thing—Da would have something to say about it, I'm sure—but right now I welcome any small bit of steadiness, even if it's unnatural.

I close my eyes as Mom drives. And then to fill the quiet, she starts to sing to herself, and my blood goes cold. I recognize the tune. There are hundreds of thousands of other songs she could sing, but she doesn't choose any of them. She chooses Owen's. He only ever hummed the melody. She adds the words.

". . . my sunshine, my only sunshine . . ."

My skin starts to crawl.

". . . you make me happy . . . when skies are gray . . ."

"Why are you singing that song?" I ask, trying to keep my voice from shaking. She trails off.

"I heard you humming it," she says.

"When?"

"A few days ago. It's pretty. Used to be popular, a long time ago. My mother used to sing it when she cooked. Where did you hear it?"

My throat goes dry as I look out the window. "I don't remember."

I follow the humming through the halls.

It is just loud enough to hold on to. I wind through the Narrows, and the melody leads me all the way back to my numbered doors and to Owen. He's leaning back against the door with the I chalked into its front, and he's humming to himself. His eyes are closed, but when I step toward him, they drift open, crisp and blue, and consider me.

"Mackenzie."

I cross my arms. "I was beginning to wonder if you were real."

He arches a brow, almost playfully. "What else would I be?"

"A phantom?" I say. "An imaginary friend?"

"Well then," he says, his mouth curling up, "am I all that you imagined?"

The moment we are home—safe within the walls of the apartment—I sit down at the kitchen table, pull my phone from my pocket, and text Wesley.

No sleepover tonight.

A moment later he texts back.

> Is everything okay?

No, I want to say. *I think Owen might be back and I can't tell the Archive because it's my fault—he's my fault—and I need your help. But you can't be here because I can't stand the thought of him coming for me and finding you. If he's even real.*

Do I *want* him to be real? Which is worse, Owen in my head, or flesh and blood and free? He *felt* real. But real people don't just *disappear.*

He's not real, whispers another voice in my head. *You've just lost it.*

Cracked little head, echoes Sako.

Broken, whispers Owen.

Weak, adds Agatha.

Finally I text Wesley back.

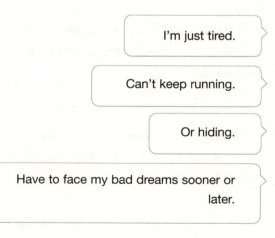

> I'm just tired.

> Can't keep running.

> Or hiding.

> Have to face my bad dreams sooner or later.

The grim truth is, I'm not afraid to fall asleep, because my nightmare is already coming true. I sit at the table waiting for his reply. Finally it comes.

> I'll miss your noise.

The numbness in my chest begins to thaw, and I turn the phone off before I can break down and write back. It takes everything I have to sit through dinner, to muster up some semblance of poise and scrounge together words about school. I only bother because skipping would lead to more worry, but the instant the dishes are clear, I escape to my room. My chest tightens when I see the open window, and I move to slide it shut. I hesitate, my fingers still wrapped around the lip.

There are three names on the list in my pocket. Part of me thinks they are the least of my problems, but the other part clings to this last vestige of duty, or at least control. I consider the climb to the apartment above, and then the drop.

"Mackenzie?" I turn to find my mother in the doorway. She's looking directly at me. "Are you all right?"

"Yeah," I answer automatically.

She continues to look me in the eyes. Her mouth opens and closes like a fish, and I can tell she's still trying to form the words: *I'm sorry.* But when she finally speaks up, all she says is, "Better shut the window. It's supposed to rain."

My attention drifts back to the drop—what was I thinking? I barely made it up that wall last night with Wesley helping me— and I pull the window closed, and say good night. Mom surprises me by pulling the door shut behind her. It's a small step, but it's something.

As soon as she's gone, I collapse onto the bed. Beyond the walls of my room, I can hear my parents talking in low voices as they shuffle through the apartment, and past them, the far-off sounds of the Coronado shutting down, the tenants retreating, the traffic on the street ebbing to a trickle and then to nothing. I realize how quiet it is in this room, without sleep and without Wesley. Some people might find it peaceful. Maybe I would, too, if my head weren't so cluttered.

Still, the quiet is heavy, and eventually it drags me down toward sleep.

And then, just as my eyes are starting to unfocus, the radio on my desk turns on by itself.

My head snaps up as a pop song fills the room. *A glitch,* I tell myself. I get to my feet to turn the radio off when the tuner flicks forward to a rock station, all metal and grind. And then a country song. I stand there in the middle of the room, holding my breath as the radio turns through half a dozen stations—no more than a few lines of each piping through—before landing on an oldies channel. The signal's weak, and I shiver as the wavering melody of a staticky crooner floats toward me.

The volume begins to turn up.

My hand's halfway to the power switch when the window next to the desk begins to *fog*. Not the whole window, but a small cloud in the middle of the glass. My heart hammers in my chest as a series of letters writes itself across the misted surface.

R I N G

I glance down at my silver band and then back up as a line draws itself through the word.

I stare at the message, torn between confusion and disbelief before finally tugging off the metal band and setting it on the sill. When I look up again, Owen's there, his reflection hovering right behind mine in the glass. I spin, ready to strike, but he catches my fist and forces me up against the window, resting his knife under my chin.

"Violence isn't *always* the answer," he says calmly.

"Says the one holding a knife to my throat," I hiss.

I can see the outline of the Crew key beneath his black shirt. If I can get it away from him and reach the closet door without him slitting my throat, I can—

He presses down on the blade in warning, and I wince, the knife's sharp edge denting the skin under my jaw. A little harder and it will slice.

"That would be a bad idea," says Owen, reading the thoughts in my skin. "Besides, the key beneath my shirt isn't the one you need." He leaves the knife against my throat and uses his other hand to pull the cord free of his collar, so I can see the too-familiar piece of rusted metal hanging from the end. It's not a Crew key at all. It's Da's key. *Mine.*

"Maybe, if you can be civilized, I'll give it back."

The knife begins to retreat, and the moment it shifts away from my skin, I catch his wrist and wrench hard. The blade tumbles to the hardwood floor, but before I can lunge for it, Owen sends it skittering across the room with his shoe. Then he catches my shoulders and pins me back against the wall beside the window.

"You *really* are a handful," he says.

"Then why haven't you killed me?" I challenge. He pulled back earlier and again just now. The Owen in my nightmares never hesitated.

"If you really want me to, I'll oblige, but I was hoping we could talk first. Your father is sitting in your living room, asleep in a chair with a book. I'm going to let go of you," he says, "but if you try anything, I'll slit *his* throat." I stiffen under his touch. "And even if you scream and wake him," adds Owen, "he can't see me, so he won't stand a chance."

Owen's hands retreat from my shoulders, and I will myself not to attack.

"What's going on?" I say. "Why can't he see you?"

Owen looks down at his hands, flexing them. "The void. It seems to have a few side effects. You helped confirm that when you first came into the storage room. I was standing right there, and you didn't even see me until you took off—"

"My ring," I say under my breath. It's a buffer, after all. A set of blinders.

"It comes in handy, I suppose," says Owen. "And all that matters is I'm here."

"But *how* are you here?" I growl. "You said you just tore your way through, but I don't understand. The doors you made, they weren't random. Why did you attack those people?"

Owen rests his shoulder against the wall. He still looks . . . drained. "I didn't mean to hurt them. I was looking for you."

My chest tightens. "What do you mean?"

The song on the radio ends and another picks up, this one slower, sadder.

"It turns out," says Owen, "the vast infinite emptiness you pitched me into isn't really empty. It's more like a shortcut without a destination. Half a door. But you can't have half a door," he says, blue eyes dancing. "You have to give it a place to go. Or a person to go to. Someone you can focus on with all your strength. I chose you."

"But you didn't find *me*, Owen. You found *five innocent people*."

Owen frowns. "Five people who crossed paths with *you*. There's a saying in the Archive: 'Strange things shine brighter.' You notice it when you read the memories in objects. But the same thing happens to the memories up here." He taps his temple. "We stand out in the minds of others more than in our own. Whoever they were, you must have made an impression. Left a mark."

My stomach turns. Behind my eyes I see them:

Judge Phillip on the verge of tears when he smelled the cookies in the oven.

Bethany clutching the silver necklace I returned.

A dazed Jason flirting to get my name and number.

Coach Metz with his gruff *good, good* when I agreed to try out for track.

And Cash? *I wasn't paying attention,* he said, *because I was thinking about you. Truth be told, I can't* stop *thinking about you.*

I wrap my arms around my ribs, feeling sick. He could have been taken, dragged through into the dark. Others *were.*

"Is there any way," I say, "to get them back?"

Owen shakes his head. "The void isn't meant for the living. It's not meant for the dead, either." Even in the dim light, I can see the way it wore on him. He looks strangely fragile. But I know better than to trust appearances.

Four people dead, for thinking about me. For caring. And how many others could have been taken? My parents? Wesley? All because of Owen. All because of *me.*

"What are you doing here?" I say through clenched teeth.

"I told you, I came to talk." Owen turns, considering the rest of the room. "I hate this place," he whispers, the words almost swallowed by the melody still leaking from the radio.

And then I remember this wasn't always my room. It was *hers*; Regina's. Owen's sister lived in here. She died in the hallway just outside. Owen looks down at the floor, where faint bloodstains still linger, worn to shadows by time. "Funny how the memory doesn't fade."

His hands, hanging loose and open at his sides, curl into fists. He should slip. If he were an ordinary History, the sight of this room and the memory of what happened here would be enough. The black of his pupils would waver and spread, engulfing the icy blue of his eyes. And as it did, he would go mad with fear and anger and guilt.

But Owen has never been an ordinary History. A prodigy turned prodigal son of the Archive. A brilliant but cunning member of Crew. A manipulator. A boy willing to jump off a roof just to die whole so he could return to punish the system he blamed.

I watch him step around the mark on the floor the way one would a body. "How long was I gone?" he asks, crouching to fetch his knife from the corner.

"Three weeks, six days, twenty hours," I say, wishing the answer didn't come so easily.

"What happened to Carmen?" he asks, straightening.

"She was reshelved," I say, "after she tried to strangle me on your behalf."

Owen turns back toward me, sliding the knife into the holster at his back. "Did she do anything else?"

"Besides waking up half the branch? No."

A grim smile flickers across his face. "And the Archive just let you walk away?"

I say nothing, and he closes the gap between us. "No," he answers for me. "They didn't. Something is different about you,

Miss Bishop. Something is wrong. They may have let you keep your memories, but they haven't given you back your life."

"At least I'm alive," I challenge.

"But your head is full of splinters," he says, his fingers tangling in my hair, his cheek coming to rest against mine. "Broken pieces and bad dreams and terror and doubt," he whispers in my ear. "So jumbled up you can't even tell real from not. Tell me, did the Archive do that to you?"

"No," I say. "You did."

His hand falls away as he pulls back to look at me. "I opened your eyes," he says with strange sincerity. "I told you the truth. It's not my fault you couldn't handle it."

"You lied to me, used me, and tried to kill me."

"And you threw me into the void," he says matter-of-factly. "The way I see it, we both did what we had to do. I didn't enjoy deceiving you, and I didn't want to kill you—I told you that then—but you were in my way. I'm here to find out if you still are."

"I will always be in your way, Owen."

A pale brow arches. "If only your thoughts were as sure as your words, Miss Bishop. But they don't lie as easily. Do you know what's written all over your mind? Doubt. You used to be so certain about your ideals—the Archive is law, is good, is god, trust in them, trust in Da—but your ideals are crumbling. The Archive is broken. Da knew—he *had* to know—and he still let them have you. Your head is full of questions, full of fears, and they are so loud I can barely hear the rest of you. And when Agatha hears them, she's going to treat you like rot in her precious Archive. She'll see you as something to be cut out before it spreads. And not even your beloved Roland will be able to stop her." He brings his hands up to the wall on either side of me, caging me in. "You want to know why I'm here? Why I haven't just slit your throat? Because unlike the Archive, I believe in salvaging what can be saved. And you, Mackenzie . . . Well, it would be a crime to let you go to waste. I want you to help me."

"Help you do what?"

The ghost of a smile touches his lips. "Finish what I started."

TWENTY-FIVE

I **ALMOST LAUGH.** And then I realize that Owen is serious. "Why would I *ever* help you?"

"Other than self-preservation?" says Owen, pushing off the wall. "I can give you what you want." He wanders around the bed to the bedside table. "I can give you back your grandfather." His fingers trail along the edge of a photo before reaching for the blue bear beside the lamp. "And your brother, Ben."

Owen's fingers close around the bear just before I slam him back against the wall. Ben's stuffed animal tumbles from his grasp.

"How dare you?" I hiss, pinning him there. "Do you think I would actually fall for that a second time? You've played this hand, Owen. It's tired. And Ben is gone. I have no desire to drag him out of sleep again. The only thing I want is to see you on a shelf."

Owen doesn't fight back. Instead he levels his infuriatingly calm gaze on me. "That won't solve your problems. Not anymore."

"It's a start."

Owen's hand flies up and wraps around my bad wrist. "So much misdirected anger," he says, tightening his grip. I gasp at the pain, but the room holds steady around me as I pull back—and to my surprise, he lets go. I cradle my wrist, and Owen crosses his arms.

"Fine," he says. "Let your dead rest. I can give you something else."

"What's that?" I snap. "Freedom? Purpose?"

Owen's blue eyes narrow. "A life."

I frown. "What?"

"A *life*, Mackenzie. One where you don't have to hide what you are or what you do. No more secrets you don't want to keep. No more lies you don't want to tell. *One* life."

"You can't give me that."

"You're right. I can't *give* it to you. But I can help you take it."

One life? Does he mean a chance to walk away? To be normal? No more lying to my family, no more holding back from Wes? But there wouldn't *be* a Wes, because Wes belongs to the Archive, Wes *believes* in the Archive. Even if I could walk away, he wouldn't. I would never ask him to, and it doesn't matter because it's not possible. The Archive never lets you go. Not intact, anyway.

"What you're promising doesn't exist."

"Not yet," says Owen. "But by the time I'm done it will."

"You mean once you've torn the Archive down—how did you put it, Owen? Branch by branch and shelf by shelf? You know I won't let you."

"What if I told you I didn't have to? That the Archive would stay, and you would stay with it if you wanted to? Only no more secrets. Would *that* be worth fighting for?"

"You're lying," I whisper. "You're just telling me what I want to hear."

Owen sighs. "I'm telling you the truth. The fact that you want to hear it means you should listen."

But how can I listen? What he's saying is madness. A dream, and a poisonous one at that. I watch as Owen crosses to the radio and switches it off.

"It's late," he says. "Think about what I've said. Sleep on it. If you're still determined to fight me, you can do so in the morning.

And if at that point I'm feeling merciful, I'll kill you whole before the Archive can destroy you bit by bit."

The Owen in my nightmares does not walk away, but this one does. He gets halfway to the bedroom door, then pauses and turns back, tugging Da's key back out from under his collar. He offers it to me, and it hangs between us like a promise. Or a trap.

"As proof," he says, "that I'm real."

Everything in me tenses when the metal hits my palm. The cool weight of Da's key—*my* key—sends a shiver through me. I loop it over my head, the weight settling against my chest. It feels like a small piece of the world has been made right. Then Owen turns, opens the door, and strides silently away.

I follow, watching light spill into the dim living room as he slips out of the apartment and into the yellow hall. Something thuds behind me, and I spin to find Dad asleep in a corner chair, a book now on the floor beside him. Even in sleep, his face is creased with worry; as I kneel to retrieve the book, I wonder what it would be like to tell my parents why I have nightmares. Why I have scars. Where I vanish to. Why I cringe from their touch.

I hate Owen all the more for planting the thought in my head, because it's not possible. A world without these secrets and lies could never exist.

But as I set Dad's book on the table and tug a blanket up over his shoulders, a question whispers in my head.

What if?

I don't remember drifting off, but one minute I'm staring at the door and the next my alarm is sounding. I should be relieved that I didn't dream, and there is a small, rebellious flicker of happiness in my chest, but it dies as soon as I remember Owen: my own living nightmare. Except I'm beginning to suspect he's not a dream.

Da's key is still pressed against my skin, and I force myself to take it off and bury it in the top drawer of my bedside table. My ring is still sitting on the windowsill, but I don't dare put it on if it'll blind me to Owen's presence. Instead I find a necklace chain and loop the band through it, sliding the silver piece over my head and tucking it beneath the collar of my uniform shirt.

It's going to be a long day without a buffer.

My list is holding steady at three names, but I can't push my luck, especially now that I know Agatha's search for Crew will come up empty. Mom's in the kitchen swearing about how she can't find her keys while the news plays out on the TV. I watch, expecting the crime scene at Hyde to be the top story, but it's never mentioned, and all I can think is that the storage room hasn't been discovered yet.

Mom, meanwhile, is still searching under papers, through her purse, in the drawers for her keys. She won't find them because they're stashed in the freezer under a bag of peas.

"I don't need you to drive me," I say. "Really. Just let me go myself."

"This isn't up for negotiation," she says, nearly upsetting a cup of coffee as she scours the mess on the kitchen table.

"I know you don't trust me—"

"It's not that," she says. "I just don't want you riding your bike until your arm's healed."

And just like that, I've got her. Hook. Line. Sinker. "You're right. I'll take the bus."

Mom stops searching and straightens: "You hate the bus," she says. "You called it a tiny box filled with germs and dirt."

"Well," I say, shouldering my bag, "life is messy. And there's a stop a block from school." I don't actually know if this is true. Luckily, neither does Mom.

Her phone goes off from somewhere under the papers she's been searching through. "Fine," she says. "Fine, okay, just please be careful."

"Always," I say, ducking out.

I'd never take the bus. Especially not with my ring hanging uselessly around my neck. The lie does save time, though, since I don't have to worry about stashing my bike before cutting into the Narrows.

Two of the three Histories go without a fight, and the third isn't a match for me, even in my current condition. I approach the boundary between Wesley's territory and mine and slide my key into the lock, hoping it turns. It does. The door bleeds into light and shape before it opens.

I'm in such a hurry that I don't think about the fact that this isn't my territory until I round a corner and nearly run straight into Wesley. I stagger back in time to avoid a collision, and he pulls up short in time to avoid dropping a coffee carrier.

"Jesus, Mac," he says, clutching his chest with his free hand.

"Sorry!" I say, holding up mine in surrender.

"What are you doing here?"

"Hunting," I say as we set off toward Hyde's door.

"I kind of got that," says Wes. "I meant, what are you doing in *my* territory?"

"Oh. Roland granted me access so I could clear my list from school."

Wes nods. "I'm glad they finally cut you some slack. Not that scaling walls isn't fun, but this seems a little less dangerous."

"Only because you don't have your stick out."

"*Bō* staff," corrects Wes. "And it's in my bag. But my list is clear, and my hands were full."

"What's with the coffee?" I ask.

He holds up the carrier. "It's for you."

"You do know my parents own a coffee shop," I say.

"That's never stopped you from taking Cash's," he says with a pout. "And I figured after yesterday's incident, you might be looking for a new supplier." It takes me a second to realize that by "incident" he means Cash's coffee making me sick, and not Cash's kiss. If he's heard about the latter, he doesn't let on, and I don't broach the subject, since it's the least of my problems right now.

He offers me a cup and I take it, careful not to let our fingers touch. The last thing I need is for Wesley to see Owen written all over my mind.

"Any word from Agatha?" he asks. "About the voids?"

The coffee turns to lead in my mouth. I try to swallow. "Not yet."

"Don't worry," he says, misreading my concern. "She'll find whoever's doing this." We reach a door with a green check mark. "How did you sleep?" he adds. "I missed your bed."

"It missed you, too," I say as he opens the door. Unlike the doors that no longer exist in the Outer—the ones tucked in cracks and folds—the Hyde School door opens not onto darkness, but onto the campus. The school is visible even from the Narrows side. I look out, scanning the green for signs of Owen's silver-blond hair. I don't see him, but that doesn't mean he's not there—and I can't afford to lead Wesley to him.

"You coming?" asks Wes.

I reach for the list in my skirt pocket as if I can feel letters writing themselves on the page.

"One more," I say with a sigh and a glance back over my shoulder. "You go on ahead."

Wes hesitates, but nods and steps out onto Hyde's grass. I close the door between us and count to ten, twenty, thirty . . . and then I unlock it with my own key and step through, beelining for the Wellness Center. I half expect to see yellow crime scene tape, but the building is quiet. The trophy hall is empty and perfectly still, and I hold my breath as I make my way toward the storage room door, bracing myself for the scene beyond the glass insert. But when I look through, the air catches in my throat. I push the door open and hit all three switches, showering the room with light.

It's untouched. Immaculate. No toppled shelves, no scattered equipment, no blood on the floor. Nothing except the void, the remnants of which still hover in the middle of the room, snagging and repelling my gaze at the same time, the only proof that anything happened here.

"I thought it would be best to clean up."

I spin to see Owen leaning against the wall, his hands in his pockets. "Good morning."

My fingers curl into fists at my sides. I hate that I'm relieved to see him. I've been dreading this moment since last night, and yet the thought of his *not* being here was in a way more frightening. But now that he's here, I need to figure out what to do. I have to dispatch him, and soon, but the questions that have been filling up my head all night are now trying to climb my throat.

Owen slides the knife out of the holster at his back. "Still determined to fight me?" I hesitate, my eyes flicking from the glinting knife to his face and back. This is not the way to beat him. I force my hands to unclench. "Ready to listen, then?" He arches an eyebrow, feigning surprise.

"You claim there's a way to live without lies," I start. "How?"

Owen smiles, returning the knife to its hidden sheath. "Isn't it obvious?" he says. "Your life is only made of secrets and lies because the Archive is. You exist in the shadows because the Archive does." His blue eyes glitter with excitement. "I am going to drag the Archive out of the dust-covered dark and into the light of day. I'm going to give it back to the world it claims to serve."

"How?"

"By opening the doors," he says, spreading his arms. "By letting the Archive out and the world in."

"The world can't even *see* the doors, Owen."

"Only because it's forgotten how. The whole world is wearing blinders. But if we take them off, eyes will adjust. Lives will adjust. They'll have to." I shake my head. "It's time for change, Mackenzie. It's messy, but the era of secrets must end. The world will adapt, and so will the Archive. It must." His brow furrows, darkening his eyes. "Think about what the Archive's secrets have cost us. Histories only slip because they wake into a world they do not know. They succumb to panic. Confusion. Fear. But if the Archive weren't a secret—if everyone knew what came next—they wouldn't be afraid. And if they let go of their fear and began to understand, then if and when they woke, they wouldn't slip. Ben wouldn't have slipped. Regina wouldn't have slipped. No one would slip."

"Histories aren't meant to wake in the first place," I counter. "And what you're suggesting—a mass awakening—is madness for the living and the dead. Crew will hunt you down before you even start."

"Not if they are with me." He takes a step forward. "You think you are the only one who doubts, Mackenzie? The only one who feels trapped? Do you know why the Archive keeps everyone isolated? It's so they feel alone. So that when one of them feels fear or anger or doubt—and they *all* do—they think they are the only ones. They stay quiet, because they know that one life doesn't matter to the Archive.

"Crew are stronger, paired minds, willing to obey or disobey as a group, but not daring enough to do so. Keepers and Crew all know: if one person or pair rises up, the Archive will simply cut them down. It can always extinguish one voice, Mackenzie. But it can't douse them *all*. Fear. Anger. Doubt. They have been piling up like kindling inside the Archive, and the whole place is ready to burn. The Archive is doing everything it can to keep the fire from starting, but all that's needed is someone to strike the match. So believe me when I tell you that the Crew will go with me. And the other Keepers, too. The question is, will you?"

I open my mouth, but I'm cut off by the sound of steps in the trophy hall beyond the door. Owen falls silent beside me as voices take shape.

"I know the official missing person mark is forty-eight hours," someone is saying, "but what with all the disappearances, I thought it best to let you know."

"I'm glad you did," replies a gruff voice I recognize at once. Detective Kinney. I press myself against the wall beside the door as the footsteps draw closer. Owen doesn't try to hide, but doesn't move, either.

"His wife called me this morning," says the first man. "Apparently, he never picked up their son from preschool yesterday, and he never went home last night."

"Does he have a habit of wandering off?"

"No. And then, when he didn't show this morning, I figured I'd better call. I wish I could tell you more."

The footsteps come to a stop on the other side of the door.

"He was last seen here?" asks Kinney, peering in through the glass.

"Coach Kris saw him in his office before the bell rang."

Kinney pulls away from the door. "We'll start there, then," he says.

The footsteps fade along with the voices as the two walk away. I let out a deep breath, resting my hands on my knees.

"This is all your fault," I say. "If you hadn't dragged those people through—"

"Really it's yours," counters Owen, "since you pushed me into the void. But who's counting crimes?"

The bell rings in the distance, and I check to make sure the coast is clear before pushing the door open.

"The detective is," I say, Owen falling into step beside me. I have to remind myself as I step onto the quad that no one else can see him. And even if they could, he'd blend in. His silver-blond hair glitters in the sunlight, and I can almost imagine what he must have looked like as a student here. His simple black attire lacks any gold piping, but otherwise he'd look just like any other senior. I don't know how much of that has to do with the fact that he is— was—Crew and how much is the fact that, even though he seems old, he's not.

Within seconds of entering the tide of students, I realize how hard it will be to keep my ring off. The path is crowded, and I'm instantly buffeted by a chorus of *what color tights should I wear tonight will Geoffrey even notice I'll never pass x to the ninth is what how many references do I need should have added art Coach Metz better not make us do sprints I'm still sore from Mom is going to kill me I'm going to kill Amelia I hate this place Wesley Ayers better dance with me why did I agree to so weird sometimes metatarsal is connected to the I wish I had cookies get it right empty house Dad is being such an ass stressed silver horns or black streaks can I pull off wings* and it's all tangled up in stress and fear and want and teenage hormones.

I grit my teeth against the crush of people's lives.

"It's time to let the world in," presses Owen beside me. He brings his hand down on my shoulder, his quiet pressing through me, and instead of talking—ostensibly to myself—I *think* the next question.

And what happens once you've done that? I challenge. *The living would, what? Be free to visit the dead?*

"Why not?" says Owen aloud. "They already do—in graveyards."

Yeah, I think, *but in graveyards the dead can't wake.*

I roll my shoulder, shaking him off before he can hear my thoughts spinning.

People aren't smart when it comes to the dead. That's what Da said, and he was right.

How many would claw their way toward their loved ones, rip them from sleep to keep them close? How long would it take for the walls to come down as well as the doors and the world to tear itself apart?

How can he not see that this is madness? Is he truly that blind to the consequences? Or is he really willing to tear the world apart just to get his way? Either way, I have to stop him. But how? Even in his weakened state, the odds aren't in my favor. Owen cannot die. I can.

I pause on the path and pretend to look through a notebook.

Owen rests his chin on top of my head, hushing everything but his voice. "Penny for your thoughts?"

If you're so convinced that everyone else will follow you, why do you need me?

Owen pulls away, and by the time he comes around to face me, his features have grayed into something unreadable. "Before I can call on anyone, there's something I need," he says. "The Archive has it, and I have a plan to take it—but that plans requires two."

My pulse quickens. But it's not fear that makes it race, it's excitement. Because Owen has just handed me the way to beat him. I might not be able to drag him back to the Archive, but I can follow him in. No one else has to get hurt. No one else has to die.

I start walking again, and Owen follows in my wake, a swell of students carrying us into the building on a wave of *was there a test what was I thinking please let this day be over.*

We move in silence through the crowded hall, and come to a stop outside my class.

"What is it we need to steal?" I ask under my breath.

Owen smiles at my use of *we.* He tucks a strand of dark hair behind my ear. I can feel the quiet spreading through me with his fingertips, feel him reading me for lies, but I've learned his tricks, and I'm learning my own. As he reaches through my mind, I focus on a simple truth: *Something has to change.*

"I'm glad I have your attention," he says, his hand falling away. "And I appreciate the collective pronoun. But before our partnership goes any further, I need to know that your heart's in it."

My heart sinks a little. A test. Of course it wouldn't be as easy as saying yes. Owen Chris Clarke doesn't gamble. He only plays games when he thinks he'll win. Am I willing to play? Do I really have a choice?

I hold his gaze as the second bell rings and the hall empties around us.

My voice is barely a whisper, but my words are firm.

"What do you want me to do?"

TWENTY-SIX

"**G**O TO THE ARCHIVE," says Owen, "and steal me something."

"What kind of something?" I ask, clenching my fingers around my backpack strap. Pain flickers through my wrist. It helps me focus.

"Something small," says Owen. "Just a show of good faith. If you succeed, I'll tell you what we're really going to take from them. If you fail, there's no point. You'll just be in my way." His eyes go to a clock on the wall. "You have until lunch," he says, turning away. "Good luck."

I stand there, watching him go, until someone clears his throat behind me.

"Avoiding my class, Miss Bishop?"

I turn to find Mr. Lowell holding the door open for me.

"Sorry, sir," I say, and follow him inside. His hand grazes against my shoulder as he guides me through, and I'm hit with *worry strange girl distant trouble at home I see the bruises quiet clutter ink stains* before I continue forward out of his reach and take my seat. Sixteen people in a classroom without the buffer of a ring make the air feel like it's singing. I sit there, wincing faintly every time a student gets too close, Owen's warped ideas playing through my head while Lowell lectures on the warped ideas of others. I'm not paying much attention until something Lowell says echoes Owen.

"Every uprising starts with a spark," says Lowell. "Sometimes that spark is a moment, tipping the scale. And sometimes that spark is a decision. In the case of the latter, there is no doubt that it takes a certain amount of madness to tip that first domino— but it also takes courage, vision, and an all-encompassing belief, even misguided, in their mission. . . ."

Owen sees himself as a revolutionary, exposing the Archive his cause. That single-minded focus acts both as his strength and his weakness. But is it a weakness I can use?

He's so fixated on his goal that he can't see the flaws. It's proof that even someone as cold and calculating as Owen was once human. People—the living and the dead alike—see what they want to see and believe what they want to believe. Owen wants to believe in this mission, and he also wants to believe that I am salvageable.

All I have to do is prove it.

The moment the bell rings I'm on my feet, moving through the halls and their mess of *sum total of silver or gold silver or gold Saturday school for purple laces if he ever hits me again I'll* out the doors and across the quad to the Narrows door set into the side of the shed, where I pull the key out from under my collar and pass through. Wesley's coding system is different from mine, but I soon figure out that he's labeled Returns with a white plus sign and the Archive with a white *X*, and I slot my key, take a breath, and step through into the antechamber.

Patrick is seated behind the desk, turning through the pages of the ledger. He pauses to write a note, then continues leafing through.

"Miss Bishop," he says, my name little more than a grumble. "Here to confess?"

"Not yet," I say. It's still hard for me to believe he's not the one responsible for the voids. I was sure he was out to get me removed. Erased. But he's not—at least, not this time, this way.

"I need to see Roland. Just for a few minutes." Patrick's eyes move up from the ledger to mine. "Please, Patrick. It's important."

He closes the book slowly. "Second hall, third room," he says, adding, "Be quick about it."

I set off through the open doors and into the atrium, but I don't follow Patrick's directions. Instead of cutting down the second hall to the third room, I head down the sixth hall, following it to the very end the way Roland did when he first showed me to his room. I half expect the corridors to change around me, the way they seem to when I trail him through the maze, but the straight line stays straight. I press my ear to the small set of doors at the end, listening for steps, then slip through into the smaller, dimly lit hall that holds the Librarians' quarters.

Halfway down the hall, I find his simple, dark-paneled door. It's unlocked. The room is as cozy as it was before, but the lack of music whispering from the wall—and the lack of Roland sitting in his chair—makes the space seem too vulnerable. I whisper an apology for what I'm about to do.

I cross to the table by the chair and slide open the drawer. The silver pocket watch is gone—surely Roland has it on him—but the old, palm-sized notebook is there. It sings beneath my fingers as I slip it gently into my back pocket, my heart twisting. I scour the rest of the drawer for a scrap of paper and pen, and when I find them, I write a note. I do not say I'm sorry, or that I will bring it back, only jot down two small words.

Trust me.

I don't even look at the paper, since lives are messy and it will be easier to hide this small deviation from the theft if it's subtle.

If Owen goes looking, I want it to be a mere whisper in my head instead of an image. Instead I focus on the very real guilt I feel as I fold the note, put it in the drawer, and duck out. My heart thuds in my chest all the way back into the atrium.

Wood and stone and colored glass, and all throughout, a sense of peace.

That's how Da described the Archive to me when I was young. As I walk through the stacks now, I grasp the calm that used to come so easily. These days it feels like a memory, one I'm reaching for and can't quite grab. Wood and stone and colored glass. That's all he told me. He didn't mention the fact I could never leave, or that the Librarians were dead, or that Histories weren't the only things to fear.

Your life is only made of secrets and lies because the Archive is.

I smother Owen's voice in my head before it can become my own. I cross back through the doors into the antechamber, sensing that something is wrong the moment I move from wood to stone, but it's too late. The massive doors swing shut behind me, and I turn to see Agatha in front of them, her hair the color of blood and her cream-colored coat like a splash of paint against the dark wood.

My eyes flick to the desk, where Patrick is sitting. Of course he would call her.

"My list is clear," I say as calmly as possible.

"But I'm out of Crew," says Agatha. Her voice has lost its velvet calm. "And out of patience." She takes a step forward. "You've run me on a chase, Miss Bishop, and I am sick of it. I want you to answer me honestly. How did you make the voids?"

"I didn't make them," I say, fighting to keep my voice steady even as I take a step back toward the door and the sentinels guarding it.

"I don't believe you," she says, tugging off a black glove as she comes toward me. "If you are innocent, then show me." I shake my head. "Why don't you want me in your head? Afraid of what I'll find? The innocent have nothing to hide, Miss Bishop." She pulls off the other glove.

"You don't have permission."

"I don't *care*," she growls, her bare hands tangling in my shirt.

"Agatha," warns Patrick, but she doesn't listen.

"Do you know how small you are?" she hisses. "You are one cog in one wheel in one corner of an infinite machine, and you have the audacity to deny *me*? To defy *me*? Do you know what that's called?"

"Freedom," I challenge.

A cold smile touches the edge of her mouth. "Treason."

I feel the two sentinels move behind me, and before I can turn, their hands clench around my shoulders and wrists. Their movements are fast and efficient, wrenching my arms behind my back, twisting up hard until my knees buckle. My pulse races in my ears and my vision starts to go dark, but before I can fight back against the men or the encroaching tunnel moment, Agatha's hands are there, pressing against my temples.

At first, all I hear is the quiet that comes with her touch.

And then the pain starts.

TWENTY-SEVEN

THE PAIN IS like hot nails in my head, but a moment after it starts it's gone, along with Agatha's touch. The sentinels let go of my arms, and I fall forward to my hands and knees on the Archive floor. When I look up, Roland's hand is wrapped around Agatha's wrist, and Patrick is standing at the mouth of the atrium, holding one of the doors open.

"What are you doing?" snaps Roland.

"My job," says Agatha icily.

"Your job is not to torture Keepers in my antechamber."

"I have every reason to believe that—"

"If you truly have every reason, then get permission from the board." There's a challenge in his voice, and Agatha stiffens at it, the smallest shadow of fear flickering across her perfect skin. Appealing to the board of directors means admitting she's not only allowed more traitorous behavior in the Archive, but that she's failed to uncover the source. "You will not touch her again without approval."

Roland lets go of Agatha's wrist, but doesn't take his eyes off her.

"Miss Bishop," he says as I get to my feet, "I think you'd better get back to class."

I nod shakily, and I'm about to turn toward the door when Agatha says, "She has something of yours, Roland." I stiffen, but he doesn't. His face is a perfect blank as Agatha adds, "A notebook."

I can't bring myself to look at him, but I can feel his gray eyes weighing me down. "I know," he lies. "I gave it to her."

Only then do I look up, but his attention has already shifted back to Agatha. I'm halfway through the door when she says to him, "You can't protect her." But whatever he says back is lost as I slip into the dark.

I don't stop moving until I reach Dallas's office. I'm early, and she's not there, but I sink down onto the couch, my heart pounding. I can still feel Agatha's hands against my temples, the pain of the memories being dragged forward toward her fingers. *Too close.* I pull Roland's journal from my pocket. The memories hum against my skin as I cradle it in my palm, but I don't reach for them—I've taken enough from him already. Instead I close my eyes and lean my head back against the couch.

"I'm impressed."

I look up to find Owen sitting in Dallas's low-back chair, twirling his knife absently on the leather arm while he watches me intently.

"I have to admit," he says, "I wasn't sure you'd do it."

"I'm full of surprises," I say drily. He holds out his hand for the journal, and I hesitate before relinquishing it. "It's very important to someone."

"Everything in the Archive is," he says, taking it from me. His hand lingers a moment around mine, and I recognize the touch for what it is: a reading. His quiet slides through my mind while my life slides through his. I can almost see the struggle with Agatha play out in his eyes, the way they widen, then narrow.

"She's angry because I won't grant her access to my mind."

622

"Good," he says, pulling away. He pages through Roland's notebook, and I'm surprised by how gentle he is with it. "It's strange," he adds under his breath, "the way we hold on to things. My uncle couldn't part with his dog tags. He had them on him always, looped around his neck along with his key, a reminder. He served in both wars, my uncle. He was a hero. And he was Crew. As loyal as they come. When he got back from the second war, I had just turned thirteen, and he began to train me. He was never the kind and gentle type—the Archive and the wars made sure of that—but I believed in him." He closes Roland's journal and runs his thumb over the cover. "I was initiated into the Archive when I was only fourteen— did you know that?" I didn't. "That night," he continues, "after my induction, my uncle went home and shot himself in the head."

The air catches in my throat, but I will myself to say nothing.

"I couldn't understand," he says, almost to himself, "why a man who'd lived through so much would do that. He left a note. *As I am.* That's all he wrote. It wasn't until two years later, when I learned about the Archive's policy to alter those who live long enough to retire, that it made sense. He would rather have died whole than let them take his life apart and cut out everything that mattered just to keep its secrets." His eyes drift up from the journal. There is a light in them, narrow and bright. "But change is coming. Soon there will be no secrets for them to guard. You accused me once of wanting to create chaos, but you're wrong. I am only doing my job. I am protecting the past."

He offers me the journal back, and I take it, relieved.

"It's rather fitting that you chose to take that," he says as I slip it into my bag. "The thing we're going to steal is not so different."

"What is it?" I ask, trying to stifle some of the urgency in my voice.

623

"The Archive ledger."

I frown. "I don't under—" But I'm cut off as the door clatters open and Dallas comes in, juggling her journal, a cell phone, and a mug of coffee. Her eyes land on me, and for a moment—the smallest second—I think they take in Owen, too. Or at least the space around him. But then she blinks and smiles and drops her stuff on the table.

"Sorry I'm late," she says. Owen rises to his feet and retreats to a corner of the room as she collapses into the abandoned chair. "What do you want to talk about? Who you're taking to Fall Fest? That seems to be all anyone *else* wants to talk about." She fetches up her journal and begins to turn through pages, and I'm surprised to see she's actually taken notes. I've only ever seen her doodle flower patterns in the corners of the page. "Oh, I know," she says, landing on a page. "I want to talk a little about your grandfather."

I stiffen. Da is the last person I want to talk about right now, especially with Owen in the audience. But when I meet his gaze over Dallas's shoulder, there is a new interest—an *intensity*—and I remember something he said last night:

The Archive is broken. Da knew—he had to know—and he still let them have you.

I'm just beginning to earn Owen's trust (or at least his interest). If this is going to work, I need to keep it. Maybe I can use Da.

"What about him?" I ask.

Dallas shrugs. "I don't know. But you quote him a lot. I guess I want to know why."

I frown a little, and take a moment to choose my words, hoping they both read the pause as emotion rather than strategy.

"When I was little," I say, looking down at my hands, "I worshipped him. I used to think he knew everything, because he had an answer to every question I could think up. It never occurred to me that he didn't always know. That he would lie or make it up." I consider the place between two knucklebones where my ring should be. "I assumed he knew. And I trusted him to tell the truth. . . ." My voice trails off a little as I glance up. "I'm just now starting to realize how little he told me."

I'm amazed to hear myself say the words. Not because the lies come easily, but because they're not lies at all. Dallas is staring at me in a way that makes me feel exposed.

I tug my sleeves over my hands. "That was probably too much. I should have just said that I loved him. That he was important to me."

Dallas shakes her head. "No, that was good. And the way we feel about people should never be put in past tense, Mackenzie. After all, we continue to feel things about them in the present tense. Did you stop loving your brother when he died?"

I can feel Owen's gaze like a weight, and I have to bring my fingers to the edge of the couch and grip the cushion to steady them. "No."

"So it's not that you *loved* him," she continues. "You *love* him. And it's not that your grandfather *was* important to you. He *is*. In that way, no one's ever really gone, are they?"

Da's voice rings out like a bell in my head.

What are you afraid of, Kenzie?

Losing you.

Nothing's lost. Ever.

"Da didn't believe in Heaven," I find myself saying, "but I think it scared him, the idea of losing all the things—people, knowledge, memories—he'd spent his life collecting. He liked to tell me he believed in someplace. Someplace calm and peaceful, where your life was kept safe, even after it was over."

"And do you believe in that place?" she asks.

I let the question hang in the air a few long seconds before answering. "I wanted to."

Out of the corner of my eye, I see Owen's mouth tug into a smile.

Hook. Line. Sinker.

"Why the ledger?" I ask as soon as we're out.

Everyone else is going to lunch, and I've chosen a path that rings the campus—a large, circuitous route few students use when they can cut across the quad—so that we can talk in private.

"How much do you know about it?" he asks.

"It sits on the desk in the antechamber. It has one page for every member of the branch. It's how the Archive communicates with its Keepers and Crew."

"Exactly," says Owen. "But at the front of it, before the pages for the Keepers and the Crew, there is one page labeled *ALL*. A message written on that page would go out to *everyone* in the book."

"Which is why you need it," I say. "You need to be able to contact everyone at once."

"It is the only connector in a world divided," says Owen. "The Archive can silence one voice, but not if it's written on that page. They cannot stop the message from spreading."

"It's your match," I whisper. "To start the fire."

Owen nods, his eyes bright with hope. "Carmen was supposed to take it, but she obviously failed."

"When do *we* take it?"

"Tonight," he says.

"Why wait?"

Owen gives me a pitying look. "We can't just walk up to the front desk and rip the page out of the book. We need something to distract the Archive. We don't need something long, but we need something bright." He gestures to the quad, where the stalls and booths and decorations are still being erected.

"Fall Fest?" I ask. "But how will something in the Outer distract the Archive?"

"It will," he says. "Trust me." Trust. Something I will never feel for Owen. Warning lights go off inside my head. The more factors, the less I can control.

"You and I, Mackenzie, we are the same." I attacked him once for that very idea, but this time I hold my tongue. "Everyone in the Archive has doubts, but theirs whisper and ours shout. We are the ones who question. We are the bringers of change. Those who run the Archive, who cling to their rules, are terrified of us. And they should be."

Something sparks inside me at the thought of being feared instead of afraid. I smother it.

"And tonight we will . . ." He trails off, eyes fixed on something down the path. Not something, I realize. Some*one*.

Wesley.

He's standing on the path, holding his lunch tray and talking to Amber. I've been clinging to the hope that even if he saw him, Owen might not recognize Wes—the boy he stabbed on the roof of the Coronado had spiked hair and lined eyes and a different manner—but Owen frowns and says, "Didn't I kill him?"

"You tried," I say as, to my horror, Wesley catches sight of me and waves before turning back to Amber.

"I saw him written on your skin, but I didn't realize the marks were so fresh," says Owen, withdrawing his knife from its holster with one hand, gripping my arm with the other. "You've been keeping a secret," he growls, quiet forcing through my head.

He has nothing to do with our plans, I think as calmly as possible. But this time, the plural pronoun does nothing to placate Owen.

"He is a tether to the life you're leaving," he says, tightening his grip. "A rope to be cut." He twirls the knife.

No. My mind spins with his blade. *He can be salvaged. If your grand scheme is for the Keepers and Crew to rise up against the Archive, you'll need every one of them you can get. And when the call goes out, he'll stand with me. Killing him would be a waste.*

"I'm not convinced of that," says Owen. "And don't pretend to be pragmatic where he's concerned."

"Fine," I say, pulling free of his touch, "if you don't want to listen to logic, then listen to this: this isn't Wesley's fight. I haven't dragged him into it, and neither will you. If you hurt him in any way, you will *never* get my help. *Trust me.*"

Owen's eyes harden. The knife stops spinning, snapping into his grip. For a second his fingers tighten on the handle. Then, to my relief, he puts the weapon away and falls in step behind me.

"Hey, you," says Wesley, waiting for me to reach him before setting off again toward the Court. My eyes go to his hands to make sure he's wearing his ring. He is.

"Why weren't you in Physiology?" asks Amber.

"Doctor's appointment," I lie.

"We were just talking about the cops on campus," says Wesley. "Did you see them?" He's asking another question underneath the words: *Do you know why they're here?*

I shake my head. "No. Amber, do you know what's up?"

"No idea," she says with a groan. "Dad's not giving me *anything.*"

"The elusive Mackenzie Bishop!" calls Cash as we reach the Court. "No lunch?"

"Not hungry," I say. Owen wanders over to the Alchemist and watches the scene unfold, and it's all I can do to keep from looking at him.

"Missed you again in gym," he says. "Another meeting?"

I'm about to go with "doctor's appointment" again, but Saf cuts in.

"Gee, what kind of meeting forces you to miss gym multiple days in a row?"

"Don't be an ass, Saf," shoots her brother. "You were sent to Dallas, like, *seven times* last year."

"It was three, jerk."

Cash turns his attention to me. "Point is, no big deal. We've all been there. Eventually your parents come up with an excuse, or the school does."

"What did they send you for?" I ask, eager to turn the attention on someone else.

"Hyperactivity," he announces proudly.

"Perfectionism," says Saf.

"Stress-induced anxiety," adds Amber.

"Antisocial tendencies," says Gavin.

All eyes go to Wesley. "Depression," he says, twisting a straw absently around his fingers. My heart aches at the thought of Wes suffering. I imagine us in bed, imagine myself pulling him in against me, wrapping my arms around him and warding off his demons. *He's worth it,* I think. *And I will not—cannot—drag him into this mess.*

"And you, Mackenzie?" asks Cash, drawing my attention back. "What have you done to land yourself in Dallas's office?"

My eyes flick toward Owen. "Apparently I have a problem with authority." I say.

"Is that why you can't go to the dance?" asks Gavin. Owen frowns.

"Actually," I say lightly, "I'll be there after all."

Wesley's eyes light up. "Really?" he asks with a smile. It breaks my heart.

"Yeah," I say, forcing myself to echo his happiness. "Really."

I'm relieved as the conversation turns toward the more innocuous topics of whether Saf and Cash will put gold streaks in their hair and what color glasses Gavin will wear. I'm no longer looking at Owen or Wes, but I can't shake the feeling that both pairs of eyes are still studying me. Wesley's pretending to listen to something Amber says, but every time I look up, I notice him glancing my way, and Owen's watching me like a hawk. And then Wesley's attention starts drifting away from me toward the Alchemist, and it occurs to me for the first time that even though he can't *see* Owen, he might be able to *sense* him. Owen seems to be realizing this, too. He stays quiet and still against the statue, his eyes narrowed in Wesley's direction. Wes returns the gaze without seeing. They both frown.

Mercifully, the bell rings.

I practically spring to my feet. But as I turn toward class, I feel Wes come up beside me. He knocks his shoulder against mine, but instead of his usual noise I'm hit with *something's off what's going on did I do something distant pulling back does she know how much I missed her noise couldn't sleep* before I can put space between us. I keep my ringless finger carefully out of his line of sight.

"Are you really coming tonight?" he asks as Owen appears at my other side.

"Wouldn't miss it," whispers Owen.

"Wouldn't miss it," I echo, stomach twisting.

"I can't believe the watch and the warden gave in."

"Yeah, well"—*they haven't yet*—"I can be very persuasive."

A pair of students calls to Wes across the quad. He hesitates. "Go on," I say. "I'll see you tonight?"

"Can't wait," he says with a smile before taking off across the grass.

"What's going to happen tonight, Owen?" I ask when we're alone.

"Why?" he challenges. "Are you having second thoughts?"

"No," I say before doubt can weaken the word. "As long as my friends don't get hurt." Before he can reach out and read the questions in my skin, I turn and walk away, telling myself I will stop this before it goes too far.

But how far am I willing to go? And how can I possibly stop it when I don't know what *it* is?

Owen shadows me all afternoon. I focus on the clock instead of his pacing form, and as soon as the last bell rings, I make my way toward the door in the shed, thinking that maybe, if I can get him to follow me into the Narrows, then—

"This way," he says, changing course when we're halfway there. My heart sinks as I follow him toward a copse of trees, where he stops and draws a key from a hidden pocket in his sleeve. His Crew key. It takes everything I have not to lunge for it. But we are nowhere near a real door, and I now know that sending him into the void isn't a permanent solution. I have to shelve him, and only one key is going to let me do that, so I still myself as he lifts it to a spot in the air and the teeth vanish into nothing.

No, not nothing. A shortcut. Right here, at the edge of Hyde. Another reminder that this was Owen's campus long before it was mine.

He turns the key and offers me his hand, and I do my best to clear my mind before I let him take it and lead me through.

My shoe hits the ground on the other side, and my heart lurches when I look up and see them. Gargoyles. We are standing on the Coronado roof. I suppress a shudder. How many of my nightmares have started like this?

But if Owen sees the strange poetry of our being here again, he doesn't mention it—only looks out over the edge of the roof and down.

"The day I died," he says, "it was Agatha who gave the order. Alteration. I remember running, thinking for a second how strange it was to be on the other side of the chase. And then I got to the roof and knew what I had to do." He looks back at me. "Would you do it?" he asks. "To stay whole?"

I shake my head. "No," I say, turning toward the roof door. "But I wouldn't go down without a fight."

Owen follows me. "Where are we going?"

"There's still one thing standing in our way," I tell him.

His brow furrows. "What?"

"My mother."

Bishop's is busy. A flock of students from the public school take up half the seats and, judging by Mom's frenetic pace, have been ordering a slew of things. Berk is on the patio, and Mom's behind the counter making drinks. Owen follows me in, his steps slowing as he sees the rose pattern on the floor. He stands there, looking down at it as I head up to the counter.

"Hey, Mom," I say, resting my elbows on the marble.

"You're home early," she says, and I'm kind of amazed she knows what time it is, considering how many orders she seems to be juggling.

"Yeah, it turns out the bus is a pretty efficient mode of transportation. Still dirty, but efficient."

"Mm-hmm," she says, clearly distracted.

"Hey, so, there's a party at Hyde tonight, and I was wondering—"

And just like that, her head snaps up from her work. "You're joking, right?"

"I just thought maybe I could—"

She shakes her head. "You know the answer to this—"

"I know," I cut in, keeping my voice low, "and I wasn't even going to bother asking, but Dallas said I should." For how often she drops *her* therapist's name, mine should carry some weight. And sure enough, Mom quiets. "I know it's a long shot," I say, hoping this doesn't sound as rehearsed as it is. "It's just . . . I want to feel normal. I want to feel *okay*, and this—the house arrest, the hovering—I know I've earned it, but it's the constant reminder that I'm not. And I know I'm not. I haven't been okay for a long time, and I know I have a long way to go before I get there, but for one night I just want to pretend I'm already there."

I watch her begin to falter.

"Never mind," I start to say, adding a small waver to my voice. "I understand—"

"Okay," she cuts in. "You can go."

Hook. Line. Sinker. My chest loosens even as my heart sinks.

"Thank you," I say, hoping my relief can pass for excitement. Then I do something that takes us both by surprise: I hug her. My head fills with *tell her tell her you're sorry can't lose her was only trying to I can't lose her too.*

For once, instead of pulling away, I tighten my grip. "But you have to check in," she adds when I finally let go. I nod. "I mean it, Mackenzie. No disappearing. No antics."

"Promise," I say, turning to go.

"A rousing performance," says Owen as we head back upstairs. I don't reply, because I don't trust myself. Just a few more hours. A few more hours and I will return Owen to the Archive.

A few more hours and this will all be over.

"Not again." Owen's voice is a low growl as we reach the third floor, and I look up from the steps through the glass insert to see what he sees. Wesley is leaning back against my door, holding a box. My stomach twists. Why is he making it so hard to keep him safe?

"Send him away," orders Owen.

I shake my head. "I can't. He'll suspect something is wrong. Just give me some time——"

"No," says Owen. "You said you wanted to leave him out of this, so do it."

"I'm not going to tell him anything. I just want . . ." I trail off. Owen's eyes bore into mine, and I would give anything in this moment to be able to read *his* thoughts.

"How many good-byes did you get to say to Carmen?" I ask. "Please. Give me one."

Owen's hand comes to rest on my shoulder, and I can feel him reading me for defiance, but I'm learning how to bury it. I am not a History. I am a human, and my life is messy and loud. I focus on the truths instead of the lies.

Truth: I am scared for Wesley.

Truth: I do not want to hurt him.

Truth: This is not his fight.

Truth: I cannot protect him from the Archive, but I can protect him from me.

Owen's hand slides away. "Fine," he says. And even if he can't feel the relief in my skin, I'm sure he can see it in my face. "I have a few finishing touches to put on tonight. Have your time with him, but don't be late. The party starts at seven. The show's at eight."

I nod and head out into the hall, feeling his eyes on me the whole way there. When Wesley sees me coming, he smiles.

"What's with the box?" I ask.

"You have a Fall Fest to get ready for," he says. "I've come to help." He clicks a button on the box, and it opens to reveal a dazzling array of makeup.

"Does this make you my fairy godmother?" I ask as I let him in, locking the door behind us.

He considers the term. "Well, yes. In this case I guess that's fair. But don't tell Cash. My cred will go through the floor."

"Where did you even get all this?" I ask, scanning the selection of pencils and shadows.

"Stole it from Safia." He sets the box on the kitchen table and starts searching through, then makes an *aha* sound and emerges with a handful of shadows and a silver liner. "Sit," he says, patting the tabletop.

I climb up, leaning forward until my face is inches from his.

His hair is still smoothed down and his eyes unlined, and at this distance, I can see the gold flecks in his hazel eyes. A strange panic fills me. I don't know what's going to happen; the only thing I know is that I want Wes as far away from it as possible.

"Skip it," I whisper as he uncaps the liner.

"Skip what?"

"The dance," I say. "Don't go. Stay home."

"With you?" he asks, smiling crookedly. I shake my head and the smile falters. "I don't understand."

"I just . . ." I start, but what can I say? What can I tell him without putting him in harm's way? "Never mind." I duck out from under his arms, feeling ill. I go into the bathroom and splash water on my face, then grip the counter and breathe.

"You okay?" calls Wes as I rifle through the medicine cabinet above the sink for some aspirin.

"My arm's just sore," I say, scanning the bottles of pills. My fingers curl around a prescription bottle I don't recognize, and as I read the label, I realize what the small blue capsules are. Sleeping pills. Not your average over-the-counter kind; the kind strong enough to knock you out in minutes. They're practically tranquilizers. These must be what Mom dissolved in my water. I hesitate, weighing the bottle, the contents, the possibility. Is this how my mother felt before she slipped them in my drink? My stomach turns, and I set the bottle back. I would do almost anything to keep Wes safe.

But not that. He would never forgive me.

"Here." Wes appears in the doorway with a small vial. "I keep some aspirin in my bag."

I take the tube with shaking hands and rinse down two while Wes assesses himself in the mirror. He pulls a small disk-shaped container from his pocket and opens it, dabbing his finger in the gel. He starts to spike his hair when someone knocks on the door.

"Coming," I call.

"Is it pizza?" asks Wes from the bathroom. "I would kill for some pizza."

"Wouldn't get your hopes up," I say. "Mom probably forgot a key."

I throw the lock, and the door's barely open before a hand tangles in my collar and wrenches me forward into the hall hard enough that the door slams shut behind me. I'm shoved back against the wood as *about time been waiting can't wait has it coming little Keeper* spills in through my head, and I hardly have time to register the noise as Sako's before a key is driven into the door and I fall back and through.

I hit the antechamber floor hard enough to knock the breath out of me and roll to my feet to see Agatha standing there, smiling grimly.

"Seize her," she says, and I feel the sentinels take hold from either side as she comes forward, holding a piece of paper in front of my face.

"Do you know what this is, Miss Bishop?" The page is written in Latin, with the Archive seal—three vertical gold bars—at the top. "It's permission," she tells me, setting the paper on the desk. I try to pull free as she begins to tug off her black gloves one at a time.

"Now," she says, setting them aside, "let's see what you've been hiding."

TWENTY-EIGHT

WHEN OWEN LOCKED me in the Returns room, my life—thrown onto the walls—began to compile, organize, and fold in. The sensation was strange and dull and numbing.

This is the opposite.

It's like being turned inside out, exposed to things I don't want to see, think, feel again. It's all pulled out of the recesses of my mind and dragged violently into the light.

The pain tears through my head as I see *Wesley in my bed my parents together on the couch looking at me like I'm already lost Cash handing me coffee Sako pinning me in the alley carved a line into my skin beating the thug's face into the park path Roland telling me to lie down and Owen stalking me through the gargoyles killing me in class lifting Ben's blue bear sitting in Dallas's chair.*

Da used to say that if you wanted to hide something, you had to leave it sitting out, right there on the surface.

"When you bury it," he said, "that's when people go digging."

I think about that the instant before it starts. I think about it while Agatha's in my mind, the pain knifing through my scalp and down my spine, all the way into my bones. I think about it after—or between—while I'm lying on the cold antechamber floor, trying to remind my body how to breathe.

There is a moment, lying on that floor, when I just want it to be over. When I realize how tired I really am. When I think

Owen's right and this place deserves to burn. But I drag myself back together. It's too early to stop fighting. I have to get out of here. I have to get back to the Outer. I have to get through tonight. Because one way or another, I *will* get through tonight.

I struggle to my hands and knees. The metallic taste of blood fills my mouth, several drops dripping from my nose to the antechamber floor.

"Get her back up," orders Agatha. The sentinels drag me to my feet, and her hand wraps around my jaw. "Why is that traitorous History streaked across your life like paint?"

Owen. I tell the closest thing to the truth that I can manage. "Bad dreams."

Her eyes hold mine. "You think I can't tell the difference between nightmares and memories?"

And then I realize something with grim satisfaction: she can't. Because I can't. She may be able to look inside my mind, but she can only see what I see.

"I guess not," I say.

"You think you can hide things from me," she growls, her fingers running through my hair. "But I'm going to find the truth, even if I have to tear your mind apart to do it." Agatha's grip tightens, and I close my eyes, bracing for another wave of pain, when the Archive door swings open behind her.

"I warned you, Roland," she says without looking back, "that the next time you interrupted me I would have you reshelved."

But the man in the doorway is not Roland. I've never seen him before. There is a kind of timeless poise to the warm brown hair that curls against his temples and the closely trimmed goatee that frames his mouth. A gold pin made of three vertical bars gleams on the breast pocket of his simple black suit.

"Unfortunately, my dear," he says, his accent unplaceable, "you cannot play judge, jury, *and* executioner. You must leave some work for the rest of us."

Agatha tenses at the sound of the man's voice, her hands sliding from my head.

"Director Hale," she says. "I didn't know you were coming."

Everything in me goes cold. A director. One of the Archive's leaders. And one of its executioners. Roland appears at the man's shoulder, and his eyes find mine for an instant, darkening with worry, before he follows the other man—Hale—into the antechamber. The director crosses to Agatha's side with calm, measured steps, each eliciting a small snap.

"Seeing as my presence has a noticeable impact on your vehemence," he says, "perhaps it's best to behave as though I am *always* in the room." His steady green eyes slide from Agatha to me. "And I'd advise you to take a little more care with our things," he says, still addressing her. The sentinels release me, and I will myself to stay on my feet. "Miss Bishop, I presume."

I nod, even though the small motion sends a wave of pain through my head.

Director Hale turns back to Agatha. "Judgment?"

"Guilty," says Agatha.

"No!" I shout, lunging toward her. The sentinels are there in an instant, holding me back. "I didn't make the voids, and you know it, Agatha."

Hale frowns. "Did she make them or not?"

Agatha holds his gaze a long moment. "She didn't *make* the doors, but—"

"I will remind you," cuts in Hale, "that I only granted you permission so that you could determine if she was behind the void incidents. If she is innocent of that, then pray tell how is she guilty?"

"Her mind is disturbed," says Agatha, "and she's hiding things from me."

"I didn't realize anyone *could* hide things from you, Agatha. Doesn't that defeat your purpose?"

Agatha stiffens, caught between outrage and fear. "She's involved, Hale. Of *that* I have no doubt. At least let me detain her until I solve this case."

He considers, then waves a hand. "Fine."

"No," I say.

"Miss Bishop," warns Hale, "you really are in no place to make demands."

"I can solve the case," I say, the words spilling out.

Hale arches a brow. "You think you can succeed where my assessor has failed?"

I find Agatha's eyes. "I *know* I can."

"You arrogant little—"

Hale holds up his hand. "I'm intrigued. How?"

My chest tightens. "You have to trust me."

Hale smiles grimly. "I do not trust easily."

"I won't let you down," I say.

"Do not let her go," warns Agatha.

Hale arches an eyebrow. "I can always bring her back."

"Give me tonight," I say. "If I fail, I'm yours."

Hale smiles. "You belong to the Archive, Miss Bishop. You're already mine." He nods to the sentinels. "Release her."

Their hands fall away.

"Hale—" starts Agatha, but he turns on her.

"You have *failed me*, my dear. Why shouldn't I give someone else a chance?"

"She has a traitor's heart," says Agatha. "She will betray you."

"And if she does, she will pay for it." His attention shifts to me. "Do you understand?"

I nod, my eyes escaping for a moment to Roland. "I do."

And then, before anyone can change Hale's mind, I turn my back on the director, Roland, Agatha, and the Archive, knowing that it won't be the last time I step *through* this door, but if my plan doesn't work, it will be the last time I walk *out* of it.

Sako is waiting. She slots her key and turns it, holding the door open for me. "I hope you know what you're doing, little Keeper," she hisses as she shoves me through.

I stagger forward into the yellow hall of the Coronado before one knee finally buckles beneath me. Pain continues to roll through my head and, desperate for a moment of true quiet, I tug my ring from the chain around my neck and slide it back on for the first time all day. The world dulls a little as I get up and return to the apartment.

"Where the hell——" starts Wes when I open the door. And then he sees me and pales. "Jesus, what happened?"

"It's okay," I say, holding up a hand before I realize there's blood on it.

Wes hurries into the kitchen to get a wet towel. "Who did this to you?"

"Agatha," I say, taking the cloth and wiping at my face. "But it's okay," I say. "I'm okay."

"Like hell, Mackenzie," he says, taking the towel from my hand and blotting my chin.

"It's *going* to be okay," I correct.

"How can you say that? Did she get what she wants? Is it over?"

I shake my head, even though the motion sends pain through

it. "Not yet," I say with a sinking feeling. "But it will be soon." *One way or another.*

"What are you talking about?"

"Don't worry."

Wes makes an exasperated sound. "You come home covered in your own blood two days after cutting yourself and say something cryptic about it all being over soon and expect me not to worry?"

My eyes go to the clock on the wall. "We need to get ready. I don't want to be late."

"Forget about the damn dance! I want to know what's going on."

"I want you to stay out of it." I close my eyes. "This isn't your fight."

"Do you really believe that?" says Wes, throwing the towel down on the table. "That just because you keep me at arm's length, just because you don't tell me what you're going through, that it somehow stops it from being my fight, too? That somehow you're sparing me anything?"

"Wes—"

"You think I haven't gone myself to every one of those crime scenes and searched for something—*anything*—to explain who's doing this? You think I don't lie awake trying to figure out what's happening and how to help you? I care about you, Mackenzie, and because of that, it's never *not* going to be my fight."

"But I don't want it to be your fight!" I dig my nails into my palms to keep my hands from shaking. "I want it to be mine. I need it to be mine."

"It doesn't work that way," says Wes. "We're part—"

"We're not partners!" I snap. "Not yet, Wes. And we'll never be, not unless I get through this."

"Then let me *help* you."

I press my palms against my eyes. Every bone and muscle in my body wants to tell him, but I can't. I'm willing to bet with my life, but not with Wesley's.

"Mackenzie." I feel his hands wrap around mine, his bass playing through my head as he lowers them, holding them between us. "Please. Tell me what's going on."

I bring my forehead to rest against his. "Do you trust me, Wes?"

"Yes," he says, and the simple certainty in his voice makes my chest hurt.

"Then *trust me*," I plead. "Trust me when I say I have to get through this, and trust me when I say I will, and trust me when I say that I can't tell you more. Please don't make me lie to you."

Wesley's eyes are bright with pain. "What can I do?"

I manage a sad smile. "You can help me put my makeup on. And you can take me to the festival. And you can dance with me."

Wesley takes a deep, shaky breath. "If you get yourself killed," he whispers, "I will never forgive you."

"I don't plan on dying, Wes. Not until I know your first name."

He hands me the towel from the table. "You get the blood off. I'll get the makeup kit."

"Okay. You can open your eyes."

Wes holds up a mirror for me to see his work: dark liner dusted with silver and shadow. The effect is strange and haunting, and it pairs well with his own look. "One last touch," he says, rooting around in his bag. He pulls out a pair of silver horns and nestles them in my hair. I consider my reflection, and a strange thought occurs to me.

When I pulled Ben's drawer open, his History was wearing the red shirt with the *X* over the heart. The one he had on when he died. And if things go wrong tonight and I die, I'll die like this: sixteen and three quarters in a plaid skirt with silver shadow on my face and glittering horns in my hair.

"What do you think?" asks Wes.

"You make a perfect fairy godmother," I say, looking toward the clock on the wall. "We'd better get going."

I head for the Narrows door in the hall, but Wes takes my hand and leads me downstairs instead, through the Coronado's door and out to the curb.

There's a black Porsche parked there. My mouth actually falls open when I see it. At first I think it can't be Wesley's, but it's the only car around, and he heads straight for it.

"I thought you didn't have a car."

"Oh, I don't," he says proudly, producing a key chain. "I stole it."

"From who?"

He presses a button on the key and the lights come on. "Cash."

"Does he know?"

Wes smirks as he holds the door open for me. "Where's the fun in that?" He sees me in and shuts the door, jogging around to the other side of the car and climbing into the driver's seat.

"Are you ready?" he asks. There are so many questions folded into those three words, and only one way to answer.

I swallow and nod. "Let's go."

TWENTY-NINE

"**A**RE YOU AFRAID of dying?"
Wesley and I are sprawled out in the garden a week and a half before school starts. He's been reading a book to himself, and I've been staring at the sky. I haven't slept in what feels like days but might be longer, and the question slips through my mind and out my lips before I think to stop it.

Wes looks up from his book.

"No," he says. His voice is soft, his answer sure. "Are you?"

A cloud slices through the sunlight. "I don't know. I'm not afraid of the pain. But I'm afraid of losing my life."

"Nothing's truly lost," he says, reciting Archive mantra.

I sit up. "We are, though, aren't we? When we die? Histories aren't us, Wes. They're replicas, but they're not *us*. You can't prove that we are what wakes up on those shelves. So the thought that nothing's lost doesn't comfort me. It doesn't make me any readier to die."

Wes sets the book aside. "This is kind of a morbid topic," he says. "Even for you."

I sigh and stretch back out on my stone bench. "Our lives are kind of morbid."

Wes goes quiet, and I assume he's gone back to reading, but a minute or two later he says, "I'm not afraid of dying, but I'm terrified of being erased. Seeing what it did to my aunt . . . I'd rather die whole than live in pieces."

I consider him. "If you could leave the Archive without being altered, would you?"

It is a dangerous question, one I shouldn't ask. It whispers of treason. Wes gives me a cautious look, trying to understand why I'm asking.

"It doesn't matter," he says. "It doesn't work that way."

"But if it did? If you could?"

"No." I'm surprised by the certainty in his voice. "Would you?"

I don't answer.

"Mackenzie?" he prompts.

"Mackenzie, we're here."

I blink to find the car sitting in the Hyde School lot. Wes is twisted in his seat, looking at me. "You okay?" he asks. I will myself to nod and offer him a reassuring smile, then climb out of the car. With my back to Wes, I slide the silver ring off and loop it on my necklace chain, wishing I could cling a little longer to the buffer and everything that comes with it. But I can't afford to miss Owen.

"Wesley Ayers!" calls Safia from the edge of the parking lot, "you look ridiculous." All four of them are there waiting for us: Saf and Cash with gold streaks in their rich, dark hair, Amber with blue ribbons and butterfly patterns on her cheeks, Gavin in green, thick-framed glasses that take up half his face.

Wes runs a hand over his black spiked hair. "You say ridiculous, I say dangerous."

Cash arches a brow. "Dangerous as in, you could probably impale a low-flying bird?"

"Love the horns, Mackenzie," says Amber.

"I thought you had a date, Safia," I say.

"Yeah, whatever, I bailed."

"She wanted to be with us," says Amber. "She's just too proud to admit it."

"Is that my car?" asks Cash.

On campus, the buildings are dark, but the light from the festival glows against the low clouds, and the air is filled with the distant thrum of music—nothing but highs and lows from here. We reach the front gate with its wrought iron bars and its sculpted *H—abandon all hope, ye who enter here*—and pass through. Then we head down the tree-lined path toward the main building and around it, the noise growing louder and the lights growing brighter as we approach. When we pass into the glowing center of campus, Fall Fest rises up before us.

Silver, black, green, and gold. The colors trail in streamers down the building fronts to every side and across the lawn, forming a colorful canopy. Lanterns hang from the trees, lights line the paths, and the grass below the streamers is filled with students and edged with booths. The music seems to come from everywhere, not the way it does when I touch Wes—not filling my bones—but simple and normal and real and loud and all around. A group of girls in brightly colored wigs is perched on a bench eating and laughing, a huddle of boys is playing booth games, and a ton of students decked out in wild makeup and glittering accessories are dancing. The air is alive with their bodies and voices.

Teachers dot the crowd, chatting with one another—none of them with face paint or fake hair, but all in dark clothes like shadows cast around the festival. Mr. Lowell and Dallas hover in front of a booth; Ms. Hill and Ms. Wellson sit on a bench at the edge of the grass dance floor. And there, leaning against a drink stand, is Eric. I tense when I see him, looking grim as he surveys the crowd. I should have known he would be here, watching. But is he still acting as *Roland's* eyes? On the other side of the lawn, Sako sits perched on the edge of another bench. *She* is definitely here for Agatha. I scan the crowd for any other vigilant eyes and spot a third—a man I've never seen before, one with dark skin and Sako's same cold grace—which means that somewhere there's probably a fourth, his partner, but I don't see her. Everyone else looks like they belong. And really, somehow, so do the Crew.

But there is no sign of Owen. Not yet. Even with the whole school here and everyone decked out with crazy hair and strange eyes, I know I'll spot him at a glance.

The party starts at seven. The show's at eight.

What is he planning? A cold shiver of dread travels down my spine. What if the gamble's too great? What if I'm making a horrible mistake?

Amber and Gavin link arms and head for the nearest food stand, and Safia grabs Wesley's sleeve and demands a dance.

"It's tradition," she says. "You always dance with me."

Wesley hesitates, clearly not wanting to leave my side. And if I'm being honest, I don't want him to leave, either. I'm struck by the sudden fear that if he does, I won't have a chance to . . . To what? Say good-bye? I won't say that anyway.

"Go on, you two," says Cash. "Mac and I will get along fine."

Safia pulls Wesley into the throng, and Cash holds out his hand. "May I?"

I accept, and my head fills with his jazz and laughter and all of his thoughts, and as we dance I do my best to let them be like music instead of words and listen only to the melody. Cash is full enough of life and energy that, as we spin and twirl and smile and sing along, I almost forget. Even hearing his voice and his music and his life in my head for one whole song, I almost forget. That is the beauty of Cash. Another me in another life would have fallen for this pretty boy who looks at me and only sees a pretty girl and helps me pretend for one song that anything could be that simple.

But even if I believed in Owen's dream of a life without secrets and lies, Cash is not the boy I'd share it with.

Soon the song trails off and a slower one picks up. A senior girl appears at Cash's shoulder and asks for a dance. Wesley appears at my side at the same time.

"Dance with me," he says. And before I can say anything, he wraps his arm around my waist and fills my head with his sadness and his fear and—threaded through it all—his ever present hope. I rest my ear against his shoulder and listen to his heart, his noise, his life. Every moment of it hurts, but I don't let go or push away.

And then, near the end of the song, I see Owen hovering at the edge of the dance floor. His eyes meet mine. My pulse quickens, and I tighten my grip on Wes, gathering up the strength to pull away. I can do this. Whatever I have to do to put an end to this— to Owen—I will do it. I have to. I let him out. I'll return him. I'll lay him at the Archive's feet and earn my life back with his body.

Owen turns and makes his way to the shadow beside the clock tower. The song ends, but Wesley doesn't let go, and I look up into his dark-rimmed eyes.

"What is it?" he asks.

"You're worth it," I tell him.

His brow crinkles. "What do you mean?"

I smile. "Nothing," I say gently. "I'm going to get a drink. Save me another dance, okay?"

My fingers begin to slide through his. He hesitates and starts to tighten his grip, but Amber grabs his other hand and pulls him toward her. "Where's *my* dance, Ayers?" she asks. Our hands fall apart. The music starts up again and I vanish into the crowd, forcing myself not to look back.

Eric's back is turned and Mr. Bradshaw is trying to strike up a conversation with Sako as I slip away into the dark. Owen is humming (*you are my sunshine, my only sunshine . . .*), and I follow the sound of it into the shadows of the clock tower, where I find him leaning against the brick side, turning his knife over between his fingers.

"Hyde School always knew how to throw a party," he says, eyes lost in the glittering lights.

"Will you tell me now what's going to happen here? When do we steal the page?"

"That's the thing," says Owen, putting away his knife. "*We* don't."

I stiffen. "I don't understand."

"There's a reason this plan requires two people, Mackenzie. One of them distracts the Archive while the other steals the page."

"You want me to create the diversion?"

"No," says Owen, "I want you to *be* the diversion."

"What do you mean?"

"You're already on thin ice with the Archive, right? Well, if they're busy dragging you to your alteration, they're less likely to notice *me*."

"Why would they be doing that?" I ask slowly.

"Because you're not going to give them a choice. You're going to make a scene. The Archive hates scenes. I've already staged it for you." He toes the grass, and even in the dark I can see wires. Fuses.

"I said I didn't want anyone to get hurt."

"You have to play your part, Mackenzie. Besides, they're only fireworks. I told you, something short and bright. Flash and show. Once you've lit the match—a literal one this time—all you have to do is be ready to run. I'll take care of the hard part."

"What hard part?"

"All eyes are on you," he continues. "Waiting for you to mess up or make a move. So that's what you're going to do. And then you're going to run, and Crew will chase you. And when they catch you—and they will—you're going to *fight back*, with everything you have, to the very end."

My mind spins. This isn't how it's supposed to go. We are supposed to go into the Archive together. I am supposed to return him. How am I supposed to do that if I'm being executed?

"You don't want a diversion, Owen. You want a sacrifice."

"Don't be dramatic."

"I am not a martyr," I snap.

"I won't let them erase you."

"Oh, well, if you won't *let* them . . ." I say sarcastically.

"I'll save you," he insists. "Trust me."

I scoff. "You want me to put my life in your hands."

In an instant, Owen has me back against the brick wall. "Your life has been in my hands since the moment I stepped out of that void," he growls.

A sickening realization dawns on me. He's already set the scene. He doesn't need my consent to make me a diversion. But the only way he'll come for me is if he thinks I'm worth saving.

But the ledger is on the desk at the very front of the Archive.

What's to stop him from walking in and taking it and leaving without me?

"I won't," he says, reading the thoughts through my skin. "I will not leave you behind. I still need you. We are the bringers of change, Mackenzie. But I need you to be the voice of it."

His hands fall away. He turns toward the festival, and the lights cast shadows across his pale skin. "Change is coming," he says quietly. "Either the Archive will evolve or it will fall."

And watching him in that unsteady light, it hits me.

It's all a lie. His promise of an Archive without secrets, his dream of a world exposed—Owen doesn't expect the Archive to survive this. He doesn't want it to. He wants the same thing he's always wanted: to tear it down. And he thinks he's found a way to do that—by letting this world do the work.

He doesn't want change.

He wants ruin.

And I will do whatever it takes to keep him from it.

My mind is spinning, but I cannot afford to let him see my panic. I take a short, steadying breath. "You should have told me sooner," I say. "For someone who scorns secrets, you sure keep a lot of them."

He frowns. "I didn't want you to overthink it," he says. "But our fates are bound in this. If you fail, I fail; and if I fail, you fail. We are like partners."

We are nothing like partners, I think, but all I say is, "Don't you dare leave me there, Owen."

He smiles. "I won't."

And then he crouches and lifts the end of the fuse from the grass. A lighter appears in his other hand. He looks up at the clock tower beside us. Five minutes till eight p.m.

"Perfect," he says, sliding his thumb over the lighter. A small flame dances there. "Five minutes from the spark." He touches the flame to the fuse and it catches, a hissing sound running down the line. *No turning back now,* I realize with a mixture of terror and energy.

"Find the spotlight." Owen steps out of the shadows and onto the path, but I linger against the building and pull the phone from my pocket. There's a text from Wesley . . .

> Where are you?

. . . and I answer back . . .

> Science hall.

. . . hoping I can at least get him out of the way of whatever's about to happen. And then I swallow and dial home. Mom answers.

"Hi," I say. "Just checking in. As promised."

"Good girl," says Mom. "I hope you have a great time tonight."

I fight to keep the fear out of my voice. "I will."

"Call us when it's over, okay?"

"Okay," I say, and I can tell she's about to hang up, so I say, "Hey, Mom?"

"Yeah?"

"I love you," I say, before ending the call.

Four minutes till eight p.m. The clock tower looms overhead, fully lit. I watch a minute tick past as students dance and laugh beneath the colored canopy. They have no idea what's about to happen.

In all fairness, neither do I.

Three minutes till eight p.m. I tell myself I can do this. Tell myself it isn't madness. Tell myself it will all be over soon. When I run out of things to tell myself, I step out of the shadows, expecting to see Owen, but he's not there, so I head toward the quad. I only make it a few strides before a large hand wraps around my arm and drags me back into the dark and *thought you were clever can't get past me thought I wouldn't see the pattern* ricochets through my head. Before I can try to twist free, a metal cuff closes around my wrist, and I crane my neck to see Detective Kinney behind me.

"Mackenzie Bishop," he says, cuffing my hands behind my back, "you're under arrest."

THIRTY

"**D**ON'T CAUSE A SCENE," he orders, pulling me away from the festival.

"Sir, you're making a serious mistake." The clock strikes one minute till eight, and I twist around, desperately searching for Owen as Kinney drags me down the path.

"Do you know the last name entered into Coach Metz's computer?" he says. "Yours. And the last number to call Jason Pinter's phone? Yours. The prints on Bethany Thomson's necklace? Yours. The only place you didn't actually leave evidence was Phillip's, but you broke into his house, so I'm willing to bet we can tie you to that, too."

"That's circumstantial," I say. "You can't arrest me for it."

"Watch me," says Kinney, pushing me toward the front gates. His cruiser is waiting, lights flashing, on the other side. But the gates are closed. Not just closed, I realize—locked. And I can smell the gasoline from here.

"What the hell?" he growls.

His grip slackens on my arm, and I wrench free, making it three steps back toward the festival before Kinney's hand comes down hard on my shoulder.

"Not so—"

But he never gets a chance to finish. The clock tower chimes eight, and the fireworks start. Not in the air, but on the *ground*.

Several high whistles, followed by the heavy booms as massive spheres of color, light, sound, and fire explode across campus. The blasts are concentrated in the quad, but one goes off much closer to where we stand, and the force is enough to send Kinney and me to the ground. My ears are ringing as a pair of hands pulls me to my feet.

"Can't leave you alone for a moment, I swear," says Owen, soot dusting his cheeks. Behind him, the Hyde front gate is engulfed in fire.

"Where the hell were you?" I snap, ears still ringing as he strides over to Kinney, who's still getting to his hands and knees, clearly disoriented from the blast.

"Busy," he says, pulling the gun from Kinney's holster. He spins the weapon and brings the butt down hard against the detective's temple. Kinney crumples to the path. Back at the quad, another round of explosions goes off. People are screaming. Owen finds the keys on Kinney's belt, unlocks my cuffs, then drags me back toward the blossoming inferno.

We pass through a wave of smoke and into a world engulfed in fire. The blasts are deafening, and the streamer ceiling of the dance floor burns and breaks, dropping flaming strips onto the students below. Everyone is running, but no one seems to know where to run because the blasts keep going off. It's a blanket of chaos.

Owen storms through it, scanning the smoke-covered ground.

"What are you looking for?" I have to shout now over the noise of the falling festival.

"I left him right——"

Just then a body slams into Owen hard, his gun skittering toward me as they both go down. Another blast goes off behind me as I scoop up the weapon, Owen and his opponent a tangle of limbs on the burning ground until he manages to snake his arm around the man's throat and pull back and up, and I see his face.

Eric. One of his eyes is swelling shut, and a bad gash carves a path against his shirtfront, and when he sees me standing there, he tells me to run. And then he sees the gun in my hand and confusion lights up his blood-streaked face.

"Shoot him," orders Owen.

I stare at him in horror. "He's Crew!"

"Right now he's in our way," growls Owen, as if this is just an unfortunate turn of events. But it's not. This was always his plan.

I'll take care of the hard part.

The fireworks were nothing but a smoke screen. They could have been an accident. But killing a member of the Archive . . . there would be no question. No hesitation. The Archive would hunt me down. They'd erase me.

"You have to commit, Mackenzie," orders Owen, struggling to gain leverage over Eric. Another firework goes off, showering us in red light. I lift the gun, mind spinning. I've come so far and risked so much. I can't lose Owen, not now. But I can't do this.

"Commit."

I pull the trigger. But I aim wide.

The blast sounds, sharp even in the chaos, the bullet zinging past them both, and between my shot and Owen realizing I missed, Eric twists free and spins. *Run,* I think, *run.* And I'm about to level the gun on Owen—it might not stop him, but it will slow him down—when he slams his fist into Eric's jaw hard enough to crack bone. Eric crumples, and before he can recover, Owen takes his head in his hands and snaps his neck.

The world slows. The smoke thins and the fire dims, and in the instant just after I hear the crack and before the light goes out of his eyes, I see Eric's life unravel. I see him sitting beside me on the patio wall, telling me to stay out of trouble; questioning Dallas in the hospital; leaning up against the yellow wallpaper, chiding me for trying to slip away; checking my hands in the park for broken bones; standing on the sidewalk, nothing but a golden shadow, a glint of light, and then gone.

I stifle a cry as Eric's body slumps lifeless onto the charred earth. No. This isn't happening. This can't be happening.

"Run, Mackenzie," comes Owen's voice as I stare down at the corpse. My fingers tighten on the gun, but by the time I manage to drag my eyes away from Eric's body and up, Owen's already gone, and I'm alone. I look around and realize that I'm standing at the very center of the chaos. There are sirens in the distance, and people are still running, shadows in the smoke and all I can think is *please let Wes and Cash and the others be among them be safe.*

And then, through the chaos, I see her. Everyone else is running *away*. But she is running *toward* me.

Sako.

And I know from the way she's looking at me that she heard the gunshot, that she can see the weapon in my hand . . . and Eric's body at my feet. The gun tumbles from my grip as two more Crew—the third I saw earlier and a fourth—appear behind her. I don't have a choice. There's only one way out now.

I take a stumbling step backward.

And then I turn and run.

THIRTY-ONE

THERE'S ONLY ONE of me and three of them, and they are all *fast*.

The third drops to a knee beside Eric's body but the other two don't stop. I sprint across the quad, not toward the front gates like everyone else, but deeper into campus, cutting through the doors of the language hall only moments before I hear them crashing through behind me. I don't look back, don't sacrifice a single step of my lead as I sprint through the building, all the way to the opposite exit and back out into the burning night.

You're going to run . . .

Smoke billows up from the burning lawn as I cut hard down the path toward the Court. I'm almost there when I realize that one set of footsteps has vanished behind me; an instant later, the third Crew steps into my way. I can't change direction before he swings, catching me across the face with his fist.

And when they catch you . . .

I go down hard, tasting blood as the world rings in my ears.

. . . and they will . . .

Just as I'm getting to my feet, Sako grabs me from behind and throws me down on the dirt path, kicking me hard in the ribs.

. . . you're going to fight back *. . .*

The force sends me sprawling onto my back, and a second later she's kneeling on my chest. Hate and anger and images of Eric's corpse roll through me.

"I'm going to kill you," she growls. I throw a punch with my injured arm, but she catches it and slams my hand back to the ground. "I'm going to take my time and make you beg, you little shit."

"Sako," says the other man. "We have orders."

"Hang the orders," she spits.

I bring my knee up hard, catching her in the stomach, but she doesn't even move, only leans forward and forces her hand over my mouth, digging her nails into my jaw. "How could you? How could you?"

All the pain and anger is written over her and pouring through me as her hand slides from my jaw to my throat. And then, out of nowhere, a metal bar appears under her chin and wrenches her back and up and off me. *No.* She rolls to the side, and Wesley puts himself squarely between Sako and me as we both get to our feet.

"Wes, go! Please!"

The fire burns bright in the quad. A few final explosions thunder through Hyde.

"You shouldn't have done that, little Keeper," Sako hisses.

"Get away from her," growls Wes.

He swings his metal bar, and she catches it the instant before it connects with her face, ripping it from his grasp. "You really shouldn't have. . . ."

"Wesley! Don't——"

The third Crew slams into me from behind, wrapping his arms around my chest, pinning mine at my sides as *try to run I'll chase love the hunt little rabbit* forces its way into my head.

"Gotcha," he says, right before I drive my elbow back into his ribs and drop to a knee sudden and hard, jerking forward and forcing him to lose his grip and tumble over my shoulder. He's catlike, up again in a blink, holding something in his hands that looks like ribbon but glints in the uneven light. Metal wire.

"You should surrender," he says, "before this has to get worse."

"I can't," I say. He smiles like he's happy to hear it. And then he attacks. His hand flies forward, and the length of metal wire expands, like he's casting it out. I dodge, avoiding the thread, ducking out of its way. Out of the corner of my eye, I see Wesley go down hard, blood streaking across his cheek. In that instant I feel the lightest touch as the cord loops around my good wrist.

"Gotcha," he says again, and with a single swift jerk the wire cinches, cutting into my skin. I try to pull free, but when I struggle it only tightens, so I grab hold of the thread and use it to wrench him toward me, even though the wire slices into my fingers. My free hand curls into a fist and catches him in the stomach, a solid enough blow to knock the wind from his lungs and send pain up my arm. I realize my mistake too late; before I can get out of reach, he's got the length of wire twined around my other wrist. He pulls, and my hands are forced together in front of me. He grins triumphantly.

Fight back . . .

I intertwine my fingers and bring my locked fists across his jaw as hard as I can, splitting his lip—which manages to wipe the smile from his face, but doesn't help me get loose. He keeps his hand around the metal thread and yanks me forward to him, forcing me off balance before driving his fist into my ribs. I double over, and before I can recover he shoves me backward and swings his leg behind my knees, sending me to the hard earth.

He drags me back to my feet, and I have just enough time to see Wesley stagger to his hands and knees—Sako picking up his metal bar and dragging it along the ground toward him—before the

Crew's fist connects with my ribs again. The wind rushed out of my lungs, and I'm left fighting for breath as he hauls me down the path to the nearest building. I try to call out to Wes, but there's no air, no time. The Crew slams me back against a side door, pulls a dark key from his pocket, and jams it into the lock, and a second later, the path and Wesley and Sako all vanish as I fall into the Archive.

I hit the antechamber floor hard. The moment I try to get to my feet, the sentinels are there, forcing me roughly back to my knees.

Agatha is waiting, the other Librarians in line behind her—and clearly they've been told what happened. Their faces are a spectrum of horror and sadness and confusion and betrayal. Patrick is on one side of Roland, Lisa on the other, and they are both holding him back. My eyes flick from his face to the golden key around his neck and back again, willing him to understand, to trust me even if he can't. Again I try to fight to my feet, and again the sentinels force me down in front of Agatha.

"I warned Hale this would happen," she says, cold triumph in her eyes. "A broken mind and a traitor's heart. Do you have *anything* to say?"

I'm sorry. Listen. Please. Trust me. This isn't what it looks like. But I can't say any of those things. I have to sell it. Everything in me wants to scream *NO* as I spit blood onto the dark stone floor and say, "The Archive is broken."

Agatha backhands me hard across the face. Pain blossoms against my brow and blood trickles into my vision. "I'll summon Hale. Take her away."

The sentinels wrench me to my feet.

Fight back . . .

I jerk forward hard and manage to twist free. It takes every ounce of will and strength, but I run into Roland's arms, pressing my bound hands flat against his shirtfront. It looks like a plea, but only because no one can see my fingers wrapping around the gold key he wears there. The one that turns lives on and off. The one only Librarians are meant to handle. A numbing pain, pins-and-needles sharp, spreads through my fingers and up my wrist, but I don't let go.

. . . with everything you have . . .

"Trust," I whisper, closing my hand over it just before they pull me off him. The snap of his necklace is buried beneath the sounds of the struggle as I'm dragged away. I palm the key, slipping it under the edge of my sleeve just before a crushing blow sends me forward to my hands and knees. Two more sets of hands— sentinels both—take hold.

. . . to the very end.

A hood is thrown over my head. Everything goes black. Even then, I try to fight.

"Enough, Miss Bishop," orders Patrick as I'm dragged through the Archive. All I can think as I'm led away is that it *will not be enough, it will not be enough, it will not be enough.*

And then I hear it.

Back in the antechamber.

Wesley's voice.

Shouting my name. Arguing with someone loudly as he storms into the Archive.

Everything in me crumples. This was never supposed to be his fight. As I'm dragged down another corridor, I hear the sound of people chasing after him, hear Patrick give a quiet order, and feel one of the sentinels pull away from my side and turn toward the commotion. Patrick's hands—hands I know well because they've patched me up countless times over the last four and a half years—take his place. He and the second sentinel force me through a pair of doors and into a room so empty our steps echo, my name still bouncing on the walls of the Archive.

Then, abruptly, it stops, and I don't know if it's because they've closed a door or because they've caught Wes, but I tell myself he'll be okay even as I try to twist free. The hands tighten, digging into the gash on my arm hard enough to make me grateful for the gold key's spreading numbness as I'm shoved roughly down into a chair. They slice the metal thread free from my wrists, but before I can get to my feet, they're strapping me down, my waist and legs and wrists cinched to the cold arms of the chair. There's no way out. I twist in the binds, but it's no use, and they know it.

"Good-bye," says Patrick, and then a door opens and closes, and the room is silent.

Totally silent.

And totally dark.

And that's when the fear finally hits. It's been chasing me all night, but now it finally catches up.

Fear that none of this is going to work.

Fear that I misjudged, that Owen isn't going to save me, that I was nothing more than a disposable tool.

Fear that he won't come in time.

Fear that he won't make it past the antechamber.

And under all of it, a far worse fear.

A fear that makes me close my eyes, despite the dark.

The fear that maybe, somehow, *Owen isn't real*. That the

nightmare never gave way to reality, that somehow it's been me—and only me—all along. That I've lost my mind. That I'm about to lose my life.

A prickling pain is spreading through my body from the Archive key pressed against my wrist, and I focus on that as I try to twist my arm against the chair, to work the metal toward my hand.

And then I hear it. The door opens behind me, and the sounds of the Archive—of hurrying feet and muffled shouts, none of them Wesley's—pour in for a moment before cutting off again. There's a short, quiet scuffle followed by a sickening crack. I struggle again with my binds, fighting with the chair until someone reaches out and grips my shoulder and the all-too-familiar quiet seeps through my skin.

"Owen?" I gasp.

"Hold still," he orders, and relief spills over me. I coat myself in it as he pulls off my hood. The room I'm in is a glaring white, nearly as bright but not as seamless as a Returns room and completely bare of shelves—of *anything* except the chair and a sentinel slumped in the corner, his head tilted at a very wrong angle. Eric flashes up behind my eyes, but I force myself to focus as Owen frees one of my wrists and drops to a knee, setting to work on my ankles, leaving me to free my other hand myself. He gets my legs unbound and circles behind the chair to find the buckle for the waist strap. The final strap falls away, and Owen rounds the chair again.

"You put on quite a show," he says, offering me his hand.

My heart races as I take it. "I know," I say as he helps me to my feet. "You were right," I add, fingers curling around the metal in my hand.

His brow furrows. "About what?"

I meet his gaze. "I just had to commit."

My grip tightens around his. Confusion flickers across his face, but before he can pull away, I drive the gleaming key into his chest and turn it. For an instant, he stares at me, blue eyes wide. And then the light goes out of Owen's face, the life out of his body. His knees buckle and I catch him, and the two of us sink together toward the sterile white floor.

I can hear the footsteps rushing down the hall, and a strange sadness spreads through me as I ease Owen's body to the ground. He kept his word. He believed in something, however misguided.

I don't know what I believe in anymore.

The only thing I know for sure is that I'm still alive.

And it's almost over.

Almost.

THIRTY-TWO

I CANNOT SEEM to escape this room.

Cold marble floors. Ledger-lined walls. The long table stretching in the middle.

It is the room I was inducted in. It is the room Wesley and I were summoned to after the History escaped into the Coronado. And now it is the room where the Archive will decide my fate.

When Roland and Agatha and Director Hale found me in the alterations room, kneeling over Owen's body, a sentinel slumped in the corner, I said only one thing.

"I want a trial."

So here I am. The remaining sentinel stands beside me, within easy reach, but mercifully hands-off. Roland, Agatha, and Director Hale sit behind the table, Roland's key on its broken cord in front of them.

I flex my hand, still waiting for the feeling to return to my fingertips after using it. Director Hale offers me a chair, but I'll fall over before I sit down in here again tonight. My gaze find Roland's. A minute ago, he paused on his way in and reached out, pretending to steady me.

"Do you regret it yet?" I asked under my breath. "Voting me through?"

A sad smile ghosted his lips. "No," he said. "You make things infinitely more interesting."

"Thank you," I said in a low voice as he turned away. "For trusting me."

"You didn't leave me much choice. And I want my journal back."

Now Roland sits at the table, gray eyes tense as Hale rises to his feet and approaches me, bringing his hands aloft.

"May I?" he asks.

I nod, bracing myself for the pain I felt when Agatha tore through my mind. But as Hale's hands come down against my temples, I feel nothing but a cool and pressing quiet. I close my eyes as the images begin to flit rapidly through my mind: of Owen and the voids and the festival and the fire and Eric. When Hale's hands slide back to his sides, his expression is unreadable.

"Give me context for what I've seen," he says, taking his seat.

I stand before them and explain what happened. How the voids were made. How Owen finally got through. How I set my trap.

"You should have involved the Archive from the start," he says when I'm done.

"Sir, I was afraid that if I did, I would be arrested for the mere fact that Owen still existed, and then Crew would go after him themselves, and everyone would suffer for it. As it is, Eric did suffer. I considered it my job."

And I wasn't entirely sure Owen was real.

"It is *Crew's* job to hunt down Histories in the Outer," clarifies Agatha.

"Owen Chris Clarke was not an ordinary History. And he was my responsibility. I gave him the tools he needed to escape the first time, and my crimes were pardoned on the assumption that he was no longer a threat." I'm surprised by the calm in my

669

voice. "Besides, I was in a unique position to handle him."

"How so?" asks Director Hale.

"He wanted to recruit me."

Hale's brow furrows.

"Owen wanted my help. And I let him believe that I was willing to give it."

"How did you concoct the plan to lure him here?" asks Roland.

"I didn't," I say. "He did." I watch the confusion spread across their faces. "I imagine," I add, "that he thought it would end differently, but the seed of the plan was his. He wanted me to be a diversion—to attract the energy and attention of the Archive while he achieved some ulterior goal."

"What was his goal?" demands Agatha.

I hold her gaze. "He wanted to attack the ledger. He promised that, in exchange for my diversion, he would rescue me before I could be altered."

"And you believed him?" asks Hale, incredulous.

"Why would he save you?" asks Agatha.

"*I* believed Owen would attack the Archive. And *Owen* believed I could be converted to his cause. I encouraged that belief in hopes that by insinuating myself into his plan, I would be able to assure his return to the shelves and end the threat he posed."

"Quite a risk," observes Hale, lacing his fingers. "And if your initial plan failed? If you had not been able to obtain Roland's key, if Owen had never come to save you?"

"I weighed it," I say. "Given Owen's skills, I believed my strategy had the highest odds of success. But I hope you understand that I was playing a part. That in order to give myself the best odds, I had to commit to it."

"I hope *you* understand that a Crew member is dead because of your charade," says Agatha.

Behind my eyes, Eric's body crumples to the grass.

"I do. That moment is scarred into my memory. It is the moment I nearly faltered. And the moment I knew I couldn't. I had started down a road, and I had to finish. I hope you can forgive me for the selfish need to end Owen's life with my own hands."

Hale straightens in his seat. "Continue your account."

I swallow. "When I was brought into the branch, I knew I had to introduce as much chaos as possible, a short burst of disorder to help ensure that Owen reached me so that I could stop him."

"I assume that's also why *Wesley Ayers* made such a scene?" offers Roland with a weighted look.

"Yes," I say, leaping on the thread. "He was acting under my orders. Is he all right?"

"He's the least of your worries," says Agatha.

"He's alive," says Hale.

"He'll be okay," adds Roland, sensing my worry.

"You do have a way of inspiring allegiances, don't you?" says Hale. "That boy running around shouting his head off, Roland here claiming he didn't even feel you take his key—"

"I was caught up in the moment," says Roland.

Hale waves him away. "And Owen Chris Clarke. You gained his trust, too. I marvel at that, the way he must have genuinely believed in your commitment."

"Owen believed in his cause," I say. "His focus was greater than my acting."

"So you never actually considered defecting?" he asks, his question close on the heels of my answer.

I hold his gaze. "Of course not," I say calmly.

Hale considers me, and I consider Hale, and silence descends on the room, interrupted only by the director tapping his fingers on the table. Finally, he speaks.

"Miss Bishop, your dedication and sense of strategy are impressive. Your method, however, is reprehensible. You circumnavigated an entire system to fulfill your own desires for revenge and closure. But the fact is, you achieved your objective. You uncovered the truth behind the voids and suppressed a serious threat to the Archive with minimal—albeit upsetting—losses." He turns to Agatha. "Your sentence is overruled."

Relief and hope begin to roll through me. Until Agatha cuts in.

"You forget," she says to Hale, "that there are *two* charges against Miss Bishop. The first is for treason. Clear her of that if you will, but the second is that she is no longer mentally fit to serve. You cannot deny me that claim."

Hale sighs and slumps back in his seat. "No," he says, "but I can consider a second opinion. From someone whose pride isn't so bruised." He waves a hand at the sentinel, who goes to the door and opens it. A woman strides in, her blond hair pulled back in a messy ponytail, blood streaking her hands and the front of her clothes, soot smudged across her forehead and jaw.

Dallas.

"Sorry I'm late," she says, wiping at the soot. "I had to take care of the body."

My stomach turns. I know she means Eric.

"What is the situation at the school?" asks Roland.

"Chaos, but it's calming." Her attention slides to me. She raises a brow. "You look like you've had quite a night."

"Dallas," says Hale, drawing my therapist's attention back. "You've had several days with Miss Bishop. What is your assessment?"

Agatha's eyes narrow at the use of the word.

"Of Mackenzie?" asks Dallas, scratching her head. "She's fine. I mean, *fine* might be the wrong word. But considering what she's been through"—her eyes flick to Agatha and narrow slightly— "and what she's been *put through*"—they shift warmly back to me—"her resilience is astonishing. She was in control of the situation the entire time. I did not interfere."

Roland's shoulders relax visibly, and I take a deep breath, allowing myself to finally believe that I've succeeded, that it's going to be okay.

"There you have it," says Hale. "I think we're——"

"There is doubt in her," snaps Agatha, pushing up from her chair. "I read it."

"Enough," says Hale, rubbing his eyes. "Doubt is not a crime, Agatha. It is only a tool to test our faith. It can break us, but it can also make us stronger. It is perfectly natural, even necessary, and it troubles me to think that you've lost sight of that." He pushes to his feet. "Give me your key," he says softly.

Her gloved hand goes to the gleaming gold below her throat. He snaps his fingers, and her jaw tightens as she gives the gold thread a swift tug, breaking it, and places the key in his palm. He considers it a moment.

And then he drives the metal into Agatha's chest.

He doesn't turn the key, but stands there, gripping her shoulder with one hand and the gold stem with the other, staring into her eyes while the room holds its breath. His lips move as he whispers something to her, so softly I can barely hear.

"You disappoint me."

And then, as quickly as he struck, he withdraws the key, and Agatha gasps for breath.

"Get out," he says, and she doesn't hesitate, but turns, clutching her front, and hurries from the room, her cream-colored coat rippling behind her.

As the door closes behind her, Director Hale sighs and takes his seat, setting Agatha's key on the table before him. The room is deathly still. Roland's eyes are on the table. Dallas's are on the floor.

But mine are on Hale.

"It may be true that nothing's lost," he says, "but everything must end. *When* is in my hands. I'd caution you to remember that, Miss Bishop." He turns to Dallas. "See that she gets home safely."

"Sir," I say. "Please. What about Wesley?"

He waves a hand at the door. "He's out there somewhere. Go find him."

It's all I can do not to shout Wesley's name as I hurry down the hall and into the atrium, breaking into a run as the antechamber comes into sight—and with it, Wesley. He's cut and bloody, swaying a little but still standing, his hands on his head. Patrick waits on one side of him and Lisa on the other, and the Crew who brought me in waits behind him, and I don't care about any of them.

I run, and he looks up and sees me as I make it through the doors, and his hands fall from his head just in time to wrap around me.

We are both bruised and broken, wincing at the other's touch even as we pull each other closer. My arms are tight around his waist, and his are tight around my shoulders. And when he presses his lips into the curve of my throat, I can feel his tears on my skin.

"You are an idiot," I say, even as I guide his face and mouth to mine. I kiss him, not gently, but desperately. Desperately, because he's worth it—because life is terrifying and short and I don't know what will happen. All I know is that here and now, I am still alive, and I want to be with Wesley Ayers. Here and now I want to feel his arms wrapped around me. I want to feel his lips on mine. I want to feel his life tangling with mine. Here and now is all we have, and I want to make it worth whatever happens next.

I tighten my grip on Wes enough to make him break off his kiss with a gasp.

"I'm sorry," I whisper, my lips hovering over his.

"I'm not," he breathes, pulling me closer and kissing me deeper. I'm still afraid of caring—of breaking, of losing—but now there is something else matching the fear stride for stride: want.

"You said you trusted me," I say.

"You said you were in the science hall. I guess we're even." He pulls me back toward him. "What happened tonight, Mac?" he whispers, lips against my jaw.

"I'll tell you later," I whisper back.

I can feel him smile tiredly against my cheek. "I'll hold you to it." His lips brush mine again, but someone clears her throat, and I force myself to pull away from Wesley's kiss. Dallas is standing there waiting.

"All right, you two," she says. "Plenty of time for that. Right now I have to get you back to school." She's standing by the desk, and for the first time I notice the smoldering wreckage of the ledger.

"What happened?" I ask.

"The only thing Owen Chris Clarke achieved was an act of vandalism," says Lisa, gesturing to the book. "He burned it."

Dallas shakes her head and gestures to the door. The Crew who dragged me is standing there, and I tense when I see him.

"No hard feelings," he says.

"I'm sure," I say, Wesley's hand tangling with mine.

"Just doing my job." But he smiles when he says it. It's not a gentle smile, and I'm reminded of the things that filled his noise—the fun of the hunt.

"I'd tell you not to be such an ass, Zachary," says Dallas, brushing him away from the door, "but it would be a waste of my breath. I don't know how Felicia tolerates you." And with that she turns her key, the door opens onto sirens and darkness, and Wesley and I follow Dallas back onto Hyde's campus.

In the Outer, Wesley's noise pours through my head, a tangle of want and love, relief and shock and fear. I don't know what's singing across *my* skin, but I don't pull away. I trust him with it.

Most of the buildings look all right—though the fire ate away a good deal of the ivy—but the field with its streamers and lanterns and booths is a charred black mess.

"Is everyone okay?"

"A few burns here, a few stitches there, but everyone will live."

My eyes slide from her face to her clothing. The black of her cotton shirt is crusted darker with blood, its stain streaking across her exposed skin. "Everyone except Eric," I say as she leads us around the scorched scene and toward the front gate. "That's why you were late."

She nods grimly. "I tried to get his body into one of the flare-up fires before the emergency vehicles got here. Make it look like an accident."

"And Sako?" I ask.

Dallas rubs her hands together, and blood flakes off to the ground below. "She took off. I sent Zachary's partner, Felicia, to find her."

"I think I broke her nose," says Wesley.

Dallas gives him a once-over. "It looks like she got in a few good hits."

"So you're Crew, too?" I ask as she leads us toward the burned remains of the festival.

"No," says Dallas. "I'm what you might call a field assessor. It's my job to make sure everything and everyone ticks and tocks the way they should."

"And if they don't?" asks Wes.

She shrugs. "If they belong to the Archive, I turn them in. If they belong to the Outer, I fix them myself."

"You make alterations," I say. "Wipe memories."

"When I have to," she says. "It's my job to clean up. I already took care of that cop, Kinney. I'll have to send Crew in to get the evidence, but at least I carved you out of his head. As far as he knows, the explosions are what knocked him out."

So many questions are rolling through my mind, but we reach the front gates, which have been pried open. Everyone's corralled there, and two firemen rush over.

"Where did you three come from?" one demands.

"These two got trapped under one of the booths," says Dallas, her tone shifting effortlessly to one of authority. "I can't believe you didn't find them sooner. Better make sure they're both okay."

And before they can ask who *she* is and what she's doing there, she turns and ducks under the yellow tape that's been strung up across the gate and vanishes into the swell of students and teachers and parents that fill the lot. EMTs pull Wes and me apart to check us out, and I slide my ring back on, amazed by how quickly I've become accustomed to the world without it.

The EMT looks me over. Most of my injuries I can blame on the booth that apparently collapsed on top of us, but the wire marks on my wrists are harder to explain. I'm lucky that there are too many people who need looking after and not enough people to do it; the EMT listens when I tell him I'll be okay and lets me go.

But Wesley is either a less convincing liar or he's in worse shape than I realized, because they insist on taking him to the hospital to be safe. The ambulance goes out of the lot before he can say much more to me than, "Leave the window open."

I've barely ducked under the yellow tape when someone shouts my name, and I look up to see the rest of the Court huddled on the sidewalk, a little singed but otherwise unhurt. There is a stream of *where were you*s and *what happened*s and *are you hurt*s and *is Wesley with you*s and *is he okay*s and *that was crazy*s before they finally settle down enough to let me answer. Even then I only get halfway through before Cash makes a crack about how this will go on his feedback card for sure—and Saf elbows him and says she heard that someone *died* in there, and how can he be making jokes? Amber comments on traumatic experiences being optimal times for levity, and then I hear my name again, and turn to find my parents pushing through the crowd toward me, and I get out half of "I'm okay" before my mother throws her arms around my neck and starts sobbing.

Dad wraps his arms around us both, and I don't need to have my ring off to know their minds, to feel their relief tangled with their desperate need to protect the child they have left and their fear that they can't. I can't protect them, either. Not from losing me—not every time—but tonight I'm here, and so I hold them tighter and tell them it's going to be okay.

And for the first time in a very long time, I believe it.

AFTER

I'M SITTING ON the edge of my bed that night in my ruined uniform, the silver horns still snagged in my hair, smelling of smoke and blood and thinking of Owen. I am not afraid of sleeping, though I wish Wesley were here with me. I am not afraid of nightmares, because mine came true and I lived through them.

I get to my feet and begin to peel off my ruined uniform, wincing as my stiff and wounded body protests every movement. I manage to tug my shirt over my head, then shed my skirt, and finally my shoes, unlacing them and tugging them off one at a time. I pull the first one off and set it on the bed beside me. When I pull the second shoe off and turn it over, a square of folded paper falls out onto the floor.

I cringe as I kneel to pick it up, smoothing the page. It's blank but for a single word in the lower right corner, written in careful script: *ALL*. I run my thumb over the word.

I wasn't going to take it.

I crouched there over Owen's body, listening to the sounds of footsteps, counting the seconds, and feeling dazed and numb. I didn't plan to take it, but one second I was just sitting there and the next my hands were patting him down, digging the folded page out of his pocket, slipping it into my shoe. The moment was easy to hide. To bury.

Now, as I stare down at the page, I consider burning it. (Of course Owen didn't just burn the ledger; he burned the *rest* of the ledger to cover the fact that this page was missing.)

The thing is, Owen was so wrong about so many things.

But I don't know if he was wrong about *everything*.

I want to believe in the Archive. I *want* to. So I don't know whether it's doubt or fear, weakness or strength, Da's voice in my head warning me to be ready for anything or Owen's telling me it's time for change, or the fact that I have seen too much tonight, that made me take the paper from Owen's pocket.

I *should* burn it, but I don't. Instead I fold it very carefully—each time pausing to decide if I want to destroy it, each time deciding not to—until it's the size it was before. And then I pull *The Inferno* from my shelf, slip the square of stolen paper between its pages, and set the book back.

Maybe Owen was right.

Maybe I am a bringer of change.

But I'll decide what kind.

TURN THE PAGE FOR A **BONUS SHORT STORY** FROM WESLEY AYER'S POINT-OF-VIEW JUST MOMENTS AFTER THE EVENTS OF THE UNBOUND.

HOSPITALS MAKE HORRIBLE music.

I don't mean the literal kind they pipe into elevators or play at background levels in waiting rooms (with the TVs and the magazines and all the other stimuli, because apparently if you give people any actual quiet they'll think about the fact they're in a hospital). No, I mean the hum and buzz and beep, the ringing phones and squeaking stretcher wheels and distant coughs that layer together to make up a hospital's sound track, the way slivers of thought and memory make up a person's noise. It sets my teeth on edge, which sends a dull pain through my head, which reminds me of the pain flickering in my shoulder and ribs, and it's a slippery slope from calm to pain to panic so I stop myself right there.

I hate hospitals.

I don't even have a good reason, like I spent too much time in them as a kid because my grandma was sick (she was already dead) or my dad worked in the ER (if anyone needed medical attention it was me, and nobody noticed). I just hate the way they sound. They're everything the Archive isn't. Well, everything it wasn't, when I still thought it was everything.

But I'm here, and I'm staring at the X-rays the doctor left tacked up on the light board. The screen's dark now but the image is still ghosted behind my eyes. Strange thing, to see your body from the inside out. People are made of so many fragile pieces.

I tick past the trouble in my mind. A few broken ribs. A cracked shoulder. A little internal bleeding (nothing serious). And behind those things, the older scars. Hairline fractures and fused bones. Only so much you can blame on a collapsing tent in a festival fire. And yet, no burns. Because I wasn't really trapped beneath a tent in a festival fire. I was fighting for my life. For Mackenzie's.

But I can't say that, of course, just like I can't say that those old wounds came from fighting Histories—an old man with a hunting knife, a kid with sharp teeth, Owen Chris Clarke—so they bring in a social worker, to make sure I'm not being hurt at home. And for a moment I'm pretty tempted to say yeah, yeah I am being hurt, because my father's a prick and my stepmother—shudder— is an evil money-grubbing bitch, but in the end I just shrug and say it must have been soccer because Dad may be a horrible person but the marks he's left are more absences than injuries, and Izzy is only an evil money-grubbing bitch in context. I probably wouldn't hate her if she was gold-digging someone else's family.

I don't think the doctors really believed me in the end, but then Dallas showed up and said something and they let the matter drop, which I owe her for, but lying here surrounded by hospital music I'm almost wishing I'd drawn it out, let Dad and Izzy take the fall so someone else could suffer. Maybe I'm just mad because I told them to go home and they listened. Didn't even put up a fight. They were dressed like I'd pulled them away from some important function—that's what they call it when you're too rich and impor- tant for words like *dinner* or *party*. Everything becomes a function, an event, a gala.

So here I am. Alone. Which is fine, it's fine, it's fine, but it's not.

An IV drips cloudy fluid into a tube running into a needle run- ning into the back of my hand. I hate needles, almost as much as hospitals. Mac would probably make fun of me if she knew, which means I'll probably end up telling her. That's a form of masochism, I'm sure, but if it will make her smile, she's worth the bruised ego. She's worth the real bruises, too. She's even worth the needles.

I picture telling her, and in my mind I'm still on my back but I'm no longer in this hospital bed. No, I'm lying with my head in her lap, looking up through her waves of auburn hair. It's just getting dark, and we're stretched on the worn stone steps of the Court at Hyde. No fire. No explosions. No Owen. Just us.

Just Mackenzie, really, and that small, hard-won smile.

"Honestly, Wes?" she'll tease, brushing her fingers across my forehead so she can see my eyes. "Not monsters or serial killers or the dark?"

I reach up and tuck a strand of copper behind her ears. No IV. No bruises. Just my hand on her skin.

"Hey, look," I'll say. "There are rational and irrational fears in this world, and last time I checked, it's not irrational to be afraid of sharp, pointy things." Especially not after being stabbed, I'll think, but I won't say that, because I'm not supposed to remember that day. It would be easier not to remember that day.

Mac will give me that skeptical look. "You sure have a lot of piercings for a guy with a needle phobia."

"I am the master of my fears," I'll say. Even though the truth is I made Cash go with me every time, and you know he's a good friend because he never gave me hell, never did anything but flip through the tattoo catalogs along the wall and wonder which design would piss his father off the most.

Fake/future/alternate-world Mackenzie bends down and kisses my forehead. My head spins.

They've got me pumped full of god knows what, and it's dulling the world in all the wrong places. It's like standing at the very edge of a dream and you can't seem to wake up, but you can't forget you're dreaming either.

And then, just as panic starts to really dig its fingers in, my cell starts buzzing on the side table. When I reach for it, pain blossoms across my stomach, but it's worth the trek. It's Mac.

"I left the window open," she says.

And just like that, the world pulls back into focus. I stop spinning and something in me cracks—not something literal like bones, thank god, but something just as deep—and I'm so ready for this damn night to end, but I don't want it to end here.

I take a bracing breath, knowing this is going to hurt, then sit up, and sure enough the pain makes light dance behind my eyes. I didn't feel it during the fight—I didn't feel anything. I didn't even feel it after, when Mac and I were back on campus. It wasn't until the EMTs pulled us apart that the pain hit me in a wave.

I perch on the edge of the hospital bed, waiting for the room to stop spinning. It hurts to breathe, but I have this trick, where I try and focus on the good, so I remind myself that things only hurt because I'm still alive to feel them. Silver linings, kids. I'm full of them.

Getting dressed takes a painful—and painfully long—time and I alternate between cursing and holding my breath in case a nurse chooses this moment—trying to balance with one leg in my pants—to come in.

But no one does.

I find a mirror in the cubicle of a bathroom, and my reflection stares back. I've looked better. My face has found a way to look pale and bruised at the same time, my eyeliner smudged into a messy shadow; my father assured the doctors it must be smoke, or face paint from the festival. Because the idea of me wearing makeup bothered him more than seeing me in a hospital bed.

I run a hand through my hair, trying to smooth away the hospital-bed head, which is even worse than normal bed head, but I give up. There's a cut above my eyebrow held closed by two strips of white tape, and I wonder if it will leave a scar, because scars are rather dashing, and then I hear Mac in my head again.

"Get over yourself, Wes," she says and I smile and it hurts.

It's late, and hospital wings really do get quiet at night, so it's easy enough to slip out. I find my key in the front pocket of my jeans, but I don't know where the nearest Narrows door is, and the grim fact is I'm in no shape for handling Histories, so I take a cab across town.

I've never been so glad to see the Coronado's creepy face, the gargoyles perched like ravens on the roof. I never told Mac but I have names for them all. Governor. Socrates. Headless. Malcolm. . . .

I stand on the curb, staring up at the three floors that stand between me and Mac's room. Or more accurately, I stare at the fourth-floor window above Mac's room, the one I used to climb down to get through her window, and realize there's no way I can make that descent tonight.

And then, the universe takes pity on my predicament. My phone buzzes again. Another note from Mac.

I left the door open, too.

My heart skips a little as I head into the lobby, and think about taking the stairs, but decide it won't be very charming if I pass out halfway up and someone finds my body in the morning, so I take the death trap of an elevator to the third floor.

3F is waiting at the end. I could kiss it.

I press my ear to the wood, and then turn the handle as softly as I can manage and step inside. The apartment's dark and I find my way by feel and memory through the living room and down the hall to Mackenzie's bedroom.

Inside, it's cloaked in moonlight and shadow. At first I think she's asleep, but as I slide the door shut behind me, she rolls over.

"You came," she whispers, her voice as tight as my chest.

"No place I'd rather be," I say softly. "I wish the entrance had been grander. The door doesn't have nearly as much style as the window and——" But I don't get any further because she's on her feet, crossing the space between us, and then her mouth is on mine, her noise thundering through my head where she grips me.

I gasp under her touch, and she pulls back, but that's the last thing I want, so I pull her close again and let my body scream. She tangles her fingers with mine and leads me to the bed, and when we get there she climbs onto the covers and makes a Wesley-size space for me beside her, and suddenly the pain means nothing because this moment is perfect.

We lie there for a few minutes, staring up at the ceiling instead of each other, only our hands tangled together. And then I turn her toward me, her stormy eyes narrowed on my wrist.

"What's this?" she asks, fingering the hospital bracelet. I'd forgotten all about it, and now she's looking at it way too hard, as if it's the most fascinating thing in the world and not an infernal piece of plastic. And then I see what she sees, and I can feel the blood drain out of my face. Can feel my stomach sink through my feet.

She squints at the writing on the bracelet, at my legal name printed on the label, and I cover it with my fingers but it's too late. I can tell she's read the name. My first name.

Templeton.

Templeton Wesley Ayers II, also known as reason number forty-five why I hate my father. Because what kind of sadistic asshole passes on a name like that?

"Mac . . ." I start, but it's too late. She doesn't just smile, she starts laughing, and I want to be angry but god, it's the most beautiful sound in the world, even better than that storm going inside her head. I would slay monsters and run through fire and jump off cliffs just to hear that sound. Which is why it takes all my strength to stifle it, and press my hand over her mouth. The laugh becomes a muffled chuckle in her chest. And then her fingers drift up to mine, and pry them gently free.

"Don't say it," I hiss, as her lips form the word. "Don't mouth it. Don't even think about it."

"Okay," she whispers. ". . . Templeton."

I groan, but she cuts off the sound with a kiss. We're gentler now, moving carefully over each other's bruised and broken bodies, the crackle of pain swallowed up by the fact that Mackenzie Bishop is letting me kiss her. Mackenzie Bishop is kissing me.

"I'm glad you told me," she says, breathlessly.

"I didn't tell you," I point out.

"Well, I'm glad I found out."

"Why's that?"

"Because now I won't laugh when we become Crew."

I go still. Not because I don't want to hear those words. But because I do. I want them to be true.

"Do you mean it?" I ask, rolling gingerly to face her.

She mirrors me, rolling onto her side so I'm looking straight into her eyes. "Yes," she says.

I can tell I'm smiling like an idiot. I don't care. "I don't suppose you have any hidden and mortifying names? Habits? Secrets?"

691

"Only one."

"And what's that?"

"I'm in love with a boy named Templeton."

The Archived

ACKNOWLEDGMENTS

To my father, for liking this book more than the first one. And for wanting to tell everyone. And to my mother, for elbowing my father every time he did. To Mel, for always knowing what to say. And to the rest of my family, who smiled and nodded even when they weren't sure what I was doing.

To my agent, Holly, for putting up with the often pathetic—but undeniably cute—animal pictures I use to explain my emotional state, and for believing in me and in this book.

To my editor, Abby, for building this world brick by brick beside me, then helping me tear it down and build it again out of stronger stone. And to Laura, for every bit of mortar added. It is a joy and an adventure.

To my freakishly talented cover designer, Tyler, and to my entire publishing family at Disney Hyperion, for making me feel like I am home.

To my friends, who bolstered me with bribes and threats and promises, and followed through. Specifically, to Beth Revis, for her stern looks and gold stars when I needed them most. To Rachel Hawkins, for brightening every day with a laugh or a photo of Jon Snow. To Carrie Ryan, for mountain walks and long talks and for being an incredible person. To Stephanie Perkins, for shining so brightly when I needed a light. To Ruta Sepetys, for believing in me, often more than I believe in myself. To Myra McEntire, for dragging me back from the cliffs of insanity. To Tiffany Schmidt, for reading, and for loving Wesley so much. To Laura Whitaker, for the tea and good talks. To Patricia and Danielle, for the kindness and the care. And to the Black Mountain crew, who helped me meet my deadline and then thrust a flask and a jar of Nutella into my hands immediately afterward.

To my Liverpool housemates, for always wanting to help, whether it was making tea or creating quiet spaces so I could work. And to my New York housemates, for not giving me weird looks when they find me talking to myself, or rocking in corners, or when I burst into nervous laughter.

To the online community, for its constant love and support.

To the readers, who make every bad day good and every good day better.

And to Neil Gaiman, for the hug.

The Unbound

ACKNOWLEDGMENTS

They warn you about sequels.

They tell you to stock up on caffeine and pajama pants. They tell you to strap yourself down against the storm. They tell you that it will all be worth it in the end. That you'll get through it.

But they never tell you how.

The answer?

People.

People who keep you grounded. People who keep you sane. Who talk plot. Talk pacing. Talk character.

People who answer hypothetical questions about really strange things without looking at you like you've lost your mind.

People who steal the delete key from your keyboard when you decide at two a.m. that maybe you should hold it down.

People who know when you need to be left alone and when you need to be dragged from the computer into the light of day (or the darkness of a laser tag arena).

People who care. Who believe. Even when you don't.

This was not an easy book, in any sense. It fought back. It dragged me through mud and thistle. There were casualties. Hours. Drafts.

But I had people.

I had my mother, who reminded me to eat and breathe, and my father, who reminded me to swim until the world felt small enough again.

I had my NYC housemates, Rachel and Jen, who knew when I needed noise and when I needed quiet (and when I needed to watch cartoons).

I had Carla and Courtney, who hauled me to my feet and dusted me off and squared me on my path.

I had my agent, Holly, who told me I would find a way, because I always did.

I had my editors, Abby and Lisa, who believed in the books, and in me.

And I had you.